Sturmtaucher T

Book 1: January 1933 – A₁

The Gathering Storm

Alan Jones

Paperback edition

ISBN 978-1-9997368-2-8

For Catrin

CONTENTS

PREFACE

This is a work of fiction. Most of the characters are drawn from my imagination but some of the characters existed: world leaders, the higher echelons of the National Socialist Party, some senior SS and Gestapo officers, and prominent clergy and military figures. I also included a few notable Kiel citizens who made the newspapers of the day - Dr. Friedrich Schumm, Wilhelm Spiegel and Otto Eggerstedt. They were truly brave men.

I also discovered Captain Wilhelm Canaris during my research. The more I read about him the more I believed that he would have been General Erich Kästner's closest friend. Apart from the private conversations he had with the General and other characters in the book, Wilhelm Canaris's story is largely true, as far as I could establish.

Many of the events in the book, or events like them, happened. Where they are fictitious, I have tried to write them with integrity, always having in mind that they could have taken place, and that none of them should distract from the truth of the terrible crimes committed across Europe during the darkest time in human history.

In a very few instances, I have changed a location or tweaked a timescale to suit the narrative, but it is rare, and I hope the historians will forgive me.

I made extensive use of maps and nautical charts from the 1930's and 40's during my research. It was the only way I could make sense of the global scale of the war, and the Holocaust. I have included a few maps and charts in the book but it would be impossible to show enough detail in them to be truly useful, but maps, charts, and diagrams are available in much larger format at www.alanjonesbooks.co.uk/maps_charts_plans_st.html

There is also a raft of other supporting material; photographs, documents, and links to other websites packed with information surrounding the events in the book, and a glossary. As a reader, I always find these resources useful, especially when reading books of the length and scope of the Sturmtaucher Trilogy.

www.alanjonesbooks.co.uk/sturmtaucher_trilogy.html

Handsell's German - English dictionary
Sturmtaucher; noun. Shearwater (Seabird)

Richsthoffen's Encyclopaedia of Natural History
Manx Shearwater [Puffinus puffinus]

A medium-sized shearwater in the seabird family Procellariidae. These birds are most common in temperate and cold waters. They are tubenose birds and have a cruciform flight, with their long wings held directly out from their bodies. They fly close to the water, cutting or "shearing" the tips of waves to move across wave fronts with the minimum of active flight. This technique gives the group its name.

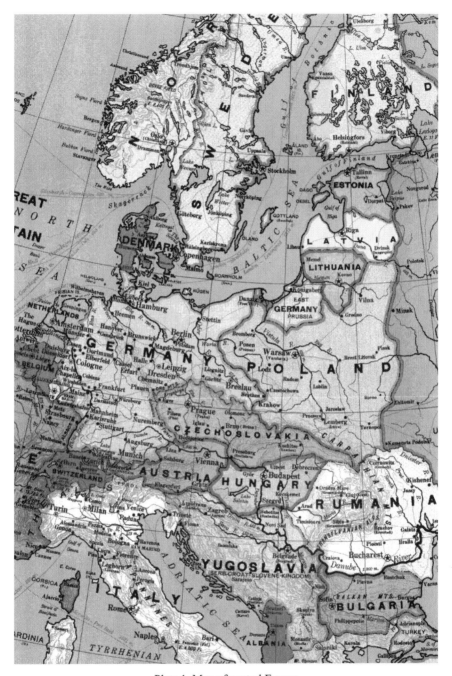

Plate 1. Map of central Europe

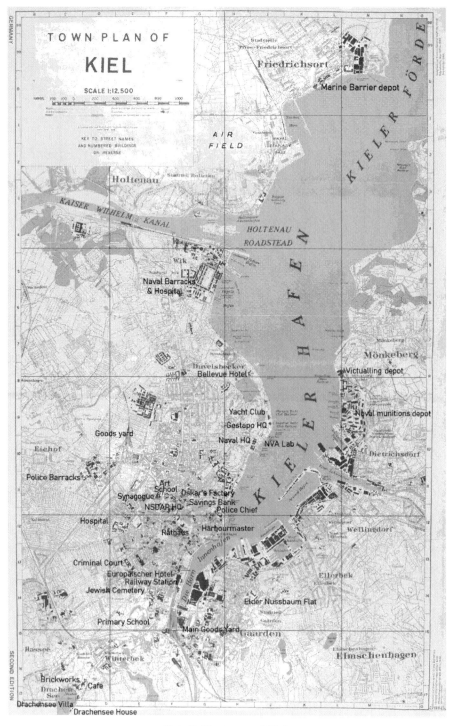

Plate 2. Street map of Kiel.

6

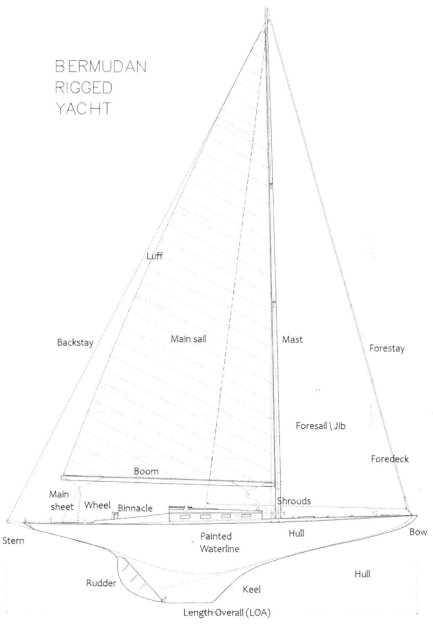

BERMUDAN
RIGGED
YACHT

Luff

Backstay Main sail Mast Forestay

Foresail \ Jib

Foredeck

Boom

Main
sheet Wheel Binnacle Shrouds

Stern Hull Bow

Painted
Waterline

Rudder Hull

Keel

Length Overall (LOA)

Plate 3. Sail plan of Bermudan rigged yacht

For detailed maps and diagrams visit www.alanjonesbooks.co.uk/maps_charts_plans_st.html

PROLOGUE

[19/05/2001 Saturday]

Maldon, England.

'It's hard to know where to begin, but I guess the day I met Adolf Hitler is as good a place as any.'

My head jerked up.

'Don't look so shocked,' Ruth said, smiling. *'I moved in very exclusive circles in those days.'*

She paused.

'He was a well-groomed man; bristling with zeal and an intensity that held every one of us in the crowd in his thrall, even myself. I was only twelve at the time, but if I'd known then what he and the National Socialists would do, I'd have pushed him off the dais, onto the cobbles below.'

A vein throbbed in her temple, and she closed her eyes for a moment.

I was interviewing Ruth Nussbaum at her home in Maldon, overlooking the quay and the salt flats beyond, as part of my dissertation. I'd heard snippets of her life as a young girl in Germany, but it wasn't until I was in my final year at the University of Lincoln, studying for a degree in English and Journalism, that I realised Ruth's story would be an ideal topic for my final paper, if she'd agree to tell me about it.

'A beautiful Kiel day,' she said. *'Bright sunshine. A fresh-to-strong breeze. Ideal conditions for racing, and I knew that the boys' boat had a great chance of winning.'*

She sighed.

'They had stiff opposition,' she continued, *'from one of the navy boats in particular, but Johann and Franz were just too strong for them, and they crossed the line half a boat-length or so in front.'*

Her eyes glistened, the memory of sixty-five years ago as fresh as if it were yesterday, and she was a young girl again.

'That's how we met The Führer, Antje and I. He presented the winners with their prizes, and we were there. I'm sure he guessed that I was a Jew.'

This time, as her eyes closed again, her mouth formed a thin, taut line across her face, and a shiver passed through her. Her hands gripped the side of the chair with whitened knuckles.

I gave her a few seconds to compose herself, watching as her body slowly relaxed and she opened her eyes again.

'Yes, that was the beginning.'

It wasn't, as it turned out, but I wouldn't know that until Ruth had finished telling me her part in the story, and I'd had a chance to flesh out the rest, with thousands upon thousands of hours of research.

I could have picked another date to start; the end of the First World War in 1918, or three years later, when Adolf Hitler became leader of the National Socialist Party. I could have chosen the Beer Hall Putsch in '23 when he and his party attempted to overthrow the Weimar Government, or the publication a few years later of Mein Kampf, his blueprint for what was to blacken Germany a decade later.

I chose to begin in early 1933. It was the day General Erich Franz Kästner retired from the German Army, and it was Ruth Nussbaum's earliest encounter with the terrible changes that were to sweep across Europe over the next twelve or so years.

I didn't use her story for my dissertation, knowing that twenty thousand words would barely scratch its surface. To this day, I can't remember what I submitted, but it secured my degree and a job in a small regional newspaper close to home. The wages and prospects weren't great, but I could live within my means and do the job without too much effort, and the resources I had at my fingertips as a member of the press allowed me to unravel Ruth's story, and that of those she loved, piece by piece. I spent two years checking the facts and immersing myself in the horror her memories had unlocked. There were trips to Kiel and Hamburg, and one to Denmark, and a visit to a Jewish archive in Berlin. I buried myself for hours on end in the reading rooms of the British Library in London, and there were journeys north to Perthshire in Scotland, then Oban. I even flew to Boston for a weekend.

Ruth died not long after reading the first draft of her story, when she'd told me that not much needed changed.

'You skimped somewhat on the passion we had,' she'd said with her wicked smile. 'I can understand that it might be a little awkward for you, being the latest generation to think sex is a new discovery, but I'm glad that I've told my story, and that you've managed to put it down so well on paper.'

They were the last words she spoke to me. A few weeks later, after her funeral, I began the second draft with her words in mind, adding more colour to her character, and those around her, fleshing out their desires, and their hunger for life, and started looking around for a suitable publisher.

This is the manuscript that I'm submitting. I'll let you be the judge of whether it's worthy of consideration.

1933

"Weighing the sacrifices of the last war, we want to be true friends of a peace which will at last heal the wounds from which all have suffered."

Adolf Hitler, Potsdam, March 21, 1933

CHAPTER 1

[28/01/1933 Saturday]

Kiel, Germany.

The party was in full swing. Miriam Nussbaum, the Kästner's cook and housekeeper, and her husband Yosef, the butler, driver, and handyman, shuttled back and forward from the kitchen with heaped plates of food; Matjes, the pickled herrings famed in Kiel, brown shrimp on toast with dill, and Leberknödel, the small liver dumplings that Miriam made better than anyone else Maria, the General's wife, knew. A buzz of conversation filled the large drawing room and the sound of children's laughter drifted from the open doorway.

General Kästner stood talking with a group of men, most of them dressed in military uniforms bedecked with arrays of medals. He saw his wife attempting to usher the throng to their seats for the first of the three courses that she'd spent weeks planning with Miriam, who was now pouring the wine for their guests.

When they finally began to drift through in small groups, Yosef shepherded the children in with his usual immaculate timing and seated them at the smaller table set up for them at the side of the large room.

The General caught his eye, nodded, and smiled.

~~o~~

In the lull that followed, Yosef escaped to the kitchen and picked up the newspaper lying on the table. He skimmed through the article about his employer.

KIELER MORGENPOST

Wednesday 25th January 1933

KIEL GENERAL RETIRES

General Erich Kästner retired today, after close to thirty years of active service in the German Army. Born in Kiel, the son of Admiral Franz Kästner, he joined the 3rd Army, 22nd Infantry Division of the Imperial German Army in 1904 and saw action in both Deutsch-Westafrika and Deutsch-Ostafrika. He rose from the rank of Major to Oberst during the Great War, serving on the Western Front, winning an Iron Cross at Passchendaele. He was promoted to General four years later, in the much reduced 2nd Division, garrisoned in Stettin. General Kästner told the Morgenpost that it had been a privilege to serve his beloved Deutschland and that, despite retiring from active duty, he hoped that his experience could still be of some use to the Reichswehr, and to his country. General Kästner is married and has four children. He and his wife, Maria, live in the Hassee district of Kiel, overlooking Drachensee. Franz, his eldest son, has been accepted as a candidate at Hanover

For a few minutes, the buzz of conversation faded to a hushed quiet, with only the clacking of cutlery on fine china and the occasional request to pass the condiments breaking the silence, as the General and his guests focused on the food. As the diners cleared their plates, the thrum of debate and gossip resumed.

Yosef laid down his paper and returned to the dining room to tend to the diners' needs.

~~o~~

'So, Erich, how does it feel being a free man? Perhaps you should at last join the navy.'

Vizeadmiral Conrad Albrecht nodded at the laughter his comment had generated around the table.

'Conrad,' the General replied, 'it feels strange. Notwithstanding my lovely wife, Maria,' he said, turning to her, and ignoring her blushes, 'I feel as if I've been married to the army for the last, well, almost thirty years.' He paused, while the murmurs of his guests subsided. 'And now we've had a divorce. The last thing I want is a mistress.'

A chorus of jeers erupted from the men of the Reichswehr, delighted with their army colleague's rebuttal, in the age-old inter-service war of attrition.

The laughter subsided, and the room soon filled with scattered conversations around the table, in their twos and threes. Even at the children's table, there were whispers about who was who in the rather imposing assembly of adults, interspersing the more mundane chatter about school, and what games they would play once they had been freed from the constraints of the dinner table.

'Old Franz will want to listen to the boring grown-ups as usual.'

Eva, the elder of the General's two daughters, teased her oldest brother, knowing that Johann, a year or so his younger, was the one who was full of mischief, and much more likely to indulge in the fun and games that always ensued when the Kästner, Böhm and Nussbaum children got the chance to play together.

The other children giggled, and Johann did a perfect impersonation of Franz trying to act like his father.

For most of the year, the Kästner children, once they reached the age of twelve, boarded, depending on their sex, at a military school for young men, or at the girls' school designed to impart the finer points of being ladies to the often unruly and resistant daughters of Kiel's officer class.

When they were old enough, the two Nussbaum children would attend local upper schools befitting the offspring of those employed in domestic service. Antje, the youngest of the General's two daughters, was still at home and was in the same *Grundschule* as Ruth. It was the school that all the Kästner and Nussbaum children attended before the age of twelve.

The General smiled, seeing his son's pained expression at the ribbing he was being subjected to by his brother. He watched him strain to listen to the confused snatches of grown-up conversation reaching him from the main table.

No matter. He'll be seventeen next year and sitting with the adults.

At fifteen, Franz was the eldest of them. Ruth Nussbaum was the same age as Antje, his youngest sister, four years junior to Eva, who was already a precocious fourteen-year-old. The baby of the group was Immanuel, or Manny, as everyone called him. He was Ruth's younger brother and they all spoiled him by including him in most of the games they played, even though, at five, he sometimes restricted the scope of their activities. Lise and Eberhard Böhm, the children from next door, sat with them.

As soon as the first course was finished, Yosef and Miriam Nussbaum cleared the empty plates and, with Maria flapping back and forth from the kitchen, they applied the finishing touches to the main courses, and relayed the brimming dishes to the dining room.

The General smiled at his wife. Despite her belief that she ran the household, he knew that it was Miriam Nussbaum's dedication that ensured that the Kästner home was kept spotless, clothes were washed and ironed, and dinner appeared on the table when it needed to.

He conceded that his wife oversaw the décor, and his social diary when he was at home, but it pleased him that Miriam let her mistress think that she was the Chef de Maison in her kitchen, as Maria liked to tell her friends.

The doorbell rang, and the children rushed to answer it before Yosef could get there.

'It's Uncle Wilhelm,' the shouts came from the vestibule at the entrance. As often, Captain Wilhelm Canaris was the last to arrive. When his young welcoming party finally released him, he gave his coat to Yosef, and waited to be ushered in.

General Kästner pushed back his chair, rose to his feet, and excused himself to greet the small man standing in the hallway, who had been his friend since the early days of their respective military careers.

'Canaris.'

'Kästner.'

They laughed and grasped each other's hands warmly.

Every conversation they'd ever had started this way. He knew that it infuriated Maria, who couldn't see why the joke that had amused them so much when they'd met as junior officers was still considered funny. She was forever asking them why they didn't use their forenames like normal people.

'You're still a captain?' the General said, with a wide grin.

'Yes, for now. The papers haven't come through yet, but I'm sure I'll be made up to an admiral next week.' Captain Canaris returned the smile. 'Are you still a general?'

'Recently retired, to fester in my crumbling ruin. How are you? Are all your little cadets behaving themselves?'

In the up-and-down career of Wilhelm Canaris, he was now the commander of the Reichsmarine training vessel, the *Schlesien*.

'Oh, these navy lot learn quickly, unlike your army rabble. They need to. We're putting them through training in half the time. There are some outstanding young officers coming up through the ranks, and I'm convinced the more intensive training brings out the best in them.'

'Ah. The Reichsmarine too. The Reichsheer is churning out soldiers as if a war is imminent. You'd think the French and the British would notice, wouldn't you?'

'Damn them. We stuck to that stupid treaty long enough. We need a strong army and a strong navy.'

The Treaty of Versailles, signed six months after the Armistice of 1918 that ended the First World War with a German defeat, limited the army to 100,000 men and the navy to just six battleships and six cruisers, twelve destroyers and no submarines. It also prohibited a German air force.

'Enough politics, Canaris, come in and meet everyone. You'll know most of them.'

~~o~~

A chorus of jeers met the pair as they entered the dining room. The captain's tardiness for social occasions was famous in military circles, tolerated because he was excellent company, with an intelligent mind, a dry sense of humour and fluency in five or six languages, which made him the darling of the diplomatic circles.

He took the empty seat next to the rather dreary wife of one of General Kästner's colleagues and proceeded to charm her, pretending that a discourse about her offspring, and a rundown on the latest garrison gossip, was of great interest to him.

As the guests tucked into the Sauerbraten, a beef dish marinated for days, then slow-cooked for twelve hours, accompanied by the traditional Bratkartoffeln, Knödel dumplings and Sauerkraut, Captain Canaris couldn't resist commenting.

'Maria, my darling, if they gave out medals for gourmet cooking, you'd have been

14

decorated a long while ago for your wonderful food. The beef is delicious; it simply melts in the mouth. And the potatoes… what can I say? May I steal the recipe from you? I'm trying to improve my wife's cooking.'

The table erupted with laughter and Maria Kästner blushed. Even if she'd been tempted to take the credit for the excellence of the food, Miriam and Yosef had just walked in with more plates piled high with traditional German food; Wiener Schnitzel, the thin, breaded, fried veal cutlet that was the General's favourite, Bratwurst, Rinderrouladen, mouth-watering rolls of stuffed beef, and a local pasta dish, Maultaschen.

The General knew that Captain Canaris was all too aware of who was responsible for the brilliance of the dishes, and that Maria's overseeing of the kitchen was more of a hindrance than a help. He stifled a laugh, trying to avoid his wife's glare, and sat back to watch her squirm.

'Oh, I can't take all the glory, Captain Canaris,' she said. 'Miriam makes such an excellent job of it. I just plan it all and keep an eye on everything.'

She put on her best smile and waved her hand in the vague direction of the spread. The General, knowing that graciousness in a hostess was essential, suffered a pang of guilt at the teasing she endured from him and Canaris, a cruelty that had been going on since they'd all first met, while the two men were young officers.

And he knew it would earn him the edge of her tongue later.

The room settled down again and, listening to the pleasant hum of chatter, and bursts of laughter, the General was content that the evening was going well. When the Nussbaums returned to clear up after the main course which, he had to admit, had been a near perfect triumph, he heard his wife speak quietly to Miriam.

'The General is going to say a few words before dessert. If you listen at the door you'll hear when he's drawing to a close, and you'll know when to start serving.'

He saw Miriam nod dutifully.

The General had already told her what he'd planned to do, but he knew that Maria liked to feel that she was in charge and, because she was, on the whole, easy to work for, Miriam was more than happy to play her part in the pretence.

Although the Nussbaums were employees, the relationship between the two families went much deeper.

When the admiral, Erich's father, had retired in 1913, he and his wife Ingrid stayed on in Kiel for a couple of years, rattling around in the big old house until Erich, now fighting on the Western Front, married Maria. The old couple had sat the newlyweds down and told them that instead of moving in with them when they returned from their honeymoon, as planned, the Drachensee house would now be theirs, to themselves.

'We've decided to live at the lodge. We love the mountains. We'll still come and visit, Erich, and you and your sister will always be welcome to come and stay with us. Fill this house with children. That's what it's for.'

The newlyweds had been dumbstruck – they had expected to start their married life as lodgers, so it was, Erich knew, both exciting and daunting for his bride to be the mistress of a grand house of her own.

Yosef's parents, Samuel and Renate Nussbaum, had worked for the admiral for nearly three decades. A couple of years after the admiral and his wife left for their mountain retreat, the elder Nussbaums had also retired and Yosef and Miriam, not long married, had taken over the servants' cottage and the domestic positions at the Drachensee house which they vacated.

Erich hadn't interfered when his new bride had insisted on a more formal relationship with her domestic staff than the admiral and his wife had deemed appropriate, but it all changed when Maria became pregnant with her third child. It was not an easy confinement and, somewhere between Eva's conception and the difficult birth, Miriam's kindness and attention to the expectant mother and the premature child left a lasting mark on Maria, and the two women had been friends since.

There were still boundaries in place, as much at Miriam's insistence as Maria's; they came from social backgrounds that were worlds apart, and there was a mistress-servant relationship to maintain.

But, when the General rose to his feet, tapping his glass with a spoon to silence the hubbub, Yosef and Miriam, as proud of the General as if they were part of the family, stood unseen in the hallway, just outside the door.

'Friends,' the General started, 'we feel humbled and privileged to have you share this evening with us. I'm not going to speak for long because I believe there are some especially delicious desserts to follow this wonderful meal, prepared by Miriam, helped, naturally, by my beautiful wife.'

There were a few murmurs, and everyone looked at Maria Kästner. She blushed a little.

'Without her by my side, I wouldn't have achieved as much as everyone seems to think I've done. If it weren't for her, and my children, none of it would have mattered.'

There was a polite spattering of applause. It was the children's turn to feel the gaze of the guests.

'I owe an incredible debt of gratitude to my parents, who supported my choices. My father's influence on me cannot be understated, which is why I joined the army instead of the navy.'

A chorus of good-natured whistles, stamping feet, jeers and boos filled the room from the army and navy contingents, and he waited for it to subside before continuing.

'In all seriousness, their care for me, and the generous gift of this magnificent house, has made our lives here full of joy.'

He paused again, while the admiral and his wife were applauded with genuine affection.

'Kiel has been a wonderful place to live and bring up children,' he continued. 'As you all know, my passion, sometimes shared by Maria and one or two of my children, has always been sailing, and there are few better places to be if you love nothing more than a fine wind and a steady cutter. We will continue to live in this great seafaring city for the rest of our days.'

A gentle round of appreciative murmurs greeted his praise for the navy town that most of them called home.

'We've made a plethora of friends here, often through sailing, but also among the naval sorts who seem to congregate in these parts. In addition, I can't forget those wonderful people I've met through my involvement in the Rotary Club and, last but by no means least, those acquaintances I've picked up over the years in the army.' He looked around the table as he said this, nodding to each group in turn as they raised their glasses to him.

'You all have what I can best describe as some questionable qualities...' He paused as gentle laughter filled the room again. 'But none more so than I, so perhaps that's why we are such good friends.

'Now, I hope to spend more of my time at home and devote myself to my family. While I do not intend to sit in front of the fire with my pipe and slippers, I haven't quite decided what I am going to do to fill my days.'

He paused and looked around the room, as if gauging each face, and weighing up their character.

'We are living in exciting times. While I don't entirely agree with all of Herr Hitler's politics, there is no doubt he is galvanising the nation. Within Germany, and within the Reichswehr, there are changes in the air which some of the older among us would have loved to have seen years ago but, now that they are happening, we have a few reservations. Still, for the greater good of our nation, we must embrace them.'

The Reichswehr, the German armed forces, was made up of the Reichsheer, the army, and the Reichsmarine, the navy. There was no air force under the terms of the Versailles Treaty.

Murmurs of assent from a few of the guests almost drowned out a subdued intake of breath from others at the table; it was unusual for Erich Kästner to make any point that was remotely political, unless to his close friends, and then only in the privacy of intimate conversation.

'So please raise your glasses to Kiel, to Germany, and to a peaceful and prosperous future. *Prost.*'

They all stood up, and clinked the bottom of their glasses together, responding with one voice, in the usual impressive German fashion. When everyone sat down, with much chair-scraping and jostling, Wilhelm Canaris stayed on his feet.

'Kästner,' he said, looking at the General, 'I've been asked to reply to your toast, the truth being that we all knew you wouldn't pass up the chance to say a few words, and these people here...' he swept his hands around the table, 'these people seem to think that I give a monkey's curse about you, and that some sort of friendship exists between us.'

The General smiled as the diners laughed, knowing his friend would never have replied with bland sentimentality.

'However,' he continued, 'I have known General Erich Kästner for a number of years and indeed, I served under his father, a true military man.'

This time the ribald response of the uniformed guests was more voluble, and Captain Canaris smiled at his audience.

'True, he fought valiantly in our African colonies, when we had some; he served on the Western Front with distinction, winning an Iron Cross and proving himself to be a clever and adept tactician who inspired his men, but at heart he was an army man and, coming from a background like his, with a deep knowledge of the sea, he must have been a profound disappointment to his father, Admiral Kästner, the white-haired and broken-hearted gentleman seated to my left.'

The room exploded with laughter. The admiral himself guffawed so much that his glasses fell off and had to be retrieved from the floor by the attentive Yosef. Most of the General's friends had tears of laughter running down their cheeks and even some of the women smiled, amused by the indulgent behaviour of their childish spouses.

'Despite that apparent stab in the back, the admiral has shown nothing but kindness for his wayward son and so, with reluctant grace, I must propose a toast. Erich, I hope your country is not finished with you yet. It would be a waste of all your experience and an extraordinary military mind, and I'm sure there will be something asked of you in the upcoming resurgence of our beloved Deutschland.'

He turned to his friend, and then to the assembled guests.

'Please raise your glasses and join me in a toast to an outstanding General and a remarkable man. General Erich Franz Kästner.'

The loud and enthusiastic echo of Wilhelm Canaris's toast reverberated around the room, and anyone passing by would have wondered if a military barracks had sprung from nowhere in the heart of the leafy and genteel Drachensee neighbourhood.

What touched Erich Kästner the most was the unprompted and sustained salutes that all the military men in the room executed, which he returned with equal fervour, turning away to hide the dampness in his eyes.

CHAPTER 2

In shirtsleeves, Captain Conrad Patzig sat at his desk. It was late, and the only light was the desk lamp illuminating the green leather writing surface.

He picked up the piece of paper from the top of the pile and wondered how things were going in Kiel. He reread the memo he'd received from the ministry nearly a week ago, and the reply he'd sent back a few days later.

~~o~~

Memo: Geh.KdoS. ABW 22/01/33 CAC0103.1

For Attention Only: Captain Conrad Patzig, Chef der Abwehr

From: General der Infanterie Kurt von Hammerstein-Equord, Chef der Heeresleitung

In the light of the unprecedented upsurge of support for Adolf Hitler and the National Socialist Party, and their possible victory in an election in the foreseeable future, restructuring and massive expansion of the German armed forces is expected. Any future NSDAP government will almost certainly utilise its own internal intelligence services, probably under the auspices of the Schutzstaffel (SS), headed by Heinrich Himmler and reporting directly to Adolf Hitler. There is some evidence that a subdivision of this organisation, Sicherheitsdienst des Reichsführers-SS (SD) will be directly responsible for national intelligence.

It is therefore of paramount importance that the armed forces retain and expand the Abwehr as an independent military intelligence organisation. In light of this, there are several appointments that need to be filled to ensure that the armed forces work together to minimise intolerable political interference. A list is attached of the new appointments necessary but one of the key positions is a naval liaison officer who will facilitate collaboration between the Abwehr, the Reichsheer and the Reichsmarine. This posting will be based largely in Kiel, within the Naval Operational Headquarters. Please search for suitable candidates and inform me of your findings by 28th January.

A person of rank greater than Colonel would be preferred as it is important that senior naval and army officers should deal with someone of an equivalent rank. An appropriate candidate may, if necessary, be promoted to said rank. [END]

~~o~~

Memo: Geh.KdoS. ABW 24/01/33 CAC0103.2

For Attention Only: General der Infanterie Kurt von Hammerstein-Equord, Chef der Heeresleitung

From: Captain Conrad Patzig, Chef der Abwehr.

After due diligence, the search has shown up two ideal candidates. Captain Wilhelm Canaris would be at the top of the list, having had significant experience of working in the field as a naval intelligence officer. However, there have been a few questions on his handling of the Lohmann affair. Despite this, I sounded him out about the position, but he has just taken command of a naval training vessel and would prefer to retain that commission at present.

The second candidate has recently retired as an active general in the Reichswehr. He lives in Kiel and has excellent contacts within both services, his father being a retired admiral. He is a close friend of Captain Canaris, and indeed, during my discussions with the captain, it was the latter who suggested that General Kästner would be ideal for the position, and that he might welcome an approach from us.

Captain Canaris also offered to make an initial discreet contact with the General to assess his interest in our proposal. He will be attending the General's retirement dinner and will report back to me as soon as possible. [END]

~~o~~

After dessert, which was noisy and good-spirited with much discussion of the speeches and the food, the men retired to the study and the women drifted through to the large drawing room which faced out onto the garden. If it had been summer, they could have walked through the French windows, and admired the view of the moonlit lake through the gap in the trees, but the bitter freeze that had settled on Kiel since mid-December kept them inside.

The children remained with the women, impatient for the moment when Maria Kästner would release them from their social constraints, and they could find places in the far-flung corners of the large house to be children again.

The youngsters were all introduced in turn to a variety of matronly ladies, fidgeting whilst being coddled over and patted on the head, studying Maria for signs of disapproval if they were anything other than polite and deferential.

Ruth saw her father approach Franz and, with a gentle hand on his shoulder, whisper something in his ear. Franz looked around, surprised, and followed Yosef out of the room.

He's joining the men, she thought, irritated, but glad that she and the others would soon be released to play, away from the stifled world of the grown-ups. *It's his own fault that he's going to miss out.*

She turned back to the tall, elegant lady with the silver hair and rather large jewels and replied with the required politeness to her questions about school, and how she was enjoying the Christmas holidays.

~~o~~

Yosef and Franz crossed the hall, and the older man opened the door to the study and guided Franz through. His grandfather spotted him, and with a beaming smile, made his way towards him.

'Franz, my boy, come, I'd like to introduce you to some fine gentlemen of my acquaintance.'

A silence fell on the room as all the men looked at Franz. He blushed under their scrutiny, but the deep hum of men discussing matters of a serious nature soon resumed, and Franz was introduced to the cream of Kiel's military establishment.

Franz glanced at the door, his eyes seeking out Johann in the crowd outside, but he knew that any resentment his brother harboured at his elder sibling's induction into the adult world wouldn't be sustained; Johann would be bored and he'd itch to run free, once the novelty had worn off.

~~o~~

A short while after Franz's departure, his mother indicated that so long as they kept the noise down and didn't disturb the adults, the children could go and play.

As the eldest, it was up to Johann to choose the first game, and Ruth was delighted when he decided that hide-and-seek would be the most fun and would keep the younger ones occupied.

When he made himself the seeker the first time, and began his count, Ruth didn't follow the others, figuring that the best spot to hide would be amongst the adults; the last place Johann would expect to find her was back in the world of boredom and monotony.

She slipped unnoticed into the drawing room once his back was turned and scuttled behind one of the long heavy drapes that hung to the floor, covering the French windows which faced the lake. The glass was cold on her back, but she suffered it, wanting to impress Johann with her cleverness.

Despite being five-and-a-bit years older and, in her eyes, tremendously grown up, he was still fun to be with, and willing to join in their childish games, forgetting that he was on the verge of adulthood, postponing the time when he could no longer exist without a care in the world.

'Don't you just think he's wonderful,' she'd confided to Antje, Johann's younger sister, in a moment of unguarded candour.

'Yuk, he's horrible, and he's a boy. You're so silly.' Antje's scathing reply hadn't dulled her admiration for Johann, but it made her cautious about ever telling anyone again about her affections for him. Fortunately for Ruth, Antje had either forgotten her words, or didn't feel the desire to needle her about it; either way, not until they were much older, would Antje mention Ruth's infatuation again.

As she waited, her mind roamed, and she imagined a future when Johann would be a famous young Reichsheer officer, and she would be the elegant young lady on his arm. She was so diverted by her imagination, that she was taken by surprise when a voice interrupted her daydream.

'Franz is such a serious and respectful young man, and they are expecting great things of him.'

She recognised the voice of Frau Böhm, the Kästners' immediate neighbour.

'Yes,' she heard a second woman reply. 'Franz takes after the General, Johann is more like his Aunt Traudl. Marrying Heiner Weib was her saving grace.'

Ruth frowned. The woman's voice sounded familiar, and she tried to put a face to it. *Who is she?*

'They say Franz will go far in the army. He's already a cadet captain.'

'I hear he and your daughter are stepping out together.'

'I wouldn't say that, although Franz does seem besotted by my Lise. He has been since Grundschule.'

'They would make a lovely couple, and it would be a good catch for Lise.'

Ruth could almost feel Frau Böhm stiffen.

'Most certainly, but quite a catch for young Franz too. My Lise was voted as the most popular girl in her form at school and she always comes out in the top three or four at her studies.'

20

'Oh, I didn't mean anything. Lise is a most beautiful young lady and I'm sure she has many admirers. But the Kästners are such a well-connected family and, needless to say, General Kästner and his father have both won the highest honours; the General has an Iron Cross, you know.'

'You're right, most assuredly, although my Eberhard... I shouldn't really be telling you this... he's been more or less told he will head his section this year, when that horrible man, Shlossberg, is gone. He's a Jew, you know.'

'You must be delighted. Eberhard has worked exceedingly hard for it, and he is of good German blood. I only hope he gets it.'

'Of course he will,' Frau Böhm snapped, then tried to cover her slip. 'It's only a matter of time. I'm sure Herr Hitler will win the next election, and after that...'

'I know, isn't it exciting. He's such a compelling speaker. I get such a thrill when I hear him on the wireless.'

'I don't think...' She paused and lowered her voice. 'I'm not sure that the Kästners are awfully keen on him. I mean, that speech the General made was hardly an endorsement.'

'I know what you mean. But then again, they are a bit cosy with their own Jews, aren't they?'

'Yes, you're right. I mean, as if having their servants' children sitting at the same table as my Lise and Eberhard Junior isn't bad enough, being Jews only makes it worse. I sometimes wonder if Lise would be better off marrying someone else, but who can get in the way of young love?'

'I wouldn't worry. The Nussbaums are very discreet; almost like real Germans.'

'I know, and if the National Socialists get into power and clean things up a bit, they could always be moved on.'

'You don't have any problems with your staff, do you? Ours are from very old German serving families.'

Ruth almost managed a grin through the tears that were running down her cheeks. The Böhms only had one maid, who came in three times a week to clean. Frau Böhm was forever complaining about her.

'Our maid is excellent,' Frau Böhm said, 'and definitely not tainted with any non-German blood. I sometimes wonder what I would do without her.'

'I know exactly what you mean. Two of our staff are from Bavaria, and they took a while to adjust to our ways, but they're fine now. The other is local, and do you know, he's probably the least reliable.'

Ruth tried hard to imagine the tight anger in Frau Böhm's face, and the victorious smirk of her adversary, then she heard someone approaching. Thinking it might be Johann, she pulled herself further against the glass, making sure that her feet weren't poking out.

'Ladies, how are you both? Did you get enough to eat? Can I get someone to refill your glasses?'

It was Tante Maria. They were only permitted to call her Aunt when they were alone, the Kästners and the Nussbaums. At all other times it was *Ma'am* or *Frau Kästner*.

Frau Böhm replied, her voice sickly sweet.

'Another glass of wine would be lovely. The food was exquisite. And it was lovely seeing all the children together. They get on so well, especially your Franz and my Lise.'

'We always try and include the children. Franz and Lise are getting so grown up now, and Franz will attend military academy next year. My baby, out into the wide world. It seems no time at all since they were all in their prams. I shouldn't fret, really; it's his chance to see more of the world.'

'I hope he doesn't forget us,' Frau Böhm said, with a brittle laugh. 'Perhaps Lise and he should exchange friendship rings.'

'I feel they're probably a little young for that, but I'm sure they'll make up their own minds.'

The third woman spoke. Ruth recognised her now. Her husband was the man who wore the chain around his neck; the mayor, or was he just a deputy, like in the cowboy films? The

21

children called them Herr and Frau Kartoffelkopf, due to the matching shape and size of the couple's heads, which resembled potatoes.

'I've been told that young soldiers like to sow some oats before they settle down; and they say that sailors have a girl in every port.'

Ruth stifled a giggle. Frau Potato-Head had just gone up in her estimation. The Böhm woman obviously couldn't conjure up a suitable response.

Frau Kästner called for the ladies' glasses to be filled, and Ruth identified the faint scent of her mother's perfume as footsteps approached. Already motionless, she froze quite still, hardly breathing, as if her mother would be able to sense her presence so close by.

'Thank you, Miriam,' said Frau Böhm, 'the dinner was quite delicious. You should be tremendously pleased with yourself. You must have worked all day in the kitchen.'

'Miriam has been on the go since six this morning. I'm sure she deserves a rest now,' said Frau Kästner. 'Miriam, fetch a glass and pour a wine for yourself, and join us.'

Ruth could imagine Frau Böhm's disapproving frown and her mother's fleeting blush.

'Thanks, but perhaps I might join you later, Frau Kästner. I'm afraid there's still too much needing to be done.'

Ruth heard her mother walk away.

'She's such an asset to you,' the deputy-mayor's wife said, but will you be able to hold onto the Nussbaums once Herr Hitler is elected?'

Ruth held her breath again.

'The Nussbaums have been with us for nearly fifty years and for two generations. They're part of the furniture. I'm sure the National Socialists will not be the slightest bit interested in them. And my husband and my father-in-law do have a little bit of influence, you know.'

'That may be true, Maria,' said Frau Böhm, 'but times are changing, and in modern Germany, things may become somewhat different from the way they are now.'

Ruth couldn't have explained how she knew, but she realised that these women who, on the surface, were good friends, disliked each other intensely. Sometimes the girls at school acted in a similar way and she wondered if it would be the same when she and her classmates became adults.

Frau Kästner excused herself and moved away to talk to another group on the opposite side of the room. The two ladies spoke for a while in rueful tones about their host's need to recognise that society was changing, then, realising that Maria Kästner was at the centre of a group of influential ladies, they sidled over to join them. In the quietness behind the curtain, Ruth didn't know what to think, but she felt that somehow her world had shifted, and she wanted to ask her parents what it meant.

'BOO!'

She jumped and screamed at the same time, tripping over the folds of the curtains and landing in a heap at Johann's feet. He doubled over with laughter, tears running down his face.

'You are rotten, Johann Kästner. You scared me.'

'That's what you get for being so sneaky, hiding in here.'

'It took ages for you to find me,' she said, her cheeks flushed, but she could see that despite the laughter, there was a grudging respect in his manner that a girl had outwitted him for so long, and one that much younger than him.

'You were the last to be found. I suppose that counts for something.'

She felt warmed by his praise and resolved that one day she would be his wife, when she had grown up.

Frau Kästner came over to see what the fuss was, and she scolded Johann for frightening Ruth and causing a commotion, but Ruth could see the smile in her eyes as she steered them out of the room to find the other children.

'The men will return soon, and I'd like you to play and sing a little for everybody before you all go to bed. If you're awfully good, we will all have a game of charades before you go.'

Franz stood and listened, fascinated. *How many cadets at my school would get the chance to be surrounded by men like these?*

The group he stood among boasted some of the most formidable military brains that Germany could muster, and the civilians scattered among them were all men of stature too. He moved around the room, listening to snatches of their conversations.

'…and the latest unemployment figures in Kiel are the darkest ever…'

'…no real recovery since the Wall Street Crash in '29…'

'Every second shop in Kiel is boarded up…'

'…even with Roosevelt elected, the Americans aren't interested in what is going on in Europe; they're not going to interfere.'

He wandered over to stand by the group talking to his father and grandfather.

'But do we have the infrastructure in place to support such an expansion?' his grandfather was saying.

'Not quite, but we are better prepared than the politicians realise.' This was from Oberst Rolf Kummetz. 'We have von Seeckt to thank for that.'

Franz looked lost, and the colonel noticed his confusion.

'My boy, you are about to enter an army that is, in one way, a shadow of the one that fought in the Great War. We lost that war, and there's no point in raking over the coals as to why that was, but the result of that defeat was a grossly punitive economic and military clampdown which suppressed any hope Germany had of recovering after the war was over and was, in the main, a sop to France and her fear of our great country. What are they teaching you about it at that military academy you attend?'

'The Treaty of Versailles,' Franz blurted, his stomach churning. 'It limited us to an army of just over 100,000 men, and a navy of twelve capital ships and the same number of destroyers. No air force or submarines.'

'Quite so, Franz. But they forgot about German ingenuity and efficiency. After the war was over, when General von Seeckt was forced to trim the army down, he retained the brightest and best officers and loaded the remaining regiments with these men, your father among them, with no sentiment for tradition or for war heroes. He concentrated his tactics on speed, aggression and the abilities of his commanders and lower officers to use their initiative and exploit opportunities. When the army gets the chance to blood its swords, in the fullness of time, this core of expertise at officer level will allow it to expand rapidly while retaining discipline and competence across the board.'

A moustached man in a colonel's dress uniform spoke up.

'He also utilised the police force to give men basic military training. When the time comes to expand the army, these men will fill the ranks of our new regiments.'

Oskar von Friedeburg, one of his father's friends, added his contribution.

'Our Soviet allies, while still a threat, have also been of immense benefit. In return for our help with their industrialisation, we have been able to develop our own engineering and chemical expertise to prepare for a massive expansion in German industrial output. We have also secured sources for all the raw materials we need, primarily through Russia and Sweden.'

'And the Reichsmarine will respond in a similar fashion,' Admiral Albrecht interjected. 'All our current fighting vessels are overstaffed with officers, but this means that trained captains, lieutenants and midshipmen will be ready and available when the need arises. The merchant navy is awash with suitable ratings to crew the new ships that they will build, here in Kiel and in Wilhelmshaven.'

'And what about submarines?' Franz said, the words out before he remembered the company he was in. 'Will we not need them?'

There was a murmur around the room.

'Ah, I see the boy is a chip off the old block, and the even older block.'

The men all laughed, and Franz blushed.

'You are quite right, Franz,' the admiral continued. 'Contingencies have been made for that, too, but let's not worry about the detail.' He paused.

'Why submarines, young man?' Admiral Albrecht said.

Franz gulped, wishing he'd kept quiet, but he saw his grandfather and father smile at him, so he answered the admiral's question.

'We have too small a navy and not enough seaports to compete with the British in the Atlantic, and Helgoland is vulnerable, so the Nordsee will still be dominated by the British. We can control the Baltic from Kiel with our surface ships but, to make an impact outside, in the Nordsee and the Atlantic, we will need submarines.'

A murmur of admiration for the boy's pluck travelled around the room. A few of the men turned to their neighbours and commented. The admiral looked Franz in the eye and smiled.

'You have got to the nub of the problem, my boy.' He looked around the room. 'If only our politicians were as perceptive as young Franz here!'

Again, laughter filled the study, and most of those present nodded in assent.

'Were you taught this, or did you come to this conclusion yourself?'

'One of our teachers, Captain Schwarz, teaches us military history. He likes to have us discuss and rationalise the past and how it affects the future.'

'This Captain Schwarz sounds an interesting man. Perhaps we should have a word with him.'

There were more laughs, and Franz's stomach lurched again.

'I hope I haven't got him into any trouble,' he stuttered, his palms sweating. 'He's one of my best teachers. It's just a small group of us he takes for these discussions.'

'Don't you worry, Franz. Far from getting Captain Schwarz into trouble, you may just have earned him a promotion. We need people like him who are willing to recognise the cream of our youth and develop them; not just into soldiers, sailors and airmen, but into intelligent and quick-thinking officers.'

Franz looked dazed from all the attention and the unexpected questions he'd been asked. The General put his hand on the boy's shoulder.

'I think my son has had enough for now, and it is time to rejoin the ladies, gentlemen; as much as I have enjoyed your company, let us move through to the drawing room.'

Franz cast a relieved look at his father, who winked at him. He felt a squeeze on his arm and looked round to see his grandfather smiling.

~~o~~

When Franz looked back, it struck him that he'd been ushered gently into the world of adulthood that evening.

They'd sat in the kitchen after most of the guests left. Antje had been sent to bed, and Eva and Johann had soon bored of the adults and their interminable dullness and had made their way up the stairs to their rooms.

Yosef and Miriam had finished clearing up and Miriam accepted a glass of wine from Frau Kästner but, as soon as they could, without appearing impolite, the Nussbaums gathered up the sleeping Manny, took Ruth's hand and headed for their own quarters in the two-storey cottage set apart from the main house. Maria and her mother-in-law also made their excuses, leaving the kitchen to the men.

And Franz.

The General opened the whisky bottle and poured four generous glasses. Captain Canaris pulled a glass towards him and added some water from the small jug on the table. Oskar von Friedeburg fetched a couple of ice cubes from the Kästner's icebox. Admiral Kästner and the General sipped the amber fluid neat from the glass.

As if in afterthought, the General poured a small measure into a fifth glass and added some water. He handed it to his son. 'Take your time with it,' he whispered.

Captain Canaris reached for the bottle, then tilted it away from him to read the label.

'Macallan, eh?' he said. 'Your tastes are getting more expensive, Kästner.'

'I'm always searching for the perfect malt. I import it directly from Fortnum and Mason's in London. It's my only indulgence. The love of Scotch Whisky is one of the many things my father instilled in me.'

The old admiral gave his son a benign smile.

'I acquired a taste for it when I visited Portsmouth, back in late 1890,' he said, 'when the British were still talking to us.'

Canaris took a sip, nodded in appreciation, and looked directly at the General.

'You shouldn't have spoken as you did earlier, in front of all your guests.'

The General wasn't surprised that Canaris had mentioned his comments. He didn't respond but waited for his friend to expand on his statement.

'First of all, I know you consider them all as friends and that you can trust them, but these are becoming dangerous times, and you should learn to trust no one.'

The General shrugged. 'So, you're saying I'm naïve?'

'More or less. Anyway, it so happens that I agree with much of what the National Socialists and Herr Hitler stand for, although I don't always condone their methods. If you must disagree, as many senior officers in the armed forces do, I would strongly advise you to be discreet about it. Sooner or later, they will take power, and they may not tolerate dissent.'

The General turned to his son.

'Franz, I first met Captain Canaris when he served as a junior officer under your grandfather. It was at Kieler Woche, in 1905, I think.'

Kieler Woche. Kiel Week. The most prestigious sailing regatta in Germany.

The admiral corrected him.

'It was 1906, not 5. I had command of the *Kaiser Wilhelm der Grosse*, and Canaris was a young upstart second lieutenant who caught my eye. The ship was back in Kiel for a refit; she was built at the Germaniawerft shipyard, you know, and I invited Canaris to watch the racing at Kieler Woche with us.'

The old man smiled at Franz.

'Your father,' he continued, 'who was a mere lieutenant back then, was racing in one of the army yachts, and we all went out for one or two drinks afterwards, and some Bratwurst, if I remember. They've been the best of friends ever since.'

The General laughed. 'And since then, he's had this irritating habit of trying to tell me how to run my life.'

'It's sound advice, my friend.'

Oskar von Friedeburg rarely said anything that wasn't of significance.

'I have dealings every day with the National Socialists,' the wealthy businessman continued. 'In my position I have no option, but I agree with the captain. They do have the drive and the ideas to lift this country out of the mess it's in, and although some of their methods and beliefs are not to our taste, we may have to live with them for the greater good. It was almost inevitable once Adolf Hitler was elected the leader of the National Socialists.'

'It wasn't as clear-cut as that,' the General retorted. 'The attempted coup of 1923, the famous Beer Hall Putsch, failed, and the party had to regroup, and start again.' Franz could see the vein in his father's neck engorge as he spoke.

He'd heard his father talk about Hitler and the National Socialist Party before, and wished he weren't quite so fervent. He and his classmates at school were all members of *Hitlerjugend*. He smiled. Being part of the Hitler Youth movement gave them all so many opportunities; the association even had a national sailing team and there were hundreds of activities and visits to go on. One of the best had been attending a rally Adolf Hitler himself had spoken at, and they'd all found the party leader mesmerising.

He hadn't risked telling his father that he'd been chosen as part of the Hitlerjugend sailing team, and that their first competitive race would take place during this year's Kieler Woche, whose races attracted boats from all over the world.

'I mean,' the General conceded, 'they have done a remarkable job; they came from nowhere to be the second-biggest party in Germany in the 1930 elections. They did remarkably well in the Federal elections last year, and they may win the coming elections in mid-March. As a German patriot, I cannot go against their policies where they're aimed at making Germany a world leader again and giving her citizens a chance to prosper. But there are things about them that don't sit well with me.'

The old admiral leaned towards his son. 'Why don't you give these people a chance. Nearly everyone I know is a supporter of the National Socialists or at least they're willing to wait and see what the buggers are going to do.'

The General thought for a few seconds and, seeing their concerned faces, relented.

'I'll say nothing more. I'll wait and see what happens after the elections. After all, I may be overreacting.'

'That would be wise, my friend.'

Canaris nodded, pleased that they had succeeded, at least in part, in persuading his friend to be a little more circumspect.

There was a chorus of agreement from the others. A sense of relief flooded the room and Erich Kästner realised that all of them, apart from maybe his son, had spoken together before deciding that they needed to intervene.

~~o~~

'Mama, why are we Jewish?'

Miriam tried to keep her voice as matter of fact as she could.

'Ruth, you know why. We're all descended from Jacob who was also named Israel. That's why we sometimes call ourselves the children of Israel. Why do you ask? Has one of the others been teasing you?'

'No, Mama. I heard a lady speaking when I was hiding. Will we be able to always live here? I like it, staying with the Kästners.'

'You shouldn't eavesdrop on people; it's rude. And anyway, you've probably picked it up wrong.'

'No, I was hiding from Johann. He was *It*. I was behind the curtains in the big front room. The woman said that we'd have to move, or Franz couldn't marry Lise.'

Miriam stiffened. As Ruth described what she'd overheard, it took all her strength of will to keep anger away from her voice.

'Don't you worry, we are staying right here. Your father and I need to look after the Kästners, who are wonderful people, but they have such a big house that they need lots of help. The General is a terribly important man, so no one is going to tell us to move. The best thing for you to do is not to listen to idle gossip, Bubbeleh.'

'All right, Mama.' The little girl still looked unsure, but Miriam knew that Ruth trusted her, and loved being called by her favourite pet name.

'Can you read me a story?'

'Not tonight, Chamudah. It's terribly late.'

She wrapped her arms around her daughter and kissed her forehead.

'Goodnight.'

'Goodnight, Mama.'

~~o~~

The General hugged Wilhelm Canaris at the doorway. He was the last guest to leave.

'You're going to miss the big one,' Canaris said, the alcohol imbuing his words with great gravitas, at least in his judgement.

'You think there will be another war?'

'Not right away. We're not ready. But Germany must be great again. And they won't be

26

able to live with that.'

'I'm not sure I'd want to be involved in another war. You forget I was in the worst of places in the last one.'

He hadn't meant to be harsh. Wilhelm Canaris had acquitted himself well in the conflict and had captained a submarine for the last year of the war, but both knew that the battlefields of France sowed the seeds of countless nightmares for those who survived the hell of its trenches.

'My friend, war *is* coming, and there will be a place for you, though maybe not on the front line. In a few days, someone will call on you. Listen to what they say, that's all I ask.'

With a flourish, he doffed his cap and turned sharply, almost falling over, and marched down the driveway to his waiting car.

CHAPTER 3

Memo: Geh.KdoS. ABW 28/01/33 CAC0103.3

For Attention Only: General der Infanterie Kurt von Hammerstein-Equord, Chef der Heeresleitung

From: Captain Conrad Patzig, Chef der Abwehr.

Further to Memo ABW24/01/33CAC103.2, Captain Canaris spoke with General Kästner but gave him no details of the appointment to be offered. The Captain reports that General Kästner would be open to an approach and that he has been told to expect contact from us. He confirms that the General's loyalty would always be to the armed forces. [END]

~~o~~

Memo: Geh.KdoS. ABW 28/01/33 CAC0103.4

For Attention Only: Captain Conrad Patzig, Chef der Abwehr

From: General der Infanterie Kurt von Hammerstein-Equord, Chef der Heeresleitung

Contact with General Kästner should be made as soon as possible, preferably tomorrow. I have inspected his Reichsheer record and concur that he would be the most suitable candidate. Please inform him that he is to be commissioned at his current rank of General and at the same pay grade. He will be nominally based at the Heer Barracks in Stadtheide, near Plön, in Schleswig-Holstein, but I expect that he will spend most of his time in Kiel, with a monthly or bi-monthly visit to Berlin. [END]

~~o~~

[29/01/1933 Sunday]

General Kästner awoke early, as always. The habit stretched back to his days at military school where reveille sounded at 0630 and bunk inspections took place at seven.

His wife lay on for a further hour after he rose, as she often did, but as soon as he went downstairs, he realised, as usual, that the house had stirred before he had. From the kitchen, he could hear Miriam filling the kettle and Yosef stoking the range with wood, preparing for breakfast. When he entered his study, he noticed that the fire had already been cleaned and backed-up, ready to light. He was tempted to set a match to it, but he knew that Yosef and Miriam would disapprove of him doing one of the tasks they saw as their own.

He sauntered through to the kitchen, wondering as ever how he had come to be so lucky to own the Drachensee house. Having been brought up in it, he knew it intimately, and loved it for the happiness it had brought him and his family throughout his life.

'Guten Morgen, Miriam, Yosef, another fine winter day,' he said as he entered the kitchen.

'Guten Morgen, General,' the Nussbaums chorused, smiling at him as they always did; their love and devotion to his family and the house was the other reason his home was such a pleasant one to live in. His only regret was that he had spent so much of his adult life away from it, for large tracts of the Great War, and on frequent postings since then, but he knew that he was now home for good and was prepared to enjoy it.

'Some breakfast, General?' Miriam asked.

'That would be lovely, Miriam, and I wonder if you could take some up to Maria around eight o'clock. She deserves breakfast after such a tiring day yesterday.'

There was a glint of mischief in the General's eyes. He knew that Miriam and Yosef had slept little more than five hours themselves, but it was a sign of how highly he regarded them that he could make a joke of it.

Miriam smiled. She prepared a tray and left it on the dresser, whispering to Yosef when he entered the kitchen not to let her forget it when the time came.

The General sat at the table and motioned for the Nussbaums to join him. If Maria had been down, they would have had breakfast in the dining room with the children, but more often than not, he sat with the Nussbaums, discussing the needs of the house for the day, and catching up on how they and their family were faring.

He sipped his coffee and buttered a slice of the freshly baked bread Miriam had made that morning.

'Thank you both for your help yesterday. The food and the service were wonderful, and all of our guests enjoyed the evening immensely.'

'Thank you, sir,' Miriam replied. 'It was quite a party. Very much like the old days.'

He thought about it. There had been fewer of these events in recent years. Perhaps they should throw big parties more often, like they did in the early years of his marriage to Maria.

A bell rang. At first, he thought it was Maria ringing for something. Most of the rooms in the house had bell pulls that rang on the board high up on the kitchen wall, but the small brass arm for the master bedroom lay flat and, instead, the indicator for the front door had tripped.

When he got up to see who was at the door, Miriam told him that her husband had already gone to answer it.

'Are we expecting any deliveries? It's early for visitors.'

'The grocery order will be here this morning, but it is usually closer to lunchtime, and Herr Hessner always brings his delivery to the back door.'

Footsteps echoed in the hall outside and the kitchen door opened. Yosef appeared.

'General, there is a Captain Conrad Patzig wishing to speak with you. I took the liberty of seating him in the drawing room. He gave me this for you.'

Yosef handed the General a small white card, which he read.

Captain Conrad Patzig
Chef der Abwehr
Berlin 23477

Canaris. Last night. So, this is the contact.

'Yosef, I will see Captain Patzig in my study. Please show him in there in five minutes.'

He considered putting on his dress uniform but realised the absurdity of such a gesture at this time in the morning. He threw on a tweed jacket and glanced at himself in the mirror of the small bathroom under the stairs. He berated himself for fussing, but he knew that it mattered.

He was sitting at his desk when Yosef showed Captain Patzig into the study. He rose from his chair, and walked over to the door, shaking the captain's hand, and guided him to a chair on the opposite side of the desk from his.

'Captain Patzig, can Yosef get you something? A coffee, perhaps? It is a little early for something stronger.' He smiled.

'Herr General, a coffee would be most welcome. I travelled overnight from Berlin.'

'My dear man, would you like to freshen up first? You must be exhausted. Have you eaten?'

'Thank you. My wife made me some sandwiches for the journey. A cup of coffee would be fine.'

Yosef took the captain's coat and left to organise the coffee.

The General waited until Yosef had closed the door after him, then turned to the man opposite him.

'So, Captain, what can I do for you?'

The man cleared his throat.

'I believe Captain Canaris spoke with you?'

'Yes, it was just last night, in fact. He vaguely mentioned about my being contacted about a proposal of some sort, at some point. I wasn't expecting it to be so soon.'

'Yes, sorry about that. It's just that the pace of events is moving so fast, and I was told to try and see you as soon as possible. Did Captain Canaris give any details of why we wished to speak to you?'

'No, he didn't even say who you were, or which organisation you represented. How is he involved?'

'Oh, he's not directly involved, but he is well known within the Abwehr; he has done intelligence work with the Reichsmarine on and off for a long time, although he currently has a naval command. We knew that you and he were acquaintances and thought that it would be useful if he sounded you out before we made a formal approach.'

'And if I weren't interested, I would never need to know anything about whatever it is you are proposing.' The General smiled.

'Quite. In our line of business, we do not advertise.'

They were interrupted by a knock on the door. Yosef entered and placed a tray with two steaming cups of coffee on the desk.

'I thought you might like another cup of coffee too, General.' He turned to the visitor. 'There's milk and sugar should you need it, Captain Patzig'

'That's excellent. Danke.' *Thank you.*

'Will that be all, sir?' Yosef asked.

'Yes, Yosef, please see that we are not disturbed.'

He waited until Yosef had left.

'So, Captain, you were saying? I hope you do not wish me to become a spy!' He laughed.

The younger man smiled, but the General wasn't sure that the smile reached his eyes.

'No, it's not an espionage role, sir. We feel it is something you are uniquely qualified, or should I say, suitable for.'

'I'm intrigued now. As far as I know my only qualification is the ability to lead men, in battle or on the barrack square.'

'We are not going to ask you to do that. I'm sure Germany is grateful for all your service in command. What we are looking for is a man with a deep understanding of the Reichsheer, but who can also relate well with the commanders of the Reichsmarine. We need someone who can liaise on the Abwehr's behalf, at a local level in Kiel, with both arms of the military, and possibly the Luftwaffe when we develop an air force.'

The General tried to hide his surprise. His job in recent years had been more and more confined to a desk, so that aspect of the position he was being offered did not concern him.

And it had always been part of his daily remit to be, at times, a diplomat, but he was perplexed as to why the Abwehr thought that he would be suitable for a job that involved nursing egos and dealing with entrenched attitudes across the two services.

He didn't speak for a while and the young captain, to his credit, did not attempt to interrupt his thoughts.

'I'd need to know much more about this proposal of yours,' he said, breaking his silence, 'but it's rather unfair of me to expect you to continue without some breakfast and, if you'd rather rest first, I would completely understand.'

'General, I would appreciate a quick bite to eat but I have no need of a rest. I will do that when I return to Berlin after our meeting. These are new and exciting times, and Germany is moving forward rapidly. I am quite prepared to make the odd small sacrifice to facilitate this.'

'In that case, if you'd like to use my bathroom first, I will have some food made ready for you.' He got up and showed his visitor where to freshen up.

He spoke to Miriam, who set the table in the dining room and, with remarkable efficiency, produced a meal of bread, cheese, ham and sliced sausage by the time the captain was shown in. The General accepted a small plate from Miriam, to put the captain at his ease, and they continued their conversation as they ate.

'I'm interested, especially as you stated that the appointment would be in the Kiel area. I have no wish to spend time away from home if it can be avoided.'

'You would be nominally posted to the nearest Reichsheer barracks, which will almost certainly be at the Stadtheide camp in Plön. You would spend no more than one morning a week there, if needed, but we would expect that the Reichsmarine would supply you some sort of office facility at their headquarters in Kiel which would function as your main base.'

'That would make sense. Most of the naval people I would be dealing with are stationed here.'

'Most of your work will be with Kriegsmarine personnel. We have people in place who liaise with the army command, in Berlin and at our regional bases. No more than once each month, you would be expected to attend a meeting of the Abwehr executive in Berlin. For logistical reasons, this would involve an overnight stay in the capital. I can vouch for the inadvisability of trying to travel there and back in one day,' the captain said, with a wry smile.

Perhaps he did have a sense of humour.

'That wouldn't be too onerous. What would my rank be, and who would I report to?'

Captain Patzig flushed slightly.

'You would retain your current rank. At present, I am the head of the Abwehr. I'm a Kapitän zur See, but I report directly to the Chief of Defence, General Kurt von Hammerstein-Equord.'

The General raised an eyebrow.

'That could be a little awkward, couldn't it.'

'Not if you can live with it.'

The young man has balls, the General thought.

'General Kästner, if it's easier for you, just think of General von Hammerstein-Equord as your superior, and me as his adjutant.'

'The awkwardness was not on my part, Captain. I just wondered how you would deal with it, and if others might find it a little strange. I can see how a position like this one might throw up some unusual command-chain issues. I can assure you it will never be a problem for me.'

'Thank you, General. If you need to throw your weight about at any time, you might be better using General von Hammerstein-Equord's authority.'

He paused and looked at the General.

'So, you agree to join us then, sir?'

'I should probably consider it for twenty-four hours and consult my wife but I'm sure it will make no difference so, yes, I will take the commission.'

Captain Patzig got to his feet and beamed.

'That's great, sir. I'm delighted. Welcome on board.'

General Kästner wondered if he'd misjudged the young captain. Genuine pleasure showed on the man's face that his offer had been accepted.

'Very apt, Captain,' he said, standing and shaking his hand.

'Apt, sir?'

'Yes, just a navy pun, Captain. On board.'

'Of course, sir.' He laughed, perhaps in deference to his rank. The General wondered how their relationship would work. For some reason, the captain seemed to hold him in some regard. Although the Abwehr was a small component in an army that was a mere shadow of

31

its former self, it must have taken a large slice of bravado for a captain to have put himself forward for the job of running its intelligence organisation. In the coming weeks and months, it would be interesting to see if the younger man would be able to dish out commands to the General, as if their respective ranks were reversed.

'In the short term, you will receive communications directly to your home until we can sort out your office in Kiel. In the meantime, I will send orders for you to report to the barracks in Plön. That should happen over the next few days. You can requisition any equipment you need there, and a staff car and driver will be assigned to you. I will arrange for the driver to take you there tomorrow or Tuesday.'

The General was amused by the speed of it all, and a little surprised.

Is there something going on that I've missed?

'I have your number,' he said. 'I will telephone if I have any more questions. Are you sure you do not wish to stay and head back to Berlin tomorrow morning? Or even this evening? You should get at least a few hours' sleep.'

'Thank you, sir, but I need to be back by tonight. Thanks again for your offer.'

The captain handed the General a sheaf of forms; confirmation of commission, pay office, Staatsgeheimnisse declaration and pension deferment. He signed them and showed Captain Patzig out, shaking hands with him again on the doorstep.

'Captain, if you don't mind me asking, why were you so keen to have me for the job?'

'Well, sir, it's your record. One of the best in the Reichsheer, and you have an Iron Cross, from the Great War, I believe. And you were available.'

The General smiled. *Was that a mild put-down?*

'Yes, but that doesn't qualify me for this job. Army liaison officer, yes, but not this.'

'I suppose so, sir, but your father was an admiral, and you've lived in Kiel all your life. You know all the top people in the Reichsmarine and, more importantly, they know you.'

The General nodded. *At least the man was honest.*

The captain saluted.

The General returned his salute and closed the door, turning to see his wife standing at the foot of the stairs, arms folded.

~~o~~

Memo: Geh.KdoS. ABW 29/01/33 CAC0103.5

For Attention Only: General der Infanterie Kurt von Hammerstein-Equord, Chef der Heeresleitung

From: Captain Conrad Patzig, Chef der Abwehr.

Further to Memo ABW24/01/33CAC103.4 I have approached General Kästner and I can confirm that he has accepted the commission with the Abwehr. I did not inform General Kästner that Captain Canaris had also been considered for the position. [END]

CHAPTER 4

[30/01/1933 Monday]

The driver held the door open for the General.

'There is a briefcase on the seat, sir. Captain Patzig thought you might be able to go through the papers on your way to Plön.'

He smiled. *Handing out orders to a General was perhaps not an issue after all for Captain Patzig.*

He glanced up at the house. Maria stood on the steps and waved, as if he were a child setting off for his first day at school. The Nussbaums stood behind her. He gave the expected wave and told his driver to get under way.

Before he opened the briefcase, he closed his eyes and thought about his wife.

She'd calmed down faster than he'd expected. He thought the only thing that annoyed her about it was the fact that he hadn't spoken with her first and that, deep down, she had been dreading the thought of him not working. He just wasn't the type to tend to the garden, or fish in the lake. In the summer, there would be sailing, but what would he do in the winter?

When she found out that he would be based in Kiel, she came round to the idea far quicker than he'd expected and had his dress uniforms laid out for Miriam to launder, even though they'd been washed and ironed only a few days before.

He opened the flap on the briefcase. He removed an envelope and a sheaf of memos and sat the briefcase down at his feet.

The envelope was addressed to him and had been stamped with the letters *Geh.KdoS.* He'd received correspondence marked with the *Secret Command* designation on countless occasions during his army career, so he broke the seal knowing it was intended for him alone. It contained a note from Captain Patzig. As the car sped along Hamburger Chaussee towards the centre of Kiel, he started reading.

General Kästner,

A couple of things I didn't mention yesterday. Once you arrive at Plön, you will be assigned an office in the barracks. We wouldn't advise you to retain any documents there; for accessibility, all files would be better kept at your office in Kiel. However, you may find the room useful for any meetings with your Reichsheer contacts, away from Kiel and the prying eyes of the Reichsmarine.

The General smiled. It was obvious that Captain Patzig had immersed himself in the Abwehr, distancing himself from his former naval colleagues. He continued reading.

I would suggest that you keep at least one member of staff permanently based in Plön to keep communications with the Army open.

As I stated, your main base will be in Kiel, within the Naval HQ building on Düsternbrooker Weg. You are to meet with a Lieutenant Bauer at 17:00 today. He will show you the office space they have put aside for you. Let me know if you consider it suitable. I have arranged a secretary for you. Frau Helene Müller. She will report to you tomorrow at 09:00.

The General supposed that the Lieutenant Bauer he was to meet was Heinz Bauer, the son of a former Korvette Kapitän, who was an acquaintance of his. The boy had even sailed on the General's yacht, on a day trip to Eckernförde a few years before.

As the car swung right onto Hummelwiese, crossed the main railway tracks, and passed the southern end of Kieler Hafen, the General's eyes returned to the captain's note.

```
You asked yesterday why we wanted you for the position. I gave
you the reasons. There was one more argument for wanting you,
above others, for this position. For reasons that will become
clear, your reservations when discussing Herr Hitler and his
National Socialist Party have been noted and were a factor in
your inclusion on our shortlist.

Please read the enclosed memos. I'm afraid there are rather a
lot of them and, although they are not all relevant to the
execution of your task, they will help to brief you on the
current position of the German Military and the Abwehr in
particular.

I have also enclosed a book. Read it at your leisure. You may
find it insightful.

Conrad Patzig, Captain
```

The General looked out of the window. They had passed through Gaarden on Preetzer Chaussee, and were now leaving the outskirts of Kiel, heading towards Preetz itself, twenty kilometres to the south. The flat, rather monotonous landscape of hedge-lined fields and small remnants of forest flew past, and the General glanced into the open briefcase. There was a brown package that he assumed was the book, but he turned first to the memos.

Patzig was right. There were piles of them. They were in date order, and he thumbed his way through them, assimilating the information they contained with ease. It was something he had been doing all his life.

Troop and ship movements; weapon, vehicle and equipment testing and roll-out; new commissions; significant political events; foreign intelligence. Some he'd seen already, in the final days before he retired from active service; most were new to him and were much more specific to his current role. As he neared the end of the bundle, he realised they were almost at Preetz, where the landscape would become a little less dull.

He picked up the last one, dated that morning and realised the significance of it at once.

Memo: Geh.KdoS. ABW 30/1/33 CAC0119.1

For Attention Only: All senior executive officers, Abwehr.

From: Captain Conrad Patzig, Chef der Abwehr.

```
President Hindenburg has appointed Adolf Hitler, Chancellor of
Germany, and the head of a coalition government of "National
Renewal". The National Socialist German Workers' Party
(Nationalsozialistische Deutsche Arbeiterpartei; NSDAP) and the
German Nationalist People's Party (Deutschnationale
Volkspartei; DNVP) are members of the coalition.

I feel that this is another step on the road to a National
Socialist Government. No action required. [END]
```

He had expected it might happen, but it still came as a shock. He prayed that Germany would not regret the ailing president's decision.

He put the note back in the envelope and replaced it, with the memos, in the briefcase. He reached in and extracted the book. He opened the packet, and a frown crossed his face when he saw the title. He wondered if it were some kind of test, to see his reaction.

He glanced at the driver's eyes in the soldier's rear-view mirror, but they were locked on the road as they approached the centre of Preetz.

He opened the book, a copy of *Mein Kampf*, by Adolf Hitler, Germany's new chancellor, and looked at the inscription inside the front cover, partly obscured by the dust cover.

He folded it back and read Captain Patzig's words.

You should read this, to know what we are dealing with.

CHAPTER 5

Yosef watched his wife through the kitchen window. She was washing the breakfast dishes and stacking them away before she started preparing the evening meal. Frau Kästner was attending a lunch with the Ladies' Guild, and the children were all at school; the older Kästner children would be gone all week, and Antje and their own children wouldn't be home until four o'clock, so there were no lunches to prepare. He supposed that, after all the routine cleaning was completed, she would catch up on the sewing and darning jobs that had built up over the last few weeks.

As he washed the Kästner family car, a gleaming Mercedes-Benz sedan which was a joy to drive, he wondered what was bothering Miriam. He finished hosing the vehicle down and, while it dried off, he cleaned his feet on the mat, mindful of Miriam's kitchen, and opened the door.

'I hope your feet are clean.'

'Yes, dear, I've just wiped them on the doormat. May I come in?'

She wasn't in the mood for humour.

'Of course you can. What a silly question. What do you want?'

He said nothing for a few seconds.

'Something is bothering you. You've not been yourself since we got up this morning.'

'I'm fine,' she snapped, but her face softened when she looked at him. 'It's nothing.'

'If it were nothing, you wouldn't be walking around with all the *Tsuris* in the world sitting on your shoulders.'

He saw her smile at his use of the Yiddish word for 'worries'. They rarely spoke Hebrew or Yiddish now, outside of their weekly outing to the synagogue on the Shabbat.

The General wouldn't have minded, he thought; as boys, he had taught Erich Kästner all the swear words in Yiddish, which he sometimes muttered under his breath, just out of his wife's hearing.

Frau Kästner wouldn't have been so comfortable with us conversing in a foreign language.

'Ach, it was just something Ruth said last night,' Miriam said. 'It meant nothing, but it upset her.'

'Did one of the boys tease her? They don't mean anything by it, I'm sure. They are terribly fond of our two.'

'No, it wasn't one of the children. She overheard two of the guests speaking at the party last night. She was hiding in the drawing room behind the curtains, playing a game. They didn't realise she was there.'

'Let me guess. The Kästner children shouldn't mix with the servant's brats. It's not the first time we've heard that one. We explained to Ruth that not every family is like the Kästners.'

She said nothing. He turned to her, a furrow on his brow. She looked away.

'What?' he asked, touching her gently on her arm.

'Yes, they said that our children shouldn't have been there last night, but it wasn't just because they were the children of domestic staff... it was more.'

Yosef sighed, and his shoulders slumped. 'It's not the first time. You know they've both had comments at school. It's part of being a Jew, I'm afraid.'

'But this is the first time they've had it here, at home.'

'Miriam, this isn't our home.'

'You know what I mean,' she said, slamming the cutlery drawer shut. He just got his fingers out of the way in time.

'I'll have a word with her. She needs to learn about real life, and how to deal with it. She'll come across worse than that when she's older.'

36

She turned her back to him. Surprised, he reached out to touch her. They almost never fought.

'Don't be angry. We're Jews. People don't always like us, but we've always lived with that.'

She turned back to him. He could see she was struggling to hold back tears. He took both of her hands.

'This isn't like you. Has something else happened?'

'Ruth asked me if we would have to leave here soon. I didn't know what to say.'

'Why would she say that? There's no reason to suppose we'd ever need to move from here. The Kästners have always been more than happy with the way we look after the house. Has Frau Kästner complained?'

'No, no. She never has anything but praise for what we do.'

'Who was it, then? The colonel's wife? They say she's a tyrant with her staff. I'm surprised you would take any notice.'

'Yosef, it was Frau Böhm. She said that maybe Lise and Franz shouldn't be going out together while the Kästners associated with Jews or had people like us in their house.' A few sobs escaped with the last of her words.

Yosef was shocked. The Böhms, from the house next door, were frequent visitors to the Kästner home. All the children played down at the lakeside together, and the two families spent at least one evening a week in each other's company or played tennis at the club. The Böhms and the Kästners even went sailing together from time to time, although the Nussbaums were never included in those outings, other than to pack the hampers for each trip.

'Are you sure? Frau Böhm has never said anything that would make me imagine she would be like that.'

'Ruth was sure. She was talking to Frau Hoffmann. Her husband is the deputy mayor. She wasn't that much better, by Ruth's account but they were both as nice as you like when Frau Kästner was talking to them. They spoke to me when I poured their drinks. It must have been just after they'd said these nasty things. They're two-faced...'

Yosef watched her struggle. As Jews, they'd been taught from a young age to turn the other cheek and not to respond to people like Frau Böhm and Frau Hoffmann.

'There has been, and there always will be, some people who hate us. We're as much a part of this country as anyone, so we're going nowhere,' he said. 'And anyway, the General wouldn't stand for anyone trying to tell us that we had to move.'

'I know, but those horrible National Socialist people, they seem to want to stir things up. Their thugs, the ones with the brown uniforms, started a riot in Altona last year, and Hamburg was never like that. A little rough around the docks, maybe, but Uncle Toder, Tante Rahel's husband, had a shop there. Never a bit of bother until then. He sold it after that. Moved to Cuxhaven.'

'It's all a flash in the pan. Herr Hitler won't last long in office. The people will see through him.'

He paused and gave a little smile.

'That being said, perhaps they shouldn't get rid of him before he sorts the unemployment levels and the railways out and deals with the communists from Russia who're always looking over our shoulders.'

The joke fell flat. Miriam shook her head.

'It's not funny. There has been a change of mood.'

'Well, all right, there have been one or two incidents, but most people are horrified.'

'Yosef, they set off a bomb in the synagogue not long ago. Someone could have been killed.'

'Feh. It wasn't much more than a firecracker. It took less than a day to clear up the damage.'

'Nothing like this has ever happened before. Frau Aisikmann says it has got steadily worse since all these new Jews have moved to Kiel from Poland, and the Ukraine.'

'Now, Miriam. That isn't like you at all. You know they had to come here. If you think we have problems, you should talk to them. They had a hard time of it. The worst.'

'I know, I'm sorry. But they don't try and fit in. It's as if they go out of their way to be different from anyone else.'

'They're just very pious. They're much stricter than we are. It's their way. Perhaps we should learn from them. They follow the teachings of the Torah better than we have ever done.'

She bowed her head.

Neither Yosef nor she was deeply religious, but they observed the Shabbat and all the holy days as far as they could and, although their diet was not always strictly kosher, they avoided flagrant digressions from it. They worked Saturdays, but only until ten. Most of the congregation at the synagogue did the same.

Yosef smiled. *How else would a shopkeeper or a doctor make a living?*

'I try to see things their way,' Miriam said, 'but they make no effort to do the same. Sometimes it feels that they are looking down on us.'

'People are all different. We have our ways and they have theirs. I mean, I was speaking to a group of them last Shabbat, after *Shacharit.* They all wish to go back to their homes one day, or to Palestine.'

'If they don't want to be here, they should go now,' she snapped, 'then they might appreciate Kiel more. I don't hear of any German Jews wanting to leave Germany for a barren desert thousands of miles away.'

'Well, there are one or two youngsters who have become ardent Zionists, but you're right, they are the exception. I admire their bravery, but for myself, I'm happy here, where we belong.'

A tentative smile crossed Miriam's face.

He knew she thought of him as her rock but, for him, his wife was the stronger of the two, and her fierce loyalty to her loved ones, including the Kästners, always humbled him.

'I'll speak with Ruth,' he repeated. 'Everything will be all right, you'll see.'

CHAPTER 6

Lieutenant Bauer was indeed the young man the General remembered being so enthusiastic on board *Schneegans*, the yacht the General had named after the snow geese that he'd seen once, on a trip to Norway.

'Heinz, my boy, so glad to see you, although I should probably stick with Lieutenant Bauer.' He snapped a salute at the young man who, caught by surprise, nearly poked out his eye in his hurry to return it.

'Sir, Heinz is fine, or Lieutenant, or Bauer, whatever you prefer. Welcome to the navy.'

He grinned, and the General couldn't help laughing.

'I should give you your proper title, Lieutenant. It might stop you being too familiar.'

'Yes, sir. I'll strive to be less familiar, sir.'

The General laughed again. He didn't mind a bit of banter between the ranks, providing it didn't get out of hand, and the lower orders knew when he was being serious.

'Your quarters, sir; they're this way.'

The young naval officer led him to a large second-floor office, comprising a large anteroom and, to General Kästner's astonishment, a bright and spacious corner room for him, with large windows facing onto Kieler Förde.

'Well, well. I wasn't expecting this. I was sure the navy would shoehorn me into a stationery cupboard in the basement, with a broken heater and one solitary light bulb. This is very impressive.'

'Sir, Rear Admiral von Heutschler died two weeks ago. They hadn't reallocated his office, so when the request came in from Berlin...'

'Right place at the right time. Poor old bugger. At least he died with his spurs on. Goodness, I was even at his funeral.'

'Yes, sir. I saw you there. I was going to say hello, but I was with the official pall-bearers, so I didn't manage to catch you before you left.'

'So, I don't even need to request furniture. Everything seems to be here. My secretary arrives tomorrow, I believe.'

The lieutenant couldn't meet his eye, and he could see a twitch at the corner of the young man's mouth.

'Sir, Frau Müller was the admiral's secretary, before he died.'

The General made an effort to keep his face straight, if for no other reason than to support the sterling effort the young man was making to do likewise. He changed the subject.

'How do I requisition supplies, etc, and where do I get coffee around here?'

'You just have to ask, sir. There is an officer's mess, but I'll make sure there are coffee-making facilities in your front office.'

'I'm still not sure why I'm getting this red-carpet treatment from the Reichsmarine. It's a tad worrying.'

'Sir, I can only tell you what I've heard. There was a bit of consternation about a senior Abwehr officer being assigned here, but once it was known that it was yourself who'd been commissioned, there was a bit of relief all round and it has been widely accepted as an excellent choice.'

'Ah, so they think I'm a soft touch, then?'

'No sir, I'm sure that's not the case. It was more the fact that most of them know you well, you have a working knowledge of the sea, and the problems the navy faces, and there's your father...'

'I hope I didn't receive any favouritism because of that old duffer. That's the reason I joined the army!'

They both laughed. The General shook the young lieutenant's hand.

'If there's anything you need, just come to me. My office is just along the corridor.'

The General walked over to the windows and looked out over the largest and the best natural harbour in Germany.

'What is that racket?' he asked.

The lieutenant stepped over to the one window that was open and closed it.

'Glockengeläut und Dankgottesdienste, sir. To celebrate Herr Hitler's appointment as chancellor. All the church bells in Germany are ringing, and they're expecting big crowds this evening at the thanksgiving services. Will you be going, sir?'

'I doubt I'll manage. I have a lot of work to get through if I'm going to get up to pace on this new job. I'm not as young as I used to be.'

'I'm sure you're still more than able, sir. I'm honoured to be of help. You do have quite a reputation, sir.'

'Thank you, but I just do a job, as I'm sure you do. How long are you going to be land-based?'

'I'm seconded to HQ for another six months. I hope that it's a return to sea for me after that.' He seemed delighted that the General had asked, and his desire to be back on board any type of ship was undeniable.

'Six months will soon pass. Make the most of your time ashore. Do you have a young lady?'

'I do. And you're right, sir. It won't be quite so easy when I'm posted away.'

'Right, you'd better be on your way. Get off to church and celebrate our new leader.'

'Oh no, sir. I have a date with my girlfriend. I'll stick to your advice and make the most of it. Good day, sir.'

He waltzed off and the General smiled, refreshed by the young sailor's exuberance and easy humour. He looked around his new workplace, with its plush seating, the large ornate desk, and the view.

Don't get carried away. You have a job to do. And this could get very, very interesting.

~~o~~

'Darling, I'm going to see less of you now than I did before. Must you go to your meeting tonight?'

He'd arrived home later than he'd have liked, dropped off by his Abwehr driver just as the family were sitting down for their evening meal.

'I have to go,' he said to Maria. 'They voted for me to be chairman when they heard I was retiring. I do enjoy the Rotary Club, and it does a lot of good for the local community. A bit like your Ladies' Guild, but without the backbiting.'

'Erich, really.'

Maria Kästner frowned.

'Antje,' she scolded, as her youngest daughter stifled a giggle, 'it's not funny.'

'Well, it's true,' the General said. 'Every time you come back, you complain about this one and that.'

She got up from the table and stomped through to the kitchen, muttering something about speaking with Miriam about the following day's meals.

He looked round at Antje. All his children loved having him home. He knew Maria was a marvellous mother, balancing softness and discipline, fun, and severity with a delicate touch, acknowledging the help she got from Miriam and Yosef, but he also knew that when he came home, the house was more alive.

The children, and Maria too, simply didn't know what would happen next. For the children, it made for a wonderful and exciting time. For Maria, the occasional sense of frustration was made worse by the ease with which he earned her forgiveness.

'I think I've upset your mother again.'

Antje giggled, out loud this time.

'I'd better go and butter her up,' he added.

40

He walked through to the kitchen and met Maria on the way out. He blocked her way and cajoled her into a waltz as he hummed a suitable tune, and the sternness in her face eased into a smile. He released her into the dining room, Antje making a face of disgust at her parents' overt display of affection.

The General continued to waltz, now on his own, towards the kitchen, his daughter's laughter following him as he spun.

He had a brief word with Yosef to arrange the car for the evening and headed upstairs to dress for his meeting.

CHAPTER 7

'Erich, now you have a new job. What have you done?'

He was the last but one to arrive at the Europäischer Hof, having sent Yosef home with instructions to return at eleven.

'I was approached to be a liaison officer between the Reichsmarine and the Reichswehr, based mainly in Kiel, and I keep my rank and pay. What would you have done?'

Uwe Müller, Kiel's deputy police chief, who'd asked the question, shrugged, and laughed.

'You have a point. But a desk job? Is that what you want? I thought you were a man of action.'

'Ach, to be honest, the last few years have been more and more office-based, or spent in one meeting after another. The further up the tree you get, the less time you get to spend on the ground.'

Uwe Müller laughed and twisted his ample moustache.

'I'm beginning to find that myself. Once Old Faithful retires, I'll apply for his job, but I suspect I'll be even more desk-bound than I am now.' He patted his ample gut. 'Not great for the figure, either.'

His friends grunted in sympathy, although none of them quite had the policeman's prodigious girth.

'You'll still manage your stint as chairman though?'

Eberhard Böhm, General Kästner's neighbour, had positioned himself as the General's right-hand man, doubtless in the hope that he would be given the chairman's job when his neighbour relinquished it. For the General it was a chore that he was willing to give his time to; for others, the attraction of it was the prestige and standing that came with it, which the General had no need for.

He reassured his friend that he would carry on in the position; because he was based in Kiel, the task shouldn't be beyond him.

Jürgen Hoffmann, the deputy-mayor, brought up the subject that was on everyone's mind.

'So old Hindenburg has given the chancellor's job to Adolf Hitler.'

He didn't seem disappointed.

'So it would seem,' the General said. 'We'll just have to wait and see what becomes of it. Surely he'll have to be more pragmatic and moderate some of his rhetoric.'

'I'm not sure,' Jürgen Hoffmann said. 'He seems to have caught the imagination of a significant part of the population. Especially amongst the unemployed and the poorly paid. They see him as their saviour. What do you think, Oskar?'

Erich Kästner always took careful note of Oskar von Friedeburg's opinion. He'd urged caution at the General's house, so his views on the latest developments were of interest to the Abwehr's latest recruit.

'He will want more power,' Oskar said, 'and he won't mind how he goes about it. Just remember to keep any criticism of the man or his party to yourselves or you might end up in Uwe's hotel.'

The men laughed. 'I can give you all single rooms,' the policeman joked.

'He has big ambitions,' the businessman continued, after the laughter had died down, 'and I don't think the world will find it easy to deal with him. I'm not saying he won't be good for Germany; it could be the exact opposite, but for some of us, it may take some adjustments.'

'Perhaps we need a politician like Adolf Hitler,' he said. 'I mean, the country is a mess, and the rest of Europe has stomped all over us for too long now. I say we give him a chance.'

'Would you join his party?'

He blushed at the General's question.

'You've joined already, Jürgen, haven't you?' The General had never been the politician's biggest admirer.

'I was forced to,' he blustered, 'The NSDAP are going to be the party of power, sooner rather than later, and if I wish to remain in my position and help the people of Kiel...' His voice trailed off.

'Ach, don't be too hard on Jürgen,' Oskar said. 'He has always had the good of the city in mind. We'll all have to give serious thought to joining the party. I'd be surprised if Uwe hasn't already joined. I hear there's been a stampede of policemen to the party offices in Gartenstraße.'

'Like Jürgen, I'm pragmatic,' Uwe Müller said. 'I just want to do my job. The chief joined and suggested that I should too. So now I'm a party member. It makes no difference to me what party is in power; they'll always need policemen.'

'What about you, Oskar? Are you going to jump on this bandwagon?'

'I may well do, General, but I haven't yet. All the public contracts in a year's time will go to party men, mark my words, and I do a lot of business with the state and central government. I hear stories of businesses, small and large, contributing to the NSDAP. My hand may be forced.'

The General suspected that Oskar von Friedeburg had a sneaking admiration for the new chancellor, and he said so.

'Think about it,' Oskar said. 'Here's a man who failed in an ill-conceived attempt to overthrow the legitimate government of this country then turned his trial for treason into a triumph of propaganda, with the prosecutor eating out of his hand and the judge practically joining his party at the end of the trial.'

'He only served eight months of a five-year sentence,' Uwe Müller interjected, 'and came out of prison as the most famous politician in Germany. That, after being found guilty of treason!'

The General shrugged. 'I won't be joining.'

'You're in a position to do that, Erich. It's not quite as simple for the rest of us,' Oskar said.

'I know. I'm sorry, friends. It's just that I don't like the man, and I'm a grumpy *alter Furz*.'

'A grumpy old fart. I'd find it hard to disagree.'

The voice came from behind the General. He spun round in his chair.

'Doc. Where have you been? We wondered if you were feeling ill.' He grinned at the tall, bearded man who faced him, and clasped his hand.

The other three greeted the new arrival. The full committee of the Kiel branch of the Rotary Club was now present.

'I'm very well. The members of the medical profession are a remarkable bunch, keeping us all so healthy.'

Doctor Speer, or 'Doc' to his friends, had a practice in Gaarden-Ost. Most of the patients he ministered to were manual workers and their families who lived in the clusters of houses surrounding the three large shipyards that lined the east shore of Kieler Hafen. The General and his family, and a selection of notables who lived in Kiel, also retained him as their doctor. He made no bones about the fact that these well-to-do patients subsidised the fees for the ones who could ill afford his services.

'Busy at the hospital?' the General asked. Doctor Speer worked three afternoons each week at the city's university hospital. The chronic shortage of doctors and the city's overstretched finances put pressure on family doctors to provide cover for hospital clinics and minor operations.

'Strange times,' he said. 'I removed a growth from a woman's foot today. It was much more involved than I expected; it should have really been done by a surgeon, but they are all busy beyond belief. If you'd told me five years ago that I would end up spending time in an operating theatre again, I would have questioned your sanity.'

43

'Brings back old memories, eh?' the General asked, rubbing his hand over the back of his head. The doctor had served in the same battalion as the General during the Great War and had seen uncountable horrors in the makeshift field hospitals of the Western Front. He'd removed a jagged piece of shrapnel from a young Major Kästner and, after the war, when the medic set up his plate in Kiel, one of the first patients to register at his practice was the same Erich Kästner, now a colonel. They had been the best of friends since.

'Ha, you're not going to say it still hurts, are you?'

The General took his hand away from the scar that ran from the back of his left ear to the bottom of his hairline.

'No, but I always like to remember it's there. Makes me realise how lucky I was.'

The Doc put his hand on his friend's shoulder.

'When I saw that clear fluid oozing out from your skull, do you know what I said to the nurse?'

Oskar von Friedeburg interrupted with a groan.

'We know. *Another vegetable for the plot.*'

Doctor Speer and the General laughed.

'Old men and our stories. I think we're boring these three with our war tales, Doc.'

'As old soldiers do, General. We've earned the right, though, for the odd reminiscence.' He paused.

'I fear it might happen again.'

'Not you too, Doc. The General here has been all gloom and doom about Herr Hitler. Give the man a chance.'

The Doc shook his head.

'I don't like all this nationalistic vitriol. It worries me. I'm as patriotic as the next man, but the National Socialist's agenda doesn't sit well with this old soldier.'

He sat down heavily in the chair Oskar von Friedeburg had fetched for him, the others shuffling theirs around to make space.

'Anyway, enough of politics. We have plans to make.'

Eberhard Böhm pulled a pad from the briefcase by his feet and began to take notes. For the next hour, they finalised the schedule for the remaining Rotary meetings and made a start on the plans for their main fundraising event of the summer, which took place during Kieler Woche, one of the biggest sailing regattas in the world.

The Rotary Club ran a fun stall during the race days and organised the event-opening parade of cars that locals decorated with flowers, collecting donations from the crowd as the procession crawled along the sea front, on Hindenburgufer, then Düsternbrooker Weg, from the Bellevue Hotel to Bootshafen. Entries were up this year and the Rotary Club charged for each one, in addition to the monies raised from the spectators.

By the time Yosef returned to collect the General, the group had long finished their task and had settled down with the familiar comfortable blend of anecdotes and gossip, lubricated with moderate quotas of Schnapps or beer and, in the General's case, malt whisky.

Constitutional issues didn't feature again, as if there was a tacit agreement between them that there was more than enough tension in the current political climate to risk a rift within the group.

~~o~~

Settling into the seat, Jürgen Hoffman scowled as the car sped along the deserted Kiel streets.

As Kiel's mayor-in-waiting, he was adept at sitting on the fence on most issues and going with the populist trend. The rise of the National Socialists had caught him by surprise, and he hoped the people of Kiel had forgotten the scathing remarks he'd made about the party, and their leader, at the time of the Beer Hall Putsch, when he was just a young council member sitting in the Rathaus.

It was nearly ten years ago, after all.

44

He wondered if he could remove a few issues of the local newspapers from the town archives, just to be on the safe side.

It's all right for Erich Kästner. I have to work with these people.

CHAPTER 8

The car rolled to a halt, the gravel crunching under the wheels. The General, perfectly able to exit the car under his own steam, waited until the car door was opened for him, knowing that it pleased Yosef to do it.

He entered the silent house; everyone else was asleep, and he made his way to the kitchen. Miriam had left a light supper for him should he be hungry when he returned. He poured himself a cup of coffee from the pot sitting on the range and sat at the table. Yosef entered by the back door, having parked the car in the garage, annexed to the servant's cottage ten metres from the main house.

'Rest your legs, Yosef,' the General said. 'Have a coffee with me.'

'Yes, sir. That would be most welcome.'

They sat for a minute, enjoying the quiet solidity of the old house.

'The events of today, sir, they are worrying.'

The General shrugged.

'I don't know, Yosef, if I'm being honest, but it does make me somewhat uneasy. I'm hoping it is just a brief aberration, that the German people will see the National Socialists for what they are. Herr Hitler has limited power for now; it is a coalition government, after all.'

Yosef hesitated for a second.

'I'm not so sure, sir. He seems to be garnering support.'

The General sighed.

'The thing is, Yosef, people are disillusioned. Unemployment is soaring, living conditions are worse than ever and our politicians are indecisive and do nothing but bicker and prevaricate. We are being bled dry and treated as pariahs by the rest of the world and our armed forces are emasculated. Is it any wonder that people see him as some sort of saviour?'

'Do you support him, sir?' There was an edge to Yosef's voice.

The General tried not to flinch.

'No, Yosef, I don't. But I can see the reasons why people might.'

'All I know, sir, is that this country has changed. Maybe it's not so bad in Kiel, but all over Germany Jewish people and other minorities are feeling terribly vulnerable; verbal abuse, physical violence and discrimination are all on the increase. And the National Socialists are stoking the fires.'

The General shook his head. 'It's not that bad surely? It's just rhetoric.'

Yosef's voice was cold and flat.

'People have been forced to move, businesses have been targeted, why, even my own children come home from school with stories of bullying and name-calling.'

The General was surprised at Yosef's anger.

'There was always a bit of it at school. Look how often we got into fights when we were at school over that sort of thing.'

'Yes, when there were comments made, you fought on my side, but I was the one the taunts were directed at, and I learned to live with them. This is different, somehow. It's more widespread and organised, and it is being legitimised by people who are now in power.'

The General's uneasiness about Hitler's rise to power had in the main been based on the man's expansionist views and his intimidating and abrasive style, but he hadn't given enough consideration to the other aspects of his politics and principles.

'Is it really that bad, Yosef?'

'Sir,' said Yosef, with a resigned bitterness, 'it even happens in your own house.'

The General stared at him, a frown creasing his brow.

Yosef told him what Ruth had overheard.

As the General listened, his face coloured, and his mouth pursed in a thin, straight line.

'Beate Böhm,' he said. 'I find it hard to believe.'

Yosef stiffened.

'Ruth wasn't lying, sir,' he said. 'She wouldn't do that.'

The General shook his head.

'No, no. I didn't mean it like that. I just find it hard to get my head around it. There's no chance Ruth could have picked it up wrong, or misinterpreted it?'

'Sir, there wasn't much to misinterpret. And she repeated the conversation to her mother, then to me. It was identical both times.'

'I'm so sorry she had to hear that, and that you and Miriam are having to deal with it. That woman will never be in my house again.'

'Sir, that would be impractical. You have to work with Herr Böhm at the Rotary Club, and what do you tell Frau Kästner?'

He had to concede that Yosef was right but doing nothing did not sit well with him. He considered telling Franz to have nothing to do with Lise Böhm, but that would be unfair if he liked the girl. On the other hand, did Franz have a right to know? What had been a German problem up until now had become an unforeseen Kästner problem.

'When you say Ruth and Manny are being subjected to insults and ill treatment, I hope none of my children are the culprits.'

'No sir, they would never do that. In fact, Franz and Johann pulled a couple of boys up for calling Ruth and Manny *Yids* at the park, a few weeks ago. Kicked their backsides, from what I was told.' He smiled.

The silence between them grew, the General trying to come to terms with the small-mindedness and cruelty of people that he thought he knew.

'Sir, there's one more thing. I hate to ask, but…'

'Go on, Yosef.'

'Well, what Frau Böhm said. Is there any truth in it?'

The General felt his face burn.

'How can you ask that? Of course there's no truth in it. You and Miriam, and your children, are part of this family. I'm disappointed you might think otherwise.'

'I'm sorry, sir. I shouldn't have asked, but I just had to be sure. For their sakes.'

The General's anger subsided as quickly as it had surfaced.

'I apologise. It's understandable that you're sick with worry. All I can tell you is that for as long as you and Miriam wish to remain here, your positions are safe. Anyway, who is going to force you to leave? You are a German citizen, a veteran of the Great War, a taxpayer and contributor to our society. You must know that.'

'Thank you, sir. We have no desire to move.'

'Yosef, listen to me. I wouldn't normally say this, but I am a general of the German Reichswehr. I have served my country for nearly thirty years. I am on first-name terms with some of the most powerful people in the country. No upstart politician with a crazy agenda of hate is going to tell me who I employ, or whom I keep as friends. You are safe here with us.'

Yosef nodded. 'Thank you again, sir,' he said.

CHAPTER 9

Memo: Geh.KdoS. ABW 3/2/33 CAC0128.1

For Attention Only: All senior executive officers, Abwehr.

From: Kurt von Hammerstein-Equord, Chef der Heeresleitung

Chancellor Adolf Hitler sought and received the support of myself as Reichsheer commander-in-chief. In a subsequent meeting, I, and other senior members of the Reichsheer and Reichsmarine expressed caution and the need to maintain an independent intelligence gathering function within the armed forces. It is our belief that the Abwehr should be expanded and be retained under the direct control of the Reichswehr minister. [END]

General Kästner stared at the piece of paper. He had hoped that the top echelons of the army and navy would have put up a little more resistance to the chancellor's overtures. Handing over control of the army to Adolf Hitler had been almost inevitable, but he'd been sure that the Chef der Heeresleitung would have been able to at least delay until the elections.
He picked up the second memo.

Memo: Geh.KdoS. ABW 3/2/33 CAC0134.1

For Attention Only: General Erich Kästner, Abwehr, Kiel Field office.

From: Captain Conrad Patzig, Chef der Abwehr.

Further to Memo ABW3/2/33CAC0123.1 I confirm authorisation of the following additional staff for the Abwehr Field Office, Kiel.

1 Hauptmann

1 Unteroffizier

3 Schützen

This is in addition to Schütze Zimmer, already assigned to you as driver.

The staff should be recruited from the Reichsmarine staff pool, Kiel or from Stadtheide barracks, Plön. If you have any difficulty, I can assign staff from elsewhere. [END]

At least now he had a few men under his command. It had felt strange being a general with no troops. He picked up the phone and dialled.

~~o~~

'Sir, you asked for me?'
The General looked up. Lieutenant Bauer's head appeared around the door.

'Lieutenant, sit down.'

The young naval officer took the seat in front of the desk and waited for the General to continue.

'I'm looking for some staff; a junior officer, a sergeant and a couple of privates.'

'Yes, sir. And how can I help?'

'Who is in charge of naval personnel here?'

'That would be Kapitän Weitz, sir, but…'

'But what?'

'Well, sir, you'd be better talking to his chief petty officer.'

The General looked at Heinz Bauer, his eyebrow raised in question.

'The Kapitän doesn't keep in great health, sir. Stabsfeldwebel Krause keeps things running,' the lieutenant replied, then looked away.

'Is the illness of the liquid variety?'

'Sir, I couldn't comment. Perhaps I can deal with the Stabsfeldwebel for you. Do you have requisition papers for the men?'

'No, but they will come through in the next week or so. I'll get them to you.'

The lieutenant nodded. He was about to speak, but the General hadn't finished.

'I want to talk to the men before anything is finalised. This isn't like being back at battalion, when I had to work with what I was given. At least there were plenty to choose from for the critical jobs. Here, I need to choose the right men.'

'Yes sir. I'll get onto it as soon as the paperwork comes through. I'll have a word before then with Stabsfeldwebel Krause.'

'There's one more thing, lieutenant.'

'Yes, sir.'

'I know it would keep you away from sea for a bit longer, but there's a captaincy in it if you're interested in joining my team. How does Captain Bauer sound?'

The General watched the young lieutenant. The man was torn, as he had intended.

Will he see the bigger picture and take the promotion, with a lengthy shore-based commission, or will he hold out for a seagoing posting with a lower rank?

The young officer hesitated for no more than a few seconds.

'Yes, sir. I'd be delighted to accept. I'll have to clear it with my commander.'

'Naturally, but I've already had a word with him. I phoned him while you were on the way down here.' The General smiled. Reading men, moulding them to his ways was what he was good at. He continued.

'If you were army, you would be Hauptmann Bauer, but I suppose, coming from the navy, that would make you a Kapitänleutnant.'

'Very good, sir. I can see what they say about you is true.' The young officer laughed.

The General thought he'd made the right choice. The young man had just the right combination of brashness and deference that he liked, and sharp with it.

'Don't bother with idle flattery. I've heard it all before,' the General warned him, but there was a hint of a smile at the corner of his mouth. 'You'll need about ten ratings and two sergeants. That should give us enough choice.'

The lieutenant made good his exit, hurrying to tell Stabsfeldwebel Krause his news and to find out which men were available.

Erich Kästner chuckled.

Captain Bauer will do just fine.

CHAPTER 10

Tuesday 28th February 1933

FIREFIGHTERS BATTLE REICHSTAG BLAZE

Over 200 firefighters from stations all over Berlin fought the catastrophic fire which started around 9pm. Despite efforts to put out the blaze, the fire was still raging as this paper went to press. Reports say that the building will be irreparably damaged. Reichstag minister Hermann Göring, who was one of the first on the scene, called for a "crackdown on communists".

The chancellor, Adolf Hitler, visited the scene shortly after, and was said to be "deeply distressed".

~~o~~

Erich Kästner threw the paper on his desk. He'd read it on the way to the office, trying to evaluate the reports of the fire in the German Parliament, and the comments of the politicians who had been on the scene remarkably soon after the blaze began, considering the late hour. He picked up the small bundle of memos that the night-duty officer had put in the basket and skimmed through the first few, which were mundane and routine, requiring no action on his part. The third memo caught his eye.

Memo: Geh.KdoS. ABW 28/2/33 CAC0139.1

For Attention Only: All senior executive officers, Abwehr.

From: Captain Conrad Patzig, Chef der Abwehr.

The Reichsheer has given assurances today that all possible assistance will be given to the Police and the Government in the apprehension of those responsible for last night's arson attack on the Reichstag building. [END]

Erich Kästner stared at it.

Von Hammerstein isn't stupid.

Nearly all the senior commanders in the Reichsheer disliked and distrusted the communist party, so this was not much of a concession. The General suspected that the NSDAP wouldn't ask for help from the army while their own de facto paramilitary force, the Sturmabteilung, or the SA for short, had the intelligence resources and capability to root out anyone with communist leanings, real or fabricated.

He passed the time before the others arrived by working on the memos and documents that only he himself could deal with and placed the rest in the basket on the newly promoted Captain Bauer's desk, on the opposite side of the large room. The young officer had proved his effectiveness in getting things done; there were now two desks in the anteroom; in addition to the secretary's, the sergeant would have his own just inside the door. It was going to get a little crowded, although the private soldiers or able seamen that had yet to be assigned would use the ratings mess hall in the basement when they weren't tasked out.

The door to the outer office opened and Captain Bauer and Helene Müller walked in, talking in low tones. Through the open internal door, they both saw the General at his desk and fell silent. The secretary hung up her coat and slipped in behind her desk.

The captain's promotion had just come through that week and he was still self-conscious about his new rank. He continued through the doorway and stopped in front of the General's desk.

'Have you seen this, sir,' he said, handing him the newspaper.

The General grunted an assent then took a second glance at the paper and picked it up.

'As a matter of fact, no,' he said. 'This is the late edition.'

He picked up his own paper and showed the captain the front page, before reading the later version.

KIELER MORGENPOST

Tuesday 28th February 1933 Late Edition

REICHSTAG BLAZE – COMMUNIST PLOT TO OVERTHROW STATE

Berlin Police have arrested Dutch communist Marinus van der Lubbe, who was found near the burning building. He has been charged with arson. A spokesman for the National Socialist Party (the NSDAP) blamed the fire on a group of communist agitators. The police are searching for three other men in connection with the fire, Bulgarians Georgi Dimitrov, Vasil Tanev and Blagoy Popov. The public are warned not to approach these men but to inform the authorities immediately if they are spotted.

In reaction to the communist attempt to subvert the German government, President von Hindenburg has decreed emergency powers to the NSDAP/DNVP coalition government under Chancellor Adolf Hitler for the Protection of People and the State.

'What do you think?' the General asked.

'What do you mean, sir?'

'Where does this leave Germany?'

Erich Kästner suppressed a smile at the young officer's sudden wariness.

'It's not a trick, Captain. I was just looking for your opinion. You are now working for the Abwehr. We are the intelligence branch of the armed forces, and technically we answer to the government, but one of the reasons the Abwehr is expanding is because the men who control the army and the navy are nervous, and they feel the need to protect the armed forces from the excesses and, frankly, stupidity of some of the politicians.'

'I see, sir. Does that not go against democracy?'

'An excellent question, Captain. Let me ask you a question. Have you ever heard of the

Kiel Mutiny?'

'Yes sir, it came up in history lessons in school. The sailors of the German fleet revolted in 1918, refusing to fight in a battle that they believed to be unwinnable and suicidal.'

'Indeed. You're right, and it triggered the revolution which brought down the monarchy within a few days. It was the beginning of the end of the German Empire and led to the establishment of the Weimar Republic. Even if it wasn't a decision by the top level of command of the navy, it was still a military decision to disregard the will of the government of the day.'

'Are you saying the army should disobey the government's orders?'

A bead of sweat formed on the captain's brow.

The General put his hand on his junior officer's shoulder.

'No, I'm not saying that. What I am telling you is that the army, and the navy, need to know what is going on, both at home and abroad, so that we can understand why we are being ordered to do something and make informed decisions on how to implement those orders. Our job here is twofold. We have to gather information from a variety of sources and pass that on to our superiors, and we have to disseminate information to the right people when we are ordered to.'

'This is all new to me. Life in the navy was a little less complicated.'

'Perhaps I should have explained more of what our remit is when I asked you to be part of it. If you'd rather not be here, I can have you transferred. I'll make sure there's nothing on your record that will hold you back.'

'No sir, I believe that I can do this. I would like to carry on.'

'That's the spirit. I didn't think I'd misjudged you. What we're doing may be much more important than anything you could accomplish at sea.'

The General showed him what he wanted done with the documents he'd given him and, while the officer worked out what was required of him, Erich Kästner spoke to his secretary, Helene Müller.

She was a pleasant, middle-aged woman who did little to hide the fact that she didn't believe that the General was ever going to live up to the standards of her previous and recently deceased boss. He passed on a sheaf of handwritten notes that he wished typed up, and a folder of documents that required filing.

He slipped out of the office, feeling a little cooped up, and decided to go out for a cup of coffee rather than sit in the officers' mess. He strolled along the waterfront; the view never failed to inspire him. The giant cranes and sheds of the shipyards on the opposite shore of Kieler Hafen filled the skyline. Almost all the slipways or dry docks harboured a vessel of the Reichsmarine, each of different size and at various stages of construction or repair. Men moved over them like ants on a discarded biscuit tin as the steel hulls grew each day from the keel upwards, transforming them into the beautiful and proud ships which lined the moles and jetties of the huge harbour.

He bought a coffee at one of the small cafés that littered the promenade and chose an outside table, despite the cold, so that he could watch the movement of boats in and out of the Kieler Hafen. Ferries, criss-crossing the Förde, delivered people from the industrial east shore to the residential and government districts on the opposite bank and from Friedrichsort and Laboe near the mouth of the Förde to the Innenhafen at the head of the harbour, right in the heart of Kiel itself.

In contrast to the shipyards and workers' homes opposite, the large houses of the middle-and-upper classes, and the leafy parks of Düsternbrook, overlooked the small boat harbours belonging to the numerous yacht clubs lining the shore. The General could almost see the mast of his own boat, moored in the most exclusive one of them all, the Kieler Yacht Club.

A tug sounded its horn as it nosed its way towards the almost completed heavy cruiser, *Deutschland*, berthed on the Deutsche Werke mole. He looked for the other tugs and saw them heading for the stern of the giant warship. The General marvelled that the men of the shipyard had put this leviathan together sheet by sheet, rivet by rivet, and that it was almost ready to leave the yard forever. He remembered the fanfare when the keel had been laid down. The *Deutschland* would be the biggest warship that the yard had ever built, they said. He supposed that the secret lay in the 10,000 men who toiled in the Deutsche Werke shipyard, the largest of the three Kiel yards strung close together along the east shore of Kieler Hafen.

Finishing his coffee, he paid the waitress and walked back to the Reichsmarine headquarters. It was one of the more imposing buildings on the Kiel seafront, built in the late nineteenth century as the Imperial Navy Academy. Now, since 1910 it had been the Baltic fleet Naval HQ.

He strode up the steps and returned to his office, to find a line of sailors standing in the corridor. They moved aside to let him enter, and passing through the outer office, he noticed another two sailors sitting across from his secretary.

As the General entered the office, Captain Bauer rose from behind his desk. The General raised an eyebrow and nodded his head in the direction of the line of sailors at the door.

'The men are here to be selected, sir. I thought you'd like to do that as soon as possible.'

General Kästner felt a brief flicker of annoyance and disappointment. He had expected his deputy to organise the staff he'd been allotted, but perhaps the young man was just being prudent, not wanting to be blamed if his choices didn't please him.

'I suppose I should be pleased. The orders came through last week. Why the hold-up?'

'Sir, the light cruiser that was in last week, *Karlsruhe*, I think. They had an outbreak of food poisoning. She needed thirty replacements immediately, as she was on manoeuvres.'

'Fair enough, we can't complain about that. At least we have them now.'

'The two chief petty officers are in the anteroom. The ratings are all in the corridor.'

'Yes, Bauer, I noticed. I thought I'd requested a sergeant?'

'Yes, sir. Stabsfeldwebel Krause thought it might be more appropriate for your role if you had a non-commissioned officer rather than a sergeant.'

'He did, did he? Well, I suppose we'd better get on with it. I'll interview the petty officers first, then you and whichever of the two we choose can interview the seamen. I only need two ratings. I want an army man for the final post, on the grounds of impartiality. I'll sort him out when I go to Plön at the end of the week. You can come with me, to see how the army works.'

The captain saluted and showed the first of the candidates through. In the end, the General chose the older of the two men, although there wasn't much between them. He left his two officers to weed out the others and left to find his driver. He was going to make the most of his new position and decided that seeing around one of the warships that were berthed at the Tirpitzhafen naval dockyard at Wik was as good a way to familiarise himself with the navy as any.

The SMS *Emden* was in Kiel for a week's furlough, crew changes, refuelling and victualling. And the General knew her commander, Otto Kohl, very well. An invitation to visit the light cruiser had been proffered at the General's retirement party. The General smiled. He was now getting paid to do something he'd have been delighted to do in his spare time.

He looked at his watch. It was one o'clock. He told the captain that he didn't need the car; he would take the tram.

On a whim, he first boarded a tram that took him in the opposite direction, to Drachensee. Antje, his daughter, and Ruth Nussbaum would be home from school, and he decided to take them with him to Tirpitzhafen. The terminus at Wik was only a short walk from the ship, and they could ride the tram all the way there from a few metres outside the Kästner front door, on Hamburger Chaussee.

As he left, the chief petty officer they'd just selected turned to the captain.

'Does he always travel by tram?'

~~o~~

'My grandpapa used to be a captain of a warship like this,' Antje said, fidgeting while her father spoke with the crew on the *Emden*'s bridge.

'I know. He's an admiral.'

'He was. He's retired now.'

'Both my savim are retired,' Ruth said.

'Savim? I thought you called your grandpapa sabba. I've heard you.'

Ruth sighed and made a face.

'We say sabba if it's only one of them, like Sabba Nussbaum or Sabba Sachs, but savim when we talk about them both.'

'Oh. I see. What about Bubbe?'

'That's simple. I have two bubbes. Bubbe Nussbaum and Bubbe Sachs.'

Antje smiled, then her face dropped.

'I only have one grandpapa. Mama's papa is dead.'

'I'm sorry.'

'You don't need to be. He died before I was born.'

She glanced at her father, still talking to Kapitän Kohl.

'I hope Papa doesn't talk too much longer,' she said. 'He promised us an ice cream.'

~~o~~

'Mama, we got to drive the biggest ship you ever did see.'

Antje Kästner did her best not to jump up and down as she imparted her news to her mother, sitting at the kitchen table opposite Miriam Nussbaum, a leather-bound ledger and a sheaf of grocery and other household receipts between them.

Frau Kästner laid down the fountain pen she was holding, took both of Antje's hands and smiled at her daughter.

'Stand still and let me see you.'

At the opposite side of the table, Ruth Nussbaum sidled up to her mother, her face as animated as her friend's.

'Now, has your father turned both our young ladies into rough-and-ready sailors?' Maria Kästner said, frowning.

'By the time they are old enough, perhaps girls will be able to join the Reichsmarine, eh?'

General Kästner had followed the running girls into the kitchen.

'Oh no, Daddy. It was wonderful to see the big ship, but I wouldn't want to work on it. It was far too loud, and everything is made of metal and they paint it horrible colours.'

'That's the navy for you. At least in the army, we use various shades of green.'

The two women laughed, and the girls joined in, still wound up from their unexpected treat.

'What about you, Ruth?' the General asked.

'Well, if I could be on the bridge, or have a cabin like the captain, I might just consider it, but I certainly wouldn't like to work anywhere near the engines.' She turned to her mother. 'It was dirty and smelly and everything we touched had coal dust on it.'

'They were refuelling. The *Emden* uses coal and oil. Most of the newer ships will use oil alone,' the General said. 'Our navy may be small at present, but it will be one of the most advanced, in a few years' time.'

'Papa knows the captain,' Antje blurted.

'Commander Kohl,' the General said to his wife.

'The captain said only Papa would bring two little girls on an inspection with him. He said that the army had some strange habits.' She giggled.

The General glanced at his wife, knowing there would be a frown of disapproval on her face. Anything that could possibly undermine his status or gravitas disturbed her. But he could live with it, so he changed the subject.

'He was very charming to the girls. He even showed them his personal quarters.'

'Oh, his cabin was lovely, wasn't it, Ruth?'

'It was tiny, for such an important man, but everything was made of wood and all the furniture was screwed to the floor.'

'That's so you two girls wouldn't steal it.'

The girls squealed with laughter at the General, and Frau Kästner took the chance to send them to the bathroom.

'Let's get these clothes off you before you leave a trail of coal dust everywhere.'

'What do you say to General Kästner, Ruth,' Miriam chided her daughter as she shepherded the girls up the stairs. She would have to hurry to the cottage for clean clothes for Ruth once she got the girls into the bath.

'Thank you very much, General Kästner,' her daughter shouted over her shoulder as she raced Antje across the landing.

~~o~~

The General sat down and picked up the paper.

He sighed as Maria turned to him, frowning.

'Whatever possessed you to take the girls to see a warship?' she asked, equal measures of amusement and annoyance in her voice.

'Ach, they loved it, and I don't see why the boys should have all the fun. They're away at school anyway. So is Eva, but she would never have gone anyway.'

'And rightly so,' his wife snapped. 'Now that the boys are too big for this sort of jaunt, you're not turning my daughter into a substitute son.'

He laughed. Sometimes he thought that his wife needed to relax a little more.

'Well, no harm done, and it kept them entertained for a while, and let you and Miriam get on in peace.'

'We were just doing the monthly accounts. We can do that with the girls here. Anyway, we still had little Manny running about our feet.'

'Ah, was he disappointed? He was just too young to take.'

'Erich, you are not a babysitter. And Manny is not one of your children.'

'He's a smart little boy though. Where is he?'

'Out playing in the garden. No doubt he'll need a bath, too, when he comes in. Miriam can take him to the cottage. We have to draw the line somewhere.'

He sighed again. She sometimes got exasperated when he treated the Nussbaum children like his own, but, in fairness to her, she made allowances because Yosef and he had been brought up in the same way, always together, like Antje and Ruth.

She's wrong though. They're not my children. I'm like an uncle to them. Just a fond uncle.

~~o~~

Later, as they got ready for bed, Maria asked him how he felt about the new posting.

'I'm enjoying it immensely. It's completely different.'

He watched her undress. It still never failed to take his breath away, after all these years. In the quietness of the bedroom, the veneer of respectability dropped from her shoulders with her dress, and she became the simple girl he'd fallen in love with as a junior officer.

'I have some staff now. Helene Müller, do you know her? She was Admiral von Heutschler's secretary before he died.'

'Yes, she was at the funeral. Herr Müller is a town clerk. Helene works with a couple of charities I help with. She's awfully nice, and quite efficient, I imagine.'

'I hope so. I also managed to persuade young Heinz Bauer to be my second in

55

command; you remember his father, Kapitän Bauer.'

'Yes,' she replied. 'Didn't you take the boy sailing once?'

He removed the webbing suspenders from his shoulders, draping his trousers over the back of his chair.

'Yes, he was very keen. Well, he's turned out to be quite an impressive young officer, so I grabbed him from the general staff. I also have a petty officer and four privates.'

'That's quite a regiment you have there. How will you keep track of them all?'

He laughed. 'I'm still getting used to having such a small command.'

'Give me a hand with this girdle. I can't seem to get the fastener undone.'

He'd unbuttoned his shirt, but he walked around the bed to help her before hanging it up.

As he undid the clip to release her underwear, she turned to him, and removed the shirt from his shoulders, dropping it to the floor beside her clothes.

'Do you have time to fit me into your oh-so-busy schedule?'

~~o~~

Memo: Geh.KdoS. ABW 1/3/33 CAC0139.2

For Attention Only: All senior executive officers, Abwehr.

From: Captain Conrad Patzig, Chef der Abwehr.

The government has commenced the mass arrests of members of the communist party, including every KPD Party parliamentary delegate.

The SA, rather than the police, made most of the 4000 arrests so far.

For information only. No action required. [END]

Erich Kästner stared at the memo. He wasn't a fan of the KPD, and part of him thought that it was no bad thing that curbs were at last being put in place to control the communists' disruptive influence.

But a small voice in his brain pierced his complacency. He picked up the phone and dialled.

'General Kästner here. Can I have a word with Herr Hoffmann, please?'

'Certainly, Herr General. Would you please hold the line for a second?'

A minute later, Jürgen Hoffmann's voice cut through his thoughts.

'What can I do for you, Erich?'

'Jürgen, how are you? Bearing up under all the excitement?'

'It's been all go here. Terribly trying, and hard to get anything done.'

'Many arrests?'

There was a short silence at the end of the line.

'A few. Just a couple of agitators. Tried to lock themselves in the chamber. They're just fixing the doors as we speak.'

'What's the mood there? Are people worried?'

'I wouldn't say that. There's as much election fever as anything else. We're expecting the party to make big strides forward. Coalitions are all very well, but Germany could do with a strong government at a time like this.'

'Quite. Are you out campaigning?'

'Without doubt. One must be seen to be enthusiastic. You should consider joining the party. It's the future, Erich.'

'I'll think about it, Jürgen. If you hear anything else, let me know.'

He gave him the phone number of his office at Düsternbrooker Weg and hung up.

Best to have him on side. As a natural gossip at the heart of local politics, he was a useful source of information.

[03/03/1933 Friday]

Yosef Nussbaum held his cap in his hands. He told himself not to be nervous; he'd known the rabbi for years. He glanced at Jakob Teubner, the man sitting next to him.

'Thank you for staying, Yosef,' the rabbi said, 'and you, too, Jakob.'

'It's no trouble,' both men said, almost together.

The three men sat in the small office at the back of the synagogue, after the evening Shabbat service was over.

'I wanted to talk to you,' the rabbi said. 'I count on you as my two staunchest supporters over my time here, and as my friends, I hope.'

Jakob went to speak, but the rabbi held up his hand.

'I'm leaving Kiel, with my family,' he said.

Yosef Nussbaum and Jakob Teubner stared at him. Neither man said anything.

'I know it will come as a shock, but I've been considering it for a while. For the sake of my family, I'm going to leave Germany.'

'But what will we do without a rabbi?'

'It's not a necessity to have a rabbi. Even if you can't find a replacement, you two can hold the congregation together.'

'I'm not sure I'd know where to start,' Yosef said, finding his voice.

'Form a committee, gentlemen, that's my advice; there are plenty capable men in Kiel to help you, but one of you should take charge.'

'When are you leaving?'

'Very soon. Perhaps a month or six weeks. I wanted to tell you two first, so that you could make plans.'

'It's a blow, for sure,' Jakob said, 'but we'll do as you ask. Where are you going?'

'Holland, initially, but we intend to travel to Palestine if we can get in.'

'You think that things will get that bad here?' Jakob said.

'Yes, I don't like the mood of the country. I've lived here all my life but if Adolf Hitler wins the election, I fear for every Jew in Germany.'

Yosef felt a cold hand take a grip of his heart.

'Surely decent Germans will come to their senses,' he said. 'Not everyone supports the National Socialists.'

'I will tell the congregation to get out, in my last sermon. That's how deeply I feel about it.'

Apart from the slow tick of the mantel clock, there was a silence in the room.

The rabbi put his hand inside his jacket pocket and brought out a photograph. He handed it to Yosef. He and Jakob Teubner looked at it.

It showed a lit menorah, framed in the window of the front room of the rabbi's home in Gartenstraße. Behind it, through the curtains, the two men could see the imposing NSDAP building opposite, with a large National Socialist flag hanging in front of it, a black swastika in its centre.

'My wife took it last Chanukkah,' he said. 'As you know, she's a photographer. She has written a message on the back.'

Yosef turned the photograph over and read the handwritten words.

Chanukkah
5692
1932
"Judea dies", thus says the banner.
"Judea will live forever", thus respond the lights.

CHAPTER 11

Erich Kästner and his sons spent the whole weekend getting the boat ready for the new sailing season. She'd been lifted out at the boatyard, scraped down, caulked, and painted, and put back in the water the week before, and the mast had been stepped.

They'd rigged the boat so often together that it had become second nature to them. Attaching the boom to the mast, they tightened all the rigging and halyards, and packed the sails in their lockers except for the mainsail, which was attached to the boom and hoisted up the mast to check that it was running free, then lowered and stowed on the top of the boom ready for their first trip.

There was a myriad of other jobs to do, but by four o'clock, it was finished. The only interruption they'd had was the hour they spent at church, at Maria's insistence. The day had started out cold and dry but, by the time they were eating the bread and sliced Mettwurst that Miriam had packed for them, the warm sun made it pleasant to sit in the cockpit without the need for a coat.

'Pass out the beers, Johann.' Erich leaned back against the coaming, feeling the satisfying fatigue in his muscles that came from unaccustomed physical work.

Johann reached over the side and, from the cold water of the dock, he pulled up the hessian bag containing three bottles of beer. He passed one to Franz, gave the second to his father and looked at the last bottle with a hopeful glance.

Erich shook his head, watching the disappointment on his son's face, then laughed.

'Go on, you've earned it. Just don't tell your mother.'

The boy excitedly opened the bottle and they sat silently for a while, content in each other's company and with the work they'd achieved on the boat.

'I'm looking forward to getting out a lot more this year; being home most of the time. We can maybe do a few of the evening races during the summer.'

The boys looked at each other and grimaced. The boat was primarily set up for trips lasting days or weeks at a time, not for racing, but there were some races for cruising yachts like their father's, involving all the sailing clubs in Kieler Förde.

'We don't mind crewing for you, but would you not be better with some old-timers like yourself? We're used to something with a bit of speed,' Franz said, grinning.

Erich laughed. 'That's very rude. I know you boys are top racing sailors but just remember who taught you to sail.'

'You taught us to sail, and we'll help you out seeing you're getting on a bit, but once you've tasted being the hare it's hard to go back to being a tortoise,' Johann replied, managing to paste a pitying look onto his face.

'All right, boys. I get the message. I'm old and I'm slow. I'll ask some of the Rotary boys if they fancy it. A few of them know a mainsheet from a fairlead. But I'm disappointed you don't want to race with me. You used to be desperate to get out on the water. Have you moved on to girls now?'

'Girls are interesting, certainly,' said Franz, 'but there's something I've been meaning to tell you…'

Erich looked at Franz, surprised. He didn't think his son would have found him difficult to talk to.

'You want to join the navy instead. Is that it?'

Franz laughed, but it had a nervous ring to it.

'No, it's nothing like that,' he said, 'although you could hardly object, could you? You joined the army despite Grandfather being an admiral.'

'You're both free to do what you like. It would amuse the old codger if one of you did join the navy. Anyway, what's the big secret?'

'Well, you know that all the boys at school are members of Hitlerjugend?'

'Yes, I can't say I'm overenthusiastic but if that's what they want to do with their spare time, that's up to them.'

'Well, I was the only one in the class who hadn't joined, and there were several events coming up, so…'

'…you joined. Look, I don't like the man, and I don't like some of his party's policies and the way it behaves, but I'm not going to come down on you for wanting to join in when all your friends are already members. What about you, Johann?'

'I've not joined yet. I was going to ask you, but after the other night…'

Erich Kästner suddenly felt old. He'd always prided himself on being open with his boys and being approachable. The last thing he wanted to be was overbearing and he always believed in allowing them to make their own judgements.

'Listen, I'm not going to try and stop either of you joining or give you a lecture about what to do. All I'll say is that you should learn a bit more about this man and his party, just so you're going in with your eyes open.'

Franz looked at his brother and nodded. 'There's more, though, Father.'

Erich Kästner sighed. 'What?'

'The reason that I can't sail with you is that I'm in the Hitlerjugend sailing team. If Johann joins up, there may be a place for him too. I've told them how good he is, and they're keen to try him out.'

The warmth seemed to have gone out of the afternoon.

General Kästner forced a smile onto his face.

'You're both great sailors, especially around the cans, and this could be a stepping stone to something much bigger, so take the opportunity while you can. You never know, perhaps you'll sail for Germany in the Olympics one day.'

The relief on his sons' faces hurt a little, if he was honest, but it hit home how much they had become young men. His only hope was that they didn't regret getting involved in an organisation with such close ties to the NSDAP. But then again, nearly everyone he knew was doing the same thing, it seemed.

He dropped the boys off at the house and left to vote. He was perturbed, but not intimidated, by the National Socialist's Sturmabteilung thugs strutting about outside the polling station, who had the temerity to smile at him on the way in, assuming that he would be voting the 'correct' way.

He cast his vote.

CHAPTER 12

KIELER MORGENPOST

Monday 6th March 1933 Late Edition

ELECTION RESULT – COALITION GOVERNMENT RETURNED

The NSDAP failed to win an outright victory in yesterday's general election. Despite making significant gains in the poll, they fell well short of the majority they needed to be the sole party of power.

After a meeting between Adolf Hitler, leader of the National Socialist Party (NSDAP) and Alfred Hugenberg, the leader of the German National People's Party (DNVP), Herr Hitler announced that a Coalition of these two parties would form a Government in the interest of national unity.

The results for the main parties are:

NSDAP 288 seats, 43.91% of the vote, up 11%

SPD 120 seats, 18.25% of the vote, down 2%

KPD 81 seats, 12.32% of the vote, down 5%

Centre 74 seats, 11.25% of the vote, down 1%

DNVP 52 seats, 7.97% of the vote, down 0.5%

BVP 18 seats, 2.73% of the vote, down 0.5%

Adolf Hitler remains the Chancellor of the Reichstag.

~~o~~

Yosef Nussbaum read the lead article twice. He felt some sense of relief. The National Socialists had not won the landslide that they'd been predicting and, even with the support of the DNVP, they barely managed a majority.

The first few pages were all about the election. An article on the second page contained local and national reactions to the result. He was surprised to find responses from across the political spectrum which he judged to be fair, if you made allowances for the absence of any comment from the Communist Party, the KPD.

The SPD, the party he had voted for, had just about held the centre-left vote, and he felt saddened that so many in the Jewish community felt compelled to vote for non-socialist parties. He'd tried to reason with them but most of them were small business owners and professionals, and they were naturally conservative. Some were even voting for the German Nationalists, the party who were making it possible for Hitler to retain his hold on government, and who had overt anti-Semitic clauses in their constitution.

'Daddy, what are you reading?'

He put the paper on the table and swung his daughter onto his knee. The kitchen of the cottage they lived in was a fraction of the size of the one in the big house, but it was warm,

61

homely, and perfect for the four of them.

'It's all about the election, Motek,' he said.

He watched as a warm smile lit up her face. *Sweetheart* was the favourite of the pet names he gave her.

'Our teacher told us about it,' Ruth said. 'Herr Hitler is going to win again, isn't he?'

'Well, the results are here. In one way, he didn't quite win, but in another, he might as well have. It's complicated.'

'Miss Brinckmann says that we shouldn't bother ourselves with it all, that we should stick to learning our lessons.'

'She is very wise, your teacher. You like her, don't you?'

'She can sometimes be stern, but mostly she's good fun, not like some of the other ones we've had. She gives the boys a row when they call Hanne, Rebeka, and me names. She made them wash their mouths with soap too.'

She giggled.

'What did the boys call you?' He could guess. There were only three Jewish girls in her class.

'The teacher told us not to repeat them, that she would sort the boys out.'

'Your teacher is clever.' He thought she was more than that, dealing with the problem without taking it outside the class.

'But you could write them down for me,' he said, trying to smile. 'That wouldn't be breaking your promise.'

She looked at him sideways, as if she didn't quite believe him, but she nodded. He opened a drawer and found a pencil.

'Write them on the bottom of the newspaper for me.'

He watched her small and innocent hand write, the words appearing like poison on the paper.

Yid
Judenschwein
Schmutziger Jude

He pointed to the first word. 'This isn't so bad. You know what Yiddish is?'

'Of course I do. It's a language that Jewish people speak. Like Hebrew. Bubbe Sachs taught me.'

Miriam's mother, Nellie, didn't see the children as often as Bubba Nussbaum did, but when she was with them, she was forever telling them stories about the old days and teaching them all she could about their Jewish heritage.

'Yes, it's mainly German with a lot of Hebrew thrown in and a sprinkling of other languages like Russian and Polish for good measure. Well, Yid is just short for Yiddish, so it's not so bad. It just means you speak an extra language that they can't.'

'What about the others? I'm not a pig and I'm not dirty, am I?'

'You certainly aren't either of those. It's just people who become fearful when someone else is a bit different from them, with maybe a bit of jealousy thrown in. Many of our Jewish friends are successful and wealthy. People lash out when they aren't doing quite so well themselves, with whatever insult comes to mind, so they call you dirty when you're not. It makes them feel better.'

She seemed satisfied with this explanation and he was going to end there, but he thought he should finish what he'd started.

'Many Jews don't eat meat that comes from pigs; it's not regarded as kosher. You know what that means?'

She nodded.

'Well, to call a Jewish person a pig is a terrible insult but, at the end of the day, it's only words, and they can't hurt you if you don't let them.'

She nodded again, her face so solemn he almost smiled, despite himself.

He tore the bottom off the page and put it in his pocket.

'Don't the girls call you names?'

'No, Antje doesn't let them. She's the most popular girl in class so they listen to her. But not the boys.'

'I'm glad. Do the girls call Hanne and Rebeka names?'

'Not Rebeka. She is Antje's friend too.'

'What about Hanne?'

Yosef knew the girl's parents; they ran a small clothing repairs shop in Kleiner Kuhberg, where a small Jewish community lived and worked. Max Weidmann was the girl's father. He had arrived from the small Polish town of Gorzów Wielkopolski, close to the German border, not long after the end of the Great War and had set up shop doing what he'd always done. When he'd gathered up enough money, he sent for his wife and two girls. A year after she joined him, Hanne was born, then two brothers for her and her sisters. They were Orthodox Jews.

'We all sometimes share our snacks, but Hanne never eats any of ours. And she never comes to anyone's house if they have a party. Her papa has such a funny beard. The boys make fun of him, and his kippah too.'

Yosef touched the back of his head. He only wore his skullcap on the Shabbat.

'He's a different kind of Jew to us. And so is Hanne. She can't eat what we eat. They are stricter than us about kosher foods.'

Sometimes, when he spoke with Orthodox Jews, mostly from the East, he felt that he'd strayed too far from the tenets of their faith, but he knew that he'd made that choice when he followed his father into service with the Kästner family.

'Because we sometimes eat at the Kästners, and we eat spare food that Mama cooks for them to stop it going to waste, we can't always stick as rigidly to a kosher diet.'

He paused, hoping he'd find a way through the minefield he'd stepped into. He ploughed on.

'But any food we cook in our house, especially for Shabbat dinner, is kosher.'

'Hanne's father never works on the Shabbat, and her mother doesn't wash clothes or do dishes either. She says it's not right to do these things on the day of rest.'

He held his daughter's hand.

'We all have different ways of worshipping God. Sometimes we must make compromises, and it's wrong for Hanne to be critical of us. Even so, do your best to be her friend. And try not to worry about the names they call you. You must learn to turn away when it happens, like your mother and I did, and your grandparents before us. Inside, they can't touch us. And besides,' he said, smiling, 'Antje will not always be there to stop them.'

He looked down at her. She looked so serious; it was a sin for a nine-year-old girl not to be laughing and smiling and enjoying life.

'Where is Antje, anyway? I thought you two were joined at the hip.'

'Daddy, you know Antje goes horse riding on Monday after school.'

'Ah, so she does. I'd forgotten it was Monday.'

'You're silly.' She paused. 'Could I go horse riding one day, with Antje?'

He sighed. He'd just tried to teach his daughter about ethics and morals. Now he was going to have to explain to her the harsh realities of economics.

'Ruth, the General has been wonderful to us and, in return, we look after him very well, but his generosity doesn't extend to paying for you to go riding, and he doesn't pay us enough to buy you a pony. What's wrong with walking, anyway?'

She giggled again and he could feel the ripples of her laughter run through her body, pressed against his. He squeezed her tight and made a note to write to his wife's cousin, who lived on a farm in Karstädt, about 100 kilometres beyond Lübeck. Perhaps they had a horse that she could ride. They could visit in the summer holidays.

CHAPTER 13

The General's first thought when he'd read the paper wasn't that Adolf Hitler had lost the election, but that if the communists had won as many seats while most of their party workers were in police custody, what would have happened had the elections been free and fair?

And his initial mild optimism based on the fact the NSDAP would have to scramble about again to find partners to govern Germany faded when he reached the office and read the first memo of the day from Captain Patzig.

Memo: Geh.KdoS. ABW 6/3/33 CAC0143.1

For Attention Only: All senior executive officers, Abwehr.

From: Captain Conrad Patzig, Chef der Abwehr.

Arrests of all the KPD delegates who won seats in yesterday's election have been ordered, along with any remaining communist party personnel, giving the NSDAP\DNVP coalition a workable majority. This has received cautious support from the Ministry of Defence and the heads of the Reichsheer and the Reichsmarine after assurances from Adolf Hitler that there will be no abuse of power and that the armed forces are a priority for the new government.

No action required. [END]

He placed the memo on his desk.

They'll have more control of the Reichstag than I'd hoped, with the communist delegates removed.

He spent the morning keeping himself occupied, trying not to dwell on the outcome of the elections, continuing to meet with the various departments of the Reichsmarine, listening to their plans for the coming year and their complaints about funding and supply bottlenecks. These weren't in his remit, but it gave him a chance to get to know the individual officers in these posts and, just as importantly, for them to meet him and feel that he was there to listen and to help where he could.

In some instances, all it took to fix a problem was a word in the right ear at the Reich Ministry or at Naval Command, which endeared him to officers just below command level and began to gain him a reputation of a man who could get things done.

And all the time, he was gathering information for the Abwehr, building up a picture of how the navy worked and thought.

By the time the captain informed him that his car was ready, just after one, the General was glad of the distraction and, an hour later, the car was purring across the causeway to Plön. The town, and its barracks a few kilometres south, were almost completely surrounded by water, on a spidery latticework of land set amidst the Großer Plöner See, the largest freshwater lake in Schleswig-Holstein, with a cluster of small lakes connected to it.

'This looks very grand,' the captain said, as they crossed the narrow, marshy strip of land that connected Plön to Sandkaten, almost an island itself.

On the right side of the road, an impressive array of white military buildings stood by the lakeside, with Kriegsmarine and National Socialist flags flying from the flagpoles at the entrance.

'Ah, that's the Ruhleben Barracks. It's a Marineunteroffizierschule for U-boat officers. The U-boat training flotilla is based here. The Großer Plöner See is deep enough. We're going to Stadtheide barracks, an army facility. It's not quite as imposing.'

Unterseeboot. U-boat. The General knew that submarines were necessary, but there was something about them that always sent a shiver down his spine.

The car swept past the submarine officer school, and its training flotilla. Three-quarters of a kilometre on, it turned left.

'I see what you mean, sir.'

Beyond the wire mesh of the entrance gate, the captain gazed at a grid of low wooden huts surrounding a barrack square.

'The only thing it shares with the Kriegsmarine barracks is a view of a lake, Captain,' the General said, smiling.

The sentry let them through, and the General and a sergeant of the guard gave the captain a quick tour of the barracks.

When they'd completed the tour, finishing at the General's office, the captain was surprised that there was only one soldier standing to attention outside.

'Sir, I thought we were going to go through a selection process, as we did back in Kiel.'

'It's not necessary, Captain Bauer. This is Private Martin Lubinus. He was my orderly for the last decade of my time in the army. I requested him for the one remaining position in our unit. Private, this is Captain Bauer, my second in command.'

The two men saluted.

After a meeting with the barracks' commanding officer, the General told Private Lubinus to fetch the satchel of army mail and documents and to meet them at the car.

'We can head back now,' he said to the captain. 'The private's bag has been put in the trunk of the car. He can ride up front with the driver. He will join us in Kiel for a few days, then return here, where he will be based, running this office for me.'

The drive back was devoted entirely to work, the General explaining to the captain how he would like the group to function.

'My job is to have regular meetings with the various naval commanders and to collate and coordinate our efforts to collect intelligence on all aspects of naval operations in Kiel. I want you to hand over most of the administration jobs to the secretary and to the two naval ratings, and Private Lubinus in Plön; train them up as necessary, but you should find that Lubinus has a real knack for paperwork. I want you and Chief Petty Officer Neuer to concentrate on each of the departments that I have already visited. I've set up meetings with all of them, at the equivalent rank level to your own.'

'What are we looking for, sir?'

'First of all, we need to do everything within our power to help the navy function as well as it possibly can, especially in areas where the Abwehr can be of benefit. We must aim to be an integral part of their operations here, to be trusted and valued by them, at all levels of command. Only then will we be able to collect and assess information about the Reichsmarine for the good of the Reichswehr.'

'Yes, sir,' the captain said, beginning to grasp what the General wanted.

'Do you know why I want us to get so involved in the day-to-day running of the Reichsmarine, Captain?' the General asked.

He paused. 'I think so, sir. You'll be able to gauge the mood and opinion of the whole navy. I mean, the admirals might try and fudge the whole thing and tell you what they want you to hear, but I'm sure that the rank and file will be more forthcoming about issues that concern them. It's very clever, sir.'

'I told you to cut out the flattery, Captain, but you're right. Do you understand our role now?'

'More and more, sir. It's not what I expected.'

'For the time being, we're simply trying to collect as much information as possible and, in the coming years, to keep it up to date. As time goes on, we'll also be expected to disseminate information at various levels throughout the navy, to help them function more efficiently, and in line with the Reichswehr's expectations. Think about it as giving them little nudges in the right direction. Now, let's do our job.'

~~o~~

Memo: Geh.KdoS. ABW 7/3/33 CSH002.1

For Attention Only: General Erich Kästner, Abwehr Field office, Kiel.

From: Captain Conrad Patzig, Chef der Abwehr.

Reports suggest that the NSDAP are now targeting delegates and members of the Socialist party, the SPD.

The Reich Ministry and the Reichsheer have continued their backing for the government's actions and the Reichsmarine has also expressed some support, but can you arrange to meet with Admiral Albrecht and his senior commanding officers to judge their commitment. Give an alternative reason for calling the meeting. This is more likely to yield information on their real sentiments. [END]

~~o~~

Memo: Geh.KdoS. ABW 8/3/33 CSH002.2

For Attention Only: Captain Conrad Patzig, Chef der Abwehr.

From: General Erich Kästner, Abwehr Field office, Kiel.

I met today with Vizeadmiral Albrecht, Konteradmiral Herman Witzell, Kommodore Rolf Boehm and Kommodore Alfred Marschall, the senior commanding officers present in Kiel. The given purpose of the meeting was to highlight the need for heightened security in the light of intelligence we have received concerning the targeting of Reichsmarine ships and shore installations. The Vizeadmiral assured me that all necessary security measures were in place. He expressed surprise that the communist movement would still have the resources to mount any sort of threat as most of them seem to have been detained. He went on to say that this was not a bad thing and that, from the Navy's point of view, it sent a message across the fleet that any form of activity harmful to the state or its executive bodies would not be tolerated.

There was no mention of the measures being taken against the SPD, so I was forced to introduce it into the conversation. There was a little more unease about this issue but, in the end, they all agreed that the SPD was merely a less extreme version of the KPD and that some form of control was justified. It was of note that none of them showed any interest or insight as to the democratic repercussions of these events and, the overriding view that it was probably to the future benefit of the Navy, and the country.

I hope this is of use. [END]

The General gave the memo to the young captain and sat for a second, staring out of the window.

Since the meeting with Admiral Albrecht and his staff, he'd wondered if there was anyone else in the armed forces, or even outside the Reichswehr, who was alarmed at the events unfolding across Germany. Needing someone to talk to who wasn't blinded to the dangers of national socialism, he picked up the phone, and dialled.

'Dr. Speer's surgery. Can I help you?'

'Yes. Is the doctor available?'

The doctor's secretary recognised Erich Kästner's voice; the General and her boss were close friends. Where possible, she knew that the doctor would expect him to be put straight through, without her usual preamble about the nature of the phone call.

'Yes, General, he's just finishing off with a patient if you can hold for a minute. I was just about to take him a cup of coffee, so he should have a few minutes free.'

The General laughed. In a polite way, he'd been given a time limit to talk to his friend. *Well, we'll see about that.*

'Erich, how are you, my friend?'

'Not great, Doc, I'm afraid, but there's nothing the medical profession can do about it.'

'Ah. The times we are living in are getting you down, eh?'

'Yes, I just needed to talk to someone else who doesn't have blinkers on.'

'My eyes are always open, Erich, as you know. Did you vote?'

'Yes, and I thought it may have done some good when I saw the results, but now I'm not so sure. You heard that they arrested all the KPD delegates in the Reichstag?'

'Yes, I heard. But that was always going to happen.'

'That's bad enough. A majority seem to think that clamping down on the communists is no bad thing, and they might be right, but now they are leaning on the SPD, from what I hear.'

The news about the SPD crackdown had been confirmed by a source in Kiel, so he didn't feel he was giving away any state secrets by telling the doctor.

'I hadn't heard that, but it's no surprise. I was told that there was nearly a riot in the chamber at the Rathaus yesterday when they arrested the KPD councilmen. Old Schmitt was removed from the chamber too.'

'The mayor? Why?' Erich was shocked.

'He objected. Tried to make a speech about democracy. He was hauled out by the police.'

'That's terrible. He's about as conservative as you can get. Why would they want rid of him?'

'Who's the deputy mayor, Erich?'

'Jürgen! So, he'll be mayor now. And he's a party member.'

'No election. Job done.'

'Scheiße.'

'I'd normally say there's no need to curse, but in this case, I think you're right.'

'Listen, thanks for the time, Doc. I'll keep in touch. Just watch yourself.'

'You too, Erich. Keep well, my friend.'

The General put down the phone. He looked at the open door of the office, wondering if any of his staff had heard him swearing.

He made towards the door, meaning to shut it, when a runner arrived and handed the latest batch of correspondence to his secretary. She sifted through them as she entered the inner office and handed a couple of items to the General, depositing the rest in the tray on Captain Bauer's desk. The General shut the door behind her. He put the weekly admin sheet to one side, for signing later, and looked at Captain Patzig's reply to his earlier memo.

Memo: Geh.KdoS. ABW 8/3/33 CSH002.3

For Attention Only: General Erich Kästner, Abwehr Field office, Kiel.

Your report is excellent. Continue to monitor opinion on this and further political matters. I feel that events may unfold rapidly regarding this government. [END]

~~o~~

Satisfied that his unit were fulfilling the role they'd been given, the General decided to follow up on the Doc's disturbing news.

He dialled the number for the Rathaus and asked to speak to Herr Hoffmann again. This time, he was left on hold for nearly five minutes before the line crackled in the General's ear.

'Erich, what can I do for you? This seems to be a regular occurrence.'

'Jürgen, I heard all the KPD councilmen had been arrested.'

'Who told you that?'

'It's in the paper, I think,' he lied.

There was a silence at the end of phone.

'I'm not quite sure, Erich. As far as I know, the KPD have boycotted the council meeting. The mayor has resigned.'

Erich Kästner knew that he hadn't, but he let it slide.

'You'll be the mayor now, won't you? You've waited a long time for this.'

'Erich, I'm merely stepping in to fill a void. I'm sure they'll hold another election as soon as the furore from this one has died down.'

'You used to be with the Centre Party, didn't you?'

'Yes, but I felt they weren't representative of the whole community.'

'Because it's a Catholic party?'

'Not particularly. I still attend mass, but I felt that the National Socialists were more inclusive; they appeal to voters across the spectrum.'

'And that won't harm your chances in a mayoral election, Jürgen.'

The man laughed nervously.

'That's probably true, I'll have to admit, but we must all be pragmatic, especially in political life. It's not like being in the army, you know.'

'No, it's not.' He bit back a caustic response. The relationship between the navy and Kiel was advantageous to both and he had to work with the local and regional politicians on a regular basis.

'I'm surprised the fracas wasn't reported in the *Morgenpost*.'

There was another pause at the end of the line.

'It couldn't have been important enough for the paper to print. Did you hear that they have a new editor?'

'No. That's strange. I spoke to Dieter Maas last week, just before I retired. He put a nice piece in the *Morgenpost* about it. And I thought he did a very fair editorial after the election.'

'He resigned today. A difference of opinion with the paper's owners. Hans Broschek has taken over.'

'I don't think I know him. A party member, I'd guess?'

'He may well be. There are more and more people joining every day. Are you sure I can't persuade you to be one of us, Erich?'

He could just imagine Jürgen Hoffmann boasting to his party friends how he'd managed to recruit such a high-ranking army officer to the party.

He laughed.

'I'll say this for you, Jürgen, you don't give up, but I'll leave it just now. The Abwehr should stay out of politics. The best of luck with the new job. Will you still manage to come to Rotary with us lowly citizens?'

The new mayor laughed.

'I'll try to be there, but my time is at a premium now, so I can't make any guarantees. Needless to say, I can promise the full support of the town council for all the sterling work that the Rotary Club does.'

'That's most kind of you, Jürgen. I'll look forward to seeing you then.'

The mayor put down the phone after muttering a goodbye. Despite appearances, both men knew that they were now on opposite sides of a divide.

CHAPTER 14

KIELER MORGENPOST

Thursday 9th March 1933 Late Edition

GOVERNMENT ACTS SWIFTLY TO QUELL UNREST

The Government has today responded to the increasing violence of the Communist Party and other anti-state agitators by appointing provisional Reich commissars to preside over several state governments as a temporary measure until control is restored. These commissars will be directly subordinate to the central government. It is hoped that in the legislatures affected by these changes, normal operations will return within a short space of time. Prominent businessmen and local politicians have praised the decisive actions of the Government. Town Mayor, Jürgen Hoffmann spoke to the Morgenpost. "Elements of the left wing and foreign influence are in danger of destroying democracy in our towns and cities, and throughout the entire country. Only the National Socialist government stands between us and anarchy".

After a number of small demonstrations, church leaders appealed for calm, and asked the people of Kiel to rally behind the elected government.

In reply to a question raised by the Jewish Council for Germany, a government spokesman gave assurances that there was no anti-Jewish sentiment in government policy. "No harm will come to loyal Jews".

'It was terrifying. One moment we were driving along, the next we are in the middle of a riot.'

Maria was almost hysterical. The General knew, from what Yosef had told him, that he'd been forced to divert from the main road in Wellingdorf on his way to take Maria to one of her charity events, this time in Mönkeberg, on the east shore of Kieler Förde, past the shipyards and the naval base.

A significant crowd of people with placards were being held back by the police and, as they sped in the opposite direction, a unit of brown-shirted SA men were running towards the disturbance.

'At no point did I feel we were in any danger, sir,' Yosef had said.

From Maria's distraught manner, he suspected she thought otherwise.

'They were probably communists,' she continued. 'I hope the police managed to disperse them or arrest them all. We can do without that sort of thing in Kiel.'

'There aren't enough communists left to protest. They're all in prison. It was more likely to be the socialists. I hear they're being harassed terribly by Hitler's thugs.'

'That's not the point. It's not right when decent citizens can't travel in safety. Some of the ladies arrived in a terrible state.'

Erich had seen some small demonstrations on his way to the office but from Yosef's description, the one on the Wellingdorf side of the harbour did seem more substantial.

He was sure that all the ladies lunching together in one of the large houses overlooking the shore would have relished the telling of ever more dramatic accounts of the lucky escapes they'd had, and of how close they'd come to being hauled out of their cars by a rampaging crowd and set upon.

He curbed whatever comment he would have liked to have made; he seemed to be doing a lot of that these days.

The sad truth, the General realised, was that the people in real danger were the protestors.

~~o~~

[10/03/1933 Friday]

'It's not even in the paper. The people were rioting in the streets, for goodness' sake.' She thrust the *Morgenpost* at him.

The General took it from her. There was no mention of the previous day's demonstrations on the front page, and, as he flicked through the paper, he failed to see anything about the protests or the National Socialists' assault on state governments that sparked them off.

He turned back to the front of the paper; a headline on it had jogged a memory. The announcement that Hinrich Lohse, who had been a member of the Reichstag since 1922, had been appointed as Oberpräsident of the Province of Schleswig-Holstein, took up a third of the front page. A vague memory of the man struggled to surface in his mind, but it eluded him. He turned to his wife.

'Maria, have you come across a man called Hinrich Lohse? He's just been made the president of the state. I didn't know that such a position existed.'

'I'm not surprised,' she sneered. 'These people are always giving themselves fancy titles.'

Erich Kästner knew that his wife enjoyed being at the centre of Kiel's social circles, but she was disdainful of minor politicians who suddenly thought they were somebody, simply by getting themselves elected. Coming from one of Kiel's old established families, she preferred to rub shoulders with her own kind, and the wives of Kiel's military elite, her mild pretentiousness not quite spilling over into overt snobbishness.

He watched as her brow creased for a second.

'He was the chairman of the Farmers' Association a few years ago,' she said, her frown easing. 'I remember meeting him and his wife at the agricultural show at Rendsburg. The Ladies' Guild had a cake stall at it. She was lovely, but he was a bit pompous.'

He remembered the man now. On a beautiful summer's day, he'd taken charge of the children while she fussed about selling cakes with her 'ladies' to raise funds for the church orphanage in Kiel. The women had excelled themselves, and the tiers of Himbeerschnitt, Bremer Klaben and Schneebälle drew the crowds. Before Maria had chased Erich and the children away for stealing from the far-too-tempting plates, Herr Lohse and his wife had visited the stall, in his capacity as honorary president of the show. Maria was right; he had been pompous and over-condescending to the children. His wife had been charming, however, almost mitigating the oily fawning of her husband.

~~o~~

When he got to the office, he found the list of tasks he'd set himself out to do that day and added finding out a little more about Herr Lohse to it. He was reluctant to meet with the man but he knew that it was necessary in his Abwehr capacity.

71

He skimmed through his correspondence. There was only one communication from Captain Patzig.

Memo: Geh.KdoS. ABW 10/3/33 CAC0152.1

For Attention Only: All senior executive officers, Abwehr.

From: Captain Conrad Patzig, Chef der Abwehr.

By the authority of the Decree of the Reich President for the Protection of People and State, the NSDAP/DNVP coalition government has suspended the German state governments. The reasons cited were the fear of public order breakdown and criminal elements attempting to subvert the authority of the state governments. Reich commissars have been temporarily appointed to oversee the individual states. They will directly subordinate to the central government.

For information only. No action necessary. [END]

He could hear Captain Bauer talking to his secretary as he hung up his coat.

After he'd come in, and the usual pleasantries had been taken care of, he gave the captain the memo.

The young officer read it and looked up at the General.

'What do you think?'

The captain was becoming more accustomed to the General's sudden requests for his opinion and had developed several strategies for buying himself some time to formulate his answer.

'Sir, it certainly is worrying. What are your thoughts on it?'

'Captain, I know my views on the matter. I'd like to hear yours,' the General said, rather drily.

Heinz Bauer swallowed, then plunged in.

'Well, sir, it gives the government effective control of all the states.'

Since the end of the Great War, Germany had been a republic, made up of seventeen autonomous states. The responsibility for much of the day-to-day running of the country rested on each of the states' legislatures, and central government had little control over large swathes of services and provisions that affected most people's lives.

'Correct. And yet, the papers barely mentioned it. Don't you find that strange?'

'Sir, I don't tend to read the papers. To be honest, I find them rather dull.'

The General raised his eyebrows.

'So how do you know what's going on in the world?'

'Sir, I sometimes listen to the wireless but often I just hear what's happening by listening to others,' the captain replied, shifting uncomfortably in his seat.

'Well, I'd recommend that you rise half an hour earlier each morning, get yourself a newspaper and read it over a cup of coffee. You need to know what's going on in the world, although, judging by today's *Morgenpost*, it wouldn't be of much help.'

'Sir, this may sound a bit stupid, but perhaps they think it's not newsworthy.'

'There are demonstrations on the streets of our city, the largest of which needed hundreds of police to contain and was dispersed by a significant number of Sturmabteilung thugs. Every state government in Germany has been taken over by central government and none of this is worth writing about?'

'Sir, when you put it like that…' the captain tailed off, with a thoroughly miserable air.

'Heinz, part of our job is to monitor the world outside the navy and the army and assess how events are going to impinge on the Reichswehr; to be their eyes and ears, in effect. We, as the Abwehr, need to interact with individuals and groups outside of the military because it's something that the armed forces don't do well. It also helps to keep the civilian authorities on our side.'

'It takes a bit of getting used to, sir. I don't know if I'm cut out for it.'

The General wondered again if it would be kinder to let Heinz Bauer return to the straightforward world of the navy. He was pushing his second in command hard to make him think for himself, but he wondered, not for the first time, if he was trying to hammer a round peg into a square hole. He didn't believe so.

'You'll do a great job here; it will just take a while to adapt. Forget you were ever in the navy. I've had to let the army go too.'

'Yes, sir. What do you want me to do?'

'Keep thinking, listening, watching. It'll all click one day, wait and see. Now, as it happens, there is something else you can do for me.'

CHAPTER 15

Yosef and Miriam Nussbaum took their usual route when they left the synagogue. Saturdays were a favourite with Ruth and Manny; once the service and the obligatory socialising afterwards were over, they often had lunch at one of the numerous cafés sprinkled around the centre of Kiel and, because everything was already prepared for the evening meal, they didn't need to be back at the Drachensee house until late afternoon.

In summer, they would spend the few hours between lunch and the long walk back home feeding the ducks in Kleiner Kiel, watching the fishing boats in the Bootshafen, or strolling along the waterfront, often as far as Düsternbrook. Once in a while, they would catch a tram all the way out to Holtenau and the canal, and watch the boats go up and down the massive sea locks, then walk all the way back along the front past the naval dockyard, where Manny would spend as long as he was permitted spotting and naming all the different battleships, even though he wasn't yet six. On wet days, Yosef and Miriam would take the children to see a film, or visit the city's Zoologisches Museum, or an art gallery.

As they reached the end of Humboldtstraße, and crossed Knooper Weg, Manny campaigned for a visit to the cinema. There was a matinee showing of a selection of Laurel and Hardy films, which both he and his sister loved; as with most Germans, dubbed films from the United States were becoming their cinema of choice.

'It's too fine a day to sit inside,' Miriam insisted. 'Would you not rather go down to the front and watch the ships? If you're really good we might even take a boat trip to Laboe, if we have time.'

She looked at Yosef, and after checking his pocket watch, he nodded. Although they couldn't afford such extravagance every week, it was such a beautiful day to be out on the water.

'We'll buy a snack from one of the stalls down at the harbour, and eat it on the boat, or we'll run out of time,' Yosef said, and they started walking down Fleethörn, Manny trotting to keep up.

Manny's excitement grew with every step. 'We're going on a boat. We're going on a boat,' he chanted, and skipped on in front.

They were just approaching the Reichsbank building when, up ahead, they could hear shouting, and Yosef could see that a crowd had formed outside the Rathaus.

Miriam shouted to Manny to come back, and hold her hand, and the boy did as he was told, huffing a little. As they drew closer, Yosef could see a cluster of the brown-shirted SA men who seemed to be ever-present these days, but he also recognised uniforms like the one he had worn during the Great War.

'These are Stahlhelm men,' he whispered to Miriam. 'Veterans of the Great War who think Germany should be ready to fight again. The only difference between them and the SA is that they believe that the Kaiser should be in charge instead of Adolf Hitler.'

He gripped Ruth's hand in one of his, and Miriam's in the other. Some of the men looked towards them and, not wanting to make an obvious U-turn, Yosef kept walking, moving out into the road to keep clear of the crowd jostling around the tall pillars of the Rathaus entrance. Another band of uniformed men stood in the town square, on the opposite side of Fleethörn, so they kept to the centre of the street, trying to avoid contact with either group.

The group that stood apart from the mass around the town house had a uniform that Yosef had never seen before; they wore the same brown shirts as the SA men, but the rest of their uniform was black, including the long wool coats that made them stand out from the rest.

He'd heard stories about an elite force attached to the National Socialist party but neither he, nor his friends, had ever seen any of them in Kiel.

'Schutzstaffel. SS,' he whispered. 'Don't say a word.'

As they walked past the Rathaus entrance, one of the SA Brownshirts peeled off from his friends and approached them. He stopped directly in front of the Nussbaums and held out his hand, like a policeman controlling traffic.

'Halt.' They stopped in front of him. Manny squinted at the man, his young curiosity aroused. Miriam gripped his hand and willed him to stay quiet.

'Where do you think you're going?' the man asked.

'We are taking the children to Laboe, sir.'

The man smirked at Yosef's deference, and looked around to see if his friends were watching. He wasn't much more than twenty.

'May I see some identification, please.'

Yosef handed him his driving licence.

'Drachensee? You live on Hamburger Chaussee?'

The man's disbelief showed in his face.

'Yes, I am General Kästner's driver. My wife is the General's housekeeper.'

Yosef's answer should have been enough explanation but, far from satisfying the man, it made him more suspicious.

'Nussbaum. Isn't that a Jewish name?'

Yosef weighed up the risks of lying and the humiliation of denial, against the worry about what the man might do if he told him the truth. The SA were notorious in their harassment of Jewish people.

Just as he'd decided to tell the truth and be damned by it, one of the SS men crossed the road.

'Hey, kleine Puppe, leave them alone.'

Little puppet.

Yosef, almost choking, bit back a laugh.

The SA thug baulked and faced the dark-coated man for a few seconds, but his eyes turned away first from the SS stormtrooper's cold stare.

'I was just telling them to be on their way,' he said.

'Well, I say it's you that should be on your way. Go back to your friends.'

The Brownshirt glared at the man for a second, then crossed the road. Yosef could see him talking to his friends and gesticulating towards the SS man. He frowned. He'd been led to believe that the SS were part of the SA, and subordinate to it.

I must ask the General.

The SS man's voice interrupted his thoughts.

'I'm sorry, but may I see your card, please.'

Yosef handed him the card and waited.

'So, I overheard you say that you work for this General Kästner, ja?'

'I do. I also served under him in the war.'

'Ah, a soldier. I thought you had a rifleman's bearing. Perhaps it would be better for you to move on, to take your children away from here.'

Yosef longed to ask the man what was taking place, but he knew that he should keep walking. He glanced at the Rathaus before turning back to the SS man.

The man laughed.

'Don't worry. Some of the councillors decided they could vote to remove the legal mayor, Herr Hoffmann. Verdammt insurrection! Along with our colleagues in the Sturmabteilung and the Stahlhelm,' he said, sneering as he named the two groups. 'We've broken up their illegal meeting. We'll secure the building until the council can be reconvened lawfully.'

He glanced at his SS companions, standing disciplined in the square, and then at the milling mass of Brownshirts and nationalist veterans.

'I apologise for them. They're an undisciplined rabble. We are here to ensure that there is no violence, that the due process of law is adhered to.'

Yosef wondered where the police were, and how the law fitted in, but he said nothing.

'Anyway, I would be on my way if I were you. Sieg Heil!'

The man snapped his heels and saluted, his right arm straight out in front of him.

'Sieg Heil,' Yosef said, raising his arm in response, before gathering up his family and walking across the square, trying their best not to look as if they were hurrying.

'What was that?' hissed Miriam when they were well out of earshot.

Yosef couldn't meet her eyes. 'It's what you must do if they salute you. Mannfred told me about it, thank God. If you don't, they think you're a communist.'

'It makes me sick.' Her voice softened, seeing Yosef's face. 'But if we must do it, we will.' She turned to the children. 'If that ever happens to you, do what your father did.'

The children nodded obediently, not understanding the full significance of the exchange but knowing by instinct that it was important.

'Now, we should head back home. It looks like rain,' Yosef said, a tremor still in his voice.

'No,' his wife said, squeezing her husband's hand and smiling, 'let's go to Laboe. We'll not let the threat of something like that stop us doing what we want.'

As they turned hand in hand into Holstenbrücke, young Manny skipping again, they both knew she hadn't been talking about the weather.

That evening, massed ranks of Brownshirts and Stahlhelm filled the town square. Around the edges, and up and down Fleethörn as far as the eye could see, townspeople packed into every available space to watch the spectacle and listen to the speeches. Spotlights had been rigged to illuminate the front of the Rathaus, and the party officials and Brownshirt leaders crowding the balcony on the first floor. Long red banners hung from the upper windows, the black-and-white swastikas stark against the blood-red cloth spilling down to the ground.

Stirring words of hate rained down on the crowd from the Rathaus's balcony to a frenzied clamour of acclaim.

The General stood at the corner of the square closest to Martensdamm and watched for a while, then turned on his heel and started to walk home.

[12/03/1933 Sunday]

'Sir, can I ask you a question?' Yosef said, placing a cup of coffee on the table in front of the General.

'By all means, Yosef,' the General said. 'Ask away.'

'The SS. Are they not part of the SA?'

The General frowned. It wasn't the sort of question he'd expected. Something about the house, perhaps, or the car.

'Why do you ask?'

'We were stopped by the SA outside the Rathaus yesterday. The man was a boor. An SS man stepped in and let us go on. It surprised me.'

'Technically, the SS is part of the SA but since Heinrich Himmler took over its command, it has become more independent, answering almost exclusively to Hitler now.'

'I see, sir.'

'You had your papers with you, I hope.'

'Yes, sir. The SS man checked them and let us go. He was more civil than I'd expected.'

'I wouldn't count on all of them being like that, Yosef. I'd avoid all of them if I were you.'

CHAPTER 16

[13/03/1933 Monday]

Ruth's hand shot up.

The teacher looked at her and smiled.

'Well, Ruth?'

'Albert Einstein, miss.'

'Very good, Ruth. That was an excellent answer.'

Ruth beamed at the teacher.

'Now, does anyone else know a famous German scientist?'

Miss Brinckmann looked around the class. Another hand was raised.

The boy was called Peter Hauer. He wasn't the smallest boy in the class but had suffered sporadic bullying because of an unfortunate stammer. Ruth, Antje, and a few of the other girls had tried their best to curtail the taunts and pranks that he was forced to endure, and to a certain degree, they'd succeeded.

It all changed for Peter when he was one of the first in the school to join the Hitlerjugend. His Gebietsführer, the head of Hitlerjugend in Kiel, had seen something of himself in the boy and, over his first year, had steadily advanced him up the ranks until he was a section leader, despite his age.

The first time Rottenführer Hauer wore his uniform into school, the teacher made him change out of it. All the boy had with him was his sports gear, and he was made to sit through the whole day in shorts and a singlet.

Two days later, his Gebietsführer visited the school and spoke with the headmaster. From then on, Peter Hauer, and the classmates who followed him into the ranks of the Hitlerjugend, were permitted to wear their uniforms if they so wished.

Miss Brinckmann never acknowledged the change in the rules, but from that day forward, the bullying stopped, and the boy's stammer disappeared.

Now, when he spoke, there was a sneering arrogance in his voice.

'Max Planck, miss, because he is a true German. Not like Einstein.'

'Max Planck is a great answer, but although Albert Einstein now lives and works in Switzerland, he was born in Württemberg and was educated in Munich.'

'Miss, Albert Einstein is not a German. He is a Jew.'

For the briefest second, the class fell silent. Then two of the boys snickered.

'What did you say?' Her voice was quiet, but it cut through the uneasy shuffling of the class.

'He is a Jew. Not a true German, miss.'

Her question had been rhetorical. She hadn't expected him to repeat his statement. A flush spread upwards across her face.

'Peter, please stand outside and I will come and deal with you.'

She would give the class an exercise to do and decide how to deal with the boy's outburst.

'No, miss. It is the Jews who should leave,' he said, his voice strong and clear, looking at the three girls sitting near the front of the class.

She moved towards him but, out of the corner of her eye, she detected an almost imperceptible movement in the boy sitting next to him, then the boy across from him. She stopped, suddenly nervous.

In front of her, Peter Hauer raised his right arm, and started to sing.

'Die Fahne hoch! Die Reihen fest geschlossen!'

Raise the flag! The ranks tightly closed!

Halfway through the first line, another boy joined in, then another, leaving their seats

78

and standing beside their desks with their arms raised, mimicking his. Before long, over half the class were singing the Horst Wessel Song.

'Stop,' she shouted, but the sound was drowned out by the boys' voices, loud and in unison, in a flawless rendition of the National Socialists' anthem. She looked around. One or two of the girls had also got to their feet and joined with the boys.

'SA marschiert mit ruhig festem Schritt.'

The SA marches with calm, firm pace.

She looked at the three Jewish girls, sitting together, staring towards the front, their bodies rigid with fear. She closed her eyes.

When the song was finished, the boys remained standing.

'Now you've had your little moment,' the teacher said, her voice cold, 'sit back down in your seats and act as children should. You will all be reprimanded, you especially, Peter Hauer.'

'No, we won't, Miss Brinckmann. Today we are honouring the leader of our country, Adolf Hitler.'

The rest of the class looked towards her, gauging how she would react. She estimated that two-thirds of her pupils were behind Peter Bauer and she conceded defeat.

'Ruth, please go to Herr Lehmann's office and ask him to come immediately.'

She realised her mistake at once.

Peter Hauer nodded, and two boys moved to the door, blocking it.

She cursed herself for choosing one of the Jewish girls. She should have chosen Antje, or one of the boys who wasn't involved.

She moved to the door and, keeping eye contact with the boys guarding it, she forced them to separate and let her pass.

As she left the room, she heard the strains of the Hitlerjugend anthem rise again behind her. She ran.

~~o~~

'The boy was primed. For the love of God, they sang the Horst Wessel Song. I've spoken to the headmasters at two neighbouring schools. Almost identical incidents happened in their classrooms.'

The headmaster had reacted to Emilie Brinckmann bursting into his room, breathless and pale, by asking the school janitor to accompany him to Fräulein Brinckmann's class, but the boys had locked and barricaded the door, after expelling anyone from the class who hadn't sang with them. One of the boys passed a note under the door. The school was to close for the day, in honour of the country's leader. After sending the remaining children home, he'd convened a meeting of all the staff.

'How do we deal with it?'

'Do we need to?' The voice came from the back of the room.

Everyone turned round. The deputy head was standing by the door.

'Sorry I'm late,' she said. 'I had a parent to deal with.'

'You think we can just let this go?'

'I don't think this will happen again. It was just the boys flexing their muscles. It's not in their interest to disrupt their schooling.'

Miss Brinckmann spoke up. 'This was an organised walkout. It wasn't just the boys behind this, and there was some hateful thing said, in front of the whole class. We can't just brush it under the carpet.'

'Miss Brinckmann,' the deputy head intoned, 'just because you lost control of a class of nine-year-olds, it doesn't mean we have to take draconian measures.'

For the first time since it started, Emilie Brinckmann felt tears well up in her eyes. Furious, she turned on the older woman.

'I can control a class just as well as you, Frau Köhler. This was something not one of you could have dealt with. If you'd been there you would understand.'

'If I'd been there it wouldn't have happened,' she sneered.

Before Emilie Brinckmann had a chance to retort, the head teacher interceded.

'Now, there's no point in recriminations and in-fighting. Fräulein Brinckmann, you are an excellent teacher for one so young, and I'm sure this is none of your fault, but you have had a very traumatic day, and it would be beneficial if you took a couple of days off to recover. I will take your classes.'

She bridled, but part of her agreed with what he was saying. She didn't want to face the children the next day.

'I will let the boys go. There's only an hour of the day left. But I will have a word with all their parents. Fräulein Brinckmann, would you please write down a list of names before you go.'

Emilie Brinckmann made her list and handed it to the principal. He put a hand on her shoulder and gave her an encouraging smile.

'Come back on Thursday. We'll sort something out.'

As she left the room, she overheard the deputy head, talking to one of the other teachers.

'…the boy had a point. Albert Einstein is about as German as the king of Denmark.'

'Will that be all, General?'

It was late. Miriam had left Yosef to tidy up the kitchen and to see if the Kästners needed anything, and Maria had gone to bed, citing a headache.

'Yosef, we're just going to have a whisky. Would you join us?'

Yosef, though polite, often declined General Kästner's invitations but that evening, he sat down and watched as the General poured two generous measures of his favourite Scottish malt and a smaller one for Franz. Johann was staying over with a schoolfriend and the girls were in bed. He added water to his son's glass while Yosef fetched some ice.

The General looked at the lines of worry on Yosef's face.

'We need to talk.'

'I know. I'm worried, General.'

'Antje spoke to me about what happened at school. I've already told Franz.'

'Ruth came home in tears. It was kind of Antje to stay and accompany her and Manny home. What kind of world are we living in when a nine-year-old boy can take command of a class and shut down a school?'

'I don't know, but I am going to see the head tomorrow. You'll come?'

Yosef smiled bitterly. 'I guess it's the only way I'll get to see anybody. I went to the school today. There was nobody available to talk to me.'

'I'm also going to see the girls' teacher. She has been given a few days' leave.'

'From what Ruth said, she tried her best. The boy had too much support from the rest of the class.'

The General turned to Franz. 'Tell Yosef what you know.'

Franz cleared his throat. 'At our weekly Hitlerjugend training, they had all the boys practising the Horst Wessel Song, more so than usual. The leaders also gave us a lecture on getting behind anyone who got up and made a stand in class. While the rest of them were brushing up on their marching drills, they took some of the senior youth ranks away for some *special instructions*.'

He paused, looking at Yosef, not able to meet his eyes.

'Franz was one of them,' the General said. He nodded for his son to continue.

'They told us to find any excuse to disrupt classes and, if possible, to engineer a school walkout. One of the boys at my school said that we couldn't do it because ours is a military school, and we would be instantly dismissed. The Stabsführer asked us if that was true, and we all said yes. He had a think about it, then said, as future officers of the Reichsheer and the

Reichsmarine, we were right to point out that discipline at a military school should be paramount, for the good of the fatherland, but we should politely insist to our teachers that we should sing the Horst Wessel Song, and salute our glorious leader. For all other schools, the plan was still to shut them down. He also said…'

He paused again, shame etched on his face.

'Go on,' the General said, not unkindly.

'…He said that if there were any Jews in the class, we were to blame them. We only have one Jew in the whole school.'

'So, what happened?' Yosef asked.

'Well, we asked the teacher and he said that we could go ahead. We sang the song and sat down. That was it.'

'What about the Jewish boy?' Yosef asked.

'He's in Johann's class. He sang it too. Nobody forced him, he just joined in. He saluted and everything.'

Erich Kästner didn't know if his son's embarrassment was for the Jewish boy's compliance or his own actions.

'It confirms what we know,' he said. 'This was a concerted countrywide tactic planned by the NSDAP using Hitlerjugend to carry it out. The day before their big marches,' he said.

'I don't want to take part now,' Franz said.

'I don't think you should pull out at this stage,' Yosef said softly.

The General looked at him, a frown creasing his brow.

'It would look bad withdrawing at the last minute,' Yosef explained. 'It would mark you out at school.'

The General thought about it.

'He's right. You'll just have to go through with it. And the sailing. You can't pull out of that now, either. You'll be leaving Hitlerjugend this year, anyway, when you join the army. And Johann will only be a year behind you.'

Franz argued for a short while, but at Yosef and his father's insistence, he agreed. He looked almost relieved, the General noticed.

'How did we ever get to this?' Yosef asked. 'Why have the National Socialists been so successful?'

The General looked at his son, wondering whether this was a conversation he wanted him to hear.

'There are a few reasons,' he said. 'First and foremost, they are telling the German people what they want to hear, and giving them someone to blame for Germany's woes; foreigners, the communists, the Social Democrats…'

He hesitated.

'…and the Jews.'

'So, nothing changes,' Yosef said. 'We have been blamed for the woes of Europe for hundreds, even thousands of years. There will always be pogroms, but I didn't expect it here, of all places.'

Yosef glanced up at the two Kästners as he spoke and gave a resigned shrug.

Erich Kästner put his hand on Yosef's arm.

'If that were all,' he said, 'they would just be another protest party, shouting their hatred to anyone who would listen. But they have three groups of people behind them, as far as I can tell. First, ultra-conservative members of the former aristocratic ruling class who think they can use Hitler and his henchmen to destroy the Republic, then replace him with someone of their own choosing; preferably a descendant of the Kaiser.'

He paused to let his words sink in.

'Then there are the wealthy bankers and industrialists, like Krupp and IG Farben. They put pressure on Hindenburg to back Hitler because they were convinced that he would be good for business, coming down hard on communism and the trade-union movement, and promising support for free enterprise.'

Neither Yosef nor Franz said anything.

'Finally, there's the military. It's also gambling on Hitler, believing his promises to tear up the Treaty of Versailles and return our armed forces to their former glory.'

'But surely the army won't be party to the way the National Socialists are behaving?'

'The army and the navy will do whatever it thinks is best for them. It may be wary of getting into bed with Hitler and, in some ways, it may still manage to keep a distance, but it will support the government if it means expansion.'

'So, there is no one to oppose them,' Franz said, shocked at his father's words.

'Oh, they have their opponents, but they are gradually getting rid of them too. Tell him, Yosef.'

'We nearly got caught up in the putsch at the town hall. The SA and the Stahlhelm took over the Rathaus and expelled all the councilmen. I was told that they were trying to reinstate Mayor Hoffmann. I thought it a bit strange; as far as I knew, he was the deputy mayor.'

'They arrested our former mayor a few days ago. Replaced him with Jürgen Hoffmann. From what I can gather, the SPD and Centre Party councilmen locked themselves in the chamber all day yesterday in protest at the arrests of the KPD councillors and the removal of the mayor. They demanded that Jürgen Hoffmann be removed. The SS, the SA and the Stahlhelm stormed the building and hauled all the protestors out and occupied it overnight, until the NSDAP, DNVP and BVP councillors convened this morning, with Jürgen Hoffmann reinstated as mayor.'

'He's your friend, is he not?' Franz asked his father, puzzled.

'I doubt it. He's a staunch party member now, and he knows how I feel.'

Franz had his head in his hands. His father felt for him, facing the cold, hard facts of the new political face of his nation.

'There's also this, sir.' Yosef picked up the paper, and opened it, pointing to the small news item at the bottom of the third page.

LOCAL LAWYER DIES – CRIMINAL CONNECTIONS SUSPECTED.

Dr. Wilhelm Spiegel, a Jewish lawyer, has been found dead at his home in Kiel. Reports suggest that he had died from gunshot wounds. The police will not confirm if they are looking for anyone in relation to the incident.

Dr. Spiegel, a social democrat, was a member of the SPD and was the board president of the Jewish Community Association. The police are looking into evidence that Dr. Spiegel was heavily involved with criminal elements of the Communist Party.

As the General finished reading it, Yosef continued.

'Dr. Spiegel was a member of our synagogue,' he said. 'He wasn't a regular attender, but he was well known within the community. He was a civil rights lawyer, and he was murdered by the SA.'

'It says here he was mixed up with the Communist Party. It's a risky business these days.'

'He was a social democrat. Last year, he defended the Volkszeitung, a regional workers' paper, against libel claims by Adolf Hitler. The paper had accused him of pursuing the objective of a civil war. On Sunday night Dr. Spiegel was visited by two men, one in SA uniform, who claimed to be the police. He took them into his study, where they shot him in the back of the head.'

Both Kästner men gasped.

'The thing is, sir; was it because he dared to oppose Hitler or was it because he was

Jewish? Did that make him an easy target?'

'They don't take easily to criticism. I would imagine it is because of his stance against Herr Hitler.'

'Then why him, and not someone at the newspaper?'

A silence filled the room.

'Is the newspaper still going?'

'They went underground and printed a few issues but that will stop. I don't read it, and neither do most of the Jewish community. Workers' rights are not our thing.'

'Have there been other attacks on Jews in Kiel?'

'There's a lot of verbal stuff, like I said before, sir, and things like serving Jewish people out of turn in most shops. It's the sort of thing that has always gone on, but it's more brazen now. It's worse elsewhere in Germany.'

He frowned.

'There was the bomb in the synagogue, a while ago,' he added. 'To be honest, it wasn't much of an explosion, but it could have hurt someone.'

'When was this? It's the first I've heard of it.'

'It happened last year. You were away sailing. There were no injuries, and the damage was superficial, but it could have been worse.'

'Listen, Yosef, I know you and the family are feeling threatened at this point in time but, for God's sake, you served your country in the war, you're a respected member of the community and you work for me. It's inconceivable that you or your family would be in any danger but, if you feel you should leave, then don't be afraid to say.'

'No sir. We don't want to leave. We haven't even discussed it. We are Germans, and we are more than happy here. It will all settle down.'

As the last of the whisky warmed its way down their throats the fears for the months and years ahead lay heavy on all their minds.

'It's ironic, sir. Yesterday was the Jewish holiday of Purim. Do you know what that is?'

'I should do, Yosef. You told me once, a long time ago. I know it's not Passover, but you'll have to remind me.'

'Sir, Purim is the day of the deliverance of the Jews.'

CHAPTER 17

It is an impressive sight.

Maria smiled, holding Antje's hand tightly as they watched the massed ranks of Hitlerjugend, followed by the younger boys of the Deutsches Jungvolk and the girls of the Bund Deutscher Mädel, as they swept past the corner where they stood. Her face lit up and she waved when she spotted Franz, then Johann and Eva. A kind gentleman standing beside them lifted Antje up onto his shoulders so that she could see her brothers and sister marching past.

Maria's heart filled with pride as she watched Franz pass. As one of the youth leaders, he carried a large swastika-emblazoned party flag which flapped in the wind as he waved it from side to side in time with the others.

He made no show of noticing her, or Antje.

Colour and sound filled the street, from the red, white, and black of the flags and banners, to the singing, amplified by the facades of the tall, elegant buildings on either side. A school band had been persuaded to march at the back, which added to the noise.

'Die Straße frei den braunen Bataillonen.
Die Straße frei dem Sturmabteilungsmann!
Es schau'n aufs Hakenkreuz voll Hoffnung schon Millionen.
Der Tag für Freiheit und für Brot bricht an!'

Make the streets free for the brown battalions,
Make the streets free for the SA man!
Already millions are looking to the swastika, full of hope,
The day of freedom and of bread is dawning!

'Do you see them, Antje?' Maria cried, pointing.

Antje shouted at her three siblings, but her yells were drowned out by the clamour behind them.

As the column marched down Holtenauer Straße, passing the headquarters of the Bund, a man shouted out.

'Fascists!'

From nowhere, half a dozen brown-shirted SA men and policemen grabbed him, protesting, and bundled him towards a police van parked around the corner in Schauenburgerstraße.

The procession continued towards the centre of town, large crowds lining the streets cheering on the children, or simply curious. The snaking column turned right into Bergstraße then into Wilhelminenstraße. Maria, following the procession, wondered at the route, surely not the most direct way to the square in front of the Rathaus, but when they turned into Gartenstraße, she realised the reason for the detour. Large flags flew from the walls of the NSDAP district headquarters and, as they passed, the Gauleiter, Hinrich Lohse, and a line of party officials, stood on the balcony and saluted, arms outstretched.

'Heil Hitler!' they barked.

From the massed ranks below, the reply roared upwards.

'Heil Hitler! Sieg Heil!'

And the column marched on to the Rathaus.

~~o~~

Franz looked around him. Everywhere, wonder lit up each youngster's face, their eyes still shining, electrified by the stirring speeches that had resounded around the square from the men on the banner-draped dais. While the march had wound its way around the Rathaus, the NSDAP leaders had made the short journey by car from Gartenstraße, ready for the arrival of the marchers.

The speeches had been fiery and full of righteous fervour, only lacking the bible-thumping of the sermons delivered by hellfire-and-brimstone preachers. Instead, they inflamed the crowd with bile and hatred, and blind nationalism.

The youngsters stood and listened to each speaker with rapt attention, each oration punctuated with a volley of *Sieg Heils* and salutes to the Führer.

As the rally ended, Franz waited, his anxious gaze searching for Johann and Eva, lost in the confusion of the crowd around the Rathaus. Collecting them together, he threaded his way homeward through the throng, his siblings trailing in his wake, looking for Yosef, in the car, returning for them after dropping Antje and their mother home.

By the time they passed the civil courts, halfway along Königsweg, the crowd had thinned, and they heard Yosef sound the horn on the opposite side of the road.

They crossed and got in, and Yosef spun the car round in a tight U-turn, heading southwards. Johann opened his mouth to speak but Franz silenced him with a shake of the head, puzzling Eva and frustrating his younger brother, still buzzing from the promises made to them by the National Socialist leadership.

'Later,' Franz whispered to him, 'Not now.'

Franz glanced up. He saw Yosef watching him in the driver's mirror. He looked away, unable to meet Yosef's gaze.

~~o~~

[15/03/1933 Wednesday]

'I'm going. That's the end of it,' Yosef stated, staring at Miriam.

His wife's arms were folded across her chest. Just occasionally, Yosef put his foot down when he was determined enough about something. If it hadn't been vital to him, it wouldn't have been worth the aggravation he would suffer but, on this occasion, he felt strongly enough about it to insist.

'There will be trouble at it,' Miriam said. 'Mark my words.'

'There won't be, but if there is, I'll keep out of the way. I just feel the community should stand together. I don't expect you to come.'

He saw her soften a little. He steeled himself.

She knows that I have right on this side of the argument.

'Be careful,' she said.

He nodded and put his hat on.

Wilhelm Spiegel's funeral was expected to draw large crowds; the Jewish community was angry and disturbed by his murder, and they would be joined by trade unionists, social democrats, and the few remaining communists who, to their astonishment, still had their freedom.

Yosef had spoken to the General; he thought it prudent to warn him that he was going. He had offered to accompany him, but Yosef dissuaded him on the grounds that, if there was to be trouble, he didn't want his employer to be involved.

He walked to the cemetery in Eichhof, refusing General Kästner's offer that he should use the car. The Eichhof tram would have taken him all the way from the centre of Kiel, but it was a crisp day, and it gave him time to think. He was touched to find hundreds upon hundreds of working men lining Eichhofstraße on both sides along much of its length who, to a man, waited to doff their hats and bow their heads when the hearse drove by, watching in respectful silence as the long column of mourners, from all walks of life, marched in protest behind the cortège.

Once in the cemetery, Yosef stood near the back, not being a close friend of the family. He was still deep in thought when the service began, and he stumbled his way through the Keriah, tearing the black strip of ribbon that had been pinned to his coat when he arrived, and chanted the words he knew so well, barely listening to the prayers and the readings from the Psalms.

Then Otto Eggerstedt stood at the graveside and began to speak. As he delivered his eulogy for Wilhelm Spiegel, the crowd sensed they were listening to something historic and significant. In all probability, it would be the only public condemnation of the National Socialists that they would ever hear. A social democrat and ex-Altona police chief, Eggerstedt was one of the few politicians remaining who was willing to speak out.

In the cold stillness, his voice hung above the crowd, the truth of it heavy on their chests. He laid bare the bones of the NSDAP and all its leaders; Adolf Hitler, Heinrich Himmler, Joseph Goebbels, Hermann Göring and Ernst Röhm, the SA chief. Each in turn was accused of lying and cheating their way to power, and for dragging the country into the blind cul-de-sac of fascism.

And, as much as anything, he blamed the German people for sleepwalking into dictatorship.

When he finished, the hundreds, maybe thousands of dark-coated men and women stood in silence.

Then, a lone voice rose to chant a prayer and, as the coffin was lowered into the ground, his Jewish friends and his family began intoning the Kaddish for him. Yosef looked around. At the gates of the cemetery, three men turned and hurried towards one of the few cars parked near the entrance. Unlike the rest of the crowd, they hadn't removed their hats in respect. As the men got into the car and drove back to the city, Yosef glimpsed the familiar flash of their brown uniforms.

~~o~~

[16/03/1933 Thursday]

Miss Brinckmann entered the classroom. The children were much younger than those in her old class; she'd been given the infants for the remainder of the year.

She wondered if her former pupils would miss her, as she would miss them. She turned to the class and told them to find a blank page in their workbooks.

'We're going to practise a few sums. Do you all know how to add?'

'Yes, miss,' they sang back at her.

She turned to the blackboard to write the first numbers and froze.

A word had been chalked in large letters, filling the whole board.

Judenliebhaber

Jew lover. She lifted the duster and, watched curiously by thirty small faces, erased the word from the board.

~~o~~

Memo: Geh.KdoS. ABW 20/3/33 CAC0169.1

For Attention Only: All senior executive officers, Abwehr.

From: Captain Conrad Patzig, Chef der Abwehr.

The SS (Schutzstaffel) has opened a concentration camp outside Munich, near the town of Dachau. The camp will be officially used to incarcerate "protective-custody" prisoners. Heinrich Himmler announced in the Münchner Neueste Nachrichten that it could hold up to 5,000 people and described it as "the first concentration camp for political prisoners" to be used to restore calm to Germany. It will be managed solely by SS personnel.

For information only. No action necessary. [END]

KIELER MORGENPOST

Friday 24th March 1933

EMPOWERMENT FOR THE PEOPLE!

Yesterday, by 441 votes against 94, the German parliament passed the Law for Rectification of the Distress of Nation and Reich. It has been welcomed as the "Enabling Act". This law allows the Chancellor, Adolf Hitler, to initiate and sign legislation into law without obtaining parliamentary consent and is in response to the perilous democratic state of the nation, and its vulnerability to criminal political elements, both within and without the country.

The Morgenpost salutes the brave stance of our leaders in protecting Germany by whatever means necessary.

CHAPTER 18

[25/03/1933 Saturday]

'Happy birthday, little Dumplingwurst.'

The admiral handed his granddaughter her present.

'Grandpapa! Thank you,' Antje said, trying not to rip the wrapping paper off, conscious that her mother was watching.

As she teased the tissue paper apart, a wooden box emerged, with a picture of a seabird in flight, soaring across a stormy sea, painted on the lid with a couple of lines of words, set in black scrolling type below it.

Der Sturmtaucher
Aquarelle des Künstlerfarben
V. Klemperer and sons.

Beneath the box of watercolours, there were a variety of brushes and mixing pots, a pad of cartridge paper and a small foldaway easel.

She squealed with delight. 'Thank you. Thank you. Thank you. A watercolour paint set! I love it. And it has a shearwater on it. Can I paint now, Mama?'

'Not just now,' Maria Kästner said, frowning, as Antje gave her grandfather and her grandmother each a big hug. 'Perhaps later.'

'You'll have to do as your mother says, and don't make a mess.'

As Antje undid the hasp on the box, he turned and winked at Maria, who blushed.

'Oh, a few messy clothes and some paint on the floor won't be a disaster,' she said, flustered.

Antje lifted out the small wooden palette and gasped at the rainbow of paint tubes below, each in its own wooden compartment.

'Look, Mama,' she said.

'We heard she was quite the budding artist. We thought she should have the proper paints, but the easel sits on the table, so she doesn't make a mess of the floor.'

The admiral smiled at Maria, who blushed again.

'Erich will be home soon,' she said, to hide her embarrassment. 'He's had to go to a late meeting, and he apologises. We've to start the birthday party without him if he's not back by seven.'

'Papa has a new job. He's working with the navy now, just like you did, Grandpapa.'

'Ha. I always knew that he would come good. Is he an admiral now, like me?'

'Oh, no. He's still a general. I don't understand how he can be a general and be in the navy though.' She shrugged and shook her head.

'He is with the army, Antje, but he is the one who talks to the navy when they need to tell each other something,' Maria corrected her.

'Oh yes, I remember now. He's a lassoing officer.'

The adults all laughed, and the admiral ruffled his granddaughter's hair.

'Grandpapa,' she asked, when she'd wriggled away from him and had smoothed her hair again, 'why did Daddy not become an admiral, like you?'

'That's an excellent question, child.' He sighed, and his face sagged with sadness. 'Your father was always a wayward boy. He never did anything he was told. When he was a little older than you, your grandmother and I thought he would follow me into the navy, as he loved the sea, and sailing, but he suddenly decided that he wanted to be a soldier. It nearly broke my heart.'

Antje looked at her grandfather, shocked. To hear such terrible things about her father, who she adored, from her grandfather, who she loved almost as much, was not what she'd expected.

'Grandpapa. You're teasing me!' she cried, seeing the twinkle of mirth at the corner of his eyes.

He grabbed her and tickled her until her screams filled the house and brought Miriam into the sitting room to see who was being murdered.

'No, Antje,' he said, when the girl's laughter had subsided, 'your father always wanted to be his own man, and not be seen to have any advantage he might have had from being in the navy, with an admiral for a father. I always respected him for that. Everything he achieved was entirely on his own merit.'

Antje found the real reason for her father's choice of career much less interesting than her grandfather's first version.

'Can I go and show Ruth my present, please,' she said, as much to Miriam as to her mother.

Maria glanced at Miriam, who gave a brief nod.

'On you go,' her mother told her, 'for a few minutes only, and bring Ruth and Manny over. We'll be starting your party soon.'

Antje grabbed her paint set and ran, before her mother changed her mind, almost colliding with Yosef, carrying a coffee pot.

'And don't open any of the paints!' Maria shouted after her. She turned to her father-in-law.

'He never would tell me why he chose to join the army, when he clearly was more at home on the water. I often wonder if he would have joined the navy if the ships still had sails.'

As the old couple laughed, a car pulled up in the driveway, the crunch of its wheels on gravel alerting Yosef, who slipped from the room. It wasn't the General. The first of Antje's invited friends had arrived, and her birthday party was underway.

~~o~~

The General winced at Doctor Speer's frown. 'You're working too hard for a man of your age,' the Doc said.

'Nonsense. Don't you know I've retired?'

The Doc laughed.

'You'll never retire. Soldiering is in your blood.'

'And you think that's why I have stomach troubles?'

'Maybe. That and a rich diet. Miriam is too good a cook. I'll prescribe you some stomach powders and I'd advise you to eat plain food for a few weeks until it settles down.'

The General slumped. Doctor Speer smiled at his crestfallen face.

'It's only for a short while,' he said. 'And, by the way, cut back on your drinking.'

'You've gone too far, Doc. Everyone knows that a little whisky before bedtime is marvellous for one's health.'

'I'm not stopping your sundowners. It's the wine with your meals and the four or five whiskies you partake of at Rotary evening that I'm getting at.'

'Oh. And you wonder why people don't seek medical attention?'

They both laughed. It wasn't often the General came to see Doctor Speer in a professional capacity, but his dyspepsia was getting to the annoying stage, and he thought he'd better get something done about it.

'I'll follow your advice,' he said. He glanced at the Doc.

'You're looking tired,' he said.

'I'm overworked too. The fools have decided to remove all female and all Jewish doctors from their posts and we're having to take more patients on.'

'Why, for God's sake,' the General said, an incredulous look on his face.

'Oh, the usual National Socialist dogma. A woman's place is in the home, producing little soldiers for the Reich. And without question, Jewish doctors are filthy, lecherous and greedy.'

'That's ridiculous. All of it. They can't do this.'

'But they have, Erich. It's not quite as bad as it sounds; the bulk of doctors are men anyway, and they've made an exception for female doctors working in midwifery. In addition, Jewish doctors can still treat Jewish patients. They've had the temerity to replace the doctors with medical students, on a temporary basis!'

'It's hard to believe. What's next?' the General asked.

CHAPTER 19

KIELER MORGENPOST

Saturday, 1st April 1933

THE FIGHT BEGINS - DEFENSIVE BOYCOTT CALLED FOR

The Chancellor, Adolf Hitler, urges German patriots to adhere to the boycott of all businesses owned by Jews. Reich Minister of Public Enlightenment and Propaganda, Joseph Goebbels, launched the anti-Jewish boycott in response to what he called "foreign propaganda", which he stated the Jews were spreading about Germany.

Julius Streicher, national co-ordinator of the boycott, told the assembled press that the boycott was to commence all over Germany at 10:00 a.m. "Uniformed guards of the SA and the SS will be deployed in front of Jewish shops, department stores, and factories to ensure that the protest remains peaceful, in the light of strong provocation by the Jewish community, both economically and politically. The businesses themselves will be marked with yellow Stars of David to identify those affected by the embargo".

The action, which includes banks, doctors' surgeries, and law firms, will be repeated on Wednesday.

"It is expected that there would be widespread support for the boycott, and condemnation of those Germans still patronising Jewish establishments".

~~o~~

Exactly a week after Antje's party, Manny's sixth birthday was a quite different affair. Miriam had enlisted Ruth and her two friends, Antje and Rebeka, to help shepherd the flock of five- and six-year-olds who were to descend on the small Nussbaum house.

Returning at noon after the normal Shabbat service, Yosef had a quick bite to eat and picked up the newspaper while Miriam and the girls busied themselves preparing for the party.

Yosef read the headline.

DER KAMPF BEGINNT

The fight begins.
He bowed his head.
At least it's out in the open now.
He put the paper down on the kitchen table, then thought better of it. He didn't want Miriam to see it.
Not on Manny's birthday.

As he left the house, he tucked it under his arm and closed the door behind him.

He parked the car in front of the house and waited. The General had told him that he would drive himself and Frau Kästner to her fundraiser, that Yosef should stay for the party, but he had insisted on driving them.

He grimaced. The thought of spending an afternoon with a gaggle of squealing infants and gossiping ladies didn't appeal but, anyway, they would be back before the party ended; he would join in with the fun then, and the Kästners would make an appearance, to give Manny his present.

CHAPTER 20

Miriam breathed a sigh of relief. The day had turned out fine, and Manny and his friends had the run of the substantial Drachensee grounds, with only the Kästner house and the driveway out of bounds. Two of the other girls' mothers had offered to stay and help.

After they'd helped to serve up the birthday picnic on the lawn and laugh as the troupe of young explorers found most of the treasure that Ruth and her two classmates had secreted around the garden earlier in the day, the three women settled down on chairs they'd carried from the kitchen and placed at the edge of the lawn.

They sat chatting, watching the children play schlagball, similar in most respects to the British game of rounders.

It was refereed by Ruth, Rebeka and Antje.

'The girls are getting big, no?' Rosa Liewermann said.

Miriam nodded. Although she liked, maybe even loved, Maria Kästner, she felt much more comfortable in the company of the two women sitting either side of her.

They were her closest friends, and both had young children around Manny's age, although Moshe, Esther Weichmann's son, was the year above him at school, despite being only six months older.

Moshe was Manny's best friend and lived close enough that the boys were able to go out and play together after school, and on weekends. Often, Shoshana, his sister, would join them if they couldn't sneak out without her.

Esther was one of the few people in Kiel that Miriam had known since childhood, both having been brought up in Altona, near Hamburg, reuniting as new brides in Kiel within months of arriving.

Miriam had met the second of her close friends, Rosa Liewermann, at the synagogue in Kiel. She had been pregnant with Ruth at the same time as Rosa had been carrying Rebeka, and they had been thrown together by the older women of the congregation, who loved to meddle, mostly to the benefit of the recipients. Her son, Fischel, was in Manny's class, the two women giving birth for the second time within weeks of each other, much to everyone's amusement.

'It's lovely to see them play. No tsuris at their age. I wish I could say the same.'

No troubles, thought Miriam. Rosa was right. It would be nice not to wake up every morning, worrying.

Esther was the one to say aloud what was on all their minds.

'I don't know where this is going to end. Itsik is worried about the shop.'

She sometimes helped out in her husband's hardware store, one of the most popular in Kiel. Her words spilled out, with barely a breath between, and a tear slipped down her cheek.

'He told me not to go in today, that his brother was going to come over; he works at the furniture factory in Annenstraße and they're closed because of the boycott. He was more than happy to help, but I'm still frightened about what will happen if people stop buying from us. It could go on for days or even weeks.'

Miriam glanced at the children, but they were too absorbed in the game to notice. She took her friend's hand between her own and gave it a squeeze.

'Take a breath, Esther. Itsik will be fine. His is the best hardware store in Kiel; everyone says you never leave Weichmann's without the item you went there for. Yosef swears he must have a storeroom that goes on forever.'

Esther tried to smile.

'He does have a lot of stock, but it's because he knows where everything is, and what it's all for.'

Rosa spoke.

'And he's so kind and friendly with all his customers, even the ones who are unpleasant.

Emil says that when the men at the factory send one of the new apprentices to him with idiotic requests for 'sky hooks', or 'left-handed brushes', he always explains gently that they've been sent on a fool's errand, then packs them off with a gift of a little something useful for their toolbox.'

'I know. One of the poor souls was sent to fetch some *striped* paint. It always gives us a laugh.'

Esther wiped her face, and when one of the little boys rushed over, dancing from foot to foot, holding himself, and blurting out that he needed the toilet, she smiled at the boy and took him by the hand into the cottage.

'It must be a worry for her, but I can't see the people not using their shop just because it's owned by Jews,' Rosa said to Miriam, while Esther was away.

'I don't know,' Miriam replied. 'Our nasty so-called leaders are whipping up peoples' fears and prejudices. I don't know where it's going to end. You saw what happened at school.'

'I know, sending them home like that, for nothing. I mean, it was a good job Rebeka was there to look after her brother.'

Miriam looked at her.

'Did she not tell you the reason they were sent home?'

'Yes, it was something to do with the march. The boys and the girls who were in that stupid Hitlerjugend club had to practise.'

Miriam looked around, then glanced towards the house. Esther still hadn't appeared.

'Rosa, that's not why they were sent home.'

She recounted Ruth's telling of the events in the classroom that led to the school being closed.

'Don't be hard on her,' she finished, 'she probably didn't want to upset you, or maybe she didn't want to talk about it.'

She'd been watching her friend's face. The initial pallor of shock soon gave way to anger.

'An evil nine-year-old boy dictated how my children are educated! I've got a mind to go around to the boy's house and tell his parents the truth about their wonderful son. Wait till I tell Emil.'

'It won't make any difference, and it might make the boys pick on the girls even more. No doubt his parents are proud of their little Hitler,' Miriam said, her voice hard but measured.

As Esther returned with the newly-relieved child, Antje ran towards them. She waited for a few seconds until Esther had taken her seat.

'Auntie Miriam, Ruth says that Manny's real birthday was on Monday, but I know that he was born on the first of April, because Mama told me.'

The three women laughed. It was Esther who tried to explain.

'Well, Monday is the day his birthday falls on in the Hebrew Calendar...'

She saw the confusion on the young girl's face.

'We have our own calendar, and although we can use both, our Hebrew calendar doesn't always match up to your calendar.'

'Manny's lucky. He has two birthdays!'

She ran off. Miriam heard her telling Ruth that she knew all about Hebrew calendars now.

And for a short while at least, the three women's fears about Germany's youth evaporated.

~~o~~

Ruth spotted Maria and the General first. They must have only just arrived back home, as they still had their coats on, but they'd come through the big house to pick up Manny's gift.

'Tante Maria,' she cried, 'come and have a piece of cake.'

'Do I not get any?' the General said, laughing.

'Of course you do, Uncle Erich.' And she took both their hands, leading them towards the table with the last remnants of the cake on it. 'We kept you a bit.'

Miriam rose from her chair as soon as she saw them.

She hugged Maria. 'I'm so glad you made it. I'll shout Manny over.'

'Leave the boy alone,' the General said. 'He's engrossed in his game. I might just join them,' he said, laughing and throwing off his coat.

The women watched as the young boys shouted with delight at an adult being a part of their game, each group of boys vying to have the General on their team. He agreed to play only if he could be on Manny's team, and the ladies smiled as all the boys solemnly nodded, a fair decision in their eyes.

As the General proceeded to be the worst schlagball player in the history of the game, flailing ineffectively at the ball, and tripping up over his feet when he finally did manage to connect with it, the boys howled with laughter, even those on Manny's team.

'Try harder, Uncle Erich,' Manny shouted as the General missed an easy catch, winking at Ruth as the ball dropped through his hands.

The girls giggled and looked away, party to the General's deception.

Miriam turned to Maria.

'Where's Yosef? He was with you, wasn't he?'

'Yes, he drove us to my fundraiser. The General said he shouldn't, but he insisted.'

Miriam smiled drily. 'Yes, that was terribly noble of him. Anything to avoid an afternoon with a bunch of six-year-olds. Peh. Men.'

She looked round again.

'He'll be putting the car in the garage,' Maria suggested but, a few minutes later, when he hadn't appeared, Miriam left the others and walked up to the cottage to see where he'd gone. The car was parked outside the garage but there was no sign of her husband. When she got back, she shook her head.

'No sign of him. I don't know where he could have gone. Did the General ask him to do anything?'

'Not as far as I know.' Maria turned to Ruth. 'Go ask the General to come over for a minute, will you, dear?'

Ruth ran over to the General, who was standing in line to bat, surrounded by excited boys. He left them and trotted over to the women, jacketless in the warm sun.

'Erich, where did Yosef go? Miriam can't find him,' Maria asked.

'Ah, didn't he tell you?' he said, turning towards Miriam.

'No, we've not seen him since you got back.'

'I thought he would have said. He was going to the shop to get a few things. I told him to take the car, but he said he'd rather walk.'

'Thanks, sir,' she said, forcing a smile onto her face.

Maria continued chatting with Miriam and her two friends, the three young girls hovering around them, hoping to hear snippets of conversation not meant for their ears.

Manny squealed with delight when the General, returning to the game, finally came good, launching an almighty hit almost as far as the lake, chased by a gaggle of boys from the opposing team. The three remaining players stranded on bases dashed round the circle, reaching home just before the General slid towards them, beating the ball by a fraction of a second, and tying the game.

Miriam looked across the lawn. *That should have been Yosef.*

Rosa touched Miriam's arm.

'What's wrong?' she said softly, out of hearing of everyone.

'Nothing. I'm just annoyed at Yosef. It should be him out there playing the fool with Manny and his friends, not the General.'

'I think the General is getting as much enjoyment from it as the youngsters. But that's not really it, is it.'

'Yosef's away to get himself involved in the boycott.'

Rosa sighed. 'I know. I guessed as soon as I saw your face.'

'He just couldn't let it go, could he. If he were going to defy the boycott, why couldn't he have done it earlier...'

'When you wouldn't have known anything about it, Miriam?'

'Yes,' she snapped. 'It's the thought of what he may do, or what might happen to him that's so worrying. And, before you say it, I know why he waited until now. He wouldn't have gone while he was driving the Kästners, even though he had two or three hours to spare. Damned duty. Peh,' she snorted.

'He'll be sensible. He just wants to show solidarity. I know how he feels; staying away when we should be there, even if I understand the reasons, just doesn't feel right.'

Miriam slumped. 'You're right, but poor Manny. Why did it have to be today?'

'Men. I'm sure the world would be a much better place if we women ran it.'

Miriam glanced at the house next door. She spotted Frau Böhm, who waved.

'I'm not sure, Rosa. I'm not so sure.'

~~o~~

Yosef hurried past the station, ignoring the scattered groups of Brownshirts. At the end of Sophienblatt, he took a left up the hill, then right onto Holstenstraße, making for the old town, where a couple of friends of his had shops, one a grocery store, the other a tobacconist.

He passed a couple of shop windows that looked exactly as they did on any other day of the year, except for the small, printed notice stuck to the glass.

```
German Christian Enterprise
```

In the window of a toy shop, he noticed a child's football emblazoned with a swastika, and frowned. Two doors up, the chemist's display included a tube of toothpaste with the same iconic symbol on its red, white, and black-coloured box.

As he reached Dänische Straße, he spotted an SS man and five SA men guarding his friend's shop. He stood for a second or two, trying to quell the taste of bile rising in his throat, then strode across the road towards the group standing outside the grocery store. As he drew close, the men, who had been chatting amicably, fell silent, staring at him.

He took a deep breath.

They were almost caught out by his direct and self-assured approach but, as he opened the door of the shop, they told him to halt.

He hesitated, smiled at them, and entered. Inside, the sweat trickling down his back, he rang the small bell on the counter. After a few seconds, the store owner appeared.

'Yosef!' he exclaimed, 'What are you doing here?'

Yosef could see confusion on his friend's face.

'I came to buy some fruit, Isaac. Why else?'

'I thought... well, you know. You're my first customer today. I was just going to close up the shutters. How did you get through that lot?' He nodded towards the doorway.

'I just walked past them.' He leaned closer. 'What are they doing now?'

Isaac Stern leaned to one side, to get a better view. 'The SS man is talking to the two Brownshirts. He doesn't seem happy.'

Yosef frowned.

'I think he's going to come in,' Isaac said. 'Yes, he is.'

He quickly straightened up, then turned and picked up a handful of apples, and deposited them in a brown paper bag. He placed the bag onto the set of scales on the counter, added a few weights until it balanced, and took a stub of pencil from behind his ear, writing a figure on a small pad in front of him.

The door burst open, and the SS Sturmmann marched in.

96

'What are you doing?' he asked.

Yosef was the first to speak.

'I'm buying some fruit and vegetables for my family, sir.'

'You must know that is not possible in this establishment. You shouldn't have even been allowed in. There is a shop in Holtenauer Straße where you can purchase fruit today.'

'But I have already picked my apples.' He turned to Isaac, who stared at him with a mixture of surprise and horror. 'Can I also have half a kilo of carrots, please.'

The SS man pushed Yosef aside, and stood in front of Isaac.

'You will not sell this man anything, Jew. There is a boycott.'

'I didn't realise that the boycott was compulsory, sir,' Yosef said. 'My apologies.'

The man, his face red, and the muscles around his mouth twitching, whirled to face him.

'Can I see your papers, please?' he demanded.

Yosef dug in his pocket, and handed him his driving licence, and army pension card.

'You are a Jew too?' he asked. Yosef wasn't surprised at the venom in the man's voice.

'I am, sir. Is that a problem?'

The man raised his arm and slapped Yosef across the face with the back of his hand. He picked up the bag of apples and grabbed Yosef by the collar, marching him towards the door.

'I'll deal with you later,' he said over his shoulder to Isaac, then opened the door and threw Yosef out, into the street. The SA men were surprised, but they quickly recovered and grabbed Yosef.

'This Jew thinks he can just waltz in and buy some fruit. I think he wants one of these apples.' He picked one from the bag, took a bite from it, and spat it out.

'Hold him. He stepped towards the now pinioned Yosef and, grabbing Yosef's jaw with his left hand, forced him to open his mouth by jamming his fingers and thumb into Yosef's cheeks. He rammed the apple between his teeth, drawing blood where Yosef's lips were forced against them.

'Here's your fruit, Jew boy.'

The SA men laughed. Behind the glass, Isaac stood frozen, unable to look away as his friend choked on the fruit being rammed down his throat.

'Teach him a lesson,' the SS man told his SA colleagues.

One of the Brownshirts pulled out a wooden baton and, while his comrades held Yosef, the man swung his arm back, the first blow connecting just below Yosef's ribcage; he would have doubled over if he hadn't been held upright by the men.

His head slumped, and when he managed to raise it again, he saw the bespectacled face and worried frown of Isaac Stern peering through the shop window. He willed his friend to get out of sight and was relieved to see him disappear as the second blow landed just above his right knee. He felt his leg buckle and the gall rise in his throat again. He took the next blow full in the stomach, and he vomited, choking until his frantic efforts to dislodge the apple loosened it. The men let him go, and he dropped to the ground, landing on his hip. A sharp pain shot down his leg and he wondered if it was broken but a kick to his side distracted him from the thought. For what seemed like a lifetime, blows continued to rain down on him.

When the beating stopped, he heard the men laughing, and the angry features of the SS man appeared a handsbreadth from his face.

'You're lucky, this time, Judenscheiße,' he hissed, spittle forming at the corners of his mouth, 'if you hadn't had an army pension card, you were for a night in the cells, or worse.' He smiled at the SA men.

'We're building places for Jew scum like you.' He stood up, clicked his heels, and threw his arm out in salute. 'Heil Hitler.'

The SA men returned his salute. He handed out cigarettes to each of them, and they watched Yosef crawl away as they smoked. One eye was swollen and half-closed, but through his good eye he could see the yellow, daubed Star of David on the glass as he pulled himself up, runs of paint from the bottom of the star trickling down to the low wall at the foot of the window, where it pooled, like yellow blood.

Next to the star, a hand-painted notice was pasted on the window.

Deutsche! Wehrt euch! – Kauft nicht bei Juden!

He limped away, supporting himself on whatever he could lean against, dragging his useless leg, hearing the laughter behind him fade as he turned the corner into Burgstraße, the words seared onto his mind.

Germans! Defend yourselves. Don't buy from Jews!

He almost passed out, but forced himself to continue, clutching the railings when he felt himself stumble. He'd almost reached Schlossstraße, turning back towards home, when a figure darted out from the shadows of the narrow lane running between the buildings.

'Isaac,' he murmured.

'Schhhh,' Isaac hissed, placing his hand gently over Yosef's mouth and guiding him into the lane.

'Try and make it as far as the shop, then we'll see about getting you home.'

He lifted Yosef's arm around his shoulder, and half carried him along the alley, knocking over a bin on the way but reaching the back door of his shop without attracting any attention.

He manoeuvred Yosef through the door and into the small office inside.

'Sit down here, and don't move. I'll go and fetch some help. Do you need a doctor?'

'No, I don't think so,' Yosef grunted, trying to convince himself, as much as his friend, although it was painful to breathe, and he could taste blood in his mouth.

'I've locked up the shop, so you don't have to worry about anyone coming in.' He shrugged. 'Nobody was going to buy from me today anyway. Except you. I'll get help.'

He gave Yosef a half-smile, patted him on the shoulder, and left.

CHAPTER 21

Forty minutes later, a car drew up at the end of the lane. Between the apartment blocks, little of the evening light reached the ground from the narrow strip of sky above.

The car door swung open and Isaac slipped out of the back seat, scuttling along in the dim light to the back door of the shop. Sliding the key into the lock, he opened the door and called out, keeping his voice just above a whisper.

There was no answer. 'Yosef,' he hissed, 'are you there?'

A sudden draught blew some invoices from the counter beside the back door. Puzzled, he panicked at the thought that Yosef, in his befuddled state, had unlocked the front door and remonstrated with the NSDAP thugs again.

He crept through the doorway that led from the storeroom into the shop itself. Some items from the window display had fallen to the floor, and the glass beyond had a jagged brick-sized hole in the centre. He ducked below the counter as one of the brown-shirted SA men sauntered past, peering in.

He heard a noise behind him, and he crept on all fours back through to the storeroom. In a corner, Yosef had hauled himself behind a row of shelves holding sacks of potatoes, carrots, and turnips, and he was now groaning in pain, and gasping heavy, rasping breaths. Isaac assumed he'd hidden when the window was smashed, terrified that the SS man, or the Brownshirts, would break into the shop and finish off the job that they'd started earlier.

'You've got to try and move,' he told Yosef, his voice so soft that he had to put his mouth to his friend's ear for him to understand.

He half dragged, half guided Yosef to the back door and once outside, he somehow managed to hoist the taller man over his shoulder. Almost doubling over with the weight, he stumbled towards the end of the lane, praying that the car was still there.

Yosef's body blocked his vision, and he could only navigate by following the back walls of the buildings. Twice he almost fell, but he managed to somehow regain his balance and found himself relieved of his burden by helping hands just as his strength was about to give out.

'You should go home,' the General told him, asking him if he could drop him off somewhere.

'I can get myself home,' he replied, 'and anyhow, I need to lock up again.'

He looked at the General. 'Danke,' he said, then disappeared back down the dim alleyway.

Yosef was in trouble. He lay on the bed in the Nussbaums' bedroom, the General standing at the bottom, deep concern etched on his face.

Miriam, with help from the General, had undressed him, cutting his trousers to get them off without hurting him overmuch.

The General stifled a smile, listening to Miriam delivering, with icy determination, a judgement on the wisdom of his foolhardy confrontation with the National Socialists as she applied tincture of iodine to his wounds. He almost pitied Yosef more for Miriam's verbal harangue than for the physical pain he was enduring, having assured himself that while Yosef's injuries were nasty, none of them appeared to be life-threatening.

On one hand, he found it difficult to disagree with Miriam's assessment of Yosef's behaviour, but a small voice at the back of his head questioned why he hadn't himself had the courage of his convictions to defy the boycott, as Yosef had. Maria's insistence that he should keep out of it was no excuse.

Despite Miriam's harangue, he could detect in her voice an element of fierce pride for

Yosef's actions, and he failed to meet her eye when she looked at him.

His first reaction when Isaac Stern had presented himself at the door of the Drachensee house had been one of irritation about the position Yosef had placed him in, but his loyalty and compassion had kicked in and forced him to do what was needed to help him.

'What's going on?' Maria had shouted from the kitchen, where she and Miriam were organising the evening meal, her housekeeper working on despite her worry about her husband.

'Nothing,' he'd replied, not wanting lengthy explanations to delay him, or for his wife to try and talk him out of it.

He'd drawn the car from the garage, picked Isaac up at the front, and driven as fast as he could to the shop. With the shop owner crouched in the back, he'd driven down Danische Straße, confirming that the SA and SS men were still there, and parked at the end of the lane.

He'd been horrified when he looked down the darkness of the lane and saw the shadowy figures of Yosef doubled up on Isaac's back, coming towards him. He'd jumped out and taken the groaning Yosef from the grocer, and bundled him into the car, deeply worried by Yosef's condition. It was nothing to the fury he felt when he'd seen the welts on his employee's body when he got Yosef home.

'I'm going to the police about this. They can't get away with it,' he told Miriam.

Her response shocked him. The police weren't to be involved and no one was to know about it.

He bit back a comment about the errors of not confronting bullies and tried to put himself in their shoes. It hit him that large swathes of the population were living in abject fear; trying to survive by keeping their heads down and hoping they wouldn't be targets.

He agreed to keep the day's events between the three of them, though he'd have to tell Maria something plausible. He'd extracted a promise from Yosef to take more care in future, for his family's sake, if nothing else.

It was with a heavy heart that he closed the door of the cottage and walked across the yard; Maria had taken Ruth and Manny to the big house when he returned with Yosef; they'd spend the night with the Kästners to allow Miriam to nurse Yosef for the first night without having to answer difficult questions.

~~o~~

[02/04/1933 Sunday]

Dr. Speer gently closed the door behind him and nodded at the General, motioning him in the direction of the kitchen.

'He'll live, but you should really have called me last night,' he said, sitting down at the table.

'Sorry, Hermann. He was pretty beat up, but it was only during the night that his breathing took a turn for the worse.'

He poured a cup of coffee for the Doc, and one for himself; it had been brewing since the medical man had arrived, so it was on the strong side.

Erich Kästner had hardly slept and, at first light he had tapped on the door of the Nussbaum cottage. The light was on, and Miriam had answered it almost before he'd finished knocking. He could see the strain on her face and, when he'd asked her about Yosef, and had observed the deterioration in his condition, he'd returned to the big house and phoned for Doctor Speer.

'I know that, in the army, you've often had to make a decision on how serious a man's injuries are, and whether he needs further medical attention, but in civilian life, there's no room for amateurs when it comes to health.'

Though they were close friends, Erich Kästner was not surprised that he was being

100

reprimanded by the Doc, and he knew that it was probably deserved. He apologised again.

'I'm sorry, I should have called you as soon as we got him home. What can you tell me?'

'Well, he has three broken ribs, and one of them must have punctured a lung, hence the deterioration in his breathing during the night, and the blood that he has been coughing up. Fortunately, it seems to have sealed, and once we get rid of the excess air that has leaked into his thorax, that's his chest cavity to you, he should quickly recover, although he'll be sore for a week or two.'

The doctor had been keen to take Yosef to hospital but, at Miriam's insistence that knowledge of his condition be limited to themselves, he'd agreed to insert a chest drain at home. It was a straightforward task, and he carried, in his bag, the tube and the trocar that allowed him to perform the procedure, needing only the addition of a large empty jar from the Nussbaums' pantry.

He half-filled it with water and pierced a couple of holes in the lid, threading the tubing through. As soon as the Doc had stabbed the trocar through the chest wall, air had started bubbling through water, with each movement of Yosef's chest, and although the water turned pink and a little frothy as the blood that had clotted in the chest cavity stained the fluid, the patient's colour and the depth and rate of his breathing improved almost at once.

Now, sitting in the kitchen, Doctor Speer outlined Yosef's care, and his prospects of recovery for the General.

'Once the drain comes out in a few days, he should be up and about. He'll need to be strapped up, and he won't be doing anything strenuous for a couple of weeks, but he'll make a full recovery.' He looked at the General.

'So, are you going to tell me how this happened?'

'He was mugged, last night. He went out on an errand and, when he failed to return home, I went looking for him. He was slumped in a doorway. I suspect it was because he was a Jew, but he hasn't said much, and most likely won't.'

Hermann Speer frowned at the General.

'Well, if that's all you're going to tell me, I'm sure you have your reasons and, needless to say, I'll keep it to myself. Confidentiality and all that.'

Erich Kästner bowed his head.

'It was the SS and the SA. The Nussbaums don't want to make a fuss. I'd imagine you might find this sort of thing becoming commonplace.'

'Last week. The demonstrations. I saw several patients away from my surgery who requested that their treatment was kept to myself. People are frightened, Erich.'

'I know. When will this madness stop?'

'I'm not sure that it will. Too many people see this as a way out of our troubles, but it is going to be at the expense of their fellow Germans, and democracy.'

He finished his coffee and stood up.

The General shook his hand. 'Thanks for coming, Hermann. Send me the account.'

'Don't you worry, Erich. All this secrecy is expensive,' he joked.

The General knew that his friend never charged enough, and he always added a few marks when he paid the Doc's bills.

'You said you'll call in and see Yosef?'

'I'll call in once a day unless he deteriorates. I'd normally send a nurse over, but...'

'Miriam is more than capable, and I'll keep an eye out too. Thanks again, Doc.'

He showed the doctor out and tapped on the bedroom door. Yosef was sitting up, and already looked far more comfortable.

Miriam looked exhausted.

'Go to your bed. I'll sit with Yosef.'

She started to protest, but he insisted, knowing she'd need to be strong for her family. She relented.

'Only until the children come over. I need to think what to tell them, before they see their father.'

'Let me know what you say to them,' he said. 'I've told Maria that Yosef was unlucky, that he was jumped by some NSDAP thugs. Perhaps that would be the line to take.'

She nodded. As she reached the door, she turned.

'Danke.'

~~o~~

KIELER MORGENPOST

Sunday 2nd April 1933

BOYCOTT CONTINUES - GREAT TRIUMPH

Julius Streicher, national co-ordinator of the boycott, told the Kieler Morgenpost that it had been an outright success and that it would continue. "It has been a Great Triumph for the German people and sends a message to the agitating international Jewry that Germany will not be dictated to".

In Kiel, the boycott was almost completely universal. The majority of Jewish businesses did not open, and of the ones that did, most closed early.

The city mayor, Jürgen Hoffmann, praised the NSDAP. "Due to the diligence of the Sturmabteilung and Schutzstaffel troopers who guarded the Jewish businesses, there were no incidents of vandalism or violence requiring the police to attend".

He added that the painted yellow stars identifying Jewish businesses were to remain in place indefinitely.

~~o~~

When Maria woke up, she reached out for her husband. It was Sunday morning, after all, and the children hadn't stirred yet. It had been a late night for the younger ones, the excitement of Manny and Ruth staying keeping Antje up until all hours.

She thought she'd heard Franz and Johann rise at six-thirty; there was a sailing event in one of the inland lakes with the Hitlerjugend team, and they were being picked up in an army lorry, of all things, at the yacht club at Düsternbrook.

When her arm found nothing but empty bed, she allowed herself a brief sulk, but presumed that Erich had gone to give the boys a lift, as if they couldn't have cycled as they often did.

She rang the bell; Miriam wasn't meant to work on Sunday mornings but, more often than not, she was there, as she was every other morning.

While she waited, she climbed out of bed and sat at her dresser, brushing her hair, and applying a little perfume. She would have breakfast in bed and entice the General back under the covers when he returned. She thanked her good fortune that he still found her attractive and was never one to miss an opportunity to show her why he'd married her in the first place.

When Miriam didn't appear, she rang the bell again but, when it went unanswered, she slipped into her dressing gown and a pair of silk slippers and made her way downstairs.

The range hadn't been lit, and there was no sign of any preparations for breakfast, which was strange. On the few occasions Miriam wasn't working, she would always let them know.

Maria lit the gas cooker, glad that Miriam had suggested having it fitted as a backup to the wood-fired range, which took an age to warm up. She filled the kettle and looked out the kitchen window towards the Nussbaums' house, surprised to see the car sitting outside the garage, and no signs of stirring from the cottage.

Where is Erich if he hasn't driven the boys to sailing?

She made herself coffee and replaced the milk in the refrigerator; even though they still used the large walk-in larder for most things, they had been one of the first families in the street to install one of the modern electric fridges, as the children called it, with its own ice compartment, that made keeping food fresh so much easier.

She was just wondering where her husband was when the Nussbaums' front door opened, and he appeared. He saw her at the window and waved. Surprised, and a little annoyed, she waited until he'd come in and sat down before quizzing him.

'What were you doing at the Nussbaums? Why were you up so early?'

'A cup of coffee would be nice,' he said, grinning in answer to her questions.

She opened her mouth to speak, but she bit back the caustic retort, and said nothing. Tight-lipped, she poured him a cup and set it down, none too gently, on the table in front of him.

She waited for him to speak.

~~o~~

Erich Kästner sighed and took his wife's hand.

'I couldn't sleep,' he said. 'I went over to check on Yosef; he'd taken a turn for the worse, so I called Doctor Speer.'

Her look of anger faded a little and was replaced with one of concern.

'Is he going to be all right?' she asked.

'Yes, the Doc sorted him out. He'd punctured a lung, and some air and blood had built up in his chest, but it's sorted now. The Doc put a tube in to drain it.'

'You should have let me know,' she said, still irritated at him, 'and yesterday, it would have been more sensible to call the police, instead of rushing off without telling anyone. You could have been hurt.'

'I should have left a note, and once I saw how bad he was, it went out of my mind. I stayed on after the Doc left, to let Miriam get a couple of hours' sleep. She's been up all night with him, worried sick. As for yesterday, it was nothing. The cowards had disappeared by the time I got there.'

He hoped she would never find out the truth about the events of the previous day, or his life wouldn't be worth living. He loved her, but he'd seen her sulk before, and it took time, and all his charm, to draw her out of it.

A little mollified, she offered to go over later and take a spell sitting with Yosef.

'I'm sure Miriam would greatly appreciate that. Now, I see you're still in your nightdress. Perhaps we could do something about that, first?'

103

CHAPTER 22

Maria spoke in hushed tones with Miriam. They sat in the kitchen of the cottage. Maria had given Ruth and Manny some breakfast and had taken them with her to Miriam. She'd stayed with the sleeping Yosef, keeping an eye on the drain and his breathing, while Miriam organised fresh clothes for the children, and had caught up on whatever chores she needed to do.

When the General returned, having slept for a couple of hours, he took his turn watching over the invalid again, giving the two women a chance to sit and talk, over a coffee.

A soft knock on the door interrupted them, and Miriam rose to answer it.

'Isaac, come in.' The small, thin man, with his mild stoop and round glasses, noticed Frau Kästner when he entered the kitchen and stood, twisting his hat in his hands, and shifting from foot to foot.

'I just came to see Yosef, to find out how he was,' he said, his head bowed.

'Oh, that's so thoughtful of you, Isaac. I was just telling Frau Kästner here that it was you who found him, after those awful men had attacked him.'

Miriam glanced at him with a slight shake of her head.

For a moment, a puzzled frown lined Isaac's face, then his eyes widened, and he nodded his agreement.

'It was a terrible thing. I despair of what is happening in our city.'

Maria Kästner thought it irrational and annoying that she should feel a sense of guilt at what had happened to Yosef. And sometimes she did wonder why the Nussbaums and their friends seemed to go out of their way to highlight their differences, a bit like the Catholics, only more so.

'Quite,' she said. 'There are far too many criminals these days.'

Miriam and Isaac Stern looked at each other. Both or either of them might have responded if the General hadn't poked his head around the door.

'Yosef would like a cup of coffee, and perhaps something to eat. He seems to have woken up with an appetite,' he said, smiling, before noticing the older man.

'Ah, Isaac, he was asking for you.'

Miriam nodded to the door and busied herself around the kitchen.

'In you go, Isaac. Tell Yosef I'll bring something in for him. I'll fetch you a cup of coffee.'

She turned to the General.

'I'll bring you one too, sir.'

~~o~~

'Sorry, I nearly blurted out what happened,' Isaac said, sitting on a chair at the side of the bed.

'Don't worry,' the General said, seeing Yosef's concern, 'I didn't tell Frau Kästner about the shop. Miriam suggested that the fewer people who knew about it, the better. She's not going to tell Ruth and Manny the whole story either.'

Yosef nodded. 'It's better like that.' His voice was weak, but it wasn't as painful for him to talk as it had been yesterday.

'How are you feeling?' Isaac peered at him over his glasses.

'I'll be fine. A couple of broken ribs and some bruises.'

'And a punctured lung,' the General interrupted, frowning.

'Yes, they gave you quite a going over. I thought they were going to kill you.' Isaac looked at Yosef, then at the General. He seemed to hesitate.

'You were lucky,' he said. 'Did you hear about Dr. Schumm?'

Yosef shook his head. 'What happened? Do I know him?'

'Yes, though you'll know his father better. He owns the furniture store.'

'Oh, Edwin Schumm. I do know him. The son is the lawyer fellow? Yes, I've seen him a couple of times.'

'He's dead. Murdered.'

He handed Yosef the newspaper. He looked at the headlines. There was nothing about a killing.

'It's all about the boycott. Where does it say about Dr. Schumm?'

Isaac leaned over and turned the page.

'There,' he said, pointing.

Yosef read it and handed it to the General. He scanned the paper and found the item midway down page three. It took up a few centimetres of the sixth column on the page and took him less than twenty seconds to read.

JEWISH LAWYER ARRESTED FOR ATTEMPTED MURDER

Jewish lawyer Friedrich Schumm was arrested last night after he shot an SS trooper outside his father's furniture store. Witnesses say that he objected to the SS and SA men protecting his father's property and pulled a gun. He shot the SS trooper in cold blood and escaped. The victim was rushed to hospital where he is in a serious condition. Herr Schumm was later arrested and charged with attempted murder. Some hours after his arrest, he was found dead in his cell. It is not known if he took his own life or died of natural causes.

'It sounds as if the man was guilty of attempted murder,' the General said. 'As much as I deplore the boycott and the intimidation and violence that characterise the NSDAP, we surely cannot condone victims taking the law into their own hands.'

'Sir, Dr. Schumm was more than wrong to pull a gun, but he didn't shoot him in cold blood, like they reported. The man has a flesh wound. I've spoken with Dr. Schumm's father, and the old man's version of the story is completely at odds with the story in the paper.'

'Well, he would tend to side with his son, wouldn't he?' the General said.

'I'm not sure he would, sir. These old Jews are honest to the point of being rude most of the time.'

Yosef murmured agreement and Isaac carried on. The General smiled grimly at Isaac's description of old Jews.

'Anyhow, his testimony has been corroborated by others.'

Isaac looked at the General, who held up his hands in concession.

'Dr. Schumm returned to Kiel on the day of the boycott,' Isaac continued, 'On attempting to visit his father at the furniture store he owned, he was stopped by SS guards, with a command not to buy from Jewish businesses. He left, annoyed, and walked round to the rear of the building, entering by the back door. After a short while, he came out of the front door, together with his father, and drew a handgun. The SS guards attempted to wrestle with him, and in the scuffle that followed, one of the SS men was shot.'

He paused. The General let his words sink in but didn't interrupt. Isaac resumed his account.

'Dr. Schumm fled at first, but later turned himself in. He requested that he be moved to a different jail for his safety, but even though the order was given, the local police dragged their feet. About an hour after he'd been arrested, they let a lynch mob of around thirty SS and SA men into the building. They shot him and left the police station without being challenged.'

'And how do you know all this?' the General said.

105

'One of the policemen who was there when Dr. Schumm was brought in is a friend of our rabbi. They play chess together.'

The General looked sceptical, but Yosef nodded.

'The rabbi is quite the chess master,' he interjected, 'and can be surprisingly secular for a man of God. He has more than a few non-Jewish friends, although he may find less of them over the coming months.'

The General flinched at the stinging bitterness in Yosef's words.

Isaac resumed his account.

'This policeman friend,' Isaac continued, 'who demanded that his name be kept out of it, told the rabbi everything that happened after Dr. Schumm was arrested.'

He paused.

'Not only that, but Dr. Schumm's father arrived at the police station just as the mob left. They were laughing and joking. The old man thought they were just a group of men, coming off shift.'

Isaac's head was bowed now. He continued, his voice heavy with sorrow.

'They wouldn't let him in to see his son. When he asked to leave him a message, the sergeant told him, in front of everyone there, that his son had collapsed, and there had been nothing they could do. The old man said that the sergeant was abrupt and dismissive, as if it were of no consequence.'

He lifted his eyes to the General and Yosef.

'They won't let him see the body.'

'I can have a word with the deputy chief. I know him well,' the General said, anger in his voice.

'I'm not sure it will do any good, sir. We've been told that the body has already been removed from the police station.'

'I'll at least try. The man did something that deserved punishment, but he had the right to a fair trial. This is murder.'

'Just be careful, sir. These are dangerous people.'

Miriam came in with three cups of coffee, and some bread and cheese for Yosef.

She saw the newspaper and frowned.

The General understood why. The last thing she'd want was for Yosef to become distressed, in his condition, but she said nothing, and left them to it.

'Despite Dr. Schumm's death and the assault on you, the boycott wasn't much of a success in Kiel. I don't know about anywhere else,' Isaac said, when she'd closed the door.

The General turned to the front page of the paper.

'That's not what it says here.'

'Sir, little of it is true. Most of the Jewish businesses that remained closed didn't normally open at the weekend or were closed until midday for the sabbath, as usual. It's true that a few shops, like mine, closed early, where there was overt intimidation. In most of Kiel, though, the boycott was poorly manned and largely unsuccessful, with a significant number of people defying it, even when the SS and the SA were present.'

The General vowed to find out for himself. It wasn't that he didn't believe Yosef's friend, but he assumed that the shopkeeper's views would be coloured by his own experience and background.

He asked himself if his efforts were truly altruistic, or was he just trying to make amends for not having defied the boycott himself.

And, as he questioned his motivation, he vowed to do what he could to help the family of the dead Jewish lawyer.

~~o~~

'Erich, my advice would be to stay well out of it. Do you know the man?'

Uwe Müller, the deputy chief, sounded very guarded.

'Well, no, but I…' said the General, not quite sure how to phrase it. 'He was a friend of a friend, so to speak,' he said.

'So, you're asking for help from one friend for a friend of another friend?'

'Well, yes, when you put it like that it seems ridiculous, but it's in the cause of justice, Uwe. Surely you can see that.'

'All this is only hearsay, Erich. I'm sure the correct version of events is the one that you've read in the paper.'

He hesitated.

'Erich, have you ever done anything in battle where you've made a decision and regretted it later?'

The General thought for a moment.

'I suppose I have. Some decisions are so much easier with hindsight.'

'I'm sure that, in the unlikely event that what you say is true, the sergeant is in that position now. I mean, how would you react if a horde of SA and SS men descended on you, demanding to interview the prisoner?'

There was an awkward silence.

'What I mean, Erich, is don't fight a battle you can't win, my friend.'

Erich Kästner read the genuine concern in the man's tone, but also the finality.

He nodded, then decided to risk antagonising his friend further.

'What about the body, then. Can the family at least have the comfort of laying their son to rest.'

'That could be difficult…'

'I can perhaps suggest a solution,' the General said.

They discussed the details, then spoke briefly about the upcoming Rotary meeting.

When Uwe Müller said he must be getting on, the General asked him if he could answer one more question.

He could sense that his friend's patience was growing thin but, in clipped tones, he was told to carry on.

'Did you get many calls yesterday, because of the boycott?'

The policeman seemed relieved.

'That's easy to answer, Erich. There were no reports of any incidents yesterday. It was all very peaceful, other than the unfortunate affair with your friend, the lawyer.'

The General thanked him, then gently replaced the handset on the telephone.

CHAPTER 23

KIELER MORGENPOST

Friday 7th April 1933

TOWN SQUARE RENAMED ADOLF-HITLER-PLATZ

In a ceremony today, Neumarkt Square, facing the Rathaus, will be renamed Adolf-Hitler-Platz in honour of the Chancellor. Town Mayor Jürgen Hoffmann will open the proceedings at 11am. It was hoped that the Chancellor himself would be present, but due to pressing matters of state, he is unable to attend.

In his place, the guest of honour, NSDAP state leader and Oberpräsident der Schleswig-Holstein, Hinrich Lohse, will officially rename the square. Representatives from the Reichsmarine and the Reichswehr, along with Kiel council delegates and local business leaders will be in attendance.

A large crowd is expected for this event, which will cement the tremendous support in Kiel and Schleswig Holstein firmly behind the leader who is restoring national pride after Germany's worst economic and political era since records began.

~~o~~

'Sir, why am I going? Surely, they would be expecting someone of higher rank to represent the Reichsmarine.'

'Nonsense, Heinz, my boy. It's a historic event, and don't forget you're a captain. If it weren't that I required someone I can completely trust, you would have your own command by now, which is far more that any of the Dummköpfe who are attending could boast. Anyway, I want you to see what a toadying bunch of Furzmaschinen they are.'

Captain Bauer laughed aloud. It would be interesting to see these 'fart machines', in action, as the General would have them. And it would also be educational to see prominent members of the NSDAP up close.

'Sir, might I humbly suggest that you do not refer to them in that way outside this office?'

The General laughed. 'As much as I'd like to call them that to their faces, you'll see the diplomatic General Kästner today,' he said, holding the door open for the captain. 'We, my boy, are going to be as nice as you like to them. Now, I want you to be at your charming best, and let's see what morsels they divulge.'

~~o~~

The 'crowd' amounted to a few hundred souls, scattered around the square. Private Zimmer, the driver, dropped General Kästner and the captain off in front of the Rathaus; the invitation included a pre-ceremony drinks reception in one of the grand rooms next to the chamber.

'Ah, General. I see you made it. I was rather doubtful you'd manage to be here for this historic moment.'

Hinrich Lohse had lost none of his cloying oiliness but it was now tempered by an arrogance and a nauseating self-assurance that the General would have loved to puncture.

'Oberpräsident, it's such a delight to see you again,' he said, in such an affable tone that Captain Bauer choked with surprise, covering it up as a coughing fit.

'You'll have to excuse Captain Bauer; he's recovering from a rather severe throat infection.'

'Indeed, it seems very unpleasant. It's not catching, I hope,' the NSDAP leader enquired, covering his face with his hand.

'No, no. He's past the contagious stage now. Just the remnants of this damnable cough.' He turned to his subordinate, who had stopped spluttering.

'Captain Bauer, this is Oberpräsident Hinrich Lohse, head of the NSDAP in Schleswig-Holstein.'

'It's an honour to meet you, sir.' They shook hands.

'Pleased to meet you, too, captain. Your ship is in Kiel?'

'No, sir. I'm based in Kiel, but onshore. I work for General Kästner.'

'I see. The Reichsmarine and the Reichsheer working together. So beneficial for the advancement of our nation, don't you think?'

'Yes, sir. We are playing a critical role.'

'You must itch for a sea-going command though, Herr Kapitän, do you not?'

'Sir, I hope to, at some point, but my place is with the General at present.'

The General interjected. 'I persuaded Captain Bauer to give me a few years of his career. I needed a man of his talents for this new unit, and I'm sure he will rise to command some of the navy's wonderful new ships not so far in the future.'

He waited, but Hinrich Lohse didn't see it necessary to respond.

'How about you, Herr Oberpräsident, how are you finding your new post?'

'Onerous, General, but really, you should call me Hinrich and, if you have no objections, may I call you Erich? Herr Hoffmann, the mayor, talks very highly of you.'

The General was in no doubt that the mayor would have spoken to Hinrich Lohse about him, but he wasn't sure it would all be flattering.

'Erich is fine, Herr Lohse. Jürgen is a dear friend of mine. I must congratulate him on his new job. I've only spoken to him by phone since he was appointed.'

'Why don't we go over and speak with him. I'm sure he would like to meet the captain. The navy is so important to Kiel, and it was good of the young man to spare us his time.'

The General felt his young assistant bristle at the sarcasm that dripped from Hinrich Lohse's words, but he just nodded as if oblivious to it, giving the captain an encouraging smile.

The NSDAP man led them over towards a cluster of men standing near the window. Introductions were made all around and, after the pleasantries had been exhausted, the mayor excused himself from the group, and put his hand on the General's arm, smiling.

'So, Erich, you're coming around to the National Socialist's point of view. We'll have you as a member of the party yet.' He put his arm around the General's shoulder. Heinz Bauer cringed, but the General returned the mayor's smile.

'I can see the benefits the government is bringing to the armed forces, Jürgen. And we must work together, even at a local level, for the national good,' the General replied.

An official tapped Hinrich Lohse on the arm.

'Herr Giesecke from the Reich Ministry has arrived, Herr Oberpräsident.'

It was an opportunity for Hinrich Lohse to escape.

'Splendid. Gentlemen, I apologise, but I must leave you to it. We don't want Herr Giesecke to report back to the chancellor that we were an inhospitable lot.'

Their murmurs of assent following him, the three men watched as he toadied up to the man from Berlin, a minor official in the National Socialist government but, importantly, one who worked at the centre of the emerging Third Reich.

'So, things are moving apace, Erich,' Jürgen Hoffman said.

'Yes, indeed. I haven't congratulated you in person for your appointment, Herr Mayor.'

The General clapped him on the shoulder and, for a second, Jürgen Hoffmann looked confused.

'Well, thank you. It is a great honour. To be honest, Erich...' He looked at Captain Bauer and then to the General.

'Go on, Jürgen, you can speak in front of the captain. He's my right-hand man.'

'Right,' he said, doubt still on his face, 'I thought I detected some disapproval the last time we spoke on the phone.'

'I will say I'm not at ease with some of the policies of your party,' the General replied, 'but we must all work together if Germany is going to recover.'

'That's great to hear. We should be able to have different opinions and still remain friends.' He looked around and lowered his voice. 'Much of the policy that you feel uncomfortable with is harmless rhetoric for the benefit of the, shall we say, more base members of the party and, in Schleswig-Holstein at least, it will be implemented with as much moderation as we can.'

'That's good to hear, Jürgen. As you know, the Reichsmarine is of immense importance to Kiel. I spoke with the minister of defence last week and, if we can believe what he says, there is to be a massive naval expansion over the next few years, and the city's shipyards will be at the heart of building these new ships, and many of them should be based here in Kiel.'

'That is truly excellent news. The unemployment figures are frightening. A flush of new shipbuilding will make a vast difference. How certain are you?'

It was the General's turn to look around. When he spoke, it was almost a whisper.

'This must only be between us, Jürgen,' he said, knowing that the mayor wouldn't be able to resist passing it on. 'Herr Hitler had a meeting with the minister in February, asking for their support. He promised a tenfold expansion of the armed forces, including the Reichsmarine.'

Erich Kästner watched Jürgen Hoffman's face perform a series of transformations as it dawned on him that his fellow Rotarian mixed in circles just one step removed from the chancellor himself.

'I'm so glad that relations between us are as they were,' the mayor said.

The General, only too aware of the man's veneration of power, took the opportunity he'd been looking for.

'I was wondering, Jürgen,' he said, placing his hand on the mayor's fat shoulder, 'in the light of the need for us to work closely with the authorities in Kiel, if it would be an idea for someone from the Reichsmarine to be temporarily attached to your administration?'

The politician looked startled at his friend's suggestion but after a moment's consideration, he seemed to recover.

'In theory, it sounds like an attractive idea. What do you have in mind?'

'Well, if I, or one of my staff, were to attend some of your council meetings, it could be advantageous for you, to have someone on hand from the navy to answer any questions you might have about our plans, and also to put across requests from our side for the city to consider.'

'I'll have to consult with my colleagues,' the mayor replied, his face beaming as he thought of presenting the idea as his own to the council, and to Hinrich Lohse.

'By all means. You can let me know what the outcome is.'

'Will it be yourself, Erich?'

'I would be honoured to do it, but I'm wondering if someone from the Reichsmarine would be better, with me being an army man at heart. The problem will be finding someone who can spare the time, with everything that is going on at present.'

The General looked deep in thought for a moment, then his face brightened, and he looked at his subordinate.

'Perhaps the captain here would be ideal. I can spare him for a few hours each week, and he could be briefed beforehand by myself or one of the base commanders, and report back to us afterwards.'

Disappointment showed on the mayor's face, and Captain Bauer looked at the General as if he'd been asked to strip naked and swim across Kieler Hafen.

'Of course, if it were to prove to be successful, it wouldn't surprise me if one of the admirals might find it advantageous to attend occasionally in person,' the General added and, seeing the man's transparent vanity, made a further suggestion.

'And, if it wouldn't be too much of an imposition, it may be necessary for you, and perhaps a few of your key colleagues, to visit the Reichsmarine headquarters to gain some insight into our plans for expansion.'

~~o~~

As the mayor made a pretence of reluctant capitulation, it struck Captain Bauer suddenly why the General had been appointed to his position in the Abwehr. He didn't quite understand the reasons for it, but he realised now that the General had just achieved his objective in attending the event.

While he was coming to the conclusion that there was more to his commanding officer than he'd appreciated, a Rathaus official entered the room, and announced that the ceremony was about to begin, and that everyone should make their way across to the square.

As they walked down the Rathaus steps, he turned to the General.

'You had that in mind before we left the office, didn't you, sir?' he murmured.

'Yes, Heinz. I did. I'm sorry for not warning you, but I wanted you to look surprised. I didn't know how much of an actor you were.'

'You certainly caught me off guard, sir. Why do you want me involved with these people?'

'Two reasons. First, get to know the councilmen; you'll not learn much in the meetings, but talk to them in the lobbies, or take them for a drink, and don't forget to speak with the civil servants.'

The young officer nodded.

'Next, your involvement will convince the NSDAP that we are fully co-operating with them.'

'And you think they'll buy this, sir?'

The General put his finger to his mouth. 'Ears,' he said, as they reached the VIP seats in the square, but he leaned closer to the young man.

'The mayor has no real power. He'll have to take my suggestion to Hinrich Lohse, which he'll try and take some credit for. The Oberpräsident will jump at it and will also invite himself to the meetings at Naval HQ.'

'But won't the brass complain about him coming? I gather the admirals have little time for career politicians.'

'They don't know there is a meeting yet. It's our job to convince them that it was their idea,' he replied, a grin at the corner of his mouth.

The young man suppressed a laugh. He was beginning to think that joining the General's staff had been one of his better decisions.

~~o~~

The renaming of the square was a big disappointment for Captain Bauer. The NSDAP had bussed in a few hundred extra supporters to bolster the crowd, who roared and saluted with righteous fervour, but the speeches lacked the fire he'd been expecting, having seen newsreel footage of Hitler, Goebbels, Himmler, and Göring inciting the masses with screaming vitriol.

As the National Socialist flag was lifted from the new sign with a fanfare over the tannoy, the thought that 'Adolf-Hitler-Platz' had a certain ring to it crossed his mind and made him smile.

As the crowd filtered away, Jürgen Hoffmann approached them.

'It went well, didn't it?'

'Yes. Excellent speech, Herr Mayor,' the captain lied, taking his cue from the General's earlier flattery.

'Thank you, Captain Bauer. We shall be seeing a bit more of each other.' He turned to the General. 'I ran your idea past Hinrich, and he was very much in favour of it. He'll also try his best to find time in his busy schedule to meet with your senior commanders.'

'It may take me some time to set it up, but I'll get the captain on it as soon as we get back. In the meantime, when is the next meeting of the council, so that he can put that in his diary?'

'There's one on Tuesday, at eleven.' He turned back to the captain. 'Come to my office ten minutes before it starts. Just ask at the main desk.'

He shook both their hands, and hurried back to the Rathaus, where Hinrich Lohse and the Berlin official were waiting for him.

As the car drew up, and the driver jumped out to open the door for the General, the captain looked at the three men, then back to the General, already ducking into the car, and smiled.

CHAPTER 24

KIELER MORGENPOST

Saturday 8th April 1933

RESTORATION OF THE CIVIL SERVICE

The government of the German Reich has issued the Law For the restoration of a national professional civil service. Civil servants may be discharged from office in accordance with the following regulations:

Civil servants of non-Aryan descent are to be retired.

This does not apply to civil servants who were already employed on August 1, 1914, or who fought during the World War at the front for the German Reich or who fought for its allies or whose fathers or sons were killed in the World War.

Civil servants whose former political activity affords no guarantee that they will act in the interest of the national state at all times, and without reservation, can be dismissed from service.

A pension will not be granted to civil servants dismissed or retired in accordance with this act.

The Reichsbank and the German Reich Railways are empowered to make corresponding regulations.

A spokesman for the National Socialist government expanded on the benefits this will bring for the German people.

"Control of the civil service, which has been usurped by unpatriotic elements, will now be returned to loyal German citizens. It is estimated that hundreds of thousands of new jobs for Aryan Germans will be created".

In a surprise move, the government also issued a law which decrees the disbarment of non-Aryan lawyers by September 30, 1933. Exempted from this provision are Jewish lawyers practising law since August 1, 1914, or who are veterans of the Great War or those with a father or son killed in action in the Great War.

The Morgenpost believes this is in response to the large number of Jewish lawyers retained by the Communist Party and its splinter groups.

~~o~~

Ruth couldn't hide her disappointment.

'I can't come over tomorrow after school.'

'That's all right,' Antje said. 'I only wanted to play. Eva is so boring now.' She grimaced and mimicked a yawn. 'Why can't you come, anyway?'

'Passover starts tomorrow. It's a big thing with us.'

'Like Christmas?' Antje said, excitement lighting up her face.

'Well, not quite, but I suppose it's similar in ways.'

'So, what do you do? Give each other presents?'

'No, but it is such fun. We eat, and sing, and dance, and the grown-ups talk a lot. My grandparents from Altona will be staying, and Mama's brother and his wife. Bubbe and Sabba Nussbaum will be there too, but they'll go back home afterwards. It will be wonderful. I could ask Mama if you could stay over.'

'I would love to.' Her face darkened. 'There won't be enough room, though, with all these people.'

'Oh, don't worry. Mama and Papa will sleep in the living room, so Bubbe and Sabba Sachs can have Mama's room, and Aunt Elsa and Uncle Nikodem will stay in the spare room. And you can sleep with me.' She beamed.

'I'll ask Mama later. No, wait, I'll ask Father. He always says yes.' Antje thought for a minute.

'Do you sacrifice a lamb?'

'No, don't be so silly. What made you think that?'

'We read about Passover in the bible, at Sunday school. It was in Egypt, when the Israelites wanted to escape from being slaves.'

Ruth was somewhat taken aback that her friend knew something about Pesach.

'We don't sacrifice anything, dopey. It's just a ritual. It starts tonight. We all clean the house and search for Chametz.'

'That doesn't sound like much fun, cleaning the house.'

It would never have occurred to Ruth to say that Antje's mother and father employed her parents to do the Kästners' cleaning, or that Antje would never be expected to help with household chores, like Ruth did, just as Antje would never look down at Ruth because the Nussbaums worked for her mother and father.

Instead, she tried to explain why the day was so special to the Nussbaum family.

'When the Jews were captives in Egypt, and forced to build the Egyptians' temples, God promised to release us, and take us to our holy land, Canaan. When the pharaohs of Egypt wouldn't let us go, God sent ten plagues on them but, until the last one, they still refused. Then God sent an angel to kill all the firstborn children of every family in Egypt, but he warned us, the Israelites, to sacrifice a male lamb and paint its blood on our doorways so that the angel knew that he should pass over that house and not kill the oldest child. The Egyptians let us go the next day, so that is why we call it Passover.'

'I remember. I remember. It's in the book of Exodus and Moses parted the Red Sea and climbed a mountain to get the Ten Commandments.' She frowned. 'It's the same story for both of us.'

'I know,' said Ruth. 'Mama says the Hebrew religion, that's another name for Jewish, is similar to Christianity, but you believe that Jesus is the Messiah, and we believe he is still to come for us.'

Antje thought about that for a minute, then curiosity got the better of her.

'So, what do you do if you don't sacrifice a lamb?'

'Well, first we search for Chametz...'

~~o~~

The sun had set, and the Nussbaums were all exhausted. The house was spotless, and every trace of yeast, or leavened bread, had been removed. They made this ritual search for Chametz fun for the children by hiding small gifts for them to find while they were helping to clean the house.

As they did, Yosef explained to Manny that when the Israelites had to leave Egypt in such a hurry, they didn't have time to let the bread rise, taking unleavened dough with them instead, but he could see that the boy was tired and not taking it in.

Once the children were asleep, Yosef sat with his wife, happy that all the preparations for Passover had been completed.

'This is the first Pesach where I've understood how those in Egypt must have felt.'

Yosef shivered, as if a draught had entered the room with his wife's words, and he gave himself a shake.

'It will get better. With every crazy law that Hitler passes, the more likely it is that people will come to their senses.'

'I'm not so sure, husband,' she said, looking at him with fondness for trying to reassure her. 'I mean, we've just had laws passed to exclude Jews from the civil service – that includes teachers, doctors, nurses and even professors. That's a lot of good people.'

Yosef tried to interrupt. 'It may all be posturing. I don't know of anyone who has been removed from a government post.'

'We'll see. I can't believe that they would pass a law and not use it to their advantage. They'll want to give the jobs to their own people.'

'We are their own people, Miriam. We're Germans, just like them.'

'I don't think we are, Yosef.'

He remained silent. But Miriam couldn't stop.

'We can't even fight the new legislation. Jewish lawyers are to be prevented from practising law. Who will stand up for us?'

'Not every Jew is excluded. If I were working for the government, I wouldn't have lost my job, and there are thousands like me.'

'Yes, I know you're a veteran and, for now, you may be protected, but your army pension card didn't help you last week.'

He instinctively moved his hand to the side of his chest. He was still heavily strapped, but he'd made a steady recovery, the pain easing every day, and he was already doing light duties in his own home and for the Kästners.

She continued. 'I don't know who's worse, the Ostjuden, whose answer seems to be to get more and more Jewish as each new law bites, or the Jews who think of themselves less Hebrew than German. For goodness' sake, the Eisenmanns were just saying the other day how the National Socialists have reduced unemployment and lowered crime on our streets, that they should be applauded for it, and supported.'

He wondered why he always seemed to be on the wrong side of the argument when he was talking with Miriam. With anyone else, he would take the stance she was taking.

'I still don't understand why the German people handed him the power, without question,' he said, his voice bitter and defeated. 'We went from a democracy to a dictatorship in a few short months, without so much as a whimper.'

'Because deep down, the German people don't really like us, and if we're the price they pay for putting Germany back on the world stage, they'll give him anything.'

~~o~~

'No, Antje. You can't go. It's not fair on Miriam. This is the time for their family; it has nothing to do with us.' Maria's arms were folded across her chest, and she faced her daughter, determined not to give in.

'Papa, please, tell Mama that the Nussbaums would be happy to let me stay over.'

The General looked at his daughter's pleading eyes, and at the set of his wife's mouth.

God, I need the wisdom of Solomon, if that isn't inappropriate.

'Antje, Mama is right. This is an important day for Ruth's family and, although they would never make you unwelcome, it would be unfair of you to impose on them.'

He knew this wasn't true. Yosef had invited the Kästners every year, but the only time he'd ever mentioned it to Maria, she'd made a poor excuse that made it clear that such an invitation would never be accepted.

He didn't know if this was a genuine desire to not disrupt the Nussbaums' celebrations or an unwillingness to take part in something she felt uncomfortable with.

Maria Kästner wasn't a devout woman, but she insisted that the Kästners attend church every week as a family and, apart from Miriam, all her friends were members of the same church they visited every Sunday morning.

The General saw the disappointment on his daughter's face but knew that Antje recognised the finality in his voice and would accept it.

'Perhaps I should take you to see one of the new cartoon films to make up for it. Would you like that?'

'I suppose so,' she said, not willing to let him entirely off the hook.

~~o~~

Ruth's eyes shone as they crowded around the table in the cottage, with barely elbow room between them. After prayers, and a blessing, Yosef read from the Haggadah, telling the fifteen steps of the story of the Jewish misfortunes in Egypt and of the exodus from slavery, the sojourn in the wilderness, and their eventual delivery to the promised land.

As the story of each of the ten plagues was recited, a drop of wine was spilt to remind them that their liberation was tinged with sadness for the suffering of the Egyptians.

It fell to Manny, the youngest present, to start the rite that people of the Hebrew faith had practised for thousands of years.

'Why do we eat unleavened bread?'

His father answered. 'We eat only Matzah because our ancestors could not wait for their breads to rise when they were fleeing slavery in Egypt, and so they were flat when they came out of the oven.'

'Why do we eat bitter herbs?' Manny chorused, and they all watched with pride.

'We eat only bitter herbs to remind us of the bitterness of slavery that our ancestors endured while in Egypt...'

Once the Seder was over, and they'd all had their fill of the food and wine that it demanded, they sang.

'It's my favourite part,' Ruth had told Antje, when her friend voiced her disappointment that she wouldn't be permitted to join them.

'The food is amazing,' she'd said. 'Lamb, to symbolise the sacrifice that saved their firstborn children; Matzah, the unleavened bread, and Charoset, a sweet paste of fruit and nuts which Papa says represents the mortar of the Egyptian temples the Hebrew slaves built. There's others, too, but they're the ones I like most.'

'I asked my father if I could come,' Antje had said, disappointment in her voice, 'but he said the same as Mama. When I am old enough to make my own decisions, I will come.'

The two girls had hugged, friends for always.

Ruth smiled. *It would have been nice if Antje had been here.*

For the next eight days, Ruth, and the rest of her family, would only eat bread that was unleavened.

CHAPTER 25

Captain Bauer shrugged. It had been a long day.

'Sir, the councillors spend hours pontificating about nothing. Most of the work is done by civil servants, who rarely seek advice from the councillors. They rubber-stamp any of the policies coming down from the NSDAP executive but by the time policies get implemented, they're pretty watered down, for now anyway.'

'Did you manage to talk to any of the councillors, individually?'

'Only a couple. They're all party stalwarts, as you predicted, but one or two seem to do a worthwhile job, your friend the mayor, for one.'

'Ah, so Jürgen makes a decent go of it then.'

'He's under the thrall of Hinrich Lohse, but in day-to-day matters, he's the one who will get things pushed through, or sorted, and he's the one councillor the civil servants like, at least for now.'

'But a party man though.'

'An opportunist party man, I'd say; not a fervent believer, like Lohse.'

'Interesting. Keep up the good work, and maybe try and cultivate one or two of the civil servants. They quite often have a better grasp of what's going on.'

'Do you wish me to try and organise that meeting, put feelers out?'

The General looked at his watch. 'There's no hurry; maybe next week. I'd like to have a word with one or two of their lordships first, and I just haven't the chance.'

The captain smiled at the lie. The General had lunch with most of the admirals or commanders at least two or three times a week.

~~o~~

Memo: Geh.KdoS. ABW 11/04/33 CAC0178.1

For Attention Only: All senior executive officers, Abwehr.

From: Captain Conrad Patzig, Chef der Abwehr.

URGENT: The Government has followed up the issuing of the Restoration of the Civil Service Act by reinforcing it with a decree defining "non-Aryan" as a person who cannot prove his parents and grandparents are all "Aryan".

It is the responsibility of every area commander to do all that they can to ensure that no qualifying civilian employees remain in position in their section by 30/04/33

This does not yet apply to members of the German armed forces.
[END]

After he'd read the memo, the General handed it to Captain Bauer, along with the *Morgenpost*. He pointed to the article on the front page.

'You want me to check, sir?' he asked, looking at the door to the outer office, dismayed.

'I doubt Frau Müller has any Jewish blood in her, but send her in.'

The captain, disturbed that the army was endorsing the National Socialist's divisive policies, did as he was asked but his mouth was tight and unsmiling. He led Helene Müller in, and sat her down in front of the General, who handed her the memo.

'I'm sorry to have to ask you this, but do you have any parents or grandparents who are

117

Jewish,' he said when she'd finished reading.

'Most certainly not, sir,' she said, her face reddening as she started to rise from her chair. 'I'm appalled that you should have to ask such a question.'

'Sit down, please, Frau Müller. I am required by the ministry to ask you the question. Unfortunately, you must sign a letter to that effect, stating what you have just told me. I'm sorry if it has caused you any upset.'

'It has indeed, Herr General, to be even thought of as anything but German is unimaginable.'

The captain watched, fascinated. As Frau Müller calmed down, she apologised for reacting so heatedly.

'I know it's not your fault, sir. I'll type a letter up straight away, and happily sign it.'

The General smiled at her and indicated that she could return to her post in the outer office.

When the door closed, the captain turned to the General.

'You knew, sir, didn't you?'

'I had an inkling that she was, let's say, sympathetic to their views.'

The captain grinned. 'We definitely know now, sir.'

'We, captain?' The General stared at his subordinate, his eyebrow raised.

The captain flushed.

'Sir, what I meant is that…' His words trickled to a halt.

'It's all right, Heinz. I'm just pleased you're beginning to see the bigger picture. Unfortunately, you seem to be in the minority.'

'Sir, I just want what's best for my country, and the German people, but I can't see how this law is going to make that possible.'

'Nobody does. We can just hope and pray that the army, when it is strong enough, will step in and stop it all. Given Herr Hitler's powers of persuasion, I despair that it will never happen.'

~~o~~

KIELER MORGENPOST

Wednesday 12th April 1933

GOVERNMENT CLARIFIES ACT – "ARYAN" DEFINED

In a bid to strengthen the recent Restoration of the Civil Service Act, the German government has issued a decree requiring civil servants who acquired their positions after August 1, 1914, to prove the Aryan ancestry or their status as World War I veterans.

CHAPTER 26

[12/04/1933 Wednesday]

Yosef pulled out of the driveway as Erich Kästner leaned back in his seat.

'Thanks for this, Yosef,' the General said. 'The captain has gone off with my car and driver, and I need to get to Plön for this damned meeting.'

'No problem, sir. I was just planting out some new shrubs. They'll do tomorrow.'

'Listen, Yosef, I haven't had a chance to apologise for doubting Isaac's account of Dr. Schumm's murder.'

'Sir, there's no need. It is hard to believe that something of that nature can happen in our country in the twentieth century.'

'That may be, but I didn't believe you and Isaac, and I should have.' He hesitated. 'I've asked around. I know a few people in the police force. They admitted, off the record, that the sergeant and his staff should not have been bullied into letting that mob in, but they are not going to pursue it any further; they're under a lot of pressure from the party to write it off as a natural death. I'm sorry.'

'Sir, the family have been told that. I think they knew that would happen. They just wanted to bury their son. Thanks for helping them do that.'

'I just made enquiries. That's all.'

'Whatever you say, sir. I'm sure they would have appreciated your efforts on their behalf.'

'You didn't mention me, did you?'

'No, sir, I presumed you wanted to keep your name out of it.' He glanced at the General in the mirror. 'The coffin was sealed. It was a condition of the release of the body.'

'That's not a surprise,' the General said, his face filled with sadness. 'Was that a problem?'

'They were only glad to get him back, sir. It might have been an issue, but Dr. Speer identified the body at the undertaker's, sir.' Yosef glanced in the mirror again. It was hard to tell if the surprised look on the General's face was feigned.

'It was fortunate Dr. Schumm was a patient of his,' the General murmured.

Yosef slowed for a bend in the road.

'Yosef, advise… no, tell the family not to try and take the matter any further. You as well, for that matter.'

'But sir…'

The General interrupted, a harsh edge to his voice.

'Listen, the SS have opened a concentration camp at Dachau. They are locking up anyone who has a dissenting voice, or who tries to fight the system. They'll end up being sent there if they persist.'

'Can they do that, sir?'

'It seems they can do anything they want, so don't give them an excuse.'

'I'll pass the message on. Are they just locking up Jews, sir?'

'No, it doesn't seem so. Anyone who is critical of the National Socialists is at risk. They seem to be trying to cleanse Germany of any opposition. How are your friends coping?'

'Just keeping their heads down. This business of everyone proving they're 'Aryan' is worrying. Where will it leave us?'

'Have there been large number of job losses in the Jewish community?'

'It seems to be a bit hit or miss, sir. Most who are government employees have lost their jobs. Only those with long service or who are veterans of the war have held onto their positions. We just don't know where the axe will fall next.'

~~o~~

The General looked out. They were passing through Plön.

The Mercedes swung into the entrance of Stadtheide barracks and stopped at the barrier.

'That's us here, sir.'

Yosef switched off the engine. The General waited, expecting Yosef to jump out and open the door for him. Instead, he turned to the General.

'Before you go, sir, I'd like to say my own thanks for…'

Erich Kästner held up his hand, and Yosef's voice trailed off. Both men nodded to each other, a lifetime of understanding passing between them.

~~o~~

KIELER MORGENPOST

Thursday 13th April 1933

CORRECTION

The Kieler Morgenpost would like to apologise for any offence caused to its readership by the wrongly typeset headline in yesterday's paper. The use of quotation marks around the word Aryan were a result of a junior typesetter's error. The headline should have read:

GOVERNMENT CLARIFIES ACT - ARYAN DEFINED

The employee concerned has been reprimanded.

CHAPTER 27

'You can tell Private Zimmer that I'll not need the car tonight.'

'Yes, sir. Going by tram again?'

A suggestion of a smile showed on his chief petty officer's face. The General chose to ignore it.

'No, I'm off on the boat with my sons. The yacht club is a five-minute walk away.'

'Excellent, sir. And how do we get hold of you?'

'I've left my intended itinerary with Captain Bauer. In addition, I will check in by telephone once daily. I trust that you will all manage until I get back?'

'Yes, sir, I'm sure we will. But you never know what might happen these days.'

'Quite. Where is the captain, anyway?'

'He's still with the mayor, sir. He'll be back shortly. It's his shout this weekend.'

The two officers took turn about to man the office at the weekend, with one of the privates to help. Rarely was there anything to do; Captain Patzig would send a despatch rider to the General's house if there was anything important or urgent enough.

'Well, enjoy your weekend, Feldwebel. What are you up to?'

'My wife has plans for me, sir. She has a lot of relatives. We seem to spend most of our free time visiting them.'

The General laughed as he picked up the small holdall he'd sat behind his desk and headed for the door.

'I'll see you on Monday morning.'

~~o~~

It was three o'clock by the time the boys arrived at the dock, and by then, the General had almost finished readying the yacht for departure. They'd stocked her up with provisions the previous evening, so, within fifteen minutes of his sons climbing aboard, they were making good way towards Friedrichsort in a freshening breeze.

As usual, they settled into their rhythm in no time, each complementing the other. Passing Bülk Lighthouse half an hour later, the General made an entry in the yacht's log.

Log Entry Friday 14th April

16:12 BÜLK LT 0.5NM, 270°. Depth 1.5 fathoms.

Weather fair. Sea slight. Visibility Good. Wind F4-5 North-easterly. Air Pressure 1010mb. Full sail, 010°M, 6.5 Knots

They were almost scraping the bottom, cutting the corner, but he knew these waters well, and he'd crossed the Kleverberg bank often, without a serious grounding.

'Ideal sailing conditions, boys, and the wind should be on the beam all the way, once we turn nor'westerly.'

His sons grinned at him.

'It's good to see you smile,' Franz said. 'You've been looking a little careworn for the last few months.'

Erich Kästner shrugged. 'Work,' he said.

I can't burden them with my worries.

They were making for the Schlei river for the first night, hoping to anchor in the bay just inside the entrance, or behind Maasholm if the wind got up. The yacht surged forwards once they'd rounded the headland that guarded the mouth of Kieler Fjord, and they were in open water.

Two hours later, they negotiated the narrow entrance to the river, ignoring the small and exposed Schleimünde harbour just inside, following the channel as it opened out into the small estuary lying behind its protective dunes. Large, shallow bays took bites from the low-lying land on each side. There was an annoying short chop to the waves in front of Maasholm, a spit of land that jutted out into the estuary, so they tucked in behind it, in three metres of water, and dropped the anchor. The yacht lay on her chain comfortably as the sea breeze died into a still, warm evening.

A meal of pork chops, Sauerkraut, potatoes, and gravy was wolfed down to the sound of hundreds of wading birds, ducks, and geese preparing to roost for the night, their calls plaintive and insistent. A bottle of wine was shared between them and the General watched on as Johann persisted in trying to bait his brother, mainly about his budding romance with Lise Böhm.

Franz just smiled, frustrating Johann, and the General saw a lot of himself in his older son. He didn't ask any questions of the boy; if he wanted to talk to him about Lise, he'd do it in his own time.

'Johann, I think you've exhausted all avenues to try and rile Franz,' he said. 'Perhaps a change of subject is in order.' He smiled at them both and Johann shrugged, admitting defeat.

~~o~~

'So, how's school?' the General asked.

'It's good, father,' Johann replied, not put out by his fun being curtailed. 'A bit dull at times, especially history and German. I like maths, physics and chemistry the most, and military studies, obviously.'

The General smiled. 'The subjects you like are essential for a future soldier but you can learn a lot about war, and peace, from history and it's important to be able to communicate well, so stick in with your German.'

Johann groaned. 'I hoped you were going to say that I needn't bother too much with them because I'm going to join the army.'

'It's only for another few years. Look at Franz – he is going to the academy before long.'

'And I bet they teach German and history there too,' Franz said, seeing a chance for revenge.

Johann's jaw dropped. He hadn't considered the possibility.

'I'm afraid he's right, Johann,' the General said, smiling, 'and they'll teach you French, and some English too.'

Johann sighed. He'd counted on escaping from the boredom of the classroom when he reached seventeen, and left school forever.

'Why do we have to know French and English? That's stupid.'

'A commander sometimes needs to confer with officers of other nation's armies. You can rely on an interpreter, but it is much more impressive and civilised to be able to speak the tongue of your enemy, or an ally.'

'I suppose so,' Johann conceded, with a frown.

~~o~~

The General knew he wouldn't sulk for long.

'But you're both enjoying it?' the General asked.

'Almost all of it, yes,' Franz said. 'There's just a little edge to everything right now. The whole Hitlerjugend thing was great to start with, but it often makes me feel a bit

122

uncomfortable now.'

'I love it,' Johann said. 'The exercises are excellent, and it's even better because they've made me a Rottenführer,' Johann said.

The General nodded. *Section Leader*. It wasn't a rank the army used but he knew that the SA and the SS did. He smiled at the pride in his son's voice.

'Franz is a Scharführer now. No surprise there,' Johann said, but his grin robbed the barb of any malice.

The General frowned.

'Wasn't that the rank of the boy in Ruth's class, Peter somebody, who started all the trouble in their school?'

'No, he was a Rottenführer,' Franz said, 'but he must have shown special aptitude at that age to be given even that rank.'

The General heard the sharpness in his son's voice.

'By the time I'm Franz's age, I hope to be a Scharführer too,' Johann said, anxious to please. 'Having a higher rank in the Hitlerjugend will help when I join the army.'

The General forced a smile onto his face. He couldn't take the pleasure that his son got from being a Hitler Youth away from him, just because he didn't like it. The organisation should have been of great benefit to German boys, if it had remained free of politics.

'That's great, Johann.' He searched for the right words. 'Just don't do anything they ask you to do if it makes you feel uncomfortable.'

He glanced at Franz. His son's head was bowed, his eyes on the table.

'What do you mean, father?' Johann asked.

'You'll know. If it doesn't feel right, tell them no.' He could imagine how difficult it would be; a young man brought up with the discipline of a military education questioning a superior officer. Perhaps it was too much to ask of the boy.

Johann nodded, but the General could see that his son wasn't convinced. He decided not to push the point.

'What about the sailing team? That's exciting, isn't it?'

He listened to Johann enthuse about the upcoming races and their intense practice sessions, his father's admonishment forgotten for the time being.

By ten, Johann was flagging, and the General suggested he should turn in for the night.

When he'd brushed his teeth, unrolled his sleeping bag, and climbed into his bunk in the forward cabin, the General turned to Franz.

'I couldn't bring myself to say too much to him,' he explained, his voice soft. 'He's so excited about everything connected with the Hitlerjugend.'

'I'll have a word with him. To be fair, I felt the same as him when I first joined.'

'You'll be out of it soon.' The General opened the forecabin door a crack and looked in.'

'Sound asleep,' he said, turning to Franz. 'So, school is fine then?' he asked.

'Yes, on the whole. We almost lost one teacher to the purge. Someone reported him as being Jewish; we don't know if it was a pupil, or a fellow teacher. After a meeting with the headmaster, he was told he could keep his job because his father was killed in the war.'

'And your Hitlerjugend leaders. What are they like?'

'Not too bad. The bulk of our battalion consists of boys receiving a military education, so they're careful. A couple of our school officers insist on meeting with the Hitlerjugend leaders on a weekly basis to discuss discipline and standards.' Franz smiled. 'There's no love lost between them, but they tolerate each other.'

'So, nothing too extreme yet? That's at least something.'

'They took us to a rally once, you know. We heard him speak. It was mesmerising.'

'What, Hitler himself? You never said.'

'I was going to tell you but, at your retirement party, you seemed so set against him. I couldn't bring myself to say.'

The General sighed.

'Listen, Franz. Never be afraid to tell me anything. Even if we disagree, I'll still listen. I might try to change your mind; you may change mine, for that matter, but whatever it is, I'll always be there for you.'

'I know, but when you said those things, it hit home, and I realised you were right. I was ashamed of ever getting involved.'

Erich Kästner put his hand on his son's shoulder.

'We all make mistakes. You're a bigger person if you can admit to them. I also thought he was a breath of fresh air when I first heard about Adolf Hitler and his party. He's extremely plausible, and he tells people what they want to hear. And he gives them a scapegoat.'

CHAPTER 28

KIELER MORGENPOST

Friday 14th April 1933

POST NOW VACANT FOR SUB-EDITOR

The Kieler Morgenpost are saddened to see the retirement of sub-editor, Benno Arndt, through ill-health. Benno started at the paper as copy boy in 1909. After a brief spell in the army during the Great War, he was invalided out and returned to the Morgenpost where he eventually rose to be sub-editor. Everyone at the Kieler Morgenpost wishes him well in his retirement.

Applications for the vacant post should be made in writing to the Kieler Morgenpost offices in Kirchofallee.

~~o~~

[15/04/1933 Saturday]

'We are sorry to be parting from you, my friends. I have been your rabbi for nine years and it is a wrench to be leaving. As you all know, we are setting off for Palestine tomorrow, and a new life there.'

The rabbi stood on the Bimah, the platform in the centre of the synagogue where the Torah was read, where other members of the congregation could deliver blessings, and where the rabbi delivered his sermons.

'During our time here, we have come to know you all very well, and love every one of you. You are a mixed bunch...' he paused to let the congregation laugh, '...but in your own ways, you are all sons of Abraham, and you love God, and the Jewish faith.'

He looked around. It was busier than he'd ever seen it and he was both touched and chagrined; they'd all come to say farewell to him and his family but, he asked himself, *why were they not all here every week?*

In fairness, most of them attended Shabbat services at some point, but the less devout didn't attend every week, and some were only there once or twice a year, at Passover and Hannukah. He knew that a sizeable proportion of Jews in the city didn't attend at all; some still considered themselves as Jews but had lost their religious beliefs; others had so assimilated themselves as Germans that they didn't consider themselves to be Jews at all.

The influx of the Jews from the East; from Russia, the Ukraine and Poland, in the main, had brought a different kind of worshipper. Fiercely devout and rigid in their adherence to the teachings of the Talmud and the Torah, these Orthodox Jews kept themselves separate from the German people, other than to serve them in their shops or through their businesses, and for the rabbi, ministering to these conservative Jews and the more assimilated secular Jews, who made up the bulk of the congregation, took the fine balance of a tightrope walker and the diplomatic skills of a Franco-German ambassador.

All things considered, I've succeeded.

He'd managed to keep friction between the two groups to a minimum but, with the squeezing of Jewish rights and freedoms by the National Socialist government, the cracks in the foundations he'd built over the years were beginning to show.

125

The secular Jews, to all intents and purposes indistinguishable from other Germans, blamed the bearded, side-locked, and black-frocked Orthodox Jews for being provocative and drawing attention to themselves and, by association, the bulk of German Jews, who wished for nothing more than to blend in with their fellow Germans.

The Orthodox Jews, who all adhered to Jewish law and to a strict Kosher lifestyle, condemned the secular Jews for compromising themselves and their religion.

It's my last sermon. I have a duty to be blunt with them.

'We are entering another chapter in the oppression of the Jewish people,' he continued. 'Some of you have come here to escape pogroms in the East, only to find the same is now happening here.'

He paused again, looking around at the faces of people desperate for guidance, both temporal and spiritual.

'I am leaving Germany with reluctance because, until recently, I regarded myself as German, and I loved this country. If it were just our leaders who were trying to impose their anti-Semitic views on the nation, I could live with that. But the German people; not all of them, but a significant proportion of them, are embracing those views and, in my view, it can only get worse.'

He could see that his harsh words were hitting home.

'I would urge you all to leave, not necessarily to Palestine. Even among us, there is debate whether Zionism has a place in our lives, but consider France, England, and the United States, even South America.'

There was a collective gasp from the congregation as he said this, and murmurs of assent clashed with a ripple of disapproval. He held up his hands to quieten them.

'I know most of you won't heed my advice, and I respect you for that, even though I consider it to be a wrong choice. But, for those that stay, please do one thing for me.'

He looked at them long and hard, making their eyes touch his.

'Stick together and look after one and other. It's your only defence against hate. Hashem yevarech.' *God Bless.*

The next day, the congregation turned out in larger numbers than he expected, to see him and his family off on the train, and the deliberations over his parting homily continued for weeks. Some heeded his advice, and a score of Jewish families left Kiel in the latest round of the diaspora, heading for destinations all over the world, often to relatives who had made the journey years before.

The Nussbaums were not among them.

CHAPTER 29

[16/04/1933 Sunday]

'Where did you go? Did you see a Sturmtaucher?'

'No, I don't think so,' the General said.

Antje, waiting at the doorway with Ruth, had given her father a huge hug as soon as he got out the car. Yosef smiled, and reversed the car into the garage.

'Can Ruth stay a little longer?' Antje asked, tugging at her father's sleeve.

The General glanced at Yosef, who nodded. Ruth and Antje followed him and the two boys into the house.

'Be back home by eight o'clock. You have school in the morning,' Yosef shouted at his daughter's receding back.

Erich Kästner barely had a chance to greet his wife and shout a hello to his older daughter when Antje had hauled him to his study and insisted on him showing her and Ruth their trip on one of the old charts he kept in his desk.

Johann followed them in, keen to show off his navigational knowledge, and the General was happy to leave it to his son to tell the girls about the journey.

He half listened, watching Franz standing talking with Maria in the hallway. His oldest son always found time for his mother, telling her what was going on in his life and listening to her latest gossip, hiding any hint that he'd rather be somewhere else. The General frowned. From the occasional glance towards the Böhm house next door, he could see that Franz was desperate to be with Lise.

Should I warn him about the girl's mother? There's no reason to believe that the daughter is anything like her.

Johann's voice broke into his thoughts.

'...so, after we left Maasholm, we sailed over here.' He was using a small steel pencil sharpener to represent the boat, and he slid it across the chart from the mouth of the Schlei river to the north-west tip of Ærø, to a harbour near the south end of the long, thin island.

'This is called Ærøskøbing. It's in Denmark,' he said. 'Father had to fill in customs forms at the harbour master's office.'

'I've been there. I've been there.' Antje jumped up and down. 'I remember seeing all the fish in boxes.'

'No, Antje, that was Marstal. We were there last year. It's not far from Ærøskøbing though.'

'Remember Mama was so disgusted,' Antje jabbered, 'because you were cooking that enormous cod in the galley; she said it would make the whole boat smell of fish for a week.'

The General glanced at the drawing room again. Franz was still standing with Maria. He saw his son's eyes drift to the window again.

'Maria, come and hear what they're saying about you,' he said, smiling.

Maria touched her son's hand and walked into the study. Franz shot his father a grateful look and slipped out of the room.

'We bought it from a fishing boat. I helped choose it,' Antje was saying.

'You bought what? When was this?' her mother said.

'Last year. The big fish. In Marstal. You remember, Mama, don't you? You didn't like Father cooking it.'

'Oh, yes. The monster cod. I couldn't stand to be in the cabin for days after it. It's a wonder I wasn't seasick.'

'When you've all finished,' Johann said, 'can we get on with this trip, please?'

Antje drew him a look but said nothing.

'Go on then,' his father told him.

'Well, we went to a tavern. I was only allowed one beer though.' He glanced at his mother, who frowned at the General.

'I thought it would be interesting for them, and they're almost old enough to go in themselves. The people couldn't have been more friendly.'

He and Franz spoke reasonable Danish, and many Danes had passable German. They'd fallen into easy conversation with the fishermen, who recommended the fish stew and fresh bread that was the tavern's staple fare.

'And there was nowhere else to eat,' the General said, embellishing the truth a little. 'It was tasty, wasn't it, Johann?'

The boys had loved the glimpse into the adult-only world of the quayside bar, with Johann in particular soaking it all in. The smell and the sounds of it all; beer, Akvavit, the local equivalent to Schnapps, tobacco smoke, the crackle of the fire in the grate, the clack of dominoes and the talk and laughter of men sloughing off the dangers of the sea; they were all intoxicating to him.

And they'd been welcomed. The older men teased the two boys, and the General spoke with knowledge and love of the sea, bridging the divide in nationality and in station.

Antje's eyes widened as Johann described some of the characters; Maria's frown deepened.

'They're joining the army soon, woman,' the General said. 'They'll see and hear much worse.' He turned to Johann. 'I think we need to hear a bit more about the sailing, and less about the nightlife.'

Johann took the hint.

'The next morning, that was Sunday, we set off after first light. We were lucky with the weather, and we had a great sail to Rudkøbing on Langeland. We were there by nine o'clock. We berthed up and Father made us go to church.'

The General turned to Maria, an innocent smile on his face. 'To make up for the debauchery of the previous evening,' he told her.

Johann and Antje giggled.

The General couldn't avoid his wife's suspicious glance. He flinched.

Surely she doesn't think I'd stoop so low as to ask her sons to lie to me?

Johann resumed his account of their journey, saving the General any further scrutiny.

'Anyway, after lunch we headed north... here, to Omø. We saw three warships. Father said he knew all their captains. One of the ships, a destroyer, gave us a blast on the horn.'

'They all know the boat,' the General said. 'It was a long sail back the next day, but the wind had swung round to the north a little, so we didn't have to tack.'

The General put his hand on his youngest son's shoulder.

'And we had a new man in charge.'

Johann looked at his mother, bursting with pride.

'Father made me the skipper for the last day. I got to boss him and Franz about. I found them to be just about satisfactory as crew,' he said, grinning.

The General gave him a playful cuff to the back of his head.

'I'll remember that. You had one of the best crews that has ever sailed. Even so, you did well enough. You're quite capable of taking charge of the boat now.'

'Can I take my friends out one day?'

'Soon,' the General replied, remembering his own father letting him take his yacht out when he was only sixteen. Franz and Johann had already been away on short trips on the boat together and, from what he'd seen, he would be comfortable with Johann taking a few friends out, for short sails to start with. Most of the boys he ran around with were familiar with yachts, and he hoped that Johann wouldn't take unwarranted risks with the boat, despite his sense of adventure.

But he saw his wife's expression turn to worry and told himself that he'd have to reassure her before he let Johann loose on *Snowgoose* with his friends.

CHAPTER 30

'Mama, what's a leave of absence?' Antje asked, lifting her head from her sketching. The evening light streaming in the drawing-room windows was beginning to fade, and they just about needed to switch on the lamps. Eva was reading, and Maria picked at the embroidery on her knee; she dabbled with needlework from time to time, as much from custom than from any real desire to be creative.

Eva answered her sister's question.

'It's when somebody is off sick, or maybe one of their family dies or something similar. Why do you ask?'

'One of our teachers has gone off on a leave of absence. They don't know if she'll ever be back.'

'Which one, Antje? I wonder if it's one of the teachers I had, when I was at Grundschule.'

'It's Frau Epstein. I had her two years ago.'

'Oh, she took us in year five, I think. She was nice.'

'Oh yes, I remember her,' Maria said. 'She was an excellent teacher. At parents' evening, she said you were an especially bright pupil, Antje, but that you were often easily distracted.' She laughed.

'And what did she say about me, Mama?' Eva asked.

'Oh, I can't remember now. I'm sure she said you were bright, too, dear.'

'I should really sulk because you always remember everything about your golden girl.'

Maria protested, but she admitted to herself that Eva had a point; as the youngest, Antje was a little spoiled.

'That's not true, Eva,' she said, unwilling to concede. 'It was just much longer ago.' She saw her daughter's smile and shook her head. 'You're a devil!'

'She was one of the better teachers though. We all liked her,' Eva said.

'Ruth says she sits in front of her at the synagogue, but she wasn't there on Saturday.'

Maria blanched.

'I didn't realise Frau Epstein was Jewish,' Eva blurted out, 'Is that why she's not…' She tailed off, catching her mother's glare out of the corner of her eye. A brief shake of Maria Kästner's head reinforced the admonishment.

They both glanced at Antje, who was adding a few lines to her drawing. She didn't seem to have noticed the exchange. Maria breathed a sigh of relief and mouthed to Eva that she would talk later, then Antje looked up and turned to them.

'I'll ask Ruth if she can find out if Frau Epstein is ill. Someone at the synagogue will surely know.'

Maria's heart sank.

'Perhaps it would be better if you didn't, just in case she's not ill. It could be that someone close to her has died, and it wouldn't be fair to go around asking about her.'

'All right, Mama. If you think so. But I'm sure Aunt Miriam would know, and she'll tell Ruth.'

'Let's see if dinner is ready,' Maria said, 'Your Papa will be home soon, and he'll be hungry. And don't say a word to Miriam, Antje.'

~~o~~

When Maria Kästner found something to worry about, the General often shouldered the brunt of her angst.

At dinner, she barely smiled when he mentioned the hapless officer who had wheeled the cadets to the right instead of the left, marching them off the end of the quay into the harbour, or at his description of the first lines of young sailors trying to stop as they reached the edge of the quay, only to be pushed into the water by the still marching ranks behind them.

Untouched by her daughters' laughter, Maria had fretted until Antje and Eva had gone to bed.

'What do we tell her?' she asked, after she'd explained to him what had happened to Antje's teacher.

'Just tell her the truth. That people are losing their jobs just because they are Jewish.' He paused. 'That's not strictly true. Other people are losing their jobs, too, because they are opponents of the ruling party but, in a dictatorship, that is what nearly always happens, so it is easier to rationalise. But targeting Jewish people is just madness.'

'We don't live in a dictatorship. This is Germany. We're a democratic country. You might not like Hitler or the National Socialists, but the country voted for him.'

'Did it, Maria? That is the question the German people should be asking themselves.'

She flared. 'Of course we voted for him.' It was out before she realised, and she watched his face for signs of anger.

Instead, she saw disappointment. She felt like a small child again, caught with her hand in the sweetie jar.

'Don't look at me like that. I'll admit I voted for them, for him. I want a better Germany, and he's the only one who can bring back the days when we were a great country.'

He sighed. 'But at what price, Maria? At what price?'

She knew that if she got into a debate with him, it would end with her tied up in knots. They rarely talked politics; as an army officer he kept his political views under wraps on the whole but, recently, she'd noticed him becoming more vocal about his opinions, and it unsettled her.

'Maria,' he continued, 'I'm not going to tell you how to vote but you should be informed enough to know what you are voting for. The Enabling Act, which the Reichstag voted into legislation a few weeks ago, allows Herr Hitler to pass any law he wants without it going through parliament. All he needs to do is write it down, and hundreds of his fanatical supporters will do his bidding.'

'Sometimes exceptional measures are needed when we live in terrible times. Once the country is stabilised, we'll return to normal, surely?'

She kicked herself at making a question of her argument.

'I wish I could say it will, but it's a forlorn hope, I'm afraid.'

She saw the bitter defeat in his eyes, and it worried her, but she was still angry at his bias against anything the government did.

'He's strengthening the army, and the navy. You must approve of that.'

'The army will support him for their own ends, and the navy too. They've both been calling for an end to the Treaty of Versailles for years, as have I. They'll give Herr Hitler support while it is in their interest. And that worries me.'

'Why? Should Germany not have strong armed forces to defend our people?'

'I couldn't agree more, but I doubt Adolf Hitler's aims stop at defence. He has expansionist ambitions and there are enough like-thinkers in the army to follow his ambitions.'

'What are you saying, Erich? There will be another war? That's piffle!'

'You think so? I hear it every day. There is a certain caginess in the higher echelons of the Reichsheer and the Reichsmarine about Adolf Hitler but there is also a lot of approval for his ideas.'

~~o~~

They sat for a while. He watched her, silent in her anger.

The General wondered if it had even crossed her mind that her two sons were set to join the army soon and, if there was a war, they'd be expected to fight. Strangely, it was something he'd always accepted. He had done so for himself, and he would do the same for his sons.

But what would they be asked to do in the name of this new Germany, the 'Third Reich', as Adolf Hitler was now calling it?

He looked across at his wife and gave her a sad smile.

Perhaps she is right to bury her head in the sand when, like me, she is powerless.

'There's nothing we can do about it,' he said. 'They're in control now. Pray that they do right for Germany, and all its people.'

'You talk to Antje,' she said, handing him an olive branch, 'but don't tell her anything that might get her into bother.'

Erich Kästner thought that her words were more damning than anything he had just said.

CHAPTER 31

Antje sat on her father's knee, at his desk. She wasn't often in his study; it was never off-limits to her, but her mother disapproved of her interrupting him when he was working, so it was a special treat when he'd called her in and lifted her up onto his lap.

She snuggled into his arms and he gave her one of the tight hugs which squeezed the air out of her and should have been frightening but wasn't.

She giggled when he let her breathe again.

'Papa, can I go in the boat with you and paint something?'

'You can, most certainly. It needs a new coat of paint.'

'No, Papa. Don't be silly. I mean paint a picture.' She giggled again, her small body shaking against his chest.

'Ah. What do you want to paint?'

'I want to paint a bird.'

'Won't that be difficult? It surely won't keep still enough for you to paint it.'

She tutted. 'I know what it looks like. I just want to see it flying.'

'Oh, I see. What kind of bird is it?'

'A shearwater. Like the one on my paint box. Don't you remember?'

He nodded. 'I do. It was ein Sturmtaucher. And it was in flight.'

He frowned.

'Why don't you just copy that one?' he said. 'It would be a lot easier.'

'I want to paint my own one. That's what real artists do.'

He started to smile, but she was being quite serious, so he hid his grin with his hand.

'It might be quite unusual to see a shearwater where we sail with you and Mama. You would have to go to the North Sea or the Atlantic to see them.'

She looked disappointed.

'You sometimes go there, don't you?'

'The boys and I, and Grandfather, have been through the Kaiser-Wilhelm-Kanal a few times and sailed in the North Sea. And we've been to Norway, but Mama says it's too rough for her. She certainly wouldn't want you going.'

'But why not? I wouldn't be scared.'

'I'll tell you what. If we go through the canal this year, I'll ask Mama if we can take you with us. Would you manage to live on the boat for more than a week without her?'

She frowned for a second but nodded at him, her solemn expression making him smother another smile.

'I suppose your Mama couldn't really complain,' he said. 'Your brothers went away with me at your age. It saved her having to go.'

Her mother would do no more than one outing a year on the boat, venturing no further than the sheltered waters around Kiel and the Western Baltic. Eva went sailing only under duress and, to avoid having a huffing teenager on the boat, she more often than not was sent to stay with her Aunt Traudl, Erich's sister, whom she adored.

'Why won't Mama go with us?' she asked.

'She doesn't like strong wind or large waves, so she only goes when the weather looks settled, and where there is easy shelter. But you'll be fine. The boys and I would look after you.'

Antje brightened up at the thought of being spoiled for a whole week by the three men in the family.

'Antje, there's something I need to talk to you about.'

She peered at him, a long-suffering expression on her face.

'Is it about babies and stuff?'

She didn't quite catch his stifled smile, but she saw him blush.

'No,' he said, 'but do you want me to explain it to you?'

'No. I'm sure Mama will try and tell me, but I know already. I read about it in the 'cyclopoedia. It doesn't mention people, but it must be just the same as it is with animals.'

This time, he laughed out loud.

~~o~~

When he'd regained his composure, he looked fondly at her.

'You're full of surprises, young lady,' he said. 'I'm sure your mama will fall off her chair if you say that to her. Perhaps it would be better not to tell her you already know. Just let her tell you about it when she's ready, listen to what she says then nod your head like a good girl.'

'All right, Papa. If you think I should.'

'Yes, I do. Anyway, that's that dealt with. What I really wanted to talk to you about was the teacher who left the school.'

'You mean Frau Epstein?'

'Yes, that's her. Well, she's not ill, but the government are replacing all Jewish teachers with Christian ones. It's not a nice thing to be happening, but there's nothing we can do to prevent it and, the thing is, it can get you into trouble if you talk about it.'

'Why do they want to get rid of Jewish people? My best friend is Jewish.'

He smiled again. She could be like a little old lady sometimes.

'Herr Hitler has something against Jewish people, and now that he's the leader of Germany, he is trying to get rid of them, to have them go to other countries.'

Her bottom lip trembled, and he could see tears well up in her eyes.

'Will Ruth and Rebeka's families have to leave too? That would be so unfair. What about Moshe's family?'

He briefly wondered what Rebeka's parents did for a living.

And who the hell is Moshe?

'I'm sure they won't,' he said. 'The Nussbaums will always have a home with us and, anyway, what would Mama and I do without Yosef and Miriam?'

His daughter smiled and sniffed. He stroked her hair and put his arm around her. He remembered that Moshe was Manny's little friend. He'd seen his mother at Manny's birthday party. Something told him he should know who Moshe's dad was.

'What does Rebeka's dad do?'

'He works in a factory, I think.'

'I'm sure he'll be fine.'

He hoped his answer didn't sound glib. He racked his brain about the identity of Moshe's father.

Weichmann's, he thought, his memory kicking in at last. Moshe's father owned the hardware store in the centre of Kiel. It was a wonderful place, where you could buy almost anything. The Kästners had an account there, although it was usually Yosef who picked up bits and pieces needed for the maintenance that he did around the house and garden.

'Moshe's dad will be fine,' he reassured her. 'He has the best shop in Kiel, doesn't he?'

He scoured his brain, trying to remember the man's name.

Itsik, that's it.

'Papa, the best shop in Kiel is the ice-cream shop at the botanic gardens, or the sweetie shop in Königsweg,' Antje said. She was smiling again, the relief evident on her face.

'Well, you might be right, although I'm sure Mama would favour one of her expensive dress shops, or maybe the jewellers.'

Chances are, both would be owned by Jews.

He knew his tailor was.

She laughed, then frowned at him.

'You're making fun of Mama,' she said, but he could see that she loved him for including her in the joke.

'What we talked about earlier, about your teacher. Best not to speak to anyone else about it. Let it be our little secret, yes?'

'All right, Papa, but if Ruth and Rebeka speak about it, is that allowed?'

He thought for a few seconds.

'Yes, but only when it's the three of you. Other children, or adults, might not understand. If anyone says anything to you, come and tell me.'

'Yes, Papa.' She hugged him and he tickled her until she squealed.

'Now, go and practise painting. You'll have to become very quick, to catch that Sturmtaucher flying across the ocean.'

CHAPTER 32

[20/04/1933 Thursday]

There were banners everywhere. Pictures of Adolf Hitler hung from almost every window and, on the walls, posters announced that it was the chancellor's birthday.

In civilian clothes of slacks, a sweater and a heavy gaberdine coat, the General stepped off the tram on Holtenauer at Waitzstraße and looked around for Dieter Maas's apartment block. The sacked *Morgenpost* editor lived at number ninety.

As he walked along Waitzstraße, he ticked off the house numbers; fifty-eight, sixty-four, sixty-eight. He crossed Knooper Weg and continued his count; seventy-two, eighty-four, almost as far as the next corner, then he saw it. He checked down the list of names on the buzzers. He spotted the one he was looking for.

Herr D. Maas

He rang the bell, and a window opened on the third floor.

'General, come on up, it's not locked.'

He pushed the door and, sure enough, it creaked open. He took the stairs two at a time as far as the first landing but then thought better of it and climbed the next two flights at a more measured pace. Even so, he was breathing hard when he made the landing. The door on the left was ajar, so he walked through it, into a dimly lit hallway.

'Hello,' he shouted.

'Through here.' The voice came from the door at the end of the hall, and he could hear a song playing in the background, so he followed the soft crackling sound of the gramophone. His nose registered the smell of freshly brewed coffee.

Dieter Maas was standing in his kitchen. A coffee pot sat on the tile slab beside the cooker, with a coffee grinder beside it. He pulled down two cups from the rack on the cupboard.

'You'd like a coffee, General?' he asked, and held out his hand.

The General shook it. 'Yes, that would be most welcome,' he said, 'and please call me Erich.'

The man, tall and thin, with a shock of dark curly hair, placed the cups and the coffee pot on a small tray and motioned for the General to move through to the lounge. The record had finished, and Dieter Maas lifted the needle and set the arm on its stand.

The General looked around. It was a well-furnished room; not large, but decorated with simple taste, and not overly adorned. A picture of a plain but pleasant woman hung in a frame on the wall.

'Your wife?' the General asked.

'Yes. Margot. She is out shopping.'

The General raised his eyebrow.

'Yes, she thought it best to leave us to it. She'll not be back before you go.'

The newspaperman gestured for the General to sit down.

'I was intrigued when I got your call, General.'

'Please. It's Erich. I meant to get in contact sooner but, you know...'

'Yes, you must be busy, with your new position. It sounds intriguing.'

'It has been. It's all completely new to me, all this diplomacy lark, trying to get the army and the navy to talk to each other.'

It was Dieter Maas's turn to look sceptical.

'Amongst other duties,' the General added.

Dieter Maas shrugged. 'So, what can I do for you... Erich.'

The General hesitated.

'We may be able to do something for each other. First, I was dismayed to hear that you'd...' he paused, '...left the paper.'

The man smiled thinly. 'It was a wrench for me too. I loved the *Morgenpost*.' He looked at the General, as if sizing him up. He seemed to come to some sort of a decision. 'I worry about it,' he added.

'I do too. It has become nothing more than a mouthpiece for the NSDAP, I'm afraid.' He studied the paper's former editor. 'I'll assume that nothing of this conversation will ever be repeated.'

'Of course. By either of us.'

'Indeed,' the General replied. 'Part of my job is to keep the Reichswehr up to date with what is happening in the province, politically, shall we say. I presume that you still have your contacts and sources. I'd be willing to employ you, to keep me informed of anything that you think might be useful to us at the Abwehr.'

The newspaper man didn't quite hide his surprise.

'Why me? There must be hundreds of informants you could pick up. I'm out of it all now, and I'll never get a job in a newspaper again, thanks to the owners of the *Morgenpost*. They're ardent supporters of the NSDAP, as you'd gathered,' he added.

'Here's the thing. I need someone with extensive local knowledge whom I can trust. I've had dealings with you in the past, and I thought your piece on the election was balanced, fair and insightful, and anyway, you'll need a job.'

'People are going to be very suspicious when I have an income again, but I don't appear to do anything.'

'I'll give you a job title. Press administrator, how does that sound?'

'I don't know. Wouldn't one of the enlisted personnel normally fill a role like that?'

The General thought about it.

'Leave it with me, I'll sort something out. Are you interested?'

'Yes, but only because you had the brass to come and ask me, knowing I was on the blacklist.'

'I didn't even know there was a blacklist, but that's exactly why I asked you. I know you're not one of them.'

'The strange thing is, I wasn't against the National Socialists to start with. Part of me wanted them to be the reformists, the movers and shakers that would lift Germany from the mire it was in. Even when their fascism became more ardent, I would still give them credit for building new roads, creating jobs and the like. But now...'

'It was the same with me. I only wish I'd noticed sooner.'

The General looked at his watch. 'I'd better go. We'll speak soon.'

He stood up and waited for Dieter Maas to get to his feet.

'You have a fine collection of books,' he said, nodding at the large bookcase that almost covered one wall.

'I like to read.'

The General glanced at some of the titles.

'You might want to have some of these less prominently displayed,' he said, 'should you ever receive a visit from our NSDAP friends.'

Dieter Maas nodded. 'I've been considering it, but I keep this in pride of place,' he said, pulling out a well-thumbed copy of *Mein Kampf*. 'For balance.'

'You've read it, I assume?'

'Yes. Of all the books I own, it's the one I think everyone should read. Have you...?'

The General nodded.

They shook hands, and the General left. As he exited the building and walked down the street, a woman, who had been standing in a doorway opposite, picked up her shopping bags and entered the building he'd just left.

~~o~~

He sat on the tram and tried not to think too much. From his vantage point he could see much more of his surroundings than he did when he was in the car. He made up his mind to do it more often. It would allow the captain to use the Abwehr car and driver sometimes, too, something that would do the young man's standing at the Rathaus no harm.

His meeting with Dieter Maas had been encouraging and, as the General watched people going about their business from his elevated situation, he was confident that he'd made the right choice.

CHAPTER 33

[26/04/1933 Wednesday]

KIELER JÜDISCHES FREIHEITSNACHRICHTENBLATT

Volume 1

Nissan 25, 5693

NEW JEWISH NEWSPAPER

This newspaper has been published in response to the lack of balanced reporting in other Kiel newspapers. For months, the Kieler Morgenpost, among others, has been printing only articles supporting the position of the NSDAP. We will strive to provide a weekly news page but due to circumstances this may not always be possible. FREIHEIT FÜR JUDEN.

ACADEMICS AND TEACHERS DISMISSED

As the Law for the restoration of a national professional civil service of 7th April starts to make its mark, a series of dismissals of Jewish academics has taken place.

Jewish Professor Kantorowicz, a teacher of Criminal Law, was dismissed from Kiel University on the 13th of April and a further nine Jewish teachers were dismissed on the 22nd of the same month, including International Law expert, Professor Schucking, the chief German exponent of the legal concept on which the League of Nations is based.

In support of the NSDAP's attack on Jewish academia, a mob of students at the university burned books written by Jews, political opponents, and liberal intellectuals.

The purge was not confined to the University, or to Jewish academics. Following on from these dismissals,

Director Bernhard Harms, founder of the Institute for the World Economy in Kiel, an internationally renowned intellectual body, was sacked for refusing to dismiss Jewish members of his staff, and for insisting on retaining books in the library written by Jewish authors. His successor, Jens Jessen, is a supporter of the NSDAP.

~~o~~

With mixed emotions, Yosef looked at the single sheet of paper in his hands. His head slumped at the news from the university but, although the fear of being caught reading it unnerved him, his heart soared with pride that Jews were willing to risk their lives to spread the truth.

Freedom for Jews.

He heard the kitchen door lock turn, and he stuffed the page down the side of the couch. The parlour door opened, and Miriam entered. She looked at Yosef and stiffened.

'What's wrong?' she asked him.

'Nothing,' he said, but he couldn't meet her eye.

'Yosef Nussbaum, I know when you are hiding something, so what is it? Are you still sore?'

He shook his head.

'I'm still a bit stiff, now and again, but I'm all right.'

He fished the newsletter out from the couch and smoothed it out on his knee before handing it to her. She looked at it, reading the first page, then turned it over and read the second page. The silence between them grew.

'Where did you get this?' she asked.

'You're better not to know. It was handed to me.'

'And you thought I'd disapprove?'

'Well, I thought you'd say it's too dangerous to have around, to be caught with a copy.'

'It might well be, but it's the only news I've seen that I could put a grain of belief in. Have you read it all?'

'No, just the first page. I wasn't in long in front of you.'

'Read the back.' She handed it to him.

JEWISH STUDENTS UNDER THREAT OF EXCLUSION

The National Socialist Government passed a law yesterday against overcrowding in schools and universities. This limits the number of Jewish students allowed in public schools. Some are expected to expel their Jewish pupils as from today but there is no information if this includes any of the schools in the Kiel area.

Jewish Religious and business leaders have met to discuss the consequences of a widespread exclusion of Jewish children and students from educational establishments, with a view to providing alternative schooling within the Jewish community.

'There's been no news from the school, has there?' he said, when he'd finished reading.

'No, but we'll see what happens when the children come home.'

'It may not come to anything. Their headmaster always seems so sensible and level-headed.'

'The school wasn't slow in getting rid of Frau Epstein.' Miriam's brow creased with worry.

'Wait and see. The universities are forever meddling with politics, and some of the students are far too radical. Schools will be different.'

'But all those professors! Who's going to teach the students? You surely can't replace people like that at the drop of a hat.'

'No, I don't suppose you can.'

He hesitated. 'I feel bad saying this, but it's a relief that neither of us is employed by the government.'

He walked over to the unlit fire, struck a match, and, touching it to the corner of the newsletter, he held the paper until it was well alight and watched as it shrivelled to ash in the grate.

CHAPTER 34

Memo: Geh.KdoS. ABW 26/04/33 CAC0169.1

For Attention Only: All senior executive officers, Abwehr.

From: Captain Conrad Patzig, Chef der Abwehr.

Hermann Göring, Minister of the Interior for the State of Prussia, has created a new agency, Geheime Staatspolizei, from the old Prussian state political police department. It is to be known by its abbreviation, the GeStaPo. He has appointed Rudolf Diels as its first chief.

As the secret police of the largest state in Germany, with access to the extensive records of the superseded Prussian state police, it can be expected to use information gathered on prominent German citizens to ensure their compliance with NSDAP objectives.

For information only. No action necessary. [END]

Erich Kästner handed the memo to Captain Bauer. When the young officer had finished reading it, he turned to Günter Neuer, the unit's chief petty officer.

'The National Socialists love an acronym,' he said, grinning. 'Even the Hitler salute has now been shortened to the Hitler greeting.'

He flicked his hand up in a parody of the truncated salute that had become prevalent, particularly with supporters of the NSDAP, who seemed to be taking note of anyone who didn't participate in the 'Heil Hitler' obsession. Even outside of the party, the 'Hitler greeting' had become compulsory in places of work.

'I heard that comment, Captain,' the General scolded, keeping a straight face. 'You're lucky I'm not an NSDAP informer. Our National Socialist government do not like ridicule of their leader.'

'The General has a point, captain,' the chief petty officer said. 'A friend of mine was arrested two months ago for telling a joke about Herr Hitler. He's still in prison. His parents have hired a top lawyer to try and have him released.'

'I've heard rumours,' the General replied. 'What was the joke, out of interest.'

He saw their faces change, uneasy now. 'I just want to know what one gets arrested for these days,' he said.

'Sir, with all respect, you never know who is listening.'

'You're quite safe with us, Stabsfeldwebel. I hope I speak for you, captain.'

'Without doubt, sir, but it is prudent these days to be careful of your friends.' He walked over to the open door, peered out, and closed it.

The General looked at his chief petty officer. 'Well…'

The man glanced at them both and shrugged his shoulders.

'There can't be any elections in the foreseeable future,' he said, his face straight.

'Why?' the General asked, playing his part.

'There was a break-in at the Ministry of Propaganda and the results for the next elections have been stolen from Goebbels' desk.'

All three men laughed. In the outer office, Helene Müller heard them, and frowned.

~~o~~

140

Captain Bauer pulled on his coat. The General was still working at his desk, but the rest of the staff had gone home. He checked his watch. Half past six. He was picking Käthe up at seven. The cinema again, then back to his small flat. His mind drifted to the night before; they had been together every night, but she always insisted on going home. He was considering asking her to marry him.

The General's voice pierced his thoughts.

'There's one other thing, captain, and I want you to deal with it personally. We have a small budget for intelligence gathering. I'd like you to arrange a monthly salary for a Herr G. Schmitt of 120 Reichsmarks.'

'Yes sir, when do you want the first cheque to be made out?'

'No cheques, Captain Bauer. Herr Schmitt will be paid out of petty cash. If you place the correct amount in an envelope, I will deliver it myself.'

The thought that the General might be pocketing some extra cash flashed through the young officer's mind before he discounted it, disgusted that he'd even considered it, however briefly.

'Yes, sir. I'll get on that first thing tomorrow.'

'And Captain…'

'Yes, sir.'

'Keep this between me and you, Heinz. Our man wants his involvement kept as quiet as possible. The fewer people who know about it, the better.'

CHAPTER 35

[27/04/1933 Thursday]

'How did it go?'

Miriam waited for Yosef to hang his coat up on the hook and sit beside the fire in the kitchen. He still gave the odd wince when he moved.

Ruth and Manny had gone to bed at nine, an hour since, and Miriam had waited in the quiet house, her nerves taut, for Yosef to come home from the synagogue. A group of the congregation's men had formed a committee to tackle the most pressing issues that were blighting the lives of most of the local Jewish population, and he was part of it.

She'd made a pot of coffee and she handed him a cup, taking her seat on the other side of the fireplace.

'What you'd expect, really,' he said. 'Max Weidmann and Isaac Stern complained about the loss of business and, in Isaac's case, replacing the window in his shop.'

He sipped his coffee, blowing on the surface to cool it.

'They also told us that they'd both had letters from the council making it their responsibility to maintain the yellow stars painted on their shops, so as not to lower the standards for the other residents within their districts.'

'And if they don't do it?'

'They can close them down. Rescind their trading licence.'

She stayed silent.

'Three more Jewish teachers have been dismissed from the university,' Yosef continued. 'There can only be a few remaining. Professor Opperman was one of those they sacked.'

Miriam and the professor's wife had met when Ruth and the professor's daughter, a couple of years older, had both taken part in a concert in aid of Jewish orphans. They weren't close friends, but they were more than passing acquaintances.

'I must go and see her. Poor woman. What will they do?'

'There are no jobs for the men, but I hear that some of their wives have taken laundry jobs, or cleaning. What skills do their husbands have besides teaching?'

'What will their students do?'

'Peh. The government doesn't want students, especially in the humanities. They are all at camps for young people, learning how to be good Aryan citizens and soldiers for the Führer.'

'What about the schools?'

'Good news and bad news. There have been no expulsions of Jewish pupils in Kiel, but almost all the Jewish teachers have been 'retired', with a pension, at least. It seems that the school boards in Kiel can't condone Aryan children being taught by Jewish teachers but can tolerate them being in contact with Jewish pupils for the time being, at least.'

Relief surged through Miriam, and she tried to ignore the sense of guilt that came with it, while other people suffered, but she kept it to herself.

'Was it bad, moving around?'

'I wasn't stopped, I didn't see any SA men or Hitlerjugend louts, but the streets don't feel safe somehow.' He paused. 'It's like we've moved to a foreign city, but it still looks like Kiel.'

She saw the hurt in his eyes and reached forward, laying her hand on top of his.

He sighed.

'It was a long evening,' he said.

They sat for a while, then she patted his hand a couple of times.

'Franz was seventeen yesterday. Did you remember? We're invited over tomorrow evening when the boys get back from school.'

'I forgot, I'm afraid. The General did mention it at the start of the week, but the Kästners haven't needed me to drive since Tuesday, so it slipped my mind.'

'I've to do some food during the day, then we've all to go over at seven.'

'He's turned into a fine young man. It's like watching his father when he was that age.'

'I hope he doesn't turn up in his Hitlerjugend uniform. Those children, marching and singing; it makes my skin crawl.'

'The poor lad regrets having joined. I don't think he had much choice, being at the school they're at. Johann still hasn't seen through the country's blind worship of Hitler yet, but Franz definitely has.'

He told her about seeing Franz's face in the car mirror when he'd picked the children up after the march.

'He was ashamed, and I could see it in his eyes that part of the shame was me seeing he and his brother in those uniforms. Johann and Eva, they didn't think twice about it, but Franz knew.'

~~o~~

[28/04/1933 Friday]

For a while, the Nussbaums were the only guests at Franz's birthday celebration. It would have suited Erich Kästner if it had remained that way, but he knew that life seldom worked like that.

As usual, Johann took great joy in teasing the younger children, until, fed up with the screams and the squeals, Maria told them all to put on their gumboots, coats and scarves and take themselves into the garden.

But when the doorbell rang, and the Böhm family arrived with a gift for Franz, the children were called in and told to wash their hands, and Maria ushered everyone into the dining room, where an array of cold platters were laid out on the sideboard.

In the resultant happy melee, by the time everyone had taken their seats, the General smiled, looking around the table.

Frau Böhm sat sandwiched between Yosef and Miriam Nussbaum and he watched his neighbour's wife as she tried to strike up conversation with them. Miriam's face was guileless, but the General knew that she would wear a mask when she needed to. Yosef sat less comfortably, his mouth a thin line of disapproval.

Franz, by luck or by design, was sitting next to Lise Böhm, and the General, with a skill honed during his years in the army, watched them at the periphery of his vision, unnoticed by the young couple.

She is beautiful, but she knows it.

His mind drifted back to his own first tentative attempts to court Maria. She had looked as good as Lise but, in contrast, she'd been charmingly oblivious to the effect she had on men, and other women.

He hadn't been as shy as his son was; he'd had a bit of bravado about him, but it had still taken a leap of faith to think that she would consider him as an appropriate suitor. But she had. Now he looked at his tongue-tied son and hoped that this girl was the right one for him.

Johann, sitting between Antje and Ruth, nudged them both, grinning. The girls glanced at Lise and Franz and giggled.

~~o~~

Sitting across the table, scrutinising Lise for hints on how to behave around boys, Eva Kästner marvelled at the ease by which the girl, although a few months younger than her, had Eva's oldest brother wrapped around her finger.

143

She seems almost a woman.

She made a mental note that a blend of being aloof and, at the same time, inviting, seemed to render young men incapable of independent thought.

She caught Lise's brother glancing at her and, although a tingle of pleasure at the attention he paid her ran down her spine, she discounted him as being a bore. Her imagination had already settled on one of Johann's friends who sometimes sailed with the boys, and it was the only reason that she found hanging around the yacht club bearable.

~~o~~

Frau Böhm shivered as another effort to make polite conversation with Miriam and Yosef faltered.

It just isn't right, sitting me next to the servants, and Jewish to boot.

She wondered if it had been done on purpose, but Maria looked over and smiled at her, with no hint of malice.

Part of her wanted to advise her daughter to cut her losses and run. She could have the pick of Kiel, and perhaps even Berlin, with her beauty and manners. Maria would have been perfect as a mother-in-law for Lise, apart from the woman allowing her husband to be overfamiliar with his staff.

But she'd heard that Franz was a high-flyer and was earmarked for a rapid rise through the ranks, perhaps even surpassing his father's achievements, and it was this that stopped her saying anything to her daughter.

~~o~~

After the meal, Franz and Lise made their excuses and left for a walk down to the boathouse. Maria watched out of the window and remembered a night almost twenty years before, a few days after she and Erich had first moved in, when he'd rowed her out onto the lake, blankets and a bottle of wine on board. She remembered the thrill of walking down to the dock, with only the light of the moon and the stars to guide them.

Since then, they'd installed lighting down the path, and by the boathouse, so she could clearly see the young couple strolling together, hand in hand. She gave a start as Beate Böhm touched her on the arm.

'Don't they look wonderful,' Beate Böhm said.

Maria, if she was honest, wasn't entirely displeased with the match between Franz and Lise, but neither was she altogether happy. She still harboured the thought that her handsome and, according to some of Erich's military colleagues, brilliant boy should hold out for a better match than Lise Böhm.

She'd sat next to Eberhard during the meal and although she considered him dull but inoffensive, he'd been effusive in his praise for Franz, telling her that he considered him to be kind and gentle, and from superior stock; an excellent match for his daughter, and that they'd known each other all their lives and were quite obviously besotted.

Beate obviously feels the same.

~~o~~

Franz, sitting at his desk, groaned as Johann stuck his head around his bedroom door.

'Can I come in, Casanova?' the younger Kästner brother said, with a malicious grin.

'Only if you promise to say nothing,' Franz replied, smiling.

Johann threw himself down on his brother's bed.

Everyone had just left, and Johann was bored again.

Franz and Lise had returned to the party after their stroll but, after the usual round of lively conversation and party games typical of the neighbours' gatherings, she'd gone home with her parents when the party ended.

'So, how far did you get, Franz?'

A book flew across the room, narrowly missing Johann's head.

'Hey, it was just a question,' he exclaimed.

'And it's one you won't be getting an answer to.'

'Not very far then, I'm guessing.'

'It's none of your business. And anyway, you're obsessed. There's more to girls than sex.'

'Is there, really? I know you spout all this love piffle, and you get all starry-eyed and romantic but, at the end of the day, you, me and the girls all want the same thing.'

'You don't understand. You have all the maturity of a five-year-old.'

'You're boring. I hoped I was going to get all the juicy details about the contents of Lise Böhm's brassiere.'

Another book flew across the room. This one caught Johann on the arm.

'Whoa,' he said, wincing and rubbing his arm, 'that's sacrilegious, throwing good books at people.'

'It's not people, it's a horrible, oversexed fifteen-year-old youth and anyway, I keep a pile of old books here just for when you come and annoy me.'

Johann picked up one of the books.

'So you do. Who would have thought someone would have had the foresight?' he said. 'Anyway, you love her then?'

'I don't know. I'm terribly fond of her, and I know she likes me. I'd want to be sure though.'

'Before you do it, you mean.' Johann ducked, ready for another literary missile but none came.

'Before I commit to her, Schwachkopf.'

'Have you never… with any girl?'

'If I had, I wouldn't be telling you.'

A hurt look briefly crossed Johann's face, then it creased into a smile.

'You haven't, have you? I knew it.' He wagged his finger at his brother, grinning. 'I'm not going to tie myself down to one girl. No matter how beautiful she looks.'

Franz shook his head. 'That's the problem with you. You might just be the shallowest person I know.'

'Better being shallow than boring. At least I have friends. And I have fun.'

Both brothers laughed. Despite their differences in temperament and outlook, they were extremely close.

'I have friends. We have fun.'

'Joachim and Michel? You never see them outside of school; you don't drink with them, or chase girls, or get into scrapes.'

'It's not compulsory to act like idiots, you know,' Franz said, still grinning.

'You'll be an old married man by the time you're twenty and I'll be the most dashing bachelor in town, with a girl hanging off each arm. And you'll be green with envy.'

Franz had seen the adoring looks his brother attracted from girls his own age, and younger.

'Do you know, I believe you, but I won't be jealous.'

CHAPTER 36

[09/05/1933 Tuesday]

'Dieter, I'm sorry to call you this early, but I've sorted something out. A friend of mine owns several companies, one of them a printing works. He has a job for you. It's not editorial, I'm afraid, and the wages aren't quite what you would have been on at the *Morgenpost*, but you'll also get a stipend from me.'

'Erich, I'm ready to take any job, to be honest. I'm not unfamiliar with the printing process.' The General heard a chuckle at the other end of the line.

'What company is it?' Dieter Maas asked.

'Baltische Buchdruckerei. You'll know of them.'

Baltic Book Printers.

'Yes, they're relatively new. Oskar von Friedeburg owns it. We did an article on the company when it started.'

'Well, they're expanding. You might not like some of their customers, but the rest of the stuff they do is commercial.'

'I'm guessing they do some work for NSDAP, yes?'

'Yes, and now the town council too. Oskar joined the party solely for business reasons, and he doesn't hide it. He cultivates a reputation as a hard-nosed businessman, so no one is surprised at him trying to profit from his association with them.'

'So, if he's a party man, why give me a job?'

'He's a friend, he's more complex and less ruthless than he seems on the surface, and don't worry, he'll find a way to benefit from your employment.'

There was a few moments' silence.

'What have you told him?'

'I said that you were an occasional sailor who I was trying to encourage to become crew for me, and that you were out of a job. I told him I'd promised to ask him if there were any work available.'

'And he believed it? I've never been on a yacht.'

'Whether he believed it or not, he knows exactly who you are, and probably thinks we are friends because of the similarities of our political views. But that isn't something that would scare him.'

'All right, so when do I start?'

'You see him tomorrow. Ten o'clock at his office. It's in Muhliusstraße. He says you can start the next day.'

'Oh. That's quick.'

'Is that a problem?'

'No, it will be good to work again.'

There was a hesitation at the end of the phone.

'I'm afraid I don't have much for you yet, Erich. I presume you've heard all about the NSDAP disbanding the unions.'

'Yes, but I didn't get much detail. All I know is that their function has been taken over by the Deutsche Arbeitsfront.'

'Yes. They're not even trying to hide the fact that it's an NSDAP-controlled organisation. Most of my union contacts have been sent to the camps, but I did manage to speak with one or two of them before they were arrested. All union assets have been appropriated by the Deutsche Arbeitsfront.'

'I presume that membership will be compulsory for all workers, and that there will be a membership fee.'

'Strangely, no. Membership is optional, but from what I hear, most people who were union members are signing up. It's hard to believe people can be so gullible.'

'Thanks, Dieter. That's the sort of information I'm looking for.'

'No problem, Erich. I'll be in touch.'

'There's one more thing, Dieter.'

'What's that?' He could hear the unease in the man's voice.

'Saturday morning, nine sharp at the Kieler Yacht Club. You're going to learn to sail.'

[13/05/1933 Saturday]

'Dieter, these two are my sons, Franz and Johann. Boys, this is Dieter. He's keen to start sailing and, since you recommended that I find some crew nearer my own age, I've invited him along for a try-out.'

The General smiled and put his arm around Dieter's shoulder.

'Come on. I'll show you the boat. Don't worry about these two. They sometimes get a bit too sure of themselves.'

The boys followed them onto the boat, grinning at each other.

Dieter hadn't been sure about going sailing but, from the moment he stepped onto the boat, he'd been hooked. The effortless way Erich Kästner and his sons worked together to get the boat underway was impressive and the feeling of speed and the sound of the rushing water when the wind caught the sails and heeled the boat over, was exhilarating.

Time seemed to fly, and they'd showed him every point of sail, tacking upwind first towards the mouth of Kieler Förde, beating past Friedrichsort into the wind on alternate tacks until the lighthouse was behind them, then a long close reach to the north-east took them to just off the beach at Strande. There, they dropped the anchor, and the boys, with a little bravado, went for a swim in the still, cool waters of the Baltic sea, diving off the boom and scrambling back onto the boat within seconds, the shock of the cold water showing in their gasping breaths and their painful grimaces.

Warmed up by coffee on the sunlit deck, the boys soon took to the ex-newspaper editor, with his easy manner and his dry sense of humour. And he'd been quick to learn, picking up the names of the lines and sails without effort, getting his head around the basic concept of moving a ten-ton boat through the water with nothing but the power of a light wind. He had a natural knack for helming, keeping the boat on a steady course into the wind without fuss and, more importantly, he seemed to love every minute of it.

They scorched across Kieler Förde on a beautiful beam reach to Laboe, where they turned for home on a downwind run, goose-winging the sails out on either side of the boat to maximise the drive the wind gave them.

Three hours after they'd left it, the yacht slid towards the dock and, as it touched, Franz jumped off and looped the stern line around the cleat on the wooden jetty and took the strain, taking the last of the speed off the boat. Johann stepped over the gunwale and tied the bowline to the cleat furthest forward on the dock, and the yacht was secure.

After they'd secured all the lines, Johann retrieved the cold beers from the bag they'd left hanging from the jetty, chilled in the cold waters of Kieler Hafen.

For politeness, the two boys hung around but, once good manners had been observed, they made their escape to the clubhouse and the friends they'd been brought up sailing with.

Once they'd gone, the General slid an envelope across the cockpit seat and Dieter pocketed it.

'We go sailing once a week. If anyone asks, we're putting a crew together for the evening races. If we need to meet at any other time, it wouldn't look out of place to meet for a drink or some food.'

Dieter laughed. 'It seems like I'm going to learn to sail then.' He took a long drink of his beer. 'Listen, thanks. I was thinking of taking any old job, just to get out of the house and bring some money in.'

The General shrugged. 'I needed eyes and ears. You fitted the bill.'

~~o~~

For a while, the two men sat back in the sun, enjoying their beers. It was the General who broke the silence.

'Now, you did well today, and it will have given you some idea about sailing, but I'll run you through the basics.'

He dipped down the companionway and returned to the cockpit with a small black wooden slate and a piece of chalk. He sketched out a rudimentary boat on it.

'A yacht can sail in any direction with regards to the wind, except for here.' He pointed to the area in front of the boat.

'Once the wind goes this far forward, the boat will stall, and the sails will flap. If we want to go in that direction, we must point as close as we can to forty-five degrees to the wind, first one way and then the other. We call that *tacking* or *beating*. Are you with me so far?'

'Yes, it's obvious that we can't travel directly into the wind. It's a bit like climbing a steep hill by zigzagging up it.'

'Ah, that's an excellent analogy, Dieter,' he said, nodding his head, 'because it is the hardest working point of sail, with the boat heeled over, almost on its side at times.'

The General held his hand at an angle to illustrate his point.

'When the wind comes from the side of the boat, or the beam as we call it, we can let the sails out a bit,' he continued. 'We call this reaching, and it's the easiest wind direction to sail in, and often the fastest. The boat doesn't heel as much either. Do you understand?'

'Yes. I think so.'

'Finally, when the wind moves round to the back of the boat, we call it running.'

'Isn't that the easiest part of sailing?'

The General shook his head.

'With the wind behind, there's a danger that a gust can catch the main sail, and snap it across the deck, not stopping until it reaches the other side. This is called an accidental gybe. The boom can kill anyone whose head gets in the way, and when it snaps tight, it can damage the mast or the rigging.'

'So, when we were sailing downwind today, that could have happened?'

'Yes, but Franz had a hold of the mainsheet. Gybing is safe, providing we remember to pull the mainsail in before we turn the boat across the wind, and then let it out slowly once the wind has passed to the other side.'

The General fetched the last two beers and handed one to Dieter.

He smiled. 'That's enough sailing theory for one day.'

He put the slate down on the seat beside him.

'So, how did you get on with Oskar?' he asked, changing the subject.

'Good. He's quite a character. He told me to keep my head down and stay out of politics. If only he knew,' he said, frowning. 'He introduced me to the foreman, who showed me around the print shop and that was it; I started the next day.'

'I'm sorry it's not the job you might have been looking for.'

'It's work. That's more than I had a week ago. There's always the chance of working my way up. As you say, the company is expanding.'

'Do as Oskar says. Keep your opinions in here.' He tapped his forehead. 'I need you to stay out of trouble with your ear to the ground.'

'I'll do that. Though it feels strange to be working for the army. I hope you know what you are doing.'

'Who does these days? I can only follow my instinct. We're in for some dark days if this continues. I don't know if we can stop it.'

'If that's the case, why are we bothering?'

'Someone needs to be a witness to all of this and, one day perhaps, write it all down. Our children, and our children's children need to know what's taking place in Germany in 1933.'

~~o~~

[31/05/1933 Wednesday]

By the end of the month, Ruth Nussbaum's tenth birthday had been and gone, and Dieter Maas was an integral part of Erich Kästner's racing crew. Doctor Speer had often sailed with the General over the years and, although he'd never raced, he had a good working knowledge of the boat. Unlike Dieter, Oskar von Friedeburg had sailed as a young man, in the years before he joined, then took over his father's business.

'We'll have you welded into a team in no time,' the General told them, to disbelieving looks.

After their practice sessions, they would sit on the boat and chat over a beer or a whisky, or sometimes retire to the bar in the yacht club if the weather was poor. It wasn't difficult for the General and Dieter Maas to manage a short conversation at some point during the sail or afterwards, when the other two men had left.

On top of these sessions, the General and Dieter snatched as many hours out on the water as they could, just the two of them. On the last of those practice sessions, Dieter remarked at how he could now, while on the tiller, comfortably hold a course and a conversation at the same time.

'Yes. It becomes second nature, with time,' the General said. He paused.

'I hear one of your former colleagues has had his employment terminated too,' he added.

Dieter Maas nodded. 'Benno Arndt,' he said. 'The sub-editor who put the quote marks around *Aryan*. He told me he did it only because it was correct grammar; that he wasn't making a political point. He was Jewish, so he wasn't expecting to survive for long in the position anyway, so he's glad that people concluded that he did it for political reasons.'

'So, it was just an excuse to get him out?'

'Retired for reasons of ill health?' Dieter Maas said, disbelief etched on his face. 'He told me he's never felt better. Not much chance of him getting a new job though. It's a good thing he only has himself and his wife to support, and she works.'

'I'm sorry. I can't help him, I'm afraid.'

'He has some savings; he tells me he's bought a small hand-operated printing press; he can earn a few Deutschmarks printing flyers and the like.'

He looked at the General, as if weighing him up.

'Have you seen the latest addition to the catalogue of Kiel newspapers?'

The General looked surprised. Dieter glanced around, extracted a folded sheet of paper from the inside pocket of his jacket, and handed it to the General.

Erich Kästner unfolded it, then, passing the tiller to the newspaperman, sat and read it. He whistled.

'I'll be damned. A Jewish newspaper. Does this have anything to do with you?'

'Hell, no. You told me to stay out of politics.'

'Then who…' He paused, and his face changed. 'Ah, I see.'

He read on.

'Maybe a tad biased, but not bad, considering the circumstances,' the General said. 'No

149

vitriol or hate, just facts, although I'm guessing it won't be the newspaper of choice for the majority of Kielers,' he said, looking up.

'I thought it was pretty damn close to the truth, Erich. And brave, given the fact that, with a few notable exceptions, most German newspapers have bowed down to the government.'

The General finished reading. He gestured towards the mouth of the Förde.

'Steer ten degrees to port. We don't want to hit that ferry,' he said, smiling.

Dieter looked up, horrified, pulling the tiller towards him sharply, veering away from one of the Kiel passenger boats that ferried the city's inhabitants up, down and across Kieler Hafen.

'Sorry,' he gasped, but the General laughed.

'Don't worry, I was keeping an eye on it. If we'd got too close the captain would have sounded the horn. Five blasts, for future reference; "get out of the way, idiot", it means.'

Dieter smiled. 'It's remarkably easy to be distracted.'

'Yes,' said the General, 'just like the German people and Adolf Hitler.'

Dieter said nothing for a while.

'I've got something else that might interest you. Do you remember a man called Wilhelm Spiegel? A Jewish lawyer, killed by the SA.'

'I read something about it. He tried to sue Adolf Hitler, didn't he? The funeral was at the cemetery in Eichhof. Yosef went to it. A huge turnout,' he said.

'That's the one. Well, I went to it. I don't know why; I'd been sacked by then, but old habits die hard, and I thought it was newsworthy. The eulogy was given by a Jewish man called Otto Eggerstedt. It was one of the most eloquent orations I have ever heard; a complete denunciation of the government, the only time in public I've seen such a demolition of the National Socialists.'

'Yosef did mention it.'

'There were thousands of workers, communists, KPD supporters and most of the Jewish community. Anyway, Otto has finally been arrested. The word is he's been taken to Esterwegen concentration camp.'

'It wasn't even in this,' the General said, holding up the newsletter.

'It's in the later edition. Some were printed and distributed before the news of the arrest was released. Spiegel's funeral was a big deal in the Jewish community.'

The General folded the paper and slipped it into his pocket. The two men sat back and soaked up the warm May sun, the gentle breeze across the deck cooling the air enough to make it comfortable.

It was the General who broke the silence.

'Tell your friend to be careful. The printing business can be dangerous, I hear.'

Dieter didn't reply.

CHAPTER 37

[02/06/1933 Friday]

'Otto Eggerstedt has been arrested.'

Yosef sat in the kitchen, reading the later edition of the *Kieler Jüdisches Freiheitsnachrichtenblatt*. He had made a complete recovery from his injuries.

'I've heard the name but can't place him,' Miriam said, looking up from her sewing. She was altering some of the clothes that the Kästners had handed in; hand-me-downs that were always welcome, the quality better than anything the Nussbaums could ever have afforded.

They all wore clothes inherited from the General and his family, and Miriam rarely bought anything apart from underwear and socks, although, two years before, she'd purchased a nice summer dress for herself, just to have something that Maria Kästner hadn't worn.

'He was the man who did the eulogy at Wilhelm Spiegel's funeral. It was the best address I'd ever heard.'

'Yes. I told you not to go to that funeral. Now they're picking people up who were at it.'

'Don't be silly. There were a thousand people there. More, perhaps. They're not going to arrest every one of us. Anyway, he'd caught the attention of the authorities long before that. He was whisked away by his friends as soon as the funeral was over.'

Miriam grunted, and continued to sew.

'They say he's been taken to Esterwegen,' Yosef said. 'Where they have all the communists locked up.'

'They're just as bad as the government. I'd lock the whole lot of them away.'

Miriam looked up. Yosef was staring at her.

'Sorry,' she muttered. 'I shouldn't have said that. I'm just angry at them all. Moderate politicians seem to have gone missing in all of this.'

'I'm sure there are a lot of sensible, fair-minded people around, but they're too frightened to speak out amidst all the bullying and intimidation that goes on.'

'People are leaving. The Bernheimers went to her brother in America last week, the Blumenthals leave today.'

'I know. I was talking to Levi Doerzbacher. He sold his shop. He goes to Palestine next week and the family will follow on as soon as his wife has had the baby.'

'The best of luck to them, but it wouldn't be me. From what I've heard, it's not a safe place to be.'

'It might not be as bad as it's made out to be, Miriam, but, even so, I'd much prefer America if we had to ever leave.'

'Perhaps we should consider it.'

'No. We're happy here. Anyway, I'm not being chased out of my country by a bunch of ignorant thugs. Have you thought much about it?'

'No, not really. We couldn't leave our families, or our friends. Anyway, none of us speak the language, and what would we do there?'

'I wouldn't want to go. This is our home, and I couldn't leave the General. And we're safe with the Kästners, no matter what happens. It's a pity there's not more like him. He's not afraid to speak out.'

She stayed silent. He looked at her again. She couldn't meet his gaze.

'What?' he asked.

She still hesitated. When she spoke, her voice was soft, almost apologetic.

'I know you and the General go back a long way and that you trust him, but I'd be a little careful, Yosef.'

'What do you mean?' He hadn't told her everything about Erich Kästner's involvement in the Schumm affair, but she surely knew enough not to doubt his commitment to them.

'He's the only person I know, outside our own community, who seems to comprehend what's happening.'

'It's not that. I suspect the mistress doesn't think along the same lines and, at the end of the day, the General is going to be influenced by his wife, no matter what he says.'

'Has Frau Kästner said anything to you? You've never told me.'

'Not in so many words, but there have just been a few small things.'

'Like what?' he said, annoyed now.

'Oh, they don't mean much on their own, but taken together…'

'For example?' he said.

'Well, she was terribly keen on Franz, Johann and Eva being in the Hitlerjugend march. I heard them talking about it on the phone when she returned from watching it. She's also let a few comments slip about the National Socialists; deep down, I think she's a supporter.'

'Many people who don't like the government still think some of the things they are doing are beneficial. It doesn't mean they are party members or condone everything they do. There are even some Jews who think that getting rid of the communists has been a great accomplishment by this government and, last week after morning service, I heard old Mendel say that the ban on the unions was long overdue and that Adolf Hitler deserved a pat on the back.'

'They're fools then.'

She picked at a stitch. The clock chimed in the hallway.

'The General will never turn his back on us, Miriam, or on Germany, even if Frau Kästner has a few sympathies with the NSDAP, which I still don't believe.'

'Maria Kästner's trouble is that she worries too much about what people think of her. Not people like us; influential people, people with as much money as them, or more. I'm sure she's uneasy about us being here, and how it looks. Most of all, she worries that the General doesn't share her views and she'll try and bring him round to her way of thinking. And she just might. All I'm saying is just don't rely on the Kästners.'

'You're wrong, Miriam. They've always been kind to us.'

'We've been good to them, too, Yosef,' she said gently, with a sigh. 'We do everything for them. Our lives revolve around their needs and their wants.' She put her hand on his. 'I'm not complaining. We chose this life, and it has its benefits. They are a fine family, and I'm very fond of them. But the only people we can truthfully trust are our own.'

Yosef didn't know what to say. He couldn't accept that Miriam was right. He would bet his life on the General, more than anyone else he knew. He had to admit that Frau Kästner liked nothing better than to mix with the cream of Kiel society and, although the General worshipped her, he often gently poked fun at her mild but harmless snobbishness. But it didn't make her one of them or make it likely that the General wouldn't stick to his principles.

'I can't accept that,' he said. 'The General is my employer but he's also my oldest friend. I know him.'

Miriam tightened her grip on his hand.

'I know you do,' she said.

~~o~~

[04/06/1933 Sunday]

'Do you know anything about this, Yosef?'

Erich Kästner handed Yosef the Jewish news-sheet Dieter Maas had given him.

After the first wave of panic subsided, Yosef remembered burning his copy, and realised that the General must have obtained his from elsewhere. He breathed out slowly.

'They're calling it the KJF, sir. And yes, I've seen it. I read every one. That's the third one you have there.'

The General gave a tight smile.

'KJF,' he said. 'That makes sense. *Kieler Jüdisches Freiheitsnachrichtenblatt* is a bit of a mouthful for a newspaper. How do you get it?'

'It just appears, sir. We don't ask any questions; they just get passed out.'

'Do you distribute them yourself?'

'Sir, I'm given a few copies, and I pass them on to friends and family. That's how it works.'

'But you don't know who prints them?'

'Nobody does, sir. It's better that way. How did you get hold of that one?'

The General dismissed Yosef's concern with a wave of his hand.

'I know some people. It was handed to me. Discreetly.'

'That's good, sir. The fewer Gent... sorry, non-Jewish people who know about it, the better.' Yosef's face flushed.

The General laughed this time.

'Don't worry, Yosef, it won't be the first time you've called me a Gentile. Remember when we were Manny's age?'

They used to call each other all sorts of names. The General would call Yosef a Yid; Yosef would retort with Gentile, or worse. Then they would fall about, laughing. But always when they were alone. Because they were friends. And because they were equal.

Yosef smiled at the memory.

'Be careful, Yosef. There seems to be more and more eyes and ears out there.'

'I know, sir. It seems like you can't trust anyone these days.'

The General looked up sharply, but Yosef's face was guileless.

The General grunted his agreement.

'I'll be careful, sir, don't you worry,' Yosef added, 'and I'll not do anything that would make it difficult for you.'

A little hurt showed on the General's face.

'I wasn't worried about myself. They can't touch me,' he said, his tone softer. He laid his hand on Yosef's shoulder.

'And tell your friends to take care,' he added. 'They're taking risks and I don't have to tell you where they'll end up if they're caught.'

'I'll pass the message on, sir. Whoever they are.'

The General smiled.

CHAPTER 38

Antje adored the two days the Kästners spent together traversing the Kaiser Wilhelm Kanal from Kieler Förde to the Elbe. It seemed like ages since they'd all been together, laughing, talking, being a family without distraction from Mama's social circle or Papa's work.

From the moment they entered the sea lock at Holtenau, at the eastern end of the canal, sharing it with a large freighter and a couple of small work boats, everyone on board *Snowgoose* seemed to unwind, and smile. Even the worry lines she'd seen on her father's face seemed to fade as he stood at the wheel, his arm around her mother.

They followed the cargo ship as far as Rendsburg, where they turned into the Ober-Eider, and berthed at the town wharf for the night. Leaving *Snowgoose* tied up, they strolled into town.

Walking back to the boat after a laughter-filled meal in the Germania hotel, overlooking the Paradeplatz, Maria took her younger daughter's hand, strolling in front of the others.

'Eva and I are only going as far as Brunsbüttel, darling. Yosef is coming to collect us. Are you sure you want to go with the boys?'

'Yes, Mama, I'll be fine. I've been sailing before.'

'I know, sweetheart, but this is the North Sea. It could get rough.'

'Papa will look after me. The boys always get to do things. I want to go, too, and he promised me.'

'All right, but don't say I didn't warn you. I'm sure if it turns really bad, or you get seasick, they'll bring you back early.' She turned to her husband. 'Won't you, Erich?'

'Yes, of course we will. We'll never be more that a day's sail from Brunsbüttel.'

He grabbed Antje up and squeezed her in a hug. 'You'll be fine, won't you? We'll be sure to look after you. Besides, we need a cook.'

She giggled. 'Miriam showed me how to bake and do a little cooking too.'

Maria's face clouded for a second. Antje noticed, puzzled, but it passed.

'Your father is only joking,' her mother said. 'I just hope you don't come back rough and ready and thinking you're a boy,' she said, glaring at her husband.

'I won't, Mama. I'm a girl. I'm there to paint seabirds, and maybe lighthouses and ships.'

'And scrub decks and climb the mast,' the General had added, grinning at her.

After a game of cards sitting out on deck, the warm evening air lit only by an oil lamp hanging from the boom, Antje's eyes started to droop, and Maria had chased her to bed.

'I'm going too,' Eva said.

The boys had spread out a set of charts on the table in the main cabin, planning the route that their father had suggested, and were in animated conversation, looking up tide tables, measuring distances, and plotting their course from one destination to the next in meticulous detail.

In the cockpit, the General sat with his arm around his wife, the gentle lap of water on the hull almost lulling them to sleep.

'You will be careful, Erich, won't you? Remember Antje is on board.'

'Have you ever seen me take unnecessary risks with any of you?'

She hesitated.

'No, but I suspect you and the boys do when we're not around. Don't forget she's only

154

ten.'

'I won't, don't you worry. The weather looks settled, and the sea fog should have gone by this time of year. The only thing worrying me is that we don't find her a Sturmtaucher to draw.' He laughed.

'Providing you bring her home safe, I don't mind.'

'You and Eva have a good time. She'll enjoy having you all to herself.'

Maria had smiled. 'I can spoil her a little. Some of the ladies are dying to get her out and about, and we'll visit Mama. She is desperate to show off her granddaughter.'

'As long as none of them are planning to find her a husband. I know what they are like. She's too young.'

She looked at him, frowning. 'Of course they won't,' she said, but they both knew that all her friends, and her mother, would love to play matchmaker.

'Anyway,' she continued, 'she already has her eye on a young man, not that you'd notice.'

'Not Lise's brother, I hope. He's a bit dull.'

And a real Hitlerjugend fanatic as well.

He'd almost said it aloud but was glad he'd kept it to himself.

'No,' his wife said, breaking into his thoughts. 'I've caught her mooning over one of Johann's friends, the Schäfer boy. The boys call him Ruti.'

The General laughed. 'My, they do grow up quickly. I'd be lying if I said I was aware of it.'

'Didn't it occur to you to ask why Eva has started hanging about the sailing club? You know she hates boats.'

'I thought she'd maybe had a change of heart. Ah, well.' He sighed.

'He's a bit wild, the boy, and a year older. We'll have to watch.'

'I'll have a word with him if you like.'

'Don't you dare. Eva would never forgive you. Just keep an eye on them.'

'I'll say to Franz. He's usually there with Johann and his friends. He's very sensible.'

~~o~~

[03/07/1933 Monday]

Antje sat on the coach roof and sketched. Maria and Eva lay beside her, stretched out on towels, sunbathing, until two workers cycling on the canal bank wolf-whistled loudly at them.

The General laughed. 'Take it as a compliment,' he said, as they scurried to cover their bathing costumes, mindful of the stream of people now passing along the towpath. When they'd started out in the bright sunshine, the canal banks had been deserted but, as the day wore on, the surrounding countryside had woken up.

'We'll be at the sea lock soon. I hope Yosef is waiting,' the General said.

'I'm sure he will be. He was told to be there by lunchtime.'

The General looked at his watch. 'We're slightly ahead of schedule. We can sit and wait if he's not there.'

~~o~~

'Are you sure you want to go on?'

Antje turned to see her father standing behind her.

'Of course I do. It's soooo exciting.'

155

He smiled at her, not doubting her enthusiasm for the trip, hoping that she wouldn't regret it. The North Sea was a much less sheltered sailing ground than the Western Baltic.

'Well, this is the last chance to go with your mother. After that, you're stuck with us.'

She hugged him. 'I'll miss Mama and Eva, but I can't wait.'

'Well, if you're sure.'

He nodded ahead. 'Keep an eye out for Yosef. We're almost there.'

CHAPTER 39

Yosef stood by the car, the sun beating down, but he didn't dare take his jacket off. There were one or two SA men, and one SS soldier, checking vessels as they entered the locks. He hoped that his chauffeur's uniform gave him some immunity from their scrutiny.

He had a good view along the canal but, as yet, there was no sign of the yacht. He was early, but he wasn't perturbed; watching the traffic entering and leaving the canal passed the time easily for him.

Through the open door, he reached into the compartment between the front seats and, from the bag that Miriam had given him before he'd left, he pulled out a small flask of coffee.

A large freighter had just emerged from the sea lock, heading eastwards, and the officer on the bridge gave him a wave, which he returned. He poured himself a cup of coffee and unwrapped the greaseproof paper package that Miriam had packed with the flask. He took a bite of the Sandtorte that she'd made that morning.

'May I ask you why you are waiting here?'

He turned, nearly dropping the cake in fright. He hadn't seen the SS stormtrooper make his way over, so intently was he watching the activity on the canal.

'I'm waiting for General Kästner. I've to meet him here. I'm his driver.'

'You're not in uniform, and this is not a Reichsheer car.'

'No, I work for the General's household. I'm also his handyman and gardener,' he said, stumbling a little over the words.

'Ah, I see. May I see your papers, please?'

Yosef leaned into the car and fished out his wallet, sitting on the small shelf beside the steering wheel. He passed his papers to the soldier.

The man scrutinised each sheet in turn, then handed them back to Yosef, retaining the document with Yosef's army pension details.

'I see you fought in the war. That is correct?'

'Yes, sir, I did. I fought at Passchendaele. With the General.'

'Ah. So, he gave you a job when you returned from the war?'

'Yes, I started to work for him after the war. 1919 it was. But my father worked for the General's family before me. Admiral Kästner.'

'And you hope that your son will work for the General's son?'

'I wouldn't object to my son working for the Kästner family, but he may decide to be a doctor or a lawyer or a teacher.'

He cursed himself for saying too much. Yes or no would have been enough.

'I see your name is Nussbaum. A Jewish name, perhaps?'

'That's right, sir.' A few beads of sweat gathered on Yosef's brow.

The man laughed.

'Your son will not be a doctor in modern-day Germany. Or a teacher. There is no place for Jews in the fatherland today, you should know that.'

'Yes, sir.' Yosef kept his head bowed, an image of the bully flailing as he fell into the canal running through his mind.

It would only take a small push.

'You are lucky that you have this paper, for now, and that you work for this General Kästner.' He spat on the ground. 'But even generals will come to realise that it is not patriotic to employ a Jew boy.'

Out of the corner of his eye, a mast caught Yosef's eye in the distance, almost hidden by the bulk of the freighter. The SS man saw his glance.

'You seem to be more interested in what's going on around you. Perhaps I should question you somewhere, shall we say, less distracting.'

'Oh, no sir, you have my undivided attention. It's just that I think that is the General's boat approaching.'

The man looked along the canal. The yacht and the freighter were alongside each other now. Yosef prayed that there wasn't another yacht in the canal that day.

'So, your general arrives by boat. Why are you meeting him?'

'I am taking his wife and one of his daughters back to Kiel. They are leaving the yacht while the General and his other daughter, and his two sons, go cruising in the North Sea for a few days.'

'I see.' Yosef could see the man hesitate. To drag him somewhere within sight of the General would be risky.

'I can see it would be inconvenient for your general if you were to cause a delay. Perhaps this is your lucky day. You may not be quite so fortunate if I have to talk to you again.'

They both watched as the yacht approached. Yosef could see Antje waving as she spotted the Mercedes parked on the dockside. He waved back. He turned to the SS man to answer him, but the stormtrooper was walking towards the wharf warehouses, where three men were opening one of the large sliding doors.

Yosef watched as he started remonstrating with them, one of the men wringing his cap and mumbling apologies.

'Ahoy, Yosef,' the General shouted. 'Catch these lines, will you.'

Yosef had sailed with Erich Kästner often as a youth, so he caught the bowline expertly and looped it over a bollard. Johann jumped off and secured the stern line.

'Have you been waiting long?' the General asked.

'No, sir, not long.'

The General peered at Yosef. 'Are you feeling all right? You look terribly pale.'

'I'm fine, sir, really. Must have been something I ate.' He tried to smile.

The General frowned, then glanced across at the SS man, now shouting at the warehousemen.

'The SS soldier was talking to you when we were coming in. Did he say something?'

'It was nothing, sir. He obviously got out of bed the wrong side today. He's taking it out on these poor fellows now.'

'We'll see about that,' the General said, stepping from the boat.

Maria Kästner followed her husband on to the wharf and clutched his sleeve.

'Erich, please don't make a scene,' she said.

'That excuse for a soldier has said something hateful to Yosef and now he's making an exhibition of himself in front of my wife and children. He's a disgrace to the German Army, if you can call their type soldiers.'

'He's not army, he's SS. I'm sure he's not under your jurisdiction,' she hissed.

'Frau Kästner is right, sir, it would be better to leave it alone,' Yosef added, frowning.

'Yosef, Maria, I have always taught my boys not to tolerate bullies. I'd be hypocritical if I let this man get away with throwing his weight about.'

~~o~~

The General walked over towards the warehouse. Franz made a move to follow but his mother put her arm out to stop him.

'Don't you get involved too. Your father will have to learn to let things go. Help me get my things from the boat.'

Reluctantly, Franz did as he was told. He took the bags from Johann and placed them in the trunk of the car. They all turned to watch as the General approached the SS man.

'Excuse me, private,' the General said, showing the man his military identification, 'is all this unseemly noise necessary? You're upsetting the ladies.'

His words carried clearly back to the group standing by the car.

The SS man turned and clicked his heels together and gave a full Hitler salute.

'Heil Hitler,' he barked.

The General didn't return his salute. Technically, he was correct, being out of uniform, but these days, it was almost a crime not to respond, even for civilians.

'And you were bothering my driver, were you not?'

'Sir, I was just doing my job. Security in this area is my concern. The man was parked in a strange place, and loitering.'

'Did he show you his papers? Give you an explanation for his presence?'

'He did, sir, but…'

'That should have been enough.'

'But he's a Jew, General.'

'He's my Jew, private. What is your name?'

'It's Hartjenstein, sir, Sturmmann Artur Hartjenstein.'

'Stormtrooper, eh,' the General said. 'Who is your commanding officer?'

Maria Kästner flinched at her husband's scathing tone.

'Sturmbannführer Kolb, sir, Schutzstaffel,' the SS man answered, smirking, expecting the usual deferential and fearful response of ordinary Germans to his use of the SS rank.

'A major,' the General said. 'And who is his commander?'

The man hesitated, looking not quite so sure of himself.

'Oberführer Richter, sir,' he said.

'Helmut Richter?'

'Yes, sir. I think so.'

'Excellent. I know him well. I'm sure he served under me. I'll have a word with him about the manners of some of the men in his command.'

The stormtrooper's face blanched.

He started to say something, but the General dismissed him. The three warehousemen had been listening to the exchange and turned away to hide their smiles. The SS man cursed them as he passed but walked on, towards the canal offices. The men gave the General nods of thanks and he gave the briefest of smiles in reply before walking back to his family.

'Right, let me say auf wiedersehen to my beautiful ladies.'

He hugged Eva. 'Look after your mother,' he said.

Maria said her farewells to the boys first, then Antje. Finally, she turned to the General, hugged him stiffly, and turned away, stepping into the car. She rolled down the window.

She nodded to her oldest daughter. 'Get in, Eva. We must go.'

'We'll see you next week,' the General said, 'I'll try and phone and let you know where we are.'

'Yes, that's fine.' Her tone was clipped, and she barely looked at him.

'Maria…' the General said, but she had already wound the window back up.

Yosef looked at the General, who shrugged.

'On you go, Yosef. We'll see you all next week.' The two men shook hands.

~~o~~

'I'm afraid I've upset your mother,' the General said, ruffling Antje's hair.

She looked up at her father and gave him a tentative smile.

Franz glanced at his father and shrugged. He'd been on the wrong end of their mother's moods on occasion.

'It was lucky you knew the SS man's commanding officer. His face was a picture,' Franz said. He stood beside his father, back on the boat, waiting for the sea lock to open.

'I didn't. I've heard the name around, and I may have seen him in the barracks in Plön. Still, the private wasn't to know, and he'll live on his nerves for the next few weeks.'

Franz laughed, and started the engine as the lock gates creaked open. He shouted to Johann to cast off once the red light on the entrance to the lock changed to white and followed two barges into the basin.

He looked back. The SS man stood by the door of one of the buildings, staring at them.

The giant sea-lock gates groaned as they slowly opened out into the wide expanse of the Elbe estuary. As much as she'd enjoyed the time on the canal, Antje's heart began to race as she looked at the swirling brown waters in front of her.

'We're going to tie up to the jetty, here, to wait for the tide,' she heard her father say. 'It's running too fast for us to fight against it but should turn soon.'

He handed her a life preserver. 'Put this on,' he told her, checking that she'd fastened it correctly.

As soon as they'd exited the sea lock, Antje sensed a change. Waves slapped the murky estuary water against the side of the boat and the eddies, although out of the main tidal stream, pushed and pulled at the yacht as she edged towards the side of the mole protecting the entrance to the canal.

Antje thought for a few seconds. 'Why is there tide here but none in Kieler Hafen?' she asked.

'Ah, that's a big question, little one,' the General said. 'I'll try and explain, but it will have to wait. You and I have to get this line onto the bollard first.'

He pointed to the top of the mole and stood by her as she stepped onto the ladder. The tide was three-quarters of the way in, so it wasn't much of a climb for her to reach the top and cast the line over the large, squat, metal post five metres in front of the bow. She threw the other end back down to her father, then ran to the back of the boat, caught the stern line thrown by Franz, and repeated the procedure. The General and Franz secured the lines, and Johann stood at the foot of the ladder while Antje climbed back on board.

'Why do you think we throw the ropes round the bollards and back to us, rather than tying them on?' he asked her.

'So that they're ready to cast off again without having to get off the boat. We just let go one end and pull the other one in, silly,' she replied, and they all laughed.

By the time they'd eaten a quick lunch of bread, cheese and cold meat, the General could see, by the ripple at the end of the mole, that the tide had turned downriver. They hoisted the mainsail, and the yacht strained against the lines as it filled. Casting off, they surged forward and, as soon as they cleared the end of the mole, the tide snatched the yacht downriver. The General stood by Antje and gave her the helm while the boys raised the foresail; it caught the wind, and the fresh southerly breeze and the strengthening tide hurried them towards Cuxhaven, and the mouth of the estuary.

The Mercedes purred along as far as Neumünster, over halfway to Kiel, before Frau Kästner broke the silence. Yosef had glanced in the mirror a few times during the first hour but, with the thin set of her mouth and her unwillingness to look at Eva or him, he thought better of making light conversation, as he would have done most other days.

He suspected that she was fuming at him almost as much as at the General, for getting into what she would have termed 'trouble' in the first place, as if he had been looking for it.

'Sometimes your father doesn't know when to let things go, when they're of no importance.'

Yosef stiffened in the driving seat but said nothing.

Eva put her hand on her mother's and gripped it.

'I know,' she said. 'I nearly died when he marched over to that horrible little man. But you did try to stop him, Mama.'

'He'll get himself into bother one of these days. He thinks because he's a general he can say or do whatever he likes. These SS people are ruthless, I hear, and he could have embroiled all of us in his silly disputes.'

'He means well, though, Mama. The man was insufferable and dreadfully rude.'

'That's not the point,' Maria snapped. She leaned forward. 'Do you not agree, Yosef?'

'Definitely, madam. I asked him not to intervene. It's not wise to antagonise these people.'

Yosef had been horrified when the General had stormed off to challenge the SS man, but part of him had been proud of the way that Erich Kästner had stood up to him, despite his wife's fury.

She's right though. One day he'll go too far, and he'll pick a fight with the wrong person.

When they arrived back at the Drachensee house, Yosef helped them out of the car, and carried their bags in for them. Maria Kästner stopped Yosef as he left.

'We'll be needing the car quite a bit over the next week. I'll let you know our intentions for each day by seven the evening before.'

'Yes, madam. I can fit the rest of my jobs around your plans. Will you be needing me tomorrow?'

'Yes, we intend to go to Hanover to see my mother. Pack an overnight bag, as we will be staying over.'

CHAPTER 40

'So, Antje, to find our speed through the water, we tow the log.'

Antje looked at the small brass torpedo with propeller blades at its rear.

'We place it in the water like this,' he said, 'and let out the line, then read the number on this dial. If we measure the distance we travel in a minute,' he added, 'and multiply by sixty, we have our speed through the water.'

He read off the distance and calculated the speed.

'Six knots,' her father said. 'But the tide is also pushing the water along, so we need to know how fast it is going too.'

He flattened out the chart of the Elbe Estuary on the cockpit floor and placed a couple of heavy metal disks on it to stop it blowing away.

'See these little diamonds marked on the chart? These and the table show us how fast the tide is going, depending on when high tide is.'

'And how do we know that?'

Before the General could answer, Johann interrupted.

'There's a large freighter crossing our bow shortly,' he said, 'but it should clear us with plenty to spare.'

The General stood up. He studied the larger boat stemming the tide upriver.

'You're fine,' he said. 'Keep the course steady.'

Franz continued Antje's navigational education.

He showed her a slim book, filled with dates, times and figures that made little sense to her.

'This is an almanac. It tells us exactly when it is high tide, and it also gives us heights of tide for any time and place we want.'

'Everywhere in the world?' she asked, her eyes wide.

'No, this one is only for Germany, Denmark, and the Netherlands – the east part of the North Sea, but there are almanacs for nearly everywhere in the world.

She struggled for a second with the enormity of the whole idea, but her eyes suddenly cleared.

'So, the tide is at a different time everywhere in the world?'

'Yes, and because the moon takes about twenty-three hours to travel around the earth, the tide is about an hour earlier each day. And there are two of them.'

'It's the moon that causes the tide?'

'Yes. It's gravity that makes the water level rise and fall.'

'So why are there two tides every day, if the moon only goes around once?'

Franz looked at his father.

'It's complicated,' the General said. 'To be honest, I don't understand all of it myself, but it doesn't matter. All we need to know is the time of high and low water twice each day.'

'And that's why you need the laminac?'

The three Kästner men laughed, but a puzzled look crossed Antje's face.

'If the tide moves around all the seas and oceans,' she asked, 'why isn't there much tide in Kiel?'

They stopped laughing. The General grimaced.

'Now that, young lady,' he said gravely, 'is an excellent question, and I'm afraid it's not easy to answer. The truth is, I don't fully understand the ins and outs of it, but some seas like the Mediterranean and the Baltic don't have much tide. It's something to do with their shape, and their depth, I think.'

'There are still some currents, and the sea level rises and falls a little, but it's due to wind and weather rather than the moon,' Franz added.

Antje smiled. 'I can't wait to tell my teacher all about this, and Ruth. I hope I remember it all.'

Franz mussed up the top of her hair.

'You'll not forget. Besides, we'll have you working out tides yourself by then.'

'That's us passed the mouth of the Oste, about two cables off,' Johann shouted. The General made a mark on the chart and, using a pair of callipers, measured the distance they'd travelled.

'Five miles,' he said. He looked at his watch. 'Thirty-five minutes.'

Antje watched their faces as they all did the calculation in their heads. It was Franz who spoke first.

'Nine knots,' he said, grinning. 'Three knots of that is tide.'

Johann and the General shook their heads, disgusted at being pipped to the answer.

'We should get there in about an hour and seven minutes,' the General said, redeeming himself.

'Where?' Antje said, jumping up and looking ahead, 'Where are we going?'

'Cuxhaven,' they all replied.

'Sorry,' Franz said, 'We should have told you. That's where we'll spend the night. Then, tomorrow, we go to the islands!'

CHAPTER 41

'The children will be disappointed. They'll be in bed by the time you get back.'

Yosef had just told Miriam that he would be driving Maria and Eva that evening.

'I'll check with Frau Kästner; perhaps I can come home after I've dropped them off, and go back for them, seeing as I'm going to be away for a few days.'

'Why are you driving them to Hanover? Frau Kästner and Eva could take the train to visit her mother.'

'Frau Fischer's driver is ill at present, and they may need a car while they're in Hanover.'

Miriam said nothing, but he heard her tutting to herself. He squeezed her shoulder gently then slipped out the door. He drove the car round to the front of the big house and waited for his mistress and her daughter to come out.

Ten minutes later, they were driving along Hamburger Chaussee, Maria excited to be taking Eva to the fundraiser that evening.

Yosef cleared his throat. 'Ma'am,' he said.

'Yes, Yosef, what is it?'

'Do you know how long you are going to be, this evening?'

Maria Kästner was a little taken aback.

'I don't know, Yosef. Why?'

'I was wondering, ma'am, if I could possibly go back home after I've dropped you off and pick you up later. It's the children. I wanted to spend a little time with them before we leave tomorrow.'

He saw a flash of irritation cross her face.

'It's only a couple of days. We'll be back on Thursday.'

'As you wish, ma'am,' he said.

A moment later, he saw her face soften.

'Well, I suppose it wouldn't do any harm,' she said. 'We'll be at least a few hours. Come back at nine, but don't be late.'

'Yes, ma'am. Thank you. I'll be back in ample time,' Yosef said, pulling up at the door of the church hall.

~~o~~

'Eva will naturally be joining the Ladies' Guild, won't you, darling?'

'Yes, Mama,' she said, polite as ever, but wondering how she could get out of it without upsetting her mother. 'When I'm older,' she added.

Eva looked around. *Mama's ladies. Kaffee und Kuchen.*

Coffee and cake. It was a weekly staple of the Guild, of which Maria Kästner was the chairwoman.

Eva turned as one of her mother's friends began speaking.

'That's delightful. My daughter joined last year, as soon as she was eighteen,' the woman said.

The ladies varied in age from a shy twenty-year-old to a brash but pleasant octogenarian. The conversation was, by and large, polite and undemanding, but Eva found herself warming to the women her mother called 'her ladies'.

They were all terribly kind to her. It might have been because her mother was the chairwoman of the Guild, but Eva didn't think so.

She concentrated on the little undercurrents that she hadn't anticipated. There were allegiances and rivalries within the group, she realised. Perhaps it would be more interesting than she'd expected.

Frau Böhm was there, and Frau Hoffmann, the mayor's wife. A low murmur of conversation filled every corner of the room, the odd comment or laugh rising above the hum.

'This is Frau Messner, and this is my oldest daughter, Eva,' Maria said, introducing her to a tall, rather severe-looking woman. 'Will you both excuse me. I must check that everyone is being looked after.'

Eva spoke with the woman for a few minutes, while her mother fussed around the company.

'I expect you're thoroughly bored, darling,' the woman said in an amused drawl. 'I'm guessing you'd rather be out and about with your friends, talking about boys, but if you listen, you may just hear some juicy tittle-tattle.' She smiled, and Eva warmed to her. 'The ladies do like their Kaffeeklatsch.'

Eva smiled. *Coffee gossip.*

'Well,' she said, 'I thought it would be dull, but Mama's friends all seem nice.'

'Ha. Don't be fooled. Underneath the impeccably-dressed and polite exterior, there lurk tigers and wolves.' The woman laughed, and Eva couldn't help chuckling.

'Call me Ingrid,' she told Eva then, as she saw Frau Böhm and Frau Hoffmann approaching, with another lady.

'Here comes the wicked witch,' her new friend whispered.

Eva stifled a giggle and wondered which one Ingrid was referring to.

'Eva, so nice to see you here,' Beate Böhm said. 'It won't be too long before you'll be able to join. Lise can't wait.'

The Kästners' next-door neighbour turned to the other ladies. 'My Lise and Eva are almost the same age. Eva's brother, Franz, and Lise are awfully keen on each other. She couldn't come tonight; she had a music lesson.'

The two women nodded. Eva caught a glimpse of Ingrid's eyes rolling and stifled a laugh.

Eva watched as her mother detached herself from the last group of ladies and joined them again. Frau Hoffmann opened her handbag.

'My husband sent this,' she said, withdrawing a cheque and handing it to Maria.

'Oh. How marvellous. He's far too kind, but it is most welcome. I shall write a note of thanks in due course.'

'He's been invited to Nuremberg next month, you know, to the National Socialist rally,' she said. 'Herr Lohse and he are likely to meet with the chancellor,' she added, in a low voice.

'All party members are invited,' Ingrid murmured to Eva. 'And they'll all meet Herr Hitler, I'd imagine.'

'Pardon?' the mayor's wife said, frowning.

'I was just asking Eva if she'd like another cup of coffee. I didn't mean to interrupt.'

'Oh. Well, anyway, they've invited me, too, and Frau Lohse. The party are putting us up in a lovely hotel for two days.'

'I would like to hear him speak,' Maria said, 'Herr Hitler, that is.'

'Oh, I thought your husband wasn't very keen on the chancellor,' Frau Hoffmann said.

Maria blushed. Ingrid rolled her eyes again.

'Perhaps Frau Kästner and the General have different views on our leader,' she said. 'That is quite allowable within a marriage, I understand.'

The lady mayor gave Ingrid a cold stare.

'My husband just needs a little persuasion,' Maria said, anxious to avoid any disagreement, 'I'm sure he'll come around. The army are benefitting enormously from the government's reforms.'

'Yes, Jürgen said the General was keen to have Herr Lohse and himself meet with the top naval commanders. Jürgen has such a position of responsibility, especially as further expansion of the shipyards is planned. Obviously, the town council will have a big say in the matter.'

Happy to have had the last word, Frau Hoffmann took Beate Böhm by the arm and guided her towards the girls serving the coffee and cake. Eva turned to Ingrid.

'I see what you mean. The wicked witch. I had to try hard not to laugh.'

'Eva! Behave yourself,' her mother scolded. 'Ingrid, you should know better.'

'The woman is poison,' Ingrid said, 'and dangerous, too, with a sliver of power going to her head. I'm going to call off going to her little soirée.'

~~o~~

'That Messner woman has no manners, speaking like that. Mark my words, the day will come when they'll regret being so disrespectful.'

The mayor's wife spoke in a low voice, just loud enough for her friend to hear.

'Frau Kästner among them?' Beate Böhm said.

'No, Maria is decent enough, were it not for her husband. I'm sure she'll bring him to his senses. My Jürgen has already had a word with him.'

'Well, I'm not sure. As for bringing Eva to this. Really! She's far too young. I thought about bringing Lise, but I decided that next year would be soon enough.'

Frau Hoffmann nodded. 'And, of course, she had her music,' she said.

Beate Böhm stared at her but could see no guile on the mayor's wife's face.

CHAPTER 42

[04/07/1933 Tuesday]

'Eva, hurry up. We're late as it is.'

From the volume of their luggage, Yosef could have been forgiven for thinking that the Kästner ladies were visiting Hanover for a fortnight and not two days.

He packed it all into the car and waited patiently for Frau Kästner to flush Eva out from the house. Ruth appeared at his elbow.

'I wish I could come with you, Papa. Have a nice trip.'

He kissed the top of her head.

'I'll be back soon. Now, run. You're supposed to stay out of sight while I'm working.'

He smiled at her disappearing back as she hurried round the corner just as Maria and Eva descended the steps. His small overnight bag was in the front footwell. It contained a change of clothes, a packed lunch, and the library book he was currently reading.

'We are ready to go, Yosef. How long do you imagine it will take?'

'Madam, it depends how often you wish to stop, but I'm hoping no more than six hours.'

'Oh, that long? We should maybe have gone by train but it's such a trouble finding a porter to help with the luggage, and then one must find a cab at the other end. And we might need the car while we're there.'

Yosef wondered if it had even occurred to her that, if they'd taken the train, he would have been able to spend some time with his family. He'd have to wait until the Kästners left for their yearly fortnight at the admiral's lodge in the Harz mountains for that.

Yosef forced his mind back to the present, and to being cordial.

'Yes, madam. At least this way you're door to door.'

'True, Yosef. Well. Let's not delay,' she said, as the two passengers finally seated themselves in the back of the gleaming Mercedes Benz.

Yosef half listened to the almost constant chatter of the two women as they journeyed southwards, only broken by his announcement that they were approaching Hamburg, and would madam want to take lunch at her usual stop at Hanstedt.

'Of course, Yosef. We are absolutely famished,' she'd answered.

After Hamburg, they cut off Bundesstraße 4 on to the narrower Landesstraße that took them down through the Lower Saxony countryside to the small village on the Aue river.

When Maria visited her mother, she always liked to break her journey at the Zu den Linden, an old inn where the proprietor, Gerd Sellhorn, liked to make a fuss of her. The food was excellent, too, and the place had such a pleasant feel to it.

Yosef sat on the bumper of the car, eating the bread and ham that Miriam had packed for the journey; he'd known that he wouldn't be dining with Frau Kästner and Eva. He washed his food down with a bottle of Miriam's home-made lemonade and thought that, if it had been the General, they would have shared Yosef's lunch or, more likely, he would have been treated to a meal at a roadside café.

He dozed for half an hour while the waiter fawned over the Kästner women, but he awoke before he was called to pick them up at the front entrance.

Three hours later, he was shown to his quarters in the small room above the garage in the Fischer house. If he weren't needed the next day, he could visit with Paulus, an army friend who lived in Hanover, who he'd only seen twice in the fourteen years since the war ended.

CHAPTER 43

Antje would never forget her first sail in the Nordsee. They'd left Cuxhaven at first light to catch the last two hours of the ebb tide pushing them out of the Elbe estuary. There was little breeze until they were almost clear of Scharhörn and Nigehörn, the flat, interconnected sandy islands at the mouth of the Elbe.

Passing at low water, Antje thought they were less like islands and more like sandbanks, with just enough seagrass on top to show that they kept their heads above the water when the tide came in.

They followed the buoyed channel until it was safe to turn west, sliding through the water in the light breeze and the steady Nordsee swell, passing the mouth of the Weser, the river that ran through Bremen, then past the entrance to Jade Bight.

'There's a warship coming out from Wilhelmshaven,' Johann shouted, pointing, his excitement lighting up his face.

'That's the *Admiral Scheer*,' his father said. 'She's the Kriegsmarine's latest battlecruiser. I was over at Wilhelmshaven last week for a tour.'

'She's magnificent!' Johann said. The ship was coming towards them and, with each minute, she seemed to double in size.

The General pulled the tiller towards him, and the yacht swung round, the foresail backing and counteracting the mainsail, stopping them almost dead in the water just outside the channel that large ships used. Hove to like this, they could keep position, without having to drop sail.

They stood staring at the battleship, now almost upon them. As the first wave thrown out by its bow reached them, the yacht rolled dramatically, forcing the General to grab hold of Antje as a precaution. Antje gazed up open-mouthed at the ominous grey hull and superstructure, looming ten storeys high above them, counting every rivet.

It seemed to take an age to pass, even at the speed it was making. A couple of sailors on the aft deck waved as the stern passed the yacht, the giant screws, or propellers, churning up a maelstrom in the sea below them.

Franz let the foresail fly and it filled with a crack, like a whip. *Snowgoose*, little by little, picked up speed as they watched the battleship disappear out to sea. It was hard to imagine she'd been so close.

'I've never seen anything quite like that,' Franz said.

'No one has. She's one of the most advanced of her kind in the world. She's heading out for her sea trials,' the General said, full of pride.

'Seeing that, I might change my mind and join the navy,' Johann joked.

'That would please your grandfather no end,' the General said, laughing. 'There will be hundreds, perhaps thousands more to follow; large, small, all types of vessels. Between Wilhelmshaven over there,' he pointed in the direction the *Admiral Scheer* had come from, 'and Kiel, we're rebuilding the Kriegsmarine from scratch, at an unprecedented rate.'

By the time the smoke from the battleship's funnels had disappeared over the horizon, it was lunchtime, and they'd reached Wangerooge.

A long, low-lying strip of land, much of it barely above sea level and almost entirely fronted by sandy beaches, it was part of the East Frisians, a string of small islands a few miles off the German coast that consisted of not much more than low dunes and marshlands, which acted as a barrier against the North-Sea storms. The Wadden Sea lay between them and the mainland, a shallow stretch of lagoons, mudflats and winding channels which changed with every hour of the tide.

The town in the centre of the island existed only to serve the needs of the thousands of tourists who flocked to the island to bathe and to play; hotels and guest houses fought for beachfront space and the custom of those with money to spend.

They sailed past the crowded beach on the north coast of the island, knowing there was enough rise in the tide to allow them to slip through the channel between the western end of Wangerooge and its neighbour, Spiekeroog, and tuck in behind the west pier to drop the anchor. Most of the pleasure boats that flocked to the island, delivering tourists in vast numbers to the flourishing resort, docked at the east pier, so they would not be unduly disturbed.

'There's a little railway. With tiny trains!' Antje exclaimed, animated, looking across at the shore.

'Yes, it runs from the west pier to the town in the centre, and to the east pier at the other end of the island, ferrying the holidaymakers about. There are even little waggons for their luggage. There are no cars on the island.' The General smiled at her excitement.

'Oh, Papa, can we have a ride on it? Please.'

'Well, I was really intending to stay on the boat, have a nice meal, enjoy the peace and quiet...' he said. Franz smiled and turned away.

'Please, Father. Johann and Franz will take me, won't you?' Antje turned to her brothers.

'He's just teasing,' Johann told her, laughing. 'He's just as excited about going on the train as you are.'

The General ruffled her hair and broke into a smile.

'If we're intending to catch the next departure,' he said, 'we'd better get the tender lifted over the side and find the oars. And pack your bathing costume, Antje. You're going to one of the finest beaches in the whole of Germany.'

~~o~~

The General held Antje's hand as they walked through the crowds in the main street. In contrast to Kiel, there were no boarded-up shop windows, or men shuffling from workplace to workplace searching for employment, or women collecting sacks of washing to eke out the housekeeping. Only those with money to spend came to Wangerooge. The General noticed that the main street had been renamed *Straße der SA* but there were few soldiers or party men about, and black-and-red NSDAP flags and banners fluttered from only the occasional building.

The journey from the south-west corner of the island to the little town that occupied most of the central portion of Wangerooge had taken about twenty minutes. To Antje, the little train seemed to float across the surface of the water, the tracks only inches above the saltmarshes, flooded at high tide.

They made their way from the station through the crowded main street to the beach, where a few coins slipped into the hand of one of the beach attendants secured them a prime bathing spot and four wicker Strandkörbe, the beach chairs popular all along the Baltic coast.

Franz and Johann grabbed Antje and carried her, fully clothed, into the water, dangling her over the crashing waves. The loudness of her squeals and the disapproving stares from the matronly women on their patch of beach persuaded them to stop teasing her and let her quickly change behind a towel Franz held for her.

The General watched, lying comfortably in his Strandkorb, and laughed at his children's exploits in the sea, the boys having also changed and following their sister into the crashing surf.

He'd almost drifted off when a voice abruptly woke him.

'Erich. How are you? What are you doing here?'

He looked up.

'Walther,' he said, scrambling awkwardly to sit up.

Oberst Walther Schneider was in uniform, looking rather incongruous, surrounded by tourists in bathing attire.

'I saw you get off the train. I thought I'd come and say hello. I presume you're anchored off the west pier?'

He remembered being told that Schneider had received a promotion to full colonel, and that he'd been assigned to one of the coastal stations. The man was from Lübeck, where he berthed his yacht. It was a rather quaint, if old-fashioned, gaff-rigged ketch that looked like a good sea boat.

'Yes, we sailed from Cuxhaven today. We'll make for Helgoland tomorrow. How long have you been stationed here?'

'A few months. Overseeing the first stage in the new defences we're putting in.' He paused. 'I could show you around if you like.'

'I'm with my family. But thank you for the invitation.'

'They're quite welcome to come. We have our own beach. They can bathe there.'

Erich Kästner saw that it was going to be difficult to deflect the man's persistence.

'We have an excellent cook in our mess,' the colonel said, pressing him. 'Much better than you'll get around here, and that's if you can find a table,' the colonel added.

'Well… if you're sure,' the General conceded.

'I insist. There's a train scheduled in an hour back to the base. Later, it's not a long walk back to the pier for you. Fifteen minutes, perhaps, or I could get someone to drive you in the truck. There is a track.'

'I'll fetch the boys, and Antje.'

'Meet me at the train station in forty-five minutes.'

They shook hands and Colonel Schneider patted the General on the back.

'It's nice to see you again, Erich.'

~~o~~

When the General told them, Antje's face clouded in disappointment, but the boys' infectious excitement at the chance to look around the military installations on the island, and the promise of a private beach, soon had her smiling again.

The train was shorter than the one they'd been on earlier; one small carriage for army personnel, a flatbed waggon, a small box car and a tank waggon pulled by the most diminutive engine Franz and Johann had ever seen.

When they got to the base, the colonel showed them the new anti-aircraft gun emplacements, the searchlights, and the heavy guns in varying stages of preparedness.

'They'll soon be all over the island. This is going to be one of the strategic outer defences for the Third Reich,' the colonel said, pride showing on his face. 'There is also a small airfield that we have permission to use at present, but the Luftwaffe would appropriate it if war were to break out.'

It was all different enough to keep Antje from getting bored but, after an hour, when the colonel suggested that a couple of his staff could show the youngsters the best swimming spot, she and the boys jumped at the chance.

'A drink, Erich?' Walther Schneider asked when they'd gone.

The General looked at his watch.

'Go on.' He smiled.

The colonel poured a whisky for the General, and one for himself.

'You remembered.' The General laughed.

'I got a taste for it in '28.'

Walther Schneider had served his second spell under the then Brigadier Kästner when he was a major and had been promoted while under his command. The General was well known for having an inclusive and informal mess, which endeared him to his junior officers, but sometimes raised a frown among the higher ranks. Despite this, his men knew the boundaries, and discipline was rarely a problem.

'Everywhere I look,' the General said, 'we're mobilising for war.'

'I can't speak for anywhere else, but the plans for this place are impressive. If they're

170

repeated up and down the coast, we will be almost impregnable from sea, and from the air.'

'From what I hear, I think you're right. I'm not sure that we're quite so well protected from the east.'

Colonel Schneider glanced at the General.

'I'd heard that there was a massive increase in recruitment in the Reichsmarine and the Reichsheer to protect our borders, from all sides.'

The General laughed. 'That's supposed to be secret,' he said. 'We wouldn't want it getting out that we were flouting the Versailles agreement.'

'We're not supposed to have an air force either but they're definitely working on plans to develop the airstrip here.'

The General sighed. 'With all this expansion of the armed forces, I feel it can only mean that the government wants to flex its military muscles.'

'Rheinland and Sudetenland should be part of Germany. I believe Adolf Hitler is working towards that.'

'If he does, we may have to go to war with France, and then who else would jump into the fray?'

'I don't believe anyone has the stomach for another war,' the colonel said, shaking his head. 'If we become strong enough, as I think we will, they will not risk confrontation, and we'll have the National Socialists to thank for that.'

'At what cost though, Walther?'

'None, as far as I can see. All these unemployed people would be better off serving in the army, or the navy.'

'Granted, I do believe in a strong and stable Germany, willing to take our place on the world stage, but I worry about where our society is heading. Concentration camps, discrimination of minorities; they don't sit comfortably.'

'Erich, I wouldn't want to cause offence, but sometimes you're too tolerant. This country will not prosper while Bolsheviks, Jews and Gypsies are permitted to live off the backs of good, honest, working Germans, and who strive to bring down our democratic rights while they do so.'

The General swallowed the bile that was rising in his throat. The man was intelligent, and an excellent soldier, and Erich Kästner was keen to hear views from a cross section of the armed forces, so he bit back a response.

'I suppose you're right,' he conceded.

'You know I am. I was sceptical at first about the Führer and his party but the more I see, the more I think he is good for the Reichsheer and good for the nation.'

The General nodded. He was beginning to appreciate how widespread the support was for the National Socialists' rearmament policies, and why it might be sensible to keep his reservations to himself.

'That's what we all want,' he said, keeping his voice as neutral as he could, and Colonel Schneider beamed.

'Your son will be joining a resurgent army, General, and I hear promising things about him.'

'Well, it's early days, but the officers at the academy seem impressed. He starts at Hanover in September.'

'I hope he enjoys his time at Die Preußische Kriegsschule as much as I did,' the colonel said, laughing. 'That was where you went, too, wasn't it?'

'Yes, a few years ago now. 1904. I wonder if the delights of Madam de Fence's girls are still round the corner?'

The famous brothel had seen a selection of the Reichsheer's high-ranking officers through its doors in their youth, over the years. Her name, real or not, had amused officer candidates since she first turned up as a young woman in the last part of the nineteenth century.

'I hear it's still there, but the madam herself returned to France some years ago. Worth a fortune, I heard. Did you...?'

The General laughed. 'I couldn't possibly say.'

'Another drink, Erich?' Walther Schneider asked, proffering the whisky bottle.

'Why not,' he replied, holding his glass out. 'Do you get much chance to get back to Lübeck for a sail?'

The colonel looked surprised. 'I keep my boat here. Did you not see her? She's on a mooring, a quarter mile further up the channel you're anchored in.'

'Ah, the twin-master. We saw her when we came in. I should have put two and two together. It's a sheltered spot.'

'Yes. There's enough water most of the time to get in and out and, generally, I can stem the tide either way in the seegats.'

The General always studied the pilot guides before sailing anywhere new and he'd read all about the seegats, the shallow channels between the islands with powerful tidal flows that could make passage through them difficult.

'I imagine they'd be a struggle in strong winds,' the General said. The combination of shallow water and wind blowing hard against tide produced horrendous breaking seas which could be lethal for any vessel caught in them.

'Yes, I wouldn't go out on the ebb in anything over a Force 4 onshore but, in the main, if you watch the weather, the sailing is great. I rope in a couple of my junior officers as crew and they seem to enjoy it. Either that or they're just trying to keep on my good side.'

The two men laughed. The colonel stood up.

'Let's go and see how your daughter enjoyed our bathing raft,' the colonel said, still chuckling.

They watched as Antje dived from the float, two hundred metres off the beach. The General's heart almost stopped as the tide seemed to sweep her sideways but her steady stroke began to overcome it, and she made progress towards him. He saw Franz and Johann and the two soldiers catch up with her, and he breathed a little easier.

She reached the shallows safely, but forty metres further along the beach from the raft.

She saw her father and ran towards him.

'Did you see me swim from the raft?' she gasped, a combination of the cold sea and her efforts leaving her short of breath.

'I did. It's a good job you're a strong swimmer. That's quite a current there.'

'The soldiers made sure we were safe. They swim out all the time. We were diving off it, down to the bottom. I collected some shellfish.'

She turned to one of the soldiers, who reached inside a drawstring bag and, grinning, gave a handful of razor clams to Antje.

'They're for dinner,' she said, her eyes shining with excitement.

'Did you catch them all?'

'No, I just got a few of them. The men got the others.'

~~o~~

The General was glad he'd accepted Walther Schneider's invite.

The colonel hadn't been lying about his cook; the meal was delicious. In addition to a beautiful fillet of beef, they were served up the razor clams gathered that afternoon. Antje said they tasted of nothing but salt, which raised a laugh, but the General and the colonel raved about their wonderful flavour.

Franz and Johann gently ribbed their father when he told Walther Schneider about his return to racing in Kiel, but the colonel was full of enthusiasm, chastising the boys for underestimating the older generation's abilities.

'That's the youth of today,' the General said, with a smile.

'Talking of which, you are both in the Hitlerjugend, surely?' the colonel asked Franz and Johann.

'Yes, sir,' Johann answered, his face beaming with pride. 'I'm a Rottenführer and Franz is a Scharführer. We're both in the national Hitlerjugend sailing team.'

'Ah, you might yet pay us another visit here on Wangerooge, then. The Westrum tower, not far from here, was completed last year. Groups of Hitler Youth come to it for special training weeks. This place is ideal. They help us upkeep the paths and tracks on the island, and assist with maintaining the sea defences, to stop the island moving any further eastwards.'

Antje waited until there was a lull in the conversation.

'Excuse me, but may I ask a question?'

Colonel Schneider smiled at her.

'Of course you can, my dear. I only hope I can help.'

'Do you see any Sturmtaucher around here? I want to paint a picture of one.'

Colonel Schneider stared at her for a second, then laughed. Seeing the puzzled looks on his guests' faces, he explained, between his chuckles.

'*Der Sturmtaucher*. That's the name of my boat. Sorry, it was just that...' He laughed again.

Antje's smile didn't quite chase the frown from her brow.

'I'm sorry, Antje, it's not really that funny. He gave her an apologetic smile. 'You mean Sturmtaucher, die Vögel.'

'Yes. The birds. The shearwaters.'

'Well,' the colonel said, his voice under control now, 'I'm no great expert on the wildlife on the island but one of our first lieutenants is quite the enthusiast and he's forever pointing out all the different birds and other sea life. I'm sure that was one of the ones he showed us. It has pointed wings and it soars just above the waves, yes?'

'That's it,' Antje said. 'It's a brownish colour with a pale underside.'

'I don't think they are here all the time, but I'm sure I've seen one or two.' He looked puzzled. 'Why do you want to paint that type of bird?'

'It's the one on the lid of my paint set. My grandfather bought it for me. He's an admiral, you know.'

He laughed. 'Yes, I've met him. A fine old gentleman.'

'I'm not so sure about that,' the General interjected, grinning. 'Maria wasn't impressed when the paint set was produced. I don't think she could see past the mess.'

'Well, if you're heading to Helgoland tomorrow, I'd say you have a chance of seeing one. They do like the open sea.'

Antje smiled and thanked him.

'That's the reason she gave for coming on this trip,' the General explained, 'but I'm sure it was just an excuse for her to come sailing with us.'

When they'd finished eating, and the two men had enjoyed a final finger or two from the whisky bottle, the colonel insisted on walking them back to the West Pier. The track across the dunes and along the top of the sea wall was quite serviceable, even though the only vehicles allowed on the island were military trucks and farm machinery.

When they reached the pier, the tender was where they had left it, hauled above the high-tide mark. As the boys carried it down to the water, the colonel made his goodbyes with General Kästner.

'I'll see if I can pull a few strings and get Franz assigned to my unit,' the colonel told his former commander. 'I'll keep an eye on him and help where I can.'

The General was not displeased. He knew that Franz would do well under Walther Schneider's command, and he voiced his thanks.

'It's nothing,' the Colonel said, 'After all you did for me. And don't forget, if you're ever short of crew for a race, and I'm in town...' he shouted, as the General pushed the boat off the sand, and climbed in.

CHAPTER 44

The big house was empty. Miriam Nussbaum, with Ruth and Manny's help, had finished the few essential chores by eight.

She'd promised to take them to Schönberger Strand; a day at the beach would be a lovely start to their holiday, even without Yosef. She was still annoyed that her husband had been asked to drive Eva and Frau Kästner to Hanover when the train would have served them just as well.

The nearest tram stop was close by, at the junction with Petersburger Weg, and they ran to catch the car that they saw approaching as they left the house. Ten minutes later, they were at the railway station, in plenty of time to catch the nine o'clock train to the coast.

Manny watched absorbed as they edged their way through the marshalling yards, skirting the districts of Gaarden, Ellerbek and Wellingdorf, stopping briefly at each of their stations to let the night workers returning home exit the train, and families travelling to the seaside take their place, buckets, spades, and hampers in hand, and noisy with it.

Each compartment had at least one child with their face pressed against the glass, like Manny's, the remainder excitedly chattering or making unnecessary trips to the toilet just for the sheer joy of being jostled as they made their way along the corridor of the rickety train.

Their excitement grew as the city gave way to gently rolling countryside and small village halts, before the line made the shallow descent to the town of Schönberg and, four kilometres further on, its beach resort.

The train pulled into the station, emptying its cargo of eager families onto the platform, a short walk to the miles of sandy beach that drew thousands of day trippers from Kiel and the surrounding towns. The weekly tourists who inhabited the four seafront hotels and the countless guest houses secured deck chairs on the most desirable parts of the beach, but most of the working men's families were happy to find a patch of sand further away from the restaurants, ice-cream parlours and souvenir shops that dominated the centre of the strand.

Ruth unfolded the blanket from the canvas satchel she'd carried from home and spread it out in the shelter of the small dunes, while Manny discarded the buckets and spades he'd been nursing for a moment and rushed to the water's edge. He tested the water for coldness, then waded in up to his thighs before turning to check that his big sister was following. Miriam placed her own bag on the edge of the blanket and sat next to it for a while, watching her children, carefree and full of the joys of life, trying hard to make herself forget the troubling months leading up to the summer.

She sat for a while, letting the tightness in her body melt away, before walking to the damp sand at the water's edge, watching Ruth and Manny splashing each other.

'Come in, Mama,' Manny shouted, but she would only hitch her dress up a little and paddle in the shallows while they ran round her, splashing her clothes as they kicked up the surf.

'Help me make a castle,' Manny demanded of her, and the three of them set about collecting damp sand in the bucket, shaping it into a miniature version of the castle on the cover of his Brothers Grimms' *Fairy Tales*; Miriam couldn't remember if it was the one from *Snow White, Cinderella* or *Sleeping Beauty.*

They dug a moat around it and Manny and Ruth rushed back and forth to the sea, collecting water for the moat that always seemed to soak away a little bit faster than they could fetch it.

Miriam called a halt for lunch and, from the packets she produced from her bag, they ate cold beef pie and bread, followed by slices of Streuselkuchen, washed down with home-made lemonade.

In the afternoon, when they'd exhausted the possibilities that the combination of sea, sand and sun presented, she treated them each to an ice cream, before boarding the 16:40 to take them home. Manny had fallen asleep by the time the train had climbed the short gradient to Schönberg, his head across her lap. Miriam flashed a smile at Ruth, who made faces, mocking her brother's sleepiness.

They watched the countryside slip past them, tired and happy but, when they reached Wellingdorf, the train didn't pull out of the station after the usual brief stop, and Miriam sent Ruth to see what the hold-up was.

'Mama, it's those men with the brown shirts again. They are walking through the train, telling people to get off.' Miriam looked out of the window, noticing for the first time the red, white, and black flags and swastika banners of the NSDAP draping the station building. She paled as she heard guttural shouting from the next carriage along. She motioned Ruth to come and sit next to her and put a protective arm around her children's shoulders, drawing them to her. Manny woke up, looking around, not quite remembering where he was.

Out of the window, Miriam saw three or four families hurrying along the platform, glancing behind them. Every face had an anxious look on it.

'Papers, please,' a harsh voice demanded. The man at the door of the compartment was short and fat, and he smelled of rancid sweat and too much cologne.

It was not obligatory to show any formal documents, but most people carried some form of identification to avoid being detained while the necessary enquiries were carried out. At Yosef's insistence, Miriam never left the house without her identification and the letter she'd been given, typed on the General's notepaper, confirming her status as his employee.

'Nussbaum,' the man stated, looking at the piece of paper she'd handed him. 'Miriam Nussbaum. And your children are Ruth and Immanuel.'

'That's correct. May I ask what is happening? Is there something wrong with the train?'

'No, you may not ask. You are Jewish. Is that correct?'

Manny opened his mouth to speak, but Miriam squeezed his arm, in warning.

'Yes, we are,' she answered, dully.

'You'll have to leave the train,' the man declared. 'This train is for German people.'

Anger briefly flashed in her eyes, but she forced herself not to react.

'We need to get to Kiel,' she said. 'I have to go to work.'

'You should have thought of that before travelling with real Germans. If I were your employer, I would fine you for inattention to your duties. Now, leave the train, and take your litter with you.'

Manny started to sob, clutching Miriam's hand.

Miriam arose, collected their bags, and ushered the children towards the door. The SA man walked behind them until they stepped onto the platform, then returned to the next family sitting opposite, papers at the ready. Miriam thought she could see a sneer on the woman's face through the window of the train as she looked back, and a righteous indignation that she'd been made to travel in the same carriage as *die Juden*.

She hurried the children down the platform and through the station building. A further two Brownshirts stood at the station entrance, *to check the papers of those entering*, she supposed, *and to prevent any of those expelled from the train waiting and catching the next one in an hour.*

She walked along the street, her face dark with shame and anger, walking in the direction of home, her eyes blinded by the tears she fought to control.

'Mama, why did the man make us get off?' Manny asked.

'There must have been a problem with the train,' she said, flustered, her eyes imploring Ruth to keep quiet.

'But not everyone got off, and the train is moving again,' he said, pointing. Sure enough, the train was already steaming towards Ellerbek, in the same direction they were walking, with people staring at them out of the windows.

'I don't know,' she snapped, instantly regretting the lie, 'but it's a nice day for a walk, and it's not really that far anyway.'

'I don't want to walk. I'm tired.' Manny snivelled, dragging his feet.

Miriam gripped his hand tighter and pulled him with her harder than she'd intended, and he whimpered a little.

'Come on,' she said. 'It won't take long, and you can have something nice to eat and a cup of hot chocolate when we get back,' she promised, cajoling the six-year-old, regretting her harshness towards him.

'We could stop at Sabba and Bubbe's,' Ruth said, her eyes pleading with Miriam.

Yosef's father and mother had moved to a small apartment in Gaarden when they'd retired, financed at least in part, Miriam suspected, by the General's father. They often visited at the weekend, and the children sometimes stayed over if Yosef and Miriam were going to be especially busy at the house. It was about a forty-five-minute walk from Drachensee, and the children thought nothing of it, often making the journey on their own when the occasion demanded it.

The elder Nussbaums' flat was perhaps halfway along the route home, and although they could have caught a tram, Miriam was worried that the SA might be checking all public transport; the German authorities tended to be very thorough and efficient when they decided on a course of action.

'We'll maybe call in for a cup of coffee,' she said, reluctant at the thought of having to explain to Samuel and Renate what had happened to them, but rationalising that she could leave the children with her in-laws for the night and return to Drachensee herself, free from the worry of walking the children home. They would be more than happy to stay with their grandparents, and she could even wait until Yosef came home the following day to collect them.

She wiped away a few tears of anger, cursing the people who'd made her think like this, quickening her pace to curtail her children's questions.

~~o~~

Yosef sat in his room. That morning, Frau Kästner had told him that he might be required after lunch, so he'd cleaned and polished the car, sleeves rolled up in the bright sunshine. The cook had provided him with a bite to eat in the middle of the day. By six o'clock, he assumed that he wasn't going to be called upon to drive, but it was too late, and perhaps not advisable, to travel to the other side of town to see his old comrade-in-arms.

He sighed, resigned to the fact that his presence at the villa in Seelhorststraße was unnecessary and that it would be better not to tell Miriam that his time in Hanover had been wasted. He hoped that the Kästner ladies wouldn't change their plans to return to Kiel the following day.

At home, he could have found himself something to do around the Drachensee house or, if he felt like it, he could even have sat out on one of the summer seats dotted around the grounds. At the villa in Hanover, the garden was much smaller, making it impossible for him to do that without imposing on the ladies who were relaxing outside.

He briefly wondered about taking a walk, but it crossed his mind that the Zooviertel was a district where a Jewish chauffeur wandering around might stick out enough for one of the well-to-do residents to phone the police. He didn't want to think about the reaction of Frau Kästner to his being arrested, or worse, the effect it would have on her mother.

He picked up his book, sat on the bed, and read.

CHAPTER 45

The wind stayed steady from the west. By lunchtime, there was enough tide for *Snowgoose* to weigh anchor and allow the Kästners to explore the tidal creeks of the mainland, almost getting as far as Harlesiel, where the ferries to Wangerooge departed from, loaded up with tourists. An hour before high water, they crept along the channel on the inside of the island, passing the colonel's boat, *Der Sturmtaucher*, then exiting into the North Sea by the eastern seegat between Wangerooge and Minsener Oog.

The boys knelt at the bow, Johann swinging the lead in constant repetition, with its heavy weight and line, and Franz probing with the long withy stick to feel for the bottom, both shouting out the depths in fathoms, yelling to their father if he should turn to port or starboard. Antje kept an eye open for other boats, calling to her father when a small, open fishing vessel appeared in the distance, but it was of shallow draught, and it kept out of their way.

Because of the tide, it was nearly three by the time Wangerooge was in their wake, but the wind on the beam, blowing across the boat, gave them almost eight knots of speed and they made the shelter of Helgoland by six.

All day, Antje had scanned the waves. They saw gulls, terns, gannets, even puffins, but not a single shearwater.

That night, they tied up against a fishing boat in the north harbour, buying some herring from the deckhands for supper. Tired from the day's sailing, they turned in before nine, hoping to rise early the next morning. The steep climb to the upper town, the General promised, was worth it for the views across to Düne, Helgoland's sister island.

[06/07/1933 Thursday]

Miriam awoke early. With Maria and Eva due to return later in the day with Yosef, she had the beds to make up and an evening meal to think about. By the time the grocery delivery had arrived, and the butcher's van had followed soon after, it was only just after ten, and another hour saw dinner prepared.

She still smarted from having to leave the children at their grandparents, and she wondered if she'd overreacted. She untied her apron and hung it up in the cupboard, checked her hair in the mirror and, grabbing her hat and her coat from the hook on the back of the kitchen door, she left the house in the direction of Gaarden. She figured that if she didn't see anything worrisome on the way there, it would be safe enough to return with the children.

The journey was uneventful, and the children were pleased to see her, much as they'd enjoyed their unexpected stay at Sabba and Bubbe Nussbaum's. She told Yosef's father in low tones that she'd seen nothing on the streets to suggest a repeat of yesterday's frightening affair, so she was going to walk back to the Drachensee house, with the children.

'Do you want me to come with you?' he asked.

'No, but thanks. I'm sure everything will be fine. It's a lovely day for a walk.'

Each time she looked back he was still standing watching them, until they turned into Kaiserstraße. As she rounded the corner, Miriam saw a tram swaying along the street towards Kiel. It drew to a halt at the stop fifty metres away, and she was tempted to board it, but the memory of being trapped on the train, waiting for the SA men, was too fresh a scar in her mind, so she ignored the children's pleading and walked on past. They turned right onto Karlstal and followed the high shipyard wall as it curved round on to WerftStraße. The deafening staccato of the riveters' pneumatic hammers on the other side of the wall drowned out the children's chatter. As they turned the corner onto Gablenzstraße, heading for the centre of town, Miriam noticed a black car sitting on the other side of the junction, its engine running. She could just make out the two men sitting in it.

She quickened her stride, ignoring Manny's grumblings, who had to trot to keep up with her. Out of the corner of her eye, she glimpsed the car turning, and she sensed it crawling along fifty metres or so behind them. She resisted the urge to turn round, imagining the men scrutinising her, discussing whether to pull over and question her. Because Manny was starting to cry, she forced herself to slow a little and breathe, fighting the rising panic.

They'd reached the bridge over the main railway tracks into Kiel Bahnhof. An engine passed underneath them, the cloud of smoke, steam and flakes of cinder shrouding the junction for a second or two as they waited to cross the road. A policeman stood in the middle, directing the traffic, and she willed him to let them cross.

Miriam could sense that the car following them had stopped not more than a few metres behind them. The policeman held up his hand and the junction ground to a halt. He waved Miriam and the children across the road and she couldn't help glancing at the black car as they crossed a few cars in front of it. The two men stared straight at her and she looked away, afraid of making eye contact. As they reached the pavement, Miriam heard the traffic starting again, but she didn't look back. A few cars passed them, then a large truck, and the rails sang and squealed as a tram heading for Schulensee hurtled past, stopping a few hundred yards up the road.

'Mama, if we hurry, we can catch it,' Manny shouted, pulling at her arm. She heard an engine behind them, ticking over, and she momentarily considered running for the tram, but she knew that if the men were following her, they'd just wait until they got off the tram at the other end.

'I told you, it's a lovely day for a walk. It will do us all the power of good to get a little exercise.'

Manny griped for a few paces but was distracted by the whistle of another train, this time on the track that branched to Rendsburg and Eckernförde.

'Lift me up, Mama. I want to see the engine.'

They'd crossed over onto Hamburger Chaussee and were almost at the railway bridge. She could see the pillar of smoke rising from the cutting as the train approached. She lifted Manny onto the bridge parapet and helped Ruth clamber up.

Manny waved at the engine driver and was rewarded with a wave in return. A rush of air, steam and smoke engulfed them for a second or two, then the carriages passed below them, each with a swish and the clack of wheels, until the last one had gone, receding round the curve of the track towards Kronshagen.

Manny jumped down and Miriam patted the dust from his trousers. Ruth started to cry, spotting smears of grime from the bridge on her dress, but Miriam told her not to worry, that it was easily cleaned.

She looked around, resigned now, expecting to see the car sitting at the kerb, the men getting out of it, coming towards her, but the road was empty, save for an old man on a bicycle, wobbling up the hill towards them.

She leant on the bridge parapet, sucking air into her lungs, her legs almost giving way. She wiped her eyes, feeling the wetness of her tears on the back of her hand, and tried to compose herself before the children noticed.

'Are you all right, Mama?' Ruth asked, her face full of concern.

'I'm fine, Schatzi,' she told her daughter, drawing her closer. 'Just a little breathless. It must have been the smoke.'

~~o~~

When they tied up in Wyk, the General showed his military identification, and the harbour master was quick to let him use the telephone in his office.

'Kiel 3457,' he told the operator and waited for the connection.

'Erich,' he heard his wife's voice, 'is that you?'

'We're in Wyk,' he shouted down the crackling line.

He heard Maria's voice, but he struggled to make it out.

'We're in Wyk,' he repeated, 'on Föhr. It's an island just off the coast.'

The line fizzed again, then, as if someone had flicked a switch, it cleared, and he heard her answer.

'You said Föhr? We were there once before, a long time ago. A nice little place, but a bit whiffy though.'

He chuckled to himself. *It does smell of the sea, and it has no shops or restaurants to speak of either. Not really Maria's sort of place.*

'We're having a great time. We were in Wangerooge, which was beautiful; we met up with Colonel Schneider; he was one of my officers when he was younger. And last night, we were in Helgoland.'

'Oh, is that not quite far out from land? I hope you're being careful.'

'It's not that far, maybe twenty miles, and the weather has been perfect. Antje loved the town on the top of the cliffs, and the lift up to it.'

'Did you find somewhere to eat?'

'No, we ate on the boat. We bought some herring from one of the fishermen.'

He could almost see her nose crinkle in distaste.

'Well, as long as you're looking after Antje.'

The General smiled. She clearly presumed that her boys could look after themselves.

'How are you and Eva getting on? Was your mother well?'

'Oh, very well indeed. She invited a few friends around for dinner. Eva was wonderful; she's becoming quite a young lady. Her grandmother was so proud of her.'

'That's good to hear. What have you done since you've been back?'

'Oh, the usual. The fundraiser for the orphanage went well. Eva was a great help. Tonight, we've been invited to a little gathering the mayor's wife is having. Everyone will be there. Eva is so excited.'

'I'm glad you're enjoying yourselves.' He put his hand over the mouthpiece and called to Antje, who was standing outside, watching the fishing boats unload their catches.

'Here's another young lady to talk to you,' he said to his wife. He held out the phone to Antje. She took the handset from him.

'Mama,' she said.

'Antje, darling. Are you all right?'

'It's wonderful, Mama. We've sailed across the Nordsee to three islands now. Today, we travelled over forty nautical miles. That's seventy kilometres.'

The General cringed. No doubt his wife would question him about the discrepancy in the distance he'd told her. He would need to make a point of showing her on the chart when they got back.

~~o~~

'I hope you're behaving yourself,' Maria said. 'Have you been brushing your teeth, and washing yourself?'

'Yes, Mama,' Antje said, with a sigh. 'I'm not a baby.'

Maria laughed. 'No, you're certainly not, but I don't want your father turning you into a tomboy.'

'I'm still a girl, Mama. I just like to do things that boys do.'

'Well, enjoy your last few days. I'll see you on Sunday. If you want to come back before then, I'll send Yosef for you.'

'No, Mama. I want to stay. Anyway, I still haven't seen *ein Sturmtaucher* yet.'

'Don't worry, darling,' she told her daughter, 'I'm sure you'll catch a sight of one before

179

you come home.'

'I don't mind, Mama. If I don't see one this week, I'll see it next time.'

Maria felt a pang of jealousy and chided herself. During his long career, when he'd been at home, Erich had always been a great father to the children, and she knew they all adored him, but the boys had followed their father in almost everything they did; their choice of career, their interest in sailing, their wicked sense of humour. Was it too much to ask that her daughters were more like her?

The General's voice interrupted her thoughts.

'She's quite happy, and doing very well, Maria. Don't fret about her.'

'That's easy for you to say,' she snapped. 'I just worry about her turning into a tearaway with no regard for being a young lady.'

'You're overreacting, Maria,' he said, knowing too late that it was the wrong thing to say.

'Am I, Erich? I'm not too sure. Just bring her back safely, that's all I ask, but she's not going on every trip you take with the boys.'

'Whatever you say, dear,' the General said. 'I have to go now. The harbourmaster needs to use his telephone.'

~~o~~

'Kiel 1358.'

The General gave the operator the number for his office at Naval Headquarters, putting his wife's somewhat curt goodbye to the back of his mind. He smiled. She never stayed annoyed for long, he knew, and she always enjoyed him coming home.

'Captain Bauer,' he said, after Frau Müller had put him through, 'Anything interesting happening?'

'Ah sir, it's you, sorry, I wasn't expecting you to call.' He paused for a second. 'Nothing much to report, sir. There's a pile of memos on your desk. I've read and filed all the ones that are routine but there are a few that you might want to deal with yourself. There are also a couple of sealed messages for you, delivered by courier. They're not marked urgent. Do you want me to get them to you?'

'No, I'll be back Monday. I informed Captain Patzig that I was on leave for a week. He would have contacted you to get hold of me if there was anything that couldn't wait.'

'I've kept all the newspapers for you, sir. And I've set up a meeting next week for the mayor and Herr Lohse, with yourself and a few of the commanders.'

'Thanks for that. I was enjoying my holiday until now.'

The captain laughed. 'Sorry, sir. The man was pestering me, and you did say that you would get to it once you returned from your trip.'

'All right, all right,' the General replied, grumbling, but there was a smile at the corner of his mouth. 'How are our noble leaders?'

'Herr Hoffmann is getting more entrenched and powerful by the day, with the backing of Hinrich Lohse and the party machine. He's gradually eliminating any dissenting voices.'

There was a silence on the end of the phone for a few seconds.

'I was sure he would just be the party's puppy. It seems he is developing teeth of his own. Good work, Heinz. Anything else?'

'Not much, sir. I've pencilled you in to attend a few meetings next week in an observational capacity – naval appropriations, the transport section and the meeting between the Kriegsmarine, the shipyards, and the city council. It's about the yard expansion and worker housing. That could be an interesting meeting.'

'Indeed. I may need you to accompany me to that one. Take notes, keep an eye on some of the stuff going on in the background, that sort of thing.'

'Yes, sir, I'll mark it in my diary.' He hesitated, waiting to see if there was anything else.

'Are you having a good trip, sir,' he asked when the General didn't respond.

'Excellent. The weather has been perfect, and my children have been bearable.' He laughed.

'That's good to hear, sir. Where did you get to?'

The General gave him a quick rundown on their route so far.

'It sounds great, sir.' The General wondered if he heard a wistful tone in the the young officer's voice and made a mental note to ask him if he'd fancy a trip at some point. It would be difficult for he and the captain to be away at the same time for more than a weekend, but perhaps he'd suggest to Franz that he should invite the young man on the next trip with his friends.

'We're heading to Büsum tomorrow, then back into the canal the day after that,' he said. He then wished his young captain a pleasant evening, and hung up.

'Right,' he said to Antje, who was sitting on the harbour wall, waiting. 'Let's find a shop and buy something nice for dinner. What can you cook?'

CHAPTER 46

'How old are you now, Eva?'

'I'm almost fifteen, ma'am.'

'How delightful. A wonderful age to come out. I remember when I was fifteen.'

The other ladies laughed politely. The mayor's wife was not from old Kiel society, but most of the women present deferred to her, as much for her husband's prominence in the party as his position as mayor.

'And do you have a beau?'

Eva blushed, and the ladies smiled at each other.

'No... no. Not yet,' she stammered, blushing. 'Mama says there's plenty time for that.'

The mayor's wife nodded along with the others.

'Very wise, but it's never too early to start looking, and be noticed, which is just as important,' a voice to her left said.

Eva turned to look. She couldn't remember the older woman's name, but she was sure her mother had mentioned that she was the aunt to the Duke of Schleswig.

'I'm sure Eva has already been noticed,' the mayor's wife said.

'Ah, but has she been noticed by the right people?'

The woman turned to Maria.

'I'm having a few people over at the weekend. It would be beneficial for Eva to meet some of them. You really should come.'

'We'd love to attend,' Maria said, aware of the envious glare from the mayor's wife.

'I'll have my man drop you a line. Frau Kästner, isn't it? Your husband is General Kästner?'

'Yes, that's correct, ma'am.'

'I believe he has raced against my husband. He's the commodore of the yacht club in Flensburg. Spends most of his time there.' She gave a shared smile of resignation.

'The General is the same. He's sailing to Helgoland with my two sons this week, and my youngest daughter.'

'Oh, dear. You don't want to let him get his grips into your little girl. My eldest daughter became dreadfully keen on sailing when she was a teenager. Ended up marrying for love, so she told us. Poor as a church mouse, despite his good looks. We rarely see her now.'

Maria was spared from having to respond to the comment when the woman's younger companion, her niece, approached them and asked them to excuse her, but she needed a quick word with her aunt.

~~o~~

'Well, really. You would think she would return the favour. I only invited her because a friend of hers asked me to.'

Maria turned at the sound of Irmgard Hoffman's voice.

'Lady Mayor,' Maria said, putting her hand on the woman's stout arm, 'I'll have a word, if you like. I'm sure she wouldn't mind you coming with us. After all, you were kind enough to welcome her here.'

Frau Hoffmann fixed a smile on Maria and Eva.

'No, don't bother, Frau Kästner. I wouldn't want to put you out.'

Maria could see that the woman was desperate for an invitation.

'Are you sure? I don't mind asking.'

'Well, if you think it would be appropriate.'

Maria approached the aristocratic woman and spoke with her. There was a small shake of the woman's head and Maria returned.

'I'm sorry, Frau Hoffmann. She said perhaps another time.'

Maria Kästner didn't know if it was embarrassment or anger, but Frau Hoffmann's face briefly reddened before a rigid smile returned.

'Thanks for asking,' she said, 'I'll remember that.'

For an instant, Maria wasn't sure if it was a threat, and if she was included in it, just for being part of the woman's shame, but she discounted it; overall, it had been a most satisfying introduction for her daughter to the upper echelons of Kiel society.

CHAPTER 47

Yosef dropped Frau Kästner and Eva at the big house, and saw them in the front door, then parked the car in the garage. He slipped into the cottage, careful not to wake the children.

Miriam was standing by the sink, strangely still. She turned when she heard him.

'Is everything all right, Miriam? You don't seem quite yourself.'

'It's nothing,' she said. 'Just my mind playing tricks.'

She described the journey back from Schönberger Strand and explained why she'd left the children at his parents. Yosef had only seen Miriam and the children for a minute or two when he'd arrived back earlier in the day, but he hadn't had a chance to speak to her. He'd driven the Kästner ladies to the shops and then to the mayor's house, waiting for over two hours outside for them to emerge, listening to their excited chatter all the way home.

He thought of the ordeal his wife and children had been through.

'It must have been terrifying. These people are animals. They don't want us as part of their society.'

'It's not just what they do to you at the time,' she said, 'it's the way the feeling of fear eats away at you for days after.'

Yosef understood. Since he'd been beaten, he saw shadows around every corner.

She told him about the car that she thought had followed them on the way back home from his parents' house.

'It might have been something or nothing, but I was sure they were going to pick us up.'

He reached and pulled her towards him.

'We need to be careful,' he told her. 'Never go without your papers, especially the General's letter, just for now.'

'When is this all going to end?'

'Soon, I hope. There are rumours that more moderate right-wing politicians are trying to curb some of the excesses, and there are always the communists. They have a lot of backing from Moscow.'

Miriam shuddered. 'Why does the choice have to be communism or this fascism that we have now. What became of the middle ground?'

'Like everyone else. They're frightened.'

~~o~~

'That was lovely, Antje,' Johann said, laughing. 'We'll make a ship's cook out of you yet.'

The General had helped a little, and had given advice when asked, but she'd cooked most of it herself.

'I've watched Miriam cook omelettes. She showed me how.'

'It wasn't quite as tasty as hers,' Johann teased.

'I might be as good, one day, if I practise,' she replied, and Johann blushed, his joke backfiring.

They sat in silence for a while, tired and full-bellied.

'We've never been here before, have we?' Johann said.

'No. Your mother and I came once. It was when you were little. You and Franz stayed at home with Miriam. Mama used to enjoy going sailing when she was younger.'

'Father and I almost made it down here last year,' Franz said, 'when you were away at camp with your friends.'

From anyone else, Johann might have thought of it as gloating, but he knew Franz better than that.

'We came through Limfjorden and down the west coast of Denmark as far as Sylt,' the General said. 'It's the next island north of Föhr.'

'What's Limfjorden?' Antje asked.

'It's a series of fjords and narrow channels that run right across Denmark,' Franz said, 'splitting the top of the country into an island. It runs from Aalborg, on the east coast of Denmark, to Thyborøn, on the west coast. It's shallow in places, and narrow, so it isn't suitable for the largest ships but small commercial vessels, fishing boats, and leisure craft can use it to avoid the exposed and often wild waters of the Skagerrak that separates Denmark and Norway.'

'It's a beautiful journey,' the General said. 'We should do that again sometime. It would also be wonderful to cross the Skagerrak to Norway again. It has breathtaking scenery like the Bavarian Alps, with deep fjords.'

'That's another trip I missed,' Johann said, sighing.

'You were too young if I remember correctly,' the General said. 'Your mother insisted you stayed at home.'

'We could do that next year, Father,' Antje said.

The General shook his head sadly. 'Your mama would kill me if I said we were taking you to Norway. You may have to wait a few years for that, when you're a little older. We could go through Limfjorden though.'

Antje, who had started to pout, smiled again.

'All right, but when I'm bigger…'

'There are plenty other places that you must see,' the General continued. 'We could go to Sweden, to the archipelago, which is beautiful, too, and safe enough to satisfy your mother.'

'That would be fantastic,' Franz said, smiling at his sister. 'We haven't been there before either.'

'And perhaps, if you're really good, you could be crew in one of our races,' the General said, putting his arm around her. 'I'm sure my friends wouldn't mind an extra crew member.'

'If you don't mind being last.' Johann laughed.

Franz thumped him on the back, creased with laughter.

'We finished third in our first race,' the General said.

'How many boats were in it?' Johann asked, grinning, ignoring his father's hurt expression, sure that it was feigned.

'Well, there were only four, but that's not the point.'

'No, it's the taking part.' Franz could hardly get the words out, and he and Johann clutched each other, shaking with laughter.

The General winked at Antje, who had a frown on her face, evidently annoyed at her brothers' cruelty.

'Since you two are so clever, perhaps we should arrange a race between our boat and yours.'

Both boys looked at him as if he were mad, then burst into another fit of laughter that rendered them speechless, tears running down their faces.

The General sat watching, expressionless, waiting while they recovered enough to speak.

'Well, when you've quite finished…'

'Sorry, Father,' Johann sputtered, 'were you being serious?'

'Yes, without a doubt. I mean, obviously there would be standard handicaps – you can't expect us to compete on a level playing field with a purpose-built racing yacht, but that aside, we'll give it a go.'

Johann had stopped laughing, sure that his father had somehow turned the tables, but he couldn't figure how.

The General continued. 'When is your next race?'

'Travemünde Woche.'

Although Kieler Woche was Germany's leading yacht racing festival, there were others. Travemünde Woche was held in Lübeck bay, further down Germany's Baltic coast from Kiel, at the end of July.

'And when are you next back in Kiel?'

Johann glanced at Franz.

'About three weeks later,' he said. 'The nineteenth, I think. The third Saturday in August.'

It was only a month away.

'Fine. We'll give you a race on the Friday night in Kiel. Call it a warm-up.'

'I can be on your boat,' Antje exclaimed, hugging her father.

'We'll have to check with your mother, but I don't see a problem with that.'

Both his sons shook their heads and Johann glanced at Franz again. Their father had clearly lost the plot. For as long as he could remember, he and Franz had spent countless hours practising, honing their skills, and winning almost every race in their class, including some of the most prestigious events of Kieler Woche.

~~o~~

[07/07/1933 Friday]

'Happy birthday, darling.'

'Thank you, Mama,' Eva said.

'We'll have a little party for you when they get back from their sailing trip, but I'll treat you to a lunch today, just you and me. I'm sure Papa will telephone tonight with his birthday wishes.'

'It's fine, Mama. Lise said we could go shopping later on, when you're at your Ladies' Guild.'

'Oh.' Maria Kästner's face fell, then it brightened. 'It will be good for you to spend some time with Lise. She's such a lovely girl, and she'll likely be part of the family, one day.'

'Mama,' Eva said, with a gentle shake of the head and a smile.

~~o~~

Yosef carried the last box in. They weren't heavy, but there were a lot of them. Unlike some of the other drivers, he hadn't complained. On the contrary, he'd found it relieved the boredom while waiting for Frau Kästner.

They'd arrived at the church to find a truck sitting outside full of supplies donated to the orphanage, with the pastor trying to explain to the driver that, despite the delivery note giving the church's address, the orphanage was on the other side of town.

The man wouldn't listen, so, in the end, the pastor had relented and allowed the goods to be placed in the store until such times as they could be moved to the orphanage.

'Well, I'm not unloading it on my own. You'll have to help,' the driver had whined. 'I've got a bad arm.'

Yosef had noticed the bandage on the lorry driver's arm and was forced to concede that, while he could probably wheel a sack barrow, the man wouldn't be much help with lifting.

'I have a fundraiser starting in a few moments with the ladies. It will have to wait until later,' the pastor had told him.

'That's no good. I must be back in Hamburg by noon at the latest. Ask some of your fine ladies to help. After all, it is for the orphanage.'

Yosef was sure that, if the pastor hadn't been a holy man, he would have roundly boxed the man's ears, as much for the sneering smile as his rudeness.

'My driver will help. I'll give him a shout,' Maria had said.

A few of the other ladies had taken their cue from Maria Kästner and offered their drivers as labourers.

Within minutes, a steady stream of boxes made their way to the storeroom, the men grumbling, but only out of earshot of their mistresses. Like Yosef, they had their sleeves rolled up, but were soon sweating in the hot sun. The pastor and his gaggle of women stood observing for a minute, until one of their friends called them in to say the coffee had been poured.

As he set down the last box, Yosef overheard Frau Kästner talking to another of the ladies.

'It's so nice when you can do something tangible for charity, isn't it?' she said.

'Indeed. It's all very well holding whist drives and raising money, but you sometimes need practical people to get the work done.'

Yosef shook his head and returned to the car.

CHAPTER 48

The shearwater had flown twenty or thirty miles already that morning. She, along with six others, was looking for a ripple on the sea, or a shadow under the waves that would indicate the presence of food. They soared a few metres above the surface, skimming the tops of the waves before swooping down into the troughs, barely visible from more than a cable away.

Antje nearly missed them but, out of the corner of her eye, she saw a white flash against the dark sea, and she stared at it, convinced that it was just a patch of froth breaking from the crest of the wave.

Then it seemed to move further along the swell, and she watched it change to sooty-brown, difficult to see against the blue-grey of the waves, but there all the same. Suddenly, she caught its shape; the cross made by the wings, their pointed tips, and the dark head with the delicately hooked beak. It was a shearwater.

'Papa,' she said softly, not wanting to frighten the bird. 'Look.' She pointed at the shearwater, which was now fewer than fifty metres from the boat.

From her pocket, she pulled out her sketchbook and began to draw.

~~o~~

The General saw the shearwater and smiled, relieved.

Franz was on the helm and he spotted it too.

'There's another one,' he whispered, 'flying behind it.'

He eased out the sails enough to take the speed off the boat without losing way.

'There's more of them,' the General murmured, just loud enough for Antje to hear. The birds circled the boat twice, then flew on past in the direction they'd been headed.

'Did you get that?' the General asked.

'Yes, I think so.' She showed him the sketchbook.

'That's wonderful,' he said, meaning it.

He took the book and showed Franz the page. The drawing was minimal, with few pencil lines, but there were three or four recognisable shearwaters, each from a different angle, and at varied points of flight. He hadn't realised how good she was, and it was hard to believe that the sketches, which she'd done in a few minutes, were the work of a ten-year-old.

Johann emerged from the companionway.

'What's all the excitement?'

'Antje's found her Sturmtaucher. Look at these.' Franz showed him the sketches and he whistled.

Franz pointed. Ahead of them, the birds had landed in the water, sitting on the surface. Every so often, one would disappear and return to the surface a few minutes later, with a small fish or a sand eel in their beaks.

'They look better flying,' the General said, but his daughter was watching the birds, the sketchbook in her hands again, the pencil strokes catching the detail of their tubiform beaks, for all the world like some strange musical instrument, and the lie of the plumage around their heads and necks.

Franz, as gently as he could, pulled the tiller towards him and brought the yacht through the wind, so that they were hove to, sitting in the water twenty metres from the birds, who seemed oblivious to their presence in their feeding frenzy.

It took five minutes for them to drift past the feeding shearwaters and during that time, Antje filled three pages with sketches. The General watched his daughter, her rapt face and her quick hand mesmerising him. He wondered if Maria knew about her talent.

Father must have had an inkling, buying her the paint set for her birthday.

He asked to see the rest of her sketchbook. He flipped through the pages. There were drawings of puffins and gannets, and a sketch of the seals they'd seen coming out of Wangerooge, on the sands of Minsener Oog.

The drawings, on closer inspection, were imperfect if judged from an adult perspective. Her quick sketches were better, as they caught the essence and movement of the creatures without overthought. Once she filled in the detail, they lost a little of the sense of shape and movement that her jottings had, but he was sure she would learn. He resolved to see Maria about obtaining the services of an art tutor for her when they got back.

As they set sail southwards towards Büsum, Antje cleared away her sketchbook and pencils. She stood at the stern and stared at the yacht's wake. Just as the birds vanished behind the crests of the waves, they took off, wheeling back the way they'd come, disappearing into the distance.

~~o~~

[08/07/1933 Saturday]

For the first time on their trip, the weather turned. Not long after leaving Büsum, a thick, early morning fog descended, and they were reduced to creeping along unsighted, Antje at the bow, eyes and ears straining for any sight or sound of other vessels.

The General spoke with Franz and Johann, his voice low.

'We have three options. We can go back to Büsum and wait for the fog to clear. We may lose the tide, though, and have to wait until tomorrow.'

The boys grimaced.

'Or we could stay in the main deep-water channel and head out to sea; it's about ten miles long, heading west, until we clear the mudflats and sandbanks, then cut across to the Elbe and back in. We'd have to stick to the edge of the channel; it could be busy, and there's a real danger of meeting other vessels in the fog.'

'And thirdly?' Franz asked.

'There's a narrow channel that winds through the mudflats all the way across to Friedrichskoog, here.' He pointed to the chart.

Johann whistled. 'That will be tricky. Will we have enough water to go all the way?'

'Yes, we should have. The only point where we have to cross the sandbank is within the first hour, and it won't be long after high water. Remember your rule of twelfths.'

'It falls one twelfth in the first hour,' he said, 'two twelfths, or a sixth, in the next hour. Most of the drop, three twelfths in each of the middle two hours of the tide occurs then, with half of the overall fall.'

'Correct,' the General said. 'So, we should have plenty of water under the keel for a couple of hours either side of high water. The beauty about the third option is that there should be little or no traffic in the fog, and anything moving will be small, like us. What do you think?'

'We can't to go back to Büsum. We'll struggle to get home by Sunday if we do that, and we have school the next day.'

'And I have work,' the General said.

'I don't fancy being run down by a fishing boat or a barge coming in or out of Büsum, or the Elbe. Let's go for the third one,' Franz said, glancing unconsciously at Antje at the bow.

The General caught his look. He shouted to his daughter.

'Antje, you'll have to stay in the cabin. If you fall in, we'd never find you.'

She nodded but looked so disappointed that Franz suggested that if she stood on the companionway steps, with the hatch open and the washboards in place, she would be quite safe and would be an extra pair of eyes and ears. The General agreed and went below to collect the relevant charts, and his navigational tools.

Johann stayed on the helm, while the General plotted a course between each of the stick

189

markers that lined the side of the channel. There was a gentle breeze, enough for them to make way at a sensible pace without having to spill wind to slow down.

Franz settled himself at the bow, using a long withy stick and lead line, whichever was most appropriate for the depth. A couple of times, they misjudged the channel, and came to a grinding halt in the soft mud, backing the main to slide off, only twice having to start the engine when the sludge got too much of a grip of the keel.

The General gave Antje the horn to blow, which she managed after a few sputtering false starts, and told her to sound it every minute. He could hear her softly counting to sixty each time, like a metronome, and he smiled.

By the time they reached the spit north of Friedrichskoog, the tide had hardly dropped, and they crossed the sandbank into the small channel that fed the Elbe, clearing half a metre under their keel.

Only once did they see another boat, a small open fishing vessel that sounded its plaintive horn in reply to their own. They watched it emerge from the fog and pass safely to port, hailing the two fishermen with a 'Guten Morgen' before it slid into the murk behind them.

As they reached the Elbe to turn for Brunsbüttel, the fog lifted like a curtain and Antje looked back at the rolling bank of white cloud on the surface of the water, astounded that they had found their way through it.

The General took a deep breath, the sun warm on his face and a sense of relief flooding through him. He allowed himself a half-smile.

~~o~~

The breeze behind them, they made slow progress eastwards up the estuary, fighting the adverse tide by creeping along in the shallows at the edge of the main channel, where the current was less, and where they could take advantage of any eddies which flowed the opposite way to the tidal stream in the middle of the channel.

By mid-morning, they were tying up on the mole at Brunsbüttel, ready to enter the sea lock.

'Well done troops,' the General said.

Franz had seen the strain on his father's face deepen during the fog, and he'd watched it recede in the bright sunshine. Now, safely tied up, he saw his father allow himself a quiet smile of satisfaction, while they waited for the lockmaster to call them in.

CHAPTER 49

Yosef listened to the talk after the Shabbat service.

More jobs gone; those who had lost work were on half-pension at best, but only if they were former serving soldiers from the Great War. Banks unwilling to give loans. Children coming home from school in tears from the cruel barbs of fellow pupils, or worse.

They discussed politics, the absence of democracy and, most of all, the National Socialists. Everything came back to the NSDAP.

Yosef was all for going straight home but, for the children's sake, he allowed himself to be persuaded to go for their usual stroll along the promenade, the day promising to be a warm one.

Until six, when he had to be back to drive Frau Kästner and Eva for their evening with the countess and her guests. He was determined that they should enjoy the day, not giving in to the NSDAP bullies.

And it should have been wonderful. The children ran ahead as usual, the family ate ice creams, sitting on a bench, looking out over Kieler Hafen and nodding greetings to fellow strollers.

'I should be enjoying myself, but I don't feel safe anymore.' Miriam spoke in low tones, even though the children were thirty yards in front. Yosef held her hand and gave it a squeeze.

'I know. I constantly look around for SA or SS men. That policeman we passed on the way down from the synagogue, he only said hello, but I flinched.'

She gave him a worried smile. 'You too? It's getting to the stage when I think everyone is looking at me.'

'Maybe we're just overthinking it all. Surely everyone hasn't become Jew-haters overnight?'

'Maybe they've always hated us, but only now do they feel they can show it.'

'I think that's harsh, Miriam. No one, other than NSDAP people, have ever done or said anything to us, have they?'

'You didn't see the woman's face on the train. The one sitting opposite. There was a mixture of disgust and anger at having to share a carriage with us and a cruel satisfaction when we were thrown off the train.'

Yosef opened his mouth to say something, then stopped. He knew she was right. Frau Böhm, the children in Ruth's class, the woman on the train; it was as if they'd been given a green light to let their hatred show.

~~o~~

Approaching the quayside at Rendsburg, the General burst into laughter.

'Father, what's up?' Antje asked him, a puzzled look on her face.

'Look.' He pointed to the wharf. It was the unmistakable figure of Captain Canaris.

'Uncle Wilhelm,' she squealed, jumping around the cockpit, waving.

'Whoa, careful. We don't want you falling in now, do we?'

The General knocked the throttle lever back and engaged reverse gear. The propeller bit into the water and slowed the yacht as it glided towards the harbour wall. The boys had seen the captain by now, a kitbag at his feet, and readied the warps to throw to him.

As *Snowgoose* gently bumped to a halt against the quay, both ropes reached him at the same time. He caught them both, and with a flick of a wrist, he snaked the bowline over a bollard five metres further along the harbour wall. Another loop snaked along the line and dropped over the first, followed by a third before he walked back, tying a bowline with one hand, and slipped the stern line over a second bollard behind the yacht.

The General started clapping, and Antje and the boys joined in.

'You just can't help yourself, can you?' the General asked, grinning widely.

'When you have an immense talent, why hide it?' the captain replied. 'Permission to come aboard?'

'Well...'

Antje couldn't wait.

'Come on, Uncle Wilhelm. We've been to the North Sea. To Wangerooge and Helgoland and Föhr and Büsum. And we sailed through an extremely tricky channel in the fog today. And we saw lots of Sturmtaucher. I drew them all.'

The captain threw his kitbag to Franz, then jumped onto the yacht, catching Antje in both arms and lifting her up, holding her out over the water.

'Will I throw her in, Kästner?'

Over Antje's squeals of laughter, which were attracting attention from the quayside, the General, chuckling, told him to do as he thought best.

Feigning reluctance, Canaris lowered Antje into the cockpit and let her go. She wriggled out of his grasp, still giggling, until he told her to go and fetch her sketches, to let him have a look.

While she scrambled down below, he shook Franz and Johann's hands, congratulating them on their seamanship and bemoaning the fact that their expertise was wasted in the army.

They grinned at him, trying to come up with a suitable response.

'Get back to me when you can think of an answer, boys,' he told them, then turned to the General.

'Kästner,' he said. 'Not bad, but you came in a bit on the slow side. It's a good job there wasn't a breeze to blow you off.'

'Canaris. If I were looking for an opinion, I would have asked an expert,' the General snapped back at him, before both men hugged, grinning. 'What the hell are you doing here?'

'Well, I had to check you'd survived your long voyage. I mean, venturing out into a real sea, at your age?'

'And not in a big lump of a ship with hundreds of lackeys to do the work for me. Have you ever tried proper sailing, Canaris?' The General's grin broadened.

Before the captain could respond, Antje climbed out from the companionway, sketchbook in hand.

He sat down, took her on his knee and got her to open the book. At each page, he whistled his surprise, murmuring the odd word of praise here and there.

'Quite the artist, Antje,' he said, glancing at the General as he did, an eyebrow raised.

The General shrugged.

'I didn't know,' he mouthed.

The boys were sent for a beer for each of them, and lemonade for Antje. They dug around in the bilges, and fished out five bottles, cooled to perfection in the depths of the boat.

'I booked a restaurant,' the captain told them. 'It gets an excellent name for its Schnitzel.' He leaned forward towards the General, sniffing. 'Maybe a bit of a spruce-up would be a good idea first.'

The General laughed and went below to wash and change his shirt. When he returned, he repeated his question, asking the captain why they were being honoured with his company.

'We're in for a bit of a refit, so I'm stuck in port for a couple of weeks, overseeing the work at the yard and catching up on all the administrative drudgery I've been putting off. I called round to your office to buy you some lunch, and they told me you were bunking off on the yacht.'

'They did? Those precise words?'

'Well, maybe not exactly. Perhaps I'm paraphrasing a little. Anyway, they said you'd be back at work on Monday, and I figured you had to be in the canal by now. I borrowed your car and your driver – Captain Bauer was most accommodating – and we drove to Brunsbüttel. The lockmaster said you'd passed through about midday. We caught up with you at the Grünenthal Bridge and assumed you were stopping at Rendsburg overnight, so we hung around at Nobiskrug until you turned into the Ober-Eider, then your driver dropped me off here.'

'Quite the detective, Canaris,' the General said, drily. 'And the reason for your visit?'

'Oh, just to catch up; to see how the new commission was suiting you.'

'Ha! Now I see. Curiosity was getting the better of you.'

The captain attempted a hurt expression. To the General it seemed more sheepish than anything.

'I'm disappointed, Kästner, that you should think me so shallow. However, I am more than interested to find out all about it.'

'We'll talk later,' the General said.

CHAPTER 50

The butler opened the door. 'Frau Kästner and Fräulein Kästner?' he asked, before showing them in.

The elegant house was set amongst woodland in a corner of the Lindau estate, the seat of the countess's nephew, the Duke of Schleswig. The journey from Kiel, passing through Eckernförde, had taken just over an hour; the roads were quiet and by the time they'd crossed over the Schlei at Lindaunis, they'd made up the ten minutes' delay at the start when Maria, seeing Eva's dress in the sunlight, had decided that the light-blue one would show off her beautiful pale skin better.

Yosef was told where to park the car and invited to join the other drivers in the kitchen around the back, where he would be offered some refreshments, and a seat. Not wanting to appear rude or do anything that would reflect poorly on the Kästner ladies, he accepted the hospitality.

~~o~~

The countess welcomed Maria and Eva with a warmth that startled them, and led them to the centre of the room, introducing them to what Maria judged to be some of the state's wealthiest and most influential residents.

After a pleasant hour, when they were served a selection of delicious canapés, and Eva was admired and complimented by everyone in the company, they were called into the even more impressive dining room and were seated, almost as guests of honour, next to the countess. Maria hid her surprise and was glad of everything she'd been taught about social etiquette as a girl, and that Eva's school in Schleswig placed such an importance on their pupils becoming young ladies.

After the meal, the men retired, and the women sat in the music room. The conversation ranged widely in a similar vein to the society gossip cherished by the ladies Maria Kästner mixed with in Kiel. A great deal of time was spent delivering advice to Eva about the desirability of a match with one of the suitable young men they would be more than happy to introduce her to.

'A couple of them are here this evening,' the countess whispered to her.

The talk turned to the current deterioration in Schleswig-Holstein society and, while the mayor's wife was not mentioned, her name was alluded to.

'Some people simply don't understand how to behave, and never will. They have risen to power from all walks of life on the tide of change that is flooding Europe, and they expect us to accept that they have become one of us. One is almost nostalgic for the old Weimar politicians who have been swept aside; at least they knew their place and didn't try and pretend to be something they weren't.'

The old woman who'd spoken, her skin wrinkled and liver-spotted, wore the most spectacular diamond necklace Maria had ever seen. She turned to listen to the countess's reply.

'One had hoped that the Nationalists, once they'd disposed of the communists and their left-wing social democrat friends, would have seen the sense in restoring the monarchy. After all, how can we return to Germany's glory days without someone like the Kaiser as a figurehead? Herr Hitler and his colleagues would never have got into power without our support.'

This wasn't news to Maria; the General had told her as much in an ill-tempered exchange on the telephone when she'd informed him of their invitation to the countess's soirée. He'd added that Germany's foremost industrialists, businessmen and bankers had been of even greater influence in the rise of the NSDAP to power, seeing the opportunities it presented for themselves to make money.

The countess turned to Maria. 'And, of course, our wonderful army and navy. I'm sure they'd support a return of the Kaiser or, at least, his son.'

Maria Kästner stiffened, not knowing what to say. She glanced around, trying to second-guess what they expected to hear.

'My husband fought in the last war,' she said. 'He has an Iron Cross and has served in the army all his days. I'm sure he wishes that those who are in power are right for Germany. He's not entirely sure about Herr Hitler.'

'Such a nasty, ill-bred little man. To give him his dues, he appears to be solving a few of the country's problems; the Bolsheviks, the Gypsies, even the Jews, but he seems to be throwing out the baby with the bathwater. Our family's tailor is Jewish; there's simply not a better one in Schleswig-Holstein. I just don't know what my nephew will do if he's forced to close.'

'You're so right. These are such difficult times.'

The countess patted Maria's hand.

'It's so nice to know that those who hold the reins of what was once the imperial army, still hold the old allegiances dear.'

Maria swallowed, her mouth dry. She hoped the General would behave himself when he finally met these new friends of hers. He had a habit of saying exactly what he was thinking, and she dreaded him alienating them before their daughter had a chance to find a husband among their young men.

~~o~~

Eva sat in silence next to her mother, glad not to be expected to contribute greatly to the conversation. When the girls at school spoke of Adolf Hitler, it was his charisma and the power of his speeches that brought a thrill to their faces. It was why they'd all joined the Bund Deutscher Mädel.

Why should the boys be the only ones to enjoy Hitlerjugend?

The League of German Girls, the BDM, was their chance to support the Führer.

She said nothing of this, and only spoke when she was asked a question, her answers demure and respectful, as Mama and her teachers had taught her.

She smiled politely at the young men she was introduced to, although if they were anything to go by, Eva wasn't sure she wanted to join the so-called elite; while Johann's friends didn't have the breeding, and perhaps the wealth that these people had, from what she'd seen she was sure they were more fun to be around.

CHAPTER 51

Johann lay in his bunk, still awake. Franz brushed his teeth, preparing to get into his sleeping bag, and Antje was sound asleep in the forepeak.

'I still don't know why we had to turn in for the night. I was enjoying Uncle Wilhelm and Father's stories,' Johann grumbled.

'They wanted to talk. Together. On their own.'

'Did Father say something to you? I didn't hear him tell us to go.'

'They're too polite to come right out with it, but there were a couple of hints that they wanted time to themselves.'

Johann changed the subject.

'Where's Uncle Wilhelm sleeping?'

'I suppose he'll sleep in the cockpit, or down here, with us. I'll sleep in one of the pilot berths so that he can bunk down in my berth if he wants.'

'I hope not. He snores.'

Franz cleared some of the gear stowed in the cramped pilot berth, the long cubbyhole above the saloon seating, designed to be used by crew when sleeping on passage, with the lee cloths tied over to prevent them falling out. He climbed up into the cramped space and made himself comfortable.

'Read a book, or something. Just stop moaning.'

~~o~~

The two friends sat in the cockpit. The whisky bottle had been cracked open, and they'd already made a dent in it. Captain Canaris offered the General a cigar.

'So how does it feel to be in military intelligence, if that's not a contradiction in terms?'

The General laughed.

'Interesting. I'm told I have you to thank for being asked to take the commission.'

'Well, obviously, they asked me first. I thought you were an acceptable second best.'

'The bitter talk of one whose rank is lower than they believe it should be.'

It was the captain's turn to laugh.

'Touché, my old friend. I have indeed been overlooked once too often. That will change, never fear.'

'I'm sure it will, Canaris,' the General said, wondering if it were true.

'To be honest, I'm enjoying commanding the *Schlesien*. Training these youngsters to be the future of the Kriegsmarine has been one of the most rewarding posts I've had.'

'Yes, you seem to be exceptionally busy. How many recruits are you training this year?'

'Many thousands, my friend. The navy are rushing through four times what they trained last year, tenfold compared with five years ago. I presume it's the same with the Reichsheer?'

'To a degree, yes. I've heard they've ramped up the intake even further since I retired, and they're being clever about it too.'

'That's not like the army,' the captain quipped.

The General smiled. 'No, but this is coming from the National Socialists who, whatever else you say about them, are shrewd devils.'

The captain made a parody of looking around, checking no one was listening.

'You'll get into trouble one of these days,' he joked, but the General sensed it was only partly in jest. He shrugged and conceded that he should be more careful. He couldn't bring himself to tell his friend about the incident with the SS man at Brunsbüttel or his involvement in the Spiegel case.

'So, how are they being clever about it?' the captain asked, intrigued.

'They're training more officers than they need for the current strength of the army so it's more or less in line with the size allowed by Versailles but, wait for this, they're trebling the intake of cadets to the police force.'

He glanced at the captain, but there was still a puzzled look on his face.

'These recruits are doing military-style exercises. If war breaks out, there's a ready pool of private soldiers just waiting to be redeployed from the police into the army. It could treble in size in a month.'

'Ah. That is clever. Indeed.'

'Have you noticed anything strange about the men you are training?'

'What do you mean? They seem pretty normal to me.'

'Are you training many ordinary seamen?' the General asked.

Captain Canaris thought for a second or two.

'Now that you mention it, it's mostly officer candidates.'

'I have it on good authority that the Kriegsmarine are doing the same as the army,' the General said, 'training up thousands of officers. The ratings will come from the merchant navy and the reserves when they're needed.'

'How do you know all this...' The captain stopped, thumping the side of his head with his palm. 'The Abwehr. I didn't give it a thought, but you must have access to some sensitive material. It's funny, I'd imagined you more as a gatherer of information. They must think you're worth keeping informed.'

'Well, it's not that sensitive. It's mainly about opening one's eyes and putting two and two together. But it takes an agile mind...'

He glanced at the captain, who grinned, then threw his face into a fair imitation of an imbecile.

'There's one other thing, that's even more ingenious,' the General said, when he'd stopped laughing. '*Hitlerjugend.*'

Canaris frowned. 'Hitler Youth?' he said.

The General watched, smiling, as the brilliance of the National Socialist's plan dawned on his friend.

'They'll have an army of ready-trained fanatical Adolf Hitler supporters to step into roles within the Reichsheer and the Reichsmarine,' the captain blurted.

The General sighed.

'Yes. Private soldiers, naval ratings, warrant officers, even commissioned officers, at every level of the service.

He paused. 'I don't know if this was all planned or if it just happened to work out for them, but it means that, within a few years, the NSDAP will have a massive number of trained youths to call on, and an increasing loyalty base within the Reichswehr.'

'Look,' Canaris said. 'I know you have your doubts, but without Adolf Hitler and the National Socialists, none of this would be happening. You and I have worked and prayed for a proper army and navy for Germany all our lives. Now we will have that, and more.'

'I keep telling myself that, and I know the NSDAP government have accomplished in a few years what the Weimar Republic couldn't do in a decade and a half, but I can't bring myself to trust them.'

'Think what else they've done, Erich. The Bolshevik threat has been nullified, unemployment is on the way down, crime has halved and the wages in your pocket are worth more than ever before.'

'We'll have to agree to disagree, Canaris,' the General said.

197

CHAPTER 52

[09/07/1933 Sunday]

By the time they got home, Erich Kästner had been forgiven; Maria could never be angry with him for long. Yosef met them at the yacht club dock and, after Captain Canaris had made his goodbyes, the navy man had shouldered his kitbag and strolled off in the direction of Tirpitzhafen, and his ship.

At the Kästner house, it took a while for anyone other than Antje to get a word in, so eager was she to tell her mother every detail about the voyage.

'At least your father didn't take you to a tavern. Thank goodness for small mercies.'

The General had watched Maria frown when Antje spoke of swimming in the strong currents off Wangerooge, and of their blind groping through the fog-bound muddy creeks from Büsum to Brunsbüttel, but at least there were no salacious tales of night-time depravity to upset her.

Later, in bed, she told him about her pride in Eva; how she'd charmed the countess and her friends and impressed the young men she'd been introduced to.

He'd had to bite his tongue, sure that these people were somehow using his wife and daughter. He'd fought in the Kaiser's army and had seen the ruling classes at their worst, using whole battalions of men as expendable pawns in what was a game to them, designed to keep them in power whatever else happened.

He'd been glad when the monarchy had been abolished by the victorious French and the English, and replaced by the Weimar Republic, but he knew that Maria came from a background where social standing was held above all else. For him, it hadn't spoiled her, but it sometimes drove her to strive for social acceptance with people like these, and it surfaced from time to time, as now, when she considered her children's prospects.

'She's just turned fifteen,' he said. 'She's still very young.'

'She's grown up for her age and, anyway, it's never too early to mix with the right people, to be seen.'

'I'm sure Eva will make up her own mind. As long as she's happy.'

It sounded glib, but it was true.

'We must guide her though; we don't want her marrying the first boy that comes along and she falls in love with.'

'You married for love, to a lowly major, my dear,' he said, gently mocking her.

'Yes,' she replied, 'but only because your father was an admiral,' she said, giggling.

He reached out for her.

'So, m'lady,' he said, in his roughest dockyard voice, 'you're trying to say that you wouldn't have been with me if I'd been of lowly stock.'

'Well...'

CHAPTER 53

[10/07/1933 Monday]

In the week before the Kästner family decamped to the admiral's lodge in the Harz mountains, the weather stayed glorious, and Johann, Eva, Antje, Ruth, and Manny hung around the lakeside most days. Even Franz joined in, helping Johann rescue the old dinghies from the hardstanding beside the boathouse, spending two days painting their hulls, varnishing topsides, and repairing the sails.

'It's been years since we've had these out,' Johann said to his brother.

'It must be three or four,' Franz replied. 'I was about twelve. We moved up to the bigger classes after that.'

'They've scrubbed up well. Let's get the others.'

Eva refused point blank to have anything to do with the dinghies. Every day, Franz took Manny with him in the red one, and Johann took the girls in the green boat. The wind was often slight, so the races they devised were as much about mucking around in the water as they were about sailing; reach the buoy, swim to the shore, and touch the tree, swim back, sail at a snail's pace to the jetty and collect a bucket and fill it with water, then attempt to empty it into the other boat. Only late in the afternoons did any sort of decent breeze get up, and they could get the little dinghies going in proper competition.

~~o~~

Around midday on the Wednesday, the Böhms appeared, fresh back from a fortnight in Bavaria. Manny began to huff when Johann told him to change places and give Lise a turn in the boat until Ruth and Antje, giving way to Eberhard, explained to him that Lise was Franz's special girl and he shouldn't take it personally that he preferred, for a while at least, to be out on the lake with her.

Johann watched Franz, expecting him to give up sailing and drift to the most secluded corner of the lake to be alone with Lise, but when Franz's dinghy surged past him and a shout of 'Loser' rang in his ear, he presumed that Franz wanted to show off first.

Clever, he thought.

He narrowly lost the fifteen-minute battle and was about to take his hat off to his brother, assuming that the excitement of the race was part of Franz's grand plan to seduce Lise, as far away from the Kästner and Böhm families as he could, when Franz made for the shore and lifted Manny back into the boat.

With the extra person on board, Franz's dinghy was just a little bit slower, and Johann and Eberhard pulled ahead, winning the second race by a couple of boat-lengths. Ruth and Antje shouted encouragement from the jetty, waving a flag made from a branch and a handkerchief as they crossed the finishing line.

Johann watched Lise as she got out of Franz's boat. Her bearing was stiff, and her face was a mixture of irritation and disappointment. He shook his head.

Franz might be older, but he has a lot to learn about girls.

~~o~~

'I got your last postcard today.'

Ruth and Antje lay on the grass, picking daisies and making chains of them. The others had all gone indoors, leaving them alone by the lake.

'I sent one from every island we visited. I thought you'd like that.'

'They're great. It all sounds so exciting. I wish I could have been there.'

'I'll ask Papa if you can come next time. I'm sure he wouldn't mind. There's room for both of us to sleep in the forecabin. That's the bit at the front of the boat.'

A flash of disappointment dulled Ruth's smile.

'I don't think I'd be allowed to go.'

'Why? It wasn't dangerous, really. Well, apart from the bit in the fog. That felt a bit scary.'

'I just know Mama wouldn't let me go.'

'Ask anyway. I can't see why she would object.'

'I'll think about it,' she said, but she knew she would never ask. She wasn't sure why, but her parents rarely agreed to let her go to anything that Antje invited her to take part in; trips to the lodge at Oderbrück, previous sailing expeditions, skiing last year in the Bavarian Alps; each time there had been a different excuse.

'Wait here,' Antje said, jumping up, and running into the house. Ruth turned on her back and watched as Antje briefly appeared at the large stair window before bounding up to her bedroom. She looked up at the sky, tracking the clouds on their route from one side of the lake to the other.

She didn't see Antje hurtling back down the stairs, so the first she knew was her best friend thudding down onto the grass beside her.

'Here,' she said, handing Ruth a piece of paper, folded.

'What is it?' Ruth asked, taking it from her.

'It's for you,' Antje said, watching her friend as she opened it, the best of her sketches of the Sturmtaucher, the one soaring above a dark sea.

'Oh, Antje, it's beautiful. Did you draw this while you were away?'

'Yes, we finally found some, on our last day in the Nordsee.'

'I'll keep it forever,' Ruth told her, hugging her friend.

CHAPTER 54

KIELER MORGENPOST

Saturday 15th July 1933

REPEAL OF NATURALISATION OF IMMIGRANT JEWS

The Law for the Repeal of Naturalisation and Recognition of German Citizenship was passed yesterday by the German government. Jewish immigrants who have been recently naturalised will have their citizenship revoked. A spokesman for the Government made the announcement and said "The Weimar Government were over-zealous in their acceptance of immigrants from Eastern Europe. The purpose of this act is to reverse those mistakes. This does not affect naturalised Germans of non-Jewish origin. As of yet, there are no immediate plans for the repatriation of any de-naturalised individuals".

~~o~~

The General finished reading the headline article. The rest of the front page and the four following pages were filled with the usual party propaganda, mixed with small snippets of local news to give the appearance that the *Kieler Morgenpost* was still a newspaper. Tucked away among the advertisements, notices and announcements on page six, the General found what he was looking for.

IN PARLIAMENT TODAY

The German parliament has issued a law making the Founding of New Political Parties illegal.

The German government also issued the Law for the Prevention of Offspring with Hereditary Diseases.

No detail, no explanation, no commentary.

A few weeks before, the General had received an interesting visit from a former soldier, a sergeant who'd served under him ten years before. The man had visited Kiel with his wife, telling his friends he'd always desired to see the city and its wonderful natural harbour. He'd hung around across from Naval Headquarters for an hour, waiting for the General to leave before approaching him.

'You'll not remember me,' he'd said as the General reached his car, turning to look at the man in curiosity.

The General had stared for a second, then the confusion on his face cleared.

'You were the battalion boxing champion, sergeant, two years running. It's good to see you. What are you doing here?'

'I came to speak with you, sir, to see if I could be of service. I heard that you were working with army intelligence.'

'Yes, I'm with the Abwehr. How can I be of help?'

'I'm a civil servant now, I work in the Reichstag.'

'Ah. I see.' The General tried to keep the surprise from his face. The man was the least likely-looking clerk he could imagine.

'I hear and see a lot of things that I don't like, sir. Some of it could be useful to the Reichswehr. I thought you'd know what to do with it.'

'You do realise that you'd be putting yourself in danger?'

'I'd like to do something, sir. It wouldn't be exactly state secrets, sir, just things that they would rather not publicise.'

'Well, if you're happy to pass these useful bits of information to me, I'd certainly make sure they got into the right hands.'

'Thank you, sir. I knew you were the man to see.'

'Can I offer you something to eat? Are you going back to Berlin today?'

'No, sir, my wife is with me. She wouldn't be comfortable... We're staying overnight, and they provide an evening meal at our guest house, but thanks for asking, sir.'

They had exchanged telephone numbers, then the General had watched the man walk across to the promenade to join his wife. She'd looked over, then the couple had turned and walked briskly towards the centre of town.

As a result of their meeting, the General now had a source of low grade, but useful information from the centre of power in Berlin and it was from the ex-sergeant that he'd learned of the three new pieces of legislation that had been rushed through parliament the day before. It didn't surprise him that only one of them had made the front page of the *Morgenpost*.

He lifted the memo he'd left on his desk and looked at it.

Memo: Geh.KdoS. ABW 14/07/33 CAC0205.1

For Attention Only: All senior executive officers, Abwehr.

From: Captain Conrad Patzig, Chef der Abwehr.

The German parliament has passed the Law against the Founding of New Political Parties.

This establishes the National Socialist Party as the sole legal political party in Germany. [END]

The fact that only one of the new laws they'd passed had been deemed important enough, or relevant, to be the subject of a memo from head office didn't surprise him either, or that it was a different one from the law considered newsworthy by the *Morgenpost*, because it was the only one that had any relevance to the Reichswehr.

Part of the army's role should have been to restore the rule of law when democracy was at risk, but the General didn't think the army would contemplate taking action in this instance, as most of the policies the government intended to implement were in line with the armed forces' objectives.

That left the third of the new laws that the government had placed on the statute book. His heart sank as he remembered the telephone call from his Reichstag source, late the previous afternoon, detailing the third piece of legislation that had been passed without being opposed.

'The Law for the Prevention of Offspring with Hereditary Diseases,' his informant had said, his voice echoing on the line from Berlin, 'mandates the forced sterilisation of people with physical and mental disabilities, as well as Roma Gypsies, asocial elements and Afro-Germans, amongst others.'

He could see the reasons why the *Morgenpost* had buried it deep within its innermost pages and why the Abwehr had ignored it.

Asocial elements could be anyone the NSDAP didn't like.

CHAPTER 55

Erich Kästner sat back and stretched, eyeing the view across the valley. The lodge at Oderbrück had been in the family since the General was a boy. Before his parents had made it their permanent home when Erich had married Maria, it had been their holiday home, where the family would spend a whole month of summer and the odd week or weekend during the rest of the year.

It had enough room for all the Kästners, even when Erich's sister, her husband, and her brood visited at the same time as the General and his family. Since the admiral and his wife had made it their full-time home, this didn't happen more than a couple of weeks a year; it was a squeeze to fit everyone in, although the children, especially when they were younger, loved bunking up in temporary beds in the basement when the house was full.

In winter, when snow covered the track, trails, and roads around Oderbrück, the family would ski for miles through the Harz mountains. In summer, they would walk the same trails, or swim at the top end of the reservoir, where the small river ran into its shallows.

'The youngsters have gone to the lake. Could I tempt you with a beer, son?'

'That would be great. I feel better having freshened up. That was a long drive.'

The admiral chuckled as he descended the cellar steps, calling behind him, 'You're too used to being driven round.'

A few moments later, he returned with two frothing beers.

'You installed a barrel, and a tap?' Erich laughed.

'One of my small indulgencies. It's amazing how much better it tastes.'

The General took a sip. 'This is excellent.'

'Maria and your mother are off admiring the new décor. As if it wasn't good enough the way it was. Women, eh?'

'Women indeed. Where would we be without them though?'

The two military leaders, past and present, sat together in the kitchen of the mountain lodge as father and son, sharing a beer. Each savoured the taste of the hops and the view, enjoying the quietness, wholly at ease in each other's company.

The admiral broke the silence.

'How are things with you, my boy. Are you staying for a few days?'

'No, I'm heading back tomorrow. We have a couple of big weeks in store. There's a massive expansion coming up in both shipyards, and in the victualling depots in Kiel. I seem to have found my niche in negotiations with the city's politicians, in addition to my liaison role within the Reichswehr.'

'How did you get involved with that?'

'I got bored, really. The position I have is a strange one; there's really not much come and go between the Reichsmarine and the Reichsheer,' Erich said, 'as yet.'

'So, you just decided to branch out?' The admiral laughed.

'No, I just made myself useful helping smooth things out around Reichsmarine Headquarters, and it gradually just slipped into my lap. You do know my role is more of an intelligence one, don't you?'

'I assumed that it was. And young Canaris dropped a hint or two.'

Erich laughed. 'Young? Canaris? I haven't heard him called that for a while. But yes, I believe he was instrumental in my being offered the post.'

'I didn't ever see you as the cloak-and-dagger type.'

'It's not really like that. It's more about collecting information that's pertinent and relaying it to my superiors, and occasionally passing information in the opposite direction. The Abwehr want to know what is going on within the navy, and to keep the navy informed of matters that may not be purely military in nature but could impact on their role.'

'Ah, so you're one of these new propaganda men I'm hearing about.'

'No. God forbid. I'm not dealing in exaggeration and gloss, just facts. The right ones in the right ears. Anyway, I figured that the Abwehr would want to know what is going on in the wider world outside naval confines, so I thought it would do no harm in cultivating a few local politicians, amongst others.'

'Ah. And you have the contacts. Very shrewd. I'm guessing you've kept in touch with the current mayor, the police chief, and one or two civil servants?'

'It works both ways. I can get them access to the right people within the Reichsmarine, who can oil the wheels of cooperation between the navy and the city, and in the process, I collect a useful amount of intelligence that I can pass on to my superiors.'

'So where did you learn all this subterfuge and diplomacy?'

'I'm a general, you were an admiral. Subterfuge and diplomacy are just part of the job. You know as well as I do that massaging egos, 'encouraging' cooperation in people and ferreting away knowledge about friends and rivals was a big part of what we did.'

The admiral laughed. 'It was a bit simpler in my day, but I agree, up to a point. Of course, the modern military is a different beast nowadays.'

'And our political masters have changed.'

The admiral's smile disappeared.

'Be careful, Erich. They are becoming extremely powerful. And they don't like dissenting voices.'

'I have to be careful. There are many in the Reichswehr who support the reforms the National Socialists are implementing and are willing to accept their less than palatable politics for the chance to rebuild Germany's military power. I only pray that they won't regret it.'

'I'm hoping that this government won't survive too much longer. There are grumblings already. It will, unfortunately, have to run its natural course; the economy will eventually implode, and the people will reject this lot and elect the next shower of imbeciles.'

'I'm not so sure. Day by day, they're tightening their grip on every facet of normal life. Even if the people wanted to change, I'm not sure they could now. And that's assuming they'd ever want Adolf Hitler out. A lot of good people have been seduced by him, even those who should know better.'

The admiral reached forward and placed his hand on his son's arm. 'People are fed up with being poor. They want to get back some national pride. And they're frightened of Russia, and the communists. Adolf Hitler seems to be the solution to all of these problems.'

Erich Kästner stared at his father and wondered if the old man's pragmatism had stretched as far as giving reluctant support for the regime.

'Look, Erich,' the admiral continued. 'I don't like the man, but I can see the effect he has on the public. I don't think you or I can change that. But we need good people to moderate some of his worst excesses, and perhaps pick up the pieces later, even if that means working away quietly, keeping their heads down, for now at least.'

'And if that means that people like Yosef, Miriam and their family are persecuted?'

He saw his father flinch.

'It's up to us to protect them, then.'

'I'm not just talking about them. I can look after my own Jews. What about their friends? Can we protect them?'

The admiral stayed silent.

'They can't touch me,' the General continued. 'I have the backing of the army, and the navy, for that matter. But I need to do something, even if it's just more of what I'm doing now, using the Abwehr...'

'Just be careful,' the admiral repeated, 'That's all I ask.'

CHAPTER 56

'I can't believe you still want to race us. I feel bad about humiliating our own father.'

Johann's face didn't betray the laughter that was bubbling up inside; he maintained a veneer of sympathy that didn't fool his father for a second.

'It's not a forgone conclusion, boys; we are using handicaps.'

'That won't help you. There's no allowance for a geriatric crew.' His voice finally broke, and he gave in to the laughter that he'd suppressed with such difficulty.

'Johann, show a bit of respect,' his brother told him, but Johann could see that Franz was struggling to keep a straight face himself.

'We'll see. Sometimes experience is more of a factor than you might think. Who's crewing for you?'

'We have Marcus, and Lise is coming along,' Johann said, his smile fading. 'She insisted. Thinks it will be exciting. As long as she doesn't get in the way…'

Johann glanced at Franz.

'She'll be fine. Stop moaning.'

The General turned to his daughter and put his arm around her shoulder.

'Come on, Antje. We'll leave these two fighting and go and find our crew.' He turned to the boys. 'Once you've all met up, join us in the clubhouse and we'll go over the rules.'

~~o~~

By half past six, both crews were in the bar.

'I'm sorry, Dieter Maas is running late,' the General said, 'but he should be here by the gun.'

He looked around. There had been a certain amount of good-natured baiting while they waited for everyone to arrive, mostly at the expense of the General's older crew.

'Usual rules, gentlemen, and ladies,' he said, looking around at the strange group. 'Five-minute warning signal, four-minute preparatory signal, one-minute warning signal, starting signal. Standard handicaps. We have four minutes, you have three.'

'A suggestion, Father. To make it more of a race, why don't we give you the time at the start, then when we overtake you, we'll be sailing in real time?'

'No, we don't want a staggered start. What about you circling the starting mark three times on the second lap? That should use up your minute.'

Franz looked at Johann.

The General imagined that they were both thinking the same thing. It might take a minute for *Snowgoose* to spin round the mark three times; their own boat could cut it to forty seconds.

He saw them nod to each other.

'Fine,' Franz said. 'We're happy with that.'

The General used the sailing club's blackboard to sketch out the course.

'Windward leg first. The start is between the end of Adalbert-Brücke and the starboard channel marker. The first turn is the port channel buoy off Mönkeberg, then come across the fjord and round the starboard marker off the Reichswehr swimming baths, then back down to the start. Two laps, and may the best boat win.'

Franz drew the course in his notebook, then shut it with a snap.

Dieter Maas arrived just as they left the clubhouse.

'Glad you could make it, Herr Maas,' Franz said, 'It's important to keep the average age of the crew on my father's boat down.'

Dieter laughed, and patted Franz on the back. 'We'll see,' he said.

As they boarded the boats, Johann couldn't resist a final barb.

'We'll get the drinks in. Just don't be too far behind.'

Franz and Johann were still laughing when their boat left the dock. Erich Kästner heard them and smiled.

Dieter Maas leaned over towards the General. 'Done,' he whispered.

~~o~~

'The bastard.'

'Don't curse in front of Lise,' Franz hissed at his younger brother, glaring at him.

'That start signal was twenty seconds early, I swear,' Johann complained. 'They set it off just as we turned away to make our final approach, and they were right at the line.'

'Are you sure?' Franz thought for a moment. 'It did seem a short minute. Did anyone time it?'

They all shook their heads.

Franz straightened the boat up and they crossed the line, heavily heeled over in the stiff breeze.

'Don't worry, we'll catch them up. They only have a twenty-second lead. And don't say anything to them when we finish. There's no point; it's our word against theirs. It will sound like sour grapes.'

'Fine,' Johann said, 'but now we definitely have to beat them, and by a reasonable margin.'

Franz laughed. Johann was the more competitive of the two, but Franz had the cooler head. They gained steadily on their father's boat with each tack, but not as much as he expected. The old man was getting the most out of the slower boat and Franz smiled.

This is going to be a race after all.

As they passed the naval victualling depot, Franz judged that they would be unlikely to pass *Snowgoose* before the mark but, if he managed to get a good turn, the nimbler boat would retain more momentum and give them a chance to take the General early in the second leg, across the wind. Even taking into account the three extra turns at the start of the second lap, providing they were ahead before they got there, they could make up the time they'd lose circling the start marker.

The General's boat made to turn but left a small gap. It looked like an error, but Franz knew that his father was giving him a glimpse of clear water to tempt him into making a dive inside and perhaps missing the mark, so he feathered the boat and stood off *Snowgoose*'s stern until they had turned round the large red steel buoy that marked the east side of the channel used by large ships heading towards the inner reaches of Kieler Hafen.

As Franz had anticipated, they turned faster and retained more speed than the boat in front, allowing them to draw level on the outside. He could see his father pulling up on the traveller to shape the mainsail, getting every ounce out of the wind, but to no advantage. Inch by inch, they crept past the older yacht, whooping and hollering as they did.

The crew of the *Snowgoose* ignored them.

It was a fast leg, and the Hitlerjugend yacht reached the mark a boat-length ahead. Franz looked back and noticed his father's crew preparing the spinnaker. His own crew was also ready and, as soon as they'd made the mark and turned downwind, he shouted for them to hoist it.

The sail billowed from the front of the boat as Marcus, an experienced foredeck man, released it from its bag at the bow and hauled up on the halyard. Johann worked the guy and the sheet at the stern of the boat, which surged forward as the sail filled, driving the yacht towards the start/finish line for the second lap.

'We must keep the boat tight doing our three turns round the mark at the end of this leg, to make them take a wide line. Use the number-two jib,' Johann shouted.

'Good thinking,' his brother replied. 'Let's get that spinnaker away in plenty time, we don't want it wrapped round the forestay.'

Between them, they managed to haul down the spinnaker and bag it and raise the smaller foresail. Lise looked on in confusion, trying to stay out of the way.

~~o~~

On *Snowgoose*, Erich Kästner watched, impressed at the boys' skill in circling the mark, keeping the mainsail sheeted and using the foresail to drive the boat round, a gybe and a tack in every turn.

Forced to take a wide line, the General's boat didn't pass the other yacht until the end of its second turn, and as he settled into the upwind leg, he looked back to see them only a few boat-lengths behind, now with their largest foresail flying.

Antje shouted to him as her brother seemed to coax a little extra speed out of the trailing yacht, gaining on them, inch by inch, tack by tack.

'They're catching us, Papa. Go faster.'

'We need a push. You're a good swimmer; dive in and give us a hand.' He laughed, loving the excitement flushing his daughter's face.

She wrinkled her nose at him.

'Here,' he said, 'you take her.'

'I can't. We'll lose.'

'Take it. Do exactly as I say. We'll not lose.'

The General glanced at Dieter Maas and grinned, then looked over his shoulder at the other yacht, now only metres behind them.

He muttered something that Antje didn't catch.

'It'll be fine,' Dieter said.

They reached the first mark for the second time, a nose in front, and took the tightest line they could, only inches from touching it.

The General shouted a warning, 'Fingers!' and they all pulled their hands away from the gunwale, but the boat and the buoy didn't touch. Franz had to slow to avoid hitting the stern of the boat in front but as soon as they'd passed the mark, he cut to the starboard side of his father, trying to pass upwind.

'He's trying to steal our wind,' the General said. 'The moment he gets alongside, we'll be in his shadow.'

He turned to Antje. 'Steer five degrees to starboard.'

She pulled the tiller towards her, and the General looked back to see Franz follow her move.

'We can't keep doing that,' he said. 'If we get too far upwind of the next mark, it will leave a big gap for him to pass us on the inside, and he can stay far enough away from us to avoid our wind shadow.'

They maintained their course for another two cables.

'Ten degrees to port, Antje.'

She pushed the tiller away, and the boat headed for the mark again. 'You keep the helm while we get the spinnaker up. Give the mark a decent offing so that there's no danger of hitting it, and head straight for the line.'

He turned to his crew. 'Doc, this time, you only need to work the guy. I'll do the sheet. Oskar, the same again; it was great the last time, but just a little faster. Dieter, that halyard has to go up in seconds.'

'Aye skipper,' they chorused, just as the nose of Franz's boat came abreast of their beam, five metres away.

'We're about to lose wind,' the General shouted, and the mainsail began to luff as the faster boat's sails choked the stream of air crossing *Snowgoose*'s decks.

'Bear away five degrees,' he added, and Antje swung the tiller.

'Won't that make it easier for him to pass us?'

'Don't worry, it won't be for long.' He grinned at her.

Antje looked at her father, a puzzled frown on her face.

She noticed him and Dieter Maas watching intently at the forward end of the boys' boat, and she glanced to see what they were looking at but there was nothing amiss, from where she stood. They were now over halfway to the last turn, and she couldn't figure any way they could catch the boys.

Just as she'd given up on the victory, a shout came from the boat ahead and she watched in fascination as their foresail suddenly flew out in front of the forestay, flapping and cracking like a whip in the wind. She watched Johann scurry along the deck to the bow, shouting for Marcus to grab the jib sheet from the water.

'Their jib sheet has come loose,' the Doc shouted, 'we can take them.'

'Steady on this course, Antje, we'll pass them to leeward.'

She looked at her father. 'How did you know…' Her voice petered out, seeing his smile.

'You always plan for every eventuality, Antje.'

They were now level with the stern of the flailing boat. Johann was struggling to gather in the loose sail; every time he seemed to have most of it in his arms, the wind would gust, and it would shoot out again. The jib sheet had become unthreaded from its fairlead, and Marcus was trying to feed it back through, but he'd taken it around the wrong side of one of the stanchions and had to redo it, losing vital seconds.

On the Hitlerjugend boat, Franz saw the carnage on deck and took a deep breath.

'Lise, take the wheel and hold her steady,' he said, showing her how to grip it. 'Turn it clockwise when I say starboard and anti-clockwise for port.'

She nodded, her face pale. Despite the clamour around him, he thought she looked wonderful.

'I'm pulling in the starboard sheet,' he shouted to Johann and Marcus. 'Be ready to tie the port sheet back on once it's tight.'

Johann jumped back to help Marcus, realising that he'd wasted time trying to hold the unruly sail.

'The sail will be on the wrong side,' Marcus shouted. 'It will stall us.'

'It will only be for a few seconds. At least we can get the port sheet tied on without it flapping.'

Franz sensed the General's boat passing them on their port side but, concentrating on getting the jib sheet fixed, he didn't see the wide grins of the opposing crew as they waved on their way past.

Johann finished tying the bowline onto the clew of the jib and threw on an extra hitch so that there was no danger of it coming out again and shouted to Franz that he could release the starboard sheet.

Franz let it go, and jumped across to the other side, frantically hauling in the port sheet until the sail filled and they began to pick up speed.

'Keep her steady at that, Lise. You're doing fine.'

He ducked his head under the foresail and watched his father's boat reach the mark, at least two hundred metres ahead, and fly the spinnaker as they turned. It was the slickest he'd seen them do it and, at that moment, he realised they'd lost. He cursed under his breath, knowing that their father would not let them forget it.

His face broke into a grin as the penny dropped.

The bastards loosened the jib sheet. That's why Dieter Maas was late!

He started to laugh.

He knew we wouldn't check. Not for a little race like this.

'What the hell are you laughing at?' Johann asked, annoyed. 'We're going to lose.'

'Let's try and catch them. At least make a race of it.'

He didn't know if Johann had fathomed out that they'd been spiked. He wasn't sure his brother would see the funny side of it, so he kept his suspicions to himself.

'Drop the foresail. Ready the spinnaker.'

Their turn was as slick as the one his father's crew had made, and as they rounded into their wake, he urged the boat on.

~~o~~

The General's crew crossed the line two boat-lengths ahead. He hadn't looked back once during the last leg of the race, but he could feel the anxious glances that his crew were taking at the chasing boat, edging closer with every minute.

A hundred yards beyond the finishing line, he told Antje to turn the boat across the wind and make their way back to the yacht harbour.

'Ahoy, *Snowgoose*. Well done.'

The General and his crew waved as the chasing boat slowed and drifted towards them. Johann looked as if he would like to sulk, but the General knew that his son wouldn't hold a grudge. He wondered if either of the boys had worked it out yet.

'Let's sail her in, boys,' he said. 'It's not a night for the engine.'

With skill, the General worked the boat, finessing it in through the harbour entrance and up to the jetty, his quiet commands given to Antje on the tiller, the Doc on the main sheet and Oskar on the jib, feathering the sails to keep just enough way on the boat to give enough steerage.

Dieter prepared the warps, and as the boat gently nudged against the jetty, he had the bowline secured and the boat sat against the dockside, held by the wind.

Franz berthed the Hitlerjugend yacht behind *Snowgoose*, equal in skill to his father under sail. He helped Lise onto the jetty and walked forward to the winning boat, his crew following him to shake the winners' hands.

The General knew the loss was hurting Johann, and his son could only bring himself to congratulate him on a 'fortuitous victory'.

'They all count,' the General said. 'We were lucky that you had that sail malfunction.'

Franz smiled wryly at his father. 'Yes, although, you know what they say. You make your own luck.'

Dieter and the General glanced at each other, and at Franz. The corners of the young man's mouth twitched in a smile, mirrored on the faces of the two older men.

CHAPTER 57

[04/09/1933 Monday]

A little over a fortnight later, Franz stood at the gates of the Kriegsakademie, being photographed with his proud family, saying his farewells.

He shuffled his feet, looking around anxiously, but the other new recruits were also standing with their parents and siblings, embarrassed, like him, at the fuss being made of them.

Two older officer candidates passed by, looking with disdain at the young men and their kitbags.

Franz could imagine what they were thinking. *Mummy's boys. We'll soon sort them out.*

His grandmother was there to see him off, joining his mother and father, and his three siblings; the officers' training school was in Hanover, so it was no surprise that she'd come to see her oldest grandson take the first steps in his military career.

'Look after yourself, Franz,' his mother said, a tear running down her cheek.

'I'll be home in three weeks, Mama,' he said, frowning.

'I know, but you're so grown up, and handsome…'

Franz blushed, hoping that none of the other recruits had overheard.

The General shook his hand.

'You'll do well, son. Just keep your head down and remember to be your own man.'

Franz smiled, then hugged his two sisters and, finally, Johann.

'I'll be here next year,' Johann said, 'and six months after that we'll be in the same *Kompanie*.'

With a final wave, Franz shouldered his bag and climbed the steps. He had no illusions about how tough it would be, but his father had been through the same classrooms and drill halls and he was confident he would not only succeed, but he would enjoy himself. Starting Monday, his initial boot camp would last six months, then he would move on to one of the regiments, to complete his officer training in the field.

He walked through the doors without looking back.

~~o~~

[22/09/1933 Friday]

It had been a gruelling few weeks, and Franz was glad to be home on leave.

But he hadn't expected to be standing in the quadrangle of Kiel University, watching with morbid fascination a scene from *Les Misérables*.

Lise had begged him to come and, with misgivings, he'd agreed to accompany her.

Despite his uneasiness, he looked around with pride; although Lise was younger than the other girls, she was by far the most beautiful. They stood next to her cousin, a student at the university, who had invited them to watch. Holding Franz's hand and ducking under his arm, she pressed against him, making his skin glow warm where she touched him. She leaned up and kissed him on the corner of his mouth.

He glanced at her, but she'd turned back to watch, her eyes shining.

Two lines of fresh-faced Brownshirts, students themselves, watched a line of young men and women file towards the centre of the quadrangle, each tossing a handful of books onto the steadily increasing pile, now the height of a man. Every so often, one of their companions would lift a jerrycan and pour some petrol onto the pyre, the fumes making Franz's eyes water. He tried to read some of the titles but, at first, they'd been academic books, few of which he'd heard of.

Then he spotted a couple of novels that he'd read. *Berlin Alexanderplatz* was there, by Alfred Döblin, and he saw Max Brod's *Schloss Nornepygge* join the pile. Both were books that his favourite German teacher had recommended. As the mound grew, he recognised a few more world-renowned German authors on their spines; Bertolt Brecht, Albert Einstein, Sigmund Freud, and Karl Marx.

And he wasn't surprised to see works by foreign writers littered among them. Novels by Victor Hugo, Hemingway, Dostoyevsky, and D.H. Lawrence were added to the pile and he wondered who had chosen the books that were to be burned.

The line dwindled, and finally halted. A young earnest man stepped forward. He started to speak, and the crowd hushed.

'Fellow students and patriots, for too long, our university has been a haven for malcontents and troublemakers. Jews, who would like us to be part of the Bolshevik empire, stole our universities from under our very noses.'

A smattering of applause from his fellow students interrupted his words.

'We would ask you to boycott those professors and teachers who preach sedition on campus or encourage those students who would promote disloyalty to our government, and to our chancellor, Adolf Hitler.'

This time, the response was louder, and there were a few shouts of encouragement. Franz looked around, but could see no dissenters, and the SA men looked relaxed, not expecting trouble.

'These books,' he said, pointing to the heap, 'have sullied our library for too long. Now, they will perish in the flames of righteous anger.'

'Heil Hitler.' His arm snapped skywards, outstretched in fervent salute. Most of the students responded. Franz, prompted by a nudge from Lise, did the same.

The young speaker nodded to one of the brown-shirted students, who struck a match, amid the cheers and chants of the student mob.

As the pyre exploded into flame, a photographer stepped forward and encouraged a few of the students to pick up books from the periphery of the pile, and throw them onto the blaze, while he flashed his camera, framing the young orator against the crowd and the buildings behind, in what looked to Franz like a scene from a pagan ritual.

He watched for a while, then, shepherding a reluctant Lise, slipped through the crowd and away, back towards the centre of town.

CHAPTER 58

KIELER MORGENPOST

Saturday 23rd September 1933

FAITH MOVEMENT OF GERMAN CHRISTIANS TRIUMPHS AT SYNOD

At the Synod of the German Evangelical Church in Rendsburg the Faith Movement of German Christians won the decisive vote to bring church doctrine in line with state thinking. "A return to the pure principals of Lutheranism is to replace the emphasis on Old Testament teaching that has crept into the church's liturgy", the newly elected Archbishop Landsbergen stated. Professor Emmanuel Hirsch, leader of the Luther Renaissance Movement, reminded the Synod that "Martin Luther had emphasised the respect for temporal or secular authority, which was reinforced by scripture in Romans, chapter 13".

~~o~~

'I'll not be at church tomorrow. You can go if you wish.'

Maria, startled, said nothing as her husband got up from the breakfast table and left the kitchen. She'd been a million miles away, planning a dinner party and wondering when to tell Erich that she'd like to invite the countess to it.

She made to follow him, wondering what he had on that was so important that he'd miss church, but something stopped her. Miriam and Yosef were at the synagogue, so she stacked the plates in the sink, and tidied up the kitchen.

She picked up the paper. The headline caught her eye. In the picture to the right of it, the new archbishop stood on the lectern of Rendsburg Cathedral, flanked by his two bishops, all in NSDAP uniforms, a large swastika flag draped behind them.

She sighed.

~~o~~

[29/09/1933 Friday]

KIELER JÜDISCHES FREIHEITSNACHRICHTENBLATT

Volume 6

Tishrei 9, 5694

JEWS BANNED FROM WORKING IN CULTURAL SECTOR

From last week, membership of the newly founded Chambers of Literature, Press, Broadcasting, Theatre, Film, Music, and Fine Arts is to be denied to citizens of Jewish origin. Being a member of the appropriate chamber is a prerequisite for employment within the cultural sector, effectively banning Jews from the workforce in these areas.

JEWS TO BE OUSTED FROM ERBHÖFE

The German government has issued the Hereditary Farm Law, stipulating that hereditary farms could only be inherited by German farmers able to document that they had no Jewish or coloured ancestors back to January 1, 1800. In an official statement, Oberpräsident Henrich Lohse stated that there was no truth in reports that farms seized from their Jewish owners would be reassigned to members of the party.

WORD OF THE WEEK

"Ahnenpaß". The identification card which must be carried by all "true Germans" to demonstrate their Aryan race lineage.

CHAPTER 59

'We finally won a proper race. Well done to my wonderful crew. Prost.'

The General held his glass aloft.

'Prost,' the four men sitting with him echoed.

'It made all the difference having young Heinz on the foredeck,' Oskar von Friedeburg said. 'The spinnaker went up and down a treat today, and that gybe round the last mark but one was a thing of beauty.' He had a big smile on his face as he thumped the youngest member of the crew on the back.

They'd been behind their rival, the boat that had beaten them in every race, with only one leg to go, in the last race of the season. Coming up to the mark, the General had noticed that the leading boat approached it a little too wide, and had gone for the gap, scraping through without touching the buoy or the stern of the other boat.

'Gybe-ho,' he'd shouted, and as the yacht whipped round the buoy, the crew, in a series of choreographed moves that impressed even their skipper, dropped the pole and flipped the spinnaker onto the port side. As the giant sail filled, it stole all the wind from the other boat, and they watched it founder, its spinnaker collapsing amid shouts and curses. By the time they'd got it sorted out, *Snowgoose* was four lengths clear, and screaming for the line, the whoops of victory from the General's crew ringing in their ears.

The skipper of the yacht they'd finally pushed into second place approached the table and proffered his hand to the General and his crew.

'Well done, gentlemen. You did for us at that final mark. A lovely move.'

'That's terribly generous of you. We've been waiting some time to see you trailing in our wake.'

'Yes, indeed. My crew are blaming me, unfortunately,' he said with a smile. 'Took my eye off the ball, they're saying.' He looked over at his own crew, standing at the bar. 'Come and join us, we'd like to buy you a drink. Gracious losers, and all that nonsense.'

Laughing, they sauntered over to join their rivals. Races were rerun and analysed, mistakes highlighted, and blame apportioned with a smile. As the evening progressed, tales of previous victories and disasters became more and more exaggerated.

The General didn't get a chance to talk to Dieter Maas until the rest of the company had decided to walk outside to see the defeated skipper demonstrate how to find one's way in the dark, using a sextant which he'd retrieved from his boat, and the North Star, which conveniently shone in the cloudless night sky. He hoped that they wouldn't find their way off the end of the dock but left them to it and sat down next to the ex-newspaperman.

'So, what gives, Dieter?' he asked.

'Oskar enjoyed the race, and the celebrations, yes?'

The General laughed. 'He did. We all did. He's as competitive as the rest of us, truth be told. How's the job?'

'Excellent. I've been promoted. More of an editing position now. I kind of miss working with the machinery. It was good to get my hands dirty again.'

'And Oskar. It's not awkward, being on the boat with your boss?'

'I rarely see him at work; he puts the right people in place and lets them get on with it. We keep our business and social lives in separate boxes.'

'And our little project?'

'Well, I thought about what you said. I'm taking notes of everything that I see around me. Just for the record.'

The General smiled. 'And what's going on?'

'You've heard the latest way the government are going to encourage good Germans to produce children?'

'No. I must have missed it. What's their plan?'

'The Unemployment Relief Act, passed earlier this month. A couple will receive a matrimonial loan of a thousand Reichsmarks when they get married provided that the wife has been in a job for six months and is prepared to leave that job, and the husband didn't earn more than a hundred and twenty-five Reichsmarks per month. If they go on to have four children, they can keep all the money they've borrowed.'

'Quite an incentive. Are families taking it up?'

'I've heard that it is proving to be extremely attractive to low-paid working families.'

'They're certainly planning for a thousand-year Reich. Anything else?'

'Back in the newspaper world, Benno Arndt would have been out of a job, even if he hadn't already been sacked.'

'Why. Have I missed something?'

'The Editors Law. Passed today. It forbids non-Aryans from working in journalism. The last few Jews, mostly copywriters and print boys, left the *Morgenpost* this afternoon, I heard.'

'When's it going to stop?' the General said.

'Not for a while, my friend. One hears grumbles about the economy, that there are plans to oust the NSDAP, that the people will reject the party at the next election, but I see no evidence for it. As far as I can see, Herr Hitler has tapped into something in the German psyche.'

'I've come to the same conclusion, I'm afraid.'

'I meet with a few groups and individuals who, shall we say, are less than enamoured with the current regime.'

The General frowned.

Dieter Maas glanced at him. 'Don't worry. I'm extremely careful, and anyway, these are all people who have been friends or acquaintances of mine for years, so it would seem more suspicious if I didn't associate with them occasionally.'

'Still, be careful, and trust no one.'

'I will, but they're a useful source of information and they're not afraid to speak in private.' He paused, then seemed to remember what he'd been going to tell the General.

'One of my friends made a comment which sums up the mood; he said that one third of the people are fanatical about Adolf Hitler and the National Socialists, one third are terrified and the rest are both fanatical and terrified.'

They both laughed, but it had a hollow ring to it.

CHAPTER 60

Mayor Hoffmann stood at the doorway of his office. It irked him that Hinrich Lohse sat at his mayoral desk while he himself stood, like some lackey, but he knew his position as the leader of Kiel's council was entirely at the man's whim, so he fixed a smile on his face.

'We are now free of Versailles and those whining French money-grabbers,' he heard the Gauleiter say.

He nodded. 'A tremendous move by the chancellor, Hinrich. We should have quit the League of Nations a long time ago.' He flinched, realising his words could be construed as criticism.

'I'm sure the timing was perfect, Jürgen,' Lohse said, glowering at the mayor. 'It was necessary to demonstrate that our military capability had grown to a level significant enough to make the French and their protectors, the British and Americans, think twice about trying to slap us down. Now, they'll skulk behind their borders and make a lot of noise, but they'll do nothing.'

'Of course, Hinrich. I didn't mean…'

'Be careful. You can be replaced. Make a mistake like that with anyone else and you might be.'

'So, do we not risk war?' the mayor asked, sweating profusely, and trying to move the conversation on.

'No, they won't dare. They haven't got the stomach for it. And in the meantime, we are preparing, mark my words. Everything you see happening here in Kiel is being replicated all over Germany. With us, it's the Reichsmarine; elsewhere it's the Reichsheer and if rumours are true, the Luftwaffe.'

'But we don't have an air force. It will take years.'

'I've been to a few social events in Berlin. Alcohol loosens tongues. We have been developing planes that are better than anything they have. The factories are ready to roll them out. And some of our commercial aeroplanes have been designed as military planes, with only simple modifications required to convert them to bombers.'

'And submarines,' blurted the mayor. 'I've seen the plans for the yard expansion. I'm not stupid. They're going to increase production as well as building more battleships, aren't they?'

Hinrich Lohse frowned, and the mayor felt his stomach lurch but when the man spoke, it was without annoyance.

'Yes,' he said. 'I believe we have been researching and developing U-boats that will outperform anything any of our enemies have, out of sight of their prying eyes. Our navy might never be as large as that of the British, or the Americans but, one day, our submarine fleet will force their surface ships to hide in the harbours they are so proud of.'

~~o~~

The General had come to the same conclusion three months earlier, even before he'd seen the work that was planned at both the Howaldtswerke shipyard and at the Friedrich Krupp Germaniawerft. A few passing comments and a chance encounter with Karl Dönitz, the soon-to-be commander of the training ship, *Emden*, planted the seed in his mind. The man had been a prominent U-boat captain during the war and had visited the Kiel shipyards on three occasions before taking up his command of the *Emden*.

Erich Kästner had bumped into Captain Canaris and Captain Dönitz at the entrance to

217

Naval Headquarters. The three men had chatted for a short while before Canaris and Dönitz had left together in a staff car. Looking out of the window of his office twenty minutes later, he saw the same car pull up onto the dockside of the Howaldtswerke yard opposite. Two men stepped out of it, and he grabbed the binoculars that sat on the windowsill, confirming that it was Canaris and Dönitz, chatting with senior yard management.

Later, Captain Canaris called in with the General before heading back to his ship, temporarily berthed in Cuxhaven.

'Canaris,' he asked his friend, 'you were involved in the U-boat fiasco in Japan, weren't you?'

'It was no fiasco, Kästner. Well, it was in a way, but the premise was good. It's no secret now, but back then, I was sent undercover to Osaka. The Japanese had agreed to let us continue to develop submarines away from the prying eyes of the French and the English. It was working well until the appropriation committee pulled the funding; something about wanting 'more cooperative' relations with the Atlantic powers…'

'And…'

'Well, I managed to arrange alternative financing. An Argentinian originally from the Rheinland and a German shipping company owner's son among them; Lohman, you remember him?'

'Yes, you told me about him at the time. That was why you got canned.' The General grinned.

The captain smiled, and sighed. 'There were some financial irregularities. Not involving me, but when the whole thing came out, I was sidelined for a while, as you know. A shore command at Wilhelmshaven.'

'I remember. You took it hard at the time.'

'I thought my career was over. It has had an impact, but I'm here now, with my own command.'

'And visiting shipyards with U-boat veterans. Most interesting.'

Captain Canaris lifted his head sharply.

'What…!' he spluttered.

'Even without the binoculars, at a thousand metres, I could see it was you. How was Herr Engel today?'

Erich Kästner had met the Howaldtswerk's yard engineer on a few occasions, a clever man with great vision and a capacity to get things done.

'You wily old fox. You were spying,' the captain said, giving him an accusatory look.

'It was hardly high espionage. I just looked out the window.' He laughed. 'Anyway, it was you who got me into this spymaster stuff.'

'I didn't realise you would take it quite so seriously.' Captain Canaris grinned at him.

'Submarines,' said the General. 'When are they planning to start?'

~~o~~

[17/10/1933 Tuesday]

KIELER JÜDISCHES FREIHEITSNACHRICHTENBLATT

Volume 6

Tishrei 27, 5694

OTTO EGGERSTEDT KILLED

Otto Eggerstedt, prominent Schleswig-Holstein politician and anti-NSDAP campaigner has been killed. He has been incarcerated in Esterwegen concentration camp since his arrest in May of this year. Camp authorities released a statement saying that he had been shot while attempting to escape from the camp during a work detail. Otto Eggerstedt was a sitting member of the Reichstag from 1921 to 1933.

Yosef read the rest of the story.

'Poor bastard,' he said, the curse slipping out.

'Yosef,' Miriam scolded. 'Mind your language, please.'

'The children are in bed, but, sorry, my love. It's Otto Eggerstedt. He's paid the price for speaking out.'

Miriam lifted her head from the socks she was darning and frowned in puzzlement.

'You know, the man who gave the Spiegel eulogy,' Josef said. 'He's been in Esterwegen since he was arrested in Altona. They shot him.'

A sadness coloured Miriam's face, but she said nothing.

Nowadays, these things are to be expected, like a man having a heart attack.

'They tried to deny it at first, but the other inmates managed to get word out that he had been shot in cold blood.'

'The poor man. And his family; it must be terrible for them.'

'It says here that he'd been inhumanely treated for months, that he was just a shell of a man. Then they took him out and shot him. The official line is that he tried to escape while he was outside the camp on a work detail.'

'Alav ha-shalom,' she murmured. *Peace be upon him.*

'HaShem yikom damo,' he replied, his voice flat and cold.

She looked up sharply. She knew that her people had, in the past, asked God to avenge the death of one of their own, but it was the first time she'd heard it spoken. And by her own husband.

~~o~~

Memo: Geh.KdoS. ABW 26/11/33 CAC0251.1

For Attention Only: All senior executive officers, Abwehr.

From: Captain Conrad Patzig, Chef der Abwehr.

The government has passed the Law against Dangerous Habitual Criminals. This gives the courts the power to imprison "habitual criminals" indefinitely if they are deemed to be dangerous to society. It also allows the authorities to castrate sex offenders. [END]

CHAPTER 61

'Daddy, can Ruth come with us to Oderbrück? It would be so much fun and I'm sure she would love it. She's never been skiing.'

The General put his pen down, pulled his chair back from the desk and sat Antje on his knee.

'Lieblingsmädchen,' he said, *favourite girl*, 'I'd be delighted if Ruth were able to come with us, but I don't think it will happen.'

'But why? She's my best friend. One of Johann's friends came last year.'

'It's complicated, Antje.' He paused. 'It would be easier if it were one of your other friends.'

'Is it because she's Jewish?'

Erich Kästner felt his jaw tighten, but he forced his voice to remain soft.

'No,' he said, hesitating, then with more conviction, 'No, it's not that. You've asked if Ruth could come with us before. Any time we've said we'd be happy to have her with us, Miriam and Yosef have always refused.'

He felt bad about putting the blame on the Nussbaums; he knew it was more complex than that. Although Maria and Miriam were close and got on very well, he knew that Miriam had reservations about her children being too dependent on the Kästners and, if he put himself in the Nussbaums' shoes, would he be the same?

And, to his shame, he also had to concede that Maria was lukewarm at best when he succeeded in getting her to agree to involve the Nussbaum children, and perhaps Miriam, sensing this, avoided any awkwardness by not allowing the children to go away with the Kästners.

He watched the confusion on Antje's face. 'You'll understand one day when you are a mother. I can't imagine it would feel very pleasant if someone else gave your children something you couldn't afford to give them yourself.'

'But then they'll not get the chance otherwise. And anyway, Mama wouldn't let me go to the Nussbaums' Passover dinner.'

Stunned by her logic, he struggled to find an answer.

'That's different. Your Mama didn't want you to be an intrusion, and the Nussbaums would have been too polite to refuse.' He hoped that was the reason.

He could see a tear of frustration in her eye, and he gave her a squeeze.

'Ruth and Manny were here for Christmas dinner. It's not fair.'

'It's traditional in our family to have everyone together at Christmas, including the Nussbaums. Yosef and I were like you and Ruth when we were young boys.'

This Christmas had been no different from any other. As soon as the food was ready, they'd all sat down to eat, the Kästners and the Nussbaums together.

'I like it when it's like that. I'll miss Ruth when we're away.'

'I'm sorry. It's just the way things are. So long as you're the best of friends, that's all that matters.'

~~o~~

Ruth tried to hide her disappointment.

'One day, you'll be able to come with us skiing, and sailing in summer,' Antje said. 'You'd love it; it's so much fun, but it's not the same without you there.'

'I don't mind, really. It does sound lovely, all that snow, and the trees, and real mountains. Did you get to go on a sledge?'

'Yes, but we mostly ski. It's quite hard work though. By night-time, you're exhausted.'

'I read in Papa's paper a couple of years ago about a woman who became the world champion of skiing. She was from Britain. Esme Mackinnon was her name. There was a picture of her. It looked terribly exciting but a bit scary.'

'That's not the type of skiing we do at my grandparents' lodge; it's Nordic skiing, not Alpine.'

'Oh. What's that?'

'We go uphill and downhill, and the slopes aren't as steep. We follow forest tracks for miles.'

Ruth frowned. 'It still sounds like fun,' she said.

'It is, and we go Alpine skiing in Bavaria sometimes,' she said. 'The slopes are much steeper. To get up, you must hang onto a rope tow, or climb up, although in some places, you can get a cable car to the top.'

Ruth's eyes lit up. She sighed, realising that she would never get the chance to find out what it was like. She tried not to be jealous.

'Do you want to play with my toys?' Antje asked.

1934

"Where they have burned books, they will end in burning human beings."

Heinrich Heine, 'Almansor', 1821

CHAPTER 62

KIELER MORGENPOST

Thursday 25th January 1934

WORKERS WELCOME GOVERNMENT LABOUR REFORMS

In a long-awaited move to improve conditions for German workers, it is now a mandatory stipulation of employment to be a member of the German Labour Front. It is expected that the new law will force employers to provide better working conditions for their employees. This is expected to impact on nearly eleven million German citizens.

German workers' groups responded favourably to the announcement. News that Jewish workers would not be admitted to the German Labour Front was broadly welcomed, although employers were quick to point out the law applied only to Jewish workers applying for new positions. Jewish workers currently in employment would, however, be ineligible for any of the new employment benefits being introduced.

~~o~~

The General shook his head.

'Yosef, Miriam, I can assure you that your jobs are quite safe. I'm surprised you felt it necessary to ask.'

Yosef pointed to the newspaper. 'It says that it affects all Jewish workers currently in employment.'

'I can understand why you would be worried, but your jobs here are safe for as long as you want them, and your pension. I've told you that before and I'm a man of my word.'

Miriam folded and unfolded the dish towel she was holding. She glanced at her husband, then at Maria Kästner.

'General,' she said, her voice quiet but determined, 'it might be out of your control. They may force us to leave. They're doing it to other Jews.'

He recognised the bitterness in her voice and sympathised with it.

'As far as I can tell, it's mainly aimed at industrial and manual workers. I'm as disgusted as you are about it, but I repeat, no one is going to force me to dismiss you. You have been with us since you were married. Yosef's parents looked after Maria and I and, before that, my parents. I won't let it happen.'

Maria Kästner had stood listening, a frown on her face.

'If you wanted to go,' she interjected, 'we wouldn't stand in your way, but only if you felt it the best thing for you and your family.'

The General glared at his wife. He wondered if the Nussbaums heard her words the way he did.

'What Maria means is that we want you to stay, but you mustn't feel compelled to remain here through some sense of duty, if you'd rather leave Germany.'

'Where would we go, sir?' Yosef asked, not requiring an answer. 'This is our home.'

'Some of our friends have gone to Palestine, others to America,' Miriam said. They all looked at her, surprised.

'Would you consider it?' the General asked.

'No, sir. We haven't even spoken about it,' Yosef replied, frowning at his wife.

'Palestine is too dangerous for the children, and we don't speak the language, so how would we survive in America?'

Maria opened her mouth as if to speak, then stopped. The General knew what she was going to say, and he was glad she'd thought better of it. He'd had the same thought, but for different reasons. They could learn a new language, and good workers always found jobs, in his experience.

'Miriam,' the General said, his voice firm. 'I would be heartbroken if you left, but I would support you and Yosef in any decision you might make. In the meantime, nothing will change. Your place here is safe.'

'Thank you, sir.'

Miriam glanced at Maria, before following her out. The General saw the look that passed between the two women. He feared that the trust between them had just been eroded a little more.

'Hard times, my friend,' the General said, when the two men were alone.

'Yes, sir. Miriam is at her wits' end. This has floored us, on top of all the other troubles that they've heaped upon us.'

'I'm sorry, Yosef. I don't know the German people anymore. Why do they not stand up against this persecution?'

Yosef smiled a sad smile.

'It's always been there, sir, under the surface. We bring out the worst in people. Talking to the Jews who've travelled here from the east, it's just as bad there. I don't know if it's the Jewish-Christian thing or something else.'

'It may be religious. The Catholics are also getting a hard time too.'

'With respect, sir, it's not quite the same.'

The General flushed.

'No, I'm sorry. I didn't mean that…'

'It's the gradual erosion of all our rights, sir. Did you know that we have been banned from all aspects of cultural life? No Jew can work in the film industry, in art or in the theatre. And as for music, sir, I don't know how they will find enough musicians for their orchestras. Half of the musicians are Jews. They even outlawed Kosher slaughter, which is fundamental to the faith of a large proportion of Jews.'

The General could only nod and let Yosef speak.

'And sir, they've forced Jews to sell farms that have been in families for generations, sometimes for a pittance. Only those without Jewish blood can farm Erbhöfe now. There are people looking for jobs everywhere, but they've banned us from most workplaces. Newspapers, factories, city councils.'

'How are people surviving?'

'We look after our own, sir. There are still a few Jews running their own businesses,' he admitted. 'They're hiring extra Jewish men or women where they can, and a fund has been set up to help those who are most needful.'

'I can give something, Yosef. It's the least I can do.'

'Oh no, sir, I wasn't looking for money. It's enough to know that there are a few non-Jewish Germans who are on our side.'

The General resolved to find a way to donate to the fund. Even a token amount would help, and at least he would feel he was doing something. Erich Kästner didn't tell Yosef but, since the boycott, he'd made a point of shopping and eating in Jewish establishments where he could, without changing the house's general suppliers. And two of them were Jewish family businesses already, as was his tailor.

He placed his hand on Yosef's shoulder.

'The National Socialists won't be around forever. One day we will return to the way we were.'

Yosef smiled again. 'I hope so, sir.'

Neither man truly believed it.

CHAPTER 63

[26/04/1934 Thursday]

'Old Franz here keeps his cards close to his chest.'

They all laughed. It was Franz Kästner's eighteenth birthday, and the four junior officers sat in a bar, gently ribbing their friend. They often referred to him as old, although he was the youngest of the four. They'd been together since the end of March, when they'd finished their basic officer training. When it came to choose which regiment Franz would apply for, there had only been one choice. He'd joined the fourth infantry, second division, his father's old regiment, and the division he'd commanded as a general.

Now they were serving under Colonel Schneider, but Franz knew better than to expect any favours for being his father's son.

The ribbing continued.

'There have been no wild stories about his sexual prowess, and we've yet to see him properly drunk.'

'Maybe tonight's the night for both?'

Franz held his hands up. 'I like a drink, friends, but I've only been roaring drunk once, and I vomited everywhere. It's not my idea of fun. I get more pleasure watching you idiots make fools of yourselves.'

They all laughed, and Franz continued. 'You must admit, you find it useful to have someone to help you find your way back to barracks. I don't know how often I've saved you all from the doghouse.'

They laughed again, and slapped Franz's back.

Fritz, the fair-haired one, spoke. 'Don't talk to me. It's a pity you weren't here when I got canned, Franz. I overstayed my welcome with an extremely accommodating Fräulein and arrived at the gate ten minutes after regulation. My boots were on the wrong feet and my coat was inside out. Seven days CB, I got.'

Confined to Barracks. They'd all been there. Apart from Franz.

'Well, you're not going back to barracks sober tonight, old boy.'

'And when's your brother arriving? You said he would be here.'

'He'll come. But he's only sixteen, and my mother will kill me if he's drunk when he gets home.'

Fritz burst out laughing.

'He'll just have to stay with us then.'

They'd rented a hotel room in Kiel. At least, two of them had, and they all intended to sneak in past the concierge. Franz fervently hoped that he didn't bump into anyone who knew him. He'd be mortified if any of his parents' friends or acquaintances saw them.

He wished he'd never agreed to show them around Kiel, but they were temporarily stationed at Plön, in the barracks his father was rostered to. They had a pass until midday, and they'd blagged a lift into town on one of the base trucks. The driver had promised to pick them up at the railway station at eleven the next day.

'I don't know why you didn't invite us to stay at your house. I'm sure your parents wouldn't have minded.'

'My father would have loved it, I'd imagine, but you don't want to see my mother on the warpath. Anyway, I have sisters.'

Ribald laughter swept round the table.

'They're too young,' Franz protested, 'and, even if they weren't, I still wouldn't let you lot near them.'

His objections were drowned out by catcalls and further howls of laughter. They were still laughing when Johann walked in.

Franz got up and ushered his brother over to the group, waiting until they quietened. Already at the sozzled stage, the young soldiers looked up at the brothers, and motioned for Franz to introduce Johann.

Johann had worn his Hitlerjugend uniform. Franz wondered if his brother would be taunted by the others for wearing it, but they'd all been in the Hitler Youth themselves, and not so long ago.

'Come and sit here,' one of Franz's friends said, 'We have a spare drink or two here. Your brother seems to be lagging. And you, my young friend, need to catch up.'

A tankard of beer and a glass of Schnapps were slid across the table to him. Johann downed the beer first then, holding up the Schnapps glass, made a rude comment about his brother's health and downed it too.

Franz's friends cheered and thumped the table with their glasses, spilling an alarming amount of beer onto the already sodden surface.

'Finally, a Kästner who can drink.'

'I take after my father. Franz takes after his mama.'

Franz joined in the laughter but didn't fall about in tears like his inebriated friends. He didn't mind being the butt of humour. In the barracks, or out in the field, they all knew he was by far the best of the officer recruits, and someone they could come to for any help, whatever its nature.

He sometimes wondered why he couldn't join in when they let themselves go; it had been the same with him and Johann; from an early age, Franz was the one urging caution and Johann was always willing to push whatever boundaries there were.

He heard someone say his name again. This time, he realised with a sinking heart, Lise was being mentioned.

They all turned to Franz.

'You've kept this a big secret. Are you ashamed of this mystery woman? Is she big and ugly, a bit of a troll?'

Again, laughter rolled round the group. When it subsided, it was Johann who spoke.

'Sorry to disappoint you, but she's one of the most desirable girls you'll ever see.' He made the usual gesture with his hands indicating that she had curves in all the right places. 'I don't know what she sees in my brother.'

'Let's see a photograph then,' one of them said, and they all joined in, pleading with Franz to show them Lise's picture.

After a few minutes of persistent drunken persuasion, a reluctant Franz opened his wallet and pulled out the picture of Lise, handing it to his friends.

'Be careful with it,' he said.

There was a silence for a few seconds, then the whistles and comments started.

'A dark horse. We have an outsider in our ranks,' one shouted.

'You're definitely punching well above your weight there, old man.'

'Here, give it back, before it gets soaked with beer,' Franz said, but they were reluctant to return the photograph. He wondered if it was because she was so arrestingly beautiful, or they didn't believe that she was his girlfriend. He could identify with that; he sometimes wondered himself.

'She's hot too,' he heard Johann saying. 'She's all over Franz like a rash, but he plays it too cool. I don't think he's even touched her magnificent breasts yet. I'd have long since investigated the contents of her brassiere if it were me.'

His friends were all looking at him, bleary-eyed and grinning.

'You're not going to draw me in with your filthy girl-talk. What happens between us is for me and Lise, so you needn't bother prying.'

'But Franz, we've got to know. What do her tits feel like?' one of his friends said.

They all dissolved in wails of laughter. Even Franz smiled, taking it all in good part.

It took them a quarter of an hour to get bored of interrogating him about her, and the extent of her sexual desires. He had no difficulty resisting their pleadings and, on a couple of occasions, he made as if he was going to divulge a snippet, just to see their faces, only to change his mind.

Soon, the talk turned to their own sexual conquests and disasters; Johann joined in, and Franz wondered if it was all bravado or was his younger brother really more experienced with the opposite sex?

Franz wasn't a virgin, but he still felt mildly ashamed of his one and only experience of sexual intercourse, with an older girl, a BDM youth leader he'd met when he was on a Hitlerjugend excursion to Munich a year or so before. She'd been comfortable having sex with him just for fun in a hotel room hired by the hour.

That's how it was, he thought.

She'd been in control. He'd felt younger than the two-year age gap between them had suggested when she dressed and left, with a wave and a smile at the bedroom door. He'd never told a soul.

With Lise, he didn't want to spoil what they had. They'd kissed, naturally, but he was acutely aware of her age and knew that he didn't want to go any further until he was one hundred per cent sure that he was in love with her, and she with him.

And, despite everything, he did have doubts. She was beautiful, soft, and gentle; she was funny sometimes, and intelligent. She was clearly attracted to him, and it was becoming obvious that she wanted him to take things further, but there was something that made him hesitate.

A voice broke his reverie.

'Old man, are you still a virgin?'

He laughed, the question catching him unawares and, on a whim, he answered that he was a virgin, but so what?

There wasn't so much laughter at that, and for a moment, the table quietened. It suddenly occurred to him that perhaps his friends weren't quite so experienced as they made out.

Wouldn't it be ironic if Johann was the worldliest of them all?

Franz stuck to beer and, after a while, the others stopped buying him Schnapps to accompany it. As the alcohol slowly glued the group together, and loosened their tongues, Franz groaned to himself when the talk turned to the German leader.

'Adolf Hitler has transformed the Reichsheer,' Artur Schweitzer said.

Franz knew, from his father, that the foundations of the current resurgence of the German Army had been laid in the twenties by General von Seeckt, with others after him building on his blueprint for a German army, with scope for rapid expansion if it was needed.

'Hitlerjugend is the future of the German Army,' Franz's fellow junior officer continued. 'Look at young Johann. In another year, the army will have thousands more brilliant young officers like him, and the same again the year after that.'

He clapped Johann on the back and hugged him.

'Here's to brilliant young officers, just like ourselves,' one of the others said, raising his glass.

They all raised their glasses and toasted each other. Franz had lost count of the salutations and pledges, but he joined in anyway. They were a good bunch of boys, and he would follow them anywhere, hoping desperately that it wouldn't lead to a brothel or some gambling den.

'Heil Hitler,' the drunkest of them said, standing up and clicking his heels together with difficulty, and giving the Hitler salute, having to fight hard not to fall over.

He cringed as they started to sing the Horst Wessel Song, looking around to see if it was going to annoy the other residents of the bar but, on the contrary, the occupants of the adjoining tables, most of them young men and women, joined in, until the whole place was singing in unison. Even the bartender was smiling.

His friends gave a roar as it finished and ordered another round of drinks.

'With Adolf Hitler in charge, we can take back the lands that were taken from us.'

This met with a raucous chorus of approval from the table and another series of toasts.

'Rheinland!'

'Saarland!'

Franz hung his head in his hands. Someone clapped him on the back and shouted that he hadn't drank enough. He looked up again. The whole group, Johann included, were on their feet, red-faced and staring wildly, the veins on their necks standing out as they thundered aloud the names of places that they felt had been stolen from Germany.

'Sudetenland!'

'Danzig!'

'Österreich!'

Franz looked around and hoped there were no Austrians in the bar. He realised that almost everyone in the place was cheering for each lost German territory and in a sudden flash of insight, he also realised that the National Socialists weren't leading the people of Germany by the nose; they were merely tapping into the latent nationalism that had been there all along, subdued by defeat in the last war, but ready and waiting to emerge when someone like Adolf Hitler, with his rousing speeches and his eye for the spectacular, lit the fuse under them.

He believed what his father and grandfather had told him; that Germany needed a stronger army to keep its own peace and not rely on others to do so, and that the threat from the Soviet Bolsheviks was real and growing.

But his father had expressed concerns that Hitler was a fanatical expansionist and that he would carry the people with him, willingly. Up until now, Franz hadn't believed him but, watching the fervour with which the crowded bar welcomed the calls for reunification of the lost territories of Imperial Germany, he wasn't so sure.

~~o~~

'Well, Franz, old man, and I mean that, really.' The young officer's speech was heavily slurred. 'I can see that you're the sensible one in the family. Your brother likes a party. We can't wait until he joins the regiment.'

'Yes, yes,' Franz said, holding the stumbling soldier as he attempted the stairs. He'd only just got him past the reception desk. They'd been lucky that the old porter had been almost deaf, and short-sighted. As Franz engaged him in conversation, the others had crawled past, a line of giggling children in field-grey uniforms.

'Just like basic training,' one had mumbled, half suppressing a laugh. 'All we need is the barbed wire.'

They'd all pretended to crawl under the jagged rolls of wire that had torn their hands and backs on the assault course, and now, Franz was helping the stragglers up the stairs, Johann among them. He considered phoning his parents but thought better of it at two in the morning.

If only that barman hadn't shut the doors at closing time and continued serving beer and Schnapps until the early hours.

He would phone first thing in the morning and send Johann on his way. The walk might clear his brother's head, ready to face his mother.

CHAPTER 64

[02/05/1934 Wednesday]

'Such lovely girls. Are they sisters?'

'No, Herr Chancellor, Antje is my daughter. Ruth is one of her friends.'

The smile disappeared, and the General thought he saw Adolf Hitler's cheek twitch, just below his right eye, but the country's leader retrieved his smile almost immediately and turned to the fawning woman next in line. The General looked away, fighting hard to stifle a grin. As the chancellor made his way to the end of the dais, shaking hands and engaging the military and town dignitaries as he went, Erich Kästner saw Hitler glance back at Ruth, just before he descended the stairway to the staff car that was waiting for him.

'That Jew-Girl should never have been in here.' The voice came from behind him. He ignored it, but it continued. 'Our chancellor shouldn't be exposed to their filth.'

He looked round at the tight-lipped woman who was staring at Ruth, her face rigid with hate.

He smiled at her and, shaking his head, stood up and spoke to the girls.

'Antje, Ruth, we're going.' He nodded to the others on the platform, estimating that the majority of its occupants had expressions of disgust at the woman's treatment of Ruth, but he could see, in the eyes of a significant few, a tacit agreement with her words of venom.

He knew the woman. She was the wife of a banker, a couple who'd embraced the arrival of the NSDAP from the outset. She wasn't a member of the yacht club, and he would see that she was blackballed if she ever tried to join. He was a past Clubkapitän of the club and a member of the committee and could, without giving a reason, prevent anyone he didn't like from joining.

The day had started well. The regatta, for members of the Reichswehr, was a new event, and the General had been given four tickets for the VIP stand, the best vantage point to watch the various rowing and sailing races that were scheduled. Maria and Eva had expressed no enthusiasm for a day watching boats, so he'd decided, on a whim, to ask if the Nussbaum children could accompany himself and Antje. Yosef had readily agreed, but Miriam had taken Manny to the doctor with an infected toe, so they'd set off together, just the three of them.

The girls had watched the action with great excitement and, when Franz and Johann's army boat crossed the line half a boat-length ahead of the navy boat, they'd looked on with tremendous pride.

Antje's brothers had climbed the steps of the specially erected dais to be presented with the trophy by the German chancellor, saluting the man with outstretched arms. In Franz's case, the General noted, it was a fraction less enthusiastic than Johann's.

After the presentation, the General had moved forward to congratulate his sons and found himself speaking to Adolf Hitler, the girls at his side. Franz had ruffled Antje's hair while the small man in his NSDAP uniform, his cropped moustache perched ludicrously on his upper lip, spoke with the General.

Then the vile woman had made her views known.

Erich Kästner shepherded the girls down the stairs at the end of the stand.

'Come on, I'll treat you to an ice-cream sundae while we're waiting for the boys to get their things together.'

As they went to cross the road, a soldier held them back.

'Just a minute, sir, if you don't mind. The chancellor is leaving.'

The General saw the long black car emerge from the crowd of onlookers and turn onto the road. As it passed, Ruth, her eyes at the level of the car's windows, caught sight of Adolf Hitler, staring coldly at her for a second, and she shivered.

He knew that it had been reckless and unfair of him to let Yosef's young daughter meet

Herr Hitler, but it had appealed to his sense of irony. If he had been less pig-headed, he would have stood with Ruth in the background while the boys were presented to the German leader.

And he was sure that his spur-of-the-moment decision to involve Ruth in their plans, cleared with her father, would annoy Maria, and Miriam too, when they found out, even more so when they heard she'd met Adolf Hitler.

He glanced at Ruth. If she'd heard the woman's remark, she'd given no immediate indication but, on the journey home, he thought she was unusually quiet.

~~o~~

Later, when Ruth had been spirited off by Yosef, Antje, in her nightdress, ran up to her father and launched herself onto his lap.

'Oof,' he said, 'you're getting too big and fat to be doing that,' he said, pretending to be winded.

'I'm not fat. Mama says I'm skinny.'

'She wouldn't know. You don't jump onto her lap like that,' he retorted, holding her up, estimating her weight. 'About two-hundred kilos,' he said, contorting his face with the effort of lifting her.

She giggled, then a shadow passed across her face.

'That woman, the one on the platform, she was dreadfully rude.'

His eyebrows rose in surprise. 'You noticed. I thought you and Ruth hadn't heard.'

'Ruth's used to it. She doesn't let on but I'm sure she's heard worse. Why are people so nasty to her?'

'I don't know. These people, Herr Hitler's lot, seem to have stirred up something in our country that I didn't think was still around. It must have been there all along, simmering under the surface.'

'At school, some of the boys and girls say that Jews aren't really Germans. I don't understand why.'

'It's like I've told you before, it's only because they don't have the same religion, and,' he admitted, 'some of them do look a little different.'

He knew she'd seen Jewish men dressed in black suits with strange hats, long beards and sidelocks, especially in and around Kleiner Kuhberg, the largely Jewish area in the centre of Kiel.

'But Ruth's parents, or the Weichmanns or the Liewermanns don't look any different from you or me.'

'It's a bit the same with the rest of us. We go to church on a Sunday, and that's enough for me. We like to think we are good Christians, and we are, but there are other Germans who are Catholics, or Jews, or Jehovah's witnesses, who may go to church more often, and have different practices to ours.'

'What do you mean, Papa?'

'Well, you'll sometimes see the Catholics make a cross, like this.' He showed her the sign. 'Like the Pastor does, at church, but they do it all the time, in their daily lives.'

'But they don't look different.'

'That's true. Perhaps you're right, maybe it's the fact that some Jewish people deliberately set out to appear so distinctive that makes other Germans nervous.'

'Hanne Weidmann's father has a long beard and wears one of those funny hats. I saw him at school, at our concert last year.'

The General remembered being introduced to the fellow, after they'd watched Antje and Ruth's class sing a traditional German song at the end of summer term the year before. The girl had been on stage with the rest of the children, all dressed in Lederhosen. The General had wondered how the man stayed cool, swathed in black in the stifling heat of the warmest summer for years.

He tried to explain a little further.

'Antje, because many Jewish Germans stick together, even the ones who don't go to the synagogue very often, or dress differently, they're all lumped together. The problem is that people don't seem to trust any group that they don't quite understand. To a smaller degree, they think the same about the Catholics. In some countries, it's the opposite way about. In Italy, for instance, the Catholics dominate, and it's the Protestants who are in the minority.'

'Protestantism started here first,' Antje said, proud of her knowledge. 'Martin Luther was the first Protestant. He was from Saxony in Germany.'

'You're a clever little piglet, aren't you,' the General said, not wanting to be drawn into a long discussion on the Reformation.

She giggled. 'I'm not a piglet,' she said.

'Oh yes you are,' her father said, tickling her until she shrieked. 'You even squeal like a little baby pig.'

The noise brought Maria running, her face full of concern, turning to annoyance when she saw her husband and daughter wrestling on the drawing-room floor.

'Really,' she said, 'You two!'

Antje and her father dissolved into laughter. And even Maria, her frown slowly evaporating, couldn't be angry with them for long.

CHAPTER 65

KIELER MORGENPOST

Sunday 13th May 1934

LAST WARNING TO THE JEWS!

In a rousing speech at the Berlin Sportpalast, Reichsminister Joseph Goebbels launched the "Campaign against Fault Finders and Grumblers".

In it, he told the audience that a minority of Germans were moaners and whingers and were holding back the next stages of the wonderful progress that the National Socialists had already brought to the nation.

He gave a last warning to the Jews. There was an unavoidable threat of a pogrom if the foreign boycott, organised and controlled by Jews abroad, did not cease.

In a conciliatory offer, he gave a promise that no harm would come to Jews "if they remain in their homes" and do not claim to be of "full or equal value".

[10/06/1934 Sunday]

'But we can't change our church. We've always gone there, and so did your parents before us.'

The General fought to keep his anger under control. He'd barely made it out of the church without saying something he would regret, Maria gripping his hand in the hope that he wouldn't explode.

'If that is being Christian, I don't want anything to do with it.'

Landesbischof Paulsen, the bishop of Schleswig-Holstein, on one of his regular visits to the Nikolai Kirche that had been the Kästner family's place of worship for almost sixty years, had delivered a sermon that extolled the Christian virtues of the NSDAP and explained why their policies and actions were compatible with church guidance.

As he'd started to rise from his seat, Maria, with a strength that surprised him, had gripped his arm and pulled him back down, giving him a look that was halfway between anger and desperation.

He'd sat through the rest of the service, fuming in silence, and he had been one of the first out of the door, aware that few of his fellow parishioners shared his outrage.

The children trailed from the church behind their parents, confused by the unfamiliar haste of their exit, more accustomed to the slow and interminable mingling and handshaking that they had to endure before being released from the tedious part of Sunday, and to freedom.

The pastor had barely made it to the back of the church to shake his parishioners' hands before the General rushed past him. Maria gave him an apologetic smile when he tried to greet her.

'General,' he called after them, 'Maria,' he added, but they'd gone, marching up the path

234

to the church gate.

'That was very rude, Erich,' Maria said, the hint of tears in her eyes not softening the anger. 'I'm sure Father Wengler is wondering what is going on.'

'If he doesn't know, or doesn't feel the same way, he should be ashamed of himself.'

'That's not fair,' she hissed, glancing round. 'The children are listening.'

He turned away and strode across the street, mindless of checking for traffic, towards their car, sitting at the kerbside. Yosef stood at the front of it, deep in conversation with the driver of one of the other cars.

Caught by surprise, he didn't have time to reach the door before the General threw it open and held it while Maria and the children scurried to climb inside. As Yosef took the door from him, the General gave him a curt nod and told him to take them home, foregoing the visit to the ice-cream shop that was the usual Sunday treat.

Not a word was said on the short journey back to Drachensee and when Yosef dropped off his tight-lipped employers, the only one who gave him half a smile was Antje.

~~o~~

'I'm sorry,' the General said later, 'I shouldn't have taken it out on you.'

'I know you're upset, Erich, and you have a right to be. The man was beastly, but Father Wengler isn't like that and I don't want to leave him and all our friends and find a new church to go to. I mean, you don't expect us to become Catholics, do you, or Baptists?'

The General had control of himself now and, for the sake of his wife, would stomach going back with his family, but he knew the church had forever lost its reassuring sense of comfort and strength for him.

At their next weekly practice, he asked Dieter Maas to look into the politics of the German Evangelical Church.

CHAPTER 66

[23/06/1934 Saturday]

Manny held his grandfather's hand. It seemed so large compared with his own, which disappeared entirely within its grasp. He had fidgeted through the Shabbat service and now skipped along beside Samuel Nussbaum, looking forward to the monthly visit to his grandparents' home; his Bubbe always had some special treat which she'd baked that morning, though never admitting to cooking or baking on the Sabbath.

Sabba Nussbaum would take him to the room he kept for making his mandolins, a hobby he used to supplement the pension the Kästners provided him with.

Manny loved to watch his grandfather work on one of his instruments. Strictly, a Saturday should be free of all work, but Samuel considered that his mandolins and his grandson were something sent to him by God, to give him joy, and he wasn't rigid enough in his faith to let it stop him doing a little sanding, gluing, or general fiddling with one of his creations, while Manny watched in rapt silence, punctuated by an occasional word between them. It could be a question from Manny, an explanation from his grandfather or just an observation from the old man about the family or life in general.

They crossed Ziegelteich, Manny and his grandfather out in front, the rest of the family following. The streets were thronged with people; it was the first day of Kieler Woche and there were stalls everywhere, with buskers and entertainers on every junction. As they rounded the corner onto Sophienblatt, a small group of people stood around a new noticeboard that had been erected that week.

Manny pulled his grandfather's hand towards it, and a space opened up as another family moved on down the street towards the Hauptbahnhof, to catch a train home.

Manny looked up at the freshly painted sign above the glass display. He was proud of his reading ability; he was one of the brighter children in the class and his parents had been teaching him to read and write since he could hold a pencil, but he struggled to read the large lettering across the top, its heavy Gothic type confusing him.

Behind the glass, a newspaper was pinned to the board but, again, Manny struggled to read the heavy, highly stylised newsprint.

He felt his grandfather try to pull him away but, in a surprising show of strength, he held his ground, staring at the words, not knowing why they fascinated him.

He heard Ruth gasp behind him, then his mother's voice telling them that they must go, just as his grandfather's pull overcame his stubborn resistance.

'What does it say?' Manny asked, but as he was being dragged away, he noticed a line in plainer lettering at the bottom of the newspaper.

Die Juden sind unser Unglück!

The Jews are our misfortune!

It struck him as odd. He knew that he was Jewish and that, in school, the other children would occasionally call him names, but he'd never seen anything so peculiar.

'Why are the Jews our misfortune?' he asked. 'And what was the funny picture?'

It was a cartoon, like he'd seen in the General's paper, which his father sometimes read. *But different.*

Miriam grabbed his other hand. 'It's the same as on the train. There's no reason for it. Some people are just born to hate us.'

'Ignore it,' his grandfather told him, glancing at Miriam, 'There are nasty people everywhere. You don't need to take any notice of them.'

~~o~~

Yosef had been watching Ruth. She'd seen it. The name of the newspaper.

DER STÜRMER

And the writing across the top of the news board.

Mit Dem Stürmer gegen Juda

With Der Stürmer against Judah

He saw his daughter's hurt frown. These street-corner billboards, or Stürmerkasten, were springing up in towns and cities all over Germany, spreading the anti-Semitic message of Der Stürmer everywhere. The combination of imaginative headlines, funny and clever caricatures and its editorial railing against Jews, Catholics, and any political enemy of the National Socialists, made it extremely popular, especially with the young.

He watched his daughter's face in horror as she read the front-page headline.

23rd June 1934

WHO BUYS FROM JEWS IS A TRAITOR TO OUR NATION

She'd tried not to react, as they'd taught her, but it was difficult to imagine what the impact such hatred would have on her young mind. He took her hand and led her away, gently squeezing it as they walked past the station, and down towards Gaarden.

~~o~~

[24/06/1934 Sunday]

'Erich, I had a word with the rest of the committee. That woman won't be welcome back.'

'Thanks, Clubkapitän. She was extremely rude in front of the children.'

'Indeed. Still, that's it all taken care of. Now we can enjoy Kieler Woche. I've been looking forward to it all year. Are you racing?'

'Yes,' the General said with a laugh, 'in the old duffers' class. I must agree though. Kieler Woche is one of the highlights of my year.'

'I see your boys are doing well, in the Hitlerjugend boat. You must be tremendously proud of them. It's such a marvellous organisation for our young men.'

'Yes,' the General said, his expression unchanged. 'but only Johann is on the Hitlerjugend boat. Franz is with the army now. They've done better than I expected. I believe both their big races are on the final day, but they also have an entry in the Star class, just the two of them. What about yourself?' he added.

'Oh, my racing days are over. What, with organising the racing programme, and everything else that goes with it, I don't think I could cram it in.'

'You do a marvellous job. Runs like clockwork every year.'

'I have a great committee behind me. And I was glad to see you signed up for it again

237

this year. So useful to have a man with military clout on the team.'

He slapped the General on the back.

The General shook his hand and made to go.

'There's just one other thing,' the Clubkapitän said.

The General turned back.

'Yes?'

'The children. Your staff's children. We're quite happy for you to bring them, for now, but there are some members who are a little bit, shall we say, anxious about these things. A bit of discretion, Erich? Not too much to ask, I hope.'

'Of course. I'll be more careful,' he said, amazed to hear his own voice, pleasant and measured.

'That's great, my friend.' The relief showed on the Clubkapitän's face. 'Enjoy the rest of the week, and good luck in the race. I'm sure Doctor Speer and Oskar will do you proud.'

As he walked off, the General recognised the inevitability of the quid pro quo. The woman would never again grace the Kieler sailing club, but he'd been served notice that the time would come when Jews would not be welcome at the club, even if they were schoolfriends of his own children.

~~o~~

[29/06/1934 Friday]

Franz turned the medal over in his fingers. It was his second Kieler Woche medal; he had another one to keep it company. He sat on the edge of the bed and wondered why he didn't feel good about it. He knew that the day's big race had been their best yet. As skipper, he was the first to give credit to his crew, but in the end, even their almost flawless teamwork was in a large part down to him, and the harsh training regime he'd insisted that they follow.

He looked at the medal again, then picked up its twin. He and Johann had won the Star class, two days before he'd gone on to win Kieler Woche's penultimate class in the Reichsheer boat. And Johann had won the youth race as skipper of the Hitlerjugend boat.

He opened the drawer of the chest next to his bed and dropped the medals in.

~~o~~

'Did you see them, Mama?'

Johann held out his hand to show her his medals.

'They're awfully pretty,' Maria said. 'Which one is which?'

'They are the same on the front, but the awards are inscribed on the reverse. This one is for the Star class win.' He pointed out the engraving on the back.

27.06.34 Race VII

She looked at the medal, trying to work out what the symbols on the front represented.

There was something mesmeric about it; a perfect square with *Kieler Woche 1934* written around the glossy black rim in silver capitals, in an almost ecclesiastical style. In the centre, there was a jagged silver triangle with a black semicircle at its centre, set in a small red square, surrounded by four chunky, white rectangles.

She turned as her husband entered the room.

'Look, Erich, have you seen Johann's medals?'

'Yes, I've seen them. The boys did a phenomenal job, winning two races each. I only wish I could claim similar success.'

She gave him an indulgent smile. 'Darling, you've won a few Kieler Woche races over the years. You're just getting a little long in the tooth to be competitive.'

'Well, that makes me feel an awful lot better. Thank you, my dearest.' He laughed.

She held up the medal for him to see.

'It's very modern,' she said. 'Quite attractive, really.'

'It's a swastika, Maria. Quite possibly with an eagle in the middle.'

She peered at it again, then she saw it.

'It's white. Swastikas are usually black. And it looks terribly squashed, but I can see it now. Did you notice it right away?'

'Yes.' He sighed. 'It's highly stylised, and not everyone notices. I was shown the design a few months ago when the committee voted for it. I'm sure there was a lot of pressure from the mayor's office, and the regional NSDAP people.'

Johann held out his hand and took the medal from his mother.

'Well, I like it. It goes well with all my Hitlerjugend medals.'

The General looked at his son and opened his mouth to say something, then stopped.

'You both did a great job,' he said, after a second or two.

He laid his hand on Johann's shoulder and smiled.

'Your wins today were as good as any I've seen,' he added. 'There wasn't much in it at the line, in either race though.'

The boy's face broke into a broad grin.

'I can't wait to show Grandfather. When are they coming?'

'Not long now. They'll be here for dinner. You can show them to him afterwards,' his mother told him, not wanting the meal to be delayed. 'The admiral will probably go on for ages about all the Kieler Woche races he has won.'

CHAPTER 67

[01/07/1934 Sunday]

The insistent ringing of the phone awoke him. The General checked his watch and wondered who could be phoning at five in the morning.

He threw on a pair of slippers and his dressing gown and hurried down the stairs to answer it.

'General Kästner,' he said, trying to keep his voice low.

'Sir, I think you should come down to the office. There's something you should see.' It was Günter Neuer, his chief petty officer. The man was unflappable, so the General didn't question the request.

'I'll be down shortly. I'll drive down myself.'

'Not necessary. I've sent a driver. He'll be with you in five minutes.'

Barely time to get dressed, he thought, putting the phone down, but by the time the car drew up outside, he was waiting on the top step, his uniform immaculate.

The General had the door of the car open before the driver had a chance to get out, and within ten minutes, through Kiel's deserted streets, they'd arrived at Naval HQ.

'What's all the fuss about?' he asked as soon as he entered the office.

'Sir, the Scheiße has hit the fan. I didn't know how it would affect us, but I thought it better that you could decide yourself. The facts are sketchy but there has been an attempted coup. From what we've heard, the SA have tried to overthrow the government. Röhm is dead, and at least three or four of his top commanders are too. Rumour has it that it was the SS who killed them, to protect the chancellor.'

'Has there been any army mobilisation?'

'Not as far as I know.'

'How did you find out?'

'Captain Bauer and I have been cultivating a few people who work with the government. I had a phone call at half past four. I called around to confirm that there was something going on, then I telephoned you.'

'It doesn't sit right. If there had been a coup, they would have called out the army. The Reichsheer is duty-bound to react, to protect the elected government...' The General paused. 'Unless the army were part of it.'

'Surely we'd have heard whispers, if that were the case, sir.'

'You're right. I'll make a few calls, but let's leave it until a sensible hour. I don't want to get anyone out of bed unnecessarily.' He grinned at the chief petty officer, who looked a bit sheepish. 'Don't worry,' he added, 'you did the right thing.'

'Thank you, sir. I wasn't sure but you always say, when in doubt...'

The General put his hand on the man's shoulder, in reassurance.

'Has anything come in from Patzig?'

'Nothing, sir.'

'Send him a memo. I'll dictate it for you. Just to let him know what we've heard, although I'm sure he'll already know.'

A pad was produced and, once the General's words had been noted down, the man left to type it up and find the duty telegraphist.

An hour later, the General read Captain Patzig's reply.

Memo: Geh.KdoS. ABW 01/07/34 CAC0308.2

For Attention Only: General Erich Kästner, Abwehr, Kiel Field office.

From: Captain Conrad Patzig, Chef der Abwehr.

Re: your communication. I am surprised that you received this information as quickly as we did here at head office. I can confirm that it is correct. As you surmised, the Reichsheer weren't approached with a request for assistance. However, the Army's commanders have been unhappy with the activities of the Sturmabteilung for some time and there have been top-level discussions between the Reichsheer and the Government over the last few months, regarding the succession to Hindenburg as president. The Army's reservations about the SA have been part of the process. This action by the NSDAP and the SS may be in response to this. Continue your excellent work and keep me posted. [END]

The General nodded. It made more sense. Hindenburg, revered president of Germany, had handed over power to Adolf Hitler a year ago, but still retained his title. It was widely speculated that he wouldn't make Michaelmas, and that was only a few months away. The NSDAP were circling like vultures, waiting to pick the last of the flesh left on the living corpse that was Paul Hindenburg.

The only defence against the National Socialists seizing the remaining vestige of power was the Reichswehr, who would, on paper at least, be compelled to support a new, independent president when Hindenburg finally shuffled to his celestial reward.

But there was a difficulty. The Reichschancellery controlled the nation's purse strings and unprecedented funds had been pouring into the armed forces' coffers so it was likely that the Reichswehr would look to their own interests and support Adolf Hitler.

Even so, they still held the balance of power. Any uprising against the National Socialists, no matter how unlikely it seemed, could well succeed if supported by the army, and he'd heard that Hitler was inclined to bouts of paranoia.

The price for the Reichswehr's support is the dissolution of the SA!

All the cards fell into place in the General's mind.

And the chancellor is using the opportunity to remove all his potential rivals in one sweeping move.

He sat, staring out of the window, both awed at the simplicity of it and dismayed at its implications.

Who would he choose as president? Himmler? Goebbels? Göring?

He asked himself which one of these seemed the likeliest, and then it came to him. He thumped the desk and Günter Neuer stuck his head in the door.

'Is everything all right, sir?'

The General waved him away. 'It's nothing, just swatting a fly,' he said.

The General rubbed his hand, wincing. The more he thought of it, the more convinced he was right.

The German people's next president will be Adolf Hitler himself.

~~o~~

KIELER MORGENPOST

Monday 2nd July 1934

ATTEMPTED COUP THWARTED – RÖHM DEAD

In an overnight operation on Friday through to Saturday, the SS and the Reichswehr arrested the leaders of an attempt to overthrow the National Socialist Government.

In an impassioned address from the balcony of the party headquarters in Munich, the NSDAP Leader told the large assembled crowd that it was "the worst treachery in world history". He went on to say that "undisciplined and disobedient characters and asocial or diseased elements would be eliminated".

An ongoing investigation by the Reich's security forces is expected to lead to further arrests. A spokesman told the Morgenpost that "no stone would be left unturned in the search for traitors, whatever rank or privileged position they hold".

A full cabinet meeting is currently in session at the Reichstag. The Morgenpost has been told to expect the release of a statement later today or early tomorrow.

~~o~~

The Kästner family sat at the kitchen table, eating breakfast. Franz was absent; he was not due home on leave for another few weeks, and the General had left early for work, the third time in as many days.

Maria tutted. *So much for him retiring.*

'Johann, it's rude to read at the table,' she scolded.

'Father does. Anyway, I'm keeping abreast of current affairs, you know,' he said, laying the *Morgenpost* aside for a second.

'I'll have none of your cheek. You're not too old to be punished, you know. You're setting a bad example for your sisters.'

Eva and Antje were observing the exchange with interest, wondering how much Johann would get away with. Since the beginning of the school holidays, they'd watched him winding his mother around his little finger.

'Father must be away early because of this,' he said, pointing to the newspaper headline.

'It's shocking,' Maria Kästner said, shaking her head. 'Like him or not, Herr Hitler is our chancellor and treason is a terrible thing. Those plotters got what they deserved.'

'Our Oberbannführer says that the SA are just thugs, that we should stick in at training and the best of us can join the SS. It was the SS who found out about the putsch and stopped it in its tracks; the Reichswehr stood back while the SS saved the chancellor's life.'

Maria looked surprised. She'd always assumed that the army would be loyal to the government.

'Perhaps it was more of a police matter, that the army didn't need to be involved,' she said, trying to be diplomatic. It wouldn't improve the General's mood if Johann were openly critical of the army, or singing the praises of the SS.

'The Oberbannführer says that there will be such a large influx of Hitlerjugend joining the regular army soon that there should be no question of its loyalty.'

Maria raised her eyebrows. She'd never given a thought to what would happen to the boys after they left Hitlerjugend. She had assumed it was just a young peoples' organisation like any other, that helped keep the teenagers occupied and taught them some discipline and good German values.

'Don't say anything to your father,' she told him. 'It will just upset him.'

Johann looked sheepish. 'He already knows. I spoke to him about it the other day about joining the SS. He says that I'd be far better off in the regular army.'

'Oh dear,' his mother said. 'I'm surprised he didn't mention it to me. Or explode.'

'He didn't seem too bothered. In fact, he sounded quite interested in what we do at HJ.'

Maria didn't like the new fashion of abbreviating everything, but she let it go, relieved that Erich hadn't given Johann a hard time.

'Well, just try not to get him riled up,' she said.

CHAPTER 68

KIELER MORGENPOST

Wednesday 4th July 1934

GÜRTNER USHERS IN SELF-DEFENCE LAW

The Law Regarding Measures of State Self-Defence, drafted by Reich Justice Minister Franz Gürtner, was passed in the Reichstag yesterday, ratifying that the execution of SA Chief of Staff Ernst Röhm, General Kurt von Schleicher and the former Bavarian Minister-President, Gustav von Kahr, was legal and justified. Röhm, and his commanders and associates, had planned to overthrow the government and only through the efficiency and competence of the security services was this treachery averted. A spokesman stated that the Government abhors taking such severe measures but in the interests of the country, no alternative course of action was possible.

The subsequent declaration from the Reichstag, exposing the despicable homosexual practices of Röhm and some of his fellow commanders, involving junior SA staff, serves to illustrate the level of corruption that existed within the command of the Sturmabteilung.

It was announced that the SA will now be commanded by Viktor Lutze. The new SA leader, former Reichstag member and Hanover police chief, was one of the architects of the SA's inception. A government spokesman said that Herr Lutze had been instrumental in the downfall of the SA conspirators and was commended for his loyalty to Adolf Hitler, the Party, and the nation.

Dieter Maas threw down the paper.

'Opponents are calling it *The Night of the Long Knives*. The government are playing it down; it's *the Röhm Affair* now. There's a media blackout, so none of the newspapers have any more details beyond what they gleaned initially, and from today's pronouncement from the Reichstag.'

He shook his head. He and the General sat in the bar, along with Captain Bauer. They didn't know how long they had before the other two arrived for their evening practice; there was no race, but they all enjoyed their weekly sail, so they usually met up, whatever was on the racing calendar.

'I don't know whether to be pleased that there was some sort of opposition or dismayed that it has been crushed,' he continued.

'I'd be dismayed about both if I were you,' the General said. 'The opposition didn't exist. There was no putsch.'

'But…'

'It was all a fabrication. Let me tell you a story.'

A group of men entered the bar, drifted over, and nodded at them, taking a seat by the window, two tables away. The General lowered his voice and his two companions leaned in to hear him.

'The SA and the army detest each other, but the army sees the SA as a useful source of raw recruits. On the other hand, Ernst Röhm, the SA leader, has aspirations that the army should become part of the SA or, at least, that he should gain control of it. In January, he asks Adolf Hitler to make him Minister of Defence, replacing General Werner von Blomberg. Hitler refuses. In late June, key figures within the NSDAP show von Blomberg, and the SS leadership evidence that Röhm and a number of his sympathisers are planning to overthrow the government. So, von Blomberg, seeing a chance to be rid of the SA forever, gives Hitler his backing. You must have seen the signed article he wrote, that appeared in the Völkischer Beobachter, in which he declared that Hitler had the full support of the Reichswehr?'

Dieter Maas and Heinz Bauer nodded.

The General went on.

'So, the SA leadership are ordered to a meeting at Bad Wiessee on the morning of thirtieth of June, ostensibly to receive a rebuke for overreaching their authority but were awakened in the early hours in their hotel and detained for questioning.'

The General paused.

'They say that Hitler personally arrested Röhm. Most of the SA command were executed immediately but Röhm was held in prison until the following day and, when he refused to commit suicide, he was shot. The SS also took the opportunity to conduct a wide-ranging purge of Adolf Hitler's remaining opponents all over Germany, even those with no connection to the SA. Evidence was fabricated to show that they were part of the Röhm putsch.'

Dieter Maas let out a soft whistle. 'Clever bastards,' he said.

'Yes. The remainder of the SA will be so terrified of the same fate that they will do as they're told. Who knows what will happen to the organisation now?'

'Discipline, sir. The NSDAP will put one of their own in charge and make it more like a private army.'

The General looked at Heinz Bauer, surprised that he'd spoken.

'I'm not sure,' he said, giving the captain an encouraging smile. 'The SA have been decapitated. I suspect it will run around for a while like a headless chicken, but it will never again have the prominence that it has had until now. Much of its membership will be absorbed into the army or the SS, depending on how loyal or fanatical they are.'

The two men sat in silence, trying to take in what they'd just been told.

'Why are you telling us, sir?'

'I'm thinking that the more people who know the truth of this, the better.'

Captain Bauer nodded, then excused himself, and made for the toilet.

'So, what happens now?' Dieter asked the General.

'Here's my prediction. The SA's decline, as useful as it is to Adolf Hitler, was his side of the bargain to get the Reichswehr to support him when Hindenburg dies.'

The former newspaper editor looked at the General for a second before replying.

'So,' he said, his eyes widening in comprehension, 'the NSDAP get to put one of their people in place as president...'

'Nearly right, Dieter. Here's my prediction, for what it's worth. Adolf Hitler will be president of Germany by Christmas.'

Dieter Maas stared at the General, open-mouthed.

'But he can't. It's not...' He stopped. The General said nothing.

'The Reichsheer won't allow it...' the newspaperman continued, then faltered again.

'Yes, they will,' the General said. 'While it's in their own interest, they'll let Adolf be whoever he wants to be.'

'It's impossible,' Dieter spluttered, as Heinz Bauer returned, with Oskar von Friedeburg and Doctor Speer in tow.

'What's impossible?' the Doc asked.

'That we'll win the next race,' the General said, 'unless we get our arses in gear and get some practice in.'

They all laughed as the General rose and steered them out from the bar. Dieter Maas sat for a few seconds, before following them.

~~o~~

[13/07/1934 Friday]

The wireless hummed, then the voice of the presenter announced that the chancellor was about to address the Reichstag.

The General looked around. The Kästners sat in a semicircle around the radio, the sun streaming in through the drawing-room windows, picking out flecks of dust floating in its beam of light. Yosef finished serving his coffee, and Miriam poured a cup for Maria. Replacing the pot on the tray, she paused, as Adolf Hitler began to speak, his voice low and insistent.

'If someone reproaches me as to why we did not use the ordinary courts for the judgment, then I can only say to them: at that hour I was responsible for the fate of the German nation, and was thus the supreme judge for the German people.'

The chancellor's voice rose a pitch or two and increased in volume.

'I gave the order to shoot the main perpetrators in this treason, and I also gave the order to burn out the ulcers from the wellspring of our nation, poisoned from home and abroad, down to the raw flesh.'

The radio crackled, and the General missed the chancellor's next words, then the static cleared, and the strident voice sang out again.

'The nation must know that its existence – and this is guaranteed by internal order and security – is not threatened by anyone with impunity!'

There was a pause, then Adolf Hitler's tirade reached its crescendo.

'...And everyone should know, for all time, that if he raises his hand to strike the state, certain death is his lot.'

In the Kästners' drawing room, no one made a sound. The General rose from his chair and turned the radio off. Yosef and Miriam stood, white-faced and still. Franz, home on leave, sat looking pensive, and gave his father a glance.

Maria, Eva, and Johann's faces shone, infused with admiration for the energy and force of will of the National Socialist leader's rhetoric. Even the General had to admit that the man could incite a crowd, and a nation.

Yosef picked up his tray and touched Miriam on the shoulder. As they walked past him, the General closed his eyes and shook his head, once.

He considered commenting on the speech, but it would just start an argument with Maria, and he could imagine the hurt and confusion in his children's eyes.

I'll talk with Franz later, and Yosef, if I get the chance.

~~o~~

[20/07/1934 Friday]

In his office, the General read an article in the *Morgenpost*, syndicated, he presumed, from one of the national papers.

Carl Schmitt, the country's leading legal scholar, had written the piece defending Hitler's speech of July the thirteenth. It was titled *The Führer Upholds the Law*.

Captain Bauer knocked, and handed the General a sheet of paper. He read it, then closed

246

his eyes.

Memo: Geh.KdoS. ABW 01/07/34 CAC0314.1

For Attention Only: General Erich Kästner, Abwehr, Kiel Field office.

From: Captain Conrad Patzig, Chef der Abwehr.

Adolf Hitler has decreed that the SS is to be an independent formation of the NSDAP. It has been placed under the command of Reichsführer SS Heinrich Himmler who will be answerable only to the Führer himself. The SS had formerly been subordinated to the SA. This makes it the prime enforcing agency in Germany and has probably been given this position as a reward for its role in the Röhm purge of June 30 - July 2.

It is the view of the chiefs of staff of the army that the SS will increasingly be used by the NSDAP leadership to ensure that its policies are implemented. This should have no effect on day-to-day matters in the Reichsmarine or the Reichsheer but Abwehr operatives should be aware of possible conflicts of interest with the SS in their intelligence-gathering activities. [END]

~~o~~

Up until now, the General had found, in his admittedly sparse dealings with both organisations, that the SS were more disciplined, professional, and less prone to thuggery than the SA.

But he wondered how long it would be before the NSDAP would wait before trying to gain control of the Reichswehr, and if they would use the intensely loyal SS to do so.

He thought about sending a memo in reply to the captain, but he wasn't sure enough of his ground to commit himself to paper. He shouted for Captain Bauer, but it was the chief petty officer who opened the door and asked him how he could help.

'Can you try and get Captain Patzig on the phone for me?'

'No problem, sir. It might take a while. I don't seem to have the same persuasive powers of Captain Bauer.'

The General laughed. 'Where is the captain?'

'I believe he is over at the Rathaus, sir. He seems to be there most days.'

The General wondered if there was a trace of disapproval in the officer's voice.

'Good,' he said, sharper than he intended. 'That's where I need him to be, keeping an eye on what the civilians are doing.'

'Yes, sir.'

'Are you overstretched here without him?'

'No, sir,' the man said, chastened. The General could see that he'd made his point, and let it go.

'Excellent. Now, Stabsfeldwebel Neuer; that phone call.'

Ten minutes later, the General's phone rang.

'Captain Patzig for you, sir.'

There was a click on the line.

'Captain Patzig, thanks for taking my call.'

'Not at all, General, what can I do for you?'

'Regarding the last memo you sent, about the SS. I had a few thoughts.'

'Oh, yes?' the captain said. The General couldn't make up his mind if he was genuinely interested or just being polite.

'Well,' the General said, hesitating, 'I'm wondering if we should be more concerned about the army coming increasingly under the influence of the National Socialists.'

There was a short silence at the end of the line.

'Go on, General,' he heard Patzig say.

'First, I suspect that the SS might start to play a much bigger role in military affairs.'

'What makes you say that? As far as I can see, they seem to be glorified bodyguards for Herr Hitler and a police force for the NSDAP.'

The General told the captain about what had been said to Johann at Hitlerjugend.

'So, you see, this so-called youth organisation,' he concluded, 'is a perfect recruiting ground and training vehicle for the party. The most fanatical, and maybe the most capable, will be siphoned off into the SS, and the army will get the pick of the rest.'

'But if the most zealous ones join the SS, the army, by inference, will get the least fanatical recruits. All the better for us, getting young conscripts with a decent basic training. We will make soldiers out of them all the faster.'

'They'll still be party loyalists. The Hitlerjugend leaders are all zealots. They're getting these boys at fourteen and indoctrinating them with their brand of nationalism.'

'Is that entirely a bad thing, General? I mean, they'll be motivated to fight for their country.'

The General's heart sank. It had been a mistake thinking that he could persuade the Abwehr, or the army, of the dangers the National Socialists posed to the armed forces, but he ploughed on.

'These young soldiers will have loyalty to Hitler first and the army second.'

There was another pause. He hoped he'd finally got through to the captain.

'We'll just have to retrain them to our needs. They're young enough for us to mould them to the army's ways.'

'It will be more difficult than you think, Captain,' the General said, satisfied that he'd managed to plant the seed in the man's mind.

'As for the SS,' he continued, while the Abwehr chief was still listening to him, 'why are they wanting so many combat-trained recruits? They must be intending to use them instead of the Reichsheer, beside the Reichsheer or perhaps even integrated within it.'

Again, the captain paused before replying.

'You've put a lot of thought into this, General, haven't you? To be honest, it hadn't figured high on my agenda. You think they're gearing up to oust the army? That's impossible.'

'You pay me to think,' the General responded, somewhat drily. 'I'm almost sure they won't get strong enough to marginalise the army, but Hitler could use the SS strategically, and the army would have to follow, especially if most of its younger soldiers are all nearly as fanatical as they are.'

'What about the SA? They're still around.'

'The SA is now firmly under Hitler's direct control. He will use them in much the same way as they have been functioning already, for bullying and intimidation, to control any civilian disobedience, and for security at large rallies and the like. They'll cherry-pick the best for the SS and the army and leave the SA with the dullards, the weak-minded and the thugs.'

'Right, General. I'm glad you contacted me. I'll have words in a few ears. I might need you to come to Berlin, depending on how it pans out.'

The General, relieved that he'd been able to convince Patzig that his concerns weren't trivial, was quite prepared to take an extra trip to the capital. He hung up and sat for a few minutes. He hadn't realised he'd been sweating, but sitting there, he could feel it dripping down his back.

CHAPTER 69

KIELER MORGENPOST

Thursday 26th July 1934

AUSTRIAN CHANCELLOR DOLLFUSS ASSASSINATED

Austrian Chancellor Dollfuss was shot dead yesterday. Despite claims that the murder was part of an attempted coup by Austrian National Socialists (DNSAP), an NSDAP spokesman in Berlin stated that this was mere speculation. A successor will be named shortly. The Austrian military has been deployed to maintain order. There have been reports of Italian military activity on the Austrian Border.

Yosef read the paper, sitting in the General's kitchen. His employer had already left. He and Miriam had tidied away the breakfast things, and the mistress was upstairs, getting ready to go out. Yosef looked at the clock, and realised he had another ten minutes before she would call for the car. He wasn't sure if the girls were to accompany her.

'This might be war,' he said, waving the paper at his wife, 'or at least the first skirmishes.'

'Don't say that. This has nothing to do with us in Germany.'

'That's how the First World War started. Archduke Ferdinand was assassinated.'

'We can't go through another one, so soon,' Miriam said, shaking her head.

'I don't know,' Yosef said, a strange look on his face. 'It might be better for us.'

She looked at him as if he'd said he'd told her there was a bear in the garden.

'If Herr Hitler is occupied fighting a war, he might leave us alone.'

'Or you might get called up again,' she snapped.

'I'm too old now. And Manny's too young.'

'You don't really think there will be another war, do you?'

'The General says there won't be, yet. But he's worried that Hitler will take us down that path in a few years' time. And he should know.'

'You sometimes put too much faith in the General. He's just human, like us.'

'He is, I know. But he's a very clever man, and he has his finger on a lot of pulses.'

The sound of footsteps in the hall put an end to their conversation. A second later, Frau Kästner's head popped round the kitchen door.

'That's me ready to go, Yosef, if you don't mind.'

'Certainly, ma'am. The car is out the front.'

'The girls are staying at home, Miriam.'

'That's fine, ma'am. I'll look out for them.'

As Yosef held the front door open, he glanced back at Miriam, but she'd turned away, and was standing at the table, reading the paper.

~~o~~

The General had heard about the assassination the night before. The communication from

Patzig had arrived just as he was finishing writing up the daily report and he'd read it with dismay.

Memo: Geh.KdoS. ABW 25/07/34 CAC0329.1

For Attention Only: All senior executive officers, Abwehr.

From: Captain Conrad Patzig, Chef der Abwehr.

The Italian Army has moved troops to the Austria-Italian border in response to the assassination of Chancellor Dollfuss. Prime Minister of Italy, Benito Mussolini, has released a statement accusing the German Government of being behind the assassination and said that "The independence of Austria, for which he has fallen, is a principle that has been defended and will be defended by Italy even more strenuously".

As for the background to the assassination, we suspect that Adolf Hitler ordered the Austrian National Socialists to create trouble in Austria, and this progressed on to an attempt to overthrow the government. Although they succeeded in murdering Dollfuss, the attempted coup failed because the Austrian military intervened to back up the government.

The Italian Government had an agreement with Chancellor Dollfuss that it would protect Austria from outside aggression. The Italian dictator, Mussolini, has now honoured the agreement and moved Italian troops to South Tyrol to deter any possible invasion from Germany.

The Reichsheer is currently on a medium-to-high level of alert but it is not expected to escalate. The 4th army is currently on manoeuvres in Bavaria and is available for instant deployment in the event of any aggression on the part of the Austrian or Italian Armies.

For information only. No action necessary. [END]

For the next week, Erich Kästner kept a close eye on the Austrian crisis. On the visit to Berlin to discuss the issue of the SS, Hitlerjugend and the infiltration of the army by the National Socialists, he was able to glean that Captain Patzig had been correct; the situation within Austria had stabilised with the appointment of the new president, and Hitler's condemnation of the ten National Socialist assassins had, to some extent, defused the tension between the two countries.

Still, he found that a sense of unease lay in his stomach that this was a prelude to something more momentous.

CHAPTER 70

KIELER MORGENPOST

Friday 3rd August 1934

PAUL von HINDENBURG DEAD. ADOLF HITLER IS FÜHRER

German President Field Marshal Paul von Hindenburg, Germany's President, has died at the age of eighty-six. In a move sanctioned by Paul von Hindenburg before his death, the presidency has been conferred on Adolf Hitler, which he will hold in conjunction with the Chancellery.

Paul von Hindenburg, President of the Weimar Republic since 1925, served with the Imperial German Army, starting as a junior officer in 1876 and rising to be Chief of the General Staff from 1916 to 1919, during the Great War. Coming out of retirement in 1925, he won the Presidency, repeating the victory in 1933. He made Adolf Hitler his Chancellor in the same year.

The following statement was issued by the German Government at 9am yesterday.

The Reich Government has enacted the following law which is hereby promulgated.

Section 1. The office of Reich President will be combined with that of Reich Chancellor. The existing authority of the Reich President will consequently be transferred to the Führer and Reich Chancellor, Adolf Hitler. He will select his deputy.

Section 2. This law is effective as of the time of the death of Reich President von Hindenburg.

General Werner von Blomberg, speaking for the Reichswehr, said that the new President had the full support of the armed forces.

Subsequent to the announcement of the new law, the German Officers' Corps and every individual in the German Army will swear a personal oath of allegiance to Hitler.

'Von Blomberg is so far up Hitler's arse he could pick his teeth clean.'

The captain stifled a laugh, then a concerned look crossed his face. He glanced at the outer office.

'Frau Müller, sir. She might take offence.'

The General opened his mouth to make an acerbic comment about his secretary, then

251

thought better of it.

'I refuse to pledge an oath to this despot. My only allegiance is to Germany.'

'With respect, General, it would be dangerous to be seen not to.'

'It is dangerous for the army to pledge such an oath. It's unprecedented, and unlawful, I'd say.'

'Just be careful, sir. They wouldn't hesitate to arrest you for sedition, no matter who you are. And there are ears all around,' he said, glancing at the door to the outer office.

'I won't swear,' the General said, trying not to sound petulant. 'Do you want to pledge an oath to Herr Hitler?'

'Not particularly, but I'll do it, if I must.' He hesitated, glancing at the General.

'I may have a solution,' the young captain continued. 'We are a small, self-contained unit. Put the Stabsfeldwebel in charge of taking the oaths individually; he could just say that all the oaths have been done…'

'I doubt if he would be comfortable with that; it may be unfair to ask him.'

'I'm sure he would be happy to do it, sir.'

The General looked at him sharply.

'Have you already discussed this, Captain Bauer?'

'No, sir. Well, not specifically, that is.'

'Mmmm.' General Kästner seemed to consider the suggestion.

'What about his oath?'

'I'll witness his pledge, sir. Whether or not he decides to make it.' He grinned.

'I suspect you two have the whole thing worked out. Just do it. Does Frau Müller have to swear? I presume she would be enthusiastic.'

'It is a different oath for civilians, sir, but similar. I believe all the non-service personnel are to make the oath together. I'd imagine Frau Müller will be in the front row.'

The General laughed.

'Quite so,' he said. 'I'll leave you to sort it all out.'

'I will do, sir. Is there anything else?'

'Yes, God preserve us. We now officially live in a dictatorship.'

~~o~~

[15/08/1934 Wednesday]

While Franz was home on leave, the General couldn't resist showing him off around Naval Headquarters, even in the knowledge that he was opening himself up to a ribbing about his son following him into the 'agricultural' wing of the Reichswehr.

Franz always came across well in company, all the more so with fellow military men. He had a quiet way of listening, the General thought, so that when he did speak, his words had credence and value.

He was deep in conversation with Captain Bauer; the two young men had known each other for years and got on very well, despite Heinz Bauer being a little older.

The General was finishing a report he'd been putting off doing; one that required a little finesse to avoid bruising the egos of several high-ranking officers, both army and navy.

'I'm off now, sir,' the captain told the General, then turned to Franz. 'Great meeting you again. I'll take you up on that offer of a sailing trip, when you can wrestle the boat from your father.'

They all laughed as the captain shut the door behind him, leaving the two Kästner men alone.

'He's a good lad. He puts up with quite a lot and he's missing out on a seagoing posting. I don't know how long I can keep him.'

'He's a captain because of you. If he does get a posting now, he's much more likely to get his own command.'

'That's the gamble he took. I'll keep him another year.' The General smiled at his son.

'Talking of which,' he added, 'how does it feel being Oberleutnant Kästner?'

Franz blushed. 'I wasn't expecting that. I assumed I'd be a second lieutenant, not a full one. I sometimes wonder if it's because I'm your son.'

The General shook his head.

'Colonel Schneider is no fool, and it's of no benefit to him to butter me up by promoting a son of mine above his station. No, you've earned it. What do your friends say?'

'They told me the same, as much as it hurt them to agree with the colonel, whom they dislike intensely.'

The General laughed. 'Nothing wrong with a commanding officer being unpopular with his junior officers. Their views will change in a year. He's a good man, and he's just riding them hard for now. They'll look back and see it was for their own benefit. How about you?'

'He's an excellent commander, I think. And he trains us well; I'm learning every day.'

'Good. So you should. I suppose Johann will want to join your regiment. It will be interesting to see what Colonel Schneider can do with him,' the General said, smiling at the thought.

'Oh, Johann will do fine. He'll get into scrapes and rub his senior officers up the wrong way at times but, in some ways, he'll make a better soldier than me.'

The General stared at his son.

Franz looked at him and smiled.

The General frowned. 'Go on,' he said.

'He'll not question anything. He'll just do what he's told and think nothing of it.'

'Will you find the oath to Der Führer hard to swallow?' the General asked gently, but there was derision in his voice.

Franz looked up, nodding, then a surprised look crossed his face.

'Oh,' he said, 'you'll have to do it too. It hadn't occurred to me…'

'…because I'm a general? We'll all have to do it.' It wasn't going to make his son feel any better if he knew that he'd managed to find a way to wriggle out of it.

'It's just words. Remember what's in here,' he said, touching his clenched fist to his chest.

'Most of the other young officers are proud to swear,' Franz said. 'I just feel sick doing it, but I have no choice. It's nothing new; we all swore loyalty to him in Hitlerjugend.'

'Many of your senior officers and rank-and-file men feel the same, but they've been at it long enough to be cynical. There will be a few alternative versions muttered during the oath, I'd imagine.'

It brought a smile to Franz's face. 'I hadn't thought of that. Verdammt!'

The General laughed. 'All heil the Rührer.'

The stirrer.

Franz laughed.

'He's certainly stirring up a hornets' nest,' he said.

He looked at his father.

'The vote will go Hitler's way, won't it?'

In four days, the country was being asked to vote in a plebiscite to ratify Adolf Hitler holding the offices of chancellor and president concurrently.

'If it's anything like the last election, yes. And it will be, I'm sure.'

'Did you hear Rudolf Hess's speech in Munich last night?'

'Yes, we listened to it. Your mother believes it's all for the good. That Germany is strong again.'

Franz's face clouded.

'She doesn't understand what's happening. It's not her fault.'

'I know, son. If I say anything, she just gets angry or sulks for a day. I've stopped discussing it with her.'

'I can't understand her way of thinking. I mean, she can see the effects it has on Yosef and Miriam.'

'She's like a lot of Germans. They're willing to overlook some of Herr Hitler's more distasteful views because he's making Germany a world power again, and promising an economic miracle, if only they support him.'

'Der höchste und einzige Führer des deutschen Volkes,' Franz said, his voice heavy with sarcasm.

The General recognised the line from Hess's speech. *The highest and only leader of the German people.*

The General put his hand on his son's shoulder.

'We can only do what we can, and hope,' he said.

CHAPTER 71

KIELER MORGENPOST

Monday 20th August 1934

PLEBISCITE LANDSLIDE – FÜHRER UND REICHSKANZLER

With a turnout of over 95%, the German people have given their resounding backing to the new Führer of the German Reich. Nearly 90% of votes cast were in favour of the greatest leader Germany has ever known holding the office of Führer of the German Reich, merging the posts of President and Chancellor.

The result was welcomed across Germany. The Mayor of Kiel, Jürgen Hoffmann told the Morgenpost that this was a landmark for the people of Kiel, and Germany. He added that as Chancellor, Adolf Hitler had ushered in a period of growth and prosperity and that, as Führer, there would be no limit to Germany's ambitions.

In a speech in Rendsburg, Hinrich Lohse, Oberpräsident of Schleswig-Holstein said that it was an historic day for the German Reich, and that this would remove any obstacles to the Führer's plans to make Germany a powerful force in Europe and bring peace and prosperity at home.

~~o~~

In the conference room at Naval Headquarters, thirty-five civilian employees stood before a staff captain, arms extended in salute. Helene Müller stood proudly in the front row. In the bright sunshine, passers-by stopped, and listened to their voices, raised in unison.

'I swear: I shall be loyal and obedient to Adolf Hitler, the Führer of the German Reich and people, respect the laws, and fulfil my official duties conscientiously, so help me God.'

A hundred metres away, in the outer office of General Kästner's unit, Privates Zimmer and Lubinus stood in front of Stabsfeldwebel Neuer, nervously reciting the oath they'd spent the morning learning.

~~o~~

On the drill square in Plön, Colonel Schneider watched as Franz Kästner and the rest of the regiment chanted the oath that was being repeated in barracks, camps, and foredecks all over Germany.

'I swear by God this sacred oath:' they intoned, in the baking midday heat, *'I will render unconditional obedience to Adolf Hitler, the Führer of the German Reich and people, Supreme Commander of the Armed Forces, and will be ready as a brave soldier to risk my life at any time for this oath.'*

'Heil Hitler!' the drill sergeant barked, and the cry, repeated by the ranks, resounded back at him.

Franz, standing ramrod straight, like the rest of his platoon, wondered if his father was

255

wrong. To a man, the soldiers surrounding him had spoken the oath in loud, clear tones, with conviction and belief that belied any doubt about their loyalty, or their willingness to fight to the death for their leader.

~~o~~

In his office, General Kästner sat at his desk, his head in his hands. He'd seen the massed naval staff stand to attention and give their oath of allegiance in front of Vizeadmiral Albrecht, and he could hear his own staff pledging their lives to the Führer outside his office door. Soon it would be the turn of the chief petty officer and the captain to join him and swear their eternal loyalty to a jumped-up Austrian corporal with a god-like belief in his own destiny.

He was glad of the arrangement he'd made with his two officers and a lump came to his throat when he thought of the men he'd picked.

He couldn't understand why only a handful of people could see it. In his new capacity as Führer of the Reich, Hitler's decisions were no longer bound by the laws of the state. He was now the absolute dictator of Germany; there were no further legal or constitutional limits to his authority.

He opened the bottom drawer of his desk and reached in as far back as he could. He pulled out a bottle of Johnnie Walker Black Label, and a small tumbler. He poured himself a generous three fingers and nursed it, taking a sip now and again. He felt the warm, familiar glow start in his belly and suffuse outwards.

When it was finished, he wiped the glass with his handkerchief and returned it, along with the bottle, to the desk drawer.

He picked up his case, turned off the light and closed the door behind him.

CHAPTER 72

[25/05/2001 Friday]

Maldon, England.

Ruth sat in the chair. It had been a gruelling six-hour session, and the effort had taken a lot out of her, and me. I expected her to want to finish for the day, but she seemed to want to continue, as if she'd reached a watershed, and she wanted to let me see beyond it.

She spoke quietly but firmly, and as always, it was mesmerising.

'At the time, Hitler's victory at the polling booths felt like the end of the world for us. The General warned my parents that there were no checks on the Führer's power, that they should seriously consider emigrating. Mother and Father hesitated; both my grandparents, the Nussbaums and the Sachs, refused to consider leaving Germany, wishing to live out their remaining days in the country of their birth and now, in their sixties and seventies, the prospect of starting over again for them was unthinkable. For my parents, the thought of leaving them behind made the decision to leave impossible.

'While we did nothing and waited, the axe that we'd all been expecting to fall stayed poised above our heads. For almost a year, the nation seemed to take a deep breath. Don't get me wrong, things didn't improve much; the constant niggling harassment of Jews still persisted but at times it seemed half-hearted, as if the playground bully had become bored, and was only tormenting his victims so as not to let his reputation slip.

'There was an expectation that trade tariffs would ease, the economy would stutter to some sort of recovery, and there was even talk at Shabbat services that people were finding jobs again, no matter that they were part-time and menial.

'Although there were others, three events spring most to mind from that year and, for once, they didn't have any immediate impact on us, or German Jews as a whole.

'In October, Johann signed up as an officer of the Reichsheer, then, at new year, Wilhelm Canaris became the head of the Abwehr, and General Kästner's boss.

'That same month, Hitler won The Saar Plebiscite, bringing war just a little closer. It also awoke in me a political consciousness or, perhaps more accurately, an inkling of how national and world politics might affect our lives.'

Ruth had that faraway look in her eyes again. I'm sure she could picture herself in the kitchen of the big house with Antje, sitting together, listening to their fathers discuss the day's news in worried tones.

CHAPTER 73

[11/10/1934 Thursday]

Kiel, Germany.

Maria Kästner had deep misgivings.

Unlike Franz, her youngest son didn't go quietly when he joined the army. Flamboyant as ever, Johann made it his goal that everyone should know he was entering the doors of the Kriegsakademie. It was also his seventeenth birthday.

In contrast to the quiet family meal the night before Franz had entered the military, the Drachensee house steeled itself for the invasion of Johann's entire school class, his Hitlerjugend squad, and the complete cadet section of the sailing club. A number of these young men had brought girls with them, and the Kästners began to regret telling their son that he could invite a few friends over for a party.

By the end of what was an exceptionally warm October evening, the adults had retreated to the drawing room as Johann and his friends pursued the celebrations long into the night.

When, at one in the morning, Maria attempted to restore peace and tranquillity to the shores of the lake, the General put his hand on her arm and led her back into the house.

'They're just letting off steam. This could be the last truly carefree night of their lives. Let the neighbours complain.'

Maria frowned.

There would be complaints.

A small fire had been lit on the only piece of lakeside that could be described as a beach, but at times it had threatened to light up the whole sky, as over-exuberant revellers added one too many dry branches to it. Around the fire, the noise of the young partygoers travelled in the still evening, and the squeals and splashes of the teenagers larking about in the dinghies would only add to the rising ire of the inhabitants of the half-dozen large houses which lined Hamburger Chaussee.

'The Böhms won't mind,' the General said. 'Lise is here, and her brother. We can apologise to everyone else tomorrow.'

'But what if they fall in?' Maria said. 'What if one of them drowns?'

She wanted to add *what will the neighbours think?* but she said nothing, knowing he'd find it petty.

'It's a shame Franz had to leave. He would have kept an eye on them.'

Franz had been at the party earlier, but Yosef had run him back to the barracks at Plön, his evening pass expiring at eleven. Once he'd gone, Lise sat in a garden chair, untouchable, holding court to an admiring group of Johann's former classmates, enjoying their adulation. If she sensed resentment from the other girls, she didn't show it.

Ruth and Antje had been permitted to attend, despite Maria's misgivings, but at eleven o'clock, when the admiral and his wife retired to the house, the girls were sent to bed.

~~o~~

In the cottage, Miriam tucked Ruth in, telling her to try and sleep. She'd draped a thick blanket over the curtain rail in the room that she and Manny shared, to try and cut out the sounds from outside.

For Manny, it had worked; he was fast asleep and didn't rouse when Ruth readied herself for bed.

But Ruth was too excited to sleep. Once Miriam had closed the door, she crept to the window and tucked herself in behind the curtain, nose pressed against the glass. Trying not wake Manny, she eased open the window just enough to hear the sounds of the party without waking her little brother up.

She watched in the light of the oil lamps that had been strung around the trees as Johann's friends ran wild. Groups of boys would disappear into the undergrowth, darting back with bottles of wine or beer, deposited earlier in the day to get around Frau Kästner's imposition of a drink limit.

And every so often, a boy would lead a girl close to the mass of trees and bushes, arms around each other, then melt into the darkness, returning after a while, dishevelled, with twigs and leaves stuck to their clothing and in their hair, flushed and giggling, to rejoin the main throng.

Ruth's heart fell when she saw Johann and the prettiest girl at the party, other than Lise Böhm, slip into the boathouse, almost stumbling as she turned her face up to his, waiting for him to kiss her.

I hope they fall in.

The moment the thought entered her head, she regretted it, but she felt cheated to be five years younger than Johann, a chasm of time at their age. But as young as she was, she recognised that he wasn't the type to settle down early and, in five years' time, she would be sixteen, him twenty-two, having left a string of broken-hearted girls behind him.

She vowed that it would be Ruth Nussbaum he would be kissing then.

In fairness to Johann, he'd been the perfect host, dividing his time in the early part of the evening between his family and his friends, charming everyone. He'd even managed to put a little time aside for Antje and Ruth, inviting them to sit for a while around the fire with his friends, eating chestnuts roasted on the flames. The boys teased them gently, but the older girls ignored them, wrapped up in their own adolescence.

Ruth wiped the steamed-up window with her nightgown, and watched Eva, now so grown-up in just a year, flirt with Rutger, the boy from the sailing club, much to Johann's amusement and Maria Kästner's chagrin. As the boy's arm crept across her back, encouraging her to lean on him, she heard Frau Kästner call,

'Eva, Kommst du.'

Eva could only ignore the summons for so long before reluctantly ducking out from under Rutger's arm.

'I'm sixteen, Mama,' Eva said, walking stiffly past her mother, into the house.

'Exactly. And it's time for bed.'

Ruth could imagine Eva stomping up the stairs at Frau Kästner's parting words, mumbling under her breath at the unfairness of it, taking one last longing look out of the landing window, gratified to see the boy still sitting on his own, looking sad.

By now, Ruth could hardly keep her eyes open. She gave in to tiredness and, within seconds of getting back into bed, she was asleep.

~~o~~

Ruth didn't see the General, aided by her father, round up the stragglers at just after two, herding them into the house, and to the camp beds that Miriam had made up earlier in the spare attic bedrooms.

The last to go was Johann. 'Thanks, Papa,' he mumbled, a little worse-for-wear, as the General sat him down on the mattress and lifted his legs onto the bed.

As he pulled the covers over him, he smiled down at his son, the soldier, a tear in his eye.

1935

"I come from a people who gave the Ten Commandments to the world. The time has come to strengthen them with three additional ones, which we ought to adopt and commit ourselves to: thou shall not be a perpetrator; thou shall not be a victim; and thou shall never, but never, be a bystander."

Yehuda Bauer,

Address to the Bundestag, 1998

CHAPTER 74

Memo: Geh.KdoS. ABW 01/01/35 CAC0361.1

For Attention Only: All senior executive officers, Abwehr.

From: Captain Conrad Patzig, Chef der Abwehr.

After long consideration and on advice from senior officials in the Defence Ministry, as from 01/01/1935, I have resigned my commission as Chef der Abwehr. My replacement will be Kapitän zur See, Wilhelm Canaris.

I trust that you will continue to provide the same level of support for Kapitän Canaris that you have given to me over the years.

Captain Conrad Patzig. No action required. [END]

~~o~~

[04/01/1935 Friday]

Erich Kästner eyed his friend across the desk.

'So, how did you manage to pull the wool over their eyes, and get them to give you the top job?'

'There was no cloth of any kind needed. They just recognised exceptional talent. They will have to promote me now.'

Wilhelm Canaris smiled at the General. They sat in the study of the Drachensee house, nursing the first whisky of the day.

'I hear Patzig was forced to resign,' the General said. 'It's a shame. He was a good man, in a quiet sort of way.'

'He overstepped the mark, Erich, it's as simple as that. He was warned, I'm told. The reconnaissance flights across the border with Poland caused a great deal of friction. The Führer ordered their termination a few months ago, after the non-aggression treaty with Poland was signed, but Patzig persisted in continuing them. It was only a matter of time before he was sacked.'

'And why did they choose you? I presume the position was in the gift of the government?'

'I suppose it was. Von Blomberg is a big supporter of Adolf Hitler so he would have a say. But strangely, it was Patzig who recommended me.'

The General looked surprised.

'A last request, so to speak?'

'They asked him who he would suggest. Once again, my name was at the top of his list. It's a recurring theme.'

The General laughed again.

'I'm still puzzled as to why they would listen to the advice of a man they'd just sacked.'

'They may have been considering me anyway. I've been a staunch supporter of the military reforms they've introduced, and of the way they have crushed the communists.'

'Yes, I hear that you give lectures to your recruits on the merits of Adolf Hitler and his party. I'm surprised you're not a party member.'

'Not yet, my friend, but I like the way he gets things done. As senior officers, we should recognise that without the Führer and the NSDAP, the restoration of German military power and military strength would not have been possible. Our duty is to make the Wehrmacht reflect National Socialist ideology. It must be our grand design, Kästner. It's far better than a watered-down government, where politicians are too frightened of the voters to do anything useful.'

The General grunted. He knew that arguing was futile.

'So, they just phoned you up out of the blue?' he asked.

'Well, not really. I'd just taken over as fortress commander at Swinemünde, when I got wind of a spat at the ministry about who should succeed Patzig. So, I made a few calls to ensure that my name was mentioned in any discussions and then dropped in on Conrad to hear his side of it. He knew he was going to be pushed, but he wanted to try and influence who would get the job. He asked me if I would consider it. He said my background in intelligence and my reputation for not being swayed by political pressure influenced his choice.'

The General raised his eyebrow and smiled.

'A loose cannon, some might say.'

'I got the impression that he didn't trust the National Socialists much. He thinks I'll be strong enough to keep the Abwehr out of their direct control.'

'And will you?'

'I don't have a problem working with the NSDAP, and I see the Abwehr supporting Adolf Hitler and his current objectives...'

'But?' the General said.

'There is a *but*,' Canaris agreed. 'Supporting the National Socialists doesn't mean that the armed forces shouldn't retain an independent intelligence-gathering capability.'

'It's a big step, taking this job. And it puts you in the firing line, close to the centre of German politics. Are you comfortable with that?'

'Listen, Erich, I was a forty-seven-year-old Kapitän zur See, with a shore posting. I was going nowhere, and too old to be considered for a seagoing command on a fighting ship. This was a chance to be a big part of Germany's resurgence, and the resurrection of our military. I couldn't, in all honesty, turn down the opportunity to be involved.'

'And you still think we're heading in the right direction?'

'Generally, yes. We need to be strong again, we must take charge of our own destiny, our own economy. Only a strong leader can do that. And in Adolf, we have a strong leader.'

'All I ask is that you keep an open mind and give your full consideration to all the material that will pass across your desk. It's not all defence-related. I know, and I only see a fraction of it.'

'Conrad spoke highly of you. I'm sure he sent you more information than he'd originally intended, just to gauge your response. For some reason, he seemed to have you down as a deep thinker.'

Erich Kästner laughed again. It felt good to talk with his closest friend and he looked forward to working with him. He hoped their different take on Herr Hitler and his party wouldn't sour their relationship.

'I don't know about that,' he said, 'but I have certain views that are in the minority within Germany. Perhaps he just wanted a balanced view of the world. He certainly took some of my opinions on board, without necessarily agreeing wholeheartedly with them. I'd like to think you'd do the same.'

'Erich, joking aside, you know I'll always value your opinion, and above that, your friendship. And I'm always open to the voices of my junior officers...'

The General roared with laughter, thumping his fist on the table. The noise brought Maria running.

She looked at the General, doubled up with mirth, red-faced and unable to speak, the tears running down his face.

'I thought something was wrong with him,' she said, turning to look crossly at Wilhelm Canaris.

'He seems to find me funny, my dear,' the navy man said. 'I can't think why.'

'I'm just...' the General spluttered in between gasps, 'I'm just laughing at one of my superior officer's jokes,' he managed to say, before dissolving once again into a fit of laughter.

His wife turned round, exasperated by their infantile behaviour, and returned to the kitchen, to finish organising dinner.

On the way out, she passed Antje and Ruth coming in, who'd also been drawn to the study by the noise.

'Uncle Wilhelm, what's up with Papa?' Antje said. 'Why does Mama look so annoyed? Were you laughing at her again? You know you shouldn't.'

Captain Canaris smiled at the little girl, whom he thought of as a niece.

'It's nothing. We weren't laughing at your mother. She just thinks we're a bit, shall we say, childish at times.'

'Well, she's probably right,' Antje said, frowning. 'You sometimes act just like Johann and his friends when you get together.'

The General, who'd almost recovered, broke down again. Wilhelm Canaris smiled, looking away.

'We're just in a good mood, Antje,' he said. 'We're celebrating my promotion. I'm now head of the Abwehr.'

She jumped up and hugged him. 'Well done, Uncle Wilhelm,' she said, clinging to him. 'Does that mean you're Papa's boss?'

'It does indeed,' the General blurted out. 'God preserve us,' he managed to say before dissolving once more into another fit of laughter. This time, it was too infectious to resist, and when Maria returned a few seconds later, it was to find the two grown men leaning back over their chairs, tears overflowing, and her daughter and her friend giggling loudly at them.

For a few seconds, she tried to retain her frown of irritation but, in the face of such unrestrained hilarity, she, too, started to chuckle.

They didn't see Miriam, passing the study door, shake her head in disbelief as she made her way through to the hall.

CHAPTER 75

For Ruth, the lead-up to the Saar Plebiscite awakened something in her young mind. At eleven years old, it was the first election she and Antje were truly aware of. Their intense and patriotic schoolteacher made a point of including every aspect of it in their curriculum, reading newspapers aloud to the class and letting them listen to the national news on the newly acquired school radio.

At home, Ruth's parents followed the progress of the plebiscite with morbid fascination, their interest closely matched by the General's. He and Yosef were forever engaged in lengthy conversations about the latest election news, often ignoring Antje and Ruth, not realising their daughters' surprising depths of knowledge on the subject.

The girls kept quiet and listened mainly, and it gave Ruth her first inkling that the General was not an ordinary German, that he was one of the few who didn't seem caught up in the whole adoration of Hitler madness.

At first, when the teacher began to explain the plebiscite to the class, Ruth and Antje had given each other knowing looks and held their hands up to their mouths in mock yawns, but as they listened, something about the teacher's fervour caught their imagination.

'The Saar, or Saarland, is a small region in Rheinland on the border with France. After the end of the Great War, the French, British and the Americans, who had fought against us, punished Germany for losing the war by taking away territory that was rightfully ours, and limiting our army, navy, and air force. Large parts of Sudetenland in the south-east were handed to…'

She saw that some of the children weren't paying as much attention as they should. She crept forward to a boy who was asleep, his head supported by his hands, his elbows on the desk. Watched in silence by the rest of the class, she raised her ruler high and brought it down sharply, and the boy's head jerked up, startled awake by the loud crack as the ruler hit the desk.

'Boy, since you know so much about history that you can afford to doze off, can you tell us which country was given Sudetenland by the Versailles Treaty?'

The boy, by the name of Claus, dropped his eyes and remained silent.

'I thought not. You can wait behind after class for punishment.' She turned to the rest of the class. 'Does any of you other philistines know the answer?'

Antje's hand shot up, then Ruth raised her hand, but slower.

'You,' the teacher said, after a moment's hesitation, pointing at Ruth.

'Czechoslovakia, miss,' Ruth answered quietly.

The teacher's face froze. Even at her young age, the realisation dawned on Ruth that the woman had asked her the question because she presumed that she wouldn't know the answer.

The teacher didn't acknowledge Ruth's response.

'The other area that was stolen from Germany was the Saar region,' she continued. 'It was given to the French in re-par-a-tion,' she said, sounding the word out. 'Does anyone know what that means?'

Ruth kept her hand down. Antje's hand shot up again.

'Yes, Antje.'

'It means we had to pay for being on the losing side.'

'Well done, Antje. I suppose you learned that from your father?' the teacher said with a smile.

'No, miss. It was Ruth who told me.'

Ruth stifled a grin. She'd known the answer, but she was sure that Antje hadn't learned it from her. All she knew was that her friend had wiped the smug smile from the teacher's face in an instant. Ruth couldn't make up her mind if Antje had done it on purpose, but it didn't matter; she loved her for it anyway.

~~o~~

Maria Kästner sighed.

'Do we have to talk politics at the dinner table?'

'Eva asked a question, darling. It's only fair that I attempt to answer it.'

Eva looked as if she regretted having spoken, but Maria wondered if she'd asked out of a need to know a little about the plebiscite, so as not to appear ignorant in the company of the countess and her cohorts. They hadn't told the General yet, but another trip to their new aristocratic friend's home had been arranged, and he had been invited.

Erich Kästner turned back to his daughter.

'You should know about it. It's important,' he said. 'The Great War finished, not with our surrender, but with an armistice, a ceasefire. The British and the Americans held the threat over us that they would attack again and, because Germany was on its knees, we eventually surrendered. The Treaty of Versailles was our punishment for losing. Part of that agreement was that the Saar, a region brimming with coal mines, was ceded to France, but only under the control of the League of Nations, and just for fifteen years. During these years, the French received all of Saarland's economic output.'

Maria yawned but she noticed that Eva appeared to be listening.

'Now,' he continued, 'as preparations are made to hold the plebiscite, or vote, the inhabitants of the Saar region will decide whether they wish to return to Germany, or retain their separate identity, administered by the League of Nations.'

'The people will surely decide to rejoin Germany,' Eva said.

'Perhaps, but it's not quite as simple as that.' He made to go on, then hesitated.

'My teacher said there are a bunch of communists there who are trying to prevent the people from making the right choice.'

They all turned towards Antje, surprised that she'd spoken.

'Well,' said the General, 'she's right about one thing. It seems that the only places where political opposition exists is in the Saar, and yes, a few of them will be communists, but most are a mix of social democrats and conservative parties, like we used to have here.'

Maria frowned. She tried to catch his eye.

He shouldn't be teaching the girls things like that.

The General ploughed on.

He's ignoring me, Maria thought.

'I fear that the National Socialists will not tolerate anything that challenges their desire for the Saarland to return to Germany.'

'Do you not want the Saar to be part of Germany again?' Maria interjected.

'On the contrary, I think it should be part of a democratic Germany, but the people should be allowed to make up their own minds.'

The children stayed silent, sensing the tension between their parents.

'Anyway, that's enough about politics,' the General said. 'Let's talk about something more interesting, like your Grandmother Fischer.'

He did a marvellous impression of his mother-in-law and even Maria joined in the laughter.

~~o~~

He'd chosen not to tell them about the widespread threats and intimidation in the Saarland that Dieter Maas had mentioned at their last meeting.

'On the ground, the NSDAP are worried,' Dieter had told him. 'There are significant

266

numbers of anti-government supporters in the Saar region who moved there after being persecuted here. They have formed a loose political group called the 'United Front'.'

He'd paused, while the General made a note of the name.

'To counteract them,' Dieter had continued, 'the Saar NSDAP supporters have formed a 'German Front' with the Catholics, aided by the Saar police and the Gestapo. The League of Nations are afraid to stop the plebiscite for fear of causing riots, even though they can see what is going on.'

The General had heard rumours, and it was good to have it confirmed, but the former newspaper editor had said more.

'I hear that the 17,000 Saarland National Socialists, who had left to go to Germany to join the SA, threatened to march back into the Saar, worried by the unexpected resistance to the NSDAP's campaign. It was only called off when Britain's Anthony Eden threatened to send soldiers in to keep the peace.'

The General's eyebrows had risen a little.

'How sure are you about that?'

'It was from a most reliable source. I'd trust it.'

The General had put it in his next report to Captain Canaris.

~~o~~

Memo: Geh.KdoS. ABW 14/01/35 CAC0371.1

For Attention Only: All senior executive officers, Abwehr.

From: Kapitän Wilhelm Canaris, Chef der Abwehr.

The Saar Plebiscite result is an overwhelming 90.3% of voters in favour of a return to Germany. Independent overseers from Italy, The Netherlands, and the USA declared that the election had been fair, and that the result was genuine. [END]

~~o~~

Memo: Geh.KdoS. ABW 14/01/35 CAC0372.1

For Attention Only: General Erich Kästner, Abwehr, Kiel office.

From: Kapitän Wilhelm Canaris, Chef der Abwehr.

Re: your report on the run-up to the Saar Plebiscite. Your comments have been noted and your observations have been confirmed from independent sources. Despite the concerns raised in your report, no action will be taken in the light of the overwhelming result and the desirability of the Saar being once again a part of Germany. It is an unfortunate and unavoidable repercussion of the rejuvenation of Germany.

NO ACTION REQUIRED [END]

Erich Kästner grimaced at his friend's dismissal of his concerns. He wondered if Conrad Patzig would have been less willing to discard his opinion but concluded that he would have acted no differently.

CHAPTER 76

Although the return of the Saar to Germany was entirely in accordance with the terms of the Treaty of Versailles, in Britain, France and the United States, worried leaders met with advisors to discuss the implications. In Germany, nearly everyone, apart from those who were categorised as non-Aryan or otherwise undesirable, celebrated long into the night.

A few days later, the General called in to Oskar von Friedeburg's printshop and asked to speak to him.

'Sorry, General, he's not in today. You should have phoned.'

Oskar's staff were used to General Kästner calling on occasion to have a chat with their boss.

'It doesn't matter. I was here to ask about a small print job, but I'll call back.'

'Oh, if that's all it is, Dieter Maas can deal with that, although I'm sure Herr von Friedeburg will want to arrange a bit of a discount for you.'

The secretary smiled at him and beckoned for him to take a seat. He thanked her and waited a few minutes when she returned with Dieter Maas.

'General, it's good to see you. What can I do for you?'

'Hello Dieter, I'd forgotten you worked here. I just need advice on a small print job. I was going to ask Oskar but I'm sure you'll be just as able to help.'

'I hope so. Come on through to my office.' He turned to the secretary. 'Could you bring a couple of coffees, please?'

The General followed him to a small office that looked out onto the print floor, high up in the roof space. The secretary arrived a few minutes later, two cups of coffee in her hands. Once she'd left, the General dropped all pretence.

'I do have a small printing request, as a matter of fact, but that will take a minute, then we can talk.'

The General handed him a piece of paper. Dieter glanced at it.

'Invitations. That should be no problem.'

'For the functionaries coming to a ship launch. I said I'd deal with it.'

'I'll get on to it this afternoon.' He looked up at the General. 'Did the result surprise you?'

'Yes and no. It was emphatic.'

'There was a lot of intimidation, as I told you. The NSDAP were terrified that there was some real opposition this time. They would have most likely won anyway, but I wasn't impressed with the League of Nations, and their observers.'

The General grimaced. "Fair and genuine". So much for international scrutiny. Where do you think that leaves us?'

Dieter Maas looked at him curiously. 'You want my opinion now? Not just information?'

The General laughed. 'I don't come across too many sceptics. There are few people I can have a frank discussion with. The Doc is too busy and Oskar...' His voice tailed off.

'At the end of the day, Oskar is a good man, but he'll do what it takes to survive. I don't think he'd knife you in the back, but he may not stick out his neck for you.'

The General laughed again. 'That's our Oskar. You're right. Deep down he's a decent fellow with a hefty dose of self-preservation.'

'Perhaps the most sensible option in the current political climate...' Dieter paused. 'For what it's worth, I think the Saar result is a bit of a game-changer.'

Apart from the slight raise of an eyebrow, the General didn't react. He waited for Dieter to elaborate.

'First, it validates the National Socialist government. It might have been skewed, but it was a free election and, more importantly, it showed that Germans living outside Germany hate the Versailles Treaty more than they fear Adolf Hitler and his regime. You only have to look at the newspaper headlines. It makes it difficult to argue that he doesn't have the overwhelming support of the German people.'

The General nodded. It was exactly the conclusion he'd already arrived at. 'Go on,' he said.

'Secondly, it boosts Adolf Hitler's personal status as a leader, and it gives him a moral authority to pursue whatever policies he sees fit.'

'There's more?'

'Yes, last of all, the League of Nations are scared witless of confronting Hitler. Even worse, Chamberlain and Daladier completely failed to notice that the National Socialists backed down when Eden threatened to send troops in.'

'Thank you. I feared I was the only one who saw what the Saar Plebiscite could mean for Germany. I didn't give as much thought as I should have to the international implications. But there is one thing you might have missed.'

'Oh, what's that?'

'Sudetenland.'

'Ah. You could be right.'

'Like Saarland, it's a largely German-speaking region and it belonged to us until it was taken away at Versailles.'

'But it was ceded permanently to Czechoslovakia, unlike the Saar. There can be no plebiscite.'

'It won't happen now, but somewhere down the line, our new Führer will want it back. And it may just start a war.'

~~o~~

[10/03/1935 Sunday]

'I've only got a one-day pass. Just my luck.'

Franz laughed. He was on a three-day furlough and could afford to gloat.

'That's probably a couple of local girls who've been saved from a life of shame,' he said.

Johann grinned at his brother. 'I can't help if I have a reputation, not that there have been too many opportunities recently; the last five months have been intense, with almost no time off base. At least it's over now.'

A voice came from the doorway.

'That's because they've shortened basic training. They want to ramp up the number of recruits going through the military academies.'

Both boys looked round as their father entered the room.

'Look on the bright side,' Franz said. 'You took a month less than me; it will get you into the regiment sooner,' Franz added.

'And just in time to deal with all the new conscripts,' the General said.

'What are you talking about? We've heard nothing about new men,' Franz said.

'It's a poorly kept secret. I'm surprised you haven't heard the rumours. They're going to pass the legislation next week. We're about to witness the biggest expansion of the army and the navy since 1913.'

'That completely rips up the Treaty of Versailles. Conscription isn't allowed under the agreement,' Franz said.

'Stuff Versailles,' Johann replied. 'We've ran a bus through it already; the new Luftwaffe, those battleships we're building. No one seems overly keen to stop us.'

'He's right, Franz,' the General said. 'Germany is going to have the army, the navy and the air force we've all been asking for, and nobody will lift a finger to stop us.'

'Good.' The table shook as Johann banged his fist down hard. 'We've been trodden on for too long. It's time Germany stood up for itself. And now that we have the Saar back, we'll have the coal to fuel it and the economy to drive us forwards.'

'It will certainly solve the unemployment problem if everyone is in the army,' the General said.

'That's not a bad thing, especially for people my age,' Johann said, missing the irony in his father's voice. 'Do you think they would let me transfer to the Luftwaffe? I would make the most dashing pilot.'

The other two laughed. They could both see Johann as the raffish airman, a girl on each arm and a sports car to match.

'It's a bit of a mouthful, though, *the Law for the Reconstruction of the National Defence Forces*. Why didn't they just call it the Luftwaffe Law?' Johann asked.

'Because they thought that no one in Britain would notice if we didn't mention an air force,' Franz quipped, and they all laughed again.

'We're going to get a new name too,' the General informed his sons. 'It's to be shortened to the 'Heer'. An official announcement will be made in May. The Reichsmarine are to be called the Kriegsmarine.'

'Not so different. Why the changes?'

'I think Hitler sees it as a new start, with a mighty new military force. And together, we're going to be called the Wehrmacht.'

'Wehrmacht,' Johann said. 'I like the sound of that.'

CHAPTER 77

Memo: Geh.KdoS. ABW 17/03/35 CAC0379.1

For Attention Only: All senior executive officers, Abwehr.

From: Kapitän Wilhelm Canaris, Chef der Abwehr.

SS Chief Himmler has created the Inspectorate of Concentration Camps, a new section within the SS.

under the leadership of SS General Theodor Eicke. This move formalises the SS takeover and centralisation of the concentration camp system that took place in July 1934.

For information only. No action required. [END]

[26/03/1935 Tuesday]

Manny cried for three nights when Ruth was moved out of the bedroom they shared, and into her own room.

There were four years between them and, listening to his classmates, he learned that older sisters were always a pain in the backside, but he'd never found that with Ruth. She did her best to look after him when their parents were busy at the Kästner house and, although she could have called them if there was any hint of trouble, she rarely did.

'When girls get to Ruth's age, they need a room of their own,' Yosef explained to him.

It wasn't much of an explanation. Manny thought of all sorts of strange reasons why this should be; he'd read all about monsters and demons in books and imagined with relish that teenage girls changed into vampires or witches at night.

He soon realised, however, that having his own room had its advantages. There was more space to hang the painted balsa-wood models he and his father made, and freedom to leave toys lying about the floor without getting into trouble from Ruth.

While Ruth missed the comfort of hearing her little brother's soft breathing as she drifted off to sleep, she was becoming aware that she felt different, and a sudden desire for modesty and privacy made going to bed in the shared room feel awkward.

When Miriam sat her down and told her that she would be getting her own room, it was her opening to warn her daughter of the changes she could expect in her body, and what they meant, and that having her own room would make it much easier for her.

Choosing wallpaper and the colour of the paint for her new room with Mama made it fun, and Manny had helped Yosef decorate the room for her, before painting the second-hand furniture she'd chosen, to make it look like new.

Moving in was exciting, but it broke her heart when she lay in her new room, listening to Manny's quiet sobbing before he went to sleep.

~~o~~

'For the last time, I'm not going. I can't stand these people.'

The General usually yielded to Maria's social demands. In return, she knew which events he would tolerate and only insisted on asking him to accompany her to the engagements where she felt his presence was essential.

He encouraged her to attend most of her events without him by behaving inappropriately when he found himself at a function that he considered a waste of his time, or where the other guests were more pretentious than usual. Rarely did Erich and Maria resort to serious argument about their social calendar.

'Erich, darling, this is of vital importance for Eva. It's her future we're talking about here.'

'Let's be clear about this, it's what you want for her future. Have you asked Eva?'

'We discuss it all the time. She's more than delighted to meet nice young men with impeccable backgrounds.'

'She also looked quite happy with her nice young man at Johann's party. Or is his background not quite good enough?'

'The boy is wild. All of Johann's friends are. It's why Johann is so unruly.'

'They're just having fun. We had fun at their age. Remember what we got up to.'

She blushed.

'We didn't do the things they do. Well, at least, I didn't.'

The General had gone through a phase as a teenager much like Johann, perhaps with a dusting of Franz's reserve thrown in. Before he'd met Maria, he'd had the odd fling, and many a drunken barracks night as a young officer, though he had to admit that Johann seemed to be making a career out of it.

'All right, they like to cut loose, but they worked hard at school, and I'm sure he'll do well in the army. I did.'

'That's not to say that this boy Rutger will be the same. She's too young to be running about with them.'

'If she's too young for them, she's too young for the Hooray Henrys you'd like her to gad about with.'

He could see her getting exasperated, and he wished there were some way he could end the conversation without being rude.

'What will I say to the countess? I said you'd come.'

'You should have checked with me first. If it's of any help to you, I have an emergency meeting with the admirals this evening.'

'Have you? It's the first I've heard of it.'

'It's the first the admirals have heard of it too,' he muttered to himself, then, to Maria, he spoke softly, regretting his harsh words.

'She'll understand. For a general, the army always comes first.'

The General could see her thinking about how his words might sound to the countess. He sensed her resolve weakening.

'And I suppose you want Yosef to drop you off first?'

'No, Yosef can take you. I'll get my army driver to come and pick me up.'

'That would be silly. We can drop you off on the way.'

He groaned. He'd imagined a night in the house, just him and Antje. Now he'd have to go down to the office. Still, he would take Antje with him; she loved his office, and they could stop for an ice cream on the walk back home.

CHAPTER 78

By the time they reached the Lindau estate, Yosef's mood hadn't improved. Arriving fifteen minutes early, Maria made him take a circuitous route around the property to ensure that they drove up to the front of the house no more than a few minutes ahead of time. He said nothing, resigned to being stuck out in the middle of nowhere on his son's birthday.

He was sure Frau Kästner hadn't known it was Manny's birthday when she organised her visit to the countess; it had just never occurred to her. He smiled to himself as a thought passed through his mind. If there had been a big party, with lots of children, mothers, and a cake, he would have been glad to stay out of the way, so perhaps he deserved his fate, even if it were galling.

~~o~~

'It's such a pity your husband couldn't join us. There are a couple of people here I'd like him to meet.'

'Oh, I am so sorry, Countess,' Maria said, 'he was called away just before we left to come here. An emergency at Headquarters. I believe the defence minister was flying in from Berlin.'

It's a harmless little embellishment.

'For him,' she added, 'the army always comes first.'

'Call me Margarethe, my dear, and you're right, we mustn't get in the way of affairs of state, must we?'

'You're so kind, Countess... I mean, Margarethe; he was most apologetic.'

The older woman put her hand on Maria's arm. 'I'm sure he was. It's a shame. I would have liked to ask his opinion on the Reichswehr's loyalty to the Kaiser.'

'I mentioned it to him.'

'And what did he say?'

'He was most sympathetic,' she lied, then, in a flash of inspiration, she added, 'It's difficult for him to talk about, he says. The work he does at the Abwehr is all very hush-hush.'

'I quite understand, my dear. One must be very careful these days.' She gave a short laugh, then turned to Eva.

'Now, young lady, I have a young man here who is dying to meet you...'

~~o~~

The car wended homewards through the dark country lanes, the light from the stars casting shadows on the occupants' faces as the vehicle swung from bend to bend.

Once they'd passed through Eckernförde, the countryside opened out and the hum of the tyres on the longer straight stretches lulled Maria into a contented sleep.

Beside her on the seat, Eva's thoughts were rattling around in her head. She was glad her mother had fallen asleep; the last thing she needed was an effusive post-mortem of the evening's proceedings. The young man she'd been introduced to, though two years older, seemed more like a boy than Rutger.

He was good-looking, well-mannered, and attentive. He was also highly educated and although there was no real arrogance to him, it was obvious from his manner that he was from an exceedingly well-to-do family. He had a swagger about him, but it wasn't the cocky, laughter-filled, I'll-try-anything strut that Rutger, Johann and their friends had; it was the self-assured belief of someone who knew their place was at the top of the pecking order.

Approaching the canal, the car passed under the railway bridge, and Yosef turned sharp left before starting the climb to cross the Levensau Bridge. As the car turned, Maria's head fell against her daughter's shoulder, and she jerked awake.

'Where are we?' she said, her eyes wide.

'We're nearly home, just crossing the canal, Mama.'

'How long have I been asleep?'

'About half an hour. Since Eckernförde.'

'It's the wine. And the food.'

Eva smiled, then groaned to herself as she heard her mother ask the question she'd been dreading.

'So, what did you think? He's awfully handsome, isn't he? And such impeccable manners.'

'He was charming, Mama. I had a lovely evening.'

She was lying. He'd asked her a few token questions about herself, but had mostly talked about his family, their estates and townhouses, and their factories and mines.

'Did he ask to see you again? He seemed terribly keen.'

'He asked if it would be appropriate to call me, if that's what you mean.'

'That's marvellous. You must have made quite an impression.'

'It wasn't a job interview, Mama,' Eva said, laughing.

'Of course it wasn't. Don't be silly. But you must see him again.' She put her arm around Eva and squeezed her.

'I told him he could call if he liked, but I'm not sure that I want to meet him again.'

Eva heard her mother gasp. In the front of the car, she thought she saw Yosef flinch.

'Why not, Eva?' her mother said, a note of testiness in her voice. 'You mustn't be rash. After all, you said you liked him.'

'I said he was charming, Mama. I didn't say I liked him.'

'Eva, you should give him a chance. He's one of the most eligible young men in the state. Most girls would die for the chance to go out with him.'

'I know, Mama,' Eva said, not without sympathy for her mother's disappointment.

For a minute, they remained silent, then Eva took her mother's hand and spoke softly.

'When you met Papa for the first time, did you feel indifferent?'

Maria Kästner turned away and bit her lip.

'No,' she murmured, turning to face her daughter again. 'I didn't.'

'Well, tonight, I felt nothing. But with Rutger…'

'There'll be others,' Maria said. 'You're too young to settle for someone like Rutger. We'll try again when you're a little older.'

Maria Kästner looked out of the window.

Her daughter sat in silence. Sometimes she found that it was the best thing to do. She glanced up at the driver's mirror to see Yosef looking at her, a sympathetic smile in his eyes.

[02/04/1935 Tuesday]

Maria Kästner hadn't slept well.

'Erich, could you please have a word with your daughter. She's going to throw her life away on that Schäfer boy.'

The General sighed.

'I had a blow-by-blow account of the evening last night at bedtime. Do we have to go over it again this morning?'

'Erich, this is important. I'm only asking for a little help.'

'For a start,' he said, 'Eva's young. This thing with Rutger will go one of two ways. It will either blow over, she'll break her heart for ten minutes and move on to the next big romance, or they'll fall in love, and in three years' time or so, they'll marry.'

'Oh, it's so easy for you to say. You don't seem to care too much for her future,' Maria snapped.

She wished she didn't get wound up by him so readily and, in her heart, Maria Kästner wondered if it was already beyond repair.

Will the countess tolerate Eva's rebuff of the young man she'd introduced her to?

The General shook his head.

'I do care,' he said, 'and if she wants to be with Rutger Schäfer, then it's fine with me. What's wrong with the boy? He's from a good family. I know his mother and father well.'

'He's a bit of a tearaway for my liking.'

'Precisely like your son,' the General retorted. 'Imagine what you'd say if some girl's mother talked about Johann like that.'

'I'd probably agree with her,' she countered, but she knew she wouldn't. In frustration, she threw her brush onto the floor. It broke into three pieces, and she started to cry.

'Maria,' he said, putting his arm around her shoulder, 'I know you only want to do your best for Eva, but you must let her have the freedom you had.'

She knew she'd lost. Then she steeled herself. She'd invited the countess over for dinner. She'd have a chance to explain, and the countess would know girls were fickle at that age. If she left it a few months before setting a date with Margarethe, the Schäfer boy would become bored and move on to his next young victim. He was too boorish to make Eva happy.

There was one problem. She'd have to find a way to tell Erich the countess was coming. And make him behave.

CHAPTER 79

[26/04/1935 Friday]

'Why can't I take my friends away for a weekend on the boat?' Johann asked.

The General put his arm around his son's shoulders.

'You can take them on the boat for a couple of day-sails at first and, if that goes well, we'll see about an overnight trip later in the season.'

'But Franz is away with his friends.'

They could still see *Snowgoose* in the distance, almost at Friedrichsort, leaning hard over in the stiff breeze.

'You could have gone with them.'

'I only have a two-day pass. It would have meant cutting short their trip. They're on a week's leave.'

'You could have gone with them for the first couple of days and caught a train back. They're going round Als, so they should be in Sønderborg, I think.'

Als was an island off the coast of Denmark, separated from the mainland by a narrow strait of water, Als Sund. It was a good day's sail from Kiel.

'I could have, I suppose,' Johann grumbled. 'I didn't think.'

'It would have been good for you. You join the regiment in July. It would have been a chance to get to know them.'

'We already met. Franz's birthday.'

He remembered. Johann hadn't come home that night and Maria had been worried sick, until he'd told her to stop fretting; Johann was with Franz and, sure enough, they'd appeared the next morning, both apologetic, Johann rather the worse for wear.

'We'll organise a sail for you and your friends next time you're on leave, then take it from there. Franz did all that last year.'

He ruffled Johann's hair out of habit, and was surprised he didn't object, being seventeen.

There's still a boy in there somewhere, the General thought.

He hadn't lied. Franz had taken the boat out quite a few times, usually for an hour or two but once for the whole day, before spending his first night as skipper away on her, anchored in the lee of Bisdorf, thirty miles down the coast, with a group of friends from the sailing club.

But, the General thought, it had been Franz's choice to take it in easy steps. The General would have been quite happy for him to take the boat away for a week, even when he was sixteen. It wasn't just the sailing; both his sons were exceptional young yachtsmen, and although Franz had an edge when it came to running a boat, navigating, and working with crew, Johann was not far behind.

What Johann lacked was the maturity that Franz had. Added to that, Johann's liking for fun might spill over into risk-taking in pursuit of thrills, or to show off.

And he needed to be sure of Johann, before entrusting him with the boat, his life, and the lives of his friends.

~~o~~

[27/04/1935 Saturday]

The sail round Als has started well, Franz thought.

The five friends had found themselves celebrating Franz's birthday at anchor in a little bay on the south-east corner of the island.

'One of us has to stay sober, in case the wind gets up in the night,' he'd told them.

'Nineteen years old, and you're acting like an old man,' Fritz Aumeier had moaned.

'I'll have a few beers tomorrow night, in Sønderborg.'

'We'll have to drink this tonight,' Artur Schweitzer had said, opening the bottle of Schnapps he'd found in one of *Snowgoose*'s lockers, pouring a generous measure in each of the four mugs he'd laid on the saloon table.

'And there's half a bottle of rum here,' Heinrich Öhlman had chipped in.

'Nobody's getting drunk tonight,' Franz had insisted, shaking his head. 'I don't want anyone falling overboard in the dark. You can have one or two, but you'll have to wait until tomorrow night to drink yourselves into a stupor.'

They'd complained, as he'd expected, but all of them had enjoyed the long sail around Als the next day without hangovers to spoil it.

By the time they'd reached Als Sund, the sun had set. They motored the last four miles to Sønderborg in darkness, and Franz could sense the tension building in the cockpit, despite his calm demeanour, and his reassurance that by following the lights on the buoys on both sides of the sound, and keeping their eyes peeled for the navigation lights of other vessels, they would be perfectly safe.

When they drifted at last into the town quay in Sønderborg, the worry on their faces melted into grins, and they clapped Franz on the back for an incredible piece of seamanship, which he accepted with embarrassed good grace.

'Let's find somewhere to eat, and somewhere to have a verdammte kaltes Bier,' Fritz Aumeier said, itching to start drinking, after a long day and the limited libation of the previous night.

They abandoned Franz to square away the boat, and when he finally found them, in a bar owned by a German from Hamburg, they'd already polished off a couple of rounds of beers between them.

'Franz, over here, man,' he heard them shout as he stood in the doorway of the third bar he'd tried.

'They do food here,' Fritz said, as Franz sat down with them. 'It's pretty basic but there's lots of it. We've all ordered Bratwurst and fried potatoes. It should be here soon.'

Franz thanked them; his stomach ached for something filling, and the smell of cooked sausage made his mouth water. He shouted to the barman, who began pouring five more glasses.

The beer arrived first. Franz took a long sip and savoured it, wondering why the first beer after a long, hard sail always tasted better.

'Das ist gut, ja?' Oberleutnant Artur Schweitzer, the only other first lieutenant in the group, held up his glass and grinned at Franz.

'Ja, das ist wunderbar. I was ready for this.'

Franz smiled broadly, loving the close-knit band they had formed. The other three were second lieutenants; Fritz Aumeier, Heinrich Öhlman, and Maximilian 'Maxi' Grabner were all from the south of Germany and they'd met each other at their respective military academies or during their infantry training, but the group hadn't coalesced until they were commissioned to Colonel Schneider's division in the Fourth Infantry Regiment.

'Great sail today, Franz. I could get really hooked on this yachting thing.'

'The weather has been kind to us. Good winds, and not too cold for this time of year. Just don't think about going for a swim; the water is still bitterly cold.'

They'd started off well wrapped up in their army gear, but the sun had shone for most of the day and, apart from the upwind stretch across the top of Als, it had been pleasantly warm.

'I wasn't too keen on that sailing blind lark at the end,' Heinrich Öhlman said. 'Do you honestly get any enjoyment from that?'

'I love it. It can be challenging, and occasionally disorientating, but it does make you concentrate, and after you've done a lot of it, you get a real buzz out of it.'

They gave him a sceptical look.

'My highlight was when that Luftwaffe plane flew low over us,' Maxi Grabner said.

'It's the first one I've seen.'

When he'd seen the plane, he'd jumped up and started waving his arms frantically, until Franz had told him that what he was doing was an internationally recognised distress signal. The plane had circled back and flown over them again, lower this time, the two black crosses on the underside of the wings clearly visible. Maxi had given the aircrew a wave again, but in a manner communicating kinship rather than a need for assistance. The pilot had flown back towards Germany, waggling his wings at them in salute.

'The Luftwaffe has only just been formed and already we have planes!' Heinrich Öhlman said, as another round of drinks arrived at the table. The Frenchies will be filling their boots with Scheiße.'

They all laughed, even Franz, but he saw that their eyes were filled with alcohol-fuelled patriotism.

'When do you think we'll get the first conscripts? I can't say I'm looking forward to that.'

'Fritz, you're just frightened you'll have to get off your backside and do some work, training the poor wretches, who've probably never seen a gun.'

Fritz Aumeier held up his hand, attempting to stop the raucous laughter.

'I'm just a very calm individual. I don't rush about like a headless chicken, unlike some of my colleagues,' he said, looking around, 'but I still get the job done.'

'Your Kompanie is the most laid-back in the army. Some days they don't even get out of bed.'

By now, tears of laughter were flowing down Franz's cheeks.

'I call them my platoon if you don't mind,' Fritz huffed.

'That's because you watch too many films. This isn't the American Civil War, you know. Don't let the old man catch you calling them that.'

'Peh. Old Schneider's a pussy. I can handle him.'

'I'll mention that, the next time I'm sailing with him.'

Franz had been sailing with the colonel on a couple of occasions. None of the others had been invited yet, but it would happen. Their commanding officer liked to take his commissioned men away on character-building sailing expeditions, often in the middle of winter.

'I don't fancy it,' Heinrich Öhlman said. 'I hear they're torture.'

'He says he can see into a soldier's soul when it gets really rough, and he can tell if an officer will make the grade,' Franz said, exaggerating somewhat. The colonel had told him that trips gave him the chance to see his junior officers up close, and to observe them under pressure and out of their comfort zone. He'd let Franz take more and more command of the boat on both trips he'd done.

Heinrich shivered. 'I hope a war starts before it's my turn. This sort of sailing is fine, but I don't do cold, wet and miserable for anyone.'

'I hope we never invade Britain then,' Artur Schweitzer joked. 'You won't be much use.'

After the laughter had subsided, the barmaid arrived with five plates of food, piled high and smothered in gravy.

Amid the wolf-whistles, she laid them down on the table and asked if they needed their glasses filled again.

'Silly question, Fräulein. We'll have another round but only you bring them over, and you stay for a little while to keep us company.'

'I'll bring your beer and, clearly, I would love to sit with you for a while, but unfortunately, I have work to do.' She patted Maxi's head and left. They all watched her walk to the bar.

'Did you see that? She's magnificent!' Fritz exclaimed.

They all nodded. The rear view of the barmaid was, if anything, even better.

'This is a great place. I hope we're not leaving too early in the morning.'

'One of the Kriegsmarine warships is anchored at the south end of the sound. We don't want to hang around too long if we want to get a close-up look at her.'

'How do you know it's there? It was dark when we came in.'

'I could see her navigation lights, and could just make out her shape, from her deck lights.'

'That's very impressive, but I still think I'll prefer the silhouette of our little Fräulein here,' Maxi said, looking longingly towards the bar.

They were still in fits of laughter when the barmaid returned, carrying two large jugs of beer.

'Beautiful jugs,' Maxi said, then burst into laughter again, his body shaking. The whole table erupted with him.

The barmaid stood with a resigned smile, waiting for a chance to put the beer on the table. Franz recovered first, holding his hand out to the girl.

'I'm sorry, we're boors. I hope we haven't offended you.'

The barmaid smiled. 'Don't worry, it won't be the last time I'll hear that. Why do you think he employs me?' she said, looking at her cleavage then nodding at the landlord behind the bar.

Franz grinned, and helped set the beer on the table.

'Let me know if you need anything else,' she said to him.

'I think you're in there, Franz,' Fritz said, when she'd gone. 'She likes you.'

'No, she doesn't. It's her job to flirt with brainless young men so that they buy more beer.'

'Good idea, Franz. More beer.' Maxi turned and shouted to the barmaid, who nodded and laid out five empty glasses on the bar, next to ones she was filling.

For a while, they talked about the characters in the regiment, which of them were going places and the others who would finish their career in their current rank.

'It's a shame about Gabriel, isn't it?' Artur Schweitzer said, serious for a moment. 'For a Jew, he was one of the best.'

'I didn't realise he was a Jew, until the army threw him out,' Maxi said. 'I suppose it was inevitable. You can't have them in the armed forces, no matter how able they might seem.' He turned to Franz. 'No offence, my friend.'

They all knew that Franz's family employed Jews, and that they treated them like family friends, but Franz rarely let himself be drawn into discussions about it. He was the best officer of the five, and a great friend to them, so they did their best to keep their opinions on Jews to themselves.

'It will come back to bite us one day,' Franz said. 'We're losing an awful lot of good people. Gabriel is one of them. Can any of us say we're a better soldier than him?'

They looked down, unable to meet his eyes. The table, from one of riotous mirth, had turned maudlin, as only a gathering of inebriated men can.

'You're as good as him, or better,' mumbled Heinrich.

'I'm not sure of that. And I can think of four or five others we'll lose through this *Wehrgesetz*. Some of them aren't even Jews, they just have a Jewish wife. At a time when the army's trying to expand, it's crazy.'

Since the German government had issued a new defence law at the beginning of the month, a stream of serving Jewish officers had been cashiered.

'Franz, let it go,' Artur pleaded, 'there's nothing you can do about it, and…' he looked round at the others, 'I'd be careful who you say things like that to.'

The other three nodded. He was sure that they'd never snitch on him, but he also knew that, deep down, they'd all swallowed the NSDAP's lies and would support most of the party's policies without question.

'If it's the price we pay to recover our economy, and our military, I'm happy to do whatever the Führer wants us to do,' Heinrich stated flatly.

Franz looked at them. He knew that Heinrich Öhlman spoke for the group.

'What's the matter with you lot, you look as if you've swallowed cat piss.' The barmaid's voice startled them.

It broke the spell. Maxi, then Fritz, broke into laughter, and the others quickly joined in. Only Franz couldn't raise more than a wan smile.

He sat for a while, half listening to the fog of conversation and laughter, his mind a million miles away.

His bladder full, he excused himself and followed the sign at the back of the bar. He stood in the cold of the privy, hoping he hadn't spoiled his friends' trip. He didn't know why he couldn't stay silent when the talk turned to the National Socialists.

He washed his hands, and stepped back into the warm room, fogged with tobacco smoke. The barmaid stood at the end of the bar, taking a few moments during a lull in service. The thrum of noise from around the room wasn't unpleasant, and it lifted his mood a little. She looked up as he passed.

'You look a little sad. Was there some sort of quarrel?' the barmaid said.

He smiled at her. 'No, not really. Not at all.'

'It's just…' She paused. 'One moment you were all laughing and joking, the next, it was as if you'd got news of a death in the family.' She looked at him. 'Oh, god, it wasn't, was it?'

'No, nothing like that. Just life in Germany at the present time.'

Why am I spilling my worries to a Danish barmaid?

'I thought it was all looking up for you.'

'You've heard nothing that would worry you about what's going on in Germany?'

'Very little. Some rumours about prison camps and political prisoners being locked up, I suppose.'

'Nothing about Jews?'

'There was something, now that you mention it,' she said, frowning. 'There have been a trickle of Jews moving to Sønderborg, mostly from northern Germany, coming to stay with relatives here.'

Franz looked at her.

The outside world doesn't know what is happening. At least, not the ordinary people.

'Your German is excellent,' he said, deciding there was no point in trying to explain. 'Did you learn it at school?'

'Yes, and I had a job for a while in Flensburg. It really helped my German.'

'Jeg taler lidt Dansk,' he said. *I speak a little Danish.*

'Det er godt,' she said, smiling. 'Tager du afsted I morgen?' *Do you leave in the morning?*

He wondered why she wanted to know.

'Ja, vi tager afsted om morgenen,' he answered. *Yes, we leave in the morning.*

She switched back to German. It was easier, he admitted to himself.

'You're on a boat?'

'Yes, a yacht. It's my father's. I'm from Kiel. The others are in my regiment.'

'I thought you were soldiers. You must be officers, yes?'

'Junior officers. As junior as you can get, really.'

'So, you must stay with the boat, and your friends?'

He blushed. 'Yes. I have a girlfriend at home.'

She laughed. 'Ah. She's a lucky girl.'

'My friends think you are beautiful. They'd say I was mad.'

'They're right. I hope she's good to you.' She leant forward and kissed him on the cheek. 'I must go. There are a lot of thirsty people waiting.'

He grinned. 'It was lovely talking to you.'

She started to walk away but turned towards him. 'If you change your mind, I finish at twelve…'

He shook his head, then, once she'd gone, he rubbed his cheek and returned to the table.

'You might at least have recommended one of us to her,' Maxi said, once he'd sat down.

'Pardon?'

'Well, let me see. You talked to her, in all innocence, needless to say, then she suggested that you might rather spend the night away from the boat. You said you had a girlfriend, she

280

said that was a shame, and you didn't think to say that your friend Maxi was a hell of a substitute.'

Franz sat looking at him blankly, mouth open for a second.

The table erupted, and they all clapped Franz on the back, remonstrating with him for having *too much honour.*

Another two jugs of beer arrived, and a cheap bottle of Schnapps.

'On the house,' the barmaid said as she placed the bottle, and five glasses in the middle of the table, giving Franz a look. She departed to another round of whistles.

~~o~~

[28/04/1935 Sunday]

The next morning, at eight, Franz steered the boat away from the wharf to pass through the King Christian X bridge when it swung open. His crew still slept soundly in their bunks.

As he passed the towering bulk of the *Karlsruhe*, Franz looked up and waved at the watch officer on the warship's bridge and was rewarded with a loud blast from the light cruiser's foghorn.

He was gratified to see his crew tumbling out from the companionway, half dressed, surprised to see that they were underway, and that the entire horizon was filled with the cold, grey steel of a Reichsmarine hull.

They dragged themselves around the deck, reluctantly following Franz's orders, complaining of the early hour, the bright sunshine, the thumping headaches, and Franz's cruel streak in not letting them sleep on.

With the sails hoisted and, watched by a growing crowd of sailors on the *Karlsruhe*'s aft deck, Franz turned the boat onto her course and headed for home.

CHAPTER 80

[21/05/1935 Tuesday]

'So, you finally made admiral, Canaris. Well, rear admiral, at least.'

'There was never a doubt, Kästner. And just call me Admiral, forget the rear bit.'

The General laughed.

'And on the very day we've officially become the Wehrmacht!' he said.

They sat at a table in a quiet corner of Café Larsen, in Kaiserstraße. They'd ordered food, and each sat with a cold beer in front of them. The place was almost empty, and the nearest people were three tables away.

Erich Kästner tried to keep the pleasure off his face, but he was delighted for his friend.

'I put in a good word for you,' he said. 'They did a poll of all your senior staff. You can thank me later.'

Canaris laughed. 'I'm sure they did,' he said.

'In all honesty, it was ludicrous having a Kapitän zur See as the chief of the Abwehr, especially as it is ten times larger than it was five years ago, and a few of your senior staff outranked you. I said the same when Captain Patzig was in command.'

'It could be awkward at times. I mean, a mere captain bossing around a revered general. How would that ever work?'

'Only if you, the good-natured general, know the meaning of the word *humility*.'

Admiral Canaris laughed again. In all seriousness, they both knew that he deserved the elevation in rank and, if it hadn't been for some untimely mishaps in his naval career, it would have happened long before.

Their food arrived, and fresh beers.

'How are you finding the job? It would be far too political for me,' the General said, between mouthfuls.

'I'm sure you'd cope. Working with the people in the Kriegsmarine, Heer and Luftwaffe is straightforward, but von Blomberg and the rest of the defence ministry need watching. Doing business with our NSDAP colleagues is like finding oneself in a nest of snakes. Poisonous ones.'

'I know. I find myself having to deal with their minions here. Self-serving, devious, and slimy. I often feel the need for a shower after they've gone.'

The admiral smiled.

'The ones I associate with are at a different level. Heydrich, the head of the SD, the Gestapo and the KriPo, is a regular visitor.'

In December '34, when SS chief Himmler unified the German state political police forces into the Berlin Gestapo office, he placed the whole organisation under the authority of his deputy, Reinhard Heydrich, who was already the head of the SD, or Sicherheitsdienst, the security service for the SS, and for the party.

KriPo, German CID, also came under Heydrich's control.

'How can you work with such people?'

'So far,' Canaris said, shrugging, 'Heydrich and I have a good working relationship. He keeps his boss, Himmler, off my back, and I keep him informed.'

The General suspected that Reinhard Heydrich's support had been critical to his friend's appointment as Abwehr chief and this was borne out by the apparently cordial relations between the two men.

'Don't trust him, Canaris,' he said. 'Despite his affability, he's as bad as any of them, from what I've heard.'

'Patzig warned me about him too,' Canaris said. 'He told me that he hated the Abwehr, that he believed that Germany's defeat in 1918 was, in part, due to the failure of military intelligence. He said that Heydrich had aspirations to oversee all aspects of intelligence-gathering in Germany but if that's the case, why didn't he try and block my appointment?'

'Maybe he thinks he can work with you, that you're a fervent National Socialist supporter.'

'He knows I'm an admirer of Hitler, that I broadly support their policies, but he also must know that I'm a navy man first, before I'm a National Socialist.'

'They're arrogant. Perhaps they think they can mould you to their ways. That's what they're doing with our young people, before they even join the Reichswehr, or Wehrmacht, as we must now call it.'

'You're not on about that again.' Canaris sighed. 'I'm not convinced. We'll do as we've always done in the army and the navy; train our soldiers and sailors to act the way we want them to fight.'

'But that's the point. It's not how they fight that is the issue. It's what they're fighting for. I've heard them. They fight for the Führer now, not Germany.'

'You're exaggerating. Soldiers will do what their officers tell them to do.'

'Yes, and most of their officers will have come through Hitlerjugend.'

'Only the junior officers.'

'Not in five years' time. Hitlerjugend has been on the go in its current form since '26. It was part of the SA before that. Think of the age that some of these seventeen-year-olds back then will be now.'

Admiral Canaris looked thoughtful. He used his bread to mop up the last of the sauce on his plate.

The General wasn't finished.

'And conscription. To me, that can only mean one thing.'

'Which is?'

'War, at some point in the future. Expansionism in the short term.'

'You've put a lot of thought into this, haven't you?'

'Yes, because I think it's important. These people have a stranglehold on Germany, and they're tightening their grip every day.'

Admiral Canaris took a long look at the General.

'I know it seems that way but, in all honesty, this country was in such a bad way, the only chance for recovery was to have a strong leader who was willing to take harsh measures to fix all the bits that were broken. You can't deny that Adolf Hitler has achieved that, can you?'

'That's a whole different discussion. I'm not convinced he's done all he's said he has. But even if he has, what has the cost been? Do you know that Himmler has created an Inspectorate of Concentration Camps, under the leadership of SS General Theodor Eicke?'

'Yes, I sent you the memo if you recall. It simply formalises the SS takeover and centralisation of the concentration camp system that took place last year.'

'Doesn't that worry you?'

'Sometimes, progress is painful. We need to make tough choices. And there are a lot of people about, even Germans, who would like us to fail.'

'What about Gestapo, the police, and the intelligence services being under the direct authority of the SS, and the NSDAP?'

'They're the government. What difference does it make?'

'Because we can never change the government.'

There was a silence. In the lull in the conversation the waiter appeared at the table with two plates of strudel, and a jug of cream. The admiral ordered another two beers.

When the waiter had left, he reached across and put his hand on the General's sleeve.

'Erich, you are my oldest friend, and I've always valued your opinion above all others.'

'But...'

'You are a little paranoid about all of this. I'm not saying some of what you say isn't true, but you're blowing it out of all proportion.'

'Why don't you sack me, then?' the General snapped, regretting his words instantly.

His friend looked around, but no one seemed to have noticed the uncharacteristic outburst.

'Don't be ridiculous. The work you do is right on the button. The admirals all wax lyrical about you, and the Reichsmarine and the Heer have never got on so well as they do today. It's just this fixation you have with the National Socialists, and the Führer.'

'Wilhelm, you know me. If I feel there's something wrong, I can't just stand by and watch. And it will be the Kriegsmarine, not the Reichsmarine, after next week.'

'Pah. It's only a name, and if it's any consolation, there are some things I'm not altogether comfortable with. And despite what you think, I don't blindly believe in everything they do. But I need to work with them, and our objectives are often the same. A strong army. A strong navy. An effective air force, at last. A right for German citizens to decide for themselves, not to be governed by an international tribunal. And I will fight to keep the armed forces independent, and anything I do will be for the good of Germany.'

'And if things change?'

'I'll weigh that up if it happens. Until then, please do me a big favour.'

'I know. Keep my thoughts to myself. Don't get into trouble. Keep quiet.'

'Yes, for me. And for your own sake.'

CHAPTER 81

Maria Kästner hadn't been at a Jewish service since Miriam and Yosef's wedding, sixteen years before. Now, back in the synagogue in Kiel, she sat, ramrod straight in her veiled blue hat, eyes fixed forward, making eye contact with no one. She sensed the General next to her, turning around, one way first, then the other, nodding to people he knew. She wouldn't look at him but could just imagine the smile on his face as members of the congregation returned his silent greeting. She heard him speak in subdued tones to the person beside him.

The nightmare had started two days before, on Ruth's twelfth birthday. They'd made their usual appearance at the cottage, Maria conscious of Beate Böhm's face at the window of the house next door. There were no other guests.

She'd heard Ruth explaining to the General that she was about to have her Bat Mitzvah, the coming-of-age ceremony that the rabbi had introduced for girls during his time in Kiel, and that there would be a Seudat Mitzvah after the service, a celebratory meal for family and friends.

'It's not as important as a Bar Mitzvah for boys,' she'd heard Ruth say. 'I don't get to read the Torah, but my father will do it for me. And there's a party afterwards.'

The girl had looked at her mother, and Miriam gave a little nod.

'You're all invited,' she'd said, her eyes lighting up.

'Why, that would be lovely,' the General had said, 'will we be able to come to the service too?'

Maria's face had blanched, and she waited, hoping that Miriam or Yosef would say it wasn't necessary.

She'd watched Ruth glance once more at her mother, a surprised look on her face, and saw Miriam nod again.

'You'd be most welcome,' Ruth had said. 'Can Antje come?'

'Of course. She wouldn't want to miss it.'

~~o~~

'You didn't even ask me,' Maria had fumed.

'I didn't think I needed to. You quite often sign me up for social events without checking first.'

'It's hardly a social event, Erich. Anyway, I take care to pick and choose the ones that you would wish to go to. I don't force you to go to anything you'd find distasteful.'

The General had raised his eyebrows, which further infuriated her.

'Distasteful,' he'd said, frowning. 'You don't have to come.'

'You're putting words in my mouth. I didn't say Ruth's Mitzvah thing was distasteful.'

'Whatever you feel, you don't have to go. Say you're sick.'

'And how would that look, if you and Antje went, and I didn't?'

'No one would mention it,' he'd said, but Maria had known that they would.

On the other hand, she'd worried that she might be seen going into the synagogue.

What would my friends think?

'I wouldn't be surprised if Antje and Ruth had planned the whole thing,' she said, 'and you fell for it.'

'I'm sure they didn't. You're reading far too much into it. It's like going to a christening. We go to the service. There's a party afterwards. End of story.'

'You know it's not the same. It's a synagogue.'

'It's still a house of God. Just a different one. You have to respect other people's beliefs.'

'But you don't have to go and worship with them,' she'd snapped, rising from the chair.

'Look, come if you want, or stay at home if you feel that strongly about it. I'm going, and Antje can come with me, if she wants to.'

'Oh, I'm sure she will,' she'd said, slamming the door on her way out.

~~o~~

When Maria walked into the synagogue, she wore a hat with a veil that covered her face. Antje squinted at it, screwing up her nose.

'It's just a hat,' Maria said, frowning.

Antje looked away. Even at her tender age, she knew that her mama didn't want to be recognised going into the synagogue.

While Maria sat in rigid discomfort, Antje looked around, her eyes wide in wonder. She'd awoken early that morning, knowing that she'd finally get to see Ruth's world, and it didn't disappoint.

As the service started, she saw Ruth at the front of the congregation in a simple but pretty blue dress, sitting next to Miriam. Yosef sat on the other side, with the men. Beyond Ruth, Antje could see the gilded Ark which took up a large part of the end wall of the synagogue. It was ornate, with a pair of heavily embellished doors on its front.

Everything happened just as Ruth had explained to her the night before.

'There's no rabbi anymore; he left for Palestine a couple of years ago, but one of the older men takes the service. After the prayers, Papa or one of the other men will read from the Torah. The Torah scrolls are kept in the Ark, which is a big cupboard at the end of the synagogue closest to Jerusalem. Each scroll is very old and has four handles which turn the pages. The men walk around the Bimah, a platform in the middle of the synagogue used for speaking from, to show everyone the scroll, then place it on the table to read from it.'

'Do you have to speak?' Antje had asked.

'No. I would have to do the reading if I were a boy, but Papa will do it for me because I'm a girl.'

'So, what happens next?'

'There will be more prayers, then one of the men, probably Herr Teubner, will deliver the Derashah, which is like a sermon in your church, I think, then there's a blessing for everyone then finally we will all sing 'Adon Olam', the last hymn.'

'It sounds like our church, but more exciting. And there's a party afterwards.'

'Yes, and I'm so excited that you're coming,' Ruth had said, giving Antje a big hug.

~~o~~

Yosef looked at the sky. The weather had looked to be changeable when he rose but, after the service, the clouds had cleared, and the heat of the sun soon dissolved the damp chill of the morning.

A large tent had been erected in the garden next to the Nussbaums' cottage, and tables had been set up inside that were now groaning with food.

'Maria has a blinding migraine,' the General told Miriam. 'She's had to go and lie down for a while.'

'Oh, what a shame. Can I do anything?'

'No, No. She's taken something for it. A few hours' rest should do the trick.'

'Well, at least you and Antje are here. It was so nice of you to come to the service.'

'I wouldn't have missed it for the world. It's been a while since I've been in a synagogue; your wedding, in fact.'

Miriam laughed. She touched his arm. 'Thank you,' she said, before moving off to make sure all the guests had drinks. The General and Yosef joined the group of men. They were listening to Ruth, who was standing with Antje, and Rebeka, the third of the three friends.

'I've been studying hard for six months,' Ruth was saying. 'My Hebrew is improving. Be'ezrát hashém,' she said. *With the help of God.*

The men all smiled and nodded. The girls heard Miriam calling and, very politely, excused themselves and ran towards the house to help with the drinks.

'Lovely young ladies,' one of the men said.

Yosef turned to the General.

'This is Edwin Schumm. Doctor Friedrich Schumm's father.'

The old man took the General's outstretched hand in both of his and, instead of shaking it, he held on, his knuckles white with the strength of his grip.

'It's an honour to meet you, sir,' he said, his rheumy eyes not leaving the General's, the sadness in them tempered with gratitude.

'And you, too, Herr Schumm. Yosef told me about the sad loss of your son. You have my sincere condolences.'

The man nodded. 'Thank you for what you did.'

He let go of the General's hand, reluctantly.

'And this is Itsik Weichmann,' Yosef continued.

The General laughed. 'Everyone knows Itsik. His has the best hardware store in Schleswig-Holstein; perhaps in Germany.'

'Thank you, sir. I've had the pleasure to serve you. I believe it was a replacement key the last time you were in?'

The men all laughed. Itsik Weichmann was not only famous for the quality and variety of his hardware but for his ability to remember all his customers, and what they'd purchased.

Yosef turned to the last two men.

'You know Isaac, of course, and you may have met Emil Liewermann. His daughter Rebeka is in Ruth and Antje's class at school.'

The General greeted Isaac and nodded to the tall, thin man on his left, and shook his hand.

'I do believe we've met. At a school play.'

'You have an excellent memory, General. It was a few years ago.'

'Please call me Erich,' the General said, 'unless I'm in uniform,' he joked.

The men laughed.

'And no saluting,' the General added. 'Even though you're all veterans.'

Yosef looked at the General, then at his friends. They looked as puzzled as he was.

I didn't tell the General they'd all served in the war.

The General smiled. 'Sorry, but you all straightened your backs when I joined you. Not quite standing to attention, but old habits die hard.'

They all laughed again. Yosef had forgotten why Erich Kästner was such a good commander of men.

He cast his mind back to the service he'd given to Germany in 1914 and contrasted it with the way he, and his family, were being treated some twenty years later. He knew that each of the four men, in different ways, was thinking the same. It was Yosef who voiced it.

'Not that you'd think it now,' he said.

The General's eyes dropped in shame.

'I can only apologise personally for the treatment that you and your families have been subjected to by a nation you were willing to risk dying for. Unfortunately, I can't speak for the rest of the country, who seem to have been infected with some sort of *beyz*.'

Evil. He's right, Yosef thought. His friends looked at the General, caught out by his use of Yiddish.

'It's better than it was,' Edwin Schumm said. 'It seems to have settled down.'

'I hope it's not the lull before the storm,' Emil Liewerman said. 'I'm holding onto my job by the skin of my teeth, and only because my boss is willing to take a risk, and because I fought in the war.'

'You work in a factory, I believe. What is it you make?' the General asked.

'We make furniture. I manage production. If I lose my job, I'll have to find a labouring job, with a fraction of the wages.'

'The takings in my shop are down fifty per cent. I've had to lay off one of my junior staff,' Itsik added.

'And my pension has been halved,' Edwin Schumm said.

'Feh. And we're the lucky ones,' Emil added, with a smile that didn't quite reach his eyes.

'They've expelled all the Jewish officers from the army,' the General said. 'My son lost a couple of men from his unit; great soldiers, he said, and a terrible loss to his battalion, just when the army is expanding.'

'What do they want from us?' Yosef asked.

'A scapegoat,' the General said. 'For all that's gone wrong in Germany.'

CHAPTER 82

KIELER MORGENPOST

Friday 28th June 1935

GOVERNMENT STRENGTHENS HOMOSEXUALITY LAWS

In response to demands from the majority of the German people, the Ministry of Justice has revised Paragraphs 175 and 175a of the criminal code with the intention of increasing the range of criminal offences to encompass any contact between men, both physical and in form of word or gesture, that could be construed as sexual. It has also stiffened penalties for all violations of the revised law.

Hinrich Lohse, Oberpräsident of Schleswig-Holstein, said in a statement that the Weimar Republic had allowed a rot to set in almost to the core of German society. "The National Socialist Government has a duty to restore the upright morals and traditional values to the nation".

As a crowd gathered outside the Rathaus to welcome this new legislation, one mother told the Morgenpost "Our sons will be safe again".

~~o~~

'If Röhm were still alive, he'd do well to stay out of prison.'

The General smiled grimly. It had been a poorly kept secret that the former SA chief, who had been executed the year before, had been a homosexual, as were a few of his colleagues in the disgraced SA command.

'This is one law that even you must be pleased about, Kästner.'

The General held the telephone handpiece away from his ear. Admiral Canaris had a habit of shouting down the phone, as if it helped the words speed along the wire and out the other end.

'Yes,' he replied. 'I always thought that the Weimar Republic's liberal sexual attitudes went a little too far. I'm all for our youth being allowed a bit of freedom but it seemed to get out of hand. I hear there have been cancellations of some theatre productions and two new films have been put on hold, while they cast replacement actors.' He chuckled, and he heard his friend laugh on the other end of the line.

'I hadn't realised how many bars there were in Berlin that catered for them,' the admiral said. 'They've closed one hundred down in the last year!'

'I'm surprised. As far as I know, there aren't any in Kiel.'

'There would have been, Kästner. You just didn't know about them.'

The General wasn't convinced.

I'll ask Uwe Müller, the next time I see him. If anyone knows, the police chief should.

'Ah, well,' the admiral said. 'Perhaps it might make the Jews feel better. Unless they're homosexual as well.'

The General didn't reply.

'Sorry, bad taste,' Canaris said. 'I shouldn't have said that.'

289

Although Wilhelm Canaris wasn't overly anti-Semitic, he had few Jewish acquaintances, but he knew and liked Yosef and Miriam, so his comment surprised the General.

'Franz was saying that they lost five or six good officers,' the General said. 'Jews, or those married to Jews.'

'I heard,' Canaris said. 'What does he think about it?'

'Oh, the same as I do. Such a waste, and dreadfully unfair.'

The phone call had been made primarily to discuss the repercussions of the Anglo-German Naval Agreement, which allowed Germany to increase its navy beyond that of the Treaty of Versailles, provided the ration of tonnage in the Kriegsmarine compared to that of the British Navy was less than thirty-five per cent.

'Quite a success for Herr Hitler,' Canaris said.

'Yes, I'm surprised the English agreed to it,' the General said. 'And the French,' he added.

'Ha. A little bird in the French Foreign Ministry tells me they didn't know anything about it.'

'Verdammt,' the General said. 'I'd have loved to be a fly on the wall in Paris when that bombshell dropped.'

'Yes, the British say they want better relations with us, and they don't think it will affect their naval superiority.'

'They have a point. We'd never match their navy, man for man.'

'Not strictly true. They do have the best fighting navy in the world, but they have a few problems. For a start, it's spread all over the globe, to keep their so-called empire under control.'

'Even so, they could blockade us in the Baltic if they needed to.'

'You're forgetting one thing, Erich, but I suppose that's understandable for an army man trying his hardest to get to grips with navy matters.'

The General smiled, hearing the laugh on the other end of the line.

'Go on,' he said.

'You'll remember I visited the Howaldtswerk yard with Karl Dönitz last year?'

'Yes.'

'And do you recall the conversation we had about my *Unterseeboot* command during the last year of the war and my work on submarine development? Well, before I took this job, I'd been working together with Karl, who is a bit of a tactical genius. He will command our new U-boat flotilla. That's what could win us a war at sea.'

The General knew that the yards were building U-boats; now he began to understand why.

'Are you sure that a few submarines can match the sheer scale of the English Navy?'

Canaris snorted. 'There will be more than a few. We're talking hundreds here, maybe thousands. According to Dönitz, with enough of them, we could paralyse the world's sea lanes.'

CHAPTER 83

[11/08/1935 Sunday]

Since the boys had left home, the General had been outnumbered by the women of the family by three to one, but he could usually rely on Antje to side with him. In mid-August, on the day before she went off to board at the same school Eva attended, it was Antje who looked to him for help.

Maria Kästner stood in front of her daughter with folded arms, a flush of anger on her cheekbones.

'You are going with Eva to school, end of story,' she said.

'But why can't I go to school with Ruth and Rebeka? I don't want to go to Eva's school. It sounds horrible and I only get home at the weekend.'

'Antje, it's a much nicer school than the one here, and you'll get a far better education,' Eva said. 'There's even an art department with easels and big windows.'

For a moment, as Antje hesitated, the General thought he'd got off the hook.

She's thinking of a beautiful art class with high ceilings, paintings covering the walls, and a view across the countryside.

Then her face flushed again.

'I can do that here,' she shouted, not falling for Eva's bribery.

'The boys went away to school too,' Maria said. 'Your father and I both did, it's what we do.'

Antje changed tack. 'I'll go if Ruth can come too.'

Maria paled, but the two red spots on her cheek remained.

'Ruth can't go,' she snapped. 'That's just plain silly.'

'Why. We could afford it, couldn't we, Papa.'

'It's not about the money, Antje,' he said, reluctant to be drawn into the conversation. 'I'd gladly pay for Ruth to go, but her education is for her parents to decide, and I'm sure they'll want her to go the realschule in Preetzer Chaussee.'

Maria Kästner flashed her husband a smile of relief. Traditionally, working-class children went to the realschule, a public secondary school.

'We could ask though,' Antje said. 'You don't get if you don't ask.'

The General stifled a laugh. Maria had paled again, and her lips tightened in a pursed straight line.

'No, you can't, and that's final,' she said.

'But Papa could ask,' she said, turning to him. 'Couldn't you?'

The General turned to her, with as sad a face as he could muster.

'It wouldn't be fair on Yosef or Miriam, or Ruth for that matter. I'm afraid it's a no, Antje.'

'Well, I'm going to her school then. You can't make me go to Eva's school.'

'Actually, young lady, we can,' her mother said. 'And if there's any more fuss, you might not even get home at the weekend.'

Antje burst into tears, and the General gave his wife a glare. She shrugged, but he could see from her face that she knew she'd gone too far.

'I'll run away,' Antje said, mumbling through the tears.

The General gently held her shoulders.

'Listen, Antje. I know this might feel like the end of the world to you but just think what it will be like coming home at the weekends and seeing Ruth. It'll be like when you've both been away on holiday, and then you come back and you're so happy to see each other.'

Antje sniffed. 'S'pose,' she said. 'But it's not fair.' She seemed to stiffen. 'Is it because she's Jewish? It is, isn't it?'

It was the General's turn to pale.

'Antje!' he said, scrambling in his mind for a response. The problem was, there was perhaps some truth in it. There had always been a few wealthy Jews who sent their daughters to the school they sent Eva to, but they were generally non-practising, secular Jews who had no outward trappings of their religion. Their daughters fitted in well, on the whole, but he'd noticed less of them in the last few years and he suddenly wondered if it was because of a more stringent selection process, or if Jewish parents were, for some reason, not choosing to send their daughters away to school.

'I'm sure it's not that,' he said. 'There are Jewish girls at your school,' he said, hoping it was true. A glance at Eva's face told him it probably wasn't, and he made a mental note to ask his older daughter later.

Antje's opposition seemed to waver, and the fight left her. Her eyes were still full of tears, but she fought to keep them under control. The General's heart went out to her, and he put his arm around her thin shoulders, drawing her in towards him.

~~o~~

'You're going to miss Antje, aren't you?'

'Yes, Mama,' Ruth said. 'She'll be away every week, apart from the holidays. I don't think she wants to go.'

'I suppose she doesn't, but all the Kästners went away, and got used to it.'

Miriam could never understand how people could bring themselves to send their children away to school. You only had them with you for a short while, so why not make the most of that time? And she wondered why you would want other people to teach your children how to behave. It was their parents' job.

'We'll still be able to spend the weekends together, so it's not so bad.'

Miriam would have liked to warn her daughter that Antje would almost certainly find a new group of friends and drift away from Ruth, mixing with girls from her own social background. She loved Antje almost as much as her own daughter, but she was pragmatic, and knew that social pressures could make or break friendships.

'Perhaps you'll make new friends at school. There will be more girls the same age as you.'

'Will there be more Jewish girls? Rebeka says there might be.'

'I suppose she's right. It's a bigger school.'

Miriam paused, lifting her head from the sock she was darning.

'What happened to the other girl in your class,' she asked. 'Hanne, wasn't it?'

'Oh, she's going too, but she keeps to herself.'

'Are you looking forward to it?'

'Yes, we can do science and maths. We can even learn English and French.' Her face clouded. 'But it won't be the same without Antje.'

~~o~~

'Keep your voice down, Erich. I don't want the children to hear us arguing.'

The General knew that his voice, accustomed to being heard on the drill square, carried further than Maria's, but she was the one whose voice was raised.

'Can we not have a sensible discussion about this. I'm not saying she should go to the realschule with Ruth, but I think we should talk about it.'

'Erich, how could you even consider sending Antje to a public school. How will she feel in a few years when she's behind all the girls her own age, and talks like a fishwife?'

'Does Miriam talk like a fishwife? Does Yosef talk like a docker?'

'That's different. They are with us most of the time. Yosef was brought up here.'

'My point exactly. He went to the local Realschule.'

'Yes, but he's not a general, is he? You went to a private school.'

'I know countless successful people who didn't go to a private school. Doc Speer for one.'

'He's not quite a prominent surgeon, is he?'

'He's a damn fine doctor.'

'That's what I mean. You can do as well as you like at an ordinary school, but it doesn't open up the opportunities that a good private school does.'

He knew she was right, but he was sure Antje was different. And for selfish reasons, now that he was home, he wanted to keep at least one of his children close to him.

'What about one of the private schools in Kiel? She could attend as a day student.'

'Erich, you know we looked into this for Eva. None of them were anywhere near suitable, and besides, living away at school will teach her discipline and how to behave, and the friends she'll make there are all people who will become someone, who will make their mark. Anyway, if it was good enough for you and I, and our other children, it should be good enough for Antje.'

'I just want her to be happy.'

'And you don't think I do? I suspect you're just doing this to spite me. I know Antje is a father's girl, but she still needs to learn how to be a lady. She will be one day, you know.'

I tried, Antje, he thought. *I tried.*

CHAPTER 84

[27/05/2001 Sunday]

Maldon, England.

I was supposed to see Ruth the following day. I was keen to hear the next part of her story; I'd become completely immersed in her telling of it, and it was frustrating to be made to wait, but she remembered a lunch she'd arranged with a group of old friends, and she couldn't pull out of it. I offered to drop by after she'd finished but, with a knowing smile, she told me that it was the type of lunch that lasted for most of the day.

The following morning, although she wouldn't admit it, she seemed a little under the weather. When I joked about her having had one too many drinks, she just laughed.

It didn't stop her carrying on where she left off, so I asked her about starting secondary school without Antje.

'It was difficult. We'd been through Kindergarten and Grundschule together, sitting next to one another in every class. I still had Rebeka, but Antje had no one. It seemed like a long week before she was home again.'

She took a long sip of water.

'I was so glad it wasn't me. I came home to Mama and Papa every night, I played with Manny and even the General used to take time to talk with me. I think he really missed Antje. He always looked sad.'

'And did you still stay friends?'

'Oh, yes. Nothing was going to break us up. We wanted to write every day, but Mama said it would be too expensive to post them all, so I could only send one letter each week, every Tuesday, so Antje would get it before she came home. She had more pocket money than me, but she said that she would do the same as it was only fair.'

'I wrote to her when the Nuremberg race laws were brought in. They were issued on a Sunday, and I didn't hear about them that day, so it was the following weekend before she spoke to me about it. She told me she'd cried when she read my letter.'

CHAPTER 85

KIELER MORGENPOST

Monday 16th September 1935

NÜRNBERGER GESETZE: DEUTSCHES BLUT UND DEUTSCHE EHRE

At a special meeting convened yesterday at the annual Nuremberg Rally of the NSDAP, the Reichstag have introduced two new laws in a bid to prevent the dilution of German racial purity.

The Law for the Protection of German Blood and German Honour forbids marriages and extramarital intercourse between Jews and Germans, and the employment of German females under 45 in Jewish households.

The Reich Citizenship Law, states that only those of German or related blood are eligible to be Reich citizens; the remainder will be classed as state subjects, without citizenship rights.

In his speech to the convened Reichstag delegates, the Führer said that "The German Reich is governed in this by the desire that, through a single secular solution, it may be possible still to create a framework on which the German people may find tolerable relations towards the Jewish people. Should this hope not be fulfilled and Jewish agitation, both within Germany and in the international sphere, should continue, then the position must be examined anew".

A spokesman for the NSDAP announced that a supplementary decree clarifying the definition of who was Jewish would be passed within a month.

~~o~~

Yosef almost dropped the coffee pot.

'German blood and German honour!' the General snarled, startling not only Yosef, but Maria and Miriam. 'I'll give them blood and honour.'

He threw the paper down on the table and stormed out of the room. It lay, face up, and they could all read the headline.

Yosef picked up the newspaper and quickly read it, then handed it to Miriam. They didn't see the irritation on the mistress's face.

'Miriam, could you bring coffee and toast through to the drawing room,' Maria Kästner said, with frost in her voice, 'I'll take my breakfast through there.'

Miriam, absorbed by the newspaper article, didn't hear her, but Yosef, suddenly aware that his employer wasn't pleased, spoke for her.

'I'll bring it through, ma'am, just as soon as it's ready.' He switched on the grill and cut two slices of bread from the loaf in the larder. 'Do you think the General will want some?'

'You can ask him,' she snapped, and stormed out. Miriam, just finishing the article, heard the annoyance in Maria's voice and turned to Yosef.

'What's she upset about?' she said, now as irritated as Maria.

Yosef checked that the coffee was ready.

'It's nothing. She was put out because we were all ignoring her.'

He buttered the toast and put it on a plate. Miriam banged a cup and a saucer onto a tray, a dish of marmalade, sugar, and a small jug of milk. Yosef placed the coffee pot on the tray, along with the toast.

'I'll take it through,' he said. He didn't want Miriam saying something that she might regret later. 'I'll find out if the General wants some too.'

'How can you be so calm? You know what this means, don't you?' she said, brandishing the paper at him.

'Yes, I know. But I'll carry on as normal. It's the only way I can.'

Her anger left her as soon as he'd spoken. She reached her hand out and touched his arm as he lifted the tray.

'It'll all work out,' he said. 'I'll speak to the General.'

~~o~~

[17/09/1935 Tuesday]

Kiel, Germany.

Dear Antje,

I know you'll have heard this by now, but I wanted to tell you myself. You may think I'm silly, but I don't care. The thing is, I can't marry Johann now. Adolf Hitler, that horrible, horrible man, has brought out a law saying that Jews cannot get married to Aryans, which Johann is. I guess you must be one too.

Mama and Papa were upset (not about Johann, they don't know). Mama cried but she didn't know that I'd seen her so don't tell a soul. I heard Papa say to Mama that we were second-rate citizens and she said we weren't citizens at all. I looked it up in the dictionary. I think it means that we're not German anymore.

I'm so looking forward to seeing you on Friday.

Your best friend,

Ruth Nussbaum.

~~o~~

[11/11/1935 Monday]

KIELER JÜDISCHES FREIHEITSNACHRICHTENBLATT

Volume 39

Cheshvan 15, 5696

NUREMBERG LAWS - THE WHOLE TRUTH

As the impact of the two new laws passed at Nuremberg on 15th September emerges, further clarification was issued yesterday, almost a month after the laws were passed into legislature.

As reported in volume 38 of the KJF, the levels of personal and state assaults on Jewish people had stabilised in the previous eight months and was declining in most areas. It was hoped that the National Socialist Party's persecution of Jews had run its course and that more moderate politicians would emerge from the sidelines.

With these laws, the NSDAP have signalled their intentions that there will be no respite in their campaign against German Jews, and a few new words have entered the vocabulary of the "Third Reich".

Mischlinge: Jewish mixed race.

Rassenschande: Racial defilement.

Ahnenpass: Document proving purity of race.

The KJF has learned that the NSDAP and the Ministry for the Interior came to an agreement that those with only one Jewish grandparent, Mischlinge of the second degree, would be allowed Reich citizenship, and those with three or more Jewish grandparents would be classed as Jewish, but factions within the Government could not agree about the status of those that fell between these two categories.

The more radical elements of the NSDAP pushed for Mischlinge of the first degree, people with two Jewish grandparents, to be classed as Jews, but a final ruling, four weeks after the announcement of the new laws, stated that they would only be considered Jewish if they practised the Jewish faith, or had a Jewish spouse.

For Jews everywhere, for those with Jewish relations and for those married to Jewish spouses, this law is an insult of immeasurable magnitude.

WORD OF THE WEEK

"Blutschande". Most commonly used for incest, literally meaning "blood shame", it has been appropriated by the National Socialists to define the adulteration of German racial purity by intermarriage with other non-Germanic races.

~~o~~

Memo: Geh.KdoS. ABW 03/12/35 CAC0412.1

For Attention Only: All senior executive officers, Abwehr.

From: Rear Admiral Wilhelm Canaris, Chef der Abwehr.

The NSDAP has issued an internal communication updating all Reich security agencies regarding the introduction of the Nuremberg Laws of 15th September, ratified on 11th November.

The first supplemental decree of the Nuremberg Laws extends the law to include Roma (Gypsies), blacks, or their offspring.

The Interior Ministry does not envisage that the laws will be immediately enforced.

In a separate communique, the NSDAP executive confirmed that venues for all events in the forthcoming Olympic Games, in August, next year, will be ready on time. [END]

~~o~~

'They can't enforce the race laws until the Olympic Games are over!'

Dieter Maas looked at the memo again. The General nodded, grim-faced.

'Correct. If they implement them now, there's a fair chance the Games would be removed from Germany, and Adolf Hitler desperately wants them here. It's his chance to put the National Socialists on a world stage.'

Dieter handed the memo back to the General, who pocketed it. If he were caught showing it to a civilian, the consequences would be grave.

The two men were sitting in the cockpit of the General's yacht, taking a break from their efforts to give the hull its annual clean.

'I've heard that German athletes are being permitted to train full time, with indefinite leave from their jobs. It's just a rumour though,' Dieter said.

'He's going to try and prove to the world the supremacy of the 'Aryan' race. I wonder if blond athletes will be given preferential treatment.'

Dieter laughed.

'I see they've extended the blood and honour law to include Gypsies and blacks. I feel sorry for my friend. He's a black, Jewish, homosexual Gypsy.'

The General joined in the ex-newspaperman's laughter. Somehow, it didn't seem offensive when Dieter said it.

'On one hand, this stay of execution is a good thing. It means the Jews should be left alone until then, but what will happen after that?' he said.

'The only difference is that there is now a legal definition of what a Jew is. There are a lot of Germans with Jewish blood in them who will welcome this legislation.'

'What?' the General said, incredulity on his face. 'They'll be happy that they are still Reich citizens, but their grandparents aren't?'

'You'd be amazed just how much self-preservation permeates this country now. Especially if you're not politically or racially pure,' Dieter said, a bitter note in his voice.

'It gives me a year to persuade Yosef and Miriam to leave.'

'Why wouldn't they go? I hear there's a mass exodus of Jews leaving for America, France, Palestine; anywhere but Germany.'

'It's more of a steady stream, I think, but the NSDAP have massaged the figures and are making a big thing about Jews deserting the country; that it proves they're not true Germans.'

Dieter Maas shook his head.

'Yosef told me his rabbi took his family to Palestine a few years ago,' the General continued. 'Before he left, he pleaded with the congregation to get out.'

'I remember the rabbi well. I played chess against him a couple of times. Clever fellow.'

The two men sat in silence for a few minutes, enjoying the winter sunshine.

The General got up from the bench, and grimaced.

'Right, Dieter. Coffee break over. This hull isn't going to clean itself.'

CHAPTER 86

Maldon, England.

Ruth seemed tired when I arrived that morning but telling her story seemed to rejuvenate her and, by lunchtime, it was her who was reluctant to stop for a rest.

'The Olympic Games saved us,' she said, starting back after our break. 'At least, that's what the General told my parents, and only for a short while. But he also told Papa that he should seriously think about what was best for his future, and that of his family.'

'So, why didn't you leave?' I asked.

She took a while to answer.

'Looking back, the decision to stay seems senseless and foolish now, but you have to understand that my parents were German, they loved Germany, and that my father had fought for Germany, and his father before him.

'And there was the General. My father had an unstinting loyalty for him, but it was more than just that. Jews fleeing the country were being forced to pay an emigration tax of up to ninety per cent of their wealth, making it financial suicide to leave, and it would have been terrible to abandon our family and friends to start afresh in a country where none of us spoke a word of the language.'

'Why didn't they consider Palestine?' I asked her. 'Many Jews emigrated there, and they nearly all survived the war.'

'You don't understand. Back then, most Jews, except for a few radical Orthodox Jews and some young men and women who felt it their duty to rebel against their parents, were anti-Zionist, often to the point where they considered those pushing for a Jewish homeland to be as bad as the National Socialists.

'You must find that terribly strange nowadays,' she added, 'but we couldn't possibly imagine the catastrophe that was going to descend on our people.'

She had that wretched look in her eyes again, that spoke to me as much as her words.

'My parents decided to stay,' she said, 'despite the General's urgings, but it did prompt them to do one thing. They sent me to learn English.'

1936

'For evil to flourish, it only requires good men to do nothing.'

Simon Wiesenthal, c.1960

CHAPTER 87

[14/01/1936 Tuesday]

Kiel, Germany

Ruth found English lessons tedious.

Her parents convinced themselves that if she learned to speak the language, she could teach the rest of the family.

The private schools that the Kästner children attended all taught English and French as core second languages, but at Ruth's school, it was only an option in the upper forms, and even then, it was at the expense of dropping French, which was much more for those living in the western margins of Germany, close to France and Belgium.

The Nussbaums decided to pay for private lessons.

Despite her antipathy, Ruth was a steady, if reluctant learner, and Manny, at an age when languages could be assimilated just by hearing them spoken, picked up a smattering of English from her, although the relevance of it escaped his young mind, no matter how much he tried.

Yosef and Miriam were hopeless.

'Ach,' Miriam would say, 'English is so difficult; it doesn't make sense. I'll learn it if we ever go there.'

Yosef learned four words. *I am from Germany.*

Ruth would practise speaking English with Antje on weekends and holidays, or with Johann or Eva, on the few occasions they were around. The General's English was workmanlike, if not convincing, but Franz was the best out of all of them.

'During my schooldays,' he told her, 'I had a teacher who spoke English well. When he saw that I was keen to learn, he would give up his time to help me practise.'

'Didn't you find it difficult?' she asked him.

'At first, but don't be put off. You're coming along well, and it will pay dividends if you get to England or America.'

Ruth's teacher was a prim Northumbrian woman who had married a German artist when she worked in one of Berlin's English schools shortly after the war. She ran her classes for girls twice weekly at her home overlooking the trees and the old graves of Südfriedhof.

The first time she went, Miriam and Manny accompanied her to the woman's house, a twenty-minute walk along Winterbeker Weg, cutting through the cemetery to save the long walk round but after the first lesson, Ruth would walk straight from school to the house on Saarbrückenstraße with the three other girls, who were a year above her at the realschule.

The girls were all Jews, and two of their families had already been given dates to leave Germany for the USA.

Ruth wondered if she and her family would be the next to emigrate.

~~o~~

Memo: Geh.KdoS. ABW 11/02/36 CAC0453.1

For Attention Only: All senior executive officers, Abwehr.

From: Rear Admiral Wilhelm Canaris, Chef der Abwehr.

On February 10, the Reichstag passed legislation confirming the role and scope of the Geheime Staatspolizei. It included the following clause:

Neither the instructions nor the affairs of the Gestapo will be open to review by the administrative courts.

In effect, this means that the Gestapo is now above the law and there can be no legal appeal for any actions the organisation takes. The Abwehr will take strong measures in support of anyone serving in the organisation who is in any way impeded by the Gestapo in the pursuit of his or her duties. [END]

CHAPTER 88

Memo: Geh.KdoS. ABW 06/03/36 CAC0457.1

For Attention Only: General Erich Kästner, Abwehr, Kiel office.

From: Rear Admiral Wilhelm Canaris, Chef der Abwehr.

** HÖCHSTE GEHEIMHALTUNG **

19 infantry and 13 artillery battalions of the German Army will enter the Rheinland at 07:00 tomorrow, 7 March 1936. 21 battalions of the Rheinland LandesPolizei will be immediately incorporated into the army, providing a defence force of 36,000 men in 53 battalions.

7 battalions will cross the Rhine but only 3 will approach close to the border with the Netherlands, Belgium and France at Aachen, Trier and Saarbrücken.

Resistance is not expected but if the French Army do attack the Rheinland, a phased withdrawal of German troops is planned to predefined lines within the Rheinland borders. [END]

The General saw the *Most Secret* flag at the top of the memo and read it with a mixture of excitement and dread. He cracked open the office door and peered out. Frau Müller was on her own, typing. He considered opening it fully and telling her that he didn't want to be disturbed, but that would be an invitation for her to eavesdrop at the door.

He lifted the receiver and requested a connection to Admiral Canaris's office in Berlin. He didn't have to wait long.

'I expected that you'd call,' the disembodied voice said, with a laugh.

'Very good, Canaris. So, I'm predictable. What do you think about tomorrow?'

'It will be fine, or we'll have a new government in a month. He's taking a big gamble.'

'I did wonder. We're not in a position to fight, if the French choose to attack, are we?'

'No, but I don't think they will, other than by posturing and placing extra troops on the border.'

'But why occupy the Rheinland now? If I were French, I'd be nervous.'

'It would be unfair of me to expect you to know, as you don't necessarily have all the intelligence at your fingertips. First, I don't think von Blomberg and von Fritsch were averse to the army entering the Rheinland; just maybe not this soon, but Herr Hitler can be extremely persuasive.'

'All right, I get that. But why not wait?'

'Two reasons, Kästner. One. The government in Paris has just fallen and a caretaker administration is in charge; they're going to be indecisive.'

He paused. Erich Kästner said nothing.

'Two. The Franco-Soviet Pact. It gives us a valid excuse to rip up the Treaty of Versailles, and the Locarno Agreements, which gave France the Rheinland.'

This time, the General interrupted him.

'But the pact was signed last May. Why now?'

'The government has taken the time to consider in full the threat that the Russian deal with Paris poses.'

The General laughed. 'That sounds like NSDAP-speak.'

'It was. Hermann Göring. Yesterday.' The General could hear the amused tone in the admiral's voice.

'I can think of a third reason,' the General said, hesitating. *How much had Canaris thrown his lot in with the National Socialists?*

'Go on...'

'There has been widespread dissatisfaction with the economy since early last year.'

'There have been grumblings, but I think you're exaggerating somewhat.'

'The government has been incredibly successful in suppressing any talk of it but there have been rumours that the underground KPD have been distributing pamphlets calling for their overthrow.'

'Where do you get this stuff?' the Chef der Abwehr said, a little tetchily.

'I have my sources,' the General said, smiling at the thought of the frown on his friend's face.

'Don't get your hopes up,' Canaris growled. 'It will take more than rumours to oust the National Socialists. Besides, I hope they get the chance to finish the job they started.'

'And what's that?' the General snapped.

'Ripping up that infernal Versailles treaty for good and retrieving our stolen territory. And leaving us with an army, navy and air force to guard it.'

Erich Kästner hesitated. How far could he go?

'But what aspirations do they have beyond that, my friend?'

There was silence at the end of the phone.

Wilhelm Canaris sighed.

'That *is* the question.'

~~o~~

KIELER MORGENPOST

Sunday 8th March 1936

WE MARCH INTO THE RHEINLAND!

Yesterday, just after dawn on March 7, nineteen German infantry battalions entered the Rheinland, with significant artillery and Luftwaffe support.

The occupation was peaceful and unopposed. The Wehrmacht troops were welcomed in the streets of the towns and villages of the region with flowers, applause, and cheers.

At Cologne Cathedral, Cardinal Karl Joseph Schulte of Cologne held a mass to celebrate and thank the Führer for "sending back our army".

In Berlin, the Italian, French, and British ambassadors were summoned to the foreign office on Wilhelmstraße, where the Foreign Minister accused France of breaking the Versailles and Locarno treaties by ratifying the Franco-Soviet Pact and, in response, Germany had no option but to renounce the Locarno Agreement and remilitarise the Rheinland.

In his address to the Reichstag, the Führer said that the

remilitarisation of the Rheinland was not intended as a threat, that he was a man of peace, and that all he strived for was equality for Germany. He offered to rejoin the League of Nations and sign a non-aggression pact with France.

The French Government has strongly hinted that military action was being considered, and the Soviet Union has denounced Germany's action.

A spokesman for the British Government was quoted as saying that "Germany had merely marched into its own backyard".

CHAPTER 89

[20/04/1936 Monday]

'He's more popular than ever, sir.'

In Kiel, Adolf Hitler's birthday had sparked off huge public celebrations.

The General looked out onto the wide promenade outside his office, with its throngs of jubilant people, and Kieler Hafen beyond. Almost every boat was decorated with flags and bunting; there was a holiday feel to the city.

Most businesses, apart from the cafés, ice-cream parlours and bars catering for the crowds, remained closed. Few Jewish stores, mindful of offending the German public, stayed open.

The General turned to Heinz Bauer. There was a bitter, resigned note in his voice.

'Yes, as popular as he's ever been, because of the Rheinland.'

Despite being sceptical of the ninety-nine per cent 'Yes' vote in the referendum, Erich Kästner had to concede that the nation's poll on their approval for Hitler's remilitarisation of the Rheinland had been emphatic.

'Taking back the Rheinland isn't a bad thing, sir. Is it?'

'No, Heinz, it isn't. Five years ago, I would have been out cheering with the rest of them.'

'Things seem to have settled down a bit, sir. There doesn't seem to be so much trouble now.'

The General turned to him with a look that could have been scathing, or one of pity.

The young captain swallowed.

'If you feel that things are getting back to normal, try taking a soapbox out there, standing up on it, and criticising Herr Hitler.'

'I didn't mean... sorry, sir. I just meant that there didn't seem to be so much violence.'

The General cursed himself for taking it out on the young captain.

'Ach, I shouldn't have spoken to you like that,' he said, his voice softening. 'It's true; harassment and intimidation on the streets has declined and so has the random violence we were seeing, but if you voice any opposition to the government, you live in fear.'

'You don't seem to, sir.'

'I'm in an enviable position, unlike most sceptics. Anyway, I do live in fear, but it's fear for our nation. And if you're a Jew, you are feeling more vulnerable and less German than ever, because all your basic rights have been taken away from you.'

'I'm sorry, sir. I didn't think. I don't know any Jews, and the race laws have been suspended. At least, that's what they're saying at the city hall.'

'It's not your fault, Captain. That's what they do, pull the wool over the country's eyes. They're just on hold until after the Olympics.'

The General saw a look of comprehension creep into the captain's eyes.

'They're worried about how it will look abroad!' he exclaimed. 'I wondered why they weren't drafting a new set of local regulations. There's usually a flurry of activity at the Rathaus when new legislation comes in.'

'Just wait until August,' the General said. He glanced at his junior officer. He looked to be getting a bit pale and soft, if that was fair. 'How are you coping with life over at the Rathaus? Are three days a week too much?'

'It's fine. Three days a week works well. I'm still here the rest of the time and I can catch up with my paperwork when I'm on duty at the weekend. I find the political stuff quite interesting in some ways, and I hadn't realised just how useful it would be to the navy.'

'I thought it might be. You're doing a great job. The chief of staff here tells me that you've sorted out any number of niggling issues in a fraction of the time they would have taken in the past.'

'Yes, sir. It helps when you know who to approach to get the job done.' He grinned.

'Quite. That's usually the case.' The General thought for a second. 'Your weekly reports. They're of vital importance too.'

'Thank you, sir. I try and include anything that might be of interest to you.'

'I've noticed. And what has impressed me is the range of topics that you've reported on. Keep up the good work.'

'Yes, sir. Will that be all?'

'Yes, for now.'

The captain turned for the door. Just as he reached it, the General called out.

'Captain, there's just one more thing.'

'Yes, sir?'

'Carry on like this and I'm sure you'll be looking at another promotion.'

CHAPTER 90

I was right.

It gave Miriam no satisfaction, but she knew that it had been inevitable.

Antje missed Ruth's thirteenth birthday. For almost the first time, she didn't come home from school for the weekend.

Miriam had seen the apologetic letter Antje had sent to Ruth.

A Bund Deutscher Mädel trip to Munich with the rest of the girls in my class. I'm being forced to go.

She hadn't said anything to Ruth.

Rebeka was at the party, of course, and one other Jewish girl from Ruth's class. Two of the students from her out-of-school English lessons came, along with Rosa, Rebeka's mother, and Esther Weichmann, accompanied by their sons, Fischel and Moshe, as company for Manny, and Shoshana, Moshe's baby sister.

The girls all sat down by the lake, Rebeka and Ruth hanging onto every word of the *grown-up* talk of the two older girls.

Moshe, Fischel and Manny disappeared into the undergrowth, appearing from time to time to annoy the girls or drink a glass of Miriam's home-made lemonade.

Miriam and her two friends sat on garden chairs on the grass outside the Nussbaums' back door. The Kästners had taken the opportunity presented by a childless weekend to travel to Berlin to see the city's Philharmonic orchestra play, so Miriam could relax, with little to do in the big house until Monday morning.

'One of Itsik's customers made an offer for the store. Less than half its market value,' Esther said, sipping a glass of red wine.

'I hope Itsik told him what he could do with his offer,' Rosa said.

'He told him he'd get back to him tomorrow. He's having a long think about it.'

'But why? It's the best hardware store in Kiel, by a mile.'

'I know, but the takings are way down; less than half of what they were a year ago. People just aren't shopping with us as much.'

'You mean, the Gentiles aren't,' Rosa said, irritated.

'Some are frightened to be seen shopping in a Jewish store, but it's not just that though. One of our wholesalers, based in Hamburg, was paraded through the streets with a placard around his neck. '*This man deals with Jews,*' it said.'

'But that doesn't mean that you have to sell the store and, even if you did, you should get a fair price for it.'

'I know. I think Itsik will refuse. It was his father's store before him, and it would feel like he'd failed if he gave up on it.'

'Quite right,' said Rosa. 'Bloody parasites.'

'Rosa!' Miriam said. 'Language. The children.'

'Feh,' Rosa replied. 'The children are out of earshot. Anyway, it wouldn't do them any harm to know what a vile country we're living in.'

'Rosa, it hasn't been as bad recently. When was the last time somebody was beaten, or even harassed?' Esther countered.

'That's not the point. There should be no question of us being safe in our own country but, then again, we're only subjects now, with no damned rights, as far as I can tell.'

'She's right,' Miriam said, 'but she should still mind her language.' She smiled, to take the edge off her rebuke.

'If Itsik could get enough for the shop, we could emigrate.'

'Good luck with that. There's a seventy per cent wealth tax if you leave the country,'

Miriam said.

'Unless you go to Palestine. Then you can take it all,' Rosa said.

'Oh, not you, too, Rosa. I'm fed up hearing about Palestine,' Miriam said.

'I'm not saying I'd go. It sounds horrible. Nothing but old ruins and desert. They even say Jerusalem's a dump. But it is an option.'

'I don't want to leave.' There were tears in Esther's eyes. 'My family and friends are all here, and how would we start all over again?'

'I'm sure if it comes to that,' Rosa said, giving Esther a smile, 'you'd manage better than you'd expect. Things could change in Germany. I hear that the government is struggling to pay even its Aryan employees. There's a bit of natural justice in that, isn't there?'

'Is that really true, Rosa?' Miriam said, trying not to get her hopes up. If the government collapsed, any replacement would surely be better. And some, or all, of the changes might be reversed.

'I don't know,' Rosa said. 'I can only tell you what I've heard.'

They were interrupted by Ruth and Rebeka.

'Can we go swimming, Mama?'

'Can all the girls swim?'

'Yes, Mama. Can they borrow some swimming clothes?'

'I'll see what I've got. You have a spare costume, and the older two can use mine. But be careful.'

Ruth and Rebeka ran into the house to collect the bathing suits.

Rosa turned to her two friends.

'Remember when we were that age? Wasn't life simple?'

They both nodded.

~~o~~

[05/06/1936 Friday]

Two weeks after Ruth's party, Miriam, Rosa, and Esther sat together in the corner of the hall at the back of the synagogue. It was decorated with flowers, and all the ladies had dressed up in their best clothes for the occasion.

A few babies and toddlers were there but most women, like Miriam, had left their children in the care of their fathers, or with their grandparents.

The coffee morning was being held to raise cash to allow Jewish families with little resources to leave Germany for Palestine. Although Miriam was sceptical about the obsession for a Jewish homeland, she always supported these events. Everyone had baked, so there was an abundance of savoury bagels, and sweet plates of Rugelach, Kugel, and apple cake, weighing the tables down until they groaned. It wouldn't be wasted. They all knew of Jewish families who were having difficulty feeding their children.

'Itsik turned down the offer.'

Miriam looked at Esther to gauge if her friend was pleased or disappointed. She judged it to be somewhere in between, by the look on her face.

'It was a ridiculous offer. Just someone trying to take advantage of the situation,' Miriam said.

'Turns out the man was a senior party member. He told Itsik that when he comes crawling back in six months' time, the offer will be half of that again.'

'Bastard,' said Rosa, lowering her voice. The other two looked around, but none of the children were within earshot.

'No one heard, don't worry,' Rosa said. 'But seriously, I'd love to see these people get their comeuppance someday.'

'Me too,' Miriam said. 'They think they can get away with anything. Including murder.'

310

'Can't Itsik sell the store to someone else? There are surely decent people out there who'd give a reasonable price for it. Even if he didn't get quite its full value, providing it was fair, it would be worth taking.'

'He has tried. Nobody has any money, other than those with influential positions in the party.'

'There must be someone, Esther,' Miriam said.

Rosa interrupted. 'It'll be a brave person who buys a business from under a party official's nose.'

Esther looked crestfallen, and Miriam glared at Rosa.

'What?' she said, shrugging her shoulders. 'There's no point in sugar-coating the truth.'

'You're right,' Esther said. 'Itsik should have taken the money.'

'Something will turn up,' Miriam said, shaking her head quickly at Rosa.

That evening, in bed, she told Yosef about Itsik, and the offer he'd received.

Yosef lay awake for a long time.

CHAPTER 91

Memo: Geh.KdoS. ABW 17/06/36 CAC0479.1

For Attention Only: All senior executive officers, Abwehr.

From: Rear Admiral Wilhelm Canaris, Chef der Abwehr.

Adolf Hitler has appointed Reichsführer-SS Heinrich Himmler as the National Chief of Police. [END]

~~o~~

Memo: Geh.KdoS. ABW 26/06/36 CAC0482.1

For Attention Only: All senior executive officers, Abwehr.

From: Rear Admiral Wilhelm Canaris, Chef der Abwehr.

Reichsführer-SS Heinrich Himmler has announced a reorganisation of the regional German police forces. He has established two main offices: [1] Hauptamt Sicherheitspolizei (HA SiPo), the security police, and [2] Hauptamt Ordnungspolizei (HA OrPo), the uniformed branch.

HA SiPo will be under the command of SS General Reinhard Heydrich and is made up of the Gestapo and the Kriminalpolizei (KriPo).

HA OrPo is to be commanded by SS General Kurt Daluege, unifying every uniformed police force in Germany.

This completely centralises control of the nation's police and security services, leaving the Abwehr as the only independent intelligence-gathering organisation in Germany. We remain in total support of the government, but I know I can count on your efforts in maintaining the Abwehr's independence. [END]

Erich Kästner looked out across the waters of Kieler Hafen.

They're tightening the noose, he thought.

CHAPTER 92

[11/07/1936 Saturday]

Maria watched from the window as Franz stepped into his car, amazed that this young man could be her son, wondering where the years had gone.

She knew her husband had helped him a little with the purchase of the car, but Franz wasn't a big spender like Johann, who frittered away most of his army pay on beer and girls.

The small open-top sports car reached the end of the driveway and turned into Hamburger Chaussee, then, a few seconds later, pulled up in front of the Böhm's house. She smiled as he stepped out, ever so handsome in his uniform. He'd wanted to wear slacks and a sports jacket, but she'd persuaded him to wear the dark-green trousers and tunic of the Wehrmacht, knowing the effect his appearance would have on Lise Böhm.

As he strode up the steps to the front door, she remembered the first time the General had called on her, and how her father had checked the young officer out before letting his daughter into his safekeeping for the evening. And the memories of the young Captain Kästner in his uniform all those years ago were still fresh in her mind.

Standing on the steps that evening, she'd blushed, as much for the way he'd looked at her, aware of the effect she had on him for the first time. She'd decided there and then that she would be the future Frau Kästner, although she hadn't let him know of her decision, figuring that it was much better if the idea came from him.

The door opened, and Maria could just see Lise's father, shaking her son's hand, before Lise stepped past him, taking Franz's arm and guiding him down the steps towards the car.

Maria was relieved that Lise hadn't worn her BDM outfit; the uniform that looked good on boys was decidedly unflattering on girls, she thought.

She was wearing a light summery dress, loose enough to be comfortable in the heat of summer, but still hugging her figure in the right places. Maria approved. She watched as her son, the perfect gentleman, held the door open for Lise, before jumping in himself.

As the car turned back on the Hamburger Chaussee, Maria smiled as the part of Lise's hair that wasn't tucked into her headscarf trailed behind her in the wind.

~~o~~

The film was the latest American romantic comedy drama to draw big German audiences. Like most of the foreign films shown, *Mr. Deeds Goes to Town*, starring Gary Cooper and Jean Arthur, was dubbed, and within minutes of it starting, Franz and Lise were engrossed.

She snuggled close to him and lifted his arm around the back of her shoulders. Where he touched her, he felt a shiver of electricity pass between them. Lise held their clasped hands on her leg, with only the thin material of her dress between his fingers and her skin.

She turned towards him, reaching her face up to his for a kiss. When their lips touched, she pressed her body against his, the swell of her breast soft and pleasing against his chest, but at that moment, Longfellow Deeds met his leading lady and Lise broke away to watch as Jean Arthur, playing a cynical reporter, attempted to seduce him.

The film so engrossed them that, throughout the entire screening, they only kissed twice but before driving her home, Franz took a short detour along Krusenrotter Weg, stopping where it passed through the woods at Vieburg to satisfy the craving they had for the touch of each other's lips and bodies. She kissed him harder this time, and her fingers carelessly brushed his leg as she reached for his hand, guiding it onto her knee.

He felt her breathing quicken at his touch, but something stopped him moving his hand from where she'd placed it. He thought he sensed her disappointment and when he looked at the little clock on the dashboard and told her that her father expected her home by eleven, she pouted, but kissed him goodnight when he dropped her off.

Parking the car, he walked into the house, ready for the questions his mother would doubtless ask, not even knowing himself how he would answer.

Yes, Lise was exciting, beautiful and everything a man could want in a woman. He'd be mad to think otherwise but she was young, and there was no rush, surely.

And at the back of his mind, there was one other thing.

During the newsreel, before the film had started, he'd watched her when Adolf Hitler's face filled the screen, his voice screaming at the massed crowd standing raptly in front of him. She'd stared at the Führer with an intensity that shocked Franz and, after the diatribe had finished, he watched as she wiped tears of joy from her eyes. It struck him, looking around, that almost everyone in the cinema was infected with a religious zeal, worshipping a new god, and his teachings.

His body screamed at him to ignore it, but he didn't know if he could square Lise's blind fervour for Germany's chancellor with his love for her.

CHAPTER 93

Memo: Geh.KdoS. ABW 16/07/36 CAC0482.1

For Attention Only: All senior executive officers, Abwehr.

From: Rear Admiral Wilhelm Canaris, Chef der Abwehr.

The SS has established the Sachsenhausen concentration camp, near Oranienburg, to the north of Berlin.

It is expected that this will ease pressure on existing camps, which are full to capacity in the aftermath of the arrest and relocation of all Roma from Berlin to the camp at Marzahn.

The legislation, passed last month, seeks to tackle "the Gypsy plague", as the Minister of the Interior for the Reich and Prussia called it. It officially sanctions the regulations and restrictions already in place at a local level regarding Roma people residing in Germany. The legislation also covers other persons who are deemed to be behaving in "a Gypsy-like manner". [END]

~~o~~

'Home now, sir?'

'Not just yet, Yosef.'

Yosef was intrigued. The General had visited a few places that morning, the latest being the small Catholic church in Wellingdorf.

As usual, Yosef had waited in the car. He watched with interest as a small van drew into the car park behind the church and reversed up to the doors of the church hall.

A couple of men jumped out of the van and two women, presumably parishioners, opened the doors of the hall, and of the van. All four went inside, to reappear a minute later carrying large steel tureens, baskets of bread and boxes of what he presumed were crockery and cutlery, judging by their weight.

The General didn't spend long in the church, and re-emerged just as the van drove off, the priest in tow. Yosef jumped out and held the door open for the General, who indicated for the priest to get in first.

'This is Father Liebehenschel, Yosef.'

'Guten Morgen, Father. Pleased to meet you.'

'And you, Yosef. But call me Father Phillip.'

'Take us to Kleiner Kuhberg, Yosef, please,' the General said. 'Father Phillip will give you directions when we get there.'

When they reached their destination, the priest directed them down an alleyway into a yard at the back of one of the buildings. The General told Yosef to park over to one side, and when he turned the car, he could see why.

The van had already been backed up to the rear doors of the building, and an orderly queue of people snaked around the other side of the yard. Yosef was shocked to see that it was made up mainly of Jews. Most were dressed in Orthodox garb; they couldn't be mistaken for anything else, but a few others were more conventionally dressed; these were the secular Jews, some of whom he recognised from the synagogue.

He turned away, not wanting to shame any of them by letting them see him.

'How long has this been going on?' the General asked.

315

'Six months,' Father Phillip said. 'We thought it better to hire this empty property and feed them here, rather than attract attention at our church.'

Yosef wiped away a tear that had rolled down his cheek.

The General turned to him then looked away, giving Yosef a moment to compose himself.

'I'm trying to source some funding for Father Phillip, from the Rotary Club,' he said. He wanted me to see what they do here. It might be better if you stayed in the car.'

Yosef nodded. 'Yes, sir,' he said, as the two men got out, and walked towards the building.

~~o~~

When the General returned, it was without the priest. The queue had almost disappeared.

'The father will go back in the van. I'm sorry you had to see that, Yosef. I thought you already knew.'

'I'd heard rumours that food was available for those who had been put out of work and had families to feed, but I always assumed it would be Jewish charity that provided it.'

'Does it matter who gives the food, as long as it's there?'

'It shouldn't do, sir, but somehow it does.'

'Stop calling me sir when we're on our own, Yosef. Anyway, I spoke to a few of them in there. They find it easier not having to face people who know them, from their own community, when they come for the food they so desperately need.'

'Sorry, sir.' He smiled apologetically. 'I'd rather stick with the "sir", if you don't mind; I might forget when the mistress is there.'

He nodded towards the doorway. 'As for this,' he added, 'we should be looking after our own people, not relying on outsiders.'

'Yosef, a few of us still believe that we are all German. There shouldn't be any outsiders.'

'But the numbers, sir, and I know these are proud people. How desperate must they be to ask for food from strangers?'

'They have families. They're not too proud to let them starve.'

'No, they wouldn't be. But it's wrong.'

'Yosef, there have been soup kitchens for ever. Only a few years ago, it was the mass unemployed queuing up at places like this, and not just in Germany.'

'The difference is that these are all Jews, sir.'

CHAPTER 94

[20/07/1936 Monday]

Lise Böhm didn't know where to look.

The Kästner table at the Ratskeller was loud. Johann was holding court, doing an after-dinner impersonation of his brother, and everyone at the table was roaring with laughter, even Franz. Especially Franz.

'I, Hauptmann Franz Eduard Kästner, do solemnly declare that I will uphold the honour of the Heer and the German nation in my new rank, single-handedly defeating any foe…'

Johann swept an imperious arm around the dining room.

'…any foe,' he repeated, 'who dares to stand up to the Wehrmacht.'

He paused for effect. The Ratskeller was empty, save for the Kästners' table, and the General could see staff hovering at the entrance to the kitchens, hoping that the evening would quickly draw to a close.

The General and his family were regular diners at the Ratskeller; they never complained about the food or the service, and they always tipped well, so none of the staff would be rash enough to rush the family out of the restaurant, no matter how tempting it was.

'This honour…' Johann pointed to the captain's insignia on the cap he'd removed from Franz earlier, '…is the first of many. Next year a major; six months after that a lieutenant colonel and the following year, I'm sure they'll make me Oberst Kästner.'

The table applauded through tears of laughter and the admiral, his grandfather, almost fell off his chair. Even Lise managed a slightly nervous smile, not quite certain about Franz being made fun of like this.

'Wait,' Johann said, holding up his hand to quieten them. 'I'm not finished.'

He looked around and lowered his voice conspiratorially.

'Not many people know this, even in the army, but there are secret plans for me. I'm afraid it won't be Brigadier Kästner, or even Major General Kästner. And the ranks of lieutenant general and general are not for me.'

He put on a doleful look, and faced the weeping audience.

'I'll be the first Field Marshall Kästner in the family!' he said, triumphant, then sat down, to howls of laughter and the clamour of table thumping from the men of the group.

Lise laughed politely, looking around at the strange family she'd become embroiled with by stepping out with Franz. Only his mother wasn't completely taken with it all, though even her shoulders were shaking a little with mirth.

She wondered how a family which was so rooted in the military could be so disrespectful to the Reich, and if she should ask her mother what to do about it.

~~o~~

KIELER MORGENPOST

Tuesday 21st July 1936

ATTEMPTED COUP BY SPANISH NATIONALISTS

A declaration of military opposition was made three days ago against the Republican government of Spain by a group of generals of the Spanish Republican Armed Forces.

The rebels have named themselves Nacionales and have stated that the left-wing Republican government of Spain has an agenda to destroy the church and turn the country into a communist state.

It is at present unclear how successful the coup has been but there are reports that Spanish Morocco and southern parts of mainland Spain are under nationalist control while the Republican Government still hold most of the major cities.

The leader of the nationalist army, General José Sanjurjo, was killed yesterday when the aeroplane he was travelling in on his return from exile in Portugal crashed. General Francisco Franco replaces him as head of the Nationalist movement.

~~o~~

[28/07/1936 Tuesday]

'What about here?' Franz asked.

'It's lovely. What a beautiful view.'

Franz opened the trunk of the car, and lifted out a thick blanket, and spread it out on the ground. The small clearing in the woods had a good view of the beach and the sea beyond, but it was secluded. They were only thirteen miles from the centre of Kiel, down a narrow track that led from the small village of Dänisch-Nienhof to the beach.

Lise sat down on the blanket and arranged her dress prettily, before kicking off her shoes. Franz looked at her sitting, her arms around her knees, looking up at him, smiling.

She's truly beautiful.

He went back to the trunk and fetched the picnic box which Miriam had packed for them. He put it on the ground next to the blanket and started to open it.

'Are you hungry?' he asked.

'Not really. Why don't we leave that just now? Come and sit beside me.' She stretched out her hand to him.

He sat down beside her, and she leaned against him, turning her face towards his. He kissed her, tentatively at first but, when she responded with an intensity which startled him, he gave in to the flood of desire that surged through him. She matched him, first with her mouth, and then, when he reached around behind her and pulled her to him, she pressed her body against his, pushing him onto the ground.

She took his hand and placed it on her knee, just under the hem of her dress. His lips met her open mouth, and he felt the tip of her tongue explore his own. She moved his hand upwards, across the soft skin of her thigh before letting it go, parting her legs as an invitation for him to explore. Her hand, now free, was suddenly in between his own legs, feeling for him. Hardly in control, he moved his hand upwards until he could feel her moistness through the silk of her panties.

She groaned as he rubbed her, gently at first. She pressed herself against his hand, guiding him, shuddering with each push. Her own hand had found him now, the feeling through the cloth of his trousers almost overwhelming, and it passed through his mind that if he didn't stop now, he wouldn't be able to.

Just as he surrendered to it, she gave a gasp and slid off him, breathing heavily. She lay beside him, still caressing him with her hand.

He groaned and realised that there would be an embarrassing mess if she continued, so he gently removed her hand, and kissed her softly on the lips.

'I can finish you if you like,' she said, but he shook his head.

Her eyes glowed, and her face was flushed from her exertions. She sat up, and just before she straightened her dress, he saw the creamy skin of her thighs and the white silk of her panties next to it.

'If we were engaged, we wouldn't have to stop, Franz,' she teased.

He laughed. 'That sounded like a proposal. I thought it was meant to be me who asked.'

'Dear Franz, a girl could wait five years to be asked if she didn't drop a little hint. You're too shy,' she said, smiling at him.

'Perhaps we should get married. We love each other, don't we, and you are the most beautiful girl in the world.'

'I'll need more than that, Franz. You'll need a ring, and you'll have to get down on one knee. I promise to act surprised.' She giggled. 'And then you'll see what it's really like,' she said, lifting the hem of her dress a little.

~~o~~

Afterwards, Franz wondered about what had taken place, then dismissed the thought that it had all been orchestrated, to push him into doing something he wasn't ready for.

With all the rest of the things that were good about her, he now knew that she was not going to be shy in bed. And that, he suddenly realised, was important. Perhaps, in time, she would come round to his way of thinking about the other things.

When his mother asked him how he had enjoyed the evening, he blushed, trying to smother the embarrassment he felt, because he was sure that she knew what they'd been doing.

'It was nice,' he said.

'That good,' she said, with a teasing smile.

'She's the same age as Eva, Mother.'

'Yes, she is, I suppose, but she's always seemed older,' Maria Kästner replied.

CHAPTER 95

'Jürgen sends his apologies,' Uwe Müller said. 'I spoke with him earlier.'

'Our mayor has bigger fish to fry than the likes of us,' the Doc said with a grim smile.

'Oh, I wouldn't be too harsh on him,' the General replied. 'He's an extremely busy man, and he does a lot of socialising; it goes with the job.'

'Brown-nosing, more like,' Oskar joked. 'He's so far up that Lohse fellow's backside he can help him brush his teeth in the morning.'

They all laughed. The four men sat in their usual spot in the bar at the Europäischer Hof. The committee meeting had taken up less than half an hour, and they'd already eaten.

'I hear that most of the Rotarians are now party members,' Doc Speer said.

'You two must be the only ones who aren't,' Oskar replied. 'It's about time you thought about it.'

'No thanks,' the two men said together, then laughed.

'No, I'm being serious. Being a party member is fast becoming a necessity. I just about wouldn't be able to do business if I weren't.'

'I don't need to do business. I'm a doctor.'

'Point taken, Doc, but there will come a time when you need to cut through red tape, and you'll wish you were part of it.'

Doctor Speer grunted, but said nothing.

'Party members are still in the minority in the army, and the navy,' the General said.

'For now, yes,' Oskar argued, 'but in three or four years' time? Nearly all the new officers coming in will have been through Hitlerjugend and, as far as I know, that makes them party members. The younger conscripted soldiers will have also been in HJ, and the older ones will do as they're told. That just leaves the higher-ranking officers. The Defence Ministry hands out the top jobs, so they'll go to party members. Those who are left are dinosaurs who have no wish to go any higher in the army. This also applies to the navy, but it will take longer to work its way through.'

'Verdammt noch mal,' the General said. 'You've got a great way of cheering me up, von Friedeburg. I'll resign my commission before that happens. It might be a while though; I feel as if I'm almost part of the navy now.'

'Yes, but you're in the Abwehr. From what I've heard, your friend Canaris is a party man.'

'He's not a party member, but he's a big fan of Herr Hitler and the NSDAP.'

'With respect, Erich,' Uwe Müller said, 'I wish you would stop that. Some people would find *Herr Hitler* a little bit disrespectful, and you need to be more careful, for your own good.'

'Thanks for the warning, my friend. I try to be careful, but I relax a bit when I'm in company I trust.'

'Just take heed. Wouldn't want to come in to work and find you in my cells.'

They all laughed.

'So, have you gone all religious?' Oskar said, looking at the General.

'Me? No, why?'

'Your suggestion for funding, during the meeting. You were pushing hard for it to go through.'

'Ah, Father Liebehenschel, St. Augustine's. I heard about his soup kitchen for the poor. I thought he was doing good work and I know they have enough volunteers, but money is tight.'

'So how did you hear about it?'

Dieter Maas had told him, but the less people who knew about the connection between them, the better.

'One of Maria's friends volunteers at it. She asked Maria to mention it to me, to see if the Rotary could help. I said I'd ask.'

'I didn't think there were any unemployed now, with conscription and all the road-building going on.'

The General sighed. 'There will always be someone who slips through the net. It's only a few years ago we had thirty per cent unemployment. You don't find jobs for all these people in such a short time.'

'You're right, Erich,' Oskar conceded. 'For every job I advertise, I still get fifty applicants. One is lulled into a false impression by the press releases from Herr Goebbels at the Reich Ministry of Public Enlightenment and Propaganda.'

The General laughed. 'I'd forgotten about that. I thought it was someone's idea of a joke when I heard it at first.'

'It's no joke,' Uwe said. 'We need to check with them before we make any major announcement in order that we don't say the wrong thing.'

The four men talked for another hour then took their leave. The General and Oskar von Friedeburg were the last to go.

'Erich,' he said, 'these unemployed people. There's nothing special about them, is there?'

'I wouldn't know, Oskar. All I care about is that they're hungry.'

'I know. But just make sure you cover your back. And trust no one.'

'Even you, Oskar?'

The businessman smiled. 'Especially me, my friend.'

CHAPTER 96

Memo: Geh.KdoS. ABW 28/07/36 CAC0493.1

For Attention Only: General Erich Kästner, Abwehr, Kiel office

From: Rear Admiral Wilhelm Canaris, Chef der Abwehr.

You are instructed to attend the Defence Ministry for a meeting with senior staff from the Kriegsmarine and the Heer on 31/07/1936 in your capacity as Chief Liaison Officer. Accommodation has been arranged for you in the Adlon Hotel, Unter den Linden for three nights from the 30th July, as further meetings may be required. For all attending, it is acceptable that spouses may accompany them to Berlin. [END]

~~o~~

[01/08/1936 Saturday]

'How did you swing this, Canaris?'

'Perks of the job, Kästner.'

The two friends sat side by side, watching the restless crowd, impatient for the ceremony to start. Their wives also sat together.

'I do so wish that these two would grow up and address each other properly, don't you, Maria?'

Maria Kästner laughed. She liked Erika Canaris and had met her often enough to know her reasonably well, and they'd both named their eldest daughters Eva, but their friendship was an occasional one.

'I constantly tell them that too,' she said. 'They've not changed at all, really. But it was wonderful of you both to think of us; imagine being at the opening ceremony of the Olympic Games!'

'We'll likely go to some of the events too. It's the one bonus about Wilhelm being posted in Berlin.'

'That would be wonderful. We'll be able to get to as much of the sailing as we like. I expect Erich will attend every day if he can, but one or two days is more than enough for me. How are the girls?'

'They're fine. Getting big. Eva will go away to school after the summer. It will be a big wrench.'

Maria Kästner smiled.

'I was the same with our Eva, when she went away. You do know that she insists you named young Eva after her.'

'Yes, she tells me every time we see her,' Erica Canaris said, laughing.

How old are the girls now?' Maria Kästner asked, as a roar rose up from the crowd.

'Eva is twelve and Brigitte is ten. How time flies! I hear both Franz and Johann are now officers.'

'Yes, in Erich's old regiment. And we're expecting Franz to get engaged any day, if he can summon up the courage to pop the question.'

'Oh, that's lovely. Who's the girl?'

'Lise Böhm. She's our next-door neighbours' daughter. A pleasant girl, and so pretty.'

'And your girls?'

'Antje has started boarding school, so she's with Eva. The house feels so empty at times.

How did we get to be this old?' She laughed.

Erika Canaris made to reply, but at that point, the massed Wehrmacht bands and three thousand choral voices struck up *'Deutschland, Deutschland, über alles'*, the first words of the national anthem, which the crowd took up with almost demonic fervour as the Führer descended the wide entrance stairway from the Marathon Gate, at the head of the Olympiad procession. Swastika banners and Olympic flags vied for prominence all around the stadium.

The two women watched transfixed as the crowd returned Adolf Hitler's salute. The sound of their chants broke around the stadium like waves on a shore.

'Sieg Heil! Sieg Heil! Sieg Heil!'

As the Führer, still at the head of the procession, walked round the track, the orchestra and the choir struck up the Horst Wessel Song. The crowd joined in and almost drowned them out. The German chancellor made his way up to the specially constructed platform which gave him, his entourage, and the IOC members their pride of place.

~~o~~

'Very impressive, Kästner, eh? You have to agree; they put on a good show,' Canaris said, sweeping his arm around the stadium.

'Yes, and the world is watching.'

Erich Kästner studied his friend. 'But what will they be thinking?'

The General had seen big differences since the last time he'd been in Berlin. Gone were the *Jews Not Welcome* signs that had been in every hotel, bar, restaurant, and shop, and the *Der Stürmer* news-stands and billboards were empty of their usual bile.

The only thing the National Socialists couldn't orchestrate was the weather, but the occasional showers and the dull, overcast sky were forgotten when the Olympic teams began to enter the stadium to the strains of the *Olympische Hymne*, played by the oversized orchestra and conducted by its composer, Richard Strauss. The sound filled the stadium until the crescendo of cheering from the crowd almost defeated it.

It struck the General that the mood of the ceremony bordered on the religious, but a man, not a God, was being worshipped, a terrifying cult of personality.

'I'm surprised so many of the teams are returning Adolf Hitler's salute,' he said.

'The Olympic salute is very similar,' Canaris replied. 'It could be mistaken for it.'

Erich Kästner wasn't convinced.

As they passed in front of the Führer, each nation dipped its flag, apart from the Americans. It gave the General a little surge of encouragement that someone had the nerve to defy Hitler, even if it was the most powerful nation on earth.

When the German team entered, the stadium erupted. Massed cries of 'Sieg Heil' once again rolled down the stands of outstretched arms in wave after wave of noise, most of the crowd crying tears of pride and joy. The General looked at Adolf Hitler, no more than fifty yards away. His face was impassive, but his eyes had a demonic craving as if he were drinking in the adoration of the crowd and drawing power from it.

~~o~~

Afterwards, eating at one of Berlin's more fashionable restaurants, the General asked his friend about Adolf Hitler, the man.

'Well, he's a great orator, if a little strident, and he didn't say much today, surprisingly, apart from declaring the Games open. His speeches are the key to everything he does. He never writes anything down these days, but when he speaks, it's up to those under him to translate his words into legislation. He likes to have each department overlapping and conflicting, vying for his attention; it keeps them on their toes. They run around like frightened rabbits, desperate to be the ones in favour; even Himmler, on occasion, needs to fawn to him, although he has more autonomy than most.'

'Have you read *Mein Kampf*?'

'No. I've seen parts of it, but I've never had the time or, to be honest, the desire to read it. Have you?'

'Yes, Patzig gave me a copy.'

'A dark horse, that one.'

'I thought he was excellent. He had a healthy disrespect for the NSDAP.'

'Unlike me, you think?' Canaris said, his eyebrow raised.

'I'm not sure. There are times when I think your aims are identical to theirs but then you'll say something that makes me wonder. Let's say that I see you as a sceptical believer. You should read it.'

Wilhelm Canaris frowned.

'What? *Mein Kampf*?'

'Yes. I'll give you the one Patzig gave me. You should know what you're up against.'

~~o~~

'Must you two talk about work all the time?' Erika Canaris interjected.

'Yes, you should be paying more attention to your wives,' Maria added, smiling.

'We certainly should, my dears,' Canaris said, a twinkle in his eye. 'What would you like to talk about? Sport?'

'Oh, for heaven's sake, Wilhelm,' Erica Canaris said. 'What do I know about sport? Why not dish some gossip about the high and mighty? You must hear interesting scraps of tittle-tattle. You are in military intelligence, after all,' she said, ending in a mocking tone, and the other three laughed.

'The General and I are sworn to secrecy, on our lives, so what I can tell you is only the minor scandals I hear in the bars and restaurants of the city.'

The head of the Abwehr proceeded to deliver an almost endless stream of mindless gossip, his wife contributing here and there to confirm, ridicule or add to the snippets he offered about the current cream of German society.

Maria felt a twinge of jealousy and wondered what it would be like to mix in the sophisticated world of Berlin, instead of the provincial and limited backwaters of Kiel, but Admiral Canaris, in his usual charming way, turned the conversation around to the Kriegsmarine elite that inhabited the naval city and, suddenly, she felt part of it.

Erika Canaris knew enough of her husband's fellow commanders, and their wives, to make for a lively, laughter-filled hour, until the couples parted at the end of a wonderful evening.

'You must stay with us and attend some of the Olympic sailing,' Maria told Erika Canaris.

'I'm afraid I'll not be able to come. Eva and Brigitte have a summer dance school on for the next two weeks, so I must stay in Berlin.'

'Oh, that's such a pity. The girls would have loved it.'

'I'm sure Wilhelm will go. He never misses a chance to go back to Kiel.'

'He'll be more than welcome,' Maria said, hugging the other woman. 'It's a shame Eva and Brigitte can't come. Both girls would love to see them. Perhaps another time?'

'For sure.'

They kissed goodnight.

CHAPTER 97

Franz had never seen so many people packed around the shores of Kieler Hafen, even during Kieler Woche. But this was the Olympics, and it might be another fifty years before they returned to Germany.

He looked around the Kieler Yacht Club stand, reserved mostly for members, their guests and a few town dignitaries who weren't quite important enough to be on the main dais next door.

All the Kästner family were present, apart from Johann, who was on a training exercise with his unit. There were two admirals in the party; Erich's father, and Rear Admiral Canaris. The three men sat together, and the two girls sat with the ladies, although Antje had engineered a seat next to her father for herself.

With the row full, Franz and Lise sat, holding hands, in the next block of seats along.

Maria, sitting with her mother-in-law, glanced over at them.

'People are saying that Franz and Lise look so wonderful together,' Franz heard her say. 'They're all waiting for them to announce their engagement. I don't think it will be long.'

Franz blushed, hoping Lise hadn't overheard.

'That would be lovely,' Grandma Kästner said, looking over. 'They make such a sweet couple.'

'Yes, they wouldn't look out of place on one of those government posters.'

Franz frowned. *The perfect Aryan couple.*

It didn't sit easy with him.

I didn't help that he could see people nudging each other and nodding towards him and Lise.

Blushing again, he turned to Lise.

'I feel that everyone is looking at us,' he said.

'What if they are? They're just jealous.'

'Of us? Why?'

'Of you, because you are so lucky to have a girl like me, Franz Kästner,' she said, giggling.

He laughed. She was right.

'So, tell me what is happening here,' she asked. 'It looks like a muddle.'

'No, it's quite simple. There are three courses; the shorter one you can see in front of us, and the second one between here and Friedrichsort are for the one- and two-man boats. The third, the longer course, is off Schilksee, and is for the six- and eight-metre boats, which have a larger crew. It's less sheltered out there.'

'But where is the course? All I see is some buoys floating about in the water, two motorboats in the centre of the fjord, and lots of little sailboats milling around.'

'They're waiting for the race to begin. That's the start line between the two boats in the centre, and the finish,' he said, pointing as he spoke. 'Around them, you can see a wide circle of eight numbered marks or buoys.'

She nodded and smiled at him.

'Before the race,' he continued, 'the committee boat will tell the competitors which marks they have to go around, and in which order. They must round each mark in the correct order, leaving it to port or starboard as stipulated. That's all there is to it.'

She still looked puzzled.

'How do the spectators know what's going on?'

'Well, if you have a copy of the racecard,' he said, fishing a small booklet from his pocket, 'and you keep an eye on the flags on the committee boat, you can work out exactly what is happening but, even if you don't, you'll see all the boats mill around the start then rush to the same mark, gradually spacing out, like a procession.'

'That doesn't sound awfully exciting.'

'There'll be lots of overtaking, and near collisions, and some boats will appeal against others for breaking the rules. If someone is to blame, they'll have to do a penalty if it's upheld.'

'How do they do that? Attach a lead weight to the back?'

He laughed. 'No, it usually means making an extra couple of turns round one of the marks. Look, here they go,' he told her.

The report of the starter's gun reached them, and the boats all crossed the line, almost together. Some chose one tack, some the other, so there were two distinct groups making their way up the course in what seemed like opposite directions. Each time they tacked and crossed, collisions seemed inevitable, but they would emerge unscathed, finally reaching the windward mark.

The races had been postponed for a couple of hours until the morning's squalls had subsided, but it was still blustery.

As the race progressed, Franz kept Lise up to date with who was who as the lead changed back and forth.

He watched her as Werner Krogmann, the crowd favourite, rounded the third mark in the lead. Her face was flushed with excitement and, as the faint sounds of chants came from the spectator barges and the stands around the bay, she joined in. Very soon, most of the spectators around them were saluting and chanting 'Sieg Heil' in unison, the temporary structure of the stands shaking as the crowd stamped their feet.

He looked across at his family. He frowned as his mother, normally so reserved in public, joined Eva by chanting and stretching out her arm in the now familiar salute with the rest of the crowd.

Of the three, only Antje kept her hand down, slightly embarrassed by her sister and her mother. She caught Franz's eye, and he winked at her.

He felt a soft jab in his side, and he turned to see Lise look at him questioningly, and he realised she wanted him to join in.

'Deutschland, Deutschland,' he shouted, to cover his lapse. She frowned and motioned for him to raise his arm.

He shook his head and continued to cheer for the German boat. As the noise reached a crescendo, the two boats reached the next buoy and, in a brilliant move, the Englishman, Peter Scott, stole inside the German's line, almost touching the mark but gaining a boat-length in the process and stealing his rival's wind, causing Krogmann's sails to flap for a few vital seconds. He never regained the lead, despite the crowd's urgings, and a disappointed groan escaped from the crowd as the British boat crossed the line first.

Daan Kagchelland of the Netherlands came in third. These three would battle it out all week for the medals.

Franz turned to Lise.

'Wasn't that a fantastic race?' he said, slightly disappointed but excited by the quality of the competition.

Lise looked away, before turning to him.

'Don't you mind that our boat lost?' she asked, her voice thin and cold.

'It would have been better if we'd won, but it's only the first race. Krogmann won't make that mistake again and he has better speed between the marks.'

It mollified her only slightly.

'Why don't you salute, like we do? You did it when you were in the Hitlerjugend; you do it in the army, don't you?'

'Yes, but I never quite feel right doing it, so I don't, unless I have to. In the Wehrmacht, only certain commanders require us to salute like that. Even the ones who do only expect us to perform a Hitler greeting.'

He did the short salute, holding his right hand up from the elbow.

She stiffened, and her eyes clouded.

'I find that hard to believe. The army should be setting an example.'

'The army are not the party. We have a degree of independence.'

'But surely the armed forces should obey the government?'

'That's true, but the armed forces' first duty is to the citizens of the nation.'

'I don't understand.'

'Let's say the government put the country in an untenable position of danger. Should the army follow them blindly, or should it say, enough is enough?'

'That's treason,' she said.

'Not necessarily.' He wondered how the conversation had reached this point.

He sighed. 'Lise, like my father and grandfather, I'm a patriot and I'm totally loyal to the army, and to Germany. But it doesn't mean I have to like what the NSDAP are doing.'

She sniffed. 'I don't want to talk about this anymore. Is there somewhere we can get an ice cream?'

'Yes, of course. I'll ask the others.'

'No, I couldn't face them. I mean, look at me.'

Franz looked at her. There was a slight moistness in her eyes but, apart from that, she looked as beautiful as ever, but a voice in his head told him to do as she asked.

As they passed his parents, he mumbled something about being back for the next race and followed her down the steps.

The ice-cream kiosk was a little further down Hindenburgufer. He bought two cones and handed one to her. They stood in silence, eating their ice cream. She wouldn't look at him.

'Let's go back,' he said, when they'd finished.

She allowed him to take her hand. During the next race, he stood and chanted with the others, and stretched his arm out in salute with the rest of the crowd. She smiled and gripped his hand in thanks. Franz couldn't look over at his father, but he could sense his eyes on him; he hoped he would understand.

CHAPTER 98

KIELER MORGENPOST

Wednesday 5th August 1936

MORE GERMAN GOLD!

Karl Hein won Germany's fourth gold medal of the Olympics in the men's hammer throw to add to the gold medals won yesterday by Gisela Mauermayer in the women's discus throw, and on Sunday by Hans Woellke in the men's shot-put, and by Tilly Fleischer in the women's javelin.

Karl Hein's winning throw of 56.49 metres, in his last throw of the final, beat his fellow countryman, Erwin Blask into silver position by over a metre. Fred Warngård of Sweden won the bronze medal.

Woellke established a new Olympic record of 16.20 metres during his victory in the shot-put.

~~o~~

Maria and Eva declined the invitation to the second day's racing and Erich's mother decided to stay at Drachensee with them.

'One day at a time watching little men in boats go round in circles is enough,' Maria said. 'We might come for the final day.'

With the extra space, Lise and Franz sat with the remainder of the Kästner family and Admiral Canaris. Antje wormed her way in between her 'Uncle' Wilhelm and her grandfather, who entertained her all day, making her giggle until she was sore. The General pretended to be annoyed at their antics, but he was as guilty as they were of teasing his youngest daughter.

'Did you see this?' the General asked, showing his father the newspaper.

'Yes, great pictures. Karl Hein and Hans Woellke are impressive brutes, are they not? Gisela Mauermayer is a big girl too, by the looks of her.'

'Yes, they did very well, and deserve all the praise that they're getting, but do you see anything missing?'

'No, we've only won the four gold medals, I think.' He paused. 'We've won a few silvers as well. It mentions one in the article. All the results are listed at the bottom. Look.'

The old admiral pointed at the full results list at the bottom of the page.

The General shook his head.

'There's a bigger Olympic story,' he said. 'One that I hear everyone talking about, but there's no headline in here. Not even a picture.'

'Ah, you mean Jesse Owens,' the admiral said, nodding. 'Maybe it's just because he's not German. The *Morgenpost* is just a local paper.'

'It's a city paper. Most of its front page is national or international. Jesse Owens has just won two gold medals, equalling the world record in the hundred-metres sprint and breaking an Olympic record in the long jump, but I've yet to see a picture in the *Morgenpost*, or even a few column inches.'

'Ach, the *Morgenpost* does what it's told. It's practically a party paper.'

'Contrast it with this.' He handed his father a copy of the *Berliner Tageblatt*. 'Canaris gets the papers sent to him every morning from Berlin. I suppose he feels he needs to keep in touch with opinion as well as fact.'

The admiral looked at the paper. A picture of Jesse Owens dominated the front page. He read through the story.

Berliner Tageblatt

Wednesday 5th August 1936

JESSE OWENS WINS SECOND GOLD IN LONG JUMP TRIUMPH!

LUZ LONG GETS SILVER.

In an exciting long jump competition, Jesse Owens, the world's fastest man, won the Gold medal, beating his German rival Luz Long with a jump to spare. Fast becoming a firm favourite with the home crowd, Jesse Owens left the best until last, and jumped 8.06 metres, having already won the Gold medal.

Up until the fifth jump, it was neck and neck between Owens and Long, each having jumped 7.87 metres at the start of the fifth round, with Owens still to jump.

Luz Long sportingly gestured for the crowd to quieten while Owens prepared to jump, and the American athlete leapt a massive 7.94 metres.

Unfortunately, Luz long failed on his final jump, leaving Owens under no pressure on his last attempt, where he broke the Olympic record.

The roar from the stadium when the distance appeared on the board was deafening and in the centre of the stadium, the two athletes embraced. It has been reported that the two men are great friends.

The result wasn't always certain - Owens only narrowly qualified for the final on his last jump. He told reporters after the final that Luz Long had given him some reassuring advice before he completed his critical qualifying jump.

In the 100 metres, the imperious Owens won the gold medal in a time of 10.34 seconds, equalling his own world record. He has a chance of two further medals; the 200 metres sprint on Wednesday and the sprint relay on Sunday although currently, neither Owens nor Metcalfe, the 100 metres silver medallist, have yet been selected for the team.

At the bottom of the story, there was a second picture, of Luz Long embracing Jesse Owens after the final. The General smiled.

'Hard to believe both papers are describing the same day at the Olympics,' the General

329

said.

Down the right-hand side of the *Tageblatt*'s front page, there was a round-up of the other events, and a prominent place was given to the four German gold medals that the *Morgenpost* had led with.

'Balanced reporting is hard to find,' the old man said. 'There are few papers that don't toe the party line. The only other one I can think of is the Frankfurter Zeitung,' the old man said.

'Yes, but for how much longer? I hear they are only being allowed to continue as a sop to foreign opinion.'

'Hmmph. That figures.' He paused. 'How are Yosef and Miriam doing? I haven't had a chance to speak with them yet.'

The admiral had known Yosef since birth and treated him, if not like a son, like a favourite nephew.

'I tried to persuade them to leave, but they refused.'

'Damn fools! Did they say why? I can most likely guess.'

'You probably can. They didn't want to leave Samuel and Renate, and the rest of the Nussbaums, and there's Miriam's family too. But there's also their stubborn loyalty to us, and their fear of starting over again in a foreign country.'

'It's a terrible situation. They shouldn't be having to make this decision; they're as German as we are. Imagine if it was our family in that position.'

'They are our family, Father.'

~~o~~

Erich Kästner had been one of the most enthusiastic committee members when Kieler Yacht Club had purchased a radio wireless set especially for the Olympic Games; the government had promised live transmissions for the whole of the fortnight and, so far, it had lived up to its pledge.

For the lucky people of Berlin, there was a daily television screening of the events in the stadium in twenty-five specially built viewing rooms around the city but in Kiel, the citizens had to content themselves with live radio broadcasts.

It was just after six at the Kieler Yacht Club; the final sailing race of the day was due to start but only a smattering of people sat in the yacht club stand, watching.

In the bar of the Kieler Yacht Club, there was standing room only, as the disembodied voice of the presenter crackled from the radio set, announcing the line-up for the two-hundred-metre final.

As in the stadium, and in public places and homes throughout Germany, the crowd cheered loudest when Jesse Owens' name was mentioned.

'Canaris, you could have been there, in the stadium, you know,' the General said.

'And miss a few days here with you, Kästner?'

The General laughed as the presenter finished announcing the runners. There were no Germans in the final, but it crossed his mind that it wouldn't have mattered; a large slice of the German people had taken Jesse Owens to their collective hearts.

'I have tickets for the final of the sprint relay. If he wins today, they'll surely put him in the team,' Canaris said.

The Abwehr chief was heading back to Berlin the next day, and the General had booked a table at the Ratskeller for eight o'clock that evening; he'd had to pull rank to get a reservation during the Olympics, but the whole family was going, on *Uncle Wilhelm's* last evening in Kiel.

He looked around. The club steward tried his best to serve drinks to tables of members but the throng of people around the bar made it almost impossible. He gave up and stood behind the bar, handing out drinks to all and sundry.

They'll settle their tabs later, the General thought, trusting the integrity of the members.

330

Everybody had one ear on the radio.

Everyone in the bar could clearly hear the chant of 'Jess-He Ov-ens, Jess-He Ov-ens, Jess-He Ov-ens' over the airwaves, and the crowd in the yacht club joined until the commentator described the starters lining up.

'Osendarp — van Beveren — Owens — Robinson — Haenni — Orr,' the voice intoned.

As the commentator announced that the athletes had crouched down in their starting positions, the stadium hushed and the hubbub in the bar slowly subsided, becoming almost silent.

From the wireless, the sound of the starting pistol was loud in the stillness, and the bar erupted. Over the radio, the commentator's voice could just be heard, as it rose in pitch with every yard of the race.

'Owens gets out of the blocks well, and after fifty metres, he's already shoulder-to-shoulder with his countryman, Robinson, in the lane outside him – as they come off the bend Owens has a two-metre lead over Robinson on his outside and Osendarp on the inside lane.'

The crowd in the bar were jumping up and down now, pushing towards the radio set, as if it would take them there, to the stadium.

'Owens continues to widen the gap with each stride – Osendarp is feeling the pain of trying to stay with Owens and is falling back.'

The commentator's voice was now feverish, caught up himself in the drama of the race. The crowd in the bar almost lifted the roof off now and the General's face broke into a grin as he shouted at the top of his voice, joining them. The commentator's voice rose to a crescendo over the last twenty or thirty metres.

'Robinson is striving to keep in touch but he's now trailing Owens by three metres – Owens is still pulling away – he's going to win – Owens breaks the tape four metres ahead – what a win – what a run – Owens has his third gold medal of these games and in some style!'

The roar of the crowd in the stadium drowned out the commentator's next words but he waited a few seconds before speaking again. Another loud cheer shook the bar the radio set was sitting on.

'The crowd have just seen the time – it's yet another Olympic record for Jesse Owens – 20.71 seconds! – the crowd are going wild – Owens is off doing his lap of honour.'

Everyone in the bar was hugging each other, and talking, all at once.

'Will the Americans let him run in the relay?'

'Can Owens make it four?'

'Will he break another world record?'

'Owens must be the greatest athlete, ever.'

The General quickly wiped his eyes and stood back, looking at his fellow Germans.

He hoped Hitler and his entourage knew that the nation was cheering for a black man, who was not only winning gold medals but was becoming a hero; this, in a nation whose leaders were trying to brainwash its citizens with delusions of Aryan supremacy.

~~o~~

KIELER MORGENPOST

Thursday 6th August 1936

JESSE OWENS WINS THIRD GOLD

Negro American runner Jesse Owens has won the Olympic gold medal in the 200-metre sprint, to add to his gold medals in the long jump and the 100-metre sprint.

In other news, Helene Mayer won the silver medal in the women's foil at the Fencing arena yesterday. Frau Mayer had won the gold medal at the 1928 Olympics in Amsterdam, and has won numerous international titles, including two world championships, in 1929 and 1931.

~~o~~

'Did you see the *Morgenpost* yesterday?' the General said.

He sat next to Franz, high up on the stands at the Kieler Yacht Club. It was a duller day, but there was a stiff breeze, so the sailing would be entertaining. Lise was arriving later; an appointment at the hairdresser had delayed her.

Antje, who hadn't missed a day, sat on the other side of her father, and Johann had phoned the night before saying that his exercise had finished, and he was trying to get an overnight pass to come and see some of the sailing, and spend an evening at home.

'Ha.' Franz laughed. 'The *Morgenpost* has finally been forced to cave into public opinion and make Jesse Owens the lead story.'

'It came from on high, my little birds tell me,' the General said. 'Right from the top; the whole nation was talking about Owens, and there was nothing in the papers. It was ludicrous, so Herr Goebbels was forced into relaxing restrictions on reporting negro successes.'

'They weren't exactly profuse in the story they ran. Terse would be a more accurate description.'

'It made my day, all the same. I hope he runs again.'

'He's not in the team, they say.'

'Everyone is calling for him to run. It's too big an opportunity for them not to give him the chance.'

~~o~~

Franz jumped up and made to kiss Lise on the cheek when she arrived, but she turned as he leant forward, and kissed his mouth.

Embarrassed, he helped her step past Antje and his father, into her seat, and sat down beside her.

'You've missed a couple of exciting races,' he said.

'I'm sure there'll be plenty more. To be honest, a whole day watching boats racing is a little too much,' she said.

'We don't need to stay until the end. Perhaps we could go for a run. I have the car here.'

Beneath her scarf, which was lying on her lap, she moved her hand and gently stroked Franz's leg.

'That would be nice,' she said, looking at him with her mouth slightly open, the tip of her tongue touching her teeth.

The familiar tingle shot up Franz's body and he lowered the day's racing programme to hide his excitement. Lise took advantage and slid her fingers across his leg under its pages, until she touched the stretched cloth of his trousers covering him.

He felt sweat trickling down the small of his back, and his breathing became sharp and fast. He glanced at his father, but the General seemed oblivious.

Franz was wondering how to stop Lise without making a fuss, when she moved her hand away, smiling coyly at him.

'Later,' she mouthed at him, taking hold of his hand and resting it on her lap. With a shock, he realised that, through her thin, summery dress, he could feel the raised band of her suspenders and noticed for the first time that she was wearing stockings.

She asked him if she might see the programme and he handed it to her, feeling almost

332

naked.

His hand seemed to burn where it touched her leg, and she rocked herself gently against him to let him know the effect it was having on her. He imagined the wetness between her thighs that he'd felt in the forest clearing and lifted his jacket onto his lap to save further embarrassment.

At the end of the next race, he offered to take her for a drink, and told the General that they might go for a spin in the country afterwards. His father nodded, and Franz wondered if he knew. Even Antje seemed to grin, but it may have been because, with their departure, she had her father all to herself.

CHAPTER 99

Franz drove to the same clearing, overlooking the beach. Again, they had it to themselves. This time, when he ran his fingers up the inside of her thigh, past the rim of the suspender belt, he was shocked to find that she had nothing on.

'I took them off when I went to the toilet,' she whispered. 'Does it feel nice?'

She was soft, warm, and very wet. He explored her gently at first but, as she became more insistent, moaning softly, he moved his fingers faster and with increasing firmness until she came again, shuddering as before, her eyes closed, letting out a low squeal of pleasure.

'Your turn,' she said, after her breathing had subsided to near normal, undoing his belt and buttons, before slipping her hand inside.

At first, she touched him through the cloth of his underpants but, after a while she slipped her hand under the waistband and gripped him firmly. He groaned, and she reached her mouth up to his, teasing him with her tongue on his lips, slowly moving her hand up and down. He came quickly, and she wiped him with the handkerchief that she'd laid on the blanket between them.

He kissed her again, while she buttoned him up, and fastened his belt for him.

'Let's get married,' he said to her. 'I'll go and see your father today, and we can tell everyone, if he has no objections.'

'Only if I say *yes*, don't forget,' she said, laughing.

'Will you marry me, Lise Böhm?'

'Of course, I will, silly.'

~~o~~

They waited until the next day. Franz made a substantial withdrawal from his savings account and purchased a pair of wedding rings, with his and Lise's name engraved inside, as was tradition.

He paid the customary visit to Eberhard Böhm.

Lise's father was delighted but cautioned them to wait a year before getting married. 'Lise will be just that little bit older then,' he added, and Franz wondered if there was a little warning in there for him.

Showing off the rings to Frau Böhm first, then to the Kästner family, was quite an event. His new fiancée on his arm, he invited the Böhms over, the Kästners having decided to turn the occasion into an impromptu party; his grandparents were still in residence and even Johann had arrived, on a twenty-four-hour furlough from the regiment. He was the first to offer congratulations to Franz, with a big bear of a hug for his brother and another for Lise, which Franz suspected went on a little bit longer than necessary.

His brother's face had hardened a little since he'd joined the army and he was already broader across the shoulders. It suited him.

~~o~~

While Lise showed off her new ring to everyone, the General, Franz, and Johann caught up with all the regimental gossip just outside in the hallway. Both had a high opinion of Colonel Schneider although Johann had, on a couple of occasions, been the subject of minor disciplinary actions on the part of their commanding officer.

'No surprise there then,' the General said, laughing, and Johann had the temerity to look hurt.

'We just like to have a laugh sometimes, and when we're off-duty...'

'Just remember it's a serious job, being an officer, and you must be an example for your troops.'

'The colonel has never criticised my command abilities; in fact, he said that he was impressed how loyal and disciplined my squad was.'

'That's excellent,' the General said, putting his hand on his son's shoulder.

'Keep up the good work and, within reason, don't lose your sense of humour,' he added, a glint of laughter in his eyes. 'How are you finding the training?'

'Our senior officers are brilliant, and Colonel Schneider is good to serve under. I've learned so much in such a short time. Some of the stuff they're teaching us is mind-blowing, this new way of fighting. We'll soon have the best army in the world.'

'We'll certainly have the biggest, per capita,' the General said, 'and one of the best, I'll agree, but there are others who would easily match us.'

'Who?' said Johann.

'The British, the Americans, the Japanese. Even the French.'

Johann snorted. 'The British think they rule the world, but they live in the past; the Americans have no stomach for a fight and the Japanese are too far away from us to be of significance; and, unlike the British, we have no empire to protect.'

'Which makes the British dangerous,' the General replied. 'They have a large and exceptionally skilled navy; ask Uncle Wilhelm; they also have a well-trained army that is honed by being regularly involved in conflicts all over the world, and they can always rely on the backing of the Americans.'

'It was the only reason we lost the last war. The Americans tipped the scale in 1917.'

'And they would again if we started another war with Britain.'

'No, they wouldn't,' Johann insisted. 'They have enough to worry about with what is going on in the Far East, with Japan and China at war, and the Japanese flexing its military muscles.'

The General wondered where Johann was getting his information from. Much of it was true but his son was being taught by someone who saw world politics in black and white. The General knew it was never that simple.

'Don't underestimate them,' he said, not wanting to curb his son's thirst for knowledge about world affairs.

'The American government would be too frightened of being thrown out of office to go to war in Europe,' Johann said, sneering. 'Unless someone attacks them, they will stay out of it.'

'Who teaches you this Scheiße, Johann?' Franz said. 'Not Colonel Schneider, for sure.'

'We have a new major in our unit. He was a Sturmbannführer in the SS but has been transferred to our regiment; five of them were appointed. They've been assigned to help the colonel's staff with training.'

Franz nodded. 'I remember a new man arriving just as my leave started. we haven't yet been introduced.'

'They don't really mix,' Johann said. 'They tend to stick together.'

'In what way do they help with the training?' Franz asked.

'You'll see when you get back. They've started political warfare classes. War is not always won on the battlefield, you know,' Johann said, his face flushed.

The General, only half listening, was casting his mind back to a conversation he'd had with his then commander, Captain Patzig.

I was right, he thought. *The National Socialists are infiltrating the Wehrmacht. It will be interesting to find out if these appointments are widespread, in both the Heer and the Kriegsmarine.*

'So, you see,' Johann continued, 'the Wehrmacht will be in a position to uphold all the Führer's demands when we take back the Sudetenland and Danzig and ally ourselves once more with Austria.'

'I don't believe the French will allow any of these things to happen, without declaring war on us,' the General said, suddenly realising what his son was saying.

'Pah. The French are all hot air. They will not attack us and, if they do, they will lose.'

'But Britain will support them again.'

'Not for minor infringements, it won't, and the French will not start a fight without Britain on board.'

The General realised that the opinions his son was glibly passing off as fact had been simmering away at the back of his own mind, and presumably Canaris' mind, for the last year or so. And the ideas Johann was repeating were being disseminated directly from the National Socialist policymakers. It confirmed in his thinking the suspicions he'd had about the government's ambitions.

'So, these political lectures; how often do you get them?'

'At least twice a week. Why do you ask?'

The General ignored the question.

'Who goes to them – all the men?'

'No, no,' Johann said. 'Only commissioned men.'

Clever, the General thought. *Teach those men most capable of instantly understanding the concepts, and they would pass it on to the rank and file.*

'We are just starting to build,' his son went on. 'In two or three years we will have the capability to take on anyone in the defence of our borders.'

'I agree. If that is our aim, we will be more than able to fulfil it,' the General said. '*If that is our aim.*'

'Whatever our plans are, I'm ready to fight for the good of Germany,' Johann said.

'You may have to, son,' the General said, shaking his head sadly.

~~o~~

'You three are being dreadfully unsociable.' Maria Kästner's voice broke the silence. She stood at the doorway, frowning at them. She walked over to Franz.

'Whatever you're talking about,' she said, 'it must be all doom and gloom. This is supposed to be a celebration of my little boy's engagement,' she said, ruffling Franz's hair.

The General and Johann grinned as Franz's face turned crimson.

'Mother,' he said, 'I'm not your little boy. I'm twenty years old!'

'You'll always be my little Franz,' she said, not in the slightest perturbed by her son's discomfort.

'You're my little one, too, Franz,' the General said, his hand on Franz's shoulder, grinning.

Franz gave up and joined in the laughter, moving back through to join the rest of the party.

Eberhard Böhm sidled up to the General as soon as he entered the room.

'Erich, isn't it delightful, our two families joining together?' he said.

'It is indeed. Lise is a great girl. I'm sure she will make Franz a wonderful wife.'

'I'm sure she will,' the prospective in-law said, putting his hand on the General's shoulder, 'and your Franz. I almost think of him as my own son.'

'They make a lovely couple. We're immensely proud of Franz, and Johann too,' he added, aware of his younger son, standing within earshot.

'I'm sure Franz and Lise would be marvellous for one of the party's posters. They look the part.'

The General drew a deep breath and counted to five. It was true; Franz and Lise looked like the ideal couple for one of Goebbels' publicity campaigns.

And he knew, without arrogance, that Franz was an exceptional young officer. The last time he'd spoken to Colonel Schneider, the company commander had told him that Franz was the most promising recruit he'd ever had under his command, and Schneider was no fool.

'I'm sure both Franz and Lise would shy away from that sort of exposure; neither of them would enjoy the limelight.'

He was amazed that he could keep his tone so light. Inside, he was seething. Was the man just stupid, or was he deliberately goading him?

'Oh, I don't know. I hear that taking part in these campaigns does no harm to the participants' career prospects.'

'I'm sure Franz will keep that in mind, although the army resists outside attempts to influence its autonomy.'

'But you must be just like us, Erich. We, in the civil service, are willing to do anything the Führer asks of us in the name of Germany. He has brought new life into the ministries and, of course, the Wehrmacht has been transformed out of all recognition.'

'We are grateful to the government for restoring the army's pride and purpose. But I do hope our boys never have to fight.'

'If that's what it takes, then fight we must,' the civil servant said, his brow furrowing.

The General's voice hardened.

'I've been through one horrendous war and survived, while millions of good men didn't. I don't want to see another generation blighted like ours.'

Eberhard Böhm's face paled, and a flash of anger crossed it.

The General had heard a few stories. When the war was at its height, Eberhard Böhm had been medically discharged after basic training, and he'd always suspected that the man's father had something to do with the decision.

Eberhard himself had done nothing to fight the ruling, and the General assumed that, at the time, he'd been hugely relieved not to be sent to the trenches.

But it had left the General's neighbour with a chip on his shoulder about those who had fought and, perhaps, thought the General, a niggling sense of guilt.

'God forbid there should be another war,' Eberhard Böhm said, but he looked away, unable to meet the General's gaze.

Deep down, he'll welcome another war, providing Germany wins, even at the risk to his own son.

A shiver of fear chilled Erich Kästner.

There will be thousands like him, millions even.

Another thought struck him.

There's me, a General in the new Wehrmacht, the holder of an Iron Cross, baulking at the thought of his sons being placed in danger, despite them having made the military their career of choice. The blind fool will consider himself the greater patriot, willing to make the ultimate sacrifice.

He put aside his dark thoughts and nodded.

'Amen to that, Eberhard, my friend,' the General said, putting his arm around his fellow Rotarian's shoulder. 'Let's hope the world's leaders show restraint and wisdom and avoid a conflict that could destroy Europe again.'

At that moment, Franz's grandfather, standing in the centre of the room, tapped his glass three times with a spoon.

'As the oldest person in the room,' he said, 'not counting my wife, who claims she is younger than me, I would like to propose a toast.'

The sound of laughter filled the room, and the admiral's wife smiled wearily at her husband.

'To Franz and Lise. Long life and happiness.'

Everyone raised their glasses.

'Franz and Lise.'

CHAPTER 100

The General jumped onto the launch and sat beside Dieter Mass. It would only take the little boat five minutes to drop them off at the barge, anchored off Schilksee, with enough seating for about two hundred people.

'Thanks for the ticket, Erich,' Dieter said. 'When you invited me, I presumed it would be at the yacht club, watching the smaller classes.'

'I just fancied a change, and I haven't seen any of the larger yachts which, let's face it, is more our thing.'

'True, though I wonder how our crew would fare against these boats.'

'We'd be last. By a good margin, I'd say, but with a bit of practice on one of these beauties, we could perhaps keep them in sight.'

'I'll take your word for it. I enjoy our club races but I'm not sure I'd commit the time for something like that.'

The General looked at Dieter.

'It hadn't occurred to me before, but I should take you all away cruising. You might just prefer it. A different harbour, or anchorage every night. Good food, fresh-caught fish, a glass of wine in a secluded bay. It's wonderful.'

'Do you know, I might be tempted to take you up on that offer, if Margot doesn't object.'

The launch had reached the barge, and once they'd negotiated getting from one to the other, they found their seats, just in time for the first race.

The General gave Dieter a quick explanation as the yachts lined up behind the starting line.

'The eight-metre class are the largest boats racing in the Olympic competition, each with six crew on board. The Swedes are out in front in the race standings, followed by the Norwegians and the Italians. Our boat is in fourth. We need a few wins.'

'So where is the course?'

The General explained the way the marks were chosen and, once Dieter understood the system, he realised that the race would be similar in structure to the ones the General's crew took part in.

At the starting gun, the ten boats, their white sails stark against the overcast sky, were an impressive sight as they jostled for position at the start of the first leg.

Towards the end of the race, only the German, Italian and Danish boats had any hope of winning but, much to the delight of the home spectators, the German boat flashed round the final mark a nose in front and surged towards the line to deafening cheers from the partisan crowd. In the end, it won by a length from the other two, who finished less than half a second apart, the Danish boat just pipping the Italians.

The two men ordered coffee and snacks, deciding to sit it out on the barge for the afternoon's six-metre race.

'Well, what did you think?'

'Very exciting. That was a great finish and a real bonus to see the German boat win.'

'Hmm,' the General said, swallowing a mouthful of Bratwurst with bread, 'that brings them up to joint second, on the same points as the Italians and the Norwegians. The Swedes are still out in front.'

'Have you followed the Games?' Dieter asked.

'Very much so. Whatever you say about the National Socialists, they've been flawless in their organisation, even if it was to put their brand of nationalism in the spotlight.'

'The world is watching, Erich, and, unfortunately, it's impressed. All right, there have been comments from abroad about the prominence of Adolf Hitler and his entourage, and there's some concern about the show of military strength at the opening ceremony but, overall, the government has scored a big international publicity success.'

'No mumblings about the regime's treatment of Jews and political opponents?'

'The Americans nearly didn't come,' Dieter said, 'on the grounds that the German government was tyrannical and that there were minorities in Germany who were being discriminated against. Avery Brundage, president of the American Olympic Committee, vetoed the NAACP's calls for a boycott and made the decision that the team should take part.'

'I'm glad they came,' the General said. 'Jesse Owens has been a great success. The German crowds love him.'

'And the NSDAP hate him. They'd envisaged an Aryan dominance of the Games, even to the point of providing leave of absences from work for some of our major athletes, and extra training facilities, but Owens has blown that myth apart.' He paused. 'Do you know what the Americans and the British call us?'

'Huns, I presume, or Fritz. That's what it was during the war. They used to shout across the trenches to us.'

'They might still do, but now they call us Nazis, short for *Nationalsozialismus*. We may be branded with that for ever if Hitler has his way.'

The General looked around, but there was no one within fifteen metres; most of the spectators had gone back to shore.

'Nazis, eh?' The General wondered how Dieter Maas was so well informed. He obviously still had some foreign press contacts.

'And what is the world saying about us Nazis?' he asked.

Dieter thought for a second.

'The international community condemns the regime's treatment of political prisoners. Jews worldwide, especially in America, are vociferous in letting the world know how we *Nazis* are treating the German Jews, but no one is prepared to do anything concrete about it, for fear of sparking conflict.'

'Yes, I hear appeasement is the order of the day. The government has the gall to gloat about it. That's why it's so important that someone like Jesse Owens succeeds, to show the people that the National Socialists are not infallible.'

'Do you think Owens will run on Sunday?'

Dieter laughed.

'There's a rumour doing the rounds about that. Avery Brundage has been heavily courted by the NSDAP. Even before the Games, they invited him over to "discuss" certain matters. From what I've heard, he's been put under pressure from the party to exclude the two Jewish runners, Glickman and Stoller, from the sprint relay team, and slot in Owens and Ralph Metcalfe. Seemingly it's less distasteful for negroes to win medals than Jews.'

'A problem we don't have in our team.' The General gave a hollow laugh.

'Well, you say that, but you know the fencer, Helene Mayer, who won a silver medal?'

'Yes, why?'

'The story is that eight or nine countries were going to boycott the Olympics because we didn't have a Jewish athlete in the team. The German Olympic committee brought her in because she was half-Jewish, she was tall and blonde, and had won medals at previous Olympics. Gold, in the Netherlands, I believe.'

'So, we had a German Jew winning a medal? That must have put the cat among the pigeons.' The General laughed, this time with genuine humour.

'The thing is, Helene Mayer emigrated to the United States in 1933 because she said she was no longer considered a German citizen. How they got around that with the IOC, I don't know.'

'Thanks for that, Dieter. Let's hope Owens wins his fourth gold, just to get up Adolf's nose.'

The newspaperman laughed.

'Any other news that might be of interest?' the General asked.

'No. Everything has been put on hold while the Olympics are on but expect a backlash once the rest of the world has returned home.'

The General shivered, and a shadow passed across his face.

The next day, the German boat won again.

CHAPTER 101

[09/08/1936 Sunday]

The entire Kästner family had gone to the yacht club; there was a gala dinner after the last race, and although Lise had been invited with Franz, she'd called off with a headache.

Franz had stoically offered to stay with her.

Once the rest had left, Lise's sore head had miraculously improved and after an hour, she was her usual self again. Franz suggested that they jump in the car and join the others at the club.

'Wouldn't you rather be alone here with me?' she asked, in a voice that left Franz in no doubt as to what she meant.

'Of course, darling,' he said, 'if you're sure about it.'

'I promised, didn't I?'

The afternoon was wonderful. Only once did they hear anyone, when Yosef's voice shouted up the stairs. Franz reassured him that he was quite well and that everything was all right, hissing at Lise to keep quiet. She obliged, but she draped herself across the bed, quite naked, while he was talking to Yosef, and Franz wondered if his voice had changed enough to give away what they were up to.

Making love with Lise was so unlike his only other experience with a woman. At first, she was surprisingly shy, but her passion soon eclipsed any reserve that she had. He was more self-conscious and when she asked him, before the first time, if he had any condoms, he flushed with shame while producing one from the bottom drawer of his bedside table, expecting her to be shocked that he had them.

Afterwards, he tried to explain.

'My father insisted on me having a few. When I was sixteen, he sat me down and told me that it was better to be prepared, that I was never to be fearful to suggest using one.'

'Your father is a wise man,' she said, raising her eyebrows. 'But don't worry.'

She opened her handbag and showed him the contents. There, in a pocket at the side, were three condoms, stored discretely in a small linen pouch.

The first time, Franz had been quick, and she'd whispered her understanding while he helped her to her own ending, his fingers somehow knowing her needs, her body wild under his hand.

They made love again, and then a third time, later, and he wondered how she'd learned about the ways they'd found to please each other. He was in no doubt that she'd been a virgin; the first time had been a little uncomfortable, and there had been a spot of blood on the sheet.

Even before they started, the room had been intolerably warm, the sun streaming through the window, and beads of sweat glistened on both their bodies in their excitement. She'd jumped off the bed in her underwear, run to the window, and pulled it upwards, trying to let in some cool air. It had refused to open.

'Here, let me do that, and for God's sake, get away from that window.'

He'd given the window a sharp tug, and it had released, opening with a loud squeak.

He'd turned, seeing her reach behind her back and, as he watched, released the catch holding her brassiere, and let it fall away.

He'd stood speechless, until she reached for him and drew him towards her.

~~o~~

Ruth Nussbaum was at a loose end. She walked down to the lake, bored, because Antje was away with the General again, watching the sailing.

She sat dejectedly under the boughs of a large tree next to the lake making daisy chains and trying to read her book. Her father was pottering about in the garage, doing something with the car, and her mother had taken Manny to the park to play on the swings; Ruth had told them she didn't want to go, feeling that she was getting too big for that sort of thing, but now she wished she'd gone with them.

She glanced up wistfully at the big house, hoping that Antje would come home early. She gave a start when she saw, in the large window on the landing, Franz and Lise, running upstairs.

She was just about to jump up and run to the house to see if Antje was back, too, but something stopped her. She stayed by the tree where it would be nearly impossible to be spotted from the house unless someone came looking for her.

Nothing happened for a while and she'd almost decided to move when, at Franz's bedroom window, Lise appeared.

Ruth's hand went to her mouth and she gasped. Lise must have taken her dress off because she was trying to open the window with nothing on but her brassiere. Ruth knew about these only because her mother had, over a year ago, explained the changes that would happen with her body, from the fine hair suddenly appearing between her legs to the development of her breasts, and nipples, that had made her go from flat-chested to having a bosom not unlike Mama's in the space of a few months during the spring. Worst of all was the monthly bleeding that had started around Easter time, that Miriam had prepared her for by giving her some of her cloth pads and explaining how they were used.

Ruth couldn't see what else Lise was wearing because she could only see her top half above the windowsill and, after a few seconds, the girl from next door disappeared back into the room and Franz appeared, also naked.

She didn't know why she was shocked; she'd seen Franz and Johann in shorts or swimwear often and thought nothing of it. She'd even seen her father and the General, discarding their shirts when working in the garden on a hot summer's day.

Instinctively, she made a connection between what she'd seen and the vague references her mother alluded to about what men and women did when they were married that produced babies, and to the whispered stories that the girls at school liked to listen to and giggle about, when they could find a quiet corner of the playground.

Franz jerked the window open, then disappeared back inside. She strained to listen and convinced herself that she could hear a few words, but she couldn't be sure. She wanted to go closer but was frightened of being seen.

Nothing happened for a few minutes and she decided that she couldn't stay there all day, so she started walking up towards the cottage, round the corner from the big house. As she got closer, she was certain that she could hear sounds coming from the open window, but they sounded more like cries. She began to worry, but they were interspersed with an occasional laugh and, at one point she distinctly heard Lise's voice saying, 'Oh God'.

That shocked her as much as anything. She knew the Kästners weren't Jews, but she'd learned enough about Christians to know that they generally didn't blaspheme.

She was intrigued, but she was almost at the cottage, and couldn't just stand there listening.

At that moment, the garage door opened and, startled out of her reverie, she saw her father come out of it, and head for the house, with a scuttle full of coal from the bunker beside the garage.

He didn't see her, so she retraced her footsteps back to the side of the lake, and leaned against her tree, watching and listening.

Through the open window, she heard Franz call; her father must have shouted upstairs to him. With sudden clarity, she knew that no good could come from her father climbing the stairs to Franz's room.

She ran as fast as she could to the back door of the big house and went in. The kitchen was deserted, so she continued through to the hall. Her father was standing at the bottom of the stairs, looking up.

342

'What are you doing, Papa?' she asked.

'Hello, Schatzi,' he said, 'I'm just going to check if Franz is all right. He didn't go to the sailing and I wondered if he was ill, and if I could get him something.'

'I'll go, Papa,' she said, surprised at herself.

'Oh, thank you. I'll put the hot water on,' he said, picking up the coal scuttle from the kitchen door, and going down to the cellar to light the furnace.

She crept up the stairs, listening all the while and wincing when they creaked. She reached the top floor and walked along the hallway, stopping at Franz's door.

She stood still, listening. Behind the door, she heard a giggle, and a small squeal, then the sounds of the bed springs squeaking. Rooted to the spot, she heard groans and at that instant, she knew she shouldn't be listening, and she turned back, walking softly so as not to be heard, before running down the stairs.

'Did he want anything, Ruth?' her father asked her.

'No, Papa. He says he's quite all right, thank you,' she lied, not knowing why, but feeling guilty and selfless at the same time.

'Come on, you can help me hose down the car first, and then, if you do a good job, we'll go and meet Mama and Manny. We might even treat ourselves to an ice cream.

~~o~~

While Lise cleaned herself up, Franz crept downstairs to Miriam's linen cupboard. He extracted a clean sheet and returned to his room, careful to fit it the way Miriam did. He bundled the damp and bloodstained one he'd removed and threw it in the furnace in the cellar, feeling terrible; fortunately, the coals were hot enough and the sheet burst into flame. He waited until every vestige of cloth had reduced to cinders, then closed the door.

~~o~~

'Do you want to go to the sailing club to listen to the race?' Franz asked.

They had dressed and had come downstairs. Lise stood at the window, looking out over the lake.

'I'd rather not,' she said. 'It's a stupid race anyway. You go if you want.'

Franz frowned, then shrugged and switched on the wireless set.

'We can listen to it here, then go and eat with the others, if you like. I just thought there would be a great atmosphere at the club, especially if Owens wins.'

'I hope they drop the baton.'

Franz stared at her.

'I don't see why everyone is so excited by these Americans,' she hissed. 'They're negroes. For goodness' sake, is everyone going mad. There are four perfectly good Germans in this race. I hope to hell they win!'

Franz found it hard to believe that this was the same Lise who had given herself so completely to him a few hours earlier.

'Well, it would be great if our boys won, but Jesse Owens...'

'Oh, screw Jesse Owens and his black friends. They're just doing it to spite the Führer. It's disrespectful.'

'Lise, how can you think that?' Franz said, shocked at her language. 'They're just trying to win. That's the whole point of the Olympics. Jesse Owens has won three medals already. Winning a fourth will make him the most successful Olympian ever. Why would you not be pleased for him?'

'Because he's not like us. He shouldn't even be allowed to compete. If he lived in Germany, it would never be allowed.'

Franz recoiled at the venom in her words.

'You're right about that. He'd probably be in a concentration camp by now,' he snapped.

'Only for the protection of the Reich's daughters. This is *not* the United States of America!'

'Well I know it. Anyway, I don't think the negro people get away lightly over there, but at least they have some rights.'

'Why do you always have to worry about other people. Why don't you concern yourself about people like us?' she shouted at him.

'What people like us?' he said, his voice cold and strained now.

'Good Germans! Aryans!' she screamed.

Franz stared at her. Her face was blotched, and her eyes flashed with anger.

'Lise, Lise. How did we get into this? Let's calm down,' he said, reaching for her hand. She pushed him away.

'It's because you and your family are Jew lovers, and now, it seems, negro lovers. I should have known but I thought you would change when we...'

Her voice broke into sobs.

'Lise...' he said, but she turned away, looking for her handbag.

'Lise, let's talk about it. You're upset, and not thinking straight.'

'Oh, you're so rational and impassionate sometimes. It wasn't when you were between my legs, was it?'

Franz looked around, suddenly appalled that someone might overhear; the Nussbaums were sure to be around, and any of the others could have returned. He checked, but no one was there.

His head dropped. He found it hard to believe the malice in her voice.

'Lise, we were making love an hour ago. How can you say these things?'

'I wish I'd never let you do that to me, Franz Kästner. I've a good mind to tell my father.'

Franz paled.

'You wanted it as much as me, Lise,' he said, his voice almost breaking.

'It was all an act, Franz. I promised, that's all,' she hissed.

Franz knew it wasn't true, but it shocked him to even consider that her actions might have been more calculated than he'd imagined.

'I don't think so, Lise,' he said softly.

It seemed to anger her more. She twisted the ring from her finger and threw it at him. It missed his face by inches and flew across the room, rattling as it hit the wall then tumbling behind the sideboard.

'You can take your ring and give it to some Jew girl, or maybe you'd prefer one with black skin. You're not a true German, Franz Kästner.'

She stormed out of the room. He heard her footsteps receding sharply down the hall, then the front door slamming hard behind her.

Franz stood, stunned, with his head in his hands for five long minutes then, fumbling like an old man, he crouched down and searched under the sideboard for the ring. Tears ran down his cheeks and dripped onto the wooden floor and the edge of the carpet. He suddenly thought of his parents coming home and what he would tell them and decided that he couldn't face them. Not yet at least.

He'd almost given up on the ring when he felt its smooth gold, still warm from her finger, sitting a fraction proud in one of the cracks between the boards, close to the back. He took a penknife from his pocket and prised the ring out. He slipped it into his wallet and collected his kitbag from his room, casting a disbelieving look around, not understanding the disconnection between the two life-changing events he'd experienced in one afternoon.

It crossed his mind to leave a note, then, remembering that Yosef had been around earlier, he left by the back door and walked over to the garage. Yosef was outside, rinsing off the car but, to Franz's dismay, Ruth was running around behind the vehicle, trying to pretend that the soaking she was getting from her father's hose was accidental.

Yosef saw Franz standing, and something in the young man's manner made him stop and tell his daughter to run in to the house and get out of her wet clothes.

Reluctantly, Ruth did as she was told, glancing back at the two men as she went.

~~o~~

Watching from the cottage window, Ruth saw her father listening intently to Franz, nodding from time to time. She was struck by the slump of Franz's shoulders and the dazed look in his eyes.

When Franz had finished, her father spoke earnestly with him, his arm around his shoulder.

She saw Franz nod once and shake her father's hand then disappear round the corner of the house, hoisting his kitbag onto his broad back.

Her father shook his head sadly and resumed rinsing the car. She didn't dare go out to ask what had happened, although her mind was buzzing with questions; she'd been told to go in and get changed and she didn't want to hear the rough edge of his tongue.

A thought played in her mind.

What does this have to do with what took place earlier?

When he came in, she was sitting demurely at the table, a cup of coffee sitting at his place, ready for him.

~~o~~

Yosef smiled and sat down, knowing that she was itching to ask him about Franz, and he was impressed by her restraint, sitting, her curious eyes watching his every move.

I am not going to be intimidated by a thirteen-year-old.

He sat reading the paper, then thanked her for the coffee and got up to put the car away in the garage and was rewarded by a plaintive voice behind him.

'Papa, what's wrong with Franz?'

He gave her a sad smile.

'You'll find out soon enough; I have to tell the General and Frau Kästner first so don't say a word to anyone, Schatzi. Can you do that for me?'

'Yes, Papa,' Ruth said, nodding solemnly.

'Come, and you can help me park the car.'

He took her hand and led her outside, not looking forward to his task when the Kästners returned.

345

CHAPTER 102

Jesse Owens ran the first leg of the relay. The Americans romped home in a world record time and, for the fourth time in the Games, the black American athlete stood on the podium in front of Adolf Hitler's box, saluting the American flag.

In the stadium, the crowd cheered for a solid ten minutes after the race, chanting Owens' name. In the yacht club, the General and his family were surrounded by members and guests who had been infected with the Jesse Owens craze; they cheered and stamped their feet during the race and congratulated each other after it had finished, as if the German team had won the medal.

The General shook his head, smiling.

~~o~~

Franz sped out towards the coast, pushing the small car to its limits, the top down and the wind blowing his hair. He turned down the familiar small track and stood on the beach in front of the little clearing so full of memories, until long after the sun disappeared behind him. He found a discarded piece of fisherman's twine on the beach and, removing both rings from his wallet, threaded the string through them and tied it with a knot. He slipped the makeshift necklace over his head and tucked it under the front of his shirt.

He got back into the car and headed back to his barracks. As he raced along, using the speed to purge the demons in his head, he wondered if Jesse Owens had won his fourth gold.

~~o~~

In the Böhm house, Lise sat sobbing at the kitchen table, her mother and father consoling her.

'He's a pig, Mama. A pig.'

Beate Böhm put her arm around her daughter. She knew to say nothing.

Unfortunately, Lise's father was not gifted with the same foresight.

'You must have said something or done something. Everybody knows that Franz Kästner is a gentleman. Can you not talk to him?'

'Shut up, Eberhard,' Beate Böhm snapped. 'Go and do something useful.'

Eberhard Böhm spluttered the start of a reply. Beate gave him a cold stare and, huffing, he left the room.

Once he'd gone Beate turned to her daughter.

'Darling, you didn't...'

'No, Mama. He tried to, but I stopped him.'

Beate took a deep breath.

'Well, that's one good thing. It would have been terrible if you two had... well, you know.'

'Mama, he's a traitor.'

Her mother gasped.

'Lise, you can't say things like that. Never repeat those words outside of this house.'

'You don't believe me,' Lise said, bursting into a fresh bout of tears.

'It's not that I don't believe you. I'm just telling you that you have to watch what you're saying.'

'He wanted those negro runners to win the race today, just to spite the Führer. And that was despite our own team running.'

Beate Böhm heaved a sigh of relief. She could give her daughter all the sympathy the girl needed while pointing out that what Franz had said was somewhat short of treason.

'Lise, I didn't want to say anything to you because I knew you were very fond of Franz, but the Kästner family have some strange allegiances; you only have to look at the way they treat their Jewish servants like members of the family. And father says that General Kästner is forever making anti-NSDAP comments at the Rotary, along with his doctor friend. Perhaps it's better that you find this out now, before your relationship goes too far.'

Lise looked at her mother, then her face crumpled again.

~~o~~

When her sobs had subsided again, Lise stood up and looked out of the window. The view across the lake was almost identical to that in the Kästner house. Even in Franz's bedroom.

Lise swallowed. She hoped her mother would never suspect what she'd done with Franz. The truth is, she'd wanted it more than anything and she'd found it exhilarating. She still couldn't believe how he'd turned on her, after their lovemaking had been so wonderful.

At least we were careful.

She started to cry again.

'There, darling. You'll look back on this as your first heartbreak, and make sure it doesn't happen again. We'll find you a nice young man with proper principles, don't you worry.'

'But I wanted Franz,' Lise howled, realising with finality that her earlier tryst would be the only time she would ever sleep with Franz Kästner, and she worried that she might regret it for the rest of her life, no matter what his beliefs.

Her mother held her, vowing that one day, the Kästner family would get their comeuppance.

~~o~~

'You chaps seem intent on taking over the world.'

Johann laughed. His English was nowhere near as fluent as Franz's, but he managed to follow the conversation and, although he left most of the talking to his father, he could answer most of the British sailor's questions, and ask a few of his own.

'We're only taking back what was ours, and safeguarding our German citizens,' he said.

Crew members from Olympic teams from all over the world had congregated at the Kieler Yacht Club the day before the finals of the sailing competition. A few of the medals had already been decided but, in every race, there was at least two or three podium places riding on the results, so few of the crews were partying hard.

Johann and his father, with their passable grasp of English, had spoken briefly with a group of British yachtsmen on their way in and, after their meal, were asked to join them in the bar. Antje sat with her mother and grandmother and watched as the Englishman who'd goaded Johann spoke again.

'So, Herr Hitler will be content with the Saarland?'

'I hope so,' the General interjected. 'The last thing Germany and Europe needs is another conflict.'

'Hear hear,' another of the English yachtsmen said. 'There's a great deal of concern about the Sudetenland, and even Austria; we hear worrying reports of National Socialist agitation in both those places.'

'I'll say this for Herr Hitler though,' an older crew member of the British boat said. 'He can put on a show. The opening ceremony was nothing short of spectacular. And these Hitler Youth chappies that help with everything; they seem ever so enthusiastic.'

'A strong Germany will make Europe safer,' Johann said. 'For too long we have been relying on others to fight the spread of Bolshevism.'

'God forbid that communism should ever be given a foothold in Western Europe,' the

347

older man said, nodding his head in agreement.

'Ach,' the third Englishman said. 'That's enough of politics. Who's going to win tomorrow?'

~~o~~

Yosef drove to the yacht club with a heavy heart, knowing he must try and hide his dismay until he could speak with the General on his own once they returned to Drachensee.

The car was full. The General, his mother and Frau Kästner sat in the back seat. Johann and Antje sat in the fold-down seats facing them and Erich's father chose to travel in the front.

'A chance to speak to someone sensible,' he said to Yosef.

'Thank you, sir. I couldn't possibly comment.'

The admiral laughed.

'This lot are enjoying themselves anyway,' the admiral said, nodding at the animated passengers in the back.

'It sounds as if you all had a good evening, Admiral.'

'We did indeed, Yosef. That Jesse Owens is a fine young man. He's certainly captured the imagination of the country.'

'Yes, sir. He's been an inspiration.'

'Can I ask you a question, Yosef.'

'Of course, sir. Fire away.'

'How's your father? And your mother?'

'They're fine, sir. In great health. You could call in with them. They'd be more than delighted to see you.'

'You're right, by God. We should have gone before. I'll get you to drop us off there tomorrow, if that boy of mine will let me borrow you.'

'I'm sure the General will be more than happy for me to do that, sir.'

'And how are you, my boy,' the old man asked.

Yosef smiled. He was forty-seven years old.

'I'm very well, sir.'

'And the family?'

'Miriam works hard as ever and keeps me on my toes. Ruth is getting big. She's turning into a young lady. Manny's just Manny.'

'You should listen to my son, Yosef.'

Yosef looked ahead and said nothing for a minute.

'I'm sorry, sir. We can't leave.'

The noise of laughter and layers of conversation filtered through the glass of the dividing screen, but the two men spoke softly.

'Listen, it pains me to say it, but Erich is one of the most astute men I know. He also has access to information that you and I couldn't even imagine. If he advises you to get your family out, do it.'

'I can't, sir. My parents; Miriam's family. This is our home; the children would never see their grandparents.'

The car swung onto Hamburger Chaussee.

'Get them out too. Start over again.'

'My parents would never leave here. Miriam's are the same.'

'Well, let them stay. You go. When things return to normal, you can come back.'

'We're not going, sir. I'm sorry.'

'Ha. Stubborn. Just like your father. Ah, well. I tried.'

'You did indeed, sir.' Yosef laughed, then his face clouded over.

'I need to speak to the General, sir. I have a message for him.'

'All right, Yosef. I'll tell him to see you in the study, once you're finished. I suspect the ladies will go straight to bed.'

'Thank you, sir. Perhaps Frau Kästner should be there as well.'

~~o~~

'What is all this cloak-and-dagger business, Yosef. It's awfully late.'

'Sorry, ma'am, I apologise, but Master Franz asked me to give you a message. He didn't want to leave a note. He was dreadfully upset.'

'What's the matter,' she gasped. 'Is Franz all right. It's that car of his, isn't it? Did he crash?'

'No, ma'am, nothing like that.'

'Let Yosef speak, Maria. Stop fussing.'

Maria Kästner glared at her husband, but he was looking at Yosef, nodding at him to go on.

'He left tonight to go back to his barracks. His engagement to Lise is off. He was too upset to face everybody.'

'Is that all?' Maria Kästner said, shrugging. 'It will just be a lover's tiff. They'll be back together in no time.'

'I don't think so, ma'am. There were some pretty harsh words between them, Franz said.'

'Did you hear any of this?'

'No, ma'am. Well, I did hear raised voices at one point, but I didn't realise then that Fräulein Böhm had paid a visit. I couldn't make out what they were saying.'

It wasn't strictly true. He'd heard some of what was said, and Franz had filled him in on the crucial bits of the argument, but he wasn't going to get involved any more than he had to, at least with Frau Kästner.

'And he's off to his unit? It's not like Franz to run away and not face things,' the General said.

'Sir, if it had been just you and Frau Kästner, I'm sure he would have waited, and told you himself. It was just with his grandparents, and Johann. I don't think he could stand the pity,' Yosef said.

'I can understand that,' the General said. 'Thanks for passing that on, Yosef.'

'There's one more thing, sir, ma'am.'

'Go on, Yosef.'

'He said he will telephone you in a few days' time, and that he apologises for running off, and for any embarrassment or awkwardness that might result from this.'

'Danke, Yosef.'

The part-time chauffeur left.

~~o~~

The General closed the back door.

'I don't see why Franz told Yosef first,' Maria Kästner said.

'He would think it better than a note. And Yosef will say to no one, not even Miriam.'

'I'm not so sure. They tell each other everything.'

The General looked at her sharply, wondering if it was a dig at him, but he knew that Yosef wouldn't tell a soul, until the General told him it was no longer a secret.

'Take my word for it. I would trust Yosef Nussbaum with my life.'

'Well, I'm off to bed. It has been a horrible end to a mediocre day,' she said, and walked out of the study.

'I'll be up shortly,' he said and waited until he heard the bedroom door shut.

He slipped through the kitchen and eased the back door open. The light was still on in the Nussbaum kitchen and he softly rapped on the door. Yosef answered it immediately.

'What was said, Yosef?'

'Politics, sir. Politics. She was out of order, sir. Franz said nothing wrong.'

'So, you did hear?'

'Only a word or two. But enough to confirm what Franz said was true.'

'And what did he say?'

'I'm sure he'll tell you himself, sir.'

'I'd rather hear it now, Yosef. You know Franz wouldn't mind. It's why he told you.'

Yosef seemed to hesitate.

'It started with Franz wanting to cheer on Jesse Owens.'

'Along with ninety per cent of the population, I'd say.'

'I think the Böhms are in the other ten per cent, sir, and Lise seems to be one of the more ardent NSDAP supporters. She more or less called Franz a traitor, before throwing her ring at him.'

'I should have told him what the mother and father are like. The mother especially. The girl is obviously just like her.'

'She called him a Jew lover and a negro lover, sir. That he wasn't a patriot, that he hated Adolf Hitler.'

The General could see how awkward it was for Yosef, having to pass on everything Franz had told him, and what he'd heard.

'He's better off without her,' the General said. 'At least it ended at this stage, before they were married. The only problem is that I will be pestered with Eberhard Böhm forever. He'll insist that the engagement can be salvaged, once we knock their two heads together.'

~~o~~

After the General had gone, Yosef argued with himself as to whether he should have said something further. It wasn't as if he knew for sure; it was merely a suspicion. If he told the General that he'd seen Lise arrive and that the young couple had spent the whole day at the house, alone, much of it upstairs, it would cause endless trouble for young Franz.

But the General was his friend, and if something came of it, and he hadn't said a word, he'd feel terrible.

He closed his eyes and shook his head.

I'll sleep on it.

CHAPTER 103

[12/08/1936 Wednesday]

On the first day of the Olympics, Antje had asked her father if Ruth could go with them.

'She can't, I'm afraid,' the General had told her. 'Remember what happened last year, when we met Adolf Hitler and that horrible woman made nasty comments to Ruth?'

'Yes, Papa.'

'I can't guarantee that it won't happen again. There are a few not very nice people in the yacht club.'

Antje had looked disappointed, but she didn't ask again.

The General, after his day with Dieter at the six- and eight-metre classes, had an idea.

He spoke with Yosef, who said he'd square it with Miriam, and Ruth was waiting in the kitchen when he and Antje came down for their breakfast; he wanted to leave early to ensure good seats in the public stands at Schilksee.

He knew that the view wouldn't be as good as they would have had on the sailing club barge, but the chances of bumping into someone he knew, or who knew who Ruth was, were minimal.

They were one of the first few to arrive and they chose seats high at the back. Saddened that he had to think that way, he figured no one would see them up there.

'The gold medal has already been won,' he explained to the girls. 'The Italians were clear victors but two magnificent wins in the last two races pulled our boat up to be tied for second with the Norwegians, so the race today is for the bronze and silver medals.'

'I hope our boat wins,' the two girls said in unison, and the General had to turn away, so that they didn't see the look of pain on his face.

As the stands filled up, a couple of acquaintances nodded to the General, but no one remarked on Ruth's presence. The General smiled as he listened to Antje explaining the course and the rules to her friend.

Once the race started, the two girls were on their feet for most of it, jumping up and down as two boats swapped the lead between them.

The General watched them. They were both at that awkward age when physically, they were becoming young women; tall, with curves starting to appear, but not yet having quite lost the carefree abandon of childhood. He smiled, thinking of the changes he would see in them both over the next few years, and was glad he'd brought them, just to watch their innocent joy at the spectacle.

The German boat lost by the narrowest of margins, with only seconds between them and the winning boat.

They watched from their lofty viewpoint as the yachts, beautifully finished out, drifted to a halt right in front of the stand where the General and the girls were sitting.

Both the skippers were thrown in the water by their crews, much to the delight of the crowd. Once they'd been retrieved, the medal ceremony took place on the large pontoon at the entrance to the Olympic harbour, when the German crew drew the loudest cheer going up for their bronze medals.

'We'll go and have a spot of lunch, then we'll head home. We can walk back, it's such a nice day.'

The girls groaned but didn't dare complain.

A plethora of snacks and drink stands had been set up for the spectators and the General let the girls choose what they wanted; both had Bratwurst on long rolls with Sauerkraut, mustard, and relish. He warned them not to make a mess of their clothes and watched with trepidation as they ate, knowing from experience the trouble he'd be in with Maria and Miriam if he returned the girls with stains on their dresses.

'We'll walk along the beach. It will be lovely.'

As they trudged along the shore, the girls dragging their feet at the thought of the long walk home, the General smiled.

An hour later, they'd reached Friedrichsort and the General suggested stopping for an ice cream. As they rounded the corner to the café, the girls squealed when Ruth spotted her father, standing beside the General's car.

Antje turned to her father.

'You tricked us,' she accused.

'Race you,' he said, beating them easily over the short distance.

'Come, my friend, let's have a coffee and look at the view,' he said to Yosef before the girls flew by, excited by the tempting pictures of fancy ice-cream sundaes displayed above the café's windows.

They found a table, and the waiter took their order, returning with ice creams for the girls, and coffees for the two men.

They sat for a while, looking out at the lighthouse, and the ships and small boats that passed in a constant stream. It was the narrowest point of Kieler Förde, and of all the harbours and docks within it, only Laboe was seaward of Friedrichsort.

'We always knew we were home when we passed Friedrichsort light,' the General said.

'Why do you call it "light", Papa? It's a lighthouse.'

'Ah, that be sailors' talk,' the General said, in his best pirate voice. 'We be shortening things to make them more easy on the tongue.'

The girls giggled and studied the lighthouse. A large ship passed, and they waved at it. An arm returned the wave at one of the bridge windows.

It was a busy waterway; as well as the merchant shipping and naval vessels whose destination was Kieler Hafen, all the maritime traffic heading for the Kaiser-Wilhelm-Kanal and passage through it to the North Sea passed this point. In addition, there were numerous leisure boats and all the usual ferries and fishing boats that regularly plied Kieler Hafen's waters.

The girls chatted away, sometimes asking questions about ships that passed, for which the General often had an answer; the girls would speculate on where a ship was heading, trying to outdo each other by naming more and more exotic locations, to the amusement of the two men.

When they weren't answering questions, Yosef and Erich sat quietly talking.

'The crackdown will start soon. Warn your people to keep their heads down and be careful. The period of grace is over or, it will be by Sunday.'

The Olympic closing ceremony would be held in four days and the General had been invited to it by Wilhelm Canaris. He was still undecided if he would take up the offer, not thirsting to see yet another sickeningly staged spectacle, designed to hammer home the National Socialist's message to the world.

Yosef looked at the General.

'They've poisoned everything, sir.'

The General looked sharply at the girls, but they were too busy chattering and looking out the window.

He put his hand on Yosef's arm and nodded at Ruth and Antje.

'I'm sorry, sir, but they're turning friend against friend, neighbour against neighbour. And now there's your Franz.'

'Franz will get over it. He may have had a lucky escape. It's your predicament that worries me more.'

'Your father gave me a talking-to last night. He thinks we should leave.'

'I agree, as you know, but I understand your reasons for not going. I just hope you don't regret it.'

'So do I, sir.' He looked at Ruth.

'If it's money that worries you, I can help.'

'No, sir. We have enough saved,' Yosef said, looking away. 'With us having a tied house, and your generosity with food and clothes for the children, we don't spend much.'

'You make us sound like a charity. It just so happens that our children are older than yours, so their clothes are passed down. And it doesn't make sense for Miriam to cook for two families separately. Anyway, your salaries were always adjusted to take account of the benefits.'

Yosef tilted his head and raised an eyebrow, but the General shrugged.

'Thank you for the offer, sir,' he said, 'but we have enough. It would allow us to start again, if we wanted.'

'It's not just about having enough money. The government will take most of it from you unless you go to Palestine. I can get it out for you if you want to go elsewhere.'

'Thank you again, sir, but we're not going anywhere.'

~~o~~

With their ice creams finished, Ruth asked if she and Antje could go and play at the beach. For a while, they ran up and down the sand, chasing the feathers shed by the seagulls and collecting shells, excitedly planning how to make bracelets with them.

Taking their shoes and socks off, they waded up to their knees in the warm summer water of the fjord.

'Is Franz all right?' Ruth asked, surprising her friend.

'Yes, I think so. Mama says he's a big boy, and he'll get over it, but Papa says his heart has been broken.'

Antje stole a glance at Ruth. 'Why do you ask?'

'I saw Franz the day he and Lise split up. He looked so sad I could have cried.'

Ruth couldn't bring herself to tell her friend what else she'd seen and heard that day. She knew that she never could.

Antje touched Ruth's hand. 'He'll be fine. Mama and Papa both say that he's had a lucky escape. She was quite nasty to him.'

'She was beautiful though. Like a princess.'

'An evil princess.' Antje laughed then, making a face and pulling her hair over her eyes; she started hissing at Ruth.

Stumbling to get away, Ruth ran along the beach, squealing, Antje in close pursuit, her arms curled in the air like talons.

~~o~~

'They've grown up so fast,' the General said.

'I know. I don't know where all that time went. It only seems like yesterday we were that age, playing on a beach.'

The General laughed.

'It wasn't yesterday, old man. We're just kidding ourselves.' He turned to Yosef. 'Come on, let's get these girls back to their mothers.'

CHAPTER 104

[13/08/1936 Thursday]

'I was there, you know, when Owens won his fourth gold medal.' Canaris smiled. 'It was an amazing moment.'

'We heard it on the radio,' the General said. 'It was quite an event at the yacht club.'

The two friends sat in Canaris' office in the Abwehr building. The General was on his monthly trip to Berlin and it always involved at least one private meeting with the head of the organisation.

'I shouldn't have, really,' Canaris said, 'but I couldn't help laughing to myself when Owens crossed the line. The crowd went wild; they took Owens to their heart, but I was watching the Führer's platform. Adolf, Heinrich, Hermann, Joseph, and Reinhard. You should have seen their faces. Five stone statues in a row with rigid outstretched arms and rigor smiles. Then, incredibly, Owens looked up and gave them a wave.'

The General laughed. 'It gives me a little faith in the German people again, the way they've embraced Owens' triumphs.'

'Don't delude yourself, Kästner. They still want Herr Hitler and his party to give them jobs, fight the communists, and make Germany great again.'

'I want all these things too. Not the rest of it though. Did you get the book?'

'Yes. It arrived. You really expect me to read it?'

'I do. It will, let's say, be educational.'

The admiral grunted.

'I've enough paperwork to get through to fill up my day five times over,' he said, 'but I'll try and get round to it, knowing that you deem it to be of such great importance.'

The General smiled. He knew Canaris would read *Mein Kampf.* Eventually.

~~o~~

[14/08/1936 Friday]

The General's phone rang. He picked it up and heard Frau Müller's voice.

'Sir, there's a call for you. It's your son.'

'Very well, please put him through.'

He heard the click as the external line was switched through. He waited a second.

'Thank you, Frau Müller,' he said.

He heard the phone click again and imagined his secretary's face, a mixture of embarrassment and annoyance on being caught out eavesdropping.

'Father,' he heard Franz say. 'Can you speak at the moment?'

'Yes. How are you? Your mother is worried sick.'

'I'm sorry. I just couldn't face everybody the other night.'

'Don't worry. These things happen. Nobody died,' the General said, then cursed himself for being flippant.

His son laughed, if only for a second.

'I know,' he said. 'In the grand scheme of things, it's not the worst thing that could happen, but I do feel numb.'

'You must do. You were very fond of her. Do you want to tell me about it?'

'I can't say much more than I told Yosef. We'd had a few disagreements about my views on Hitler and his party, and it escalated into a full-blown argument. I tried to calm her down, but she said some awful things and threw the ring at me.'

354

The General smiled as he imagined the scene, then a sense of guilt stopped him.

'Your mother thinks you'll be back together once it all blows over. I'm guessing that's not on the cards.'

'No, there's no going back. I find it difficult to believe that someone who was so loving could turn out to be so… vindictive.'

'She probably gets it from her mother.'

'What do you mean?'

The General told Franz about the conversation Ruth had overheard.

The phone was silent for a few seconds.

'That explains a great deal. It's strange how you live next door to someone for years and you don't know what they're really like. I suppose I ignored the odd thing or two with Lise that should have warned me.'

'No one could have seen it ending up like this. Don't be harsh on yourself.'

'I'll be more careful in future, if there is a next time.'

'Don't let it put you off women. I can't imagine life without having met your mother. Just give yourself time to get over it. Have a binge with your friends if that helps, but remember, if you ever need to talk, I'm here.'

He heard his son's mumbled thanks, then the phone clicked once more. He put the receiver back on its cradle and sat back, thinking.

CHAPTER 105

Erich Kästner found the atmosphere at Kieler Woche rather strange.

So soon after the Olympic sailing events in Kieler Hafen, it could easily have been anticlimactic, but it seemed as if the people of Kiel were determined to show the world that the regatta was not in any way diminished by its proximity to the Games.

The daytime crowds were down; many of those who would usually attend had taken holidays during the Olympics and were now back at work, but mothers took the chance to take their children for the afternoon races, and the evening events were as popular as ever.

The General saw little of the racing. From his office window, he could just about see part of the course and he got into the habit of taking the short stroll to the sailing club at lunchtime to catch half an hour if there was a race on. The food was good, too.

Even his evenings weren't free, other than the one when he and his crew raced in the veteran class.

It was marred by another incident which filled him with disgust at his fellow club members, and the committee.

They'd raced, and had finished a more than respectable second out of eight boats, each of whose crew's ages totalled in the hundreds of years.

When they'd squared up the boat, they sat in the bar, and he'd taken the opportunity to speak with Dieter Maas, catching up on the latest news that the ex-editor had for him.

As it happened, there wasn't much to report and they ended up talking about sailing, provisionally planning a couple of days away in the boat together, perhaps with the others, if they could all spare the time.

'Oskar. Doc,' the General said, leaning across and tapping both men on the shoulder. 'How do you fancy a trip, just the four of us? A reward for your stoic efforts,' the General said, beaming.

'Forty-eight hours cooped up in a boat with you three!' Oskar said, grinning. 'You must be mad.'

'Don't be so cantankerous, Oskar,' the Doc said. 'You'd love it, if only you could pull yourself away from work for a day or two.'

'Oh, I can relax, Doc. I'm just not sure I'd choose to spend my precious free time with two *alte Fürze* like you. Dieter, needless to say, is excluded from that classification.'

Dieter laughed, and the General and Doc Speer rolled their eyes in mock outrage.

'Well?' said the General, after the laughter had subsided, 'Joking apart, are you up for it?'

Oskar shrugged. 'Why not,' he said. 'I'll have to forgo a wonderful weekend with the lovely Johanna, but one must make sacrifices, I suppose.'

Oskar was a confirmed bachelor, always threatening to settle down but never quite committing himself enough to any of the beautiful women that had adorned his arm over the years. Johanna, a lithe twenty-seven-year-old brunette with startling eyes and a figure to match, was his latest companion.

'The poor girl,' Doctor Speer said. 'Some time to herself might prompt her to reconsider the type of fellow she has got herself entangled with.'

'I take exception to that, Doc. I'm on good terms with all my ex-girlfriends.'

'No doubt. Smarm or charm, I'm never quite sure.'

The General knew that the Doc gave Oskar a hard time about his women, but the constant good-natured bickering hid a strong, if unlikely, friendship. It wasn't, the Doc admitted, that Oskar cheated on any of his women; it just seemed to him that eighteen months was the natural length of Oskar's attention span for members of the opposite sex.

They all presumed that Oskar would like to have children one day; someone to pass on his not insignificant fortune to but, so far, there was no indication that he was desperate for an heir.

Just as the businessman was about to make a stout defence of himself, raised voices from the lobby of the club interrupted him. The General, the only committee member present in the bar, was out of his seat almost immediately and, without appearing to rush, was through the door in seconds.

A man and a woman, whom he vaguely recognised, were being escorted out of the door by one of the club stewards, and the man was resisting, arguing forcibly in a raised voice.

The steward was trying to placate the man, while guiding him towards the door.

The General walked over to the group and, opening the committee room door at the opposite side of vestibule, gently shepherded the couple into the room, which was bedecked with signal flags, racing cards and various other racing paraphernalia. He told the steward to wait where he was and stepped into the room.

He closed the door behind him.

'Please, take a seat.'

The man nodded, and the General pulled out a couple of chairs for them to sit on.

He pointed to the door. 'I'm just going to have a word with our steward. If you don't mind, could you give me a minute?'

The woman answered that it would be fine, so the General went out, leaving the door open. He nodded to the steward who followed him into the kitchen area. Three or four kitchen workers were finishing clearing up, and he told them to leave for a few minutes.

'Now, Albert. What is this all about?'

'I'm sorry, sir. I was asked by the Clubkapitän to escort the lady and gentleman from the upper balcony.'

'Did he give a reason?'

'Well, no, but I heard the conversation beforehand. They're Jews, sir. At least, she is.'

'I didn't realise there was a ban on Jews in the club.'

'No, sir. I mean there isn't, but some of the members have been complaining, and the committee decided that it would be better for all if members did not bring Jewish guests to the club.'

The General was seething. The committee had met without informing him, knowing his views, and hoping that, presented with a fait accompli, the General would not cause a fuss.

'You were only doing what you were told, Albert, but could you not have done it with a little more empathy? These are people, just like us.'

The steward dropped his eyes. 'I know, sir. I felt bad doing it, but the gentleman didn't take it well, especially when I refused to answer his questions. You saw the result.'

'All right, Albert, I'll deal with this from here. Is the Clubkapitän still in the building?'

'No, sir, he was on his way home when he told me to show the couple out.'

'And are the members still here, whose guests these people were?'

'They were embarrassed, sir. They walked out in disgust and tried to persuade their Jewish friends to go with them. The woman went and made no fuss, but the man refused.'

'Right, I'll speak to the couple and I'll have a word with the Clubkapitän tomorrow. I'll contact the members later. Who were they?'

The steward told him, and he made a note of it in the little diary he always carried.

'Sir, can you please tell the Clubkapitän that it wasn't my fault?'

'Don't worry, Albert. I'll make sure there's no trouble for you. On you go.'

The General went back to the committee room. The couple were still there. The man was speaking to his wife when the General entered and was still agitated. They stood up.

'This is intolerable,' he shouted at the General.

'I agree with you, sir. Unfortunately, this club has a significant number of bigots who are members, and some of these are on the committee. They have decided, behind my back, to exclude people of Jewish faith from this club, which I deplore. It's with deep regret that all I can do is apologise and ask you not to cause a fuss; not because I'm concerned about upsetting or embarrassing the members, but because they will contact the police if you insist on trying to stay. In the current climate, as much as I admire you for making a stand, it would be better if you avoided coming to the attention of the authorities.'

The man stared at the General. He looked as if he were about to remonstrate once more but his wife tugged at his sleeve.

'He's right, love. I can't afford to be involved with the police. We've got to let it go.' She turned to the General. 'It's General Kästner, isn't it?'

'Yes,' the General said, holding out his hand to the woman.

'I've heard you're a fair man,' she said, shaking his hand. 'I'm a Christian, like my husband, but some of my family still attend the synagogue and they have spoken of you highly. We don't want to cause trouble,' she added, her eyes pleading with her husband.

'I understand, ma'am, and once again, I apologise. I'm going to take this up with the committee, but I don't have high hopes, I'm afraid.'

'We wouldn't want to come back to a place where decent people aren't welcome anyway,' the husband said, petulant now more than angry. He took his wife's hand and moved towards the door.

'Thank you,' the woman said to the General, before walking down the steps of the club, hand in hand with her husband, with a dignity the General marvelled at.

He walked back to the bar. The onlookers had long since become bored when nothing dramatic happened, but a few people looked at him when he crossed the room to where his friends were still sitting. He ignored their curious glances.

The Doc raised his eyebrow in question as the General took his seat.

'It's nothing. Just a misunderstanding,' he said.

~~o~~

[18/08/1936 Tuesday]

'It's a good parade again this year.'

Oskar and the General stood watching the brightly decorated cars, swinging round the corner in a long line. Each of the twenty vehicles was bedecked with flowers of all kinds and they sounded their horns as they passed the crowds lining Hindenburgufer.

As they reached the signal tower, they stopped, and the crowd of people following them milled around, inspecting the cars, and chatting to the drivers.

'Kieler Woche wouldn't be the same without it. Look at the crowds.'

The parade was popular with both the townspeople and visitors attending Kieler Woche for the sailing. It started each year in the Kösterallee, making its way along the shore of Kieler Hafen in slow procession.

Once they'd reached the tower, the Rotary Club members collected the one mark fee that each car had to pay to be part of the parade and the levy that the stallholders paid for a pitch.

Jürgen Hoffmann had, *with regret*, found himself busy with mayoral duties; he rarely attended any Rotary events these days, and Uwe Müller, the police chief, had a small crisis on his hands, and had sent his apologies.

It was the General's group's turn to do the flower parade this year, so he mustered his men and split them up into two. He sent Doc Speer and Eberhard Böhm to collect the fees and round up donations from the crowds, while he and Oskar manned the stall, at which the public could come and play several games of chance, having their small change removed from them for the privilege.

The encounter with Eberhard Böhm, which might have been awkward, passed without either man commenting on Franz or Lise. When the Doc and Eberhard had left with their little tin collection boxes, Oskar turned to Erich Kästner.

'That could have been difficult,' he said, wiping his brow for effect.

358

'Yes, it could have, but fair play to Eberhard, he could just have cried off today or played the injured party, but he was just his usual self.'

'I noticed. I don't think Frau Böhm will be quite as forgiving.' He smiled. 'I don't suppose you want to talk about it?'

'Not really, Oskar. I've only managed a quick word with Franz. Apparently, his politics didn't quite match up to those of a patriotic German husband. That's all I know.'

'Ah. A chip off the old block, then. One day, they will get the better of you, these principles of yours.'

'Don't you ever feel bad, working with the Schweine?'

'All the time, Erich, but I'm a pragmatist. What good would falling on my sword do? In my own way, I can do a little here and there to help people, like your Dieter fellow, and a few others.'

The General raised an eyebrow.

'I have a bit of clout with the party. They like doing business with me and I can get things for them that they would find it difficult to get elsewhere. In return, I'm allowed a little freedom in the way I conduct my business.'

'I see. I'll keep that in mind.'

'I'll not take risks though. At the end of the day, I intend to survive this regime's time in office and, if possible, prosper.'

The General laughed.

'Talking of which, I did a little research into this church charity that you've been so enthusiastically propounding of late. I was wondering if a few of us could come down and see the work that it does. I'm sure the good Father would be delighted to show us his enterprise.'

The General looked at his friend.

'I'd be delighted to arrange that. Perhaps you and Doc Speer?'

'Not the mayor, or our friend Eberhard?'

'I'm not sure they would have the ability to see the good that the Father and his helpers do in this particular instance. I'm not even sure it's worth you taking time off from your busy schedule, Oskar. Perhaps you should just trust my judgement.'

Oskar shook his head.

'Just be careful, Erich. You're beginning to be whispered about already. This would just add fuel to the fire. Keep your distance, that's my advice.'

He put his hand in his pocket and pulled out a small envelope.

'You might find this useful.'

The General took it, and lifting the unsealed flap, looked at the contents then put it in his inside pocket.

'Thank you, Oskar. That will help greatly.'

'I can give you a little each month. But it will be cash, and I'll deny ever having anything to do with it. That's what you should do. Step away.'

'I am careful. I have little contact with them.'

'Good. Now, here are our first customers…'

For the next two hours, the stall was busy, and when they counted the cash after it had all quietened down, including the money from the cars and the collection boxes, they'd raised nearly one hundred Reichsmarks.

The Doc had to rush off, and Eberhard Böhm said that he would also need to leave them to it; the family were heading off for a day at the seaside. 'We all need a break,' he said, and Oskar put his hand over his face to hide a smile.

'Let's get this cleared up then,' Oskar said to the General, nodding at the stall.

He'd used one of his company flatbeds to transport the stall that morning and, with the General's help, he loaded it on the back of the truck.

'Do you want a hand unloading it at the other end?'

'No, I'll leave it in the yard and a couple of my men will unload it tomorrow.'

Oskar generously allowed the Rotary Club to use a corner of one of his warehouses to store the various pieces of fundraising apparatus that they used throughout the year.

He jumped into the cab and was about to drive off.

'Oskar,' the General called. 'Just before you go, there's something else I meant to mention.'

'Oh, sounds intriguing. Am I in trouble?' He laughed.

'No, more of a proposition that might just interest you…'

CHAPTER 106

Once Oskar had left, the General strolled down to the sailing club. He'd seen the Clubkapitän's car parked in his reserved space when he'd passed earlier.

'Is he in?' he asked the barmaid, after he'd checked the committee room.

'He's in the storeroom,' she said, nodding behind her.

He slipped through the bar and made his way down the short corridor to the store. He knocked, then entered.

The Clubkapitän had a clipboard in his hand, and the manageress was counting boxes of catering supplies.

'Sorry to interrupt you,' the General said, 'I wondered if I could have a word.'

'Certainly, Erich. What can I do for you?'

'A word in private, if you don't mind.'

The Clubkapitän glanced at the manageress and nodded to her.

'Could you give us a minute, please.'

After she'd left, the Clubkapitän sat down on one of the spare chairs and gestured for the General to do the same.

'Carry on, Erich,' he said.

'There's a couple of things, and they're both connected. I was in here the other day, and a couple, one of whom was Jewish, were being rather noisily ejected.'

'Yes, I told the steward to ask them to leave. I'd had a few complaints from others in the club.'

'Yes, Albert said that. They were guests of one of our members. Would it not have been sufficient to ask our members not to bring them back?'

The Clubkapitän bristled. 'Are you criticising my handling of the situation, Erich?'

'As a matter of fact, I am. It was all very heavy-handed, which brings me to my second point. Why was it decided behind my back, that we don't allow Jewish people into the club?'

'It wasn't decided behind your back. You just weren't at the meeting.'

'Was this one of our scheduled meetings?'

'Well, no. It was a specially convened meeting. You were informed about it.'

'How was I supposed to have been informed, and who informed me?'

'I think it was the secretary. Most likely by telephone, old boy.'

'I'll ask him. But I certainly didn't know about it.'

'It wouldn't have made any difference if you'd been there. The vote in favour of the resolution was eight to three.'

'I-would-still-have-wanted-to-be-there,' the General said, in his best barrack-room voice.

The Clubkapitän flinched.

'I do apologise, Erich,' he said. 'It won't happen again.'

'It's too late for that. Anyway, don't apologise to me, but to the members whose guests you treated rather despicably.'

The man bristled again, but the General stared him down, until he turned his eyes away.

'And Clubkapitän,' he said, opening the door. The manageress stood in the corridor. The General caught the glance that passed between the two of them.

'Yes,' the man said, irritably.

The General took a pencil from his jacket pocket and handed it to the Clubkapitän, a look of disgust on his face.

'The next time you do a stocktake, I would strongly recommend that you use some form of writing implement.'

~~o~~

DEUTSCHE REICHSPOST

TELEGRAMM

21 AUGUST 1936

MADE 1ST LIEUT STOP CATCHING FRANZ STOP CAPTAIN NEXT STOP JOHANN END

CHAPTER 107

KIELER MORGENPOST

Friday 28th August 1936

CRACKDOWN ON DEFIANT JEHOVAH'S WITNESSES

The Government has been forced to take action against the Jehovah's Witnesses church after widespread defiance of the ban on holding services.

A spokesman for the state police said that the organisation was attempting to foment insurrection and have been doing so since 1934, when they declared political neutrality, rejecting what the Government insisted were reasonable restrictions on the practice of their religion.

The organisation has been banned since 1935, due to the Jehovah's Witnesses' refusal to swear allegiance to the state; their religious convictions forbid an oath of allegiance to any temporal power and prohibit members serving in the armed forces.

There have been a number of arrests.

~~o~~

KIELER JÜDISCHES FREIHEITSNACHRICHTENBLATT

Volume 47

10th of Elul, 5696

JEHOVAH'S WITNESSES' MASS INCARCERATION

An estimated 6000 Jehovah's witnesses have been arrested by the Gestapo in a countrywide crackdown of the religious organisation. Most of them have been detained in concentration camps located throughout Germany.

An underground spokesman for the organisation told the KJF that meetings of small groups of believers would continue to be held wherever "two or three are gathered together in my name".

The clampdown comes after years of stubborn resistance to the National Socialists by the Jehovah's Witnesses. No member of the church can take an oath, other than to the church, and they are not permitted to be part of the armed forces.

"We answer only to God, not to man", the spokesman said.

The KJF believes that these mass arrests could herald similar sweeping crackdowns on other religious groups, including the Jewish and Catholic communities.

'At least someone else is getting persecuted now.'

'Miriam!' Yosef said. 'That's not like you.'

'Well, they've never spoken out about us being hounded and victimised, only about their own religious freedoms, so perhaps it is understandable that we're not weeping and tearing our hair out for them.'

'All I can say is that I empathise with anyone who has the guts to stand up to these monsters.'

Miriam grunted. She knew it was a bit of *Schadenfreude*, the deriving of pleasure, or relief, from someone else's misfortune, but she was beyond caring.

'Nobody stood up for us when they took our citizenship away, or our jobs.'

'People are too frightened.'

She gave him a sceptical look.

'What have they got to be frightened of? We're the ones who can end up in jail if we break the pettiest of laws.'

'There are plenty of non-Jewish Germans in concentration camps for standing up against the National Socialists. The communists, for instance.'

She sighed. 'Yes, I know, but they're still German citizens. And they're in those places because of the threat they pose, not for who they are.'

'What about the homosexuals? Or the Romany people?'

She snorted. 'Homosexuality is illegal, and perverse, and the Gypsies are mostly habitual criminals. They're used to being in prison.'

'Miriam, you can't say that. I don't believe it's right for two men, or two women, to be together but I don't think they should be in prison for it. And the Romanies – their wives and children are in these camps. How can that be right?'

'I'm sorry. I just find it difficult to empathise with people who've not uttered a word against the way we're treated. Then again, there's no one else in this God-forsaken country who does help.'

'What about the General? He stands up against the government. He's helped friends of ours. And he's helped us.'

'It's easy for him,' she snapped. 'He's in a position of power. How can he know what it's like for us when he hasn't experienced the persecution we have?'

'How can you say that? He risked his life when I was hurt.'

'No, he didn't. They wouldn't have dared touch him. It might have been a bit embarrassing for him if he got caught, but it wouldn't have made any impact on the Kästner family's way of life.'

'All I know is that he's a friend to us, and he hates Hitler and his party. That's enough for me.'

'Hmmf,' she grunted. He wasn't sure if it meant that she grudgingly agreed, or if she was just being dismissive. He tried changing tack.

'The General's father spoke to me. He said we should consider leaving.'

'I'm not going unless all my family go, and your mother and father.'

'You know they won't leave.'

'Then I'm not going.'

Yosef Nussbaum made to speak, then shook his head.

~~o~~

[17/09/1936 Thursday]

Miriam raised her wine glass.

'Shanah Tovah.'

The three friends sat in Rosa Liewermann's kitchen. It was Rosh Hashanah, the Jewish New Year and, even though it was a Thursday, they'd forgone their usual coffee for something a little stronger. In the street outside, Rebeka and Ruth were playing a game of *Himmel und Hölle*, a variation of hopscotch, and were trying to teach the younger children how to play.

Moshe, Fischel and Manny were picking it up with no difficulty. Shoshana, Moshe's younger sister, was having a little more trouble kicking the stone up the court with any accuracy.

'Shanah Tovah,' Miriam's two friends echoed.

There was a hollow ring to the traditional new year greeting. Each of the three women had their own fears and worries for the year ahead, some of it concerning their children, who were playing outside without a care in the world.

'I wonder what's in store for us?' Miriam said, saying aloud what they were all thinking.

'It surely can't be any worse than this year,' Esther replied, and her two friends glanced at each other.

'I'm not so certain,' Miriam said, shaking her head. 'I think we should prepare for the worst.'

'God save us. If you're saying that, I'm really worried.'

Miriam always tried her best to shield Esther from the worst of Rosa's rather stark observations, who felt that having your eyes open was the best defence against being taken unawares in life.

'I do have some good news,' Esther said.

Miriam and Rosa looked at her, surprised.

'The shop has been sold. We can leave.'

'Oh, Esther,' Rosa said. 'That's wonderful. Where will you go?'

Esther's smile faded a little.

'Itsik wants to go to Palestine. He says we have enough money to start a new shop, a better shop, and there are great opportunities because it is a young country with an expanding population.'

'It's also full of Arabs,' Rose said, 'who aren't going to be pleased at all of us turning up, taking their land.'

'Rosa!' Miriam said. 'For goodness' sake, try to be more helpful.'

'There's no point in looking at it with rose-coloured spectacles. I'm just trying to help Esther make the right decision.'

'Don't argue, you two,' Esther said. 'I'm not stupid, and anyway, Itsik will make the decision. He favours going to Palestine because we can keep what he calls our *hard-earned* money. Anywhere else and we lose most of it in emigration tax.'

'When would you go?' Rosa asked.

'The sale will go through this month.' Esther's voice began to break. 'The new owner has asked Itsik to stay on as manager until he can train up new Aryan staff. Itsik has promised to give him three months, then we'll leave.'

She started to cry.

Miriam and Rosa put their arms around her.

'We'll come and see you one day. For a holiday,' Rosa joked.

'You should get out too,' Esther said, between the sobs.

They waited until she stopped crying.

'Who bought it?' Rosa asked. 'It must be someone with big balls...'

'Rosa!' Miriam interrupted. 'The children. You really are the limit.'

'Pah. My children hear worse. You should hear Emil and I arguing.' She laughed, and her two friends joined in with her.

'But who did buy it, Esther?' Miriam said, her curiosity piqued.

'Oskar von Friedeburg. He owns a lot of businesses, and he's highly connected with the party bosses, Itsik says. And he paid seventy-five per cent of what Itsik thinks it's worth.'

The other two women didn't hear Miriam's sharp intake of breath.

~~o~~

Miriam waited until Yosef was at his most vulnerable. They were never the most demonstrative of couples, and she sometimes cringed when she glimpsed Maria and Erich Kästner flirting with each other when they were in company, but when she knew that they had complete privacy, Miriam Nussbaum could be as passionate as the fiery Rosa Liewermann and as provocative as the sophisticated Maria Kästner.

'Yosef,' she said, just as her husband, sitting on the edge of their bed, kissed her neck and started unzipping her dress, 'did you hear that Itsik and Esther have sold the shop? They're thinking of moving to Palestine.'

Yosef stopped, and looked up at her.

'Keep doing what you're doing. You can talk at the same time, can't you,' she said, laughing gently.

'I did hear a rumour. Is it definitely true?' he asked, mumbling a little as his lips crept lower.

'Yes. Do you know who bought it?'

Yosef stopped again. Miriam's dress slipped off her shoulders and lay crumpled around her waist. She reached behind her and undid the strap of her brassiere.

'No. Probably some party official.' His voice broke a little and rose half an octave as she let the restraint fall from her breasts. 'Did he get much for it?'

'Esther says he was pleased enough. Not the full market value, but closer to it than they had hoped for.' She shivered as Yosef took one of her nipples in his mouth, rolling his tongue gently around it. He made a sound that she took to be an acknowledgement that he'd heard her.

'It was Oskar von Friedeburg,' she said.

For a second, his tongue stopped moving, then, with barely a flicker of change in his breathing, it started again.

'The General is a good friend of his, is he not?' she said.

Yosef glanced up at her again. She looked at him through half-closed eyes and waited for an answer.

'More of an acquaintance, I believe,' he replied. 'He's in bed with the National Socialists.'

He transferred his mouth to her other nipple. She began to rock her body gently against him.

'I don't suppose you mentioned Itsik's problems with the sale of the shop to General Kästner?' she asked, wriggling her dress down over her knees, dropping it onto the floor.

'I may have, in passing. We tend to chat a lot when I'm driving him around. He often sits in the front with me.'

She stood up and peeled her stockings down to join her dress on the floor. She reached out and unbuttoned his shirt before opening the buckle on his belt.

'You and the General, you're quite a pair, aren't you?' she said, lying back on the bed, and pulling him down to her.

'You should have seen us at sixteen, chasing girls,' he said, losing himself in her softness.

She giggled.

'I love you, Yosef Nussbaum.'

~~o~~

The two friends sat at the corner table in their usual café. It was one of the few places where

Jews didn't get dirty looks from the owners.

'Have a look at this,' Rosa said, passing Miriam something under the table.

Miriam took it. It felt like a folded piece of paper. She went to glance at it, but her friend gripped her arm.

'Not here, you fool,' she hissed. 'Slip it into your bag and read it at home. Don't get caught with it. Emil got it from a friend. He said to let Yosef see it.'

~~o~~

Miriam opened her bag and pulled out the folded piece of paper. She glanced around, but she was alone in the cottage. She pulled the kitchen blinds down.

She started reading. As she did, tears began to run down her face.

The pamphlet said that it had been printed in Lucerne.

That's in Switzerland, she thought. It went on to say that two hundred thousand copies were to be distributed in Germany, and it had been written by an international committee of Jehovah's Witness representatives, some of whom had escaped from the NSDAP's clampdown.

It soundly condemned Adolf Hitler, the Third Reich, and the German people for abolishing religious freedom and for the persecution of the Jewish people, the Gypsies and the regime's political opponents.

It called for international action to stop the widespread violence, intimidation, and wrongful imprisonment of people on the grounds of their race, religion, or political views, and vowed to fight for the rights of all the dispossessed in Nazi Germany.

Nazi was a new word to her, but it was obvious what it meant.

She finished reading. The leaflet called for all good people in Germany to stand with those that were being victimised.

She felt a deep sense of shame. Tears continued to fall from her face.

Rosa had written a note along the bottom.

Someone is standing up for us!

She refolded the pamphlet and put it in her apron pocket.

~~o~~

'I'm sorry,' she said later, giving the folded paper to Yosef.

He unfolded the pamphlet and looked at it.

Noticing the tears in her eyes for the first time, he opened his arms and took her into his grasp.

'Don't be sorry. This may be small, but it's what it means that counts. We're not alone.'

'I was wrong about them. And I was wrong about the General. How can you forgive me?'

'Hush, woman. You're not a bad person. It's these brutes who take away our ability to feel.'

'You're a good man, Yosef Nussbaum.'

'I know,' he said.

He felt her sobs turn to a stifled laugh from deep within her chest, and smiled.

CHAPTER 108

Memo: Geh.KdoS. ABW 01/10/36 CAC0501.1

For Attention Only: All senior executive officers, Abwehr.

From: Rear Admiral Wilhelm Canaris, Chef der Abwehr.

General Francisco Franco has been declared Generalissimo of the Nationalists and Jefe del Estado of the free state of Spain.

It is expected that the General will be a good friend to Germany, especially in the fight against communism that is threatening to engulf Western Europe.

The Nationalists have made significant inroads into Republican strongholds, but the conflict is delicately balanced. Reports that floods of foreign volunteers flocking to Spain from other countries on the European mainland and from Britain and Ireland, to fight the Nationalists, have been received.

The German government is currently in talks with General Franco regarding the provision of assistance in his fight against Bolshevism. [END]

~~o~~

Later that day, the General spoke to Admiral Canaris, by telephone.

'Did you hear what the British said?' The admiral laughed. '*The sun is going down on Europe.* If Franco wins the Spanish war, they'll swallow their pride and make tracks to his door, wait and see. In the meantime, expect them to beef up the garrison in Gibraltar.'

'Will we be getting involved?' the General asked.

'When will we be getting involved would be a better question. Hitler and his chiefs of staff have already offered our assistance. It's only a matter of time. Our boys are going to get some practice!'

The General's stomach lurched, and he cursed himself. For all the years he'd been in the army, at war or in peace, it was only now that his sons were involved that he began to worry about the threat of conflict.

'Don't worry,' Canaris said. 'They're talking mainly about naval and air support.'

He must have read my mind, Erich Kästner thought.

'And it goes without saying, of course,' Canaris continued, 'that our intelligence operatives are active in the area. I may well be able to furnish my good friend, the Generalissimo, with some useful information.'

'You know him?' he said.

'Yes, I've met him quite a few times. The first was during my 'daring' escape from internment in Chile, after the *Dresden* was scuttled, and then I was posted to Madrid, with naval intelligence. I worked loosely with him for a few months.'

The General knew the remarkable story of Canaris's flight from Chile, and his being in Spain during the war. It helped that Spanish was one of the six languages he was fluent in.

'What is he like?'

'Clever, ambitious, but personable. I like him. You may well get to meet him some day.'

~~o~~

'Oskar, thanks for taking the call.'

'For you, Erich, always. What can I do for you?'

'Nothing. I was just telephoning you to say thanks.'

'For what? I do so much for you. You'll have to be more specific.'

The General smiled.

'You do cheer me up, Oskar, but that's not what I'm grateful to you for, this time. Itsik Weichmann's hardware store. Thanks for purchasing it.'

'It's me who should be thanking you, Erich. It's an absolute goldmine, and a snip at the price. I hope you weren't under any illusions that I was being charitable.'

The General laughed. Although there was some truth in what Oskar said, he knew that he'd opened himself up for criticism for buying it from under a party official's nose.

'You might say that, but your friends might not be best pleased.'

'If they ask, I'll plead ignorance. *I'm so sorry, I didn't know you had an interest in it. If I had known, I would never have considered it...*'

The General laughed again. He could just imagine Oskar's hands spread wide and the most innocent look he could engineer.

'You make it sound trivial,' the General said. It wasn't for Itsik and his family.'

'Ach, you're making me out to be a hero. Don't forget I do very well out of your need to interfere. Look at Dieter Mass. I've got myself a top editor for the price of a print man.'

'Piffle! You're paying him the going rate.'

'For a low-grade commercial editor. I'm getting the benefits of an experienced news editor. He's made quite an impact.'

'All right, so I'll concede that you've done well out of it,' the General argued, 'and you'll make a decent return on Itsik's shop. But you didn't have to give him a job while he was waiting to emigrate.'

'General,' Oskar von Friedeburg said, like a teacher with a backward pupil, 'you are completely missing the point. It's Itsik that is doing me a favour, seeing through the transition, training my new manager, introducing us to all his smaller suppliers and more importantly, his customers. He's been a godsend.'

The General laughed, this time in resignation.

'I give up. You're just too quick for someone of my age. Let's just say I owe you a beer.'

'Now that's something I will take you up on sometime, old man.'

CHAPTER 109

[11/10/1936 Sunday]

If Franz was his father's son, there was no doubt that Johann was Maria's favourite. He had the ability to wind her up, frustrate her and wrap her around his little finger in equal measure, but she found him far easier to talk to than Franz.

So, when he called in to see her on his birthday, on the way back to barracks from a weekend's leave spent in Hamburg with his latest girlfriend, she took advantage of having him all to herself by asking him about his brother.

'Ach, on the surface he's fine,' Johann said. 'He works harder than anyone else and excels in nearly everything he does. You'd think others would be envious or resentful but that's the sickening bit; the whole regiment admires and respects him, from the lowest private to Colonel Schneider, and probably the more senior staff too, truth be told.'

She felt a surge of pride, but worried that Johann might sense it.

'Don't you get annoyed?' she said with a smile.

'No. I'm used to it. I had it all through school, remember?'

She laughed.

'He doesn't really talk about what happened,' Johann said, and Maria's smile disappeared. She'd hoped Franz had confided in his brother.

'Does he talk to anyone?'

'Not as far as I know. His friends say he just gets on with it. He doesn't go out much with them, and when he does, he doesn't enjoy himself. They've stopped asking him, and I can't blame them; I've been out with them a few times and Franz just nurses his drink and listens, rarely taking part.'

'I wish there were something we could do.'

'I don't think there is. Only time will help, probably, but I think he's mad, wasting the best part of his life. He should be out having fun.'

'Like you, you mean?'

He grinned.

'Yes. Life is for living, Mother. I just make sure I don't miss anything.'

She tutted. She wished he'd pick on one girl and settle down, but she despaired of him ever surrendering to a humdrum life of domesticity.

'Just don't get caught out by the wrong type of girl,' she said.

That was as close as she would get to warning him, and he took it with good grace. She was sure he fully intended to comply; the last thing he'd want would to be saddled with responsibility when there was a world of beautiful women out there, just waiting for him.

'I'm always careful,' he told her, laughing at her.

She blushed and covered it up, trying to be stern.

'Just don't come complaining to me when one of them turns up on your doorstep with a little wailing bundle.'

~~o~~

[15/10/1936 Thursday]

It was a shock for Eva and Antje when one of their teachers was dismissed from her position at school for having a Jewish husband. She was a favourite with all the girls, and with the other teachers. She'd been working at the school for eight years.

She was known as a teacher who had her pupils' interests at heart and was one they always turned to if there was ever a problem, but in a school of its standing, educating high-ranking Wehrmacht officers' children, and more recently, the offspring of senior party members, the staff had to be above reproach, and she had to go.

Eva had seen her leaving and had at least been able to say goodbye to her. The headmistress had done her best to keep her but when it became obvious that the matter was out of her hands, she'd treated the young woman with respect and dignity, allowing her to speak with her young charges before being driven home, a cheque for six months' wages in her handbag.

~~o~~

At Ruth and Rebeka's school, the contrast could not have been starker.

Yosef and Miriam dragged the whole story out of Ruth when she came home crying. Miriam tried to console her daughter, but it took her father's protective embrace to soothe her.

'Frau Baumgärtner and Frau Fleischmann were paraded in front of the whole school, with placards around their necks,' she said, sobbing gently. 'Judensau.'

Jewish Sow.

Her parents glanced at each other but said nothing.

She took a big breath. 'They made us all stand in two long lines from the front door to the school entrance. They made us…'

She broke down again.

'Hush, hush.' Miriam wiped her daughter's face. 'Take your time.'

'They made us shout *Juden! Juden! Juden!*' while they walked down between the two lines. Some of the children spat on them.'

Ruth's parents looked at each other again, their faces pale with anger.

'I'm going to see the headmaster tomorrow,' Miriam stated, looking at Yosef. 'Ruth's not going back to that school. She can stay here with you.'

Ruth started crying again, hearing the ice-cold anger in her mother's voice.

'No, please, Mama,' she said. 'Don't go to the school. It will only make it worse.'

'She's probably right, dear,' Yosef said. 'People who act like that aren't going to listen to reason. And what are you going to accomplish? The teachers won't get their jobs back and it could make it more difficult for Ruth.'

Miriam stood up and paced the room.

'How can they get away with it? They're nasty, small-minded people who take pleasure in the pain they cause.'

'They'll be punished one day for this,' Yosef said.

'Will they?' Miriam said. 'Will they really?'

'I have to believe that they will. Surely God will punish them for what they are doing to his people.'

'God doesn't have a great record of wreaking revenge on those who persecute us. What makes you think he'll start now?'

'Miriam!' Yosef said, his eyes wide with shock.

Miriam realised that she'd gone too far. Even Ruth was looking at her in disbelief. It occurred to her that she was spending too much time with Rosa Liewermann.

'I'm sorry. I just don't know how much more we can take of this incessant harassment.'

'Send Ruth to school tomorrow. See what happens. It will all die down. I'll see if the committee at the synagogue can help the two teachers.'

'Thank you, Papa,' Ruth said softly, and Miriam realised her angry comments and her threat to visit the school had given her daughter a fright.

Turn the other cheek, they'd always told her.

~~o~~

As autumn fell away into winter, and the biting wind blew into Kiel from the fast-freezing Baltic, Ruth and Rebeka made the daily trip to the Realschule in Preetzer Chaussee not knowing what was in store for them, or the fifteen other Jewish children who attended the school.

Even on a normal day, the least they could expect were cruel taunts from their fellow pupils and perhaps a derisory insult concerning the deviousness of Jews, or their greed, from one of their teachers.

On a bad day, Ruth, or one of her fellow Jewish pupils would be forced to stand out in front of the class, next to a gross caricature of what the National Socialists maintained was the average Jewish person.

The teacher would point out the similarities, which Ruth knew, for her and most of the other Jewish children, didn't exist.

'Now, the nose is one of the biggest giveaways,' the teacher would say, a cruel smile on his face. 'It is large, with a prominent bridge, resulting in the omnipresent Jewish hooked nose that is so obvious on this diagram.' The teacher would point to the heavily exaggerated pronounced nose on the caricature, then the wooden cane would be placed on the Jewish pupil's nose, often none too gently.

'The nose is of great importance to a Jew. They use it to sniff out money!' the teacher would declare. 'One of us in this class could have a gold coin in their pocket and this Jew, if trained by its elders, could find it by the sense of smell alone.'

The rest of the class would 'ooh' and 'aah' in practised familiarity and Ruth would be forced to walk around the room, sniffing, while the children chanted 'Juden Nase. Juden Nase. Juden Nase.' *Jew Nose.*

On other occasions all the Jewish children would be lined up in front of the assembly and be told to recite the poem they'd been made to learn.

We are little Juden pigs
We wallow in our swill,
We carry all the diseases that
Make German children ill.
We are little Juden pigs
We take, we beg, we steal,
And when we're caught and punished
Like all fat pigs we squeal.

There were further verses; the teacher made them learn a new one each week.

Ruth and Rebeka, like most of the Jewish children, learned to say nothing, even to their parents. But Ruth did confide in Antje.

'I just want to go to school and learn,' she told her.

CHAPTER 110

[08/12/1936 Tuesday]

The bottle crashed against the grey steel of the ship and disintegrated, the champagne exploding in a cloud of glass and foam, while the Kriegsmarine chaplain intoned a blessing.

For what seemed like an age, the battleship, the latest of the new capital ships that signalled the restoration of the German Navy, remained poised on the slipway. Then, with a groan, the hull began to move, almost imperceptibly at first.

Miriam Nussbaum felt the ground shake beneath her feet as the giant ship began to rumble down the slipway.

The General had arranged the visit to the Deutsche Werke shipyard as a treat for the Kästners and the Nussbaums to see the *Gneisenau*, the Kriegsmarine's new pride and joy, being launched. Manny stood between Ruth and Antje, jumping up and down with excitement.

They had an unsurpassed view, seated in the area cordoned off for invited spectators.

'It's soooo big,' Manny squealed. 'How will it float?'

The others all laughed, and Manny looked pleased to be the centre of attention.

'They've thought of that, silly,' Ruth said. 'Obviously, it will float.'

'It's heavy, Manny, and big, but it's full of air. That's what makes it float,' the General explained. 'They've launched hundreds of big ships here, so they know the water is deep enough.'

Miriam Nussbaum looked around uncomfortably, nervous of being in such a prominent spot, waiting for the tap on the shoulder and the angry shouts of 'Geh raus! Juden sind hier verboten!' *Get out! Jews are forbidden here!*

But nothing untoward happened. She heard Manny ask another of his endless questions.

'Where is it going? Far away?'

'No, it's just going over there.' Yosef pointed to the fitting-out berth a few hundred yards away. 'These tugs will move it over because its engines aren't working yet.'

Manny looked disappointed but brightened up as he watched the six tugs jostle and pull the shell of the battleship round to its new resting place.

'It will take another eighteen months of fitting-out before the ship would steam out of Kieler Hafen for her sea trials,' the General said, 'and another year after that before she'll go on service.'

The excitement over, the Kästners and the Nussbaums turned and walked through the factory gates onto Werftstraße and made their way back towards Hamburger Chaussee and Drachensee. They hadn't brought the car; it wasn't an onerous walk, and driving would have been almost impossible in the large crowd that had flocked to both sides of Kieler Hafen to watch the launch.

Maria Kästner walked ahead with Eva and the two younger girls. Yosef held Manny's hand tightly, bringing up the rear of the group, leaving the General and Miriam walking together in the middle.

'Thanks for the invitation, sir,' Miriam said. 'Manny adored it; he'll be talking about it for weeks.' She smiled.

'It was my pleasure. The job has a few perks,' the General replied, smiling. 'How is he doing at school?' he asked, concern in his voice.

'He and Ruth don't say much, but I know they get a hard time, from the teachers and the pupils. But they're tough children.'

'I wonder where they got that from?'

She smiled at him, then a serious look crossed her face.

'I'd like to apologise,' she said.

He turned to her with a surprised look.

'For what?' he said.

'I didn't really trust your motives, General.' She hesitated. 'I mean, you talked as if you were on our side, but I thought you were just doing it to make yourself feel better, to ease the guilt you felt about the way we were being treated by our country.'

The General raised his eyebrows but said nothing.

'I know what you did about Itsik's shop,' Miriam said, not put out by his silence, 'unless it is one enormous coincidence.' She smiled. 'And Yosef let it slip that he'd been to Kleiner Kuhberg,' she continued. 'He didn't mention you were involved but you are, aren't you?'

'Miriam, I just do what I can; what I think is right. It's not much, I'm afraid. My only hope is that the bubble bursts soon, and Hitler and his hangers-on are thrown out, and we can go back to muddling along without striving for German greatness.'

'They are worrying times,' she said, 'but we keep hoping people will come to their senses.'

'I wish I could reassure you, but I have great concerns. That's why I advised Yosef to consider leaving. It would break my heart to see you go, but for the children's sake...'

'We can't leave our families behind, General. And this is our home. We just keep hoping the people of this country will come to their senses.'

'There are more than a few who believe that what we are doing isn't right, but they're just too frightened to speak out; they've seen what happened to those who've opposed the National Socialists.'

'If enough people spoke out...' she said.

'You may be right,' he continued, 'but a significant proportion of the German people support all of this; the rampant nationalism, the desire for a greater Germany, the sabre-rattling and making you, the Jews, the scapegoat for everything that was wrong with Germany. They welcome it with open arms, and it shames me.'

'You've nothing to be ashamed of,' she said.

'General,' a voice behind them said, 'Manny wants to know how much the ship cost.'

They looked around. Yosef was smiling at his son, who had a comical frown on his face.

'Well,' said the General, leaning down and picking Manny up with both arms outstretched. He dangled him for a second.

'If you were solid gold,' he said, 'You wouldn't even buy a tiny little piece of the ship. You'd have to save up a lot of pocket money to buy it.'

Manny's young face creased in concentration. 'Then who pays for it?' he asked.

The General smiled. 'We all do, Manny. We all do.'

~~o~~

[23/12/1936 Wednesday]

'I hear they're calling you Moses,' the General said.

Canaris laughed.

'And where did you hear that, Kästner?'

'Oh, here and there. You know. When did you meet with Herr Heydrich?'

'On Monday. At the Reich Ministry.'

'What sort of temper was he in?'

Wilhelm Canaris had been summoned for a meeting with Reinhard Heydrich to clarify the respective areas of counter-espionage responsibilities between the Gestapo and the Abwehr. The resulting document they signed formalising these arrangements had become widely known within the intelligence community as the *Ten Commandments*, the first one being *Thou shalt not step on the Gestapo's toes*, according to wags within the Abwehr.

'Heydrich was in an expansive mood. He agreed that we should share as much intelligence as possible and demanded that the Abwehr should stay well out of domestic intelligence matters. I agreed, needless to say.'

'Obviously,' the General said, chuckling.

'He also agreed that the Gestapo will not investigate matters pertaining exclusively to the Wehrmacht and if they are investigating Wehrmacht personnel in any other capacity, they will inform us.'

'And you believe that?'

'Not any more than he believes we will not be collecting intelligence on civilian matters that could have an impact on the armed forces.'

The General laughed.

~~o~~

[25/12/1936 Friday]

Christmas at the Drachensee house in 1936 was the usual Maria Kästner production, with exquisite food, beautiful decorations, and wonderful presents for everyone, but it didn't quite match up to years past.

There was a slight pall over the whole yuletide season; the Nussbaums looked worried, the General seemed to have a constant weight on his mind, and Franz didn't come home.

'He's on exercise, Maria,' the General explained. 'You of all people should know that a soldier's life is at the whim of the army. God knows how many Christmases I missed over the years.'

'It's the first year for a long while without the whole family together. It just seems sad, and with Franz being the way he is, I get worried.'

'This has nothing to do with Franz's state of mind, it's just the generals flexing their muscles, letting their soldiers know that they belong to the army, whether they like it or not.'

He laughed.

'I've done it myself,' he added.

'I suppose so. I just worry about him.'

He put his arm around her shoulder.

'He's finding his own way through this. I've spoken to him, but he doesn't say much; he wishes to deal with it in his own manner, and in his own time. It's up to us to be there when he needs us.'

'But when will that be?' she asked.

'Just have patience and try to enjoy yourself. It all looks magnificent, as ever,' he said, looking around the wonderfully decorated room and the table filled with all sorts of delights.

Maria hurried off to check with Miriam that everything was almost ready.

Johann had been standing quietly, listening to his parents.

'He volunteered for this one, you know.'

'I suspected as much. Just don't tell your mother.'

Johann grinned.

'How much is it worth, old man?'

'Well, let me put it this way. I'm on good terms with Colonel Schneider. How would avoiding two weeks' latrine duty suit you?'

They both laughed, then the General spoke quietly again.

'Don't give up on him. Talk to his friends, keep taking him out for a drink now and then. He'll come out of it when he's ready. If you watch him closely, even though he doesn't take part, I'll wager he has a quiet smile at all your antics.'

'I will. I do keep an eye on him, honestly.'

Erich Kästner put his hand on his son's shoulder.

'I know you do, son.'

1937

'First they came for the socialists, and I did not speak out.

Because I was not a socialist.'

'Then they came for the trade unionists, and I did not speak out.

Because I was not a trade unionist.'

'Then they came for the Jews, and I did not speak out.

Because I was not a Jew.'

'Then they came for me, and there was no one left to speak for me.'

Martin Niemöller, Lutheran pastor, c. 1950

CHAPTER 111

[04/01/1937 Monday]

'It's ridiculous.'

The Clubkapitän of the Kaiserlicher Yacht Club was on his feet, thumping the table.

There was a murmur of agreement from around the room.

Erich Kästner closed his eyes.

The Imperial Yacht Club, or Kieler Yacht Club to most of Kiel's inhabitants, had been in existence since 1891, when Kaiser Wilhelm II became commodore of the Naval Regatta Club and the club changed its name in honour of its new patron.

Although the Kaiser had been in exile in Holland since the Versailles Treaty and the founding of the Weimar Republic, he was still the honorary commodore of the yacht club, which was why the pompous man at the head of the yacht club in Kiel was called the *Clubkapitän* and not the commodore, as in most other yacht clubs.

'We're being forced to merge with sailing clubs across Germany to become the *Yacht-Club von Deutschland* in the name of unity, by God.'

There was a chorus of 'shame' and 'foul' from around the table.

'Our commodore, the Emperor Wilhelm II, is to be stripped of his honorary title.'

In an instant, every man around the room was talking at once. There were no women present. The Clubkapitän let them argue for a minute, then he silenced them with a couple of taps of his pipe on the table.

'Gentlemen, it seems we do not have much choice in the matter but, if you wish, I can send a formal complaint to the government.'

The mood suddenly became less combative; eyes that had been blazing with indignation a few minutes earlier, now looked away.

'This is what happens when you hand over power to a small group of people.'

Everybody's head whipped round. When they saw that it was the General who'd spoken, most rolled their eyes, but a few murmured 'hear, hear.'

'It's not particularly helpful to be making a political point at this juncture, General Kästner.'

'I didn't intend it to be helpful, but I am making a point. It seems that the tremendous enthusiasm that some members of this club had for the policies of the National Socialists was acceptable until they started to impinge on their own personal freedoms.'

'We all know that you are an outspoken critic of the government, when we should all be supporting them, in their efforts to give Germany its place in the world back again.' The Clubkapitän didn't try to hide the irritation in his voice.

'So, bow before this edict and meekly accept that the Imperial Yacht Club is finished,' the General replied, in a measured but firm tone.

'We don't have much choice,' the Clubkapitän said, a trace of a whine to his voice. 'If we don't comply, they'll just remove us and implement the changes anyway. We may as well accept the change and try to retain as much control as possible. All Agreed?'

'Agreed.' The murmur of assent came from everyone in the room except the General.

'Is there any other business?'

'Yes, Herr Clubkapitän,' the General said, prompting more curious glances.

'Well, carry on.'

'Thank you. I would like to hand in my resignation.'

A murmur ran around the room.

One of the oldest committee members spoke up.

'Well done, General. Resigning from the committee is the best way to protest this decision. I should really join you.'

'That's not why I'm resigning. The Clubkapitän knows my reasons. And I'm not just leaving the committee; I'm resigning my membership of the club.'

There were gasps from around the table. The General had been a stalwart of the Kaiserlicher Yacht Club since he'd first set foot in it as a junior cadet, sailing dinghies at the age of six. He, like his father before him, had been a longstanding member of the committee and a former Clubkapitän.

'But why?' the old man said.

'Ask your Clubkapitän. I'm sure he'd be able to enlighten you. My boat will be removed from the club harbour by the end of the week. Here are my keys.'

He placed the keys on the table and walked out.

There was silence in the room, then it erupted with noise. The Clubkapitän stood up and rapped again on the table.

'Wait here. I'll be back a minute.'

He caught up with the General just as they reached the entrance door.

'Herr General,' he said, 'wait.'

The General, one hand on the door, turned.

'Yes,' he said curtly.

'Can we go somewhere private to talk about this?'

'No, here will do. I don't have anything to say that can't be said here.'

The man looked around, uncomfortably.

'You can't leave just like this. The committee will think I've forced you out. They still regard you as a vital asset, you know.'

'I'm sure they do. In name only. I wasn't important enough to be consulted about who's allowed into the club.'

'I've apologised for that.'

'Listen, Herr Clubkapitän, you're a small man in a small-minded club. I want no part of it.'

The man flinched, then drew himself up in indignation.

'How dare you. I've a mind to report you to the authorities for aiding and abetting Jews.'

The General gave a harsh laugh.

'Try it. I'm a Wehrmacht General. Who do you think they'd listen to?'

'I'm a party member. One day, you'll find that we will not have to bow down to people like you.'

'I hope that day never comes. I fear for Germany if it does. Anyway, go ahead and report me, but perhaps you should consider this. I have signed letters from two members of staff concerning your employee-cum-lady-friend from the storeroom. I'm sure the committee, and perhaps your wife, would find them an interesting read.'

The General wondered if he'd gone too far. The man's face had turned puce, and he briefly considered the possibility that he was suffering a heart attack, but his skin paled as the General's words sank in.

'You wouldn't...'

'Try me.'

He turned to go out the door. At the top step, he paused and looked back.

'Goodbye, Herr Clubkapitän, and good luck with the whole Yacht-Club von Deutschland thing.'

He strode down the steps, whistling, seething inside but knowing, at all costs, that he couldn't show it.

He chuckled. *Signed letters.* He liked that. It had been a spur-of-the-moment thing, but Herr Clubkapitän would always wonder.

His smile disappeared as a thought crossed his mind.

Where the hell am I going to berth Snowgoose?

~~o~~

The next day, the General stood on waste ground, not half a mile from where the *Gneisenau* sat; a hulking monster, the men swarming over her like ants on an anthill, slowly transforming her from a hollow shell to a cutting-edge fighting ship.

He stood beside two admirals, the managing directors of the Deutsche Werke and the Krupp Germaniawerft yards, and Hinrich Lohse, the Oberpräsident of Schleswig-Holstein. In front of them, Gustav Krupp, the head of Europe's largest engineering company, stood with his son Alfried. The General remembered the younger Krupp, having sailed against him in Kieler Woche, and had followed his exploits as an Olympic sailor.

They listened as Jürgen Hoffmann, the mayor, spoke at length about the strong and historic ties between the workers of Kiel and the Kriegsmarine, and how the rightful expansion of Germany's navy was at the heart of everything the residents of Kiel strived for.

'And here today in Gaarden-Ost, we are laying the foundation stones for this magnificent residential complex that will eventually provide 2,500 new homes that these workers deserve, for the dedication they show to their city, their country and the Führer.'

He threw out his arm.

'Heil Hitler.'

The crowd returned his salute. They were mostly shipyard workers who had been given an hour off work to attend, along with their families. Most of the local NSDAP officials were also present, along with a smattering of Kiel's notable citizens, curious to see how the city was expanding to cope with the increased output of ships and submarines that was expected of it.

'They're awfully proud of themselves; providing these homes in such a magnanimous gesture,' one of the admirals whispered to General Kästner.

'I'm sure they'll earn a tidy profit from them when the workers move in.'

'Not as much as they're making from the navy. Have you seen Krupp's mansion, Villa Hügel, and his 'modest' holiday home on Sylt?'

'Sadly, I haven't yet been invited.'

The admiral laughed.

'I've been to Villa Hügel,' he said. 'A misnomer if ever there was one. It's more of a grand palace.'

The General looked over at Krupp. Like a clutch of his fellow industrialists, the man had been one of Adolf Hitler's staunchest backers and had done well out of it.

'I've never been to his place on Sylt,' the admiral continued, 'it's only the elite who get invited there. It's a very exclusive island, I hear.'

'I've sailed round Sylt,' the General said. 'It's a beautiful area. I'm not surprised the man would want a house there.'

'You've met Krupp, haven't you?'

'Only briefly. We were introduced at a meeting about shipyard security.'

'I'm going to have a quick chat with him once this is finished. You can come along if you like. There's a reception for the great and the good, once the workers have been sent packing back to the yards.'

The admiral paused. Jürgen Hoffmann had a spade in his hand, and he was asking Hinrich Lohse to cut the first sod of the new complex.

'Maybe these two are going to do some real work, for a change.'

The General laughed. 'I think it's just symbolic.'

They watched as the Oberpräsident tried to make a dent in the hard ground, but he found it difficult to do more than scratch the surface.

'You'd have thought they would have loosened it up a bit beforehand, so that he could slide the spade in easily,' the admiral said.

'Ha. They probably thought about it, then decided to let him make a fool of himself. No doubt someone will suffer for this.'

The admiral smiled. A large workman walked over and took the spade from the pasty, somewhat plump NSDAP man, and standing on the blade, drove it into the ground with apparent ease. He leaned back on the spade and, when it started to break the soil, he stood back and motioned for the Oberpräsident to complete the ceremonial breaking of the turf.

The crimson-faced NSDAP man stepped forward again and, this time, managed to excavate the first spade of soil of the development.

There was a smattering of polite applause, a few isolated cheers, then the workers stood in line to receive a bottle of beer each.

As the yard men trudged down the road to the shipyard gates, the admiral guided the General to the line of cars that would take them to the Dietrichsdorfer Hof, across the Schwentine.

'How is the sailing going, anyway? I was surprised when you came out of retirement. I'd expected you to make the most of it and sail round Europe, or to the West Indies.'

'It had crossed my mind, but this job has meant that all my grand plans for the boat have been put on hold. If I'm honest, I don't think I was ready for retirement. My current problem with the boat is where to put it.'

The admiral raised an eyebrow.

'I thought you kept it at the yacht club?'

'I resigned,' the General said, 'and told them I'd be taking the boat elsewhere.'

'I thought you were one of the founding members?'

'Hardly. I'm not quite that old, but my father was. Anyway, I had a run-in with the current Clubkapitän. The man is a pompous jackass, as the Americans would say.'

'I may be able to help you,' the admiral said, a thoughtful look on his face. 'Why don't you use our jetty?'

The Naval Headquarters had two piers; a larger one for the Kriegsmarine work boats, and a smaller one for the launch that the admirals used for getting around the harbour.

'We only use one side of it, and the depth is adequate if you don't try and tie up too near the shore.'

'Will no one object?'

'Not at all. A few of our predecessors kept boats of various sorts there. And you're in effect an honorary admiral, despite your choice of the wrong branch of the service as a youth.' The admiral smiled.

'I might take you up on that. It would be ideal. Perhaps too convenient.'

'That's that, then. I'll tell the warrant officer in charge of the dock. Or you can. You seem to know everyone around here.'

'Well, I've lived here all my life.'

The car drew to a halt.

'We're here, sirs,' the driver said, and got out to open the doors.

~~o~~

'I hear you're a man who gets things done.'

The General looked at the man speaking to him. Krupp seemed like the type of person who was used to things being done when he asked.

'I like to make myself useful to the navy. It helps to dispel their poor opinion of the army.'

Gustaf Krupp gave a perfunctory laugh, but his son's smile was warmer.

'I believe we've met, General,' the younger Krupp said.

'Yes, I remember you flying past us. Kieler Woche, 1928, I think.'

'Don't be so modest. It was the tightest race we had that year. We only won by a nose. I hear your sons are making their mark.'

The General couldn't quite hide his surprise. Alfried Krupp smiled.

'I watched a couple of their races in the Hitlerjugend boat,' he said. 'We helped a little

381

with the financing of the team.'

'Ah. That's kind of you.'

'We're always happy to assist the Führer, and what better way to help than to invest in the development of our exceptional young people.'

His father interrupted.

'If you spent a little less of your day talking about yachting and more time concentrating on building ships, it would be of much greater benefit to the Reich.'

Gustaf Krupp's words lacked any real venom, and although his face showed little trace of a smile, the General presumed his comment was what passed for good-natured banter between them.

'That's what we all want,' the admiral said, beaming. 'More of your marvellous ships.'

CHAPTER 112

'Itsik Weichmann left for Palestine today.'

Yosef's head rose from the *Morgenpost*.

'I know. I went to see him yesterday. I meant to tell you.'

'It was hectic. It must have slipped your mind.'

Miriam often made excuses for her husband, and she was rewarded with a grateful smile.

'I should have told you,' he said. 'I helped Itsik and Abel load up the lorry.'

Itsik and Abel, his brother, had bought a lorry and were making the perilous overland journey to Palestine with as many of their belongings as they could fit in, and enough stock to get their new shop started.

'When I left,' Yosef added, 'they were tying things to the roof, the back and the sides, just to get it all on.'

Miriam gave him a half smile. She could just imagine the truck bristling with the bric-a-brac of modern living; brushes, ironing boards, garden implements, children's toys. And not forgetting the all-important stock to kick-start their new venture.

'Esther and the children are going to follow on,' she said, 'once Itsik has found a place to stay. His brother is going to send for his wife too.'

'Yes, they're going into business together. One day, they told me, they'll be the biggest chain of hardware stores in Palestine.'

She smiled again, but Yosef could see that it was an effort for her.

He stood up and put his arm around her.

'I know it's going to be hard for you, with Esther going.'

'It won't be easy for Manny, either. Moshe and he are like that.'

She crossed her fingers to show how close they were.

'I hadn't thought of that,' he said. 'Manny's young. He'll get over it.'

'I'm not so sure. With everything else that's going on...'

'What do you mean?'

'At school. They're both struggling. All Jewish children are the same.'

He frowned. 'They haven't said anything.'

'No, they won't. They're frightened of how we'd react.'

'Then how do you know?'

'Mothers talk to each other. We hear the odd thing, and piece it all together.'

She told him of some of the things that she'd learned. As she spoke, he could see her face changing, tears of anger in her eyes.

'What can we do?'

'Nothing. If we take them out of school, we could get in trouble with the authorities and anyway, they both still want to go to school, to their credit.'

'One day,' he said. 'One day, there'll be a reckoning. And I want to be there.'
She put her hand on his arm, in support.

~~o~~

KIELER MORGENPOST

Sunday 28th February 1937

GERMAN STREETS SAFER – PURGE ON CRIMINALS

In a welcome move, the Kriminalpolizei are clearing our towns and cities of convicted offenders and incarcerating them in concentration camps. Large numbers of arrests have been made in the last twenty-four hours, and this is expected to continue for the next two weeks.

A spokesman for the Reich Ministry of Justice said that these criminal elements were being removed from society to make the streets safer for ordinary German people.

Most had multiple convictions and were habitual offenders. The Reich Minister for Justice, Franz Gürtner, was quoted as saying: "This order came directly from the Führer himself. We are fortunate to have a leader who is willing to make the tough decisions for the good of the country".

Discussions are ongoing within the Government, but an announcement is expected shortly about further expansion of the concentration camp system.

It is expected that the crime rate, having gradually crept up, will fall again after this initiative.

~~o~~

'Thanks for the help. I could have moved it on my own, but it's far easier with two.'

Erich Kästner and Dieter Maas sat on the deck of the boat, well wrapped up against the cold; the bright February sun had no real warmth, but it was pleasant. They'd just moved *Snowgoose* from the yacht club to the admiral's quay.

'It was no bother. It broke up a slow Sunday afternoon. Does it not bother you that you've had to leave the yacht club?'

'A little. For me, it's always about people and there are still some good ones in the club. The trouble is, it's run by those who think themselves better than everyone else.'

'You've certainly got an exclusive spot here.'

The General's boat sat on what looked like a private jetty.

'It is indeed. Courtesy of the Kriegsmarine.'

The General nodded at the newspaper that was sitting on the coachroof, with its crime-stopping headline.

'At last. They're finally putting people in the camps who deserve to be there.'

Dieter Maas laughed.

'I suppose so,' Dieter said. 'That's if they're all guilty,' he added.

The General poured two coffees from the flask he'd brought.

'Oh, these are all guilty,' he said. 'Uwe Müller assures me that the ones they're picking up now are the repeat offenders who cause most of the crime in the city. He'd have loved to have been able to do this years ago. I suppose it is a small consolation for the end of democracy and our justice system.'

'The problem is, while everyone is behind it, even you and I, where does it end?'

'What do you mean?'

'Well, as things stand, the ones they're picking up are the scum who prey on other people, who make our lives a misery by breaking into our houses or assaulting innocent citizens or even molesting our children. Everyone is happy to see them incarcerated. But will it stop when they've got them all? Who's next? Train-fare dodgers? Litter louts? Businessmen who fiddle their expenses?'

'What would be the point of them doing that?'

'They're setting a precedent of imprisonment without trial. Previously, you had to be a member of a political party or a protest group to be arrested. Now, any one of us could be snatched off the street or from our homes on a trumped-up charge that would never see the inside of a courtroom. It gives them carte blanche to do what they want, and we'll have sleepwalked right into it.'

'But they could do that anyway.'

'Yes, but this way, they have everyone on their side and, before we all notice that it's not just criminals who're being taken into custody, it will be you or me; just another routine arrest, and people will say that you must have done something if the police have taken you away. And then you'll disappear, and no one will care.'

'I never thought of it like that. I'll have a word with Uwe; see what he thinks.'

'I'd be careful. I think Uwe is decent enough; he was always fair and approachable when I worked at the *Morgenpost*, but he'll be under a lot of pressure to toe the party line. I wouldn't depend on him for favours or confide in him too much, for that matter.'

'That would be a sad day. I like Uwe.'

'They're all sad days, General.'

CHAPTER 113

As far as Manny was concerned, it was the worst birthday he could remember. Everyone tried to make it as much fun as it should have been, but a dark cloud hung over the whole day.

And it was all because of the Weichmanns.

Although Moshe was a year above Manny at school, in all other respects they were equals. Being six months older, he was a little bigger and stronger, but Manny was faster, and the better climber of the two.

They both had a wicked sense of humour, and their ability to get into scrapes was legendary. It was fortunate that, most of the time, their parents never found out about their exploits.

But it was all about to come to an end. Moshe was leaving for Palestine in less than two weeks.

If it was hitting both boys hard, their mothers weren't faring any better. They'd known each other since childhood and, apart from Rosa, Esther was Miriam's only true close friend.

'This is the last time we'll be together, like this, with all the children,' Esther said, trying not to cry.

'Don't say that. You'll be back here for a visit when this is all over. Either that, or we'll join you in Palestine,' Rosa said, making a face that implied it was unlikely that it would happen, even if hell did freeze over.

'It might not be that bad,' Esther said. 'I'll let you know what it's like. You shouldn't discount it completely.'

'Esther, no harm to you, and I love you dearly, but can you imagine me in the middle of a desert? Really?'

The three women laughed. Rosa Liewermann was an out-and-out city lover. The thought of her slumming it anywhere remotely uncivilised was comical.

'Are you all ready to go?'

'Yes, the house has been sold.' She sniffed. 'We didn't do so badly out of it. One of Itsik's customers bought it. Of course, he has a bargain but considering what we might have been offered…'

She tailed off.

'Have you somewhere to stay?' Miriam asked, concerned.

'Yes, we'll stay with Itsik's mother until we leave. It will give her some time with the children before we go.'

She started to sob.

'I said I wouldn't cry,' she said, her face flushing in exasperation. 'Now look at me.'

'It's all right to cry,' Miriam said, putting an arm around Esther's shoulder. 'It's a big wrench to leave the people you love behind, not knowing when you might see them again.'

'I know, that's the hardest bit. Itsik is going to try and get his mother and father out once we have the business up and running.'

Esther was closer than usual to her in-laws. Her relationship with her own mother was questionable; Esther's father had died when she was barely in her teens, and her mother had remarried soon after, which didn't sit well with the fourteen-year-old. As soon as she was of age enough to leave, she moved to Kiel and entered domestic service with a wealthy Jewish couple.

They'd taken a shine to her and, through them, she'd been introduced into Jewish society in Kiel. When she'd met and later married Itsik Weichmann, no one was more delighted than the old couple, even if it meant losing their beloved housemaid.

She later admitted to her friends that, from the moment she met Itsik, she not only fell in love with him, but with his parents. Within months, the couple were engaged, and Esther felt that for the first time in years, she had a mother and father.

'Having them with you would make it so much easier for you and Itsik, and his brother. It'll be great for the children too,' Miriam said, smiling. 'See, it's all going to work out.'

Esther managed a smile through the tears.

'I know,' she said. 'But I'm going to miss you two so much.'

'Us too, honey,' Rosa said. 'Once there are cities, and running water, I'll come and visit, I promise.'

The three women laughed and Yosef, standing with the General, shook his head.

'One moment crying, the next laughing,' he said. 'Who will ever understand women?'

~~o~~

Manny, Fischel and Moshe sat in the den they'd made in the dense bushes at the foot of the garden, close to the lake. It had three escape routes: the one they'd entered by, accessed by moving a hanging branch on the side, another by clambering up the branches of the tree whose roots formed the gnarled seats of their hideout and in real emergencies, the do-or-die option of dropping into the shallow water of the lake at the back of the den and wading ten metres along to the beach.

Moshe, the oldest, had a penknife in his hand, and he was sharpening it with strokes of the blade on a stone he'd picked up from the water's edge.

Manny and Fischel's eyes grew larger with each metallic caress of the blade on the hard, abrasive surface of the rock, hoping that they wouldn't cry.

'Take one of these leaves,' he told them, handing them one and showing them how to rub the ball of their thumbs with the succulent plant to sterilise it.

Then, he turned his hand up so that they could see the fleshy part of his thumb and pressed the blade onto it. With a slight pull backwards, a small line of blood oozed onto the surface, and he handed the knife to Manny.

Manny took a deep breath and copied him. The first time, he didn't press hard enough and the small scratch he'd made didn't bleed. Steeling himself, he repeated the stroke and this time, he was rewarded with the same line of bright red beads that had appeared on Moshe's thumb.

Fischel looked as if he was going to faint but Moshe reassured him with a hand on his shoulder, and Manny watched him force himself to press the knife down onto his flesh.

'Go on,' Manny said as Fischel froze. 'It only hurts a little.'

'Do you want me to do it for you?' Manny asked, impatient to get it over with, and not a little worried about the drip-drip-drip of blood from his own thumb.

Fischel shook his head and, taking a deep breath, drew the knife back. They all looked as the cut began to ooze.

Moshe held his hand up, the flesh of his thumb towards the other two, and they did the same, pressing their three thumbs together.

The hairs on the back of Manny's head tingled with the warm stickiness of oozing blood and the sting of the cut being pressed against the others' flesh.

'Blood brothers!' Moshe intoned. Manny suppressed a giggle, fearful that it would spoil the moment.

'Blood brothers forever,' he said.

'Blood brothers till death,' Fischel said, and the other two looked at him, impressed.

Moshe removed his thumb and, sticking it in his mouth, sucked the wound to remove any grit from it that might have been on the blade. He then wrapped it with one of the long ornamental grass leaves that they'd brought with them. The other two copied his actions.

They waited until the bleeding had stopped, then, just to reinforce the secrecy of the ceremony, they left by the more discreet route along the water's edge, carrying their shoes and socks until they reached the beach.

Manny's wound had started seeping again, so he crept into the house, raked about in the kitchen drawer, and found what he was looking for. From a small metal tin, he took out a Hansaplast and, peeling off the backing tape, stuck it over his wound. He was about to put the container back, when he hesitated, then took two more plasters before returning it to the drawer.

'We'll have to be careful,' he said, giving the other two a dressing each. 'Don't let the grown-ups see our thumbs. They'll smell a rat.'

Manny smiled. There was nothing more satisfying than finding a use for a line from one of the Saturday matinee American films that they were treated to once a month.

~~o~~

[19/04/1937 Monday]

The Weichmanns left on a Monday.

The nineteenth of April, Miriam thought, etching it into her mind. *Esther's last day in Kiel.*

Miriam kept Manny from school and walked to the Bahnhof to see the Weichmanns away. Rosa and Fischel were there too. The boys were in a different class from Moshe and their mothers figured no one would find it strange that both were off sick the same day.

It was the Führer's birthday the following day, and in the streets around the station, and in the station itself, large banners of Adolf Hitler were being put up alongside the red, white, and black swastika flags and the bunting.

The train was packed and Esther and her children, being Jews, had been relegated to sitting on their cases in the baggage compartment for the first part of the journey, while the train was busy. If they were lucky, they might get a seat later.

Miriam had borrowed the General's camera, and one of the porters took a photograph of the three friends and the children, standing on the platform in front of the train.

Then, as shouts from the guard had everyone scurrying into the carriages, Esther gave her two friends a last hug.

'I'm not going to cry,' she said, a tear running down her cheek, turning and ushering her children onto the train. They stood at the door, Moshe's hands on top of the rolled-down window, his eyes peering over it, Shoshana in her mother's arms.

'See you next year,' Esther shouted as the train pulled away in a cloud of smoke and steam, its whistle loud under the glass roof of the station.

They walked down the platform after her, waving and blowing kisses until the bend in the track took her out of sight.

'I wish we were going too,' Manny said, then Fischel spotted a discarded box lying on the platform and the two boys started kicking it back and forth to each other as they walked down towards the ticket barrier.

Miriam and Rosa looked at each other and smiled.

CHAPTER 114

'Let her go.'

The General watched as Dieter and Oskar slipped the lines, and the Doc shoved off, stepping aboard once the boat was clear of the jetty.

Through the heavy drizzle, they could just about see the other side of Kieler Hafen but, as it widened out, they soon lost sight of both shores, and the General steered by the compass.

He handed the tiller over to the Doc and went below to mark their course on the chart. He picked up the trailing log, and once the boat had settled, he lowered it over the stern and let out ten metres of line, then read their speed on the dial. Pulling it back in, he returned it to its box, and noted the speed in his notebook.

Back in the cabin, he plotted a distance to the Friedrichsort light, and wrote an estimated time beside it.

'All right, Doc,' he said, coming back on deck. 'Steer zero-one-five degrees. There's no wind, so it's the engine, I'm afraid.'

'Zero-one-five degrees,' the Doc intoned, confirming that he'd heard the General's command, adjusting his course accordingly.

'Right, gentlemen, let's keep an eye out for the first port hand mark. Once we've found that one, we can just follow the channel northwards.'

Within five minutes, Oskar had spotted it. By the time they passed it, they could just see the next one through the smir.

'Why did you bother plotting a course,' Dieter asked, 'when you knew we could follow the channel markers?'

'If the visibility worsens, and we lose sight of the buoys, we'll still know where we are.'

'You can be that accurate?'

'Well, you have to allow for a little error, and it's only as good as the man on the tiller...' The General glanced across at the Doc.

'Within a few metres, my boy. I'd be surprised if I'm even that far out.'

'Scheiße!' Oskar von Friedeburg shook his head.

The General laughed.

'You don't believe us, Oskar?'

'You're full of it, boys,' Oskar said, grinning.

'How about a wager, then?' the General said.

'How much are we talking? Can you afford to lose?'

'What about ten Reichsmarks? Would that be enough to make it worthwhile?'

'Let's call it twenty Reichsmarks, but the winner nominates a charity of his choice that the loser has to donate to.'

'Done!' said the General. 'Right, just to make it fair, I'll stay down in the cabin. I'll instruct the Doc to steer and tell Dieter when to check the speed. We'll start from the next mark.'

Oskar sat back in the cockpit. The drizzle had faded to almost nothing but, if anything, the visibility had reduced further as a thick fog descended in its place.

'Listen everybody, we'll all have to keep our eyes open and our ears pricked for any ships. I'll be keeping her out of the main channel but there's no guarantee another small boat won't be doing the same. Shout to me when we pass the mark.'

He pointed ahead at the red port can appearing out of the mist, then disappeared below.

He handed up a small brass horn with a black rubber bulb on the end of its handle.

'Give that a squeeze every two minutes, Oskar,' he said. 'It lets everyone know we're here.'

As they passed the buoy, Dieter called down to him.

'That's the mark, General.'

'All right, Doc, steer zero-two-five degrees.'

He noted the start of his course on the chart, and checked that it cleared the point at Kitzberg, on the east shore, and that it kept them out of the main channel.

The longer they continued in the same direction, the more nervous Oskar and Dieter became. After a quarter of an hour, the General asked the former newspaperman to swing the lead, then watched him lower the weight over the side, counting the depth stops on the string until it hit the bottom.

'It's knotted in fathoms,' he said. 'It gives us an early warning if we're going aground but, because the depths are marked on the chart, it also helps us know where we are. Shout them out for me, Dieter.'

Dieter called out the soundings.

'Twenty fathoms.'

'Fifteen fathoms. Eleven fathoms.'

The yacht surged on.

'Eight fathoms. Six fathoms. Four fathoms.'

Oskar started looking over the side, anxiously.

'How much is a fathom?' he said.

'Just under two metres,' the General shouted up, unconcerned.

'Three fathoms,' shouted Dieter.

'It shouldn't go much lower,' the General said.

'Three fathoms.'

The boat continued to slice its way through the water. They could hear the sounds of the shore, close by, unseen.

'Two fathoms.' Dieter's voice rose a tone or two in pitch.

'Doc,' the General said, his hand reaching for the throttle.

'Yes?' the man on the tiller replied.

'Three fathoms,' Dieter called.

'Carry on, Doc,' the General called up. 'Zero-two-five degrees.'

'Four fathoms.'

The Doc smiled at Oskar.

'We know where we are, now. Almost perfect.'

'Six fathoms.'

'Thanks, Dieter. That will do for now. Can you check the log, please?'

Dieter stowed the lead line and took a reading with the trailing log.

'Five knots, Erich.'

'Thanks, Dieter. Doc, steer zero-three-five degrees.'

'Zero-three-five degrees.'

'You'll be on that course for twelve minutes. I'll call the next turn. It will be zero-one-zero.'

'Aye, skipper,' the Doc replied.

Oskar looked at the Doc and gave him a wan smile. He turned to Dieter.

'The old codger had balls, for sure,' he muttered. 'As for the General...'

Dieter said nothing, staring ahead into the fog, straining to listen.

'Anyone want a coffee?' the General shouted up. 'The kettle's just boiling.'

Oskar turned to the Doc.

'He's boiling the verdammte kettle while we're nearly on the shore?' he whispered. 'Is he mad?'

The Doc laughed.

'No, I don't believe so. He does some crazy things though.'

Dieter and Oskar looked at each other and shook their heads.

At the turn, the General repeated the course alteration, and the Doc brought her round.

'Five minutes,' he said.

They all peered forward.

'Keep your eyes peeled and listen out for ships,' the General told them. 'We're crossing the channel.'

'It's going to be a long five minutes,' Dieter whispered to Oskar, looking at his watch.

There wasn't a sound, other than the swish of the boat through the water and the soft thump of their own diesel engine.

'Dieter, have the lead line ready, would you?'

'Yes, skipper,' he said, unravelling the cord. He checked his watch again.

'Three minutes,' the General said.

'The mist is beginning to clear,' the Doc said.

They all peered ahead. Dieter thought he could see a glimmer of light in the mist in front of them, but it was difficult to tell.

'Two minutes.'

Dieter half got to his feet then sat down again.

Oskar strained to listen. He thought he detected a change in the sound of the engine, then wondered if he'd heard another boat.

'One minute.'

The boat broke out of the fog bank. A few hundred metres in front of them, the lighthouse shone green and white in the bright sunshine.

'Zero-four-five,' the General told his helmsman, poking his head out from the companionway.

As the boat swung round, two or three people, standing on the beach in front of the lighthouse, waved.

Dieter, feeling a little light-headed, waved back.

'Here, take these,' the General said.

Oskar sat open-mouthed as Erich Kästner passed out two steaming cups of coffee and bobbed back down for the other two. By the time he'd handed them up, and seated himself in the cockpit, the yacht had cleared the small spit of land that the lighthouse sat on, jutting out into Kieler Hafen.

'Steer zero-three-five, Doc, if you don't mind.'

'I can do that, Erich.'

The General handed the Doc his cup.

'Once you've finished your coffee, one of you can give the Doc a rest, and have a spell on the helm,' the General said to Oskar and Dieter.

'I'll have a go,' Dieter said. He'd never been out of Kieler Hafen before and already he could feel the slight swell of the open water under him.

Oskar finally broke his silence.

'I wouldn't have believed it if I hadn't seen it with my own eyes.'

'Me neither,' Dieter said.

'It was worth the twenty Reichsmarks just to see it,' Oskar said. 'Which charity do you wish the donation to go to?'

'Just the usual, Oskar. You know.'

Oskar smiled, and nodded.

'Where to, Erich?' the Doc asked.

'Well, there's no wind to speak of just now, but the fishermen are talking about easterlies over the next few days, so if we head towards Lübeck, there's a good chance we'll have a fair wind on the way back.'

He went down into the cabin and brought up the chart showing the area to the east of Kieler Hafen.

'We've another hour before we're clear of Kiel Fjord, then it's about twenty-five miles due east to Fehmarn.'

'I've been on Fehmarn a few times,' Oskar said. 'Never stopped there; always just jumping ferries on the way to Copenhagen on business.'

There were two ways to get to Copenhagen from Hamburg, or Kiel. The longer route, via Odense, only required one ferry trip, but was over 400 kilometres. The second was more than 100 kilometres shorter, but there were three ferry crossings involved. The third ferry, across Storstrøm, was soon to be replaced by a bridge, but it wasn't due to open until September.

'I thought you'd take the easy route,' the Doc said.

'I often do but, on occasion, I like the to indulge myself,' he said with a shrug. 'The child in me enjoys the ferry rides.'

He smiled and turned to the General. 'Where will we berth tonight? Lübeck?'

'No, it's too far. We'll tie up in Burgstaaken. It's on Fehmarn, not far from the ferry slip. It's a quiet little fishing harbour but they don't mind yachts lying alongside.'

'Is there a restaurant?' Oskar asked.

'Well, maybe that's pushing it a little. It's only a small place. If there's nowhere to eat, we can cook on the boat. We have beans, tinned ham and potatoes.'

Oskar groaned.

CHAPTER 115

A few miles away from the General and his friends' berth in Burgstaaken, in Reinhard and Lina Heydrich's summer home on the other side of the Fehmarn, Wilhelm Canaris nursed a glass of brandy, listening to the head of the Sicherheitsdienst and KriPo complain about his boss, the SS-Reichsführer, and how he was expected to put into place all the proposals Heinrich Himmler came up with.

The food had been superb; Reinhard Heydrich, a rising star in the Reich, always brought his own chef with him when he visited his house on Fehmarn, which he'd purchased on his elevation to high office in the NSDAP.

Canaris and his wife occasionally had dinner with the Heydrichs in Berlin; they were close neighbours, and the invitation to the house on Fehmarn had resulted from one of these dinner parties.

On the day, Erika had been forced to call off, one of the girls being sick, so the admiral had travelled alone. A few other high-ranking party members were present, and the evening was one of self-congratulation and mutual flattery, and toasts to the wonderful successes of the National Socialists.

Canaris realised why he'd been invited. The party was desperate to justify its actions to the Abwehr and, through it, to the Wehrmacht as a whole.

As the drink flowed, he was careful to limit his intake of alcohol, unlike most of the other guests. By engaging them in conversation and passing on his ready supply of mindless gossip, he was able to extract several useful pieces of information from them in return, which he filed away in his brain for future reference.

But it was tiring; both being civil to people he despised, and watching what he was saying, left him exhausted by eleven. He made his excuses and left the party not long after midnight. He was asleep by one.

~~o~~

The General sat on the coachroof, drinking his first coffee of the morning, watching the fishing boats leave for the day. Although they were all up by seven, there was no rush to leave.

'There doesn't seem to be much wind again today,' he told them. 'I was going to suggest going round the island, but without a breeze, it could be a bit of a slog, especially after yesterday's long motor, and the fact that we might all be feeling a little delicate this morning.'

He smiled.

'It was a wonderful evening,' the Doc said, 'despite the food. And do you know the best thing?'

'No, but you're going to tell us,' said Dieter.

'There were no politics.'

They all murmured their agreement.

'So, what are we going to do? Stay here?'

'No,' the General said, 'we're going to do some exploring.'

He could see he'd pricked their interest.

'On the south-west corner of the island, there's a small bay, two to three miles across, which looks interesting. It has a couple of small harbours in it, and wonderful wildlife, I'm told. I've never been in there, so it will be new to us all.'

~~o~~

Standing on the passenger deck of the ferry, Admiral Canaris was glad of the fresh air. The cloying adoration of Adolf Hitler, the single-minded addiction to the purity of the German race and the personal ambition of Heydrich and his friends had left him feeling claustrophobic and numb, and he'd been thankful to leave.

And their ready talk of expansion, and a greater Reich, had perturbed him.

His mind drifted to the conversation he'd had with Erich Kästner, only the week before.

'I'll make no excuses for being a patriot,' he'd said to the General. 'I want Germany to be strong again, *but within its borders*, and I hate communism and its creeping hypocrisy.'

'I know, Canaris, but we each have a great deal of respect for the English, especially their navy, and we both know that Germany, if it were to be drawn into another war with Britain at the present time, would nearly certainly lose.'

'You're right, but that's where we differ. In some respects, I admire the way the National Socialists have, in a few short years, torn up the Versailles treaty and discarded a raft of subsequent agreements designed to keep Germany on its knees.'

'I have no beef with that, but I suspect you're as uneasy as me at the steps they've taken to root out the unions, the Bolsheviks, the criminals and the so-called idle.'

'Drastic times require drastic measures, Kästner.'

The ferry had reached the halfway point and he came out of his reverie.

The day was windless and the only blemish on the surface was the ferry's wake. The sun, reflected on the glassy sea, almost blinded him, and it took a minute to glimpse the mast of a boat coming towards them.

By the time the ferry was berthing at the mainland, and the announcement on the tannoy advised passengers to make their way to their vehicles, the yacht was clearly visible, passing behind them through the sound of Fehmarn.

With a start, he realised that he recognised the boat; it was the General's. There were four people on board, but he was too far away to make out individual faces. Someone waved and, for a moment, as he waved back, he was envious.

He thought about his friend and smiled grimly. They differed in their beliefs but deep down, like the General, he knew he didn't trust the National Socialists, and he certainly didn't like them. And above all, he knew he could never be one of them.

He took a last glance of the yacht, motoring westwards.

He made a vow to himself to take time, and sail with the General and his friends, sometime soon, then turned and made his way aft to the stairs for the car deck.

~~o~~

Snowgoose made Heiligenhafen by mid-afternoon. The Orther Reede had been fascinating; they'd poked their noses into the two small harbours, Orth and Lemkenhafen, and they'd crept into the shallows behind Krummsteert, the long spit of grass-covered dunes that protected the west part of the bay and made it a haven for waterfowl and waders. They'd anchored within sight of the lighthouse, almost touching the bottom. Not another boat was in sight, and they could have been 1,000 miles from the nearest civilisation.

After a lunch of freshly caught fish, and bread, they headed across the short channel to the mainland.

Heiligenhafen was a bustling fishing port full of boats of all shapes and sizes. They found a space and tied up on the outside of a tan-sailed fishing smack.

The harbour, and the town behind it, had much more bustle about it. The four friends took the chance to stretch their legs as they strolled up the main street. The NSDAP office and the town hall were bedecked in swastika banners and national flags. It brought them sharply back to the present.

'Isn't it nice to be back in civilisation?' Dieter said, rolling his eyes, as they crossed Marktplatz.

'There aren't many places you can get away from this stuff,' the Doc said, staring at the banners hanging limp in the still air.

He turned to Oskar.

'How the hell can you be part of this?'

'Doc, keep your voice down,' Oskar said under his breath, gripping Hermann Speer's arm.

'That tells you something, when a party member warns you that saying something like that can get you in trouble.'

Oskar looked around and pointed to a bar, up one of the side streets that ran from the town square. It had a few tables outside, in the alleyway beside it.

He made for one of the tables, the furthest one from the street, and sat down, beckoning for the others to do the same.

'Are you sure this is discreet enough?' the General said, grinning.

Oskar shook his head.

'The less people who hear the Doc speaking like that, the better,' he said.

Hermann Speer bristled. He opened his mouth to reply, but Oskar held up his hand.

'Listen,' he said, 'I dislike all this Scheiße as much as you, but you can't do business in Germany nowadays without being a party member. Not good business, at least.'

'Do bad business then,' the Doc said. 'You'd still make a living, wouldn't you?'

'Doc, leave it,' the General said. 'Oskar's on the right side. Take it from me, I know.'

Oskar sighed.

'No, Erich. He's right. I made a choice.'

The barman came out and asked what they'd like to drink. They ordered four beers, and when the man had left, Oskar continued.

'Bad business means winning no contracts, laying off staff, closing factories, warehouses and putting good people out on the streets. And losing money.'

'If it's that bad, just sell up and get out,' the Doc said.

'It's not that simple. I joined when the party was just coming to power. To be honest, it looked as if they were trying to sort out all the problems which held business back. Unions, the communist threat, a morbid economy, a mass of unemployment that meant no one risked spending the little money they had. And for the first few years, things improved dramatically. The NSDAP government delivered. My staffing levels increased almost threefold, my profits shot up, and I was able to expand significantly.'

'So, the National Socialists have been good for you.'

'If I left the party now, what do you think would happen?'

The General interjected. 'Your businesses would fail, your employees would lose their jobs, and you might end up in a prison.'

'Yes. And believe it or not, the first two are more important to me. Anyway, I'm not as brave as you three.'

'We're not brave,' Dieter said.

'Yes, you are. You printed a scathing indictment of National Socialism in the *Morgenpost*. It got you sacked and it's a wonder you're still a free man. And as for you two,' Oskar said, nodding at the General and the Doc, 'you're forever mouthing off about the government, and the General here, is always trying to meddle, helping those affected by their policies and, more often than not, poking the National Socialists in the eye.'

He frowned.

'Sooner or later,' he continued, 'you're going to end up in one of these camps.'

'They wouldn't dare,' the General said. 'Anyway, if it happens, so be it.'

'You wouldn't say that if you knew what the camps are like,' Dieter said.

'You've seen one up close?' Oskar said, surprised.

'No, but I've talked to people who've been in them. The conditions for the inmates are appalling.'

'Listen,' the General said, 'I'm not going to end up in one, so you can strike that worry off your list.'

He turned to Hermann Speer.

'Doc,' he said, 'Oskar has helped me out on numerous occasions, and has taken risks to do so, so I don't think we can be too critical.'

'Thanks, Erich,' Oskar said, 'it's nice to know that not everyone is on my back.'

Dieter held up his hands. 'Not me. I'm one of those you helped.'

The Doc glared at them.

The barman arrived with the drinks, and nothing was said until he'd disappeared inside again.

'Oskar, I'm only saying these things because I'm your friend,' the Doc said, with an apologetic shrug.

'You've got a funny way of showing it sometimes.'

'Look, I just don't want you to get too deep into something you'll regret for the rest of your life.'

'I'll not. They all know I'm not a diehard supporter, but they value my shrewdness in business, and they quite rightly think Germany needs men like me to build the economy. It means they have to treat my sort of people with a degree of tolerance, providing we don't openly criticise them.'

'Oskar knows what he's doing,' General Kästner said.

'Just don't sell your soul to the devil,' the Doc said.

Back at the quayside, the atmosphere was a little strained but, sitting on the boat, watching the fishing smacks come and go, the warm day had a soporific effect on the four men. As each boat unloaded their catch, then filled up with ice before heading back out, the friends whiled the time away playing cards. By late afternoon, the Doc and Oskar were good again, their brief rift forgotten.

A few more yachts arrived, gravitating naturally towards the part of the harbour where *Snowgoose* was tied up. Good-natured introductions were made and loose arrangements to meet later in one of the town's taverns were voiced.

The last boat to berth was *Der Sturmtaucher*. It lay against another fishing boat fifty metres along the quay.

'That's Colonel Schneider's boat,' the General said. 'He's Franz and Johann's commanding officer. From Lübeck. The last time I saw it, he had it moored in Wangerooge.'

'That's near Wilhelmshaven, isn't it?' the Doc said.

'Yes, it's one of the Frisian Islands. We cruised there last year. He was stationed on the island. Pleasant fellow, and most hospitable.'

'It's an old-fashioned-looking boat,' Dieter said.

The General laughed.

'It's probably younger than *Snowgoose*, but it's much more of a traditional build. A man called Colin Archer designed them, and they were built as rescue boats for the wild seas of Norway.'

'He doesn't sound very Norwegian.'

'His father was Scottish, I believe.'

'It has two masts, and a strange-looking main sail,' Oskar said.

'It's a ketch. The second mast is a mizzen-mast. It divides the sail area up more evenly and balances the boat and the other sails don't need to be as large.'

'So, what's that extra boom on the mainsail?' Oskar asked.

'That's the gaff. It's a way of reducing the height of the mast, and therefore how strong it needs to be. The gaff is hoisted first, like an extension to the mast. It gives the sail a peculiar shape, but it's a rig that's been used for centuries, on working boats all over the world. The fishing boat we tied up against last night was gaff-rigged.'

'I've seen something like it on old sailing barges,' Dieter said. 'Remember the three that berthed in Kiel last year?'

'That's right,' the General said. They'd come over from the Netherlands, through the canal. Heading for Sweden, I think.'

'So why, in the days of modern rigs, would someone choose a boat like that?' the Doc said.

'Well, not everyone wants a boat that can race, like this one. His boat is an out-and-out cruising vessel, designed to be sea friendly and less tender than *Snowgoose*. All the sails are smaller and easier to handle, and he can use different combinations of sail for different conditions. The hull is heavier, with a deeper keel, so it holds its line better; it will practically steer itself. It all means it is much easier to sail short-handed, by either one or two people.'

'So, it's like a bus, rather than a sports car?'

'That's not a bad analogy, although a little unfair. It does sacrifice some speed, but in heavy conditions, it will be a much more comfortable boat to be in than this one. And it has a real connection with every working boat that sailed since man first put a mast on a dugout canoe and rigged a stretch of canvas from it.'

'It doesn't look as beautiful as some,' said Oskar.

'That, my friend, is in the eye of the beholder. Personally, I think it looks wonderful. And I'm sure Colonel Schneider will tell you why he chose it. Here he comes now,' the General said.

They watched as Colonel Schneider climbed off his boat and strode along the quay towards them.

'You couldn't take him for anything other than a military man,' Oskar said.

The General smiled. He wondered if people thought about him in the same way.

'General,' the colonel hailed him when he was twenty metres away.

'Colonel Schneider. It's great to see you. Come aboard.'

Oskar, Doc Speer, and Dieter shuffled over to make a space in the cockpit. Colonel Schneider stepped over the gunwale and the General made the introductions.

'Where are you headed, Colonel?'

'Oh, back to Lübeck tomorrow. Just one night away this time, I'm afraid. What about yourself?'

'We were in Burgstaaken last night. A lovely little place.'

'I've never been. There's nothing there.'

'Sometimes it's nice just to find somewhere peaceful,' the General said.

'I prefer somewhere you can get a good choice of eating places, preferably with some shops for the wife, if she's aboard, eh?'

'Your wife is accompanying you?' the General asked, laughing.

'No, not this time. I have a couple of my officers on board. You might know one of them,' he said, smiling.

'Franz? He's with you?'

The colonel shook his head. 'Johann,' he said. 'Franz is looking after the regiment!'

They all laughed.

'I'm joking,' he continued, 'but to be fair, he might just manage, for a few days at least.'

'Would you all like to join us this evening?' the General asked.

'I was about to ask you the same thing. We have a table booked at eight. I can tell them there are four more for dinner, if you like.'

The General turned to his friends, who nodded.

'Eight it is then.'

~~o~~

The colonel turned out to be as sociable as the General had predicted, and the three young officers injected an element of fun into the evening which extended into the small hours when they all decamped from the restaurant to *Snowgoose*'s cockpit and, as it became cooler, her main cabin.

It came with a heavy dose of patriotism.

'If the colonel is anything to go by, the army will support Adolf Hitler to the death,' the Doc said, once their guests had left, having emptied the General's bottle of rum in a series of toasts to the Heer, the Kriegsmarine, the Luftwaffe, the Führer, and bizarrely, the exiled Kaiser.

'There are thousands like him in the army. After all, Herr Hitler has given the Heer back its pride and restored its capabilities. Career army men don't see much past that. While our glorious leader uses the SS and the SA to do the dirty work, the army will be quite happy to fight his battles abroad, when he finally decides to act.'

'You think he'll take us to war?' Oskar asked.

'Yes. I do. I listened to Johann and his friends tonight. They're eager to get into a fight, and I despair. They don't know what's ahead of them.'

The Doc put his hand on the General's shoulder.

'We got through it. So will they.'

'We were the lucky ones,' the General said with a sigh. 'Too many of our comrades didn't make it.'

'I didn't fight, but I was a junior reporter at the time, and did one tour at the front,' Dieter said. 'It was hell on earth, and I was only there for a month.'

'I wouldn't have survived,' Oskar said. He had been too young for the draft, and even if he hadn't been, the General was sure that his father would have bought him out of it.

'You'd be surprised. You're a tough character, with a strong survival instinct.' The General glanced at Oskar and smiled. 'You might just have made it.'

'I'm certainly going to survive the next one if it comes. I'm fortunate to own several engineering companies, and that puts me on the list of reserved occupations.'

'I hope I'm past the age of conscription,' Dieter said.

'It depends on how bad a war it is,' the General said. 'We'll be the last to be called up, but when they get desperate, they'll come for the old ones.'

They all laughed.

Then Oskar spoke.

'I think Hitler will only enter a war if he knows he can win. He won't confront France, England, or the Americans, but he'll nibble away at territories which we have some sort of claim on. And he'll sit back and wait, watching how the world reacts.'

The General was impressed. It was almost identical to his own line of thinking.

'And in the meantime,' the General added, 'the army, the navy and the air force will be growing all the time, and no one will want to stand up against him.'

'Here's to peace!' Dieter Maas said, raising his glass.

They all did the same. 'Peace.'

CHAPTER 116

[25/04/1937 Sunday]

The encounter couldn't have been engineered if they'd tried. With the boat tied up in Kiel, their bags on the promenade at the shore end of the jetty, the General's three friends shook his hand and thanked him for a great trip.

'At least we got a decent sail on the way back,' the General said, pleased that the wind had got up, and from the east, as predicted.

They hadn't flown the spinnaker; it was a little gusty for it, but they'd run goose-winged all the way home, with the foresail poled out on the opposite side from the main, surfing down the swell that grew steadily behind them as the day went on.

It wasn't until they'd turned southwards into Kieler Förde that Oskar had commented on just how strong the wind was.

'While we were sailing downwind, we were travelling with it,' the General had explained. 'Now that it's on our beam, we are feeling its true speed, but it is still comfortable, and it's the fastest point of sail. Colonel Schneider's boat, thrashing into the wind and the waves, will have had a much harder time tacking upwind until they rounded the headland and were able to sail southwards.'

'I'm glad the wind wasn't coming from the west then,' Dieter had said.

'We wouldn't even be halfway by now,' Doc Speer had said, the only one of the crew with any experience of passage-making.

Once in the shelter of Kieler Förde, the waves had died, and they'd scudded along the last few miles to the General's berth.

Standing on the jetty, it was Oskar who noticed the Böhm family first. No more than 100 metres away, they were walking along the promenade from Kiel in the direction of Wik. Beate and Lise walked together, arms linked, and behind them, Eberhard Böhm Senior and Lise's brother, Eberhard, in his Hitlerjugend uniform, strolled with a young SS officer, deep in conversation.

Oskar nudged the Doc, who looked up and grimaced.

'Verdammt,' he said, under his breath.

~~o~~

By now, Beate Böhm had spotted the General and his friends, and stopped.

She turned around and spoke sharply to her husband, whose head jerked up and looked towards the General.

Seeing the four men, Eberhard Böhm's first instinct was to smile; three of them were long-standing friends of his, after all, and, if his wife or daughter hadn't been present, he would have acknowledged them as usual, despite the awkwardness between the two families.

But, realising that his wife and his daughter were watching him, he frowned, wiping any remnant of a smile from his face.

He reddened, realising that there was no way, other than turning round, of avoiding the group standing on the jetty and it would have been a severe breach of social etiquette to walk by and completely ignore his fellow Rotarians, so he walked past his wife, and stopped as he reached the four men.

He greeted them with as little enthusiasm as he could muster.

'Good afternoon to you, too, Eberhard,' the General said, taking the sting out of the situation by being the first to respond.

The three others murmured their greetings.

'Were you racing today?' Eberhard Böhm asked.

'No, we were away for a weekend cruise,' Doc Speer replied. 'Just as far as Fehmarn and Heiligenhafen, but it was a most enjoyable trip.'

'It sounds exciting.'

'It was, although the wind was poor until today.'

Beate and Lise had held back from coming across, but Eberhard Junior and the young SS officer had come to a halt next to Lise's father.

'My son Eberhard, who most of you have met.'

The four men shook the young man's hand.

'And this is SS-Untersturmführer Rudolf Mey, a family friend.'

The young SS officer stepped forward, clicked his heels, and saluted.

'Heil Hitler,' he said.

'Heil Hitler,' Oskar said, returning his salute.

The young SS officer frowned.

Dieter and the Doc reluctantly mumbled the required response and raised their right hands in a perfunctory manner.

The SS man glared at the General who, in civilian clothes, had no need to salute anyone.

'Well, we must be going,' the older Eberhard Böhm said, and with a brief nod, walked towards his wife and daughter, who turned and continued along the promenade. Young Eberhard and the SS man followed them.

~~o~~

'Phewww.' Dieter let out a breath. 'That was awkward,' he said.

He knew about Franz and Lise's break-up; even if the General hadn't already confided in him, it was the talk of Kiel.

'It shouldn't be,' the General said. 'Eberhard Böhm is an old friend of ours and, despite the problems the split up of my son and his daughter have caused between Eberhard and I, there's no reason for the Doc and Oskar's friendship with him to change. I'm happy to have Eberhard Böhm as a friend; it's entirely up to him how he wants to deal with it and, so far, that has been with dignity.'

He sighed. 'It must be difficult for him,' he added. 'I'm sure his wife and daughter will put pressure on him to have nothing to do with me, and most likely, the Rotary Club. But there's nothing I can do about that.'

'That's if there is a Rotary Club for much longer; here, at least,' Oskar said.

'Oh,' said the Doc. 'Have the NSDAP banned us as a political organisation?'

'No, I was talking to one of my business contacts, who is in the Dresden branch of the Rotary. They've been told that the organisation in the United States and Britain are considering the appropriateness of having part of their organisation in National Socialist Germany.'

The General whistled. 'It shouldn't be a shock. There's been some disquiet for a while from abroad. I must contact Marcus Klein. He's the head of the Rotary Club in Germany.'

'The honourable thing to do would be to dissolve the German Rotary clubs voluntarily, before we're asked to leave,' the Doc said.

The General and Oskar nodded their heads.

'It will be a sad day for us all,' Oskar said.

'And even sadder for some of the charities we support,' the General said.

~~o~~

'Did you have to be so pleasant to them. You'd think you wanted to remain friends,' Beate Böhm's voice hissed in her husband's ear.

'I still have to work with them at the Rotary Club,' Eberhard said, head bowed.

'You should resign,' Beate said.

'Do you think so?' her husband said, genuinely surprised at her suggestion.

'Yes, I do. I presumed you would do that anyway. General Kästner is the president, is he not?' She lowered her voice, conscious of Rudolf walking behind them. 'Have you forgotten what his son did to your daughter?'

He glanced across at Lise, who gave him a withering look.

'No,' he said. 'It's just that...'

'It's just what?' Beate said, venom still sharpening her voice.

'Well, I was due to become president next year.'

A strange look came over his wife's face and she took a few seconds to consider his words.

'Perhaps you shouldn't be too hasty,' she said. 'You deserve to be president, and we'd make damn sure that you'd be more successful than that man has been, and support more deserving causes too.'

Eberhard Böhm's heart sank. Becoming president of the Rotary Club was a position he'd always aspired to, but he winced at the thought of his wife becoming involved, even in the background.

'I'll think about it,' he said, wondering which choice had the worst pitfalls.

'Did you see them when Rudolf saluted?' Lise interjected. 'Herr von Friedeburg was the only one who returned it with any enthusiasm. The General didn't salute at all, just like his son,' she added with a sneer.

'To be fair, the General was out of uniform,' Eberhard Junior said. 'He wouldn't normally return a salute. It was in a book I read about the Reichswehr.'

'Be quiet, Eberhard, whose side are you on?' his mother snapped. 'It's ridiculous. Any true German citizen would have responded. The whole family are no worse than anarchists.'

Young Eberhard flinched and looked away from his mother's icy stare.

Support came from an unlikely quarter.

'Young Eberhard is technically right,' the SS-Untersturmführer interrupted.

Beate Böhm's head jerked round and Lise glared at him. He lowered his eyes.

'But it's still most disrespectful to the Führer,' he mumbled.

Eberhard Senior felt a little sorry for the young man's abject embarrassment.

'Well, I think it's shocking,' Beate said, 'and I hope that family get their comeuppance someday.'

The Böhm family walked on in silence, the three men following the two women, watched by the General, a puzzled look on his face.

~~o~~

On the way home, the General thought back to the encounter with the Böhms. The young SS officer perplexed him. He'd never heard Eberhard mention him before, and it was the sort of thing his neighbour would have brought up, even if only to impress him.

After they'd dropped Dieter off, he tapped on the glass screen between him and the front seat.

Yosef slid the window across.

'Yes, sir?'

'Did Eberhard Böhm ever mention a young SS officer?'

Yosef's face blanched a little and the General, seeing his alarm in the mirror, hurried to reassure him.

'Don't worry, it's nothing to do with you. He was with the Böhms today, and Eberhard said that he was a friend of the family.'

'I can't recall Herr Böhm ever mentioning him,' Yosef said. 'I would have remembered,' he added.

'And neither yourself nor Miriam has seen him around next door?'

'Again, sir, it would have stuck in our minds.'

'I suppose so. Not to worry.'

'When did you bump into them, sir?' Yosef asked.

'Just before you arrived to pick us up; they were taking a walk along the promenade.'

'That must have been a little awkward, sir.'

'If it had only been Eberhard, and his boy, I think it would have been fine but with Lise and her mother present, I sensed a definite frost in the air.'

Yosef laughed, and the General joined in.

He sat back as the car rolled along Hamburger Chaussee. Just as it turned into the driveway of the Drachensee house, it came to him.

The young SS officer is going out with Lise!

Suddenly, it all made sense, and he wondered how long the relationship had been going on. If it was more than a few weeks, Lise certainly hadn't wasted any time pining for Franz.

Do I tell him? he thought.

Not until I'm 100 per cent sure.

CHAPTER 117

[26/04/1937 Monday]

'I hope Franz telephones today,' Maria Kästner said. 'I wanted to wish him happy birthday and find out who he wants to invite on Friday.'

'I spoke to Johann at the weekend,' the General replied. 'He was sailing with Colonel Schneider. He says that Franz doesn't want a fuss for his birthday.'

'It's his twenty-first. We must have a party. I've already said to a few people.'

'Maria, just have family over. The boy's still hurting over Lise. Johann is quite worried about him. The last thing he needs is a whole houseful of people asking how he is.'

'But…'

He shook his head.

'Johann told me that Franz is miserable,' he said, 'and, apart from throwing himself into his work with a manic intensity, he does nothing but eat and sleep. Even his friends can't get him to snap out of it.'

'It's that little hussy next door who's to blame. I know Franz can be stubborn when he wants to be, and his views on the National Socialists are almost as dangerous as yours, but there was more to it than that.'

The General knew that his wife blamed him for Franz's dislike of the NSDAP, but she'd never said it outright. He toyed with the idea of telling his wife about his suspicions that Lise had a new boyfriend but decided against it.

'Maria, I'm sure that there were faults on both sides, but the bottom line is that she's a clone of her mother, with her inherent hatred of everyone who's not like them, and a sickening sense of racial superiority.'

'But nearly everyone agrees with her. You've no idea how difficult it is when people say that you and Franz are somehow anti-German.'

'We are not against Germany, just the way its government and its citizens are acting. Anyway, this isn't sorting out Friday evening.'

She opened her mouth to argue with him, then shook her head.

'If he's that unhappy, I'll just invite your mother and father, and my mother. Johann will surely come home too.'

'Yes, the colonel said the boys would both be on leave this weekend. And Johann confirmed that he'd come, although he did say that he might have something on the next day, so he may not stay over.'

'Of course he'll stay,' Maria said, 'it would be ludicrous for him to leave the same evening. He can just get up early and go where he needs to go.'

From what Johann had hinted, the General deduced that he was intending to meet up with a girl he'd met the last time he was home after making an appearance at the Drachensee house for Franz's birthday. He was sure his youngest son didn't intend to return home that evening.

He kept his suspicions to himself.

'You can talk to him when he arrives,' he said. 'I wouldn't be too hopeful though.'

'Sometimes I wonder what this family is coming to,' Maria huffed, as she left the room.

~~o~~

[01/05/1937 Saturday]

Although it was just family, Maria had made sure everything was just so for her oldest son's birthday. Miriam had slaved most of the day preparing food and, the day before, the Nussbaums had cleaned the house from top to bottom, Miriam doing the inside, Yosef cleaning the windows and making sure the garden was perfect.

The General stayed in his study, out of the way.

Franz and Johann arrived mid-afternoon and, despite Maria's protests, Johann insisted that he could only stay until eight.

'I just couldn't get out of it, Mother,' he said, using the lost-boy look he'd perfected to his advantage, 'Major Breit is having an evening for all his junior officers in the mess, and it was made quite clear that our attendance was not optional. I'll probably still be confined to barracks for being late, but I couldn't miss my older brother's coming of age.'

The blatant lie hardly raised a smile with Franz, even though he knew that Johann was using the excuse to cover up a tryst he had arranged with his latest conquest. He'd told him on the way over that 'tonight was the night' and that, with apologies, he wouldn't be passing up the chance of exploring her glorious body for anybody's birthday, even if it was his brother's.

'Oh, at least you came, darling,' Maria said. 'I hope you don't get in too much trouble.'

Franz, as always, marvelled at how Johann always got away with it, turning a potential pitfall on its head, and earning praise for it.

Maria turned to Franz. It was what he had been dreading.

'How's my Franz,' she said, wrapping her arms around him. 'I hear you've been terribly down about your break-up with Lise.'

'I'll be all right, Mother,' Franz replied. He knew that she loved him, and she had only his interests at heart, but he couldn't face a protracted post-mortem of his failed engagement. 'I just want to put it behind me.'

'That's the best thing to do,' she said, 'but what in heaven's name happened to you two? You looked wonderful together.'

'I know. I thought we had something special. But it wasn't to be.'

'Looking back, there was something about her that was just too good to be true, don't you think?'

'I'm sure Franz would like to get his things upstairs,' the General interrupted. 'Then we can all have a drink.'

Franz flashed his father a quick look of gratitude.

'Yes, I could do with a wash. I was officer of the guard last night, and I didn't get a chance to shower before leaving.'

He headed up the stairs. The General saw the leaden footsteps and the hunched shoulders, and his heart went out to his son. He turned to Maria.

'Just give him a little time. He'll open up to us when he's ready.'

'I know,' she said, 'it's just so hard to see him like that, and it would help to know what went on.'

'All we need to do is be there for him and, if he wants to, he'll talk to us.'

The kitchen door opened, and Miriam came out.

'Sorry to interrupt, ma'am, but how do you want the dessert served tonight?'

Tutting, Maria walked into the kitchen with Miriam, and the General listened for a few minutes as she explained exactly how she wanted the dishes to look.

The General smiled. Miriam knew well enough how her employer liked the dish served.

CHAPTER 118

[17/05/1937 Monday]

Miriam looked at the envelope. It had a strange postmark.

```
Haifa
Palestine.
```

She ripped it open and recognised Esther's neat handwriting.

Afula,

3rd May

Dear Miriam,

We arrived safely after a ghastly journey, but at least Itsik was there to meet us at the port, thank God. I don't know what I'd have done if he hadn't been there!

Palestine is hot and dry, but there's often a breeze. The house is small. Itsik says we will build our own larger house in a few years but, in the meantime, it is difficult with two families sharing three rooms.

We live in Afula, and Itsik's shop is here too. It is about 20 miles (that's 32km) inland from Haifa, the main port. It is not much of a town; just a large village, with nothing in it but a few basic shops. Itsik says it is expanding quickly and will be a wonderful town one day. The countryside around is very barren, but a few settlers are planting trees and digging ponds. Water is scarce. It only runs for a few hours a day and the privy is basic, although Itsik has promised to make a new one. We have to bathe with a bowl in the kitchen, which is cramped.

Land here is much cheaper than in Haifa so we'll have room to build once we can afford it.

The shop is small, but the land goes back a long way, so he can add to it as we need more space. Itsik is finding it difficult to get stock for the shop imported into Palestine, so he spends much of his time in Haifa, talking to importers. His contacts in Germany have been a lifesaver, and he's hoping to get a shipment of goods very soon. It's ironic that the German government are so keen for companies to export to Palestine to earn foreign currency.

Itsik is also looking to buy a shop in Haifa, with an apartment above it. His brother, Abel, will run it and Itsik will give him a share in it. Once Abel and Leah move to Haifa, it will make things easier.

The children go to school in the village, next to the synagogue. It sounds grander than it really is; both are just one-room buildings next to each other. There are nearly 100 children at the school, so they use the synagogue as an extra classroom, but all the children are Jewish! Moshe has settled in well, but he misses Manny and Fischel. He seems to have made a few friends already though.

There aren't many shops. Rosa would hate it here! Even those in Haifa are poor. I've heard you need to go to Tel Aviv to find shops like the ones in Germany, but although it's less than 100km away, the roads aren't like ours, and some parts aren't very safe.

I've written to Rosa too. I miss you both terribly. The ladies are nice here but it's just not the same. I'm awfully homesick for Kiel, too, and I miss Itsik's parents more than I ever imagined I would. I wish they could come but there's no room for them yet.

All my love,

Esther

P.S. there's a letter for Manny too, from Moshe.

Miriam folded the letter and returned it to its envelope. She would read it again later. She tucked the second letter into her apron for Manny, when he came in from school. She was delighted that Moshe had written to him, hoping it would pull her son out of the mood he was in. She would have loved to have known what he'd written.

She would reply to Esther when the children were in bed.

~~o~~

3rd May

Manny,

Mama said if I wrote you a letter, she would post it with hers.

Wow! The journey was ace. We were on the train forever through Czechoslovakia, Hungary, and Yugoslavia to Greece, then we got on a big steamer ship that took us to Haifa. We had a storm halfway there and Mama took ill, but I looked after her. Papa met us at Haifa.

We live in Afula. It's like a place in a cowboy film. Small white houses with flat roofs and big mountains and lots of desert. There aren't many trees and green fields, unlike Germany. Arab men wear funny scarf things on their heads and the women hide their faces, even the young girls. I don't think they like us much. There is sometimes a little trouble here, but it feels better than at home.

School is great. There are no Gentiles. Everyone gets on well except for one boy who tried to hit me. I punched him back. My Hebrew is coming on well.

I joined the football club. It has three teams, and we are the youngest. They also have classes for settlement defence. Some of the older boys practise with guns. One day, I will do that too, but don't tell your mama that.

They told us we were part of the Diaspora. That's Jews who left Palestine long ago, but now we're the Aliyah, those coming back home. They told us to tell as many Jews to come here as possible.

Mama sometimes cries. I think she misses Kiel, and your mama.

Your best friend,

Moshe

~~o~~

[23/05/1937 Sunday]

Ruth's fourteenth birthday was a very muted affair. Instead of the usual small party at Drachensee, the Nussbaums decided to visit Miriam's parents in Altona.

It surprised Yosef just how hard Esther's departure had hit Miriam, but he supposed that he should have known. They'd been childhood companions and, by luck, had ended up living in the same city, carrying on a lifetime's friendship.

They shared a lot; both were older mothers; Esther had even been taken for Shoshana's grandmother once, to her deep embarrassment, and to Miriam's and Rosa's amusement.

'I'm a heel, running off to Altona and leaving Rosa in the lurch,' Miriam said.

'Rosa will understand,' Yosef reassured his wife. Miriam had been a little nervous about travelling by train, but it was by far the easiest way to get there.

'I know, but it still isn't right. I should have just stayed and invited her and the children over, and a couple of Ruth's friends, but I just couldn't face it without Esther.'

'You can have Rosa over during the week. I'll take the children somewhere and you two can have a good heart to heart.'

She smiled at him.

'It doesn't matter about the children. Ruth and Rebeka look after themselves and the boys disappear into the bushes, so we hardly see them.'

'You really miss Esther, don't you?' he said, watching the green countryside fly past the train window.

'It's like part of me has been chopped off. It's silly, but I feel that something is going to happen to her, that I'll never see her again.'

Yosef shivered.

'Don't say that. It might take a while, but I'm sure it won't be forever.'

He hesitated.

'We could follow them out there.'

'No. As much as I love Esther, it sounds like hell. I'm too old to be living in a frontier town, with shootings and army patrols and the like. We'd always be looking over our shoulders.'

'The cities would be different. Did Esther not say that Abel was going to live in Haifa, and that it was better there.'

'No, she thought it was a dump compared with Kiel. She says that Tel Aviv is supposed to be nice though.'

'Well, we could go there then. If the schools are good...'

'We'd be just as bad over there, missing a whole different group of people, and judging from what Esther says, travel around Palestine isn't always easy, so I'd see little of her anyway.'

'Well, have a think about it.'

Ruth and Manny appeared.

'Did you find the toilet?' Yosef asked.

'Yes, Papa. It's only at the end of the carriage.'

It had taken all his willpower not to accompany them. Ruth was old enough to look after her little brother, but he knew that, on a train, there could be snap identity-card inspections. It wouldn't do to be separated, but he'd let them go, knowing that he was being overcautious.

He wondered how long it would be before he could stop thinking that way.

CHAPTER 119

[09/06/1937 Wednesday]

The telephone rang, and the General picked it up.

'It's Herr von Friedeburg for you, sir.'

He waited for the measured tones of his friend to come on the line.

'Erich, how are you?'

'Very well. And you?'

'In the rudest of health. I sometimes wonder why I've been so blessed.'

He laughed.

'What can I do for you, Oskar?'

'Ah. It's more like what I can do for you. You asked me the other day if I could make a few enquiries about a certain young lady and an SS soldier.'

'Yes, I remember.'

'Well, it seems they are an item, and have been for some time, but they kept it under wraps.'

'Some time, you say?'

'Before Christmas, at a Hitlerjugend rally, I believe.'

'Thanks, Oskar. I don't know if it will help, but it might.'

'You do know what they call the BDM, don't you?' Oskar said. The General could detect a note of amusement in his friend's voice.

'No,' he said, smiling, 'but I'm sure you're going to tell me that it's not the Bund Deutscher Mädel.' *The League of German Girls.*

'No. They're calling it the Bund Deutscher Matratzen,' Oskar said.

Erich Kästner guffawed. *The League of German Mattresses.*

He heard his friend laugh too.

'Thank you, Oskar. I needed a smile.'

They spoke for a few minutes more, before hanging up.

The General, satisfied that he'd been right, wondered what to do with the information.

Esther tore open the letter and read it quickly, drinking in the first words from home. It had been nearly six weeks since she'd written. After she finished, she read it again, slower this time.

18th May

Drachensee, Kiel.

My dearest Esther,

I'm sorry it has taken so long to respond. I didn't get your mail until yesterday. It seems that the postal service from Palestine is not the fastest.

It was so good to hear from you. I'd been so worried; I didn't know if you'd got there safely so it was a relief to receive your letter.

It sounds as if you are beginning to settle in. It will always be strange at first, especially living in less than ideal conditions. I'm sure you'll feel better once Itsik's parents arrive.

It has been a bit misty and damp here, so your constant sunshine sounds wonderful, and it seems as if Itsik and Abel have a great opportunity to do well, especially if the place is growing at such a fast rate.

No shops, no bath, and a primitive toilet! Rosa would die, but I'm sure Itsik will make it a priority to build a wonderful new home for you all.

I'm glad Moshe has settled in so well at school. Manny says that Moshe is now in a football team, so he will have a raft of friends in no time at all, and Shoshana will be the same, starting school soon. I'm sure you will also make friends before long; give it time. Once you get to know some of the mothers, I'm sure they'll be very supportive. Remember that most of them will have been through the same thing as you.

We miss you badly. I have to put up with all Rosa's curses and moans on my own now. I don't really mean that; she has been a rock since you left, as I have found it impossibly hard without you.

Life here is much the same. Ruth, Manny, and Rosa's two get a tough time at school, but they don't complain. Reading the newspapers is depressing; there's something new every week to worry us. You did the right thing by going.

Yosef asks after Itsik and was fascinated to hear all his news. Tell him that the new manager is making a decent job of the store, and that Oskar von Friedeburg keeps a close eye on it.

One day, we will be able to visit you, and see each other again.

Until that time, you are always in my thoughts,

Miriam

~~o~~

Moshe,

Palestine sounds amazing. Have you had much chance to explore? Are there caves? And horses?

You're learning so much stuff over there. I wish I could come but Mama and Papa would say no.

They ganged up on Fischel at school and pulled his trousers down and threw pebbles at his thingy. They said it had lost its hat, but I don't know what they meant. I tried to stop them, but I got pretty beat up but not before I'd hit a couple of them and then a teacher came out and stopped it, but he was laughing all the same.

That's all folks, as they say in the cartoons.

Ha ha.

Manny.

CHAPTER 120

Afula,

11th June

Dear Miriam,

I loved reading your letter. It made me cry just to hear from you. I'm sorry that Manny and Ruth are finding it tough at school. The schools here are so refreshing and yes, Moshe has joined a local football club. It feels like freedom after the last few years.

Itsik has also bought a small shop in Haifa, with an apartment. It's in Derekh Yafo, in the heart of the commercial area of the city. Abel is keen to start and, when Abel and Leah move to Haifa, we will have more space, although we will miss them. They will visit us every Shabbat though. Itsik's parents are coming over once Abel and Leah move out, so we won't have the house to ourselves for long, but I am looking forward to seeing them again.

The Arabs are revolting! I don't mean they're disgusting, although some of them are. They're rebelling against British rule and protesting about Jewish immigration. Itsik says it has died down a lot and that it was mainly strikes and political demonstrations. Some of the Arabs are rude and surly when we go into Haifa but here, in Afula, they are friendly enough and, anyway, most of our neighbours are Jewish, like us.

Having said all that, Itsik has an Arab driver who works for him – he knows all the roads and the areas not to go, and his wife is very pleasant. They live in the village too. We will also employ Arab labour when we start the new house.

I am going for lunch with a few of the ladies whose sons are in Moshe's class but I'm a little worried. They are all so happy here and deeply zealous about Palestine. They all look as if they work in the fields all day even though most of them don't.

Once we have a new house you would be more than welcome to come and visit. It would be too cramped at present.

All my love,

Esther.

Esther sealed the small envelope and placed it in a larger one, with Miriam's address on it.

'Moshe,' she yelled, 'have you finished writing to Manny yet? I'm posting my letter to Miriam.'

'No, Mama. I'll do it tomorrow.'

'No-you-will-not, Moshe Weichmann. You will sit down and do it now.'

Moshe, grumbling under his breath, did as he was told. Five minutes later, he handed her his sealed envelope.

CHAPTER 121

Memo: Geh.KdoS. ABW 12/06/37 CAC0562.1

For Attention Only: All senior executive officers, Abwehr.

From: Rear Admiral Wilhelm Canaris, Chef der Abwehr.

Reports are emerging that soviet leader Josef Stalin has instigated a purge of Red Army generals.

On June 11, a special military tribunal of the Soviet Supreme Court was convened to try Mikhail Tukhachevsky, Marshal of the Soviet Union for treason. Eight Red Army generals will stand trial with him.

There have also been a series of arrests across the Union of Soviet Republics within the Communist Party itself. It is not known if these are connected.

It is not expected to impinge on the current dialogue between Josef Stalin and Adolf Hitler. [END]

~~o~~

[12/06/1937 Saturday]

20th May 1937

Afula, Palestine.

Herr von Friedeburg,

You asked me to write to you, keeping you informed of our progress in Palestine. We have settled here well. I have purchased a house and a shop in Afula, a small town inland from Haifa, the main port. There are no hardware shops here, so I am hopeful that we will do well. So far, it has been encouraging, even with the limited stock we've been able to get hold of. Everyone is building houses or developing land, so they'll always need hardware.

I have also purchased a small shop in Haifa itself, for my brother and me. It has a small apartment above it for him and his wife to live in, and they both run the shop.

I am struggling to get enough stock, but my previous suppliers in Germany are doing their best to try and arrange shipments.

Our son has settled well into school, and my daughter will go next year, when she is old enough.

My parents are coming out within the next month or so, and we have you to thank for all of this. Without your help, we wouldn't have had this chance. You will forever have the gratitude of our family.

Itsik Weichmann

~~o~~

[12/07/1937 Monday]

'There's a letter here for you, Manny.'

    'Did you get one too, Mama?'

    'Yes, Esther wrote to me. They're beginning to settle in, but it sounds very primitive.'

Manny opened his letter and quickly read it.

Manny,

Thanks for your letter. I'm just going to play football.

When I'm not kicking a ball, I help Papa in the shop. I even went to Haifa one day with him, to the new shop, and down to the port. It was so-oo exciting, seeing all the big ships. It reminded me of Kiel, but smaller.

I hope you and Fischel are doing well. Sorry about your beating. You should emigrate here. It's the best ever. Ask your parents if you can come. My mama and papa could look after you.

There are lots of caves, but they won't let us leave the village because of Arab bandits. There are also soldiers here, and we heard shots, once, in the night.

Moshe.

'It's only short,' he told his mother. 'He says it's great and that we should come too.'

    'You know we can't. Perhaps one day we can visit them.'

    'I could go and stay with Moshe.'

    'Don't be silly. Anyway, would you really want to leave us?'

    Manny stared at her, then looked away.

    'No,' he said, 'I suppose not. But at least we wouldn't get made fun of at school over there.'

    'Things will get better here,' she said.

CHAPTER 122

[14/07/1937 Wednesday]

'Tell him, lads. Tell him he's mad.'

'We've tried, Johann,' Maximilian Grabner replied, looking sadly at Franz, wedged between himself and Johann. 'Believe me, we've tried.'

Artur Schweitzer, Heinrich Öhlman, and Fritz Aumeier sat on the opposite side of the table shaking their heads.

The six young officers had located a table right at the back of the bar, not far from their current billet in Neumünster barracks.

'Leave me alone, you lot. I don't know why I came,' Franz said.

'We kidnapped you, that's why. It was the only way we could get you here to talk some sense into you.'

Franz made to get up, but Johann and Maxi each put a restraining hand on his shoulders and sat him back down.

'This has gone on long enough,' Johann said.

'We're your best friends,' Fritz Aumeier said, 'apart from Johann, obviously, who's your brother…'

'Get on with it, you fool,' Maxi said.

'All right, all right,' Fritz said. 'We're worried about you. We just want to help.'

'Most of us can't understand what you've gone through, because we get dumped by women all the time, or we dump them, but Artur has been in love once, and he says it can be painful.'

Fritz looked at Franz.

'For a few days,' he added brutally, 'but not for a whole year.'

'You don't understand,' Franz said.

'You're right, we don't,' Heinrich agreed, 'which is why it's difficult for us to help you. But we're going to try.'

'We're not letting you out of here until you've explained it to us,' said Maxi, and the others all nodded solemnly.

'I can't explain it, it's just the way I feel.' He looked around at them. They were his friends, and he knew they were trying to help, in their own way.

'Try,' Johann said.

'I really loved her,' he said angrily.

'We know. But you can't go on pining for her. You know she's moved on, don't you?' Johann said.

Franz, who'd bowed his head, looked up. 'How did you know?'

'Father told me,' Johann said. 'Did he tell you, too?'

Franz shook his head.

'I saw her,' he said. 'With him. In Hamburg. She didn't see me.'

'Well. There you are. There's no point in letting her ruin your life, is there?'

'I suppose not, but I just can't talk about it, can you understand that?'

'We can,' Fritz said. 'You don't have to tell us anything, unless you want to, but just have a drink and a laugh. Put her out of your mind for a little while. We're not letting you back to barracks until you do, even if we all have to go AWOL.'

'This is insubordination,' Franz said. 'I'm a captain and you're all first lieutenants.'

They all sat stunned for a second. Then a hint of a smile appeared at the corner of Franz's mouth.

'You bastard,' Heinrich Öhlman said, as they all started laughing. 'You were leading us on?'

For the first time in nearly a year, Franz joined in.

'I thought I'd play you along for a while tonight,' he said.

'So now he finds something funny,' Artur Schweitzer complained.

'I always find you funny,' Franz said. 'I just wasn't in the mood to smile.'

'A round of Schnapps,' Maxi shouted.

'A double round!' Johann yelled, louder.

The barman heard and nodded, reaching for the bottle and a dozen glasses.

'So, you feel better now, really?'

'No, but I suddenly realised that you're right. There's no point in locking myself away.'

He looked around at them. Apart from his family, they were the closest people to him.

'It still hurts, and don't expect me to act like a clown the way you all do, but I'll try my best.'

They all beamed at him. Johann thought he saw a tear in his brother's eye but, just when he began to worry that Franz was going to give in to his emotions, the barman arrived with a tray loaded with the Schnapps.

'Here you are, gentlemen,' the barman said, placing it on the table.

Johann and Maxi handed out the small tumblers, two to a man.

'To love!' Maxi shouted, and they all downed the first glass.

'To friendship!' Johann bellowed.

The empty glasses rattled simultaneously on the table.

'Herr Ober, mehr Bier bitte,' Artur said, as the man gathered the glasses on to the tray.

He smiled at them, knowing that a table like this encouraged everyone in the bar to drink.

More beer, indeed.

~~o~~

The noise in the bar grew louder. Johann listened to their friends good-natured ribbing about the respective merits of each of their units, and he tapped his brother on the shoulder.

'Let mother and father know you're over the worst. They were worried, you know.'

'I know. I just couldn't face their sympathy, and mother's questions. I'll go and see them.'

'And don't let her put you off women.'

Franz started to protest, but Johann held up his hand.

'I know you're not like me. Or the rest of them. But one day you'll find someone to fall in love with again. In the meantime, why don't you just enjoy women for what they are?'

'And what's that, Herr Expert?'

'They're beautiful, desirable and there are too many of them for one man,' Johann said, and Franz laughed.

'I can't treat them like you do,' he said, 'and anyway, I'm definitely not ready for another relationship yet.'

'You should take a trip to *Dänemark*,' Johann said, smiling.

Franz looked at him, a puzzled expression on his face.

'How did you know?'

'Maxi told me. We were talking in the bar one night, and he complained that it was such a waste that women seemed to be drawn to you, not to him, when he was always available and eternally grateful, if only they took the time to find out.'

Franz laughed.

'He said that there was this one girl in Sønderborg,' he continued, 'when you all sailed to Denmark. He said she was out of this world. Those were his exact words.'

'She was a lovely girl,' Franz said.

'So, if you're ever there again, just remember you're single.'

'I'll probably never be back. And she'll be gone now, anyway.'

'That's not my point,' Johann said, irritably. 'It could be any girl.'
'Not for me it couldn't,' Franz said.

~~o~~

[15/07/1937 Thursday]

KIELER JÜDISCHES FREIHEITSNACHRICHTENBLATT

Volume 52

7th of Av, 5697

BUCHENWALD - ANOTHER CONCENTRATION CAMP OPENS

The Inspectorate of Concentration Camps has opened the
Buchenwald concentration camp, near the city of Weimar, to ease
pressure on the National Socialists' concentration camp system,
which is at twenty per cent overcapacity.

Increasing numbers of Jews are being incarcerated and some
Jewish groups are claiming that it is disproportionate to the
General population, but this is difficult to confirm.

What the KJF can say for certain is that most of the Jews who
are currently being held in camps have not yet been tried and
convicted, and of those that have, some of the charges are
plainly ludicrous.

We spoke to one woman whose husband had been arrested for the
"deliberate and flagrant undercutting" of prices in his bakery,
causing a neighbouring Aryan bakery to go into liquidation. The
conviction was made under the Weights and Measures Act. The
woman, who asked not to be named, has not been permitted to see
her husband, and has not yet been told which camp he is in.

CHAPTER 123

The black car drew up in front of the Drachensee house, and a policeman stepped out. He walked up to the door and knocked loudly, ignoring the bell push.

Miriam answered the door and told the man that none of the Kästners were home.

'I'm not looking to speak to anyone called Kästner,' he said. 'I'm looking for a Frau Nussbaum.' He looked at his notes. 'Frau Miriam Nussbaum.'

Miriam's stomach lurched, with a mixture of dread and bewilderment.

'I'm Frau Nussbaum. Can I help you?'

'Is there somewhere we could talk?' the policeman asked.

Miriam had a sudden appalling vision of the General or the mistress coming home and finding a policeman in their home, interviewing their housekeeper.

'This isn't my house, Inspector. I work here.'

The policeman frowned.

'I'm not an inspector, Frau Nussbaum. Just a constable. And this was the address I was given. This is the Drachensee house, Hamburger Chaussee, is it not?'

'Yes, but I and my husband work for the Kästners. We live in the cottage, over there.'

She nodded in the direction of the cottage.

'Would you rather talk there?'

'Yes. I think I would. Can you tell me what you need to speak to me about?'

'I will, but we can talk over there.'

Miriam closed the door of the big house and led the policeman round to the cottage, wishing she could ask him to park the car out of sight.

She opened the door and let him into the kitchen, offering him a cup of coffee as he removed his hat. She wondered how she was able to remain so calm.

He refused the coffee but indicated that she should take a seat at the kitchen table, then pulled out a chair and sat down opposite her.

'I'm here because of this.' He pulled an envelope out of his pocket and, with a stab of dread, she recognised her own handwriting, and Esther's address.

The policeman looked at her, not without sympathy, she thought. Her first feeling was of relief. Since he'd arrived, she'd assumed that Manny had been caught doing something bad, perhaps illegal, and had been taken to the police station. She almost didn't hear the policeman when he spoke again.

'Deutsche Reichspost has been directed to open a random selection of international mail. Yours was one of those chosen, and it was found to contain a defamatory comment.'

'Can they do that?'

His face hardened.

'That is none of your concern. You should be more worried about what I'm going to do with this.'

He waved the letter in front of her.

'Did you write this?'

She saw no point in denying it.

'Yes,' she said. 'I was writing to my friend, who has recently emigrated to Palestine, but there's nothing in it that would…'

'She is a Jew, yes?'

'She is. That's why she moved to Palestine.'

'And you are also Jewish?'

Miriam straightened her back.

'Yes,' she said. 'I am.'

'You stated that your son and daughter were…' he looked at the letter, '…getting a hard time at school, from the other pupils, and from the teachers.'

'Yes. I did. They are constantly being picked on.'

'That might be so, but you cannot say things like that, especially to someone outside of Germany, even if it is to another Jew.'

Miriam looked at him. He didn't come across as being unkind.

'So, what happens now?'

'Your mail will be monitored from now on. I would strongly advise you not to make any further remarks that could be construed as derogatory in your letters. We'll be checking all the mail from Kiel.'

He hesitated.

'In fact, I would strongly advise you to stop writing to your friend. Sooner or later, you will say something that will get you into trouble.'

Miriam gasped.

'I can't just stop writing to her. She is my oldest friend.'

'Listen to me, Frau Nussbaum, this time your file will not be passed to the Gestapo but if you persist in writing, any letters you send will be opened, and you will be investigated further. It will not be possible to avoid Gestapo involvement.' He lowered his voice. 'Stop writing. At least directly.'

She made to say something, but he shook his head.

He stood up and thanked her for her time.

She showed him out, and he turned at the door.

'Just remember what I said. I don't want to have to visit again.'

He handed her the letter.

'Thank you,' she said, and watched as he walked round to his car. She heard the crunch of its wheels on the gravel, and caught a glimpse of it on the road, heading back into town.

Ten minutes later, Yosef drove the Kästner car into the driveway, arriving home with Maria and the two girls.

Miriam leaned her head against the kitchen door and breathed deeply.

~~o~~

[18/07/1937 Sunday]

'Esther, read this.'

Itsik handed his wife a letter, which had arrived a few days before.

He watched her face as she started to read the neatly typed words.

```
12th June

Itsik,

I was delighted to hear from you. I had wondered how you and
your family were getting on. It seems that you have not wasted
any time in getting your new venture up and running, but that's
no surprise.

The shop is extremely busy. As you suspected, it's now trading
at the same, or a slightly higher level than what it was doing
a few years ago, and while it is good for business, and my bank
balance, it saddens me to think that takings had gone down at
all, just because of who owned it.

However, I'm unwilling to profit excessively from your
```

417

misfortune, and I have put aside what we'll call a small post-sale performance bonus for you. As it would be difficult for me to get the money to you, I have deposited it with one of your old suppliers, and you can draw it as exported stock; he tells me you have already been in touch with him to purchase goods from his company.

I have also put him in touch with a couple of government officials who I've found to be more than useful in facilitating export permits.

And before you protest about this money, it is not a gift. I am making a more than healthy profit on my investment in your shop. I know I paid a low price for it, which was fair enough as I was taking a risk that it might not perform well, but now that the risk has not materialised, I feel that it's only right that you should receive this payment as a reflection of its true value.

Good luck with your new enterprises. I won't be in contact with you again, but if you drop a note to Yosef Nussbaum in a year's time, I will certainly be delighted to receive an update on your progress.

Yours,

Oskar V.F.

Tears welled up in Esther's eyes, and ran down her cheeks, but Itsik could see that she was smiling.

'Do you know how much?' she asked.

'Three thousand Reichsmarks. I telegrammed the supplier.'

Esther's hand flew to her mouth.

'That's a lot of money.'

'Yes. But it means more than just the money. If it solves our problems with supplies...'

'I know.'

'You can tell Miriam,' he said.

CHAPTER 124

'Frau Kästner, how nice to see you.'

Maria's heart slumped. The last person she wanted to meet was the mayor's wife. Especially while shopping for a dress for the big August Kirchenfest, which all the ladies would be at, including the countess.

'Frau Hoffmann,' she said. How nice to bump into you, too. It's been a long time.'

'I know. I'm just so busy with all the official engagements in Kiel and we're just back from Berlin again. We've been there three times this year. The party is determined to listen to the views of its regional supporters.'

'That's marvellous. Berlin is so exciting. We attended the Olympic opening ceremony with Admiral Canaris. We sat almost within touching distance of the Führer.'

'He's such a brilliant man. Did I tell you we met him?'

'I believe you mentioned that you were going to the Nuremberg Rally the last time I spoke to you. You went with Frau Lohse, I believe?'

'Yes, it was a wonderful event, especially in the company of the Oberpräsident and his wife. We got to hear the Führer speaking. It was awe-inspiring to listen to, and then we were introduced to him. It was the proudest moment of my life.'

Maria was torn between wanting to get away from the insufferable woman and genuine curiosity. Within her own family surroundings, Adolf Hitler was rarely discussed in flattering terms and, unlike her husband, Maria Kästner had a growing admiration for Germany's chancellor.

'What was he like?' she said, her inquisitiveness overcoming her dislike of Frau Hoffmann.

'He had an aura of greatness, and a magnetism. Everyone there was enthralled.'

'What did he say to you?'

'He just asked us where we were from. We introduced ourselves and he told us we were doing critical work for the party and the fatherland, and that we should be proud. Then we were moved on.'

'My sons met him. He presented them with the winners' trophy in the army versus navy race last year. Johann said it was such an honour.'

'What about your Franz? What did he think?'

Maria froze. *Of course. The vile woman has an agenda.*

'Franz was delighted too,' she lied.

'That's not the way Lise Böhm tells it,' the mayor's wife said, her voice flat.

She's taking great pleasure from this, thought Maria.

'You can't believe everything Lise Böhm says. The girl is bitter about the break-up.'

'Distraught is what I heard. From what she says, your son isn't quite as white as snow as he makes out.'

'What do you mean by that?' Maria Kästner said, looking around and lowering her voice, but there was a cold, hard edge to it.

'Well, Franz is what, twenty-one, and Lise's only nineteen, and inexperienced. Seems he tried to move things on a little too fast for Lise. It turns out he wasn't happy when she said no.'

The colour left Maria's face, and she saw the triumph in her adversary's eyes.

'That's not true. My Franz would never do that. She's lying.'

'You're his mother. You would think that. Why the sudden break-up, then?'

She knew the woman had her. To defend Franz, she would have to condemn him as being critical of the government. In desperation, she tried to think of a way out.

'Your husband, the mayor.'

'Yes, what about him?' the woman said, suddenly wary. 'What does he have to do with this?'

'Erich tells me he and Herr Lohse have both been involved in the steering committee for the development of the naval facilities in Kiel.'

'Yes, it's important for the navy that they're involved.'

'I'm guessing that my husband wouldn't value Herr Hoffmann's participation in the light of these malicious rumours his wife is spreading. He's in a position of great influence in the navy, you know.'

Maria was glad she'd listened to the General's grumbles about Jürgen Hoffman, about his standing with Hinrich Lohse, and the party, and how it relied on his usefulness to the Oberpräsident, especially with regards to the Kriegsmarine.

Jürgen is desperate that the Kriegsmarine steering committee should go ahead.

Frau Hoffmann suddenly looked less sure of herself.

'He wouldn't dare interfere,' she said, the hint of defiance not quite masking the trace of doubt in her voice. 'It would cause too much upheaval if he tried to oust my husband and Herr Lohse.'

'Oh, don't think General Kästner would meddle in Herr Lohse's affairs, but let's say for instance that the admirals were to hear a rumour about your husband, and Herr Lohse was presented with a dilemma; his right-hand man being replaced, or the committee being quietly shelved. Which would he choose? I mean, any one of the higher-grade civil servants will know the workings of the city as well as your husband does, or better; wouldn't such a person be just as useful on the committee, or even more so?'

Maria Kästner could see that her words had hit home.

She knows that if Jürgen loses his influence with the Oberpräsident, he will be marginalised. No more Berlin trips.

'You wouldn't dare,' Irmgard Hoffman hissed.

'For my son, I'll do anything. Do you understand?'

The mayor's wife faced Maria Kästner for a few seconds, then looked away. Maria had no idea if the General had the authority to carry out her threats, and she doubted if he would use his influence even if he were able to, but she could see that the mayor's wife believed her threat.

'I... I... didn't mean anything by it. I was just warning you what Beate Böhm and her daughter were saying about your son.'

'And I thank you for warning me,' Maria Kästner said, an idea suddenly springing to mind.

'I'm having the countess over to visit next month. I know you're extremely busy, and I hesitate to ask, but would you be interested in coming?'

'The countess? She's coming to visit you?' the mayor's wife said, her mouth dropping open.

'It hasn't been confirmed, as yet,' Maria Kästner said, the first truthful words she'd spoken for a while. 'Eva and I are calling on her this week, and I was hoping to finalise a date for her visit and have a few of the more influential ladies over at the same time. Clearly, in the light of what you've told me, Beate Böhm is unlikely to figure high on my list of invitees.'

She saw the desperate need for acceptance by the upper classes on Irmgard Hoffmann's face and knew that she'd won.

'I'm sure I could fit that in if you give me enough warning,' the woman said, the hunger in her eyes belying the offhand nature of her words.

'I'm so pleased to have bumped into you today,' Maria Kästner said with a beaming smile. 'Wasn't that simply perfect?'

'Indeed. I'll await your call, Frau Kästner.'

'And Beate Böhm and her daughter?'

'Oh, I rarely see them. But I'll make sure they are warned about what they say.' The mayor's wife pretended to deliberate for a second. 'And I'll have a word with some of my friends. Let them know that Frau Böhm's malicious rumours are nothing more than sour grapes.'

'Oh, don't put yourself out, but I'd be most grateful if you could have a word. I'd do it myself but I'm sure it would sound much better coming from you.'

She kissed the mayor's wife on both cheeks and started to turn away.

'There's one other thing,' the mayor's wife said.

Maria stiffened.

What other concession is the woman going to try and extort from me?

'What is it?' she asked, trying to keep the annoyance from her voice.

'Well, I'd rather you heard this from me, as a friend...'

Maria Kästner's interest was piqued, and she let it show.

'Young Lise has moved on. An SS officer, older than your Franz.'

Maria was shocked. Despite her dislike for the girl, she'd imagined Lise being just as devastated as Franz.

'How do you know?' she asked.

'Her mother told me. Beate confided in me they've been going out for a few months, but Lise let it slip that she'd met him at a youth rally in Neumünster. I checked. The rally there was in late November.'

Maria Kästner's face paled in anger. She smiled at Irmgard Hoffman.

The woman is revelling in being the first to tell me.

Her voice remained polite, but a hint of ice edged her words.

'What she does is her business,' she said, 'but thanks for telling me.'

Maria Kästner kissed the mayor's wife again and walked out of the shop, trying to look imperious and relaxed at the same time.

Outside, she paused and took a deep breath. She suddenly became aware of the drip of sweat in the small of her back. Then she straightened, fixed a smile on her face, and strode down the street.

CHAPTER 125

[12/08/1937 Thursday]

20th July

Afula

Miriam,

I'm sorry to write again when you haven't replied to my last letter, but I just needed to talk to you, and this is the next best thing.

We have been pretty much confined to the house for the last few weeks, which has been difficult. There have been a few incidents on the road to Haifa and a Jewish family were attacked. The husband is going to recover but his wife died. The son was uninjured. The British have closed the road, other than for three convoys a week for essential supplies and for people who must travel for business reasons. Itsik hasn't even been able to get to Haifa but Abel seems to be coping well on his own.

There is an armed guard at the school and some British soldiers are stationed in the police station for the duration. We hope that the trouble here will be over soon. Itsik was supposed to be taking us to Tel Aviv for a night to go shopping but it had to be cancelled.

We got our first big delivery in from Germany, and our supplier promises he can send us more on a monthly basis. Abel managed to get half of the goods sent up with one of the convoys.

Oskar von Friedeburg, the man who bought our store in Kiel, wrote to say he was going to pay us a sort of performance bonus because the business was going so well. It wasn't just a token sum, and it has allowed us to import far more stock than we otherwise could have. He has been a true friend to us.

We hear the news from home, and it sounds as if things are getting slowly worse. People are so mean, and I suppose that it shows that good Germans like Herr von Friedeburg are outnumbered by the bad ones. Otherwise, why would we be in this mess?

Please consider getting out. If not here, go somewhere else, if you can.

Much love.

Esther.

Miriam put down the letter. A cold sweat made her shiver.
> *What if the Reichspost had opened it?*

~~o~~

[10/09/1937 Friday]

'Do I have to go?' Eva complained.
'Yes, you do. You know your grandmother loves to see you all.'
'But there's a party on this weekend; after the end-of-season junior prize-giving at the sailing club, everyone's going to Marta's house afterwards.'

'I'm surprised you'd want to go to the sailing club. Your father's rash decision to leave has meant that I can't show my face there now, not that it was my favourite place anyway.'

'They don't really know me there because I don't sail. I just go because everyone else does.'

Maria could empathise with her daughter. When she was Eva's age, being with the right people was the most important thing in life.

'I do sympathise with you, but your grandmother is expecting you. If you do this, I'll see about having a party for all your friends.'

'And Johann's too? That would be amazing.'

Maria bit back a retort. She'd hoped Eva had got over her infatuation with Rutger Schäfer. She'd been invited again to dine with the countess, and this time she hoped that Eva would take a shine to one of the young men she'd almost certainly be introduced to. And she had to have a reason for the countess to want to accept an invitation to Drachensee.

'We'll see,' she said, thinking of a way to settle on a date when Johann's friends wouldn't be available.

'So why are we going to Lübeck first? It seems like a silly detour.'

Maria's eyes rolled upwards. 'Oh, your father wants to travel on the new autobahn. Antje's all excited about it too. I swear he's trying to turn her into a boy.'

Eva laughed.

'Don't worry. She still likes pretty clothes, and when she's a bit older, she'll forget about being a tomboy.'

~~o~~

'Whatever you think of the National Socialists, sir, it is an amazing piece of engineering.'

'I can't deny that, Yosef.'

The General sat in the front, much to his wife's disgust; he knew she considered it unbecoming, but he wanted a good view of the new motorway.

'I think you're making such a fuss over what is, after all, only a road.'

'Darling,' the General replied, smiling indulgently, 'it's not just a road. It's the future.'

'Oh, come now. I'm sure that's a bit of an exaggeration.'

'No, not at all. Because it has two lanes each way, with a central barrier, it is safer and easier to overtake, so hold-ups will be banished forever. And, because junctions are so much safer, with cars all joining in the direction of travel, slotting into the stream of traffic should be effortless, with no queues. It's marvellous.'

'Not if you have to travel a hundred kilometres in the opposite direction to get to it,' Maria muttered.

Eva sniggered.

'What was that, my dear?' the General said.

'Nothing, Erich. Just you concentrate on your autobahn.'

'Well, I think it's impressive,' Antje said, taking her father's side as usual.

'You would,' hissed Eva, but she was laughing at her sister.

'How long is this going to take, anyway? I'd like to get to my mother's before dark.'

'We'll be in Hamburg in ten minutes, ma'am. Around two and a half hours from there to Hanover.'

'Don't be so silly, Yosef. We've hardly left Lübeck.'

'Ha. See,' the General said. 'That's how wonderful this road is. We're there in no time at all. Just imagine what it will be like when we get an autobahn from Hamburg to Hanover. You'll be able to visit your mother every week.'

'Don't be so smug, Erich.'

CHAPTER 126

SS-Untersturmführer Rudolf Mey moved his hand gently in circles, and Lise moaned.

She'd brought him to an isolated spot on the Baltic shore and, to be fair, she seemed enthusiastic, and for someone so young and inexperienced, she wasn't shy.

But in some ways, it was frustrating. Each time he'd been out with her, he got a little further, but she always stopped just when he thought she'd lost control. He'd hoped by now that she might go all the way with him.

It's not as if I'm going to leave her once I've had her, he thought.

She moaned again and flinched a little when he pinched her nipple.

Maybe a little too rough.

He moved his hand to the other side, continuing his circling motion, cupping her breast occasionally for the thrill of feeling its fullness.

He didn't want to force it; he would do anything to keep Lise, having seen the envious glances of other men. He revelled in the comments of his fellow officers about his beautiful girlfriend, and how lucky he was.

She took his other hand and placed it between her legs, in the fold of her dress. He tried to move down and pull the hem up, but she held his wrist and pressed his hand against her.

He took her hint and began moving his fingers, feeling her shape through the dress and her underwear. She adjusted her position, and moved her hand onto his, encouraging him to press harder.

He felt her rocking as he moved his hand, and tried to be more vigorous, but she gripped his wrist again, this time more tightly, and he slowed his movement. Her hand relaxed again, but the motion of her body became more pronounced.

~~o~~

Lise wondered how long it would take to teach him to do it properly, and it briefly crossed her mind that Franz had somehow known how to pleasure her without such prompting.

Then, with a flash of annoyance, she tried to put her ex-fiancé out of her mind.

It was a mistake to come here, to our clearing.

She concentrated on the feeling that was spreading from between her legs to her stomach, and upwards to her breasts. He seemed to be finally getting it when she felt his thumb moving to snag her dress and pull it up again.

'No, not yet,' she murmured, trying to hide the irritation she felt at his clumsiness. 'It's nice through the dress. Plus, you don't want to get your fingers all sticky,' she said, and smiled as his eyes rolled upwards. She wondered if she could make him ejaculate just by talking like that to him but realised it would be a waste. She wanted him to feel her hand on him the first time she made him come, to know what she could do for him.

She slowly gave in to the pleasure, forcing his hand more firmly against herself, gripping it with her thighs and squirming as she finally let herself release with a long, satisfied moan.

She turned and kissed him on the mouth, exposing her flushed throat to his hungry eyes.

'Untersturmführer, now it's your turn,' she said, with half-closed eyes.

She moved her hand down his chest to his belt, briefly toying with it then sliding down past it to the tight cloth of his trousers and the hardness within it. She teased the straining cloth with her fingernail, then, using the palm of her hand, she started gently rubbing up and down his length, watching his face, the tip of her tongue playing on her lip.

At least he's not small. That would have been unfortunate.

She slowly increased the rhythm of her strokes but suddenly, without warning, he let out a groan of satisfaction and maybe, she thought, of embarrassment, and a damp patch appeared beneath her hand.

Flushing crimson, he apologised.

'Don't be sorry,' she said, giving him a tissue from her bag.

'I know it's a bit late, but it might help,' she said, smiling at him.

He got up and turned away from her. She bit back a laugh. He cleaned himself and disposed of the tissue deep in the bushes. When he came back, she could see that the damp patch was still obvious, and she had to cover her mouth to hide her smile.

He looked down and reddened again. 'Scheiße,' he said.

'Don't worry; it will dry. I had the tissue ready, but it all happened so quick.'

'Look at the mess,' he said, whining a little.

'Go down to the water and wipe it with your handkerchief. It will dry quickly if we leave the windows down in the car.'

Rudolf's car wasn't as glamorous as Franz's; although it was a sports car, it didn't have a soft top, and she missed the thrill of the wind through her hair. Rudolf had explained to her that he'd traded in his convertible because it wasn't suitable for winter.

And I thought that Franz was the sensible one.

Rudolf was three or four years older than Franz and she'd had to work hard to convince her mother that he wasn't too mature for her when she'd brought him home for the first time.

They'd met at a National Socialist youth rally, where his unit had been assigned to help the organisers with supervision and logistics, although the real reason they were at the event, he knew, was to impress the teenagers with their smart uniforms and their air of superiority, encouraging the pick of the HJ boys to join the SS, and to give the older girls of the BDM the chance of being chosen by one of the elite young SS soldiers as a mate.

Lise smiled. In the view of the party, a girl should have no higher ambition than to provide sons or daughters for the glory of the fatherland.

One of the lectures at the rally had been aimed at BDM girls of seventeen or older who had reached the end of their schooling and, with few options for higher education or meaningful work in the male-dominated employment market, were offered the chance to *give the Führer a child.*

Lise had smiled sweetly when the BDM leader had looked at her and her friends in anticipation.

As if I'd choose to do that.

The woman had described how *Lebensborn* worked.

'Any girl who signs up will be given a battery of medical tests,' she'd said, 'along with a thorough investigation of her racial purity for evidence of any Jewish taint. She will then be expected to choose a partner from a group of SS officers at one of the special Lebensborn residences, and once impregnated, she will be looked after until the child is born.'

It had all sounded rather exciting to Lise, apart from the impregnation bit.

'The child will be taken from the girl when it is two weeks old,' the woman had continued, 'to be raised as a loyal servant of the Führer in a special home for all the Lebensborn babies.'

I'll serve the Führer in other ways.

There had been no pressure for her to join and, although a few of those in Lise's squad chose to be part of it, most opted for the more traditional route of being a wife to an SS man, and the mother to his Aryan children.

Even outside the Lebensborn program, there were financial incentives to produce a raft of children for Deutschland, but Lise had already decided that she would never be the brood mare that the party was looking for, despite her love for Adolf Hitler.

She looked across at the SS officer she'd chosen as a husband, primarily for his blond good looks, and his rank. A brief comparison with Franz flashed through her mind, but she swatted it away.

425

He was concentrating on negotiating the narrow track that led to the main road, but she moved her hand to touch his leg and she heard him breathe a little faster.

'You know, if we were engaged, we could go a little further,' she said.

He gulped.

'Further?' he said. 'How much further?'

'You do want to touch me, to feel all of me, don't you? And for me to feel all of you?'

'Yes,' he croaked.

'Are you too shy to ask me to marry you?' she said.

'I was going to, but I was afraid.'

She looked at him, a puzzled frown appearing on her face.

'Why?' she asked.

'I feared you'd say no,' he blurted, turning to look at her.

'Don't be silly,' she said, moving her hand up his leg. She noticed the damp patch was almost dry and she giggled at the thought of repeating her actions while he was driving.

He stopped the car, and she wondered if he'd read her mind. He wouldn't be the type of person who would risk losing control of the car in a moment of sexual abandon, but after he pulled in, he reached into the glove compartment and pulled out a small leather-covered box, which he handed to her.

As she opened it, she heard him speak.

'Will you marry me, Lise?' he asked.

He picked the ring out of the box and lifted her hand up.

'Well?'

'Of course I'll marry you.'

She kissed him; it was a rather more chaste kiss than her previous kisses, which she thought was more appropriate for the occasion, and he slipped the ring on her finger. She lifted the second ring from the box. She was glad he'd followed tradition.

'Now it's your turn,' she said.

Both rings fitted perfectly.

She looked around. They were a little too near the road. Someone might pass.

'Find somewhere else to park,' she said.

~~o~~

Afterwards, when they'd tidied themselves up, she sat down opposite him on the picnic blanket.

'I can't let you...' she hesitated, an embarrassed look on her face, '...go all the way,' she finally said.

Rudolf took her hand.

'Are you frightened?' he asked her softly.

She gave a nervous laugh and blushed.

'No, it's not that. I promised my mother that I wouldn't... you know, give myself completely to anybody before I was married.'

She hesitated again.

'I've been hurt before, you know.'

'I heard,' he said. 'Hauptmann Kästner.'

Her head jerked up.

'How do you know that?'

It was his turn to look embarrassed.

'I asked around, after meeting you at the rally.'

She shrugged. 'It's not a secret. We got engaged, then I found out he was a traitor.'

She spat the final word out and he was shocked at her vehemence.

'I looked into him as well. His commanders think very highly of him. He's an army man through and through and is expected to go far and, although he has a few strange political views, he doesn't broadcast them, so he's tolerated.'

'He should be castrated.' She paused, stifling a sob. 'He wouldn't take no for an answer. I was lucky to fight him off.'

A tear overspilled from her eye and ran down her cheek.

'He didn't…'

She stared at him, and he wondered if he'd gone too far, but she looked away.

'No, I managed to stop him,' she said, sniffing, 'but I'm sure he would have.'

He found it hard to believe, but he loved her, he was sure, so he trusted her. And he resolved never to do anything against her will, even if it drove him crazy to have to stop.

CHAPTER 127

'This was delivered to Abel. There was a note in it asking him to pass it on to you.'

Itsik handed Esther a small package. He had just returned from Haifa, the first time he'd been able to get in and out of Afula since the attack on the main road.

Esther took it from him, puzzled. There was an opened outer packet, addressed to Herr Abel Weichmann, with two smaller sealed envelopes inside. She lifted them out. One had Moshe's name on it, the other was addressed to her. She recognised the handwriting.

She laid Moshe's letter aside and ripped open her own.

14th August

Esther,

I hope this letter reaches you. The last one didn't. I posted it but a few days later we had a visit from a policeman, who said my letter had been opened in a random check of foreign mail by the Reichspost, and that it had been confiscated because of some of the comments I'd made in it.

I've been holding off, frightened to write, and then your letter arrived, and I realised how worried you must be about why I hadn't replied. I got Yosef to post this when he was driving Frau Kästner to Rendsburg.

As far as I could see, there wasn't much in my letter that was critical of the government, except that I did say something about Manny and Fischel being bullied at school, but that was all.

I was glad Yosef wasn't at home when the policeman came because he might have said something rash to him. The man wasn't rude or nasty, in fact, he was quite apologetic about it. He said that in this instance, my letter wouldn't be forwarded to the Gestapo, but any further infringements would result in them being alerted.

So, I can't write to you direct, and you shouldn't send any more letters to this address. Rosa's mail hasn't been interfered with so can you post any further letters for me to her house for the time being, and she will give them to me.

I addressed this to Abel Weichmann at the hardware store in Derekh Yafo, Haifa in the hope that you would get it. Thank goodness you told me where the shop was! Just to be safe, Yosef posted this in Rendsburg, when he was driving Frau Kästner to visit a friend.

Where to start! It's wonderful that you have the Haifa shop. It sounds much busier than Afula. Would you not be better to all move there?

I'm terrified that you are in the middle of a war zone. You might even be safer back in Kiel. Even so, thanks for your invitation but you know we can't leave. Moshe wrote to Manny and asked if he could come alone but he realizes it's only ten-year-old boys talking.

It is great that you have people who really know how to survive out there. I'm sure you will become great friends with them.

Manny came home from school with a black eye; he said he'd been in a fight and the other boy was worse off but I learned that he stood up for Fischel when he was being bullied and got a punch in the face for his trouble. I've half a mind to take him out of school but I'm sure we would get into trouble with the authorities.

It is wonderful that Herr von Friedeburg has paid the extra money for the shop. I have seen him once or twice when he visited the General's house and he always seemed the decent type, although, (and I shouldn't say) he is a bit of a playboy!

As you say, he is one of the good people here today in Germany. The General is another, and he seems to have instilled that into his children, but they are in the minority. Most people here either don't care or they delight in our misfortune.

I shouldn't go on about our troubles which sound petty compared to yours.

I will try and write soon but I am frightened of being caught again. The Gestapo have a fearful reputation and I'm wary of falling foul of them.

With all my love.

Miriam

P.S. Yosef was asking after Itsik. He says they are missing him at the synagogue.

She looked at the letter again. No address. She smiled.

~~o~~

14th August

Moshe,

Mama says no. Not even for a visit. So, I guess I'm not coming. I didn't even ask Papa.

There are lots of soldiers here too. The ordinary Heer soldiers are all right. I mean, the General is one of them, and so are Franz and Johann, and they're fine, but we keep clear of the SS if we can. The SA men are the worst of the lot. We try and keep out of their way because, if they suspect you're a Jew, they'll take great delight in making a fool out of you or giving you a beating.

The autobahn was opened between Lübeck and Hamburg. My papa drove the General and his family on it and he says you had to see it to believe it. Two lanes each way with a barrier in the middle and roads that join at each side without crossing the carriageway. I've not been to see it, but Papa says he'll take me some day when he's driving the General, if I behave.

Shana Tova, Moshe. It's not new year for a couple of weeks here but it might be by the time you get this. Mama says it takes up to three weeks for the post to arrive in Palestine.

Fischel and me were in the hideout by the lake today. It's not the same without you but we made some small improvements which you can see when you come back for a visit next summer.

Manny

CHAPTER 128

The day after Maria and Eva's second visit to the countess's house on the Lindau estate, Maria sat in the General's study, waiting for him to come home. She looked out of the window, suddenly nervous.

The countess had accepted an invitation to the Drachensee house despite Eva's lack of interest in the young man who'd been one of the countess's guests, and Maria wondered why the older woman persisted in befriending them.

Once again, Eva's apathy to the grandson of a real duke had frustrated Maria, but the countess had shown enormous patience and fortitude in the face of Eva's rejection of her latest choice of suitor, all the more so because Eva had told the countess that she was starting university the next month.

Maria heard the front door open and close again, and the General's footsteps come down the hall. He paused at the door of the study when he saw his wife sitting in the chair.

'I need to talk to you,' she said, getting up, and pouring him a glass of whisky.

The General sat on the corner of the desk and waited for her to speak.

Flustered at his silence, Maria lifted her glass, a gin and tonic, and took a sip.

'I've invited the countess for dinner,' she said, watching his face.

He grimaced but said nothing.

'There will be a couple of other guests as well, but I'd like you to be there too. The countess would so like to meet you.'

'Fine,' he said, giving her a thin smile, 'If I must. When is it?'

'Next Saturday,' she said, relieved that he hadn't exploded, or refused to be there.

'I presume I have nothing else on?'

'I've checked. It's clear.'

She began to worry that it had been too easy, and she had a premonition of the General having another naval emergency on the day of the countess's visit.

'You'll not cry off at the last minute, will you?'

He smiled.

'No. I'll be there.'

She hid her surprise at his compliance and took his glass to refill it.

'So, who's all coming to this dinner. The duke, the dowager queen?'

'Don't be facetious,' she said, ignoring his grin. 'It will be the countess, a friend of hers, and a couple of ladies I know.'

The General raised his eyebrow.

'Do I know these ladies?'

'Yes, you know Frau Schmitt. And the mayor's wife is coming.'

He groaned.

'Jürgen's wife's a social climber, and a bore. She's worse than him.'

She hesitated.

'I know you don't like her, but it's important. Don't ask me for details, but she's been useful in combatting the slander Beate and Lise are spreading about Franz.'

He frowned, but she shook her head.

'Is Jürgen coming?' he asked.

'No, just Frau Hoffmann.'

'Perhaps I should invite a friend too?' he said.

'You're not inviting Canaris, if that's your plan,' she said, and he laughed.

'I wouldn't subject him to it, my dear. I was thinking of Captain Bauer, or perhaps Oskar.'

She thought for a second, then realised he would end up ignoring the ladies and chat about war or politics with whoever he invited.

He probably just suggested it to goad me.

'Perhaps another time,' she said, forcing a smile, 'but the countess is particularly looking forward to speaking with you. She takes a keen interest in the army and the navy, you know.'

'Ah,' he said, grinning again, 'maybe she's a British spy. I hear the ruling classes are all related.'

'You are in an amusing mood today, aren't you?' she said, arching her brows. 'But seriously, she is fascinated, and would like to talk to you.'

She recognised his sceptical face, but he didn't comment, surprising her.

Perhaps he's a little intrigued by the countess's interest, she thought. *That would be wonderful. It might mean he'll behave.*

'Right,' he said, 'that's settled. Now, what are we doing tonight? There's a good film on at the Nordpalast. We haven't been to the cinema in a while.'

'What's on? Would Antje like it?'

'Oh, it's not her type of film. I thought that it might be nice for us to go on our own. Perhaps have a bite to eat? Eva can look after Antje.'

She smiled at him. It had been too long since they'd been out, just the two of them. It was one of the things she loved about him; he would sometimes spring a surprise on her. She felt a flutter somewhere in her stomach, and she was glad he could still make her feel like that.

'I'll go and speak to Miriam. Can you tell Antje?'

~~o~~

[25/09/1937 Saturday]

Maria had arranged the table so that the countess was sitting between the General and herself, to avoid the risk of Frau Hoffmann monopolising her and causing the elderly patrician to die of boredom halfway through the main course.

Instead, she sat herself next to the mayor's wife, with Frau Schmitt, an old friend of hers who could be trusted to shepherd any guest through an evening with charm and wit, on the tiresome woman's other side. Completely neutralised, Frau Hoffmann would be able to join in the general table talk in what was an intimate dinner, but not prevent the countess from being able to engage the General and Maria in more intimate conversation.

She placed the countess's friend between Frau Schmitt and Eva, content that it would make for pleasant company for all three.

She smiled, pleased with her own ingenuity.

Frau Hoffman can hardly complain. Simply being invited here is enough, and she'll get the chance to speak with the countess once we retire to the drawing room, after dinner.

Even then, Maria knew she'd have to harness all her social skills to limit the time the elderly aristocrat would have to endure the mayor's wife's fawning.

And the General would withdraw to his study after what he considered an appropriate length of time but, by then, the countess and he would have had the chance to get to know each other a little.

It was important to Maria that they did. *For Eva's future.*

~~o~~

Miriam had excelled herself. By the time the coffee was served, Maria could see from the glances they gave each other that the countess and her companion were impressed.

The General had been in good form. During the telling of one or two of his favoured

431

stories, which Eva and Maria had heard once too often, everyone at the table had stopped to listen, laughing and gasping in the right places.

And while she'd had to converse with Irmgard Hoffmann more than she would have liked throughout the meal, Maria was pleased to see that the General was being suitably attentive to the countess, and that Eva and Frau Schmitt had kept her friend entertained.

She was glad she'd managed a word with the countess when she'd first arrived.

'Margarethe,' she'd said, resting her hand lightly on the countess's arm, 'Can I apologise in advance if Frau Hoffman is a little…'

'Clingy?' the countess had said, smiling.

'I was going to say forward,' Maria had replied, with a muted laugh, 'but you are right.'

'I presume that you invited her this evening for a reason…?'

'You're most perceptive, Margarethe. It's… well, let's say she's been most helpful with a small problem that has arisen. I won't bore you with the details.'

'Oh, come now. You must confide in me. When we get a chance to speak quietly, you can tell me all about it.'

The countess had put her hand on Maria's and had given her a sympathetic smile.

And during the meal, she played her part.

'Frau Hoffmann,' she said, during a lull in the conversation, 'Did you enjoy Berlin?'

The countess's question caught Irmgard Hoffman by surprise, but she quickly recovered.

'It was wonderful, my dear countess, but Nuremberg was better. I must tell you about meeting the Führer. He was the most amazing man I've ever met.'

'It sounds extremely… interesting,' the countess said.

'I accompany my husband, the mayor, every time he goes to Berlin on official party business. The National Socialist Party makes a tremendous effort to include the wives of its officials in everything they do. It makes us feel we're part of a big family.'

'It sounds lovely,' the countess said, turning to Frau Hoffman's companion.

'And Frau Schmitt. It is lovely to meet you. Maria tells me that you're the backbone of most of the fundraising activities in Kiel. How marvellous.'

Frau Schmitt smiled and thanked the countess.

'Frau Kästner is too kind, but I help where I can. Perhaps if we could persuade Your Ladyship to put your name to one or two of our charities, it would raise our profile somewhat, and make it easier to raise money.'

The countess laughed.

'I'm sure I'd be delighted, as long as you don't expect me to run about the street with a collecting can in hand. I'm getting too old for that sort of thing.'

'No, ma'am. It would be in name only, although we'd be delighted to have you at any of our events. We're always looking for someone of your standing to open our larger fundraising affairs.'

'Speak to me after dinner, Frau Schmitt. My schedule, limited as it is, gets terribly cluttered.'

She was saved from having to make any further excuses by the desserts arriving.

'My dear,' the countess's companion said to Miriam, 'these are quite simply the most delicious things I have ever tasted. Indeed, all the food was marvellous. I must congratulate yourself and Frau Kästner for such a wonderful spread.'

As the guests finished eating and waited for the coffees and liqueurs to be served, Maria Kästner looked around, content. She'd done more than enough over the last few months to assure the countess that she was quite capable of holding her own in their society, and this little dinner had been as pleasant as anything she'd been to in the Lindau house, even if the guest list wasn't quite as notable.

She watched as the countess placed her hand on the General's arm, laughing, pleased that he'd made such an effort. She was desperate to ask him what they'd talked about, as she'd only caught brief snatches of their conversation; between Frau Hoffmann's incessant chatter in one ear and the need to keep an eye on all her guests' needs, she hadn't said more than a few words to the countess.

432

She glanced across at Eva, charming the two ladies she was seated with. Pride filled her heart, and she knew she'd succeeded in bringing her older daughter up correctly.

She'll hold her own in the countess's world.

She imagined a life spent in the rarefied heights of old German society, somewhat more refined than the world of Kiel's upper echelons, away from the likes of Irmgard Hoffman and Beate Böhm.

A cloud darkened her thoughts.

Will the countess be understanding when she hears Lise's terrible lies? Or when Eva rejects another of her young men?

She tried to ignore the whispering voice in the back of her mind telling her that somehow the countess and her friends were using her, and Eva, for their own ends.

The countess, as if she'd read Maria's thoughts, put her hand on her arm.

'Your husband is a very interesting man,' she said.

~~o~~

The countess was impressed. Maria Kästner had handled the evening with refined elegance.

Retiring to the drawing room after the meal was finished, the countess was happy to converse for a while with the insufferable Frau Hoffman and her rather more pleasing companion in the knowledge that the hostess wouldn't suffer the woman monopolising her for longer than was bearable.

And when Maria rescued the countess by suggesting that Eva should show the mayor's wife around the house, the elderly aristocrat allowed herself a quiet smile.

She watched as Irmgard Hoffmann trotted after Eva, accompanied by Frau Schmitt, around the elegant Kästner's lakeside residence.

After the General had politely withdrawn, Maria chatted with the countess and her companion for a while, until Eva returned with the two Kiel ladies.

'You have a beautiful home, Frau Kästner,' the mayor's wife said.

'You must come back during the day, Frau Hoffmann. The view down to the lake is lovely.'

A hint of amusement graced the countess's face as she watched Maria Kästner play the mayor's wife, admiring her skill, and she wondered again why the wife of a General was making the effort to butter up the ghastly bore of a woman.

Overall, she was delighted. She'd done what she'd set out to all these months ago; speaking with the General had been interesting, if not entirely satisfying, but she felt that he still might be useful at some point in the future, if the loathsome boor of a man in charge of Germany were ever to be removed. And he was well connected within the military.

Maria Kästner and her daughter had been a bonus. She genuinely liked them, and while they didn't come from breeding like her own, their backgrounds and their manners were more than acceptable.

She was sure she could, with time, find Eva a husband who would elevate her from her middle-class mire, and Lord knew, her own class needed a little fresh blood in it if they weren't to become inbred.

'My driver will be here shortly,' she said to Maria. 'It has been a wonderful evening and we shall meet again soon.'

She was surprised to see a tear at the corner of Maria Kästner's eye when she embraced the younger woman and kissed her on both cheeks.

'We'll catch up very soon,' she said.

'That would be lovely.'

Maria turned and asked Yosef to fetch the ladies' coats.

'All the coats, ma'am?' he asked.

'Yes. Frau Hoffmann and Frau Schmitt's car is also here.'

It was so elegantly done, that neither the mayor's wife nor Frau Schmitt would have thought of taking offence, and the countess smiled again to herself.

'Now, Eva,' she said, gathering the elegant young lady into a soft embrace, 'we will have the pleasure of your company soon, I hope, and I'll try my best to invite a few more people your own age. I suspect you're getting weary of our set ways and our rather dull conversation.'

She laughed, despite Eva's protests.

~~o~~

Irmgard Hoffman watched the easy manner between Maria Kästner and the countess with envy.

The warm embrace. The pretended affection. The almost open invitation to the countess's estate.

She forced a smile, knowing that, for the time being, she needed the likes of Maria Kästner if she wanted to mix with these people, but she hoped it wouldn't be too long before the new order, with her husband at the centre of it, meant that it would be the countess and her set who would be paying court to the party, and to those who held its reins.

She looked around. The house was so far removed from what she was used to, at least for now. Elegant, tasteful, with a sense of history, or gravitas.

Perhaps the General will go too far, one day, with his outspoken views, and his peculiar loyalty to his Jews.

She walked down the steps, where the car was waiting.

This house will be mine, with patience, she thought.

~~o~~

It was the next day before Maria Kästner had a chance to speak to her husband. When the guests had left, she'd poked her head into his study before going to bed, noting with surprise that he was working.

She had, over the years, developed an instinct for knowing when not to disturb him, so, despite being desperate to know what he and the countess had talked for so long about, she'd curbed her curiosity and told him she was heading up to bed. He'd given her a smile and a cursory nod and told her he'd be up when he finished.

She hadn't remembered him coming to bed; the worry about how the evening would go had exhausted her, and she'd fallen asleep almost as soon as her head touched the pillow.

~~o~~

He was already up when she woke the next morning, and when she joined him at breakfast, Eva sat at the table with him, and Miriam and Yosef were bustling about, serving up bread, cheese, and a tureen of scrambled eggs.

Antje had stayed over with Ruth the previous evening; she hadn't needed any persuasion to miss the dinner party. She'd breakfasted in the kitchen of the cottage with the Nussbaums and was now out playing in the grounds of the Drachensee house with Ruth and Manny.

It was nearly eleven by the time Maria Kästner managed to get the General to herself, but only by suggesting a stroll down to the lakeside.

It was a beautiful late September morning, and there was just the crisp of frost on the grass as they walked arm in arm towards the boathouse.

'Well?' she said, squeezing the General's arm after he'd said nothing for the first few minutes.

'Well, what?' he replied, teasing her, she knew.

'What did you both find so interesting to talk about? I hardly got a chance to speak to her.'

'Oh, this and that. You asked me to be nice to her.'

'And you were.'

She leant over and kissed him on the cheek.

'Thank you,' she added. 'So, what did she say?'

'Oh, nothing much. She asked a lot of questions about the army and the navy; she seems genuinely interested. Both her husband and her father held commissions in the army, so she was quite knowledgeable about the old Deutsches Heer. I suspect she was simply curious to know how the modern armed forces have changed.'

'Oh,' Maria said, disappointed. 'Is that all?'

'She told me a bit about her husband; I've met him once or twice; he's the commodore of Flensburg Yacht Club. And she spoke about her background, and life on the northern bank of the Schlei river.'

'She has been looking forward to meeting you. I just thought there might have been something to it. You know, getting a commission into a good regiment for a nephew, or something.'

'The army doesn't work like that now, my dear.'

She raised her eyebrow.

He frowned.

'Franz and Johann chose to go into my old regiment, but they got in on merit,' he said. 'I didn't get involved when they applied for their commissions.'

'Maybe not, but the commissioning officers knew exactly who they were, I'm sure.'

He shrugged.

She smiled again. It was as close as he'd come to conceding defeat.

~~o~~

The General sat at his desk. He smiled, thinking of the conversation he'd had with the countess. The old bird had been surprisingly entertaining and knowledgeable, and the evening hadn't been as onerous as he'd expected.

'General,' she'd said, lowering her voice a little after they'd been chatting a while, 'I'm a little curious as to how the army stands on Germany's future.'

'It's hard to say, Countess. There are elements of the "old army" who crave for the days of the Kaiser, but they are in the minority now.'

'And if push came to shove, do you think they would follow Herr Hitler blindly?'

'If you'd asked me a year ago, I'd have said no, but now, I'm not so sure.'

'And if there were a credible alternative, would the armed forces support it?'

'No. The National Socialists are too embedded in the Wehrmacht now. Any dissenters will be in small, isolated groups.'

He'd looked at her, his eyebrows raised.

'Have you been sent to sound me out?'

She'd hardly blushed, but he noticed it. He'd looked around. The others were all engrossed with their own little groups. Only Maria glanced at them occasionally.

'I'll be honest,' the countess had said. 'When my husband heard that I was going to have dinner with you and your wife, he did ask a few questions.'

'And this wasn't part of a grand plan, involving my wife and daughter?'

The countess didn't flinch.

'The truth is,' the countess said, 'I find both your wife and daughter charming, and a breath of fresh air.'

'And no matter what my answers are, they will still retain your friendship?'

'I enjoy your wife and daughter's company very much, if that worries you.'

He'd frowned. He'd half-suspected she might dangle her friendship with Maria in front of him as leverage for some unnamed favour.

'So, what do you want from me?' he'd said.

'Nothing, I merely wished to pick your brains.'

'Why me? You surely have much better contacts in the upper reaches of the army.'

'I've heard that you don't march with the crowd, that you have an independent mind and, more importantly, you have a unique insight into the Heer *and* the Kriegsmarine.'

'Can I be frank, Countess?'

'Yes. Please do.'

'I think you and your friends backed Adolf Hitler, supposing that he was going to restore an Imperial Germany, and now you wish you hadn't.'

Again, she'd hardly flinched, but she'd arched an eyebrow.

'They were right about you, General Kästner. You have a shrewd mind.'

He'd laughed, and she'd put her hand on his wrist.

'And my daughter?' he'd asked. 'Why are you so keen to find her a husband?'

'Because I like Eva and I think she would have no difficulty fitting in.'

'My wife would be delighted if that were to happen.'

'And you?'

'I only wish for Eva to be happy, whoever she ends up marrying.'

'Contrary to popular conception, I'd be the first to agree.' She'd put her hand on his wrist again.

He'd given her a genuine smile. She would never be in his circle of friends but who knew what alliances might be needed one day to put an end to the National Socialists.

He hadn't told her that since the First World War, he'd despised the Kaiser and the bulk of the aristocracy, and he'd welcomed the Weimar Republic with quiet satisfaction, even if it did come with the humiliation of Versailles in tow.

He'd made his excuses and left the company after coffee, shaking the countess's hand warmly. He'd done his bit. If it gave Maria and Eva satisfaction to be part of their world, he wouldn't be the one to spoil it for them.

CHAPTER 129

[01/10/1937 Friday]

Eva was one of the lucky ones to get a place at university. It surprised the General; places were mostly reserved for the offspring of party stalwarts.

There were fewer admissions than ever, especially for women; nearly all courses in the arts and humanities had disappeared from the prospectus. The degree in foreign languages, however, was one of the survivors, and Eva had always excelled in French and English, and she'd picked up enough Russian from one of the girls who boarded at her school to convince the admissions board that she would be the ideal student.

The school she'd attended, Schloss Klosterhof-Schule für Mädchen in Schleswig, didn't harm her chances either.

The General dropped her off the first day on his way to work, but when he offered to pick her up, she shook her head.

'I can get the tram,' she told him. 'It runs from the campus into town, then I can catch one out to Drachensee.'

He smiled. She was nineteen now, and independent. But when she walked away into the crowd of students, he felt a pang of loss.

~~o~~

KIELER MORGENPOST

Friday 15th October 1937

LOCAL ROTARY CLUB DISBANDED

At a packed meeting in the Europäischer Hof, the members of Kiel Rotary Club were told that the German Rotary Club had embarked on voluntary dissolution of the organisation.

General Erich Kästner, the current chairman, made the announcement after returning from a meeting of the national Rotary Club committee, where the decision was taken.

The Kiel branch of the Rotary club, a global charity that raises funds for a variety of worthy causes, was formed in 1932, and has donated over 40,000 Reichsmarks in the five years of its existence to local charities.

Club chairman, General Erich Kästner, said that it was a sad day, but in the light of current differences between national governments, it has become untenable to remain part of the International Rotary Club.

Mayor Hoffmann, a past chairman of the club, did not attend the meeting, and was critical of the national leadership.

In a statement issued by the Mayor's office, Herr Hoffmann said that this decision smacked of bowing to international pressure, primarily orchestrated by American Jewry. He placed no blame on any of the local Rotary Club members and was confident they'd done all they could to prevent the demise of such a sterling institution but had been let down by their leaders.

The final distribution of the remaining donations will be completed this week. Oskar von Friedeburg, prominent local businessman and a member of the committee, appealed for the people of Kiel to maintain their generosity and continue giving directly to local charities.

~~o~~

[08/11/1937 Monday]

'Frau Böhm. How lovely to bump into you.'

'Frau Hoffmann. The pleasure is all mine. It has been a while.'

'Yes. My schedule has been so hectic. We were in Munich last week.'

'Ah. So were we. Eberhard took me for the weekend. It's a shame we weren't able to meet up.'

'That would have been difficult. Jürgen was there on official business, and the Party organises the itinerary for all the wives.'

'I think it's marvellous that the party pays so much attention to detail. I hear that even minor officials are well looked after.'

'Indeed. Although we were allocated far superior accommodation to most of the others. Kiel is rather an important city to the government.'

Beate Böhm smiled thinly.

'Did you see Der Ewige Jude when you were in Munich,' she said. 'It's wonderful, and so educational.'

'Yes, they had a private opening for party members and their wives, with a champagne reception. We all found it enormously enlightening.'

The Eternal Jew, a new exhibition that had opened in Munich, was due to tour the country at some point in the new year. Beate had presumed that she would have been one of the few people in Kiel who had visited it.

'I didn't realise that the Jews played such a large part in the Bolsheviks attempts to take over Germany.'

'That's why the exhibition was commissioned. Ordinary people must be taught about the threat that Jews represent. I believe that a book is to be published, and the curator told us that a film might also be made.'

Ordinary people. Beate Böhm bit back a retort.

'You must come over sometime,' she said. 'You know where we are.'

The mayor's wife's eyes narrowed.

Beate Böhm smiled.

Did she think I didn't know about her visit to Drachensee House?

'It's going to be difficult,' she heard Irmgard Hoffman say, 'but I'm having an evening next week for a group of Kiel's more influential ladies. Would you like to come along too?'

'That would be nice, but is Frau Kästner going? I don't think I could stomach being in the same room as her, after what her son did to my Lise.'

'She'll likely be there, I'm afraid. And the countess. We had dinner recently, and I feel it would be rude not to ask them. Possibly some other time, yes?'

'Perhaps I should come. I shouldn't let the Kästners dictate what I do. May I bring Lise?'

'Why, of course, my dear. The more the merrier. I must meet that young man of hers, sometime. It's so nice of him, helping her get over the break-up of her engagement to young

438

Herr Kästner.'

Beate Böhm's face reddened.

'I don't know what I'd have done if Rudolf hadn't come along. For six months Lise just stayed in her room, crying. If I hadn't insisted that she went to the BDM Rally in April, she would never have met him. He's an Untersturmführer in the SS, you know.'

'Oh, I must have got it wrong. I understood they met at a party event before Christmas. I do apologise.'

'Oh, no. I believe they were both at that rally too, by sheer coincidence, but they weren't introduced until April.'

'If you say so, my dear,' Frau Hoffmann said. 'I'll let you know about the date for my little evening thing once it's confirmed.'

As the mayor's wife walked away, Beate Böhm unclenched her fists and looked at her hands. There were four red marks on each palm where her nails had dug into the flesh.

CHAPTER 130

Memo: Geh.KdoS. ABW 17/11/37 CAC0582.1

For Attention Only: Rear Admiral Wilhelm Canaris, Chef der Abwehr.

From: General Erich Kästner, Abwehr, Kiel office

** HÖCHSTE GEHEIMHALTUNG **

At a meeting with Admiral Raeder, I was passed a personal transcript of a conference that took place on 11th November. Those present were Adolf Hitler and all his key military and foreign policy leadership:

The Reich Foreign Minister, Baron Konstantin von Neurath; the Reich War Minister, Field Marshal Werner von Blomberg; the Army Commander, General Werner von Fritsch; the Kriegsmarine Commander, Admiral Erich Raeder; and the Luftwaffe Commander, Hermann Göring.

Hitler's military adjutant, Colonel Count Friedrich Hossbach, kept minutes for the meeting but, according to some of those present, those minutes have not been circulated to the participants. The information below has been assembled from personal notes made immediately after the conference by Admiral Erich Raeder and passed to me verbally. The main points are:

- The Führer stated that on his death, the resolutions made at the conference were to be considered as his political legacy.

- In Hitler's view, the German economy is failing and the only way to prevent living standards for the German people plummeting severely is to embark on an immediate policy of aggression, sooner, rather than later, to provide sufficient resources. This could be achieved by seizing Austria and Czechoslovakia.

- Britain and France are unwilling to accept a strong Germany and are blocking German foreign policy aims at every opportunity. At some point in the next three to four years Germany would have to make further annexations of Ethnic German areas in Eastern Europe to prepare for a possible war with the British and the French. These include parts of Lithuania and Poland.

- This limited military expansion should be done in such a way to avoid at all costs going to war with Britain and France before the end of 1939, the year when rearmament would be advanced enough to make such a conflict winnable.

- After the conference, Werner von Blomberg, Werner von Fritsch, and Admiral Erich Raeder tried to persuade the Führer that the foreign policy he had put forward was too risky, as rearmament hadn't been fully implemented.

In my opinion, this is a declaration of intent to go to war.
[END]

~~o~~

Memo: Geh.KdoS. ABW 17/11/37 CAC0582.2

For Attention Only: General Erich Kästner, Abwehr, Kiel office

From: Rear Admiral Wilhelm Canaris, Chef der Abwehr.

** HÖCHSTE GEHEIMHALTUNG **

With reference to your Memo CAC0582.1, it is imperative that you not share your information with anyone else. I will circulate it to those who need to know. I will be in contact to arrange a meeting to discuss the ramifications of this conference. [END]

CHAPTER 131

'Here. It arrived this morning. There's one for Manny as well.'

Rosa handed Miriam both letters. Miriam put them in the pocket of her apron.

'You can read it now if you want. I'll make us a cup of coffee.'

She'd arrived at the Nussbaum's cottage early, after the children had gone to school, her breath condensing in clouds in the freezing late-November air while she waited at Miriam's front door.

While Miriam read the letter, Rosa busied herself in Miriam's kitchen, brewing a pot of coffee and finding some home-made biscuits to accompany it. She presumed the contents of Miriam's letter would be similar to that of her own.

She watched her friend while she read, Miriam's face giving away the surge of emotion each of Esther's words were stirring.

30th October

Miriam,

I got your letter at last. I hope that this one gets to you with Rosa's letter.

Don't take any chances with the mail. No matter how much I wait for your letters, I wouldn't want you to put yourself in danger. Don't risk having the Gestapo investigating you. Even in Palestine, we hear terrible stories about them.

We wouldn't move to Haifa; Afula is better for us. Property is cheaper so we can afford a bigger plot of land than we would in Haifa, so we get more room for the children, and a bigger garden. Also, they're building houses all around so the potential for the business is great, and even the Arabs are starting to use the shop. We have lots of stock in both shops, thanks in no small measure to Oskar von Friedeburg. Itsik is delighted with the way things are going.

Abel is quite happy with the flat in Haifa, and there should be enough business there to allow him to buy a house in five or six years' time.

It doesn't feel like a war zone here, but we do have to be careful, and there are a lot of restrictions to put up with. I miss you and Rosa so much, it sometimes hurts, and I miss all the greenery. Sometimes, I'm even homesick for the snow on the pavements and the ice in the Hafen. And to think I used to complain about the cold in winter!

So far, there is no news about Itsik's parents' visas, but it will be soon, I hope.

It's a shame about Manny but tell him I think he's a brave young man, standing up for Fischel.

There are some sporadic outbreaks of violence here and there, but the British seem to be in control of it, although the District Commissioner for Galilee, Lewis Andrews, was assassinated in Nazareth last month by Arab gunmen, so we can't take anything for granted.

But the thing is, we don't feel like second-class people here. The British are fair with us, overall, and the Arabs we know are generally decent. Our biggest worry is what is happening at home.

I must go. I hope Rosa and you will have a gossip when she gives you the letter. Just pretend that I'm there!

With all my love,

Esther.

~~o~~

'So, why didn't you tell me?'

Miriam looked surprised. There was no anger in Rosa's voice, but she looked a little tearful.

'About Manny and Fischel,' Rosa said, when Miriam didn't reply.

'Oh. Did Esther tell you?'

'Yes, she did. In her letter. Why didn't you tell me?'

'I didn't want to worry you. It was nothing much.'

'Fischel never said a word.'

'They don't. It's to stop us worrying. We hear almost nothing from Manny or Ruth.'

'Rebeka didn't say, either. I'd like to go and wring all their necks. Who knew that children could be so evil?'

Miriam looked up, surprised at Rosa's choice of words.

'What?' Rosa said, shrugging. 'These children are evil.'

'I suppose so. I always thought that children could never be evil, just bad or naughty.'

'They get it from their parents, and the teachers.'

'The worst part is that we're powerless. It feels as if there's nothing we can do.'

'There is something we can do,' Rosa said. 'I've started keeping a diary.'

'How will that help?'

'One day, all these people will have to face up to their actions. Keeping a diary will help me remember.'

She looked at Miriam.

'I have to believe that,' she said, tears coursing down her cheeks.

~~o~~

Shalom Manny,

Sorry I haven't written in a while. As you might have suspected, I'm one of the better football players here for my age. You would be too. We used to play on the waste ground at the back of the shops with the Arab boys. Some of them are good, too, but now we've been told to use the new pitch by the school, and the Arab boys aren't allowed.

So, we found a new place, near where most of the Arabs live, so we can still play. We don't tell our parents, so keep this to yourself. Blood Brothers!

Some of my friends' parents don't like the Arabs but Papa has nothing against them. They come into his shop and buy stuff, so it's good for business. They used to have to wait until the pedlars came round with their mules. One even has a camel! I've seen it but didn't get too close because it spits. Somebody shot the British Commissioner. It was an Arab. Papa says the Scheiße will fly now.

Everyone really likes the German goods that we have brought in from home. They keep saying that the quality is better, and Papa says the shops are getting an excellent reputation. We are quite busy.

443

School is great. I can talk Hebrew now. Well, enough, anyway.

Got to go. The boys have just come to get me. I'm the new Ernst Lehner – the best right-winger in Palestine!

Moshe

CHAPTER 132

~~o~~

[20/11/1937 Saturday]

'Nothing better than a crisp winter day out on the water, Canaris.'

'I've done watches in much worse conditions, Kästner.'

'I'm sure you have, but we don't have a nice warm wardroom to stay cosy in.'

'Ha. And neither of us are as tough as we were back then.'

'We'll not stay out long but, you must admit, it's a safe place to talk.'

'I'll grant you that, Kästner. I'm surprised that your boat is still in the water.'

'It's coming out this week. It would have been out last month, but I had to organise a corner in the small yard we have here, and a crane to lift her.'

The admiral nodded.

'The information from Admiral Raeder,' he said. 'How did it come about?'

'He telephoned me the day of the conference; told me that he had some interesting information. I arranged to meet him that evening and he told me he was worried that Adolf Hitler was going to take us hurtling into a war that we were ill-prepared for.'

'Do you trust him?'

'I think so. I can't see anything he had to gain from lying or embellishing the truth although it was impossible for me to corroborate what he'd told me.'

'Why you, Erich?'

'Raeder knows me and knows my views,' the General said. All the admirals do. He knew he'd find a sympathetic ear, but also that I'd be able to pass it on to you if I saw fit.'

'And why didn't he just get in touch with me directly?'

'He said that I would know how to put it over to you; to convince you that something needed to be done.'

'He did, did he? Well, he's right about one thing.'

'What's that?'

'We're not ready for a war with France or Great Britain,' Canaris said. 'Nowhere near it.'

'What do I say to Raeder?'

'Tell him that his information has been of utmost importance; that if he hears anything else, he should contact me immediately. I will arrange a meeting with him later this week, but I wanted to speak with you first.'

'Does it not worry you that we at the Abwehr are the last to be consulted? Surely if you are planning to go to war, military intelligence is one of the key pillars in the process?'

'We feed an enormous amount of information to the chiefs of staff and also to the senior members of the government, but they don't necessarily feel that they need us to know their intentions. It's short-sighted but, they always come to us eventually with their plans.'

'And you will work to prevent us going to war?' the General asked.

'Yes, or at least to postpone it. Adolf is far too set on expansion for us to stop it. And I'll tell Raeder that.'

CHAPTER 133

None of the Kästner family had been invited. The cars began arriving at the Drachensee villa, the Böhm's home, early in the afternoon.

'The Böhms are either having a party,' Yosef muttered to Miriam, 'or they're being arrested en masse by the SS.'

Miriam laughed nervously.

'Don't joke about things like that,' she told him.

He looked out of the window. There were three black sedans parked in front of the Böhm's house, and she counted at least six SS uniforms. Another black car drew into the driveway and he watched as a seventh black-coated SS officer got out. He was, surprisingly, followed by a woman in a long, fur-trimmed coat and high heels. The officer held her arm, helping her across the driveway to the steps of the house. She carried a handbag, a gift-wrapped box, and a small envelope. Once they'd reached the front door, he returned to the car and, from the front seat, he collected a bouquet of flowers, and nodded to the driver.

The car exited the driveway, and Yosef saw it speed off in the direction of Kiel. *Not a senior officer,* he thought. If it had been a high-ranking SS man, the car and driver would have waited for him.

'What do you think it is?' he asked.

'Dummkopf,' Miriam said, but not unkindly. 'It's Lise. She must be getting engaged today.'

'Oh, Lord. Isn't Franz coming home this evening?'

'No, it's next week, thank goodness. I must go and say something to Maria.'

'I wish you'd stop calling her that. It will slip out when other people are around.'

'I always call her by her first name when we're alone.'

'I know, but it makes me nervous. I don't call the General Erich, even though I was brought up with him. I stopped as soon as I started working for the Kästners.'

'She'd be annoyed if I stopped.'

'She'll be even more annoyed if you call her that in front of the countess,' he whispered.

She tutted at him. 'You're such a fusser,' she said. 'I'll be careful. Anyway, if it's all right with you, I'll go and tell Madam what's happening next door.'

Yosef sighed, and returned to sorting out table settings for the evening meal.

The party was in full swing. The strains of a Strauss waltz drifted over to the Kästner house and Maria could hear sporadic laughter and the rise and fall of animated conversation.

The General came up behind her.

'Quite a party, eh?' he said.

'Trollop,' she said.

He laughed.

'She certainly didn't pine for Franz quite as long as he did for her, did she?'

'She jumped out of Franz's arms into that man's bed without much delay.'

'Now, now. You can't say that.'

'I've watched her. She's a woman, not a girl.'

He supposed you could sometimes tell the difference, but you could never be sure.

'Maybe she and Franz…'

'I hope not, but it wouldn't surprise me,' she said, sharply.

'I'm just happy to have the old Franz back,' he said.

It had been such a relief when Johann had telephoned them, back in July, saying that his brother was on the road to recovery.

And every time they'd seen him since, he'd been better; more like the son they'd known.

'Johann doesn't think he's fully over it yet,' the General said. 'There's no sign of him taking any interest in girls.'

'He'll come around. He's smart, handsome, and they would fall over themselves for him, if he weren't so reserved. Sooner or later the right one will turn up.'

'I'm surprised you've not tried to find him a girl,' he said, smiling.

She blushed.

'You have, haven't you?'

Her protests fell on deaf ears.

~~o~~

Eberhard Böhm had been overwhelmed at first. He was comfortable with Rudolf and didn't think of Lise's boyfriend in terms of his SS rank anymore, but the young Untersturmführer's commanding officer had turned up at the engagement party, along with a dozen officers from Rudolf's company, and, as a group, he found them unsettling.

Many of them had brought glamorous women with them, one or two in rather revealing dresses that, in his opinion, bordered on the shameless.

As the evening wore on, and he had a few drinks, he began to relax and see them for what they were; ordinary young men at heart, with only a hint of arrogance that came with being part of such an elite organisation.

He glimpsed young Eberhard, hanging on Rudolf's friends' every word, flattered by their attempts to convince him to join the SS after leaving school and the Hitlerjugend.

As the party grew louder and louder, older uncles and aunts of Lise made their excuses and left, and Lise's father found himself talking with Rudolf's commanding officer, the only other guest remotely near his own age.

'Don't worry, my friend,' the Hauptsturmführer had said, 'your daughter has found herself a fine young man. He's a credit to the company. They all are.' He waved his arm around the room.

~~o~~

Over in the corner, Lise's mother was sitting talking to three of these fine young men, who were unashamedly flirting with her. She laughed at them but, deep down, she was flattered and more than a little thrilled that they should find her attractive.

She knew she could still turn heads occasionally, and that her figure was better than she could expect at her age. Eberhard rarely took notice, but it didn't much bother her; it had been a long time since he had stirred any real excitement in her belly, and it briefly crossed her mind to imagine what a night with one of Rudolf's friends would be like, for her, and for them.

She saw her husband in conversation with the Hauptsturmführer and shivered. There was something about Rudolf's superior officer that made her uneasy, and it wasn't merely the uniform. She was getting used to the all-black clothing with its SS runes and its Totenkopf insignia, the high boots and the red, white, and black swastika armband on the tunic, and the dark greatcoat. In fact, she rather liked it.

On Rudolf and most of his fellow officers, it looked raffish and handsome but on their commanding officer it seemed to flag danger, and she shivered as a ripple of fear, or something else, stirred within her.

She'd heard stories about the SS but, until she'd met the Hauptsturmführer, she'd dismissed them as ludicrous. She gave herself the merest of shakes. While he kept her husband occupied, she could indulge in harmless games of seduction with these young men who seemed to think she was worth their attention.

~~o~~

Most of Rudolf's fellow officers had met Lise, often wondering aloud how the hell their friend had managed to snag such a beautiful creature. He'd accepted their incredulity with good grace, but he'd never told them about her appetite for sexual intimacy, or her willpower in making him wait for their wedding night before making love.

Twice in the last month he'd found a prostitute in a bar, just to take the sting off his frustration, but it hadn't made any difference and, each time, the pain of guilt had added to his misery.

He'd spoken to her father before they'd announced that they were engaged, hinting that the wedding would be sooner rather than later, citing the possibility of his being sent abroad. He said this while tapping his hand gently on the side of his nose, to indicate to his future father-in-law that he was a man in the know.

He saw Lise excuse herself, escaping the admiring looks of Rudolf's friends. She made for the stairs, informing him in passing that he should come to her bedroom.

'Leave it long enough so that no one is suspicious,' she whispered.

He'd waited ten minutes exactly, by his watch, before casually leaving with a glass in his hand, as if to refresh his drink.

He crept up the stairs, terrified that one of Lise's relatives, with a legitimate reason for being upstairs, might meet him halfway down, but he reached the top without mishap, before realising he didn't know which room was Lise's.

He crept along the corridor, listening for a few seconds at each door. They were all closed, and he couldn't hear anything behind them. As he came to the last door on the left-hand side, he saw that it was open a crack, so he pushed it gently, enough to see that it was Lise's parents' bedroom, with its own dressing room and bathroom off to one side. Curious, he opened the door a little further, and stepped through. It was a large room and besides the bed, it contained two bedside tables, a couple of wardrobes, and his and hers dressing tables, one on either side of the room.

He didn't hear the footsteps behind him, and he jumped as a hand grabbed his shoulder. He turned in fright.

'Lise!' he hissed. 'You scared the hell out of me!'

'What are you doing in here?' she whispered back. He couldn't make out if she was annoyed or amused, or both.

'I didn't know which room yours was,' he said. 'This was the only door that was open.'

She giggled. 'My room's opposite. I thought you knew. What kept you?' A little irritation had crept back into her voice.

'You told me to wait a while.'

'Yes, but not half an hour. I was beginning to think you weren't coming.'

'It was ten minutes. Anyway, I'm here now. Show me your room,' he said, moving close enough to kiss her lips.

She looked around. 'We could just stay here,' she said. 'No one will come. Papa is too interested in what your Hauptsturmführer has to say and Mama is getting moist just talking to your friends.'

Rudolf gasped. She could still easily shock him.

'Lise!' he said.

'It's true. Why not say it as it is? Anyway, it's harmless. She's just having a little fun at their expense. Who knows, my father may reap the benefit, here, later.'

She pointed to the bed and giggled again.

He didn't know what to say.

449

She took his hands and placed them behind her back, then did the same with hers, and pulled him to her.

He sensed the heat of her body against him and felt himself harden.

'Do you notice anything,' she asked him, between kisses.

He leaned back and looked at her, puzzled, frantically trying to think what could be different about her.

She reached behind her and moved his hands down, past the small of her back and onto the slope of her flesh below.

Leaving his hands on her, she ran her fingers down as far as his thigh. When she reached the seam of his underpants, she followed the raised ridge it formed under his trousers, back and forth.

His breathing quickened and he moved his hand down into the cleft between her cheeks, feeling the soft skin through the material of the dress. She looked up at him.

'Well?' she said.

Confusion swept his face again, and his hands faltered, so she reached around and took his hand again, this time bringing it between them and placing it on her belly.

She guided his hand down across the ridge of her pubic bone and onto the soft mound between her legs. Instead of stopping there, as he'd expected, she continued to move his hand down the inside of her thigh until he felt it reach the hem of the dress, and touch her skin, just above the knee.

She hooked the edge of her dress around her thumb, and moved his hand upwards, across the soft flesh of her thigh. She watched his face and, sticking the tip of her tongue out, she parted his lips with it. He opened his mouth, inviting and his tongue met hers.

A bead of sweat formed on his forehead.

She continued to move his hand upwards, exploring his mouth with her tongue as she did, still using her fingernail to follow the lines of his pants.

He felt a spreading heat under her dress, growing as she moved his hand upwards. He sensed he was close to touching the triangular mound between her thighs and waited, holding his breath, for the thrill of touching her silk panties, but instead, with a shock, he touched wetness, soft flesh, and hair.

She giggled again, then moaned as he gently explored her.

She pulled her mouth back from him.

'Well,' she whispered, 'do you understand, now?'

'You're not wearing anything…'

She laughed.

'It's my little engagement present to you.'

Keeping hold of his hand between her legs, she swivelled round and leaned back against him, closing her eyes. He brought his other hand, which had been pushed away when she turned, round in front of her and slid it up to her breast.

'I'm sorry. I had to wear my brassiere,' she told him. 'People would have noticed.'

It took him a second to grasp what she'd said.

'You m-mean, you weren't wearing anything underneath, earlier? Downstairs?' he stammered.

'Did you think I'd taken them off up here?' she asked him, her eyes still closed, her voice soft, with a gentle huskiness to it.

'Yes,' he said. For a while, neither of them said anything and the only sounds in the room were her soft moans, rising towards a slow crescendo.

He looked up. They were standing in front of the dressing table. In the mirror, he could see her in front of him, her head leaning back against his neck, her hair falling over his shoulders.

His gaze followed his arm down, his hand disappearing inside the gathered folds of her dress, her thighs white in the soft light of the bedroom. She moved slowly as his fingers worked, then faster still until she shuddered and leaned forward, her body bent at the waist, letting out a long slow breath between pursed lips.

Then she leaned back again and relaxed into his arms.

They stood still for five minutes, his hands still on her. Then she tilted her head up to his.

'We can't do that for you, here,' she said, gently, taking his hand and leading him across the corridor.

~~o~~

Beate Böhm stood undressing in front of the mirror. She heard her husband enter the room.

When the last guest had left, Eberhard Böhm had breathed a sigh of relief and slowly climbed the stairs, following her up. Lise had long since gone to bed, citing tiredness, and Rudolf had joined his friends and their companions to continue the party at a nightclub in town the Böhms had never heard of, but it sounded too decadent for people of their age.

As she slipped out of her dress, he hung up his jacket and moved to his dressing table before removing his collar and tie. She undid her brassiere and hung it over the mirror and stepped out of her panties. She looked in the mirror, turning slightly.

'Do you think I have a good body?' she said.

'It's lovely, my dear,' he said, without looking up. 'It always has been.'

She looked over. He'd removed his suspenders and his trousers, and was standing in his socks, unbuttoning his shirt. He removed it and reached for his pyjama jacket, on his pillow. As she watched, he sat down on the edge of the bed and removed his socks.

She looked at her reflection in the mirror for a moment or two, then back at her husband. Standing now, he dropped his underpants to the floor and stepped out of them, into his pyjama trousers. She noticed that his belly hung over the waistband and realised for the first time that he was truly corpulent.

With a grunt, he sat on the bed again, and swivelled his body onto it, pulling the covers over him as he did. He didn't look over at her.

She turned again to look at herself. She saw the slight roundness of her belly, the nipples that didn't quite point upwards the way they used to, and a wrinkle or two round the base of her neck. She smiled, pleased with how she looked, and lifting her nightdress, slipped it over her head.

As she slid into bed, she heard his first snores and wrinkled her nose in disgust.

She lay for a while then, remembering the young men who'd paid her so much attention. Her hand moved to her breast, the other across her belly and down between her legs. It had been a while, but she gave in to it, her mind wandering to what might have been if, in the fantasy she allowed herself, she'd left with one of her young admirers at the end of the evening.

~~o~~

In her bedroom, Lise stood at her window. She watched the reflection of the moon on the still water of the lake and, to her left, the side of the Kästner house that she could just make out in the gloom. There were no lights on, but she could see the shadow of the chimney against a moonlit cloud and her eyes followed it down. She knew Franz's window was just below it, at the front of the house, and she wondered if he was at home.

Then she sat on the bed and punched her pillow, until her arm hurt.

451

CHAPTER 134

Franz was pleasantly surprised. The exercise had been a good one.

They were back at the barracks at Plön, following the debrief from Colonel Schneider and the SS colonel who'd been in command of the joint exercise between the two battalions.

As the two groups of soldiers milled around outside the mess, hungry after a hard morning, Franz and Johann stood next to two SS men.

'That went well,' Johann said. Franz smiled. It usually fell to Johann to break the ice.

'Yes,' the taller of the two men said. 'Your battalion has excellent discipline, I think. I'm SS-Untersturmführer Wessler; this is SS-Untersturmführer Mey.'

Franz and Johann returned the perfunctory Hitler greeting that they used when a full salute was deemed unnecessary, but Franz hadn't expected that SS soldiers used it too.

'I'm Lieutenant Johann Kästner and this is my brother, Captain Franz Kästner.'

Johann and Untersturmführer Wessler launched into an animated conversation about their relevant roles in the exercise, which had mainly involved wading through wetlands and swimming between the small islands within the lattice of lakes which surrounded Plön, all in full kit, trying to keep their gear as dry as possible. The last part of 'Operation Beerwolf' had seen both battalions fight it out to occupy a small, densely wooded hillock.

'I'm not sure just how realistic these exercises are,' Untersturmführer Mey said to Franz, the two men standing to one side, somewhat awkwardly.

'They're useful, but we'll not know how prepared we are until we first go into combat,' Franz said.

'I agree, but we must go through the motions.'

'Don't get me wrong,' Franz said, 'I think it's important to repeat everything we do until it's second nature.'

'You are right, most certainly.'

Franz thought the man looked pensive and he was about to ask if something was troubling him when the Untersturmführer spoke, his words coming quickly.

'You don't know me, but I've heard a lot about you,' he said. 'I'm Lise's fiancée.'

'Oh,' Franz said, taken aback.

'When I saw you and your brother, I thought I'd come over and introduce myself; to save any… awkwardness, later on.'

'That was good of you,' Franz said, meaning it. 'And congratulations,' he said, not knowing how he managed to get the words out.

'Thank you. I didn't want us to end up possibly fighting together with things unsaid.'

'I'm glad you did, Untersturmführer,' Franz said.

'Call me Rudolf, but perhaps not in front of Lise,' the Untersturmführer said, laughing nervously until Franz smiled.

The doors to the mess hall opened and they began filing in. Franz and Rudolf Mey stood back to let the others in. Franz turned to the SS man before following the others and offered his hand. Rudolf grasped it and shook it firmly without a word, then turned and made for the table his unit was sitting at.

'You looked to be having a rather serious conversation about tactics with the Untersturmführer,' Johann said, as Franz squeezed into the seat beside him.

'He's Lise's fiancée,' Franz said, and Johann half choked on a mouthful of food.

Franz patted him on the back.

'Scheiße,' Johann croaked, still coughing.

'It's all right. He's a decent sort of fellow. None of it is his fault.'

'That's true. It was brave of him to talk to you. Six months ago, you might have hit him.' Johann grinned.

Franz shook his head.

'It did tell me something,' he said.

'What? Lise has a thing for men in uniform?'

Franz laughed.

'No. I know now that I'm over Lise. In fact, I'm glad she's moved on.'

'Attaboy,' Johann said.

'You've watched too many films,' Franz said, shaking his head.

~~o~~

KIELER MORGENPOST

Wednesday 15th December 1937

LAW'S NOOSE TIGHTENS ON HABITUAL CRIMINALS

From the Reichstag today:

The Decree on Preventive Suppression of Crime was carried unanimously.

It's architect, Reichsführer-SS Heinrich Himmler, in a law designed to follow on the success of February's operation to remove criminal elements from the streets of Germany, has facilitated the arrest and incarceration of any person deemed to engage in repeated asocial behaviour, and of habitual criminals or those who make their living from criminal activity.

Local police chief, Uwe Müller, in an interview with the Morgenpost, assured citizens that the law would only be used as a last resort and for the safety of the people of Kiel, but that the increase in crime necessitated drastic action.

Mayor Hoffmann told the Morgenpost that it was high time that the state's criminals feared the consequences of their actions again. "At a time when every good German is making sacrifices to ensure that Germany's borders are secure again, and provide a safe and prosperous place to bring up their children, there is no place in society for those who would live off decent citizens' backs, or steal food from their bellies".

The Act comes into force with immediate effect.

~~o~~

'The Decree on Preventive Suppression of Crime,' the General read aloud, yet another new law grating with him.

'Quite a mouthful,' Franz said.

The General looked at his son, his captain's epaulet catching the low winter sun streaming through the window.

'It's quite a piece of legislation,' the General said, pointing to the *Morgenpost* article. 'It

453

effectively gives the security forces the power to arrest and imprison people, most likely in concentration camps, without evidence of any criminal activity; merely the suspicion of someone engaging in a crime will be enough to put them behind wire.'

'They've been doing that already, have they not?'

'Yes, but on a limited scale, and it was always sold to us as only applying to the worst of criminals; those who refuse to be rehabilitated. And there was always the possibility of a legal challenge to it, if a person was innocent, although I doubt it ever happened. This is different.'

'Why? Because it's written in law? When do they ever worry about law?'

'Oh, but they do. That's why we have a raft of new legislation every month. They need to justify and sanitise everything they do. But that's not why it's so dangerous.'

'Then why?'

'Because it's so imprecise and unclear. It can define anyone they want as a criminal. You, me, your brother or your sisters; any one of us could, if they wanted, be suspected of doing something wrong.'

'But surely there would be an outrage if they started arresting respectable citizens.'

'Look what they've done to Yosef and Miriam. They've taken away all the rights they had. They've taken away their citizenship. And they were respectable citizens. Did you see much outrage?'

Franz bowed his head.

'They'll start with the easy targets. The pimps, the petty thieves. No, wait, they might leave the pimps. And the brothels. As the army grows, they'll be needed.'

Franz laughed, but it had an edge to it.

'Eventually, everyone in Germany, apart from the ones at the top, and those that follow them blindly, will fear this law,' the General continued. 'Maybe even those who think themselves immune to its consequences.'

'Do you know the worrying thing?' Franz said. 'Most people won't see the full significance of it. I didn't.'

~~o~~

'Merry Christmas, Kästner.'

'Merry Christmas to you too, Canaris.'

Both men laughed. The line crackled and the General held the receiver away from his ear for a second.

'The family?' Canaris said.

'All fine. And yours?'

'Fine too.'

Erich Kästner heard his friend's muffled voice say something to his wife, and a few moments later, he was back on the line.

'Erika's gone to make a pot of coffee. I don't like to say too much in front of her. Are you alone?'

'Yes. Wait a minute.'

He got up and closed the study door, then picked up the receiver again.

'That's better. What's going on?'

'Just following up on Raeder's notes on the Hossbach conference that you sent me.'

'They're calling it the Hossbach conference?'

'Yes, after the man who took the minutes, for some reason.'

'They'll be calling the next one after the cleaner,' the General said.

'I now have a copy of his minutes,' Canaris said, ignoring the General's joke. 'There are a few minor differences but otherwise, Raeder's notes were almost identical.'

'I thought they might be useful.'

'They were. I only got the minutes this week, so it gave me quite an advantage having the admiral's information the day after the conference. And things have moved on.'

'Oh, how?' the General said, intrigued.

'Well, there has been a whole raft of diplomatic activity going on between Berlin and Vienna. Austria is on a knife edge. There's rioting in the street, with the imprisonment of the Austrian National Socialist leaders, and Kurt von Schuschnigg is desperately trying to fight off calls from Germany, and from his own people, for an Austrian-German Union.'

'Politicians in both countries have been talking about it for years. It would have happened long ago if it weren't for Versailles.'

'I agree. And the support in Austria and Germany for it is high, although the idiotic Austrian National Socialist thugs have dented that backing in Austria, with their violence and intimidation. Heydrich says they're out of control and Hitler would like to get rid of them all.'

'So, what are the Führer's plans?'

'The strange thing is, it's not Adolf who's pushing for this; it's Hermann Göring. He has become extremely powerful within the regime during the last year or so. He's very astute and, while Adolf's motivation for wanting to expand our borders is for reasons of racial dogmatism, Hermann's is much more to do with German national power.'

The General's breath quickened. *Franz and Johann!*

'Are we going to invade?' he said, trying to keep his voice level.

'Not yet. Since Kurt von Schuschnigg replaced Dollfuss as chancellor, the NSDAP have been undermining his position, a little each day, and, because Mussolini has taken his Italian government into alliance with Hitler, he has lost any support he had from abroad.'

'He must be worried that he's going to share the same fate that Dollfuss did.'

Von Schuschnigg had taken over as chancellor when his predecessor had been assassinated, by Austrian National Socialists.

'Yes, he's abolished Austria's one-party state to try and gain popularity.'

'Do you think it will work?'

'I don't know. He's under pressure from all sides. If Göring gets his way, he'll not last until spring.'

'Let me know if it all kicks off. I have a vested interest.'

'Ah, the boys,' Canaris said. 'I wonder if our parents felt the same? We never gave it a thought at the time.'

1938

'My good friends, for the second time in our history, a British Prime Minister has returned from Germany bringing peace with honour. I believe it is peace for our time.'

Neville Chamberlain, British Prime Minister.

CHAPTER 135

[06/01/1938 Thursday]

KIELER JÜDISCHES FREIHEITSNACHRICHTENBLATT

Volume 54

4th of Sh'vat, 5698

NO HIDING PLACE!

The Government has passed a decree which bans any Jew from changing their name. It also allows the authorities to revoke any name changes that had been approved prior to the enactment of the legislation.

The Law on the change of family names and given names comes into force immediately, and it effectively removes the ability of any Jewish person who wishes to disguise his or her "Jewishness" with a non-Jewish name.

The Kieler Jüdisches Freiheitsnachrichtenblatt believes that this is to make it easier for Jews to be identified by the Government and by the civil service. This worrying development raises questions about the Government's intentions for the Jewish population.

WORD OF THE WEEK

We bring you not a word this week, but a phrase. It has been appearing on posters all over Germany, featuring the German Führer.

Ein Volk, ein Reich, ein Führer.

~~o~~

[20/01/1938 Thursday]

6th January '38

Dear Esther,

It's good to hear that things are looking up for you and Itsik. You still sound a bit low at times. How is it going with the other women in the village?

I'll start with the gossip. You remember Franz, the General's son, and Lise, the girl next door, who got engaged then broke it off the next week. You were there one day when Franz was at home and you said you'd never seen someone with a heart so broken.

Well, she got engaged again. To an SS man, of all people. Thank goodness the Kästners and the Böhms don't socialise anymore! I'd be terrified if he came into the house. Yosef says that there's talk that Lise started going out with him just a few weeks after she and Franz broke up.

Anyway, enough of the Kästners. Yosef is worried about this new law. It means people can be arrested and put in prison if the Gestapo suspect them of doing something wrong, whether or not they have any grounds to be suspicious. It's very concerning.

Ruth won a prize at school for one of her essays. Her new teacher, who she really likes, gave her the award, but one of her classmates complained to her parents who approached the school, and the headmaster reprimanded the teacher, who was made to take the prize away from Ruth. She was dreadfully upset.

There's a lot of trouble in Austria. It's all over the newspapers and there's talk of our soldiers going in to sort it out. Yosef says that this could be the start of another war.

The National Socialist Party are ramping up their rhetoric. Their latest campaign features posters of Adolf Hitler on every wall. 'One People, One Empire, One Leader' is the caption.

They think of him as a god.

I hope you are all well. It's always lovely to hear from you.

All our love,

Miriam

~~o~~

Moshe,

Ha ha. Ernst Lehner. You wish. You're too slow.

We're not permitted to play football with other boys in the school team now, but we can play in the playground with them, or after school. Some of the boys are nasty and call us Jew-pigs and stuff (you'll know the ones) but because I'm a good footballer most are all right with me, and I can stand up for myself.

Holy Scheiße, Lise got engaged. The beautiful girl next door, you remember. Everyone here is upset at what she did to Franz. One day I'll have a girlfriend like her. There is one girl in my class who I like but Fischel says not to even think about it because she's not Jewish, and I'll get beat up if the other boys find out.

Blood Brothers Forever!

Manny

CHAPTER 136

Memo: Geh.KdoS. ABW 27/01/38 CAC0598.1

For Attention Only: All senior executive officers, Abwehr.

From: Rear Admiral Wilhelm Canaris, Chef der Abwehr

General Werner von Blomberg has resigned as Chief of staff of the Army High Command, citing personal reasons. It is expected that General Werner von Fritsch will succeed General Werner von Blomberg. [END]

~~o~~

Yosef stood in front of the mirror.

'I feel foolish,' he said.

'The General told you to wear them,' Miriam said, frowning. 'Just do as he says.'

The three medals pinned to Yosef's jacket glinted in the light of the lamp on the dresser. Miriam had made him polish them.

'I don't see what difference it will make. If they want to harass us, they'll do it anyway.'

'The General is right. They'll be more likely to leave you alone if you're a veteran.'

'Or it will annoy them further to see a Jew wearing medals,' Yosef said.

'No. There's still a little protection, even in law, for those who served, or whose father served in the war.'

'I suppose. I feel strange wearing them. They don't even regard us as citizens of this country. I'm not even sure I think of myself as German now.'

'You might be right, but we are German, no matter what they say. What are we, if not?'

'We're Jews. That's all.'

~~o~~

Memo: Geh.KdoS. ABW 04/02/38 CAC0607.1

For Attention Only: All senior executive officers, Abwehr.

From: Rear Admiral Wilhelm Canaris, Chef der Abwehr

General Werner von Fritsch has resigned as acting Chief of Staff of the Army High Command as a result of being accused of offences under Paragraph 175 of the criminal code.

General Walther von Brauchitsch has been appointed as the new Chief of Staff. [END]

~~o~~

Memo: Geh.KdoS. ABW 04/02/38 CAC0608.1

For Attention Only: All senior executive officers, Abwehr.

From: Rear Admiral Wilhelm Canaris, Chef der Abwehr

The Oberkommando der Wehrmacht (OKW) has been established by decree subordinating the roles of Chief of Staff for the Heer, the Kriegsmarine and the Luftwaffe High Commands to it, replacing the Reich War Ministry, which has been dissolved.

This brings the OKW under the direct command of the Führer and it will be led by General Wilhelm Keitel in the rank of a Reich Minister, with Alfred Jodl as Chief of the Operations Staff. [END]

~~o~~

Erich Kästner picked up the paper and frowned. Changes at the very top were coming thick and fast. After the flurry of memos, he supposed it should have been no surprise.

KIELER MORGENPOST

Saturday 5th February 1938

VON NEURATH REPLACED BY von RIBBENTROP

Konstantin von Neurath has been replaced as Reich Minister of Foreign Affairs by Joachim von Ribbentrop. He has held the post since 1932 and served as Foreign Minister under President Paul von Hindenburg, Chancellors Franz von Papen and Kurt von Schleicher, and Adolf Hitler.

In a reshuffle of The Führer's cabinet, Herr von Neurath becomes minister without portfolio and has been named as president of the Privy Cabinet Council.

He finished his coffee and shouted goodbye up the stairs to Maria. His driver, as always, had his army car waiting at the front door. When he reached the office, he hung is coat on the rack and picked up the pile of memos from the desk. The first one was another one from Canaris, and it was brief.

Memo: Geh.KdoS. ABW 05/02/38 CAC0621.1

For Attention Only: General Erich Kästner, Abwehr, Kiel office

From: Rear Admiral Wilhelm Canaris, Chef der Abwehr

I will be in Kiel on 10th February. Please be available at your office from 13:00 hours onwards. [END]

~~o~~

[10/02/1938 Thursday]

'How good is the soundproofing in here?'

Erich Kästner sat behind his desk. Opposite him, Rear Admiral Canaris sat with his right leg crossed over his left, leaning back in the chair.

'It's adequate,' said the General, 'if you don't shout, and Frau Müller doesn't have her ear pressed to the door.'

The admiral frowned. He rose from his chair and walked softly to the door and yanked it open.

Frau Müller, sitting at her desk, gave a small cry of fright.

'Goodness, Admiral Canaris, you gave me such a start.'

'My apologies, Frau Müller. I was wondering if you could arrange two coffees, and maybe a cake for the General and I. Would that be possible?'

'Well, I…' she stammered. 'The General asked me to type these letters and I…'

'You can finish these when you get back.' He smiled at her. 'I always work better when I have something in my stomach. Get one for yourself and take it out of petty cash.'

'Yes, sir. Thank you, sir,' she said, putting her coat on.

Admiral Canaris closed the door.

'She'll be away for a while.'

'So, von Neurath, von Fritsch, von Blomberg and the OKW. I suppose that is what this is all about?'

'You're very perceptive,' Canaris said, his eyebrows raised in mockery.

'It's a gift,' the General said, laughing. 'So, what happened? I've heard nothing but rumours.'

The admiral paused and took a deep breath.

'I'm meeting with all my section heads individually. I want to talk to you all off the record.'

The General nodded.

'You know that von Neurath, von Fritsch and von Blomberg were all sceptical of the Führer's plans for expansion?'

'Yes.'

'Well, now they're gone,' Canaris said. 'Just like that.'

He clicked his fingers for dramatic effect.

'But von Blomberg resigned,' the General said. 'You're insinuating that he was pushed.'

'Oh, he resigned all right. That fell right into Herr Hitler's lap, but he made the most of it.'

'How?'

'So, von Blomberg got married to Erna Gruhn; January the twelfth, I think it was, I'm surprised you didn't hear. Hermann Göring was his best man, would you believe, and Hitler himself was a witness at the wedding. Turns out she was a convicted prostitute; she'd worked in cities all over Germany.'

'Sweet Jesus!' the General said, with a whistle.

'It gets better. She also had criminal convictions for posing for pornographic images into the bargain.'

'Old von Blomberg must be seething!'

'Well, Adolf insisted that the marriage should be immediately annulled, to avoid scandal.'

'And von Blomberg refused!' the General said.

'Yes. Göring threatened to expose her. My guess is that she was so good in bed that he didn't care what happened to his career. Hell, maybe he realised that his days were numbered anyway.'

'So, what about von Fritsch. It was said he was being investigated under Paragraph 175. He's a homosexual?'

'I doubt it, but who knows? They're all at it in the Reichstag. From what I can gather, Heydrich had done a number on him in '36, accusing him of "criminally indecent activities between men". At that point, it was suppressed by Hitler but, once von Blomberg had gone, Heydrich unearthed it and gave it to the Reichsführer. Himmler presented von Fritsch with the evidence and he resigned the next day.'

462

'Two down, one to go. What did von Neurath get caught doing?'

'Nothing. He was moved sideways in a cabinet reshuffle; Minister of nothing and president of the 'Privy Cabinet Council' which, according to Hermann Göring, only exists on paper.'

'And conveniently, von Ribbentrop, the new man, is a fanatical supporter of Adolf,' the General said, shaking his head sadly.

'That brings us to the OKW,' Canaris said.

'Yes, the wonderful new Oberkommando der Wehrmacht.'

'Nominally, it oversees all three arms of the Wehrmacht, and because Keitel will never stand up to him, Adolf is effectively in control, but…'

He paused.

'What's stopping him?'

'The rivalry between the Kriegsmarine, the Luftwaffe and the Heer, most likely. Göring is an out-and-out Hitler man but Walther von Brauchitsch's appointment as head of the Heer is strange; von Fritsch recommended him as von Blomberg's successor, and Hitler agreed to it. He's a bigger supporter of Adolf's more aggressive foreign policies than von Blomberg, but he's an army man through and through.'

'And what about Raeder? He's no NSDAP patsy.'

'Admiral Raeder is no pushover but, at the end of the day, even though he might not always make it easy, he'll do what's necessary to keep the growth of the Kriegsmarine on track.'

'I'd imagine they'd have difficulty getting rid of him, even if they wanted. He's seen to be a very steady pair of hands around here, but I suspect he wouldn't be averse to some military muscle-flexing, which will endear him to the Führer.'

'The encouraging thing is, he doesn't think the Kriegsmarine are anywhere near ready, so he will try and put the brakes on Hitler's plans with regards to a war at sea.'

The General turned and looked out of the window, towards the yards. There were naval vessels at every stage of construction.

'Where does that leave us?' he asked eventually.

'I've persuaded Heydrich that the Abwehr should continue its work in support of the Wehrmacht and, to my astonishment, he agreed.'

'That's a relief. And what about you?'

'That's even more of a surprise. He says Adolf is happy with the way the Abwehr is being "managed" and wants me to say at the helm…'

'Is there a 'but'?'

'Yes, he wants his department copied in on all our paperwork.'

'Oh.'

'So, if you have anything contentious to tell me, don't write it down. Try and speak with me, personally. Put nothing in a memo that shouldn't be there. Is that clear?'

If it had been anyone else, the General might have taken offence.

'Quite clear, but in exceptional circumstances, I have a couple of people I could trust implicitly to deliver a verbal message.'

'The circumstances would have to be more than exceptional. It would be better kept between us.'

The General nodded.

'Things seem to be moving swiftly in Austria,' he said.

'Von Schuschnigg's position is becoming just about untenable. He's making compromise after compromise to stave off Austria being absorbed. There's talk of him holding a plebiscite to try and prevent annexation.'

'Does he think he'll win?'

'Perhaps. It seems to be running somewhat in his favour as we speak, because of the activities of the pro-Hitler Austrian National Socialists. He might just pull it off, which would make it much harder for us to go into Austria and force the matter.'

'And if we do go in, the army will do as it's asked?'

'I'm almost sure it will,' Canaris said.

There was a pause, then the General spoke.

'Do you remember our discussion in that little café in Kiel?' he said.

'Café Larsen, was it? Yes, I remember.'

'I said back then that I worried about the army's independence. That with the SS fighting alongside, and the gradual infiltration of the Heer by Hitlerjugend graduates, we'd lose it to the National Socialists.'

Canaris smiled.

'Yes. You seemed to get on your high horse. Asked me why I didn't sack you.'

'Well, it's even more pertinent now.'

'Why?' The admiral sighed.

'Because Hitler is tightening his grip on the upper command of the Wehrmacht and strengthening his support in the lower to middle ranks. The only ones preventing him having his own private army are a few middle-ranking officers, and we are too frightened to speak out.'

'Unfortunately, my friend, I think that for once, you might have a point.'

CHAPTER 137

[04/03/1938 Friday]

'You might be interested in this.'
    Dieter Maas handed the General the newspaper.
    'This is from last July,' the General said, puzzled.
    'Yes, I kept it.'

Berliner Tageblatt

Friday 2nd July 1937

BERLIN PASTOR ONE OF HUNDREDS ARRESTED!

Pastor Martin Niemöller, rector of the Jesus Christus Kirche in Dahlem, Berlin since 1931, was arrested in a countrywide sweep of the Confessing Church, an organisation he helped set up in 1933 to oppose the imposition of National Socialist ideals onto protestant churches.

He has spoken out vociferously in criticism of NSDAP policies and has declared that the Aryan Paragraph in much of their legislation is incompatible with the Christian virtue of charity.

'So why are you showing me it now?'
    Dieter handed the General a second newspaper.

Berliner Tageblatt

Thursday 3rd March 1938

BERLIN PASTOR RE-ARRESTED!

Martin Niemöller, Pastor of a local Berlin church, was released from custody following his trial today, and was almost immediately re-arrested.

Incarcerated since his arrest on the 1st of July last year, he was recently tried by a "Special Court" for activities against the State. He was fined 2,000 Reichsmarks and given a sentence of seven months imprisonment. Having already served a prison term longer than the sentence, he was released under the time-served rule but, as he left the courtroom, he was arrested again by the Gestapo.

No statement has been yet issued by the security services about further charges.

Dieter waited until the General had finished reading.

'You asked me to find out about the German Evangelical Church. Nearly all the members of the Synod are in bed with the National Socialists; most are party members, though some individual priests are willing to be critical, or help out people who suffer as a result of this government's policies.'

'Pastor Niemöller is one of a group of priests and pastors who formed a breakaway church, the Confessional Church, that called for independence of protestant churches in Germany, with no state interference. He was particularly outspoken and was one of the first they detained back in July of last year.'

Dieter Maas picked up the paper.

'I read about his arrest,' he continued, 'and, because I keep a copy of anything that I consider of interest, I looked it out when I heard about the trial, and him being picked up again. I presume that someone in the party found the sentence too lenient and decided to take further action.'

'His church sounds like the sort of place I'd rather go,' the General said. 'At least they're brave enough to stand up to the government.'

'Well, yes, with a small caveat.'

'Go on…'

'Well, the young Martin Niemöller was a national conservative and a war hero and was openly critical of the liberal policies of the Weimar Republic. From what I've learned, he welcomed Hitler's election win in 1933, believing that they would restore Germany's nationhood, but he gradually became disillusioned when the National Socialists forced changes on the church, and he was vociferous in his damnation of the expulsion of Christians with Jewish ancestry from the church.'

'Like most of us, he was taken in by Hitler's promises, but that doesn't make him bad.'

'I'm not saying he is. I'm just not so sure he's against the NSDAP's Jewish policy per se; it seems that his only concerns with it are when it affects those who have converted to Christianity.'

'Even if that's true, the worst you can say about him is that he's looking after his own. At least he had the balls to stand up about it, and he's paying the price for it.'

Dieter Maas handed him a sheet of paper.

'This is from one of his sermons.'

What is the reason for their obvious punishment, which has lasted for thousands of years? Dear brethren, the reason is easily given: the Jews brought the Christ of God to the cross!

'That's not good, I'll admit. What do you think?'

'Mmmm. I think he's a brave man who stood up for what he thought was right. He has flaws, but don't we all. He'll have plenty time to think about it.'

'You think they'll keep him in prison?'

'From what I hear, he has been interned in Sachsenhausen. Indefinitely.'

The General flinched.

CHAPTER 138

KIELER MORGENPOST

Sunday 13th March 1938

DER ANSCHLUß VOLLZOGEN!

Hundreds of thousands of Austrians lined the streets yesterday to welcome the soldiers of the Wehrmacht's 8th Army as Austria finally became part of the Greater German Reich. There was no resistance from the Austrian army, who had been told by President Wilhelm Miklas to remain in their barracks.

The Wehrmacht had been invited in by new Chancellor, National Socialist Arthur Seyss-Inquart after the resignation of former Chancellor, Kurt Schuschnigg, to quell the riots that were threatening to engulf Austria in civil war.

By early afternoon, the situation in Austria was declared under control, and Adolf Hitler crossed into the newest territory of the Third Reich at Braunau am Inn, the place of his birth, with a 4,000-man personal bodyguard.

The Führer and his party were greeted by cheering crowds of Austrians with NSDAP flags and flowers, saluting and chanting "Heil Hitler!", and "Sieg Heil!" He is expected to tour the country over the next few days, to allow its citizens to meet him.

A meeting between Adolf Hitler and Chancellor Seyss-Inquart will take place during the Führer's visit to Austria.

~~o~~

The General put the paper down.

'So, the Anschluss is complete, according to our wonderful press.'

'It would seem so, sir,' Captain Bauer replied, 'and with no casualties on either side. It's remarkable. I'm surprised just how strong the welcome has been for our troops, considering the protests and rioting that there were beforehand.'

'That's possibly because most of the violence and unrest was caused by the Austrian National Socialists,' the General said, 'and now they have what they want.'

'That could be true, sir.'

'I must concede that the Austrian people seem to have almost universally welcomed the idea of their country becoming a German state. It will be interesting to see what happens over the next days, weeks and months.'

'Were your sons involved, sir?'

'No, it was the 8th Army who got the job. Franz and Johann are with the 4th. Johann is distraught to have missed it; he would have been especially keen to make the acquaintance of some of these Austrian Fräuleins who were out in force to welcome the triumphant heroes.'

They both laughed.

~~o~~

[01/04/1938 Friday]

Vizeadmiral Wilhelm Canaris turned to General Kästner.

'Let's get out of here as soon as it's polite to leave,' he said, under his breath.

The reception was being held in one of the larger rooms at the Kriegsmarine building, looking over Kieler Hafen. There were four admirals present, and countless other naval officers of every rank, all friends and acquaintances of the newly promoted Vizeadmiral.

They'd been standing for the best part of two hours, Wilhelm Canaris taking care to speak with everyone in the room.

Although it had been a couple of years since he had held a naval commission, having transferred to the Abwehr, he'd been around the Kriegsmarine since before the Great War, and had served in various branches of the navy, including the submarine fleet. As a result, he was well known and respected, and despite his wish for the function to be over, he'd been flattered that they'd all turned up to see him receive the elevation in rank that most felt he deserved.

'I have a bottle and a couple of glasses in my office. Slip along in another ten minutes. I'll see you there. Anyone remaining after that will be too drunk to notice you've gone.'

The General made his way over to the door and let himself out. As he reached his office, Chief Petty Officer Neuer emerged from it, almost running into the General.

'Sir, I was just coming to see you before I sign off for the evening. There was a telephone call for you. It was your son.'

'Which one?'

'Hauptmann Franz, sir.'

'Is he still on the line?'

'No, sir, but he left a message. He said that he and his brother are passing through Kiel in an hour, and they would call here, if you were still about. I said you most likely would be.'

'Thank you, Günter. I'll see you on Monday unless anything happens over the weekend.'

'Like we decide to invade somewhere else, sir?'

The General burst out laughing and looked at his chief petty officer with a new appreciation.

'Very good, Günter. Very good indeed. Just don't let Herr Hitler hear you say that.'

~~o~~

He was still smiling ten minutes later, when Admiral Canaris let himself into his office. Two glasses of whisky had already been poured, and the two friends sat down on opposite sides of the desk.

'So, the Führer has done it again, eh,' Canaris said. 'You surely can't still be sceptical about his achievements for the Fatherland.'

'The newspapers are certainly full of it,' the General replied. 'Adolf Hitler and the Wehrmacht have been welcomed with open arms. A tactical genius, they say. Britain and France powerless to save the Versailles Treaty and Germany once more a nation to be reckoned with.'

Despite the Anschluss delivering a fatal blow to France and Britain's efforts to keep Germany militarily and economically weak, neither of the two nations' leaders had reacted, other than to condemn the union of Germany and Austria as unacceptable.

The admiral looked surprised.

'It sounds as if you're impressed with the Führer, Kästner.'

'I can't deny the man's uncanny abilities. Or his popularity, even in Austria. The

Austrian people invited us in.'

The admiral chuckled.

'Well, that might not be quite the way it happened. It was our Ministry of Propaganda who issued the press reports about riots breaking out and that most of the Austrian population were calling for German troops to restore order. I've heard since there were no riots to speak of.'

'But Kurt Schuschnigg resigned, and Seyss-Inquart called for help when he took over as chancellor.'

'Seyss-Inquart wasn't made chancellor until after midnight. President Miklas wouldn't swear him in. The telegram for help, a few hours earlier, was a fraud.'

The General shrugged.

'At the end of the day,' he said, 'the Austrian people welcomed Hitler, and the union, with open arms.'

'Even the Führer was surprised at that. From what I hear, he'd intended to leave Austria as a puppet state with Seyss-Inquart as head of a pro-NSDAP government. However, the overwhelming reception he got made him change his mind and absorb Austria into the Reich.'

The two men had tracked Hitler's journey through Austria in the press and on radio, a triumphal tour that climaxed in Vienna on the fifteenth of March, when around a quarter of a million cheering German-Austrians gathered around the Heldenplatz to hear Hitler declare that 'The oldest eastern province of the German people shall be, from this point on, the newest bastion of the German Reich.'

'So, there was an element of luck, and some sleight of hand,' the General said. 'It doesn't really matter. Hitler now has his raw materials and the extra manpower to accelerate rearmament. Where next?'

'Sudetenland. He's already making speech after speech about the plight of *dem Deutschen Volkes* in Czechoslovakia. Then it will be Poland. But he'll regroup for a while first. He won't find the Czechs or the Poles quite as willing to invite us in.'

'Sudetenland I can see, but surely not Poland?'

'You'd be surprised. There are a vast number of Germans in Polish Danzig, and in isolated East Prussia. And, in case you haven't noticed, we're getting very friendly with the Soviets.'

'Yes,' the General said, with an ironic smile, 'the same evil Bolsheviks that only the National Socialists could protect us from.'

'You know what they say. Keep your friends close and your enemies closer.'

The General grimaced and filled up both glasses.

There was a sharp rap on the door, and it swung open before the General could say anything. First Lieutenant Johann Kästner burst into the room.

'Have you ever heard of being invited in?' the admiral said, with a smile.

'I knocked, didn't I, Franz?'

His brother followed him in, shaking his head.

The two men rose to greet the new arrivals and a round of hugs was followed by a search for two more glasses.

'What brings you here?' the General asked.

'We're on our way to Plön. We're being mobilised.'

The General gave the admiral a look.

'Where to?'

'We're off to Austria. To beef up the 8th Army.'

'There's trouble?'

'Not as far as we know,' Franz said. 'It's about the transport, from what we've been told. The 8th Army haven't been fully modernised yet. Too many horses and not enough trucks. Our unit and three others are being sent to assist with the supply chain until the 8th get their new vehicles.'

'It will only be for a month or so, Colonel Schneider told us,' Johann added. 'I wish we'd been part of the first wave though.'

'I suppose all the best Fräuleins will have been snapped up,' the General said, laughing at the indignant pout on his son's face.

'You think I'm that shallow?' he asked.

'Let's say you've talked of nothing else,' his brother said.

'Et tu, brother,' Johann said. A smile betrayed his wounded expression.

Franz changed the subject.

'Uncle Wilhelm, I hear congratulations are in order,' he said, turning to his father's oldest friend.

'Oh, stop calling me uncle. You're both young men now,' he said. 'Feel free to call me Vizeadmiral.'

The boys laughed.

'Yes, sir,' Franz said. 'That makes Father and you equivalent in rank, doesn't it?'

'Almost,' said the General. 'And it did take him a good while longer.'

They all laughed this time.

'I had to work my way up,' the admiral said. 'I didn't do it on nepotism and privilege.'

The boys looked from one to another, enjoying the latest round in the sparring match between the two men that they'd watched since childhood.

'And one day, you might make full admiral and, you never know, I might be demoted from Generaloberst, and I'll have to call you Sir.'

Wilhelm Canaris threw back his head and roared. It wasn't often the General had the last word.

When he'd settled down, his shoulders still shaking a little, he turned to the two Kästner sons.

'So, what does the army think?'

'There is a buzz about the regiment,' Franz said. 'There's no doubt this Austrian business has instilled a confidence, and a feeling that the army is back at the centre of things.'

'We're ready for anything,' Johann interjected, not noticing the frown that briefly crossed his father's face.

'What about your commanders? What are they saying?'

'They're telling us to train harder,' Johann said, his eyes bright, his face animated. 'They say that there will be great opportunities for us as the army expands. We had sixty new recruits last month in our company alone, and they all need to be brought up to speed.'

'Yes, your father told me that you're a first lieutenant already, and that Franz is now a captain. It only seems yesterday that I held that rank.'

'It was only yesterday,' the General interjected.

'Boys, your father is being disingenuous. I must explain that the captain's rank in the navy is somewhat different from that in the army.'

The three Kästner men stood grinning at him.

'A Kapitän zur See, which I was before becoming a rear admiral only a few months ago, is the equivalent of colonel in the army. Incidentally, that was when I took command of the Abwehr, and became your father's boss.'

'Now, now, Wilhelm, the General said, patting his friend's back, 'there's no need to be so defensive about this. We all have great respect for you, whatever rank you hold.'

Wilhelm Canaris looked at the three Kästner men and gave in.

'Oh, bugger the lot of you,' he said, making for the door, his head held high.

'I think you've upset Uncle Wilhelm,' Johann said.

'Oh, don't worry about him. He has an urgent meeting somewhere. He just likes to make a dramatic exit.'

He stuck his head out of the office door and shouted down the corridor.

'I'll be in touch. Sir.'

He heard Canaris's laugh echo down the corridor.

CHAPTER 139

'Mazel tov!'

'A freylekhn Geburtstag.'

Manny stood beaming in the centre of the group of men, accepting their congratulations and birthday greetings. They stood in the vestibule of the synagogue, and his father was among them. He was half their size, so he had to crane his neck to look at them when they spoke to him. Ruth and his mother were still inside, talking with the other women.

'Shkoyekh,' he said, politely. *Thank you.*

He spoke enough Yiddish to get by, but he wasn't fluent. Unlike some of the families in the congregation, Yosef and Miriam didn't speak much Yiddish at home, so Manny picked up more of the language from the Orthodox Jewish boys he mixed with, and from his grandparents.

His birthday greetings over, Manny listened intently as the men talked.

'This Anschluss is not good,' one of the eastern Jews said. 'It gives Hitler more power and feeds his ego.'

'It might not be so bad,' Manny heard his father say. 'There is a chance that it will satisfy their hunger for success. Remember what it was like after the Saarland was taken.'

'Yosef's right. It seemed to put them in a good mood.'

'I'm not sure. My wife's brother's uncle in Vienna says there are beatings and intimidation, that Jews have been put out of their homes by mobs of Austrian National Socialists.'

The conversation died. Even at eleven, Manny imagined the horror of the newly homeless.

'Emanuel Bandmann was taken last week.'

They all turned to Jakob Teubner. He was one of the small group of men who had stood at the Bimah and led Shabbat services since the rabbi had emigrated.

'Why?'

'He's retired, but they caught him helping an Aryan family with their son. He used to be their doctor.'

'The old fool. Did he not know this would happen?'

'He knew the risks, but the parents pleaded with him. The new doctor wasn't able to help the boy.'

'Did the Gentiles report him when the boy didn't get better?'

'No. The boy made a complete recovery. The family were grateful enough. It was the Aryan doctor who reported him, and the parents.'

'What happened to them?'

'Nothing. A ticking off from the Gestapo, that's all.'

'Where was Emanuel taken?'

'His family haven't been told. They're trying to find out. They have money, so they've managed to find an Aryan lawyer who agreed to represent them, but he says that it's not certain that he can help. It cost them 200 Reichsmarks to hear that.'

'At least the lawyer spoke to them. Few will consider a Jewish client.'

The men looked around as their wives began drifting out of the door.

'Next week, then?' Yosef said, taking Manny's hand.

'No, there's a meeting Wednesday night. Can you make it?'

'I'll be there if I can.'

~~o~~

Afula

13th March

Dear Miriam,

It's terrible! Itsik's parents have been refused permission to come to Palestine. Itsik and Abel are beside themselves and I'm completely heartbroken. They say there's no hope of an appeal, but both his parents pleaded with us not to try and return, that the one comfort they have is that we're all out of Germany. The children are taking it hard – we promised them that their Bubbe and Sabba would be here soon.

I'm sorry – it's hard to even write about anything else because worry about them fills my every thought.

You asked about the other women here. They couldn't be nicer to me, and I'd be lost without them now, but I see them looking at me sometimes as if I should just get on with it and stop moping.

We heard about the Anschluss. I hope it make things better at home. Itsik has cousins in Austria so perhaps his parents can go and stay with them. It might be safer there.

The post has not been collected here for weeks but Itsik has managed to get on a convoy to Haifa. Moshe is out playing football (again – it's all he seems to do) and he didn't leave a letter to enclose for Manny but I'm sure he says hello to him, and I'll make him write next time.

Your dearest friend,

Esther.

PS If you have time, and it's not too difficult for you, is there any chance you could visit Itsik's parents and check that they are well. They live in Jungmannstraße, just off Holtenauer. The building number is 34. Theirs is flat 5.

CHAPTER 140

'Yosef, leave what you're doing until later. I need a trip to the nursery.'

'Yes, ma'am. I'll draw the car round to the front.'

'Put a couple of wooden trays in. I'm going to buy some plants.'

'Certainly, ma'am. I'll do that first. I'll let you know when I'm ready.'

Twenty minutes later, the car swept into the Bauernhof Ahrling Gärtnerei, the nursery that the Kästners favoured.

The proprietor saw Maria Kästner step out of the door, Yosef holding it open for her, and rushed over.

'Frau Kästner, it's so good to see you. Can we tempt you with some lovely bedding plants today, or perhaps one of our new bushes that have just arrived?'

'No, Herr Ahrling. I'm here to buy some vegetables.'

The man looked puzzled. Yosef could understand why. As far as he knew, the Kästners had purchased a few fruit trees over the years, but he couldn't ever remember them buying vegetables to plant.

'I'm doing my bit for the nation,' she said. 'Blut und Boden. I'd so like to impress the ladies of the Guild with some beautiful fresh vegetables.'

Blood and Soil. Yosef turned away to hide his disgust. It was the latest NSDAP propaganda scoop, and it was splashed all over the front of *Der Stürmer.* He remembered Frau Kästner commenting on it earlier in the week. He could feel the bile stir in his stomach.

Maria Kästner took a piece of paper from her handbag.

'I'd like to plant onions, leeks, turnips, parsnips, celery, beetroot, cabbages and lettuce to start with.'

'Frau Kästner, might I suggest starting with three or four varieties to begin, and build up to a larger vegetable plot? It would let you dip your toe in the water.'

'I don't want any dipping of toes. I want a proper vegetable garden. We should also add cauliflower to that list.'

'Whatever you think, ma'am. I'll show you what we have.'

As they walked past the rows of flowering plants and bushes, the man turned to Yosef.

'Have you got a plot prepared?' he mouthed.

Yosef shook his head.

'No, we haven't,' he muttered, 'I'll get started when we get back. How quickly do the plants need to be in?'

'A day at most, for the young plants. For seeds, it wouldn't matter, but to get the benefit of summer…'

'I'll sort it out. I'll end up looking after it anyway, after a few weeks.'

The man grinned, but glanced at Maria Kästner, now ten metres in front of them.

'What is this Blut und Boden anyway?' he said, under his breath. 'I've sweated plenty blood and I've been up to my armpits in soil for the last twenty years. Do I get a medal now?'

'Perhaps. She just wants to do something patriotic to impress the ladies of the Guild. It won't last.'

Maria Kästner had reached the rows of vegetables.

'They all look the same, Herr Ahrling,' she called over.

'They do at that age, madam. Would it be satisfactory if I give you twenty seedlings of each variety, and seeds for the ones we don't have growing?'

'That will be fine. I'll wait in the car.'

The two men looked at each other. The nurseryman handed Yosef a metal container.

'Hold this. I'll dig the plants.'

~~o~~

[19/04/1938 Tuesday]

Two hard days later, Beate Böhm had watched from her window as Yosef Nussbaum planted the last of the seeds.

The sight of Yosef clearing a plot close to the wall separating the Kästner and Böhm houses had puzzled her at first, and she hadn't been any more enlightened when he planted row upon row of vegetable seedlings and erected six brand-new cold frames next to the tilled earth.

But at the Guild meeting later that morning, Maria told the ladies of her latest project.

'My gardener and I have sacrificed part of our beautiful garden to grow vegetables for the nation. We are expecting our first crops in about two months' time.'

Beate Böhm cursed. The woman had upstaged everyone, again.

The worst of it was that the ugly, raw, upturned patch of earth, with its unedifying rows of unattractive plants, was just in the right position to detract from the Böhms' view, but it could hardly be seen from the Kästner house. She wondered if Maria Kästner had done it on purpose.

~~o~~

A week after his first visit, Yosef was back at the nursery, for more seeds.

'Your mistress has started a trend,' the proprietor told him. 'I'm nearly out of vegetable seedlings until the next batch germinates. Have a look at this.'

Yosef looked at the newly painted sign the man had erected in the area he was growing his vegetables.

In large red-and-black letters, it read *Blut und Boden*.

CHAPTER 141

[22/04/1938 Friday]

Miriam almost didn't hear it. She passed the foot of the stairs before the sound registered. The sobbing was barely audible, and her first assumption was that Manny had had another nightmare. She climbed the stairs and listened at his bedroom door but could hear nothing. She turned the handle as quietly as possible and entered the room, the door creaking a little as she opened it.

He was sound asleep.

Then she heard the crying again, but it was behind her, from the room opposite. She crept out and opened Ruth's bedroom door. On the bed, she could see the shape of Ruth's body under the covers, her body shuddering in time to the quiet sobs.

As gently as possible, she sat down on Ruth's bed and placed her hand on the form of her daughter's body.

'Shush,' she said, so as not to frighten her, and she leaned down and covered Ruth's body with her own. She felt the tenseness in her daughter's body slacken, and the sobs began to abate a little.

The pillow was soaked with tears, and Miriam briefly sat up and turned it over, gently laying Ruth's head back down, her hand stroking her dark-brown curls.

'What's up, Schatzi,' she said.

'Nothing. Just things.' Ruth sniffed.

'Tell me, Ruth, sweetie. I can help.'

'I don't think you can, Mama.'

'Is it school. Are you getting bullied?'

'No. Well, a little, I suppose. It's nothing I can't handle.'

'Then what is it?'

'The teacher is making us read this.' She reached under the bed and lifted out a book.

Miriam looked across the corridor to Manny's room. He was still sleeping. She looked at the book.

Der Giftpilz. By Ernst Hiemer. The Poisonous Mushroom.

She flipped it over. Published by Stürmer. Julius Streicher's publishing house.

I should have guessed.

'He said we've to read it to celebrate the Führer's birthday.'

Miriam opened it. Each page had a cartoon picture, with an accompanying caption. She looked at the first one.

It showed a pretty, young, blonde-haired woman in traditional German dress, picking mushrooms in a forest with a young boy, her son perhaps, or her younger brother. The boy was kneeling on the ground, holding up a green toadstool he had picked, proudly showing it to her. The cartoon showed her in the act of admonishing him.

She read the caption.

```
Just as it is sometimes hard to tell a toadstool from an edible
mushroom, so too it is often difficult to recognize the Jew as
a swindler and criminal...
```

She felt her face burn hotly and her breathing shallow as she turned to the next page.

```
How to Recognize a Jew: The Jewish has a bent nose. It
resembles a number six...
```

She flicked through the rest of the book. It was all in a similar vein.

Another one caught her eye.

How Jews torment Animals: The animal falls once more to the ground. Slowly it dies. The Jews stand around and laugh.

She snapped the book shut.

'You do not have to read this... this... hateful filth,' she said, her raised voice causing Manny to stir.

'I'm going to show it to your papa,' she added, whispering now. 'It's the last straw. We will go and see your teacher about this.'

Ruth's eyes widened in fear.

'No, no, Mama,' Ruth begged, her eyes pleading with her mother. 'I'll get into trouble. It will be worse for me.'

'I'll not have you standing in front of the class with the other Jewish children reciting this filth.'

'It won't be too bad. The others will be with me. If you complain he'll make me stand there on my own.'

Ruth started to cry again.

'There, hush now,' Miriam said, folding her daughter in her arms. 'We'll see what Papa says. We won't do anything to upset you, but at some point, we'll need to make a stand. Perhaps I'll talk to Rosa, and the other Jewish mothers.'

'Please don't, Mama. I don't want Rebeka or the other children to get into bother because of me. Please don't say anything.'

She looked up at Miriam with imploring eyes.

'All right, Schatzi. I promise.'

She was almost too old to be called these pet names but, deep down, Miriam still saw Ruth as her little girl.

~~o~~

Later, when she showed Yosef the book, he paled, then anger flushed across his face.

'She's asked us not to say anything about it,' Miriam said. 'She was frantic with worry that we would go to the school and make a fuss. What kind of world are we living in when school can provoke such fear in a child?'

'The Germany of the National Socialists, that's the kind of world we've found ourselves in. We should give serious thought to leaving.'

Her eyes clouded.

'You know we can't. Until we all agree to leave. And my parents won't, I'm sure; neither will yours.'

'They're stubborn. Like you.'

She gave a tired smile.

'So, what do we do?' she said.

'We do as she asks. Say nothing. Do nothing. Hide in our little hole.'

She cringed at the bitterness in his voice, but she knew he was right.

CHAPTER 142

[26/04/1938 Tuesday]

KIELER JÜDISCHES FREIHEITSNACHRICHTENBLATT

Volume 56

25th of Nisan, 5698

FURTHER RESTRICTIONS ON JEWISH COMMUNITY

Two new laws passed within the last week are putting further pressure on the Jewish community in Kiel.

On the 22nd of this month, a law was passed in the Reichstag forbidding Jewish-owned businesses from changing their names. This decree has been brought in to prevent the "camouflage" of Jewish businesses from "real" German citizens.

And from today, the government requires all Jews to register assets over 5,000 Reichsmarks. The KJF expect that this is to enable the Government to tax these assets at a later date.

It is probable that there will be a scramble to look for ways to hide money, jewellery, and other valuables, to avoid their possible confiscation, but it could be a risky strategy, as the authorities will heavily fine or, more likely, imprison those caught trying to conceal assets.

~~o~~

'Sir, what are we to do?'

In all his years, the General had never seen Yosef so agitated.

'We'll find a way to sort it out. The main thing is not to panic. Where do you keep your money?'

'In the bank, of course.'

The General thought he could detect a note of exasperation in Yosef's voice.

'No, I mean, which bank?'

'Oh, I see. Städtische Sparkasse, on Lorentzendamm.'

The City Savings bank. Good.

The General knew the bank well.

'Let's go and get your money, now,' he said.

'I have some with some Jewish friends too,' Yosef said, bowing his head.

'What do you mean?'

'They lend money, sir, just like the banks. Other people's money.'

'Loan sharks, you mean.'

'No, no, sir. It's not like that. The interest rates are reasonable, while still giving a decent return on people's investment.'

'I'll take your word for it,' the General muttered. 'They'll need time to call in their loans but, on the other hand, their debtors, who are largely Jewish, I presume, will be pleased to offload any spare cash they have before they lose it.'

'And then what, sir?'

'Yosef, do you trust me?'

'Yes, sir. Of course. Why?'

'Give the money to me. I'll keep it for you. You can get it whenever you want.'

'That might work, sir. Would they not be suspicious?'

'Keep enough just to satisfy them when they come for it; give me the rest. I'll keep it safe for you.'

'I'll have to talk to Miriam first. I'll let you know. I'm sure she'll agree.'

'That's settled then. There can't be any paperwork for this. A verbal contract only.'

'That's fine with me, sir. You wouldn't let us down.'

'I won't say anything to Maria. Better she doesn't know.'

'What will we do if, God forbid, something happens to you?'

'I'll leave a sealed note for Maria and ask my lawyer to keep it with our wills.'

'And if something happens to us?'

'I'll see that your children are looked after. I would have done that anyway.'

'I know, sir.'

~~o~~

Yosef came out of the bank, ashen-faced, and got into the car.

'They wouldn't give me my money,' he blurted out, before the General had a chance to ask him.

'Why? It's yours.'

'They offered me 200 Reichsmarks. Said I could get the same tomorrow. It's a new rule for all Jewish account holders.'

The General cursed.

'How much do you have deposited with them?

'Nearly 12,000 Reichsmarks,' Yosef said, his voice low and strained.

The General whistled through his teeth.

'Sweet Jesus,' he said. 'How did you manage to save that much?'

'With a tied house, and because we don't need to spend too much, we've managed to save well. We have half that again with our Jewish friend. We wanted Ruth and Manny to go to university. And we hoped to buy a small house one day, when we retired.'

The General was impressed.

'We'll not let the bastards get their hands on it; I've got an account here and I know the manager. Come on. Just do as I say.'

He got out of the car and Yosef scurried to follow him.

Ten minutes later, they were back, the money from Yosef's account in the General's briefcase.

Yosef started up the car. The General watched in the mirror as a smile crept onto Yosef's face, despite his best efforts.

'That was genius, sir,' Yosef said, 'if you don't mind me saying.'

The General had asked to see the manager and demanded that all of Yosef's money be withdrawn.

'We can't, General Kästner. Rules are rules.'

'You'll find that the accounts I hold at this bank here are good enough reasons to make it advisable for you to make an exception here.'

The manager had squirmed, arguing that the repercussions could be serious if he flaunted the law.

'Listen, let's call it a loan repayment. We will furnish you with paperwork confirming that Yosef Nussbaum is repaying a loan in cash that I made to him several years ago which, including interest, comes to 11,678 Reichsmarks and twenty-two Pfennigs.'

The manager's head, which had been bowed in supplication, shot up.

'Ah. I see,' he said, seeing a possible way out of the predicament he was in. 'That might be suitable,' he continued. 'And the remaining 200 Reichsmarks?'

'Herr Nussbaum is going to withdraw that now, as far as I know, and close the account. If the details of the account happened to be misplaced, who would be any the wiser?'

'Very good, sir.' The man sounded relieved but the General, underneath his bravado, knew that the transaction would not stand up to thorough scrutiny by the security services.

As the car sped across the thin strip of land that divided the two small lakes of Kleiner Kiel, the General acknowledged Yosef's compliment with a shrug.

'Sometimes, you just have to show people a way out. Now, remember and talk to that friend of yours. Get the money in cash, not a cheque. And if the Gestapo ever asks, I'm a greedy, money-grabbing employer who took advantage of your predicament.'

'I'll go and see him later today. It would be better if I were on my own.'

CHAPTER 143

[28/04/1938 Thursday]

Miriam signed her reply to Esther's letter and sealed it in its envelope. She left to visit Rosa, hoping that God would forgive her for a couple of tiny lies. By the time she'd arrived at her friend's house and given Rosa the letter to enclose with her own, she'd justified it to herself, knowing she'd done the right thing.

There was no point in worrying her friend.

~~o~~

[03/05/1938 Tuesday]

'So, how were the Fräuleins in Österrreich, Johann?' the General asked.

The Kästner boys had a day's furlough on their return from their short posting in Austria, and they'd used it to visit their parents.

'He's in love,' Franz said. 'Well, for a few weeks, at least.'

'What's her name?' the General asked, smiling.

'Oh, leave it out, you two. She's a lovely girl, but I doubt I'll ever see her again. She said she'd write, but…'

'He didn't even manage to spend a whole night with this one,' Franz said, 'She lived with her parents, but we hardly saw him. As soon as we were off duty, he disappeared.'

'Nonsense. I drank with you a few times.'

'Only when she was working.' Franz laughed.

'So, what was it like?' the General said, interrupting his sons' verbal jousting. 'Are the Austrians as keen to be German as we've been told?'

'Definitely,' Johann said. 'Even more so if that were possible. It's as if they've been waiting for years for this to happen.'

'In a way, they have,' the General said. 'It's been talked about for a long time now.'

He paused. 'So, there's no trouble?' he asked.

'Not really,' Johann said. 'We've had nothing to do apart from move soldiers and materials around for the 8th Army.'

'There's no political unrest,' Franz said. 'The only street violence we saw is directed against Jewish people and their property. It seems more vicious than it has been here.'

'It was just a few isolated incidents,' Johann said. 'The authorities will clamp down on it.'

'I'm not so sure. The police stood back and did nothing, as far as I could tell. They told us not to intervene. And the Gestapo are there in force.'

'It will all settle down,' Johann said. 'It has back here.'

The General couldn't argue with his son. It had been a while since he'd heard of any real violence against Jews, or Jewish businesses. Instead, it was the government's persistent erosion of their rights that was hitting the Jewish community the hardest.

He was about to say something to Johann but thought better of it.

Let him see for himself.

When Johann heard his mother's voice, and went to talk to her, the General turned to Franz.

'How bad is it?'

'It's bad. Johann closed his eyes to the worst of it. There are beatings and looting every day. The people are forcing Jewish families out, and the police won't intervene. All that hate

480

must have been simmering under the surface, and now that they've been given a free rein to do what they like with impunity, they're making the most of it.'

Franz shook his head gently and half closed his eyes.

'We tried to intervene on one occasion,' he told his father. 'The police told us to stay out of it. We pushed them aside, then the Gestapo turned up. They're difficult to argue with. All sorts of threats were made.'

'Really? Like what?'

'*Think about your families back home, imagine what it would be like to be cashiered, and so forth.* Empty threats, perhaps, but I could see my men weren't happy to take that risk, so we backed off. It felt terrible, and the look in the faces of the family being terrorised will stay with me for a long time.'

'The Gestapo are getting a fearsome reputation here. As bad as the regular SS.'

'Strangely enough, the SS aren't as bad as they've been made out to be. At least, not the ones we've encountered.'

Johann came back into the room. He grinned.

'I got a lecture from Mama again about women.'

'She's right. You should settle down with a nice girl.'

'Not while there are so many beautiful ones about. Why be stuck with one?'

'If you don't get a girl in trouble first, you'll fall hard one day, mark my words.'

'Not me. I'm extremely careful, believe it or not and, unlike my older brother here, I don't still have the original packet of condoms that you gave me when we had our little chat.'

His father shook his head.

'What were you saying about the SS?'

'Franz was just saying they weren't too bad.'

'No, we get on all right with them,' Johann said. 'They take themselves a little too seriously at times, but other than that...'

'Do you still have SS men in your own units?' the General asked.

Franz looked at his father.

'Why do you ask?'

'No reason. It's just that you mentioned it the last time.'

'Oh. I see.'

'The answer is yes,' Johann said. 'They've been seconded to the battalion. It's a two-way thing. We teach them how to fight and they tell us what we're fighting for.'

He laughed.

'Are you going back to Austria?' the General asked.

'No,' Johann said. 'Unfortunately. A whole batch of trucks and half-tracks arrived for the 8th Army just as we left.'

'So, that's the end of another romance?' his father said.

'Yes,' Johann said, with a rueful smile.

'So, what's next for you two?'

'Back to barracks and hope the next action is ours,' Johann said, smiling. 'The Führer seems to be putting some pressure on the Czechs. I hope we get a chance to prove ourselves when he decides to take action.'

The General grimaced.

You might just get what you wished for.

~~o~~

[06/05/1938 Friday]

Sitting in his study three days later, once Maria had gone to bed, the General caught up with the day's news in the *Morgenpost*.

481

Or what passed for news.

There was a soft knock on the door.

'Come in,' he shouted.

The door opened, and Yosef came in, carrying a tray with a frothing cup of hot chocolate on it.

'I thought you might like a drink before you retired, sir.'

The General thanked him, and he picked up the cup, expecting Yosef to take the tray and leave, but he remained standing in front of the desk.

'Is there something...' The General's voice tailed off as Yosef handed him a thick envelope pulled out from the waistband at the back of his trousers.

'The remainder of the money, sir.'

'Ah, I see. Your friend paid out.'

'Of course, sir. It took him a little while to gather the cash together but there was never any question...'

'Sorry, Yosef. It just seemed like such an informal way of doing business.'

'Like this, sir?'

The General laughed.

'You have a point,' he said.

'Please count it, sir.'

'How much is there?'

'7,000 Marks, sir. I mean Reichsmarks.'

'I'll take your word. I don't need to count it.'

'Thank you, sir. I'll leave you to it.'

'No, sit down, Yosef, and chat for a while.'

Just like the old days.

But now, the conversation was about Austria, and what would happen in the Sudetenland, and the latest laws restricting the Nussbaums, and their friends.

'Try and persuade Miriam to consider leaving,' the General said. 'It's only going to get worse.'

'I know, sir, but she won't hear of it. I'm not even sure I'd go.'

'Well, start thinking about it seriously. For your own sake.'

CHAPTER 144

[08/05/1938 Sunday]

'Now, that was a sailing trip.'

Oskar sat on the General's boat, rocking gently on her berth in front of the Kriegsmarine building. Dieter sat on the opposite side of the cockpit. The General handed three bottles of beer up, then climbed out of the companionway to join them. All three men looked somewhat dishevelled.

'A bit of a contrast to the last one,' the General conceded.

The three of them had set out on Saturday morning for Marstal on Ærø, thirty-odd nautical miles to the north-east of Kiel across the bottom end of the Little Belt, *Lillebælt* in Danish, the stretch of water that separated Germany from the Danish Islands. The wind had blown cool, brisk, and northerly, and they'd had to beat into it most of the way, putting in a couple of short tacks to clear the bottom end of Ærø and make Marstal's harbour entrance, just round the corner.

After a pleasant evening in good company, despite the absence of Doc Speer, they'd set off the next morning to return to Kiel on their reciprocal course, only to find the wind had shifted round to the west, with just enough south in it to mean they had to tack all the way back, fighting hard for every mile towards their destination.

Now, tied up, they savoured a well-earned beer with half-closed eyes and faraway looks.

'I must be going,' Oskar said, draining the last of the bottle, gathering his things together into the large holdall that he always brought, whatever the length of trip. 'I have an early meeting in Hamburg tomorrow, and I feel some sort of sleep would be useful after today. You didn't explain that sailing could be such hard work. I'm almost inclined to ask for a refund!'

'Oh, stop moaning, Oskar,' the General said, laughing. 'You loved it.'

He'd watched Oskar on the helm when the gusts were at their worst, and he'd seen the tense determination on his friend's face to steal as much from the wind as possible without stalling the boat, and the look of triumph on his face when he succeeded.

The General and Dieter shook Oskar's hand, and he was gone, his lolling stride disappearing up the path towards Düsternbrooker Weg to hail a taxi.

'I'll make sailors out of you two yet,' the General said.

'That was enjoyable but at times it seemed like we were getting nowhere.'

'Tacking back and forward, with the wind on the nose, you travel twice the distance. That's why it took us over nine hours to get back.'

'It felt longer than that,' Dieter said, but he was wearing a tired smile.

'It's colder, it's wetter and it's more physically demanding. But you both coped admirably.' He smiled.

After a silence that lasted a few minutes, Dieter spoke.

'I'm hearing bad things from Austria.'

'I've heard a few stories. It seems to be worse than in Germany.'

'They've brought in all the laws that we have in place, with immediate effect, but there's more to it than that. It's the people themselves who seem to be embracing the opportunity for a pogrom.'

It was a word the General had first heard in talks with Yosef, mostly about Russian and Slavic Jews. It was the first time he'd heard it with respect to German-speaking Jews.

'It might rekindle the violence here,' he said, 'when the thugs at home see what their Austrian friends are getting away with.'

'The Jews here have more pressing things to worry about at the present time.'

'I know,' the General said, 'like having to register their assets. How can people think that it's right to treat our own citizens like this?'

'Because it's been so gradual. A slow drip-drip-drip of pressure, removing every right they had, little by little. Thousands of Jews are leaving, you know.'

'I've heard. I tried to persuade Yosef and Miriam, my household staff, to leave, but they refuse point blank.'

'It would be the sensible thing for them to do. Even with the punitive emigration taxes that they have to pay.'

'I've heard it goes up from eighty to ninety per cent next month. Unless they leave for Palestine.'

'If they stay, they'll lose it all anyway,' Dieter said. 'It's the only explanation that makes sense for the government needing to know how much they're worth.'

'It's an easy source of money for Adolf. And he needs it. The country is bankrupt, and we're still spending on rearmament as if we have limitless pockets.'

'The Anschluss will have helped. Money and raw materials are pouring in from Austria to the coffers at the Reichstag.'

The General nodded.

'I'd heard that', he said, 'but, of course, the unemployment figures keep coming down, and the people love him.'

Dieter laughed.

'They've taken women out of jobs and out of the count; it's the same with the Jews. No wonder the figures are so impressive. And the Gestapo and KriPo have just rounded up over 1500 people 'unwilling to work' and incarcerated them in concentration camps.'

'It's a wonder there's any room in them,' the General snorted. 'I hate to think of the number of people who must be behind wire.'

'Don't lose any sleep over it, General. The SS have just opened a new camp, at Flossenbürg in northern Bavaria.'

'How many are there now?'

'I've lost count, to be honest.'

Both men sat, lost in their own thoughts. It was Dieter who broke the silence.

'This goading of the Czechs. It could spark a war, couldn't it?'

'It could, easily. From what I hear, there are some extremely nervous senior Wehrmacht commanders. They think we're not ready to take on the Czechs, never mind the French, who are massing on our borders, ready to jump in if we cross into Sudetenland.'

'What about the Russians?'

'At the present moment, they have the troops, but they're grossly under-equipped. I think they would only attack if they saw that we were struggling in any conflict with the Czechs.'

'I just get the feeling we're building up to something. The whole country is on edge.'

'I know what you mean. That's what happens when the country is led by a madman.'

Dieter gave a hollow laugh.

The General looked at his watch. He looked across the Hafen.

'There's a squall coming. We should really be going.'

'Yes,' said Dieter, 'I need to soak in a hot bath.'

He held out his hand.

'Until the next time.'

CHAPTER 145

28th April

My dear Esther,

It's truly awful about Itsik's parents. I can't imagine what you must be feeling right now. I went round to see them and they're holding up well, considering, although they are dreadfully disappointed.

They told me that I was to persuade you not to even think about coming back home, even for a visit. They say that the peace of mind they have from the fact that you are away from all of this is worth the world to them. Even though they have concerns about the situation in Palestine, they think you're better off where you are.

I don't want to worry you, but can you make Itsik's parents find somewhere safe to put their money (if that's possible) before the government get their hands on it. We've all had to declare any assets over 5,000 Reichsmarks, including jewellery and other valuables, to the authorities. Yosef says that can only mean they're going take it from us, whatever way they think up to do it.

We're lucky, because our savings are less than that, and we live in a tied house. Still, a lot of people are extremely concerned about it, and more and more people are trying to leave.

Despite Itsik's parents being refused, expect a flurry of new arrivals in Palestine. It's the only place anyone leaving Germany can still go to, with most of their money intact. Everywhere else and the emigration tax is eighty per cent, going up to ninety next month.

I found Ruth in tears the other night. She was being made to read this vile book for school. Der Giftpilz, it's called, and you wouldn't believe the disgusting things they say about Jews. It's published by that horrible man who's behind Der Stürmer, and it's just as bad. Ruth nearly had hysterics when we said we'd go to the school about it, so we decided not to take it any further. There's a real climate of fear here now.

Manny doesn't say much but he feels it too. He's a deep one, and I feel that we need to keep an eye on him. I hear stories of young boys getting into bother.

Still, other than the doom and gloom, not much else is happening. I'll call round and see Itsik's parents again this week.

I hope this letter finds you well,

Your loving friend,

Miriam.

Esther sighed when she'd finished reading the letter. No matter how dejected she was about Itsik's parents, it was good to know that they were coping, and that Miriam was looking after them. It didn't stop her feeling bad for Miriam and Rosa, and the children. She put the pages aside to read again later, every word precious to her.

~~o~~

Miriam rang the bell of the Jungmannstraße flat. Since they'd been refused permission to join

Itsik and Esther, Miriam had visited Itsik's parents every week. Standing at the doorway, she felt a sudden stab of guilt about the untruths she'd told Esther.

Itsik's mother answered the door. She'd been crying again. Miriam had lied about how Itsik's parents were bearing up. Usually, on her visits, Herr Weichmann was morose and hardly said a word; Itsik's mother mostly cried, and spoke of life not being worth living, separated from her sons and her grandchildren, and her wonderful daughters-in-law.

Miriam had pleaded with the older woman not to tell Esther or Itsik of their despair, knowing that it might precipitate one or both brothers coming back home, and she'd played her own part by telling Esther that everything was fine.

She'd also lied to Esther about the savings that she and Yosef had managed to put aside over the years. Yosef had impressed on her that no one, other than themselves and the General, should ever know about their financial arrangement and, with the possibility of one of her letters being opened by the police looming large in her mind, she didn't even consider hinting to her friend that they had a comfortable reserve hidden away from greedy government fingers.

Miriam sighed and listened to the older lady's woes, forgetting her own for a while.

'Did you see our star?' Mama Weichmann asked.

Miriam nodded, closing her eyes. It had been a shock to see the yellow paint daubed on the front door of the flat. *The Star of David.*

'It was a neighbour from downstairs,' the old lady said. 'He's some sort of official with the NSDAP.'

'Is he allowed to do that?'

'He said it was his civic duty.'

CHAPTER 146

Maldon, England.

Ruth shook her head and closed her eyes. I tried to imagine what it must have been like for a fifteen-year-old Jewish girl back in Germany in 1938.

'That was the first of them, but soon they were everywhere. Over the next few weeks, the yellow stars that, up until then, we'd seen only on Jewish shops, began appearing on flats and houses all over Kiel. The new edict that all Jewish homes must have a painted star was eagerly pounced on by small-minded council and party officials, and ordinary people.'

'My grandparents' house in Gaarden was one of the first. Some streets had so many yellow stars, it was clear that Jewish people liked to live near other Jews and, the poorer they were, the more evident it was.'

She took a sip of her water and continued.

'Most of the Ostjuden lived and worked in Kleiner Kuhberg and the surrounding area near the centre of Kiel but further little enclaves of Jews lived in the working-class areas of Wellingdorf and Ellerbeck on the east side of Kieler Hafen, and even in the more well-to-do areas of Damperhof and Brunswick, there were small Jewish neighbourhoods.'

'Only the richest Jewish businessmen and professionals chose to live among the true Germans in Düsternbrook on the city side of the fjord, or in Holtenau, north of the canal.'

I flinched at the bitterness in her voice, but I said nothing.

'But no matter which ward of Kiel a Jew lived in,' Ruth continued, 'a yellow star appeared on their door, sooner or later. Some even painted it on themselves, hoping for a neater or less obtrusive star than one done by an enthusiastic but uncaring council employee or party man.'

'When they came to do our cottage, the General refused permission for the doorway to be daubed with paint. Papa tried to reason with him, not wanting to draw the attention of the authorities, but the General argued that the house was his property, and on his land, and that he was a close friend of the mayor.'

I saw a flicker of a smile cross her face at this small, remembered victory, but it faded almost as soon as it appeared.

'The men came back the following day, accompanied by a policeman. Again, the General refused, and the man threatened to bring the Gestapo the next time. When the General saw the look on my parents' faces, he relented, but he made Papa fetch a plank of wood and nail it to the door before he allowed the official to paint the yellow star on it and leave, satisfied.'

'He tried his best for us, the General,' she said.

CHAPTER 147

[19/05/1938 Thursday]

Kiel, Germany.

'We can take it off in a couple of days and put it back on if needed,' the General said.

'Yes, sir,' Yosef said. 'Perhaps we should leave it for a week or so, as they're likely to come back and check.'

'That's sensible. We'd better make it a fortnight. These *Schmeckel* have long memories.'

Yosef laughed at the Yiddish insult, but he knew, as did the General, that the star would have to stay where it was. There was never a warning these days of a visit to a Jew's home by some government official or another. And if the police or, God forbid, the Gestapo called, and the star was missing…

~~o~~

[11/06/1938 Saturday]

On a warm day in June, SS-Untersturmführer Rudolf Mey married Lise Böhm.

Understandably, neither the Kästners nor the Nussbaums were invited, but Maria, Miriam and the girls all watched from an upstairs window as Lise left the house and climbed into the wedding car, a picture of elegance, attended by her proud father.

At Nikolaikirche, when the bride and groom emerged at the end of the service, Rudolf's platoon, in crisp black uniforms with polished buttons and badges, formed an SS guard of honour, their swords crossed above them. Lise instinctively ducked her head as she walked under the blades, arm in arm with her new husband.

The reception was in the Bellevue Hotel, looking over the waters of Kieler Hafen to Mönkeberg on the opposite shore. On such a fine day, it was a beautiful backdrop for the newlyweds' photographs.

Of the men present, over half wore the uniforms of the Schutzstaffel. At Lise and Rudolf's request, the photographer gathered all the SS men together in a large semicircle with Lise in the centre, being cradled by Rudolf, his commanding officer and two or three junior officers.

Rudolf's parents travelled down for the wedding. She was a mousy, devout woman; he looked harried and careworn. Because of them, Beate chased away the young officers she'd teased at the engagement party when their charm overstepped once more into blatant flirting.

'Kamerad Mey, congratulations,' Rudolf's commanding officer, SS-Hauptsturmführer Arnulf Eicke, said, taking the groom aside. 'I must say, your new wife is quite the most beautiful woman I have ever seen… except for my own wife, that is.'

'Yes, sir. Thank you. Lise is the most beautiful girl I've ever met… apart…'

'It's all right, Mey, I don't expect you to find my wife more attractive than yours; it's a polite formality in case she is listening.'

He laughed, and Rudolf joined in, glad to break the tension. Like all the others, he always felt nervous around the Hauptsturmführer, who could be charming one minute and spewing spite and venom the next.

'Thank you, sir. I must introduce you. She'd be thrilled to meet you.'

'It's all right, Rudolf,' he said, surprising the young officer by using his first name, 'We've already met; at your engagement party, if you remember. It would be nice to speak with her again though. She is such a charming girl.'

Rudolf almost flushed with pride.

'Thank you, Kamerad Hauptsturmführer,' Rudolf said, clacking his heels together in a crisp Hitler greeting.

~~o~~

'What's with all this Kamerad business?' Beate Böhm said. 'I noticed it at the engagement party.'

'Shhh,' Eberhard Böhm said, putting his finger to his lips. 'They might hear you.'

'Pah. They're just little boys.'

'They're little boys who are officers in the SS, and not to be trifled with. Especially him.'

He nodded towards Rudolf's commanding officer.

'I thought you two got on like a house on fire last time?'

'We had a long chat, but I'm still uncomfortable around him.'

'Don't be such an old woman. Anyway, you were saying about this Kamerad thing.'

'Oh, yes. It's an SS tradition. They don't call each other Herr Oberst or Herr Untersturmführer; it's Kamerad this or Kamerad that. The Hauptsturmführer said it was because they're such a tight-knit regiment who would die for each other, and for the Führer.'

'It's all a bit strange, but boys must be boys, I suppose.'

'I wish you'd be more careful, dear. These people are the elite of the elite, and not to be taken lightly.'

'I'm fed up being careful. Sometimes I think I've spent my entire life worrying about doing the right thing.'

Eberhard Böhm frowned at his wife, but she was miles away in thought.

He looked around. The reception had cost him a fortune, but he knew his Lise was worth it, and the kudos that came with his daughter being married to a young SS officer with great prospects more than compensated for him having to forgo a new car that year.

~~o~~

'Liebe Frau, might I be permitted to tell you that you look divine? Quite simply the most beautiful woman I have ever laid eyes on.'

Dear lady. Not Fräulein. Lise felt a rush of heat on her face, and she took a long breath to control it.

'Thank you, Herr Hauptsturmführer. You're far too kind. I'm sure that your wife is excluded from that sweeping statement. She is lovely.'

'Ah. You are very diplomatic, but it is allowed for a man to make comments about women without having to contrast them with our wives. They stand on a pedestal all of their own.'

He smiled, and she gave a short laugh.

'My young Untersturmführer is a lucky man,' he continued. 'I just hope he realises how privileged he is. Most of the men here would sell their mothers to be in his shoes right now.'

She blushed again, cursing herself. She felt the familiar warm glow of arousal, not understanding why; the man provoked fear in almost everybody; she could see it as he circled the room. Only her mother seemed unaffected, but she hadn't engaged him in conversation yet.

'I'm awfully lucky to have him. He's kind and generous, and so handsome in his uniform, don't you think? And I hope he has great prospects, Herr Hauptsturmführer.'

He smiled at her.

'I'm sure he does, Frau Mey. He's an exceptional young soldier, and I'm confident he'll go far,' he said, looking over to where the groom was standing with his fellow officers, 'especially with such a supportive wife.'

He turned back to her.

'And do call me Arnulf, Frau Mey,' he added, 'I'd be honoured.'

She blushed again.

'I'm sure it would feel far too forward for me to do that, Herr Hauptsturmführer,' she replied.

It was the correct answer, and she tried to remain composed, but he seemed determined to have her call him by his first name.

Why?

'I insist,' she heard him say. 'Just between you and I. And I'll call you Lise.'

She suppressed a giggle. His name sounded ludicrous for the cold and cruel SS officer she'd heard he was, and she hoped she could say it without laughing.

'I'd be honoured, Arnulf, just this once, but I must call you Hauptsturmführer Eicke from now on in case it slips out at the wrong moment.'

'Thank you, Lise. And, if you should ever tire of young Rudolf there...' he turned and nodded as the group of young officers broke into laughter, 'you know where I am.'

Stunned, she watched him take her hand and lift it to his lips. She felt the soft brush of his mouth on her fingers and the warm glow in her loins returned as he walked away.

The man is dangerous. In more ways than one.

She stood for a little while, then walked over to Rudolf and put her arm through his. He turned and gave her a smile that lit up his face.

~~o~~

The Hauptsturmführer walked over to Lise's parents. Eberhard Böhm shook his hand warmly and thanked him for coming.

'It is my pleasure, Herr Böhm. It has been a privilege to see such a handsome young couple start their new lives together.'

'Why, thank you, Herr Hauptsturmführer. I do rather like the young man, and I'm sure he'll look after Lise as well as we have.'

'He'll have you and I to reckon with if he doesn't,' the SS man said, laughing and gripping Eberhard Böhm firmly by the arm.

'Indeed,' the bride's father said, wincing.

He glanced at his wife.

'I'm sure you remember Hauptsturmführer Eicke, my dear,' he said, then turned back to the SS man. 'And you've met my wife, Beate.'

The Hauptsturmführer reached for Beate Böhm's hand and repeated the gesture he'd charmed Lise with only moments before.

'I can see where Lise gets her beauty from,' he said.

He watched her. She didn't blush like her daughter.

He looked at Eberhard, then at Beate.

She has the same sensuality as the daughter. But it's hidden. And wasted.

'Thank you,' she said with a smile, 'but it's a while since I looked like that.'

'I'm sure that's merely a matter of opinion. The eye of the beholder, I'd say.'

'I doubt it,' Beate Böhm replied. 'I'd love to meet your wife. You should introduce us.'

'I'd be delighted,' he said, more guarded now. 'I see she is talking with some of my junior officers. It helps when they sing my praises to her.'

They both laughed, and she turned to her husband.

'Be a dear and refresh my drink, would you? And perhaps our friend would also like a refill?'

'That would be marvellous,' the SS man said, handing Eberhard Böhm his glass.

'I wasn't making small talk, by the way,' he said, when Eberhard Böhm left them.

'I'm sure you weren't, and it's flattering, but you do that to every woman you meet.'

He laughed.

'Only the beautiful ones,' he said.

Beate looked over at her daughter. She was holding Rudolf's arm and whispering in his ear, making him blush.

'I never quite looked like that,' she said, without envy.

They watched as Lise walked to the door. Her bridesmaid rushed to assist her, but Lise dismissed her with a smile.

'Rudolf is an extremely fortunate young man,' Arnulf Eicke said.

'He is, but Lise is lucky too. His devotion is touching. It would be a shame if anything were to jeopardise it, wouldn't you say?'

'I couldn't agree more. Unfortunately, a war is coming, and they'll have to be strong.'

'Please look after him then, for her sake. I would be most grateful.'

He looked at her, but her face was guileless. It was almost unheard of for him not to be able to read a woman, but Beate Böhm was one of them.

'Come,' he said, taking her hand. 'I'll introduce you to my wife. I'm sure you two will get on like a house on fire. I can't fathom either of you.'

As they walked across to greet his wife, the Hauptsturmführer saw Rudolf detach himself from the group and follow in Lise's footsteps.

CHAPTER 148

[17/06/1938 Friday]

'Dieter, what's new?'

'Nothing that you don't know already, more than likely.'

'Go on, you always tell me something fresh.'

Dieter laughed.

'We'll get our seats first. I don't want to miss the first race.'

The 1938 Kieler Woche appeared to be bigger than ever. The General didn't have access to the Kiel Sailing Club balcony, so he'd purchased four tickets for him and his crew on the public stands further along the shore. Doc Speer and Oskar had yet to arrive.

'Great seats,' Dieter said, looking down on the stand as the rows below them filled up.

'I like to be up at the back. One can speak without fear of being overheard, and it gives the best overall view of the course, even if it is a little more distant.'

He looked around. They were at the end of a row, the two spare seats beside them not yet occupied by Oskar and the Doc. The row in front was empty, apart from three seats at the opposite end.

'What have you got for me,' he asked.

Despite the surrounding empty seats, Dieter lowered his voice.

'It's not getting any better for the Jews. Hungary has emulated Germany and has adopted comprehensive anti-Jewish laws and measures like ours. Most of its Jews have already been excluded from the professions.'

'When was this? I hadn't heard.'

'The end of last month. It wasn't in any of the papers. I got it from a couple of Jewish newspapermen who had worked there for a few years after being thrown out of work in Kiel. They've returned now that they've lost their jobs in Hungary. They say they might as well be unemployed at home. One of them is going to get his family together and make for Palestine.'

'I'm surprised I didn't get a memo about it. Maybe I missed it. There are so many. Anything else?'

'Another purge of the so-called *Arbeitsscheue*. 9,000 this time, all sent to concentration camps.'

'The work-shy,' the General said, with a snort. 'Another drop in the unemployment figures.'

'Even more so when you consider they need to employ extra guards to man the camps.'

'I suppose so. There's nothing new in this though.'

Dieter Maas shook his head. 'A thousand of them are Jews. It's the first time they've been targeted. Until now, it has been criminals, the homeless and the mentally ill. Although there were some Jews among them, these were ones who had come to the attention of the authorities for one reason or another.'

'But this thousand are just ordinary Jews? Nothing more?'

'Ordinary Jews. No criminal records, just unemployed because there aren't any jobs they're permitted to do.'

A voice interrupted them.

'What are you two whispering about? Do you have a tip for this race? Should I put a bet on?'

'Don't be so vulgar, Oskar. We don't bet on sailing races.'

'No? Really? Try telling that to the bookmaker standing down at the back of the stand. You only have to ask him for the odds.'

The General laughed and stood up to shake Oskar's hand, and that of the Doc, who followed in his wake.

Both men carried two cups of coffee and, from a hip flask removed from an inside pocket, Oskar added a nip of Schnapps to each.

'Here's to an entertaining day,' the General said, raising his cup. 'Let's see if we can learn something. Our race is on Sunday afternoon.'

CHAPTER 149

'It's a bit poky,' Lise said.

'It's all I could afford, for now at least.'

Rudolf gently laid her down. He'd insisted on carrying her over the threshold of their new home, a small flat in Lange Reihe, not far from the railway station.

Their honeymoon had lasted only four days. It was all they could fit in to his five-day leave from the regiment. The wedding had taken up one of his precious days away from the army.

But for him, it was the best five days of his life. He couldn't even begin to compare his new wife with any of the women he'd been with. Beautiful, and full of fun; it filled him with pride just to walk down the street with her. And, in the bedroom, he found it hard to believe the depths of her desire for him, and the way she was so unabashed about showing it.

From the moment at the reception when she'd whispered the room number in his ear, the day, which had been wonderful up until then, became etched into his memory.

He'd followed her up, finding the door of the room slightly ajar and had pushed it open with a puzzled frown. She'd been standing waiting for him and, as soon as he'd entered the room and closed the door, she'd embraced him.

'I'm not waiting for tonight. I want you now,' she'd said, breathless, kissing him with a hunger that made him almost forget where they were.

He broke away. 'We can't. By the time we get the dress off, and back on again, people will notice we're gone.'

She stared at him, a smile on her lips.

'It doesn't need to come off. She reached down and gathered the cloth at the front of the dress, lifting it up.

When he moved to touch her, she stopped him.

'There's no time,' she said, 'and anyway, I'm ready.'

He'd undone his belt and trouser fasteners, his fingers clumsy and inept, and, as she lay back on the bed, he entered her. He'd expected to feel more resistance but, although she gave a little cry, he was sure he'd done nothing to hurt her. Even as she began to move under him, he knew he wouldn't last long. He felt her thighs gripping him and her hands pulling him into her, her groans growing louder. He looked down at her face, almost hidden by the folds of her dress and, as she looked back at him, her eyelids rolled closed and she shuddered. With a last push he felt himself go and collapsed on top of her.

He tried to apologise, but she hushed him.

'Don't be sorry,' she said, 'It was wonderful. I made you wait so long, it was always going to be quick, the first time. And I finished too, don't forget.'

He looked at her, surprised. It usually took longer for her than for him.

~~o~~

She'd been sick with worry that she might see the Hauptsturmführer's face instead of Rudolf's that first time, but his hard, blue eyes and square jaw hadn't appeared in her mind, even at the end when she'd closed her eyes. Worse still, it might have been Franz she'd thought of, lying back on the bed.

But Franz hadn't entered her mind, and she knew she'd done enough to make Rudolf believe that it was her first time.

Waiting for Rudolf to come to the room, she'd thought of him inside her while she touched herself and, by the time he arrived, she knew it wouldn't take her long to reach her climax; she hadn't lied when she told him they'd finished together.

She'd known he'd panic about the dress, afraid that it would be stained, with blood or his own fluid, but she quietened him and reached for a towel that was sitting on the bedside table.

'Put that under me before you come out,' she told him.

He did as he was told.

'Get yourself sorted while I go downstairs,' she said, 'before anyone notices.'

The dress was a little damp on the inside, but she was happy that its underskirt prevented it from being noticeable. She sprayed a little perfume on it and left him to finish putting his clothes back on. Dropping the towel in the laundry bin on the landing, she made her way back to the reception.

~~o~~

For the briefest moment, when he walked into the room a few minutes after Lise, Rudolf had a peculiar sense of being stared at but, glancing around, he saw that the guests were all absorbed in the thrum of happy conversation that characterised an occasion such as this.

He breathed out slowly, then his eye caught that of his Hauptsturmführer, and he shivered, despite the warmth of the room, and his recent exertions.

His superior gave a curt nod, and a smile that seemed to Rudolf to be bereft of humour, and he was seized by an acute sensation of shame that the Hauptsturmführer had seen them, and that he knew.

~~o~~

For their honeymoon, Rudolf had splashed out for his new bride and taken a room in the Excelsior on Askanischen Platz, and had shown her the sights of Berlin, eating leisurely lunches in Café Bauer or Café Kranzler on Unter den Linden and dining every night in the Zur letzten Instanz on Waisenstraße because they fell in love with its old-world charm on the first day.

He took her to the Reichstag, on the off-chance that they would catch a glimpse of the Führer arriving or departing but, other than a steady stream of minor officials, no one of note appeared. She'd encouraged him to wear his uniform on their wanderings around the city. He presumed, like him, it gave her a thrill to watch the reactions of passers-by, varying in nature from respect and adoration to fear and loathing.

'What do you enjoy the most,' she said, as if reading his mind. 'Those who fear the uniform, or those who idolise it?'

'Both,' he said, 'but I like to imagine the cold sweat that runs down the backs of Jews and other criminals when they see me or one of my fellow officers and scurry back to whichever hole they hide in.'

On his part, his heart burst with pride at the glances they attracted; the indulgent smiles of older couples, the grudging looks of harried parents and the awestruck stares of their charges but, most of all, he relished the envious looks of other men when they saw the way Lise held his arm, and the way she turned to look at him.

In between lunches, sightseeing and stepping out in the evening, they spent much of their time in the large bed at the centre of their hotel room, drinking in as much of each other as they could, in the knowledge that the Schutzstaffel would take him away once they returned to Kiel.

As he lost himself in her body on their first night in their new home, he began to count in his head the days until his next leave.

CHAPTER 150

'Gentlemen, it will be a pleasure racing against you. I've heard so much about the Kästner Brothers.'

The three young men stood on the *hard* beside the Olympic Hafen, the gathering point for the sailors taking part in Kieler Woche.

Kapitänleutnant Rainer Schulze of the Kriegsmarine held out his hand. Franz gripped it and shook it firmly. Johann did the same.

'We've also been looking forward to racing against you,' the younger Kästner brother said. 'How have you found the change from lake racing to sea racing?'

'Ach, it is much the same.' He turned round, sweeping his arm across Kieler Hafen. 'It's just a big lake here.'

Rainer Schulze had been a dinghy sailor but had graduated a year ago to racing keelboats and had taken to it as if he'd sailed them all his life. To everyone's surprise, the second navy crew, which he'd been given charge of, had outstripped the top Kriegsmarine boat in every single race, bar one. Both navy boats had been entered into the eight-metre class in Kieler Woche, along with the Kästner boy's army yacht and three other privately owned yachts.

Johann laughed.

'Kieler Hafen is sheltered, but don't underestimate it,' Franz said. 'Remember the first day of the Olympics. Thirty-five-knot winds. They were lucky it was from the south-west and didn't kick up much of a fetch. The eight-metre boats struggled for a while.'

'Out at Schilksee, any wind over twenty knots with a bit of north in it, and you'll know you're not on a lake,' Johann added.

Rainer Schulze smiled.

'I'm fooling with you, gentlemen. I spend my life at sea. I respect it, especially when it gets close to the land, where it's at its most dangerous. It will make the racing all the more interesting if we have some wind and some waves, no?'

Franz and Johann laughed.

'It will be interesting whatever the weather,' Franz said.

'I hope so,' Rainer Schulze said. 'But for now, let's have a drink and you can tell me how two army boys got to be such great sailors.'

~~o~~

[24/06/1938 Friday]

By the last race of the eight-metre class, there were only two boats that could still win. Just two points separated Rainer Schulze's *Helga-II* and the leader, *Brünhilde*, the army boat skippered by Franz Kästner.

The lead changed three times during the race, which took place in moderate westerlies, but *Helga-II* shaded it by a length on the finishing line, to win the eight-metre class.

At the Olympic Hafen, Franz was the first person on the dock to shake Rainer Schulze's hand and congratulate him. Both crews hugged each other and pledged to meet for a drink after the formalities of the prize-giving were finished.

As the navy crew entered the Kieler Yacht Club building an hour or so later, Franz's crew were already at the bar, and the barman was pouring five beers for the victors. Franz nodded for the man to put them on his tab and turned to join in the applause for Rainer Schulze and his crew.

'This is my father,' Franz said, introducing the winning skipper to the General, who had joined them for the after-race party.

'I'm honoured to meet you, sir,' the Kapitänleutnant said. 'You're a true friend to the Kriegsmarine.'

'Oh, I don't know about that. I do my best to help the navy where I can and try and keep the peace between your lot and the Heer. It's not always easy.'

'My father likes to pretend he's modest,' Franz joked, 'but I'm sure he enjoys all the praise that's heaped on him.'

Rainer Schulze turned and addressed the General again.

'I hear you finished a close second in your race. Like father, like son.'

The two Kästner men laughed.

'I did have the pleasure in competing in my twenty-sixth Kieler Woche,' the General said. 'I missed more than a few because of my postings, and the last two or three have been in the old-duffer class.'

'Ha. I watched your last race,' Rainer Schulze said. 'It was as competitive as ours, and you got the tactics spot on. But for that last wind drop, you would have caught them.'

While Oskar had been unperturbed, Dieter and the Doc had cursed when the wind deserted them just as they drew level with their rival's stern. The momentum of both boats took them over the finish, but the General had lost the advantage by then and they crossed the line a nose behind them.

'That's racing, my boy,' the General said, putting an arm on each of the younger men's shoulders. 'We survived to race another day.'

'Here's to that,' Franz said, raising his glass.

~~o~~

[25/06/1938 Saturday]

'How are you feeling, Franz? You don't look good.'

The General clapped his son on the back and pulled out a chair at the kitchen table, guiding him to sit down on it. He poured a mug of coffee from the pot and put it down in front of him.

The General had left his sons to their post-race party after a few drinks, but he'd heard them stagger up the stairs well after two in the morning. He'd been up since seven, and it surprised him that Franz had got up an hour later.

'Big night?'

Franz groaned.

'I don't do it all that often, but I keep telling myself that it will be the last. I don't know how Johann does it every week.'

'He doesn't seem to suffer the same. He'll sleep until eleven and come down and eat a hearty breakfast. Then do the same again tonight.'

'Ugh. The thought.'

'You certainly seemed to be having a good time when I left.'

The General put his hand on Franz's shoulder.

'They are a great crowd.'

'Despite the hangover,' the General said, 'It's good to just let go, once in a while.'

'It's fun at the time, but I wish I'd stopped three drinks sooner.'

'Or maybe six.' The General laughed. 'Rainer Schulze seems a decent enough young fellow.'

'Yes. He is. But we'll beat him next time. He made a couple of mistakes yesterday, and we didn't capitalise on them. He did it in the first race too. I'll be ready next year.'

'I'm sure you will. It was a great race to watch.'

'Do you know what I like about him? He doesn't do politics.'

The General raised an eyebrow and waited for his son to elaborate.

'Well, what I mean is, he's obviously a diehard navy man and, despite being young enough to think that the National Socialists are the answer to Germany's problems, he keeps it to himself. No *Heil Hitlers*.'

'And I presume you didn't bring politics up either?'

'No. We talked about sailing, and he told me all about serving on a fighting ship; I bored him with tales of army life. He seemed to be fascinated by you, for some reason, so I told him all your faults, just to paint a balanced picture.'

The General laughed.

'I'm sure you did. Just as well. I find having this reputation with the navy a little embarrassing. They must have had such a low opinion of the army that, when they finally worked with one of us who wasn't a congenital idiot, they thought I was a genius.'

Franz laughed.

The kitchen door opened, and Johann walked in.

'Guten Morgen,' he said. Franz looked at him, then at the clock, and flinched.

'I thought you'd be in bed until lunchtime,' he said to his younger brother. 'How can you be so…'

He struggled to find the word.

'Fresh?' Johann said. 'Why waste the day? Is Miriam about?'

'No,' the General said. 'She's away to the synagogue but help yourself to breakfast. The bread's in the larder. There's plenty of cold meat and cheese, and the coffee's fresh in the pot.'

Franz watched aghast as his brother filled a plate and wolfed into it without a hint of nausea. It made Franz's stomach turn.

'What are your plans, Johann?' the General asked.

'We're meeting up for lunch at that new café in Alter Markt. Are you coming, Franz?'

'Does it involve drinking alcohol?'

'We'll likely have a few beers, maybe a Schnapps or two.'

'Then count me out. I'll have a quiet day here.'

Franz turned to his father.

'Where are Mama, and the girls?'

'Yosef dropped them off first thing. Eva and Antje are giving her a hand with her stall at the parade. They've taken over the job of the Rotary club at Kieler Woche. Eva didn't seem to mind but Antje wasn't too impressed.'

Johann laughed. 'A day in the company of mother's friends won't put her in the best of moods,' he said.

The General smiled. If she couldn't be with Ruth, Antje would rather spend time with him.

'They'll be back around three,' he said. Franz always made time for his mother and his sisters when he came home. With Johann, they just had to take their chances.

'Are you going to be back for dinner, tonight,' the General asked, as Johann made to leave.

'I should be, but we'll probably go out later,' he said, as he put on his coat, and left.

CHAPTER 151

[16/07/1938 Saturday]

2nd July '38

Dear Miriam,

It was so good to receive your letter and although we are still heartbroken, it is comforting to know that you are keeping an eye out for Itsik's parents and that they are doing well. Itsik's mother doesn't say much in her letters and his father doesn't write but hey, men!

Itsik is still trying everything he can to overturn the decision.

Things are bit tighter now on the security front, so I didn't get to go on my trip to Tel Aviv but Itsik promises as soon as it's safe, we'll go. I still miss both you and Rosa terribly; the other ladies have been really kind, but they'll never be the same to me as you two are.

Moshe is becoming a little Palestinian. He's never at home and has skin the colour of coffee! He's growing up so fast. Shoshana is almost as bad; she has her friends over to play with her dolls (Itsik has made two more since we arrived, and I made clothes to dress them. It keeps me busy, sewing and knitting.) Sometimes she goes to their houses and comes back with stories about them having guns in their porches, just in case. I asked Itsik if we should have one, but he laughed and said that they're just scaremongers.

I hope things over there are improving. We keep hearing rumours and it's very worrying. Be sure to tell me anything that could affect you, or Itsik's parents.

The shops are doing well, and Itsik has bought a plot at the edge of town. He has a builder friend we know from the synagogue, but we'll be using mainly Arab labourers. Itsik knows them so it should be all right, and he hopes that building can start soon. I'm looking forward to having a bigger house, but it will be painful to have all that extra room if Itsik's parents aren't with us.

I must go now, and chase Moshe to write to Manny. They're terrible. The best of friends and they can't be bothered to sit down for five minutes and put pen to paper. Boys, eh?

Take care – don't take any risks.

All my love, Esther.

~~o~~

Manny,

Sorry I missed writing last time. I'm sure you understand. There's so much to do. The grown-ups have more time. Well, Mama does, anyway.

Even though it's been a while, I haven't forgotten your comments. Although you may have just been faster than me when we left, I'm almost sure I could take you for speed now. I've taken a growth spurt and I'm one of the quickest, even amongst the older boys.

I had to dig out your last letter, to see what you'd written. I've kept them all in a tin with our ticket from the boat and a few other things.

I remember that Lise one. She was hot. (That's what we say here when the girls are, you

499

know, good to look at.) Have you kissed one yet? Hanna Yashbum let me kiss her behind the toilets in the school playground. To be honest, it wasn't as good as I'd expected but she seemed to like it. My papa says keep away from girls until I'm in my twenties. I told him not to worry, that I just want to play football.

If you see my grandparents, say hello from me. They won't let them come over here. Maybe they think they're too old for Palestine but there are some people as old as them out here, so I don't think it's fair.

BBF

Moshe

~~o~~

[03/08/1938 Wednesday]

KIELER JÜDISCHES FREIHEITSNACHRICHTENBLATT

Volume 59

6th of Av, 5698

We apologise for the late appearance of this edition of the KJF. This was due to circumstances outside our control.

US REFUSES TO OPEN DOORS TO REFUGEES

Delegates from 32 countries and refugee aid organisations attended a conference in Evian, France to discuss the Jewish refugee crisis.

Despite calls to settle Jewish refugees fleeing National Socialist oppression in Germany and Austria, the United States and most other nations showed no inclination to ease their immigration restrictions.

JEWISH DOCTORS STRUCK OFF

Yesterday, in a bizarre move by the German Medical Council, all Jewish doctors have been struck off the Medical Register. Jewish doctors were all removed from their posts in 1933 but have been permitted to remain as doctors until now. It is unclear whether Jewish doctors can continue to treat Jewish patients, but it can be assumed that their access to medicines and other medical supplies will be withdrawn. This is expected to have a huge impact on the health of the Jewish community as most non-Jewish doctors are unwilling to risk falling foul of the authorities by treating Jewish patients.

INTRODUCTION OF IDENTITY CARDS

All Jewish and part-Jewish people are to be issued with identity cards, Kennkarte, which will allow access to those hotels, swimming pools and other public facilities that choose to accept Jews. There will be severe penalties for any Jew found not to be carrying this identification.

Kennkarte will also be issued to male Aryan German citizens

over the age of fifteen. The KJF hasn't been able to confirm it, but it is suspected that Jewish Kennkarte will be marked with the letter 'J', similar to the way Jewish passports are identified.

~~o~~

Memo: Geh.KdoS. ABW 07/08/38 CAC0639.1

For Attention Only: All senior executive officers, Abwehr.

From: Vice Admiral Wilhelm Canaris, Chef der Abwehr

SS authorities have opened the Mauthausen concentration camp near Linz, Austria.

For information only. No action required. [END]

CHAPTER 152

[12/08/1938 Friday]

'We're on the move,' Canaris said, putting down the telephone in the General's office.

'So, is this war, sir?' Captain Bauer asked, surprising the General. Usually, he didn't speak unless he was asked to, when Canaris was around.

'Well, not quite yet. But it brings it a tad closer.'

'What did they say?' the General asked, nodding towards the telephone.

'That was the chief of staff's adjutant. The order to mobilise came an hour ago. They'll have started to make for the border now,' he said, looking at his watch.

'It was only a matter of time. I'd hoped that the Czech government's agreement with all the SdP's demands for equality would be enough to prevent further action.'

'Who are the SdP, sir?' Captain Bauer asked, then wished he hadn't.

'What did I say to you about reading the papers?' the General said. 'It's the Sudetendeutsche Partei, the National Socialists by another name. Try and keep up, young man.'

'Sorry, sir. I've been snowed under with all this council business. Did you see my report?'

The General winced, cursing himself for being sharp with the captain in front of Canaris, and for not noticing that the young officer was struggling under his workload.

'I've read it, Captain Bauer. It's an excellent piece of work. I'm sorry, I've been remiss. I'll see if we can find a way to cut back on the hours you spend over there. You'll have enough contacts there by now to take a step back, and still keep your finger on the pulse.'

'Really, sir? That would be great. Not that I mind doing it, but it is sometimes a bit tedious.'

He left the room with a spring in his step.

The General saw the admiral smiling and frowned at him.

'That young man needs to go to sea.'

'I know, but I don't want to lose him. He's a real asset.'

'These Sudeten Germans are stirring it, aren't they?'

'Yes, it's a repeat of what happened in Austria. Local National Socialists cause deep unrest; the authorities clamp down; we step in to protect the German-speaking *Volk*.'

'I'm surprised we didn't go in earlier,' the admiral said. 'The Czech Army mobilised back in May.'

'You couldn't really blame them,' the General retorted. 'The British with us. That's the reality of it. What was it that Adolf said? "*It is my unalterable decision to smash Czechoslovakia by military action, in the near future*". If that's not outright aggression, what is?'

'How did you hear that? That was said in a private meeting.'

'My little Berlin mole. He overheard it. How did you hear of it?'

'Franz Halder. He was there. He's not happy with the Führer's gung-ho approach. Neither is Erich von Manstein.'

The General knew both the OKW commanders. They were old army, through and through, and weren't Hitler sycophants, like Wilhelm Keitel, the Wehrmacht chief.

'Can either of them put the brakes on Hitler?' the General asked.

'Perhaps. Just be ready if I contact you. Your job, if anything happens, is to keep the Kriegsmarine on board.'

Erich Kästner stared at Canaris, his head tilted to one side.

'Are you saying what I think you're saying?'

'I'm saying nothing. This is all hypothetical. The only thing I can say with certainty is that we're not well prepared enough for war.'

The General sat at his desk for a long time, thinking.

~~o~~

[17/08/1938 Wednesday]

'Have you changed your name yet?'

A few of the men nodded, but most shook their heads. The new *Law on the Alteration of Family and Personal Names* required that German Jews with first names of non-Jewish origin must adopt an additional middle name: *Israel* for men and *Sara* for women.

'I'm all right,' Yosef said. 'My name is on the list.'

'So is mine,' Jakob Teubner said.

'It's going to get confusing,' an older man said. 'Just imagine the conversation: *Israel, how are you? I'm fine, Israel, how's your brother Israel getting on? He's fine. He has a son now, you know. What did they call him? Israel.*'

The men all laughed, but Yosef noticed the nervous glances that had become second nature in these difficult times.

Even laughing is dangerous now.

~~o~~

'So why do we need to carry one of these, and Antje doesn't?' Ruth said, 'That's not fair.'

Yosef turned over Ruth's new Kennkarte, her identity card, in his hands. It was stamped with a large letter 'J'.

'I know it's not fair. It's because you're a Jew, and Rebeka's a Jew, it's the law. I have one, and Mama has one too. Even Manny will get one, when they get around to giving it to younger Jewish children. Never go anywhere without it.'

'But the General has one. And Franz and Johann. Why doesn't Antje have one?'

'It's different if you're not Jewish. Only males over fifteen need to carry them, although that may change.'

Johann had shown Antje and herself his own card the day before. Instead of a large 'J', his was stamped with the Reichsadler, the eagle insignia of the Third Reich.

'And why have they given me an extra middle name?'

'That's the law now too. Every Jew must have Israel or Sara added as a middle name to identify them as Jews. It could have been worse. You could have been Ruth Israel Nussbaum.'

Ruth barely smiled.

'One of the girls at school, in the year below, is going to Palestine soon. She says her passport also has a 'J' stamped on it.'

'They just want to make it easy for us to stand out from the rest, to be seen as being different.'

'But why are they doing all this? What have we done to them?'

'We've done nothing. They're looking for scapegoats, and we're easy targets.'

He hesitated. She was fifteen now, and bright.

'Listen, throughout our history, people have persecuted us. The Egyptians and the Romans, thousands of years ago. More recently, in Eastern Europe and Russia, we've been the victim of pogrom after pogrom, but Germany always seemed different. We became Germans, we were welcomed as part of the community, and we contributed.'

He paused again, far away in thought.

'Then Adolf Hitler came, and his followers, and it all changed.'

'Then why don't we leave, like others are doing. Like Aunt Esther did?'

'Do you want to leave? Neither your Bubbe and Sabba Nussbaum or your Bubbe and

503

Sabba Sachs would ever leave. And you'd lose all your friends.'

Ruth started to cry.

'Here,' he said, wrapping his arm around her. 'That's why it's difficult for Mama and me to think about leaving; we'd lose almost everyone we love.'

Ruth sniffed. 'Manny says that the government won't let Moshe's grandparents go and live with them in Palestine.'

'I know, and they can't risk coming back, even to visit. Your mama and I don't think we could live like that.'

'I suppose not. I just need to remember to carry my card.'

'And don't lose it either,' he admonished.

CHAPTER 153

'So, Franz, I've decided to put you in charge this weekend.'

Colonel Schneider looked at his junior officer's face and laughed.

'Not of the army, Franz, although it wouldn't surprise me if you ran the battalion as well as me. No, I was meaning the sailing trip. You're the skipper on this one.'

'Aren't you coming, sir?'

'Yes, I am, but just as crew. You'll be in charge.'

'Thank you, sir.'

'Ha. Don't thank me yet. We're taking three of the new junior officers, and none of them have sailed before. I want to see how you get on knocking them into shape.'

'I'll try my best, sir. When do we leave?'

'Tomorrow evening. I'll let you plan our trip. We need to be back Sunday, and I want you to include at least one night-sail, even if it's only a few hours.'

'I'm happy to do that. Do you want me to provision the boat, sir?'

The colonel nodded.

'Yes, good thinking. Take a driver this afternoon and buy what we need.'

~~o~~

The colonel kept his word. Not once did he try to take charge and, from the time they left Lübeck until they returned three days later, he did only what he was asked by his young skipper. Franz commanded the yacht, moulding the three young officers into useful crew by the time they'd completed a tricky overnight passage in pitch-blackness from Großenbrode to Wismar, with its narrow, winding channel, the moon not emerging until they dropped anchor behind Walfisch island, tired and relieved.

The colonel had smiled with quiet satisfaction; he knew that it would have taken all his skill, knowledge, experience, and concentration to have done any better than the young man who had become such an important part of his command.

And it hadn't taken Franz long to get the measure of sailing the heavy, two-masted yacht. The gaff-rigged main sail and the running backstays were new to him, but he soon learned how to set and reef the traditional sail arrangement that had its roots in sixteenth century working barques. The colonel nodded to himself as he watched his young protégé grasp the usefulness of the mizzen, a smaller version of the main sail, aft of its bigger brother, and the long, jutting bowsprit with its twin foresails, in balancing the boat's canvas.

By the time they returned to Lübeck, Franz was handling the heavy boat with ease, even at close quarters, though he admitted to the colonel that it would take years to learn her every nuance.

The three young officers gathered their gear and saluted the colonel on the quayside and made for the lorry that had come to pick them up and take them back to their barracks. They looked relieved to have passed some sort of test. Franz shook the colonel's hand and saluted.

'Thank you, sir. That was excellent. She's everything you'd want in a boat.'

'Ha. Not quite enough speed, perhaps, for your liking, but she's steady, and as solid as you like with the wind howling and the sea running.'

'Yes, sir.'

Franz turned, and made to follow the others. Colonel Schneider stopped him.

'Tell them to go on. You can ride back with me. I have a car coming in half an hour. We'll have something to eat on the way. I'd like a chat with you.'

Franz did as he was asked and spoke to the driver of the lorry, and to the other officer, already in the back.

As it drove off, Franz frowned.

He helped the colonel square away the boat, stowing all the gear and making sure the lines were all neatly coiled, sails were packed away and the warps were all doing their jobs, securing the yacht to the jetty.

Speeding back towards the barracks in Neumünster, the colonel didn't enlighten Franz as to why he'd asked him to accompany him.

It wasn't until they stopped at an inn on the outskirts of Bad Segeberg that the colonel spoke.

'You must be wondering what I wanted to speak to you about,' he said.

Franz gave a nervous laugh.

'I couldn't think of anything I'd done which would warrant a talking to, sir,' he said, 'and Johann hasn't got himself into trouble for months.'

The colonel smiled and shook his head.

'It's nothing like that. I've been watching you for a while, Franz. I'm impressed with the way you handle men, and the way nothing seems to fluster you. You also have an eye for the bigger picture, and although you follow orders as required, you question them when you think they may be wrong, but you do quietly, and with discretion. Most of my officers are too frightened to do that and, on the whole, I don't want their opinions.'

'Yes, sir. I don't know what to say, sir.'

'Well, I'm sure you'll say something when I tell you that I'm going to expedite your promotion and make you up to major.'

'Sir, I'm not sure I'm ready for that–'

The colonel interrupted him.

'You are. There's no question in my mind, and I'm a good judge of men. I know they all laugh at these sailing trips, but I learn a great deal about my officers every time we go out. And it's not about how well they sail; it's how they handle themselves, and others, and cope with whatever the trip throws at them.'

Franz tried to speak but the colonel held up his hand.

'This weekend, I put you in charge of a boat that you'd hardly sailed; a gaff-rigged ketch with a raw, untrained crew, and then I asked you to do a significant night passage with them. I wouldn't have faulted you if you'd told me it was too dangerous; that you felt it would jeopardise the boat or the crew.'

'I would have said so, sir, if I believed it was true, but the wind suited us, and the weather was decent. And it was a well-marked channel.'

'All the same, you took two days to turn them into a working crew, you prepared them as well as you could for sailing in the dark, and you made them work, looking for lights, taking their mind off their uneasiness. And then you made it look like you did it all the time, as if it were nothing.'

'I didn't think it was nothing, sir.'

'You know that, and I know that. But they didn't, and that was the important thing.'

He hesitated.

'Listen, Franz. War is coming. Ask your father; he'll confirm that, I'm sure. We need good men, good young men, and in senior positions. It will be an opportunity for you to advance through the ranks quicker then most because that always happens in war, to those who are willing to grab the chance. And I need an adjutant, a right-hand man.'

'Sir, I'm sure you're right about a coming war, but none of us can imagine what it will be like. How do you know I'll be up to it?'

'Because of the way you train your men and the way that you can see things that others don't. You remind me of myself at your age, but better and, if you're anything like your father, you'll excel in battle. He did. He was the most inspirational commander I've ever served under. He taught me most of what I know and I'm glad I've been given the chance to do the same for you.'

'Thank you, sir. I'll do my best not to let you down.'

The colonel laughed.

'I'm sure you will, but if I can offer you a little bit of advice?'

'Of course, sir.'

'Try and have a bit more fun. Relax a little. I know you've had a hard time in your personal life, and you'd rather not talk about it, but don't let that spoil your best years. Take a leaf out of your brother's book. You just have to find a way to strike a balance.'

'I'm not my brother, sir, but I do enjoy myself, in my own way.'

The colonel put his hand on Franz's shoulder.

'I'm just saying. You're only young once. Enjoy it.'

He picked up his hat and stood up.

'Right, we should go. Your new posting will come through within the next month or so.'

The colonel was wrong. The promotion did come, but it took nearly three months. And by that time, for Franz, his beloved Germany was a different place.

CHAPTER 154

[20/08/1938 Saturday]

```
KIELER JÜDISCHES FREIHEITSNACHRICHTENBLATT

Volume 60

23rd of Av, 5698

CENTRAL AGENCY FOR JEWISH EMIGRATIION OPENS IN VIENNA

The Government has opened the Zentralstelle für jüdische
Auswanderung in Vienna. The KJF hopes that this is in response
to the increased Jewish Emigration demands fuelled by the
reported violence against Jews in Austria, which has been on
the increase since the Anschluß.

SS-Obersturmführer Adolf Eichmann has been appointed as the
head of the new department.
```

~~o~~

'Maybe this means that they'll set up a similar unit here. There's a three-month waiting list to even get your case heard, and half the people applying get turned down.'

Isaac Stern held up the *Kieler Jüdisches Freiheitsnachrichtenblatt* as he finished speaking. The grocer who'd rescued Yosef with the General's help stood in the meeting room at the back of the synagogue. Five other men sat on chairs scattered around the room.

'I hope so,' Jakob said. 'Many of my friends are trying to get out.'

'You can still get to Palestine, I think, but everywhere else is becoming difficult, even if you have relatives living there. The United States turned down pleas from Jewish relief organisations to let more of us in.'

'Even Palestine is becoming more difficult,' Yosef said. 'They won't let Itsik and Abel Weichmann's parents join them.'

'I heard that,' Isaac said. 'It's as if they did it just to be cruel; let the younger people go and torture them by keeping their loved ones here.'

'Is anyone here trying to leave?'

There was a chorus of denials.

'Is anyone thinking about it?'

This time, all of them looked at the floor, except for Jakob.

'I don't blame you all. You should be, even if I'm going nowhere. The Schmeckles aren't going to make me do anything I don't want to.'

'Jakob, remember this is God's house,' a tall, pious-looking man said. His name was Siegmund Eliasowitz.

'Ach, God will forgive me, but he won't forgive those Goyim.'

They all laughed, apart from the man who'd taken it upon himself to criticise Jakob, who frowned.

'Well, I say we should invite this Eichmann fellow here and see if he can speed things up a little,' Isaac said. 'Then, at least, we can leave Germany if we decide to.'

CHAPTER 155

KIELER MORGENPOST

Friday 30th September 1938

JUBILATION IN SUDETENLAND – THE FÜHRER WINS PEACE!

In a last-minute turnaround, the British and French leaders, Prime Minister Chamberlain and President Daladier, capitulated to Adolf Hitler's demands that the Sudetenland be returned to Germany, averting the threat of war.

At the conference in Munich, the Sudetenland concession was made with the proviso that the German Government agreed not to make any other territorial demands in Europe.

A spokesman for the Reich Chancellery said that the Führer had finally won freedom for the oppressed German Volk in the Sudetenland and, in doing so, had restored Germany to its rightful place in the world.

~~o~~

'Maria, sit down, will you.'

Maria Kästner recognised the tone in her husband's voice. She sometimes thought that he used the same tone when commanding his men, but she never dared say. She sat down.

He took her hand.

'The boys have been mobilised to go into Sudetenland.'

Apart from a slight stiffening, she didn't react.

'Now, we're not expecting much fighting, but it is possible, I suppose. The Czechs have conceded to British and French demands that they wouldn't oppose the occupation and that they'd withdraw to their original borders.'

'I'm sure they'll be fine. The radio and the newspapers say that the government has handled this remarkably, avoiding the threat of war.'

'That's right,' the General said, relieved. 'I just thought you should know. And I didn't want you to fret if you heard it from someone else.'

'That's unlikely, dear. Who would I be speaking to who would know about troop movements?'

He laughed. 'I suppose that's true. I only knew as soon as I did because Canaris telephoned me, although it would have come through on a memo in time. He thought we'd like to know.'

'Tell him thank you, but I'm not sure I want to know every detail of where they are fighting. I didn't when it was you, during the war in France.'

'That's true, but you had a good idea where I was. We didn't move for months. Sometimes years.'

She noticed the distant look in his eyes again. She hadn't seen it for a long time, but the scars were still there. She remembered the first few months after he'd come home from the war to her, when he'd wake up in the darkness, sweat-soaked, shouting words which chilled her. She'd hold him tight, his body wracked with sobs, until he quietened. Sometimes Franz, not much more than a toddler, would wake up and come into the room, frightened, and she'd shush the child back to bed, telling him that everything was fine. Johann always slept through it all, and Eva, just a baby, would stir with all the fuss, and she'd have to nurse her until she went to sleep again.

She sometimes wondered if that was why her older daughter was the one closest to her.

In the mornings following his night terrors, Erich would wake up with no recollection of them and, over weeks and months, they slowly subsided until they'd gone, and all that was left was that faraway stare of his, when he thought of his time in that place.

She touched his shoulder gently, and he started.

'You were back there, weren't you?' she said.

'I will never forget them,' he answered, and she knew he was talking of the men he'd lost, and she thought of her sons.

'You came through, God be praised, and our boys will too.'

She stroked his hair and he leaned back into her.

She wondered if perhaps she would be the strong one where the boys were concerned, and he the worrier. The irony of it made her smile. She leaned down and kissed him.

~~o~~

'I'm afraid of what this means,' Miriam Nussbaum said, sitting at the kitchen table. Yosef was next to her and Ruth sat reading at the opposite end of the table, her head held up by one arm, supported by her elbow, her nose almost in the book.

'I'm sure it will make no difference,' Yosef said. 'After all, annexing Austria didn't seem to have any effect.'

'Papa, the girls at school say there's going to be a war, and we will win. Is that true? Will you have to fight alongside the Kästners?'

The Nussbaums turned to Ruth. Neither of them had realised that she'd been listening, engrossed as she was.

'The threat of conflict is less now. And no, I most certainly wouldn't be called to fight, but Franz and Johann would. So, let's pray that there's not another war.'

'Perhaps a war is the only way we'll be rid of Adolf Hitler,' Miriam said.

'Miriam, be careful,' Yosef said, looking at his wife sharply, then glancing at his daughter.

'She's fifteen, and old enough to know. And she won't say a word to anybody.'

She turned to her daughter.

'Will you, Ruth?' she asked.

'No, Mama. We don't speak about things like that. One of the Jewish girls in the school said that she didn't want to be called Sara, and she was taken out in front of the school and told to tell everyone why she was called that now.'

Yosef could feel his wife stiffen, and he didn't have to see her to know the look on her face.

'What did she have to say?'

'"I'm a dirty Jew. We dirty Jews are all called Sara or Israel. So that everyone can see that we are dirty Jews".'

Miriam's hand slammed down on the table.

'How can they get away with it?'

'Because we're powerless, and they can do what they like.'

He turned to his daughter. 'What about you?'

'I said nothing.'

'You did the right thing. Keep your head down, work hard, don't speak unless you really need to, then just say what they want you to say.'

'Yes, Papa.'

'How can you say that?' Miriam said. 'To your own child. Have you no pride left?'

'They're taking children away from people like us if they show any sign of what they call "delinquency".'

'You know this? For a fact?'

'Yes, Isaac told me about a family he knew. The boy spat at another boy, who wasn't Jewish. They told the parents that they were taking him away to a reform school, but Isaac thinks they put him in a camp.'

Yosef shuddered, thinking of his own family. He'd need to have another word with Manny, tell him about the camps. It would maybe keep him out of trouble.

Ruth's voice interrupted his thoughts.

'I'm good, Papa, and so is Manny. They'll not take us away.'

Yosef put his hand over his daughter's.

'I know you're good. You're the best daughter we could have. And Manny is the best son. We know it's hard for you but as I told you before, we Jews have been treated like this for centuries, and we've learned to bend in the wind, like a blade of grass.'

Miriam sat shaking her head, mumbling.

'It's not right. It's just not right.'

Yosef drew them both to him.

'What was the war like, Papa?' Ruth asked.

'It was unspeakable. Like nothing human. I wouldn't wish it on anyone, for any reason.'

Miriam couldn't meet his gaze.

'I'm sorry. I shouldn't have wished for war. But I can't help thinking that the German people deserve it, for what they're doing to us.'

'And the Kästner boys?'

Her head dropped again.

'No. I wouldn't wish it on them.'

'I don't want Johann to fight,' Ruth said, 'or Franz,' she added, blushing.

Yosef allowed himself a smile inside. He'd guessed that his daughter had a schoolgirl infatuation for Johann, but he could never let on to her that he knew.

'They chose to be soldiers, like their father,' he said. 'If there's a war, they'll be the first to fight. In their favour, they're professionals, and they're highly trained. We were just working men who volunteered, with no experience of combat, just desperate to fight for our country because we felt it was right.'

'And what did that patriotism get you?' Miriam said, her eyes blazing.

Yosef didn't respond.

'Nothing. Worse than nothing,' she said, answering her own question. 'But I'll still pray for the Kästner boys.'

'We'll all pray if war comes. Please God it doesn't.'

CHAPTER 156

THE LONDON EVENING TELEGRAPH

Saturday, October 1st, 1938

"YOU MAY SLEEP QUIETLY –

IT IS PEACE FOR OUR TIME."

Large crowds greeted the prime minister, Mr. Neville Chamberlain, as he returned home from his mission of peace in Germany last night.

Many thousands of people greeted him first at Heston Airport, where he landed from Munich. From there, he went straight to Buckingham Palace, where he and Mrs. Chamberlain joined the king and queen on the balcony to salute the large crowd that had gathered at the gates.

When he finally returned to Downing Street, a throng of people had waited outside Number Ten. From an upper-floor window, the prime minister said:

"This is the second time in our history that there has come back from Germany to Downing Street peace with honour. I believe it is peace for our time."

It is reported that Mr. Chamberlain has been invited by Mussolini on board his private yacht next week for new talks, and that French premier Dalardier may be present as well.

~~o~~

Major Anthony Plenderleith turned to his wife.

'I do believe Mr Chamberlain has made the most awful mistake.'

'I have to agree with you, dear. The man's English is appalling for someone who purports to be our prime minister.'

'I wasn't talking about his diction, woman, although you do have a point; *that there has come back from Germany* doesn't scan too well. No, I was talking about his embarrassing appeasement of this Adolf Hitler fellow.'

'They're saying that he prevented the start of another war.'

'Poppycock. That awful man is determined to take over Europe. Sooner or later, he will need to be stopped. We've sold the Czech people down the river if you ask me.'

'You're retired. I don't think anyone is asking you, dear. That's the problem.'

He shook his head, then started when she sat bolt upright.

'If there is a war, you might be called up,' she said, her eyes wide.

'I'm on the reserve list, dear,' the major scoffed. 'They won't call me up.'

'I wouldn't be so sure. They called up older men than you in the last war.'

'This war will be different. It won't last long. Germany is surrounded by enemies.'

'Not completely. Hitler and Mussolini appear to be on jolly good terms. And he has even softened his hostility to Stalin.'

'You're dreadfully knowledgeable about Adolf Hitler all of a sudden, Marjorie.'

'I might not read the papers, the way you do, but I listen to the radio,' she said.

Her husband had detested the radio set from the moment they'd purchased it, and he avoided listening to it, immersing himself in newspapers and magazines instead.

'Well, I still think it will kick off if he does this to Poland, or France.'

He poked the paper with his finger and read it out to her.

'German troops go in at noon,' he said. 'Zero hour in Adolf Hitler's march on Czechoslovakia has been fixed for noon today. Final preparations for the invasion along several sectors on the south-west frontier were made at the headquarters in Linz last night.'

'Even if it does, dear, I don't think they'll send you to fight the Nazis.'

The major sighed.

'One can only hope not, my dear. One can only hope.'

~~o~~

[02/10/1938 Sunday]

KIELER JÜDISCHES FREIHEITSNACHRICHTENBLATT

Volume 62

7th of Tishrei, 5699

GREAT BRITAIN AND FRANCE BETRAY CZECHOSLOVAKIA

The German army are moving into Czechoslovakia to occupy the Sudetenland, as agreed on September 30th at the Conference in Munich involving the leaders of Germany, Italy, Great Britain, and France.

The governments of Czechoslovakia and of Russia were not invited.

The Czechoslovakian leader, President Beneš, and his Government were faced with the stark choice of resisting a German invasion, with no possibility of support from France or Britain, or conceding the Sudeten territories to Germany.

It further strengthens Adolf Hitler's hold on power and bodes badly for the thousands of Czechoslovakian Jews living in the reclaimed areas, like their Austrian counterparts. It is expected that many of them will flee into Czechoslovakia itself.

All four leaders are being vaunted in their own countries for their success in avoiding the threat of another European war.

~~o~~

'We, and the Czechs have been sold out. The British were our last hope.'

'Jakob, what choice did they have,' Yosef said. 'They could do nothing.'

'The French could have threatened to move into Rheinland, and the British could have sent troops to help. That would have made Adolf think twice.'

'It would have started another war. It is just twenty years since the last one ended. We all know what that was like.'

'Jakob is right,' Isaac Stern interjected, 'We are on our own, but Yosef is right too. It wouldn't have done any good. Only the Russians could have made a difference in Czechoslovakia, and they didn't lift a finger.'

'You'd better watch those piles of yours, Isaac,' Jakob said, 'sitting on that fence.'

There was no real rancour in his comment, and the group all laughed. They'd met to discuss the latest developments, and how it would affect the Jewish community.

'There are still the Americans.'

'Yosef,' Jakob said, in a patient voice, like the one used to teach a small child an important, but obvious, life lesson, 'the Americans are over 3,000 miles away, and that's exactly where they'll stay. They have no stomach to become involved in yet another European conflict.'

'He's right,' Isaac said. 'They won't even open their doors to take those wanting to leave.'

'I've applied to go there,' one of the other men said. 'I'm told I may have to wait a year.'

'England is not much better,' Jakob said. 'A friend of mine has been waiting for six months, and nothing.'

'If you want to go, apply for France, or one of the low countries. I hear they're taking Jews. You'll be penniless, but you'll be away from all of this.'

'I'd like to put some water between Adolf and myself,' the would-be American immigrant said, and they all laughed again.

'It might not do you much good,' said Jakob. 'I hear the Führer can walk on water.'

This time, the laughter was more raucous, and a woman cleaning the synagogue poked her head in the doorway to see what they found so amusing.

'Ach. We'll just have to do as we always do,' Isaac said. 'Turn our cheek to our tormentors and our face to God.'

'Amen,' they all chorused.

CHAPTER 157

'Jürgen. How nice to see you. Have you met Admiral Canaris?'

'I've not had the pleasure, but I'm delighted to make your acquaintance,' Jürgen Hoffmann said, nodding to Wilhelm Canaris as he shook his hand.

'The pleasure is all mine, Herr Mayor. I've heard a lot about you from the General. Is the Oberpräsident with us today?'

'No, I'm afraid he has had to travel to Berlin, and then on to Sudetenland, as part of the celebrations.'

'How exciting for him. Perhaps I'll see him. I'll be there the day after tomorrow. I'm travelling overnight on the sleeping car when we get back from our sailing trip.'

The admiral turned to the General. 'Perhaps your driver will drop me off at the station when we return.'

'Consider it done,' the General replied.

He beckoned to Captain Bauer and spoke to the young officer, then dismissed him.

'The captain will organise it.'

He turned to the mayor, resplendent in his full regalia of office.

'Jürgen, you must be delighted with events.'

'The Führer has surpassed himself. Who would have thought that the British and the French would have backed down so readily? If I'm honest, I was more than worried about the prospect of war.'

'As were all of us,' Canaris said.

'The man is a genius. He seems to have such an incredible grasp of foreign policy. On every occasion he has stood up for Germany, he has emerged triumphant.'

'I can't argue with that,' the admiral said. 'He is the master of brinkmanship.'

The lunchtime reception in the town hall was being held to celebrate the return of Sudetenland to Germany, and the mayor had been delighted when the General had accepted his invitation, especially so when he learned that Admiral Canaris would also attend, although both men would only be able to stay a short time.

'It's a pity you can't stay longer,' Jürgen Hoffmann said.

'Yes, it's unfortunate,' the General said, 'But we're leaving for Eckernförde for a short trip. We meet the rest of the crew in an hour to make the best of daylight.'

Jürgen Hoffmann saw the General glance at his watch.

'Come,' he said, 'I must introduce you to my wife, and some of our councillors before you go...'

~~o~~

'Well, that was scintillating,' Canaris said, sitting in the cabin of the General's boat, steaming mug of coffee in hand.

'Jürgen's not so bad. More of an opportunist National Socialist than a fervent believer. The trouble is, there are thousands like him, which is part of the reason they have such a stranglehold on power but having him onside is immensely useful for the navy, and for the yards supplying us with ships.'

'The people's love for their Führer will have reached new heights now that he's brought the Sudetenland back under our control. And probably with good cause. I don't think anyone else would have had the balls to take on the French and the English at high-stakes poker.'

'No, you're right, and a small part of me applauds the restoration of our national boundaries and even, at a push, the Anschluss, if it weren't for all the other Scheiße that came with it.'

'There's nothing for it but to sit back and watch what happens next.'

'How close did it get?'

'Going to war, or for disaffected parties within Germany to take action?'

'Both, I think.'

'I'd say that Adolf read it right. Neither the English nor the French had the stomach for it. And without them, there could be no attempt to resolve the problem at this end.'

'But he'll push for more, surely.'

'Yes. Success will inflame his desire to do one better, again and again. It's like sex. The more you get, the more you want.'

The General burst out laughing.

'That's a novel way of putting it, Canaris.'

'Well, would once ever have been enough for you, Kästner?'

Still laughing, the General shook his head.

'No, you're right. And his craving for power and glory seems to be getting worse.'

A shout and a knock on the coachroof interrupted them.

'Ah,' the General said. 'That will be Dieter.'

'Come aboard,' he shouted up, sliding the hatch back.

He deftly caught Dieter's bag, and the newspaperman followed it down.

'Dieter, Admiral Canaris; Canaris, Dieter.'

Both men shook hands, measuring each other up.

'Stow your gear and let's get going. We have the best part of six hours sailing ahead of us, if this wind stays.'

'Why, where are we going?' Canaris asked.

'I'm not sure yet. It depends on the wind.'

'I thought you sailor types always planned ahead?'

'I've a rough idea, if the wind holds.'

~~o~~

It held up, and more. Dieter Maas had never felt wind like it but in the shelter of Laboe, it howled over the top of them.

What had been a strong breeze when they left the General's berth had turned into a near gale by the time they could see the Kiel lightship, just beyond Kleverberg at the mouth of Kieler Förde. It had swung round to the north east, and the waves were breaking over the bow and washing back along the coachroof and the side-decks into the cockpit.

'Even if we get past Kleverberg sands,' the General shouted above the roar, 'it's going to be wild out there and there's no shelter until Eckernförde, a good four or five hours away.'

'What can we do?' Dieter said, the water running down his face.

'We'll have to turn back. Ready about.'

The General ducked as another wave broke, and he turned the yacht away from the wind.

'Lee ho,' he shouted, and the admiral and Dieter let the port foresail sheet go and hauled in the starboard one.

They already had the smallest of the three foresails hoisted; only the storm jib would reduce it further. There were three reefs in the main and, although the General had a tri-sail for storm-force winds, it would have been foolhardy to persevere in conditions where it might be needed, when there were options to turn back.

They ran downwind towards Laboe, a small fishing harbour tucked in on the east shore of the fjord, just outside the Friedrichsort narrows. Travelling with the wind behind them, its ferocity subsided, and they could hear each other speak.

'It's amazing how much calmer it is when we turn downwind,' Dieter said.

'Don't be fooled,' Canaris replied. 'The wind hasn't changed, and these waves can still cause us problems.'

Dieter looked behind them. The waves were bigger than anything he'd ever seen and

516

threatened to break over the back of the boat or, even worse, broach her by lifting the stern up and throwing it to the side, but the General managed to keep her straight, and surf the wave to stop them being swamped.

By the time they'd reached the entrance to Laboe, they'd found themselves in the shelter of the higher land behind the village. The wind, although still strong, had lost the worst of its anger and the waves had subsided to a vicious chop. With some relief, they dropped the sails and motored in, to tie up next to one of the harbour's many fishing boats.

'It feels as if we've travelled further than we actually have,' the admiral said, the whine of the wind high above their heads, reminding them that the storm was still raging as they sat drying out in the warm cabin.

'We're four miles away from our berth in Kiel,' the General said, 'which, incidentally, will not be as comfortable as this one, with the wind howling down the fjord.'

Dieter, more relieved than the others, never having experienced such a change in the sea before, shook himself.

'What will we do for food?' he asked.

'Well, I have some cans of stuff,' the General replied. 'Potatoes, stew, cabbage. They're just about edible. But we may find somewhere to eat. Laboe is quite fashionable now, since the Olympics, and lots of tourists come to see the memorial tower.'

'Let's take a walk,' growled the admiral.

~~o~~

They found somewhere reasonable; a tourist spot, open for the last week of the season before closing for winter. The menu was limited but adequate, and the clientele sparse, so service was quick. Back on the boat, the General lit the small charcoal heater to take the chill off the October dampness and, in the small cabin, it soon became warm, and they snuffed the glowing coals.

'So, Dieter, Erich tells me you're one of our sources.'

'Yes,' Dieter replied, surprised.

'It's all right, Dieter. Canaris and I go back a long way. I trust him completely.'

Dieter relaxed a little.

'I'm not sure I provide anything of much use to you. In the main it's common knowledge or plain gossip.'

'Hardly, Dieter,' the General said, smiling. 'You have sources who wouldn't dare being seen talking directly to us.'

'I suppose so, and their reticence will only get worse; the Gestapo are clamping down on people who have any hint of dissent in their past. They're opening mail, questioning colleagues and neighbours, and putting surveillance on anyone it suspects of not being quite as enthusiastic about National Socialism as they should be.'

'You're being watched?' the admiral asked.

'Not me. I don't think so, anyway, but some of the people I speak to have told me to keep my distance, and we've arranged to communicate in other ways, or through third parties.'

'Don't put yourself at risk, Dieter,' the General said.

Dieter could see genuine concern on the older man's face.

'We're all at risk, Erich. Even you. Maybe especially you.'

He paused.

'How safe is it to use the telephone?' Dieter continued. 'It's something I'm getting a little nervous about.'

'We think, on balance, public telephones are safe to use,' the admiral replied. 'The SD or the Gestapo don't have a widespread enough monitoring capability, nor are they sophisticated enough yet to be able to pick up on random telephone calls, but if you have been drawn to their attention, they can and will listen to any calls to or from your own telephone line.'

'Do you think your telephone is tapped?' the General asked.

'How does one tell?' Dieter said. 'There are no clicks on the line, or any delays in connecting.'

'Always assume they are monitoring it, just to be on the safe side.'

'I do. I only meet face to face or by using public telephones, but the latter is rare. All my contacts are old friends; people I'd be expected to keep in touch with. I've deliberately not cultivated anyone new, so that I don't attract attention.'

'Good work, Dieter. Now what's the word on Herr Hitler's latest triumph?'

'The majority, even those that detest this regime, admire him for taking back the Sudetenland and doing it without having to fight. Any real opposition to the National Socialists has just gone even further underground.'

'Not a surprise. The feeling of euphoria in the country is remarkable.'

'I'm hearing stories of almost immediate repercussions for Sudetenland's Jews, much like in Austria and...'

The former editor hesitated.

The two Abwehr men waited, not interrupting, so he continued, a little unsure of the ground he was treading on.

'...I heard that there was a potential coup planned, had war not been averted. It wasn't much more than gossip, but it came from a few different sources.'

Neither the General nor the admiral reacted.

'I think we'd have heard about it,' the admiral said, 'if anyone in the military had planned it.'

'I didn't say it was just within the armed forces,' Dieter said.

'No, but one assumes that only military intervention would have any chance of success,' he said.

'Anything else?' the General asked.

'Not really. There's something brewing though. There's a tenseness pervading everything. People are becoming more cautious, and less trusting. There are reports of neighbours informing on neighbours, using the Gestapo to settle old scores. There's a climate of fear.'

'The National Socialists have always used fear and intimidation as weapons,' the General said. 'It's the stick to offset the carrots of national pride, greater prosperity and German prestige.'

'The Jewish community are worried, especially about what is going on in Austria. They're scared it might spread here.'

'I don't think it will,' the admiral said. 'These are isolated incidents that have been blown out of proportion; looters and local thugs, getting carried away. If it were going to happen here, it would have happened before now.'

'I'm not so sure,' said the General. 'The Jewish community here are deeply concerned.'

'It's up to the local police to stop any violence, or intimidation.' the admiral argued. 'They've brought it under control in Austria, and they will in Sudetenland. People just took advantage of the disruption. It will all settle down.'

Dieter and the General looked at each other.

'Then what would your advice be to the Jews living in Germany today?' the General asked.

'Sit tight, and it will pass,' the admiral replied, 'especially if there's a war. They'll need all the manpower they can get, even if it's just to fill the jobs that non-Jewish men vacate as they are drafted into the army.'

'And you, Dieter?'

'I'd tell them to get out while they can. If they can.'

Canaris looked at the General.

'And you?' he said.

'I'm with Dieter on this one. My advice is to get out.'

'Oskar, how are you?'

The businessman leant back in his chair, and swung his feet up onto his desk, the telephone handset held between his shoulder and his ear.

'I'm fine, Jürgen. What can I do for you?'

'Nothing, but perhaps I can be of assistance to you. I heard you were looking for some factory space.'

'That's correct. Business has picked up considerably, and we're bursting at the seams. There's simply nothing available, and most of the building contractors are working on government or municipal jobs, so getting somewhere built is almost impossible.'

'I might be able to help you out. I have just acquired a small factory, on Neuenrade, just off Uhlenkrog.'

'I know where you are. Is it empty?'

'Yes. The owner has emigrated.'

'Ah. You've just bought it? It wasn't on the market then?'

Oskar knew that it hadn't been on the market. He'd been on the lookout for such a place.

'No,' the mayor said. 'It was a private sale. I helped them out with some red tape.'

Oskar had seen it so often, in recent times. Properties or businesses owned by prosperous Jews would be purchased at knock-down prices by party officials in return for easing the process of getting them and their families out of Germany with at least a small fraction of their fortune intact.

'What's its square metreage?'

Jürgen Hoffmann told him, and what the rent would be.

'I'll take a look at it,' Oskar told him. He suppressed the twinge of guilt that he always had on these occasions.

If it weren't me, someone else would snap it up.

CHAPTER 158

[03/10/1938 Monday]

'Do you think they'll go back and look at past transactions?' Yosef said, his face a mask of worry.

The government had just announced the introduction of the Decree on the Confiscation of Jewish Property, which allowed the authorities to seize any Jewish assets and appropriate them in the interests of the German economy. Crucially for Yosef and Miriam, it also regulated the transfer of assets from Jews to non-Jews.

'I wouldn't rule it out,' the General said, 'but it's been six months since we retrieved your money and, don't forget, the manager recorded it as a loan repayment in his ledger. There's a good chance that will pass scrutiny even if they do check it out.'

The General saw a flash of relief temper Yosef's anxious frown.

'It doesn't state that there will be any retrospective action,' he continued, 'and anyway, I don't think they'll have the manpower, for now at least.'

'I hope not, sir. I'm glad you had the foresight to suggest this, all that time ago.'

'It was you who came to me. It was the only sensible thing to do.'

He smiled.

'We couldn't have Hermann Göring, the commissioner for the Four Year Plan, getting hold of it, could we?'

Yosef returned the smile, then his face turned grave again.

'It's going to get worse, sir. I can feel it.'

The General bowed his head.

'I'm afraid it will, Yosef, which is why you should start putting a bit of pressure on Miriam to think about leaving Germany.'

For a second or two, Yosef didn't answer, and the General wondered if his repeated suggestions that the Nussbaums should leave were irritating him.

'I will,' he finally answered in almost a whisper. 'When I mention it now, she isn't dismissing it out of hand.'

For a moment, the General was taken aback.

'That's good. Well, it's a start, at least. Where would you go?'

'England, most likely. The United States would be best, but they say there's a twelve month wait to get a visa. It's less than half that for Britain.'

'So, you've looked into it then?'

Yosef gave a wan smile.

'Not really, but it's all Jews talk about these days. There has always been a lively rumour mill in the Jewish community. Now, it has become indispensable.'

~~o~~

KIELER MORGENPOST

Wednesday 5th October 1938

JEWS MUST SURRENDER PASSPORTS

All Jews resident in Germany must surrender their passports to be stamped to identify the holder as Jewish. This will consist of a large "J", similar to that on Jewish identification cards.

All new passports issued to Jews will be pre-stamped to comply with the new law.

The Government has stated that withholding a passport will result in severe penalties, including imprisonment and a substantial fine.

~~o~~

[11/10/1938 Tuesday]

'Happy birthday, old boy.'

A chorus of greetings filled the small bar, a large crowd of soldiers in the uniform of the Wehrmacht mingling with Czech-German girls, only too happy with the influx of a new and somehow more interesting batch of young men for them to mix with.

Johann climbed up onto one of the tables.

'Thank you, gentlemen, and ladies,' he said. 'My mother will be terribly disappointed that I'm here in Teplice, in the wonderful *German* Sudetenland, and not at home to celebrate my twenty-first birthday…'

He paused while the group cheered and thumped the tables.

'…but it is my privilege to spend it here with my brother Franz,' he continued, sweeping a drunken arm around the room in his elder sibling's direction, 'and with all of you, my Wehrmacht colleagues, and those of you who will shortly be joining that happy band that I call my friends.'

A further bout of cheering ended when he fell, to be caught by his fellow soldiers and propelled across the room at head height to the bar, where Franz stood, shaking his head.

'You do like to make a spectacle of yourself, brother,' he said.

'Ach. I just like to enjoy myself. And the Fräuleins love me.'

As he spoke, a chestnut-haired girl of about eighteen or nineteen grabbed him and planted a kiss on his lips.

'You see, Franz,' he said, as he held her in one arm, the other around his brother, 'they can't seem to help themselves, and you're just a little jealous.'

Franz grinned.

Whatever anyone said, it was fun to be around Johann. Even his own friends had become more of his brother's group of peers than his, not that he minded. It often gave him an excuse to escape when he'd had enough of their hedonistic madness.

'You should take a leaf out of my book,' he continued, nodding at three girls standing laughing a few feet away.

Franz shook his head and smiled.

'I'm going to head back to the billet. Don't get too plastered. Remember you're on patrol in the morning, and old Schneider's keeping an eye on you.'

Johann watched him go, his face serious for a second, then, as the chords of a guitar broke through the cloud of noise, he turned to his companion.

'Come, my little peach. Let's go and have a sing-song.'

CHAPTER 159

Ruth's eyes were on the floor. She didn't dare look at the teacher or meet with the hateful eyes of her classmates. Her right arm extended upwards, rigid, in salute to the Führer.

Hanne Weidmann stood between her and Rebeka, flanked by two Jewish boys, all in the same pose.

Ruth had always loved mathematics but, since the start of the school year, she had come to dread the subject more than any other.

This, like all their lessons, had begun with the pupils standing to attention and saluting the Führer, shouting a sharp 'Heil Hitler' in unison before sitting down.

In most of her classes, it was almost perfunctory, done to cover the teacher against allegations of being anti-party.

But for the mathematics master, in his Hitlerjugend leader's uniform and shiny black boots, it had to be executed with precision and zeal, and any deviation from perfection was severely punished.

On the odd occasion, Aryan children were the victims of his watchfulness but, in the main, it was one or two of the Jewish children who were selected to stand out in front of the class to receive a rattle of the cane round the back of the legs and a humiliating lecture.

'Weidmann!' he shouted. 'Straighten your arm.'

He turned to the class.

'I apologise for having to interrupt your lesson to deal with these disrespectful Jewish scum. It was only a matter of time before all five of them stood here before you.'

A few of the pupils, the one or two who were still friendly with the Jewish children, held looks of guarded sympathy on their faces, but the majority of their classmates had anticipatory grins, the thrill of watching the ritual humiliation of their fellow pupils much preferable to getting their heads around the complexities of trigonometry or algebra.

The boy next to Ruth shuffled his foot and the teacher's cane flashed out, slashing across the back of his legs. He flinched but maintained his position, forcing himself not to react. The other boy in the line allowed himself a small smile of relief that it hadn't been him who'd received the first blow.

'Boy,' the master hissed. 'Do you think it's funny to disrespect the Führer?'

'No, sir,' the boy mumbled.

'I didn't hear you,' the teacher said, his voice low and menacing.

'No, sir. I don't think it's funny,' the boy shouted.

The cane flashed again, this time across the front of the second victims' legs. The boy almost stumbled but managed to regain his balance and stand straight.

'Don't drop that arm a centimetre, Nussbaum,' Ruth heard the repulsive little man say. 'You neither, Liewermann.'

The teacher was smaller than some of the taller boys in the class and Ruth wondered if this was one of the reasons for his ritual bullying. Not that it mattered.

'I think you ungrateful Jewish brats should show a little reverence for our great leader. Let us see if a little practice makes perfect. You can have the privilege of saluting the Führer until the end of the lesson.'

He walked around behind Ruth and prodded his cane into the small of her back.

'Stand up straight, Jew,' he said, then, to her relief, he moved on.

'Hanne Weidmann. Perhaps it should be your father standing here, with his long hairy chin and his bushy sidelocks and that absurd little bowl he wears on his head.'

He paused while the class laughed.

'What do you say to that, Weidmann?' he added, with a poke of his stick in her side.

'Yes, sir,' Hanne said.

Ruth knew that Hanne Weidmann's mother had taken her aside, in defiance of her father, and told her always to agree with any Goyim in authority. Her own father had told her the same, and her mother had reluctantly agreed. It made it easier to bear and, while part of her wanted to stand up to this horrible man who tormented them at every opportunity, she never quite found the courage to do so.

Ruth glanced at Hanne and gave a muted smile of comfort. She saw the girl's eyes form a smile in reply. A blow of the cane caught Ruth across the back of the head, and for a brief second, she thought she was going to pass out. She tottered and took a step forward, but instinct told her to stay on her feet and, fighting back tears of pain and anger, she steadied herself.

'Do you think your little gesture of support for your Jew-slut friend was a clever idea?' she heard in her ear, the hissed whisper designed to be heard by the whole class.

'Perhaps her father and you are more than friends?' the teacher added, drops of angry spittle spotting her skin.

He sniggered, and some of the class laughed, but Ruth caught a glimpse of others looking down at their desks, unable to meet her gaze.

Neither girl said a word, but a tear slipped down Ruth's cheek and she chided herself for letting them see she was hurt.

'Now, class, we're going to do some work. If any of you see any of these Jewish arms dropping, put up your hands and tell me.'

Ruth risked a glance at the clock. There was forty-five minutes to go. It would be a long and painful wait.

~~o~~

Between the five, they received eleven further blows of the cane before the bell released them to the refuge of the corridor, the teacher's venomous words following them.

Ruth rubbed her arm. She'd taken three of the stinging slashes, two across her back and one at the top of her leg but it was her arm that was the sorest for now. It had sounded simple to hold the salute, right arm extended in honour of the Führer but all of them, at some point, had given in to the deadening pain of fatigued muscles and had dropped a few centimetres, or bent their arm a fraction.

Each time, a forest of hands shot up and pointed out the miscreant and the cane slashed its arc onto an arm or leg. By the end of the lesson, all but one of the boys had wept, and Ruth looked at him in admiration while they walked to the next lesson.

'How do you manage not to cry?' she asked.

'I don't know. I just do.'

'I try, but I can't stop it happening sometimes.'

'I know,' he said.

~~o~~

[14/10/1938 Friday]

Esther opened the letter with shaking hands. It had been three months since she'd written to Miriam.

She looked at the date on the letter. 31st August. It was now the middle of October. *Six weeks. Why had it taken so long?*

She sat down to read.

31st August

Dear Esther,

It was lovely to receive your letter, which arrived yesterday. It seems such a long time since your last one.

I'm glad Moshe and Shoshana are enjoying life out there. It must be nice for them to have no trouble at school; for that alone I could put up with the heat and the dust.

It is still tough for Manny and Ruth, and all the other Jewish children but, as ever, they don't complain much. I notice the odd bruise and see the look in their eyes when I mention school.

It's wonderful that your new house has been started. It won't be long before you move into it, with all the space you need. Please send pictures of it, and of you and the children, and Itsik, too, of course.

I still check once a week on Itsik's parents. His father was poorly for a while, but he'd picked up a little the last time I was there.

Itsik's mother asked me if the General could help with their case for emigration. I've told Yosef to ask him next time he's speaking with him, but I warned her not to get her hopes up. Perhaps Itsik could write to Oskar von Friedeburg, the man who bought your shop. He seems to have quite a lot of influence and Yosef tells me he's a decent sort.

We now have new middle names! All of us have had to add Israel, for men, or Sara, for women, for anything official. We also have been issued with identity cards, which we must always carry. They have our new names on them and are stamped with a big yellow 'J' to make sure everyone knows that we're Jews although according to the Der Stürmer posters, we all have big noses, so they should know anyway!

I must go. I hear Yosef coming in for his dinner.

Love you dearly,

Miriam.

Esther sat, the tears running down her face. She couldn't risk telling Itsik about his parents, and how Yosef was asking the General for help, and she dare not get her hopes up.

She felt for Manny and Ruth, and for Rebeka and Fischel; Rosa had told a similar tale in her letter. She could sense that the situation for Kiel's Jews was worsening by the week. Part of her was glad they'd made the move to Palestine, as much for the children's sake as anything else but she missed the city, her family, and her friends with an ache that was almost unbearable at times.

And she wondered if it would ever get any easier.

CHAPTER 160

Yosef stood in a doorway near the junction of the corner of Kleiner Kuhberg and Treppenstraße. He was taking a risk; there were Gestapo, police and Brownshirts everywhere. He carried his ID card, the folded letter that the General had given him, and his veteran card, which afforded him the last few vestiges of privilege that a Jew could still expect. He also wore his medals, hidden under his overcoat.

He watched as the police led two Jewish families out of the building on Kleiner Kuhberg, a street that housed much of Kiel's Ostjuden population, along with its neighbouring street, Waisenhofstraße.

He recognised the family; they attended the synagogue every week, but he couldn't recall their name. It left him with a vague feeling of guilt.

The police, not unkindly, helped them up into the back of an army truck. They each carried one suitcase, and Yosef's heart went out to the little fellow who couldn't have been more than four, carrying his tiny case, trailing along behind his parents and his older sisters.

Yosef paled.

This is happening all over Germany.

One of the policemen went to lift the little boy up into the lorry, his mother already in the truck and reaching out for him, but his father shook his head and said something to the policeman, who nodded and stood back. The man picked his son up and handed the boy to his wife.

Yosef had been collecting a parcel for Frau Kästner in Knooper Weg when he'd overheard a young Jewish boy tell his father that the Gestapo were removing people from houses in Kleiner Kuhberg, and a grim desire to know who was being taken made him make his way there, slipping through the churchyard behind the Rathaus.

The lorry's engine growled, and it moved forward, stopping in front of a house two doors up. Seven or eight policemen and SA men walked with it, and when the door was opened to their loud knocking, they entered the house in single file. The two black-coated Gestapo men stood on the pavement, talking from time to time with the three or four policemen who guarded the truck.

Two minutes later, two of the SA men appeared at the top of the steps, manhandling a woman, none too gently.

Yosef bowed his head and closed his eyes for a second.

Frau Weidmann. Her daughter is in Ruth's class.

As the Brownshirts hauled the woman down the stairs, two policemen appeared with her husband, who tried to wrestle his way back into the building until an SA man behind him brought a black baton down on his head.

The fight left him, and he was half dragged, half marched to the lorry, and hefted up onto it, cursing under the SA men manhandling him. The older Gestapo officer told his wife to get up after him, and keep him quiet, or they'd both be shot. He flicked his coat aside, exposing his holstered pistol, to hammer home the threat.

Yosef's gaze jerked back to the house when he heard a child crying from the direction of the doorway, and a girl in her teens emerged, holding a young boy close to her, maybe eight or nine, who was weeping uncontrollably. Another girl followed. Although it was difficult for Yosef to tell, he thought that she was younger, but similar in looks, to the girl in front. She also had a small boy in tow, trailing behind her. The policemen, who appeared to be less brutal than the SA men, shepherded the group towards the waiting lorry, to join their parents.

Yosef frowned.

The girl. Ruth's classmate. She's not there.

A flicker of hope welled up in him, and he deliberated on whether he should wait around after they'd gone, to see if she was hiding.

Miriam wouldn't want me to leave her.

He saw an SA man emerge from the building and speak to the two Gestapo men. The taller of the two checked a clipboard then began remonstrating with him. Yosef strained to hear their voices, but they were too far away.

The SA man shouted to one of his colleagues and the two men re-entered the house. Five minutes later they emerged again, dragging the girl Yosef recognised as Ruth's schoolmate, Hanne, and his heart sank.

Struggling, she tried to elude their grasp, but the men were too strong and laughed at her attempts to wriggle free. They heaved her up into the truck like a side of meat, making ribald comments to their companions. Yosef just caught the words 'Jew-bitch' and something about a lesson.

Three of the SA men climbed into the truck with the prisoners, and the remainder waited at the kerbside until a second truck pulled up. They climbed in, and the two trucks roared off.

The Gestapo men took a last look around and, as they glanced in his direction, Yosef tried to melt into the doorway he'd been standing in. For a moment, he thought he'd been spotted but after a second, they strolled arrogantly over to a black car parked on the other side of the street and got into the back. The car pulled out and headed up Kleiner Kuhberg in the direction the trucks had taken.

Yosef eased the door closed behind him and glanced through from the kitchen to the parlour. Miriam, sitting darning, saw him put a finger to his lips, then beckon her with a nod.

She checked that the children were engrossed in their homework, and got up from her seat and, entering the kitchen, closed the door behind her.

'What's wrong?' she asked.

'It's the Weidmanns. They've been taken.'

'Oh no. God help them. What do we tell Ruth?'

'Nothing just now, until we have some idea of where they've gone.'

'She'll notice Hanne's not at school,' Miriam said.

'She'll just think she's off sick, won't she?'

'You know how quickly news travels. It would be better if she heard it from us. Not at school.'

Yosef sighed. Miriam was right. It would give Ruth's fellow pupils great pleasure to be the ones to tell Ruth about Hanne, or it could be a teacher, cruelly taunting her by announcing the deportation in front of the whole class, just to watch her break down.

'You're right. I'll tell her.'

He opened the parlour door and, when Ruth looked up and smiled, he nodded for her to come through. She got up and passed by him, a puzzled look on her face. Manny continued to colour in his picture. To his horror, Yosef noticed that it was a drawing of the town hall, with crude banners draped from the balcony. Manny had coloured them blue, the swastikas pink.

A cold hand took hold of his heart, but he followed Ruth through, his attention torn between what he was going to say to his daughter and how to tell Manny that he'd have to change the colours of his picture or suffer the consequences at school.

Miriam stood, biting her bottom lip while Yosef motioned for Ruth to sit down at the table. He took a chair opposite and put his hand over hers.

'The Weidmanns have been arrested,' he said, seeing Miriam's frown, but there was no point in trying to soften it.

'Hanne too?' Ruth asked, her voice so quiet as to be almost inaudible.

'Yes. Hanne too. I'm sorry.'

'Where have they been taken?'

'I don't know, my love. They were driven away in a lorry, with some other Jewish families. They were all Polish Jews. They may just be sending them back to Poland.'

'But they can't. Hanne and her little brothers were born here. They're German.'

'I'm sorry, Ruth. The government revoked the right of all Ostjuden to stay in Germany. At least they'll have relatives to go to in Poland, and they'll be safe. Does Hanne speak Polish?'

'A little. Maybe more, at home with her parents.'

'There you go. She'll soon be able to speak fluently.'

'I suppose. I'll miss her, in a way.'

'I thought you two weren't that close.'

'We weren't, while Antje was about; she kind of kept herself to herself, but since Antje went to a different school, we've become friends.'

She wrinkled her nose.

'Though she doesn't really approve of Jewish families who aren't as strict as they are.'

'She has a point,' he said. 'We are a bit lax about some things, although I like to call it pragmatic,' he added, with an embarrassed smile.

'I wouldn't want our family to be as strict as hers. There are too many things she can't join in with.'

'She shouldn't impose her views on you,' Miriam said, having stayed silent, 'but anyway, she's gone, and it's a crying shame.'

'The maths teacher will be happy,' Ruth said.

'Oh, why?' Yosef said.

'He hates all of us, but he hated Hanne the most.'

~~o~~

'I'm going out for a while,' Miriam said.

Yosef's eyebrow shot up.

'To see Rosa,' Miriam added. 'Tell her about Hanne.'

'Ah. That's wise. I'll stay here until you get back.'

CHAPTER 161

14th October

Tel Aviv.

Miriam,

As you can see, I've finally made it to Tel Aviv. I am sitting in my hotel room writing to you. Well, it's a guest house, I suppose. We are staying here for two nights. I am to have a whole day's shopping for bits and pieces for the new house, and a few things for ourselves and the children. Abel and Leah are back in Afula, looking after them. They have an employee in Haifa now because the shop is so busy, and he's ever so reliable. This is the first time they have left him on his own to run the shop.

I thought we might not get here – twelve days ago there was a massacre in Tiberias. It's a lovely little place on the shores of the Sea of Galilee, about forty kilometres away from us, so it was a little too close for comfort.

Arab rioters killed nineteen of our people, including eleven children, and set fire to the synagogue and many Jewish homes. Those who died were mostly stabbed to death; may their memory be blessed.

Seemingly there were about seventy of the attackers, and there were only fifteen Jewish guards. The area has always been quiet, so the British weren't even nearby, but they shut the whole place down afterwards.

I feel guilty for saying it but, fortunately for us, the coast road from Haifa to Tel Aviv stayed open, and they lifted the restrictions on the road from Afula to Haifa yesterday, so we got here after all.

The foundations of the house are finished, and the first bricks are being laid. I'll try and get some photographs of the new house as it goes up, and of the family. I'll buy a camera tomorrow! The old one is nearly impossible to use.

Thank you, a thousand million times, for looking after Itsik's parents. Mama Weichmann says you are wonderful; that you help with some of their shopping, and deal with any officials for them. I could kiss you for being such a true friend.

Itsik says he can't write to Oskar because he'd made it plain in his last letter that, with the money he'd sent, that was the end of it, and Itsik is always a man of his word. I feel embarrassed about Yosef asking for the General's assistance, but I know he's helped other Jews, so I'm swallowing my pride and hoping it is God's will that it might do some good.

Miriam Sara and Rosa Sara. I'm going to change my name too. Esther Sara. Just to fit in when we meet up again!

The weather is getting cooler here. It's almost comfortable at night now! It's still horribly hot and dry during the day but not as bad as July and August were, and we even had a shower of rain last week.

I must go. Itsik is taking me out for a meal. There are hundreds of kosher restaurants here. There's so much choice! I wish you and Rosa were here to see it.

Lots of love and affection.

Esther.

~~o~~

Miriam dropped the letter to her lap and sighed. She turned to Rosa, who was looking at her.

'It's hard,' she said, 'reading this, thousands of miles away, knowing that it may be years before we can see her.'

'I know, honey. Still, she seems to be happier. It makes me feel better.'

'Would you think about it?' Miriam asked.

'What? Palestine? I'd go mad in days, although maybe Tel Aviv wouldn't be so bad, from what Esther says. I keep hoping all this madness will stop, and we can go back to the way it was before. Then she can come back, perhaps.'

'I don't know if they'd ever come back and besides, Yosef thinks Hitler is stronger than ever.'

'Emil's the same. He keeps hinting that we should leave, but I don't think his heart is in it. He wouldn't want to leave his parents, or his brother.'

Rosa hesitated and looked at Miriam.

'What about you? Would you leave?'

'If you'd asked me a few months ago, I would have dismissed it out of hand. Now, I find myself wondering what it would be like to not worry about what was happening about the children at school, or if our money is going to be taken from us.'

'Would you go to Palestine though?'

'No, if I went, it would have to be America, or Britain at a push.'

'Why there?' Rosa asked.

'They seem to be more tolerant of Jews. Anywhere else is either too close, or they won't take us.'

'You really have thought about it then?'

'Only because Yosef keeps harping on about it. Even the General keeps telling us to get out.'

'He maybe wants Aryan staff,' Rosa said, laughing.

'No,' said Miriam, frowning and shaking her head. 'As much as I sometimes hate how reliant we are on the Kästners, the General is one of the few who stands up for us.'

'And Frau Kästner?'

'I sometimes wonder if she sees our Jewishness as inconvenient, but she's not too bad.'

'Well, let me know if you decide to go,' Rosa said. 'I don't want to be left here on my own.'

'I'm going now. Manny will be home from school soon. I'll see you tomorrow.'

Rosa laughed. 'Shalom, Mentsh.'

Miriam turned to her sharply.

'I'm not a Mentsh.'

'Esther told me what you do for Itsik's parents. That makes you a good person in my book.'

'Pah. It's what anyone would do.'

She waved her hand dismissively, and walked away, not displeased.

Rosa watched her walk down the street, glancing at every corner for policemen, Gestapo or Brownshirts.

Is this what we've come to?

CHAPTER 162

Franz smiled and shook his head.

When Johann was home, everyone knew about it. The house reverberated with his presence; shouts and laughter, Antje's squeals when he tickled her, even at fifteen; Maria's screams when a piece of rag shaped remarkably like a spider appeared in a sideboard drawer when she opened it; his father's curses when one of his books was missing from the library, propping up a stilt-legged table in Johann's room.

'It's like he's still fifteen,' the General complained to Franz. 'God knows how he commands a platoon of soldiers.'

'It may come as a surprise, but he's good,' Franz said, smiling at the chaos Johann was causing. 'His men are fiercely loyal and would do anything for him.'

'He leads them into trouble, I'm guessing,' the General said in exasperation, now looking for his favoured pen.

'No, not really,' Franz said, shaking his head. 'He doesn't get his men into scrapes, just himself. On these occasions, it's they who find him, and bring him back to barracks.'

Franz watched his father search about on his desk, opening and closing drawers, looking under piles of paperwork.

'If it's your silver pen you're looking for, Johann had it in the kitchen, writing to his latest flame in Teplice. He borrowed some of your notepaper too.'

He grinned.

'Johann,' the General shouted, striding towards the door.

'He's down at the lake, with Ruth and Antje.'

His father stopped.

'Whatever for?'

'They were going to take a spin in one of the dinghies, as far as I know.'

'Is he crazy? It's November.'

'It's not that cold today, he told me, and there's a nice breeze. They're well wrapped up.'

'As long as no one falls in. We'd better go down and see that he doesn't drown anyone.'

Franz knew that the pen was forgotten for now and, when they got to the lake and saw the small sailboat with Johann with the two girls in it, sails flying, his father turned to him.

'Come on. Jump in,' he said, opening the boathouse door and untying the second wooden dinghy out to the dock.

'Are you mad too?' Franz said, laughing.

The General grinned.

'Lift the mast up and I'll attach the forestay. The jib is in the locker.'

Franz jumped to help and within a few minutes, the boat was ready.

'Can I come?'

They turned at the sound of a child's voice, and saw Manny standing on the bank, next to the boathouse.

'Where did you come from, Manny? Does your mama know you're here?'

'Yes, she said I could go and watch the others, but not to go too close to the water.'

'Of course, you can come with us,' the General said, beckoning the young boy to come down onto the jetty.

'We'd better ask Miriam first,' Franz cautioned.

'It'll be all right. He's with us. Come on.'

Franz looked towards the cottage. Miriam was at the window, watching. He waved at her, then pointed at Manny, and at the boat. She waved back.

'Right. Let's go and catch these girls,' he said.

He turned to the eleven-year-old.

'Manny, you steer.'

The boy looked up at him, surprised.

Franz winked.

'Just do what I tell you. You'll be fine.'

He turned to the General.

'Now, Father, you take the mainsheet, and try and not get in the way.'

The General pretended to be annoyed, and Manny looked from Franz to the General, then back to Franz, unsure.

Franz winked at him again and watched as the General turned away to hide his grin.

He pulled in the jib sheet and told Manny to straighten the tiller. The little boat surged forward out into the lake, the wind catching the sails and heeling her over. The two men leaned out to stop the dinghy capsizing and looked around for the sails of Johann and the girls.

~~o~~

The General hung his jacket up over the back of a chair to dry.

They all sat in the kitchen, the oven doors of the range open to heat the room up, each of the cold sailors hugging a piping cup of Miriam's hot chocolate. Despite wrapping up in warm clothes, their ears and faces had suffered the biting chill of the November air, belying Johann's dismissal of the bitter wind.

The two dinghies had chased each other around the lake for nearly an hour, each boat's capabilities delicately balanced despite the disparity in their crews. Johann's boat was lighter, but the greater weight of the General and Franz was offset by their combined experience.

As the boats became more competitive, there were a couple of near collisions and the General, fearing that someone would end up in the water, finally called a halt. By that time, the cold had permeated through their clothes and, apart from Manny, who seemed impervious to it, they all welcomed the chance to warm themselves, inside and out.

'I haven't done that for years!' the General said, beaming.

'And the more fool you, at your age,' Maria scolded, but the others laughed.

'It certainly blew away the cobwebs,' her husband said, grabbing her and, unbalancing her, sat her down on his knee.

'Erich!' she said, glaring at him, but he saw a hint of a smile on her lips, and at the corner of her eyes.

'You should have come down. It was great fun.'

'I'm happy to occasionally go with you all in the yacht, but there's no chance I'll ever be in one of these glorified rowing boats.'

'Mama, they are sailing dinghies,' Antje said.

'Whatever they are, I'll not be in them. Now, unhand me, Erich.'

The General let her go and planted a soft palm on her buttock as she got up, causing her to colour.

'Can we go and play in my room?' Antje asked.

'Yes, providing you take Manny with you,' her mother said.

'Come on, Ruth,' Antje said, draining the last of her hot chocolate.

Ruth gulped her drink, nearly choking.

Johann patted her on the back.

'Careful,' he said, smiling at her.

She blushed, wiping her mouth with her handkerchief.

'My sister had no patience,' he said to her. 'You take your time and enjoy it.'

She blushed even more.

'You were great out there, both of you. We must teach you both to sail in summer. You'd love it, and then you could use the dinghies on your own.'

'That would be nice,' Ruth mumbled, hiding behind her hair.

Antje stood, grinning and pulling faces at her in the doorway. Ruth scrambled to get up from the chair, rushing past her, giving her a glare on the way out.

'You have an admirer,' said the General, after Ruth had beaten an embarrassed retreat up the stairs with Antje and Manny.

'What, Ruth? She's just a child,' Johann said, with a dismissive grin.

The General laughed.

'They're both growing up fast. It will be boys next. I only hope they both avoid a wastrel like you.'

Johann got up, searching in one of the cupboards for biscuits.

'Are there no chocolate ones?' he asked, opening a packet of Leibniz-Keks, dropping biscuit crumbs everywhere.

'Mind the mess,' his mother told him, ushering him back to the table. Miriam fetched a brush from the cupboard.

'I think you're all a bit harsh,' he said, trying to look indignant. 'It's not my fault that women find me attractive. What do you expect me to do, become a monk, like Franz?'

'Do you never feel any need for a relationship that lasts more than a few weeks?' Franz asked him.

'I can do without all this soldier's talk about women,' Maria interjected. 'In my own kitchen too. Go through to the study if you want to continue in that vein and let Miriam and I plan for the week ahead. I presume you will both be eating here?'

'We'll be home until Friday. Then we're back off to camp.'

'Oh, that's a shame. I'd hoped you'd still be here at the weekend. I was going to invite your grandparents down. I'll telephone them and see if they can come in midweek.'

'That would be lovely, Mama,' said Franz, getting up to leave the two women in peace.

Johann and his father rose to follow him, hustled out by Maria.

'So now you see why I don't want to get tied down to one woman,' Johann said as they made their way through to the study. 'Nag. Nag. Nag.'

The General shook his head. 'That's your mother you're talking about.'

'I know, and I take it as a warning,' he said, laughing as they entered the General's study.

When his sons had taken a chair each, the General opened his drinks cabinet and lifted out a bottle, and three glasses.

'Scotch?' he asked them and, when they both nodded, he poured three glasses.

'If you want water, you'll have to fetch a jug from the kitchen.'

When neither son got up, he lifted his own glass.

'Here's to your first action,' he said. 'Prost.'

'Prost,' they repeated.

'How did you find it?' the General asked.

'We drove across the border without any resistance,' Franz said. 'The guard posts were deserted. All the Czech soldiers had been moved back to their new frontiers.'

'In every little hamlet, the whole population came out to greet us,' Johann said, his face lighting up at the memory of it. 'It felt as if we were freeing a nation.'

'Our advance was slow,' Franz said, 'but not because of any fighting. The colonel had told us that it was as important to interact with the people as it was to get to our objective, so we stopped for an hour or two in each place. I don't know if I've ever drank so much coffee, and I had to stop my men from accepting glasses of beer, or wine.'

'Our objective was Teplice,' Johann interjected. 'It was only five kilometres from the Czech border, but we crossed at Reitzenhain, sixty or seventy kilometres further west. It took us all day.'

'And not a shot fired?'

'No. Not one,' said Johann, disappointment etched on his face.

'That's good,' said the General, not unkindly. 'Any advance by an army that doesn't involve bloodshed on either side is the most successful type of action there is.'

'The only violence we saw was in the weeks afterwards,' said Franz. 'It was the same as in Austria. The Sudeten Germans seemed to think it was their chance to terrorise their Jewish population.'

'It was an isolated incident or two…' Johann said, his voice fading away.

'You know it wasn't. What about the old couple? They burned down the house in front of them, and the barn. We got there just too late to stop them.'

Johann swallowed.

'They're not bad people. They've just had a hard time of it. They've been under Czech oppression for years, and they told me that the Jews sided with them.'

'Do you really believe that? These are German-speaking Jews we're talking about. They were under the same restrictions as all the other German residents.'

'I suppose you're right,' Johann conceded sullenly, 'but everyone was so relieved to see us, there must have been something to it.'

'They might have been a minority living under a government that didn't make them feel welcome but, from what they said, they were never mistreated the way they are now abusing the Jewish population.'

Franz turned to his father.

'There were hundreds of groups of Jews on the road, heading in the direction of Prague. Some had horses and carts, others were on foot. I'm sure the locals stopped them using buses or trains and, whenever they passed through a village or town, children, and sometimes adults, would taunt them, and throw things at them.'

'You know what youngsters are like,' Johann said, frowning. 'They can be cruel.'

'They were just taking the lead from their parents.' Franz sighed. 'Listen, it was only a minority, but no one stepped in to stop it, except, in a few instances, our soldiers.'

The General raised an eyebrow.

'Our boys stepped in, did they?'

'We did, in our unit and, speaking to a few others in passing, it wasn't just us. But we were quite thin on the ground, and it was by no means universal. I heard of quite a few occasions when our soldiers either stood by and watched or, at worst, helped the locals force the Jews from their houses.'

'Magdalena, the girl from Teplice I'm seeing… was seeing… she told me some of the Jews were informants on the German Sudetens, getting them into trouble with the Czech authorities.'

'And you believe that?'

'Why would she lie?'

'Perhaps she thought it was the truth. Look at the lies the National Socialists say about Jews here.'

'I still think there must be something to it. Why would people react that way, otherwise?'

'Johann,' the General said, shaking his head sadly, 'people sometimes behave in a way that is hard to understand. Imagine that those Jews you saw being expelled from their homes and treated like that were Yosef and Miriam, and the children. How would you feel about that?'

Johann's face paled a little.

'Obviously, I'd be angry. But that's unfair. They're not the same people.'

The General shrugged and held out his hands.

'Why not?'

Johann looked at his father, and at Franz, and shook his head, angry now.

'I played my part in stopping them when we saw people being mistreated. That's all I could do, but it's unfair to use it to spoil the success we had, that Germany had, thanks to the Führer's brilliance. You said it yourself, it was bloodless.'

He got up and left the room. Franz rose to follow him.

The General held his hand up.

'Leave him. He's not ready to see it yet, but he will, some day. I only hope it's not when they come for Ruth and Manny.'

CHAPTER 163

KIELER MORGENPOST

Tuesday 8th November 1938

ATTEMPTED ASSASSINATION OF GERMAN DIPLOMAT BY JEW IN PARIS

Ernst vom Rath, a German diplomat stationed in the German embassy in Paris, was shot yesterday by Herschel Grynszpan, a so-called German Jew of Polish origin. The cowardly attack took place when Grynszpan, a vagrant, walked into the building, saying that he had important information to give. When the unsuspecting and innocent junior embassy officer ushered him into his office, the Jewish attacker pulled out a gun and shouted "You're a filthy German. I act in the name of thousands of persecuted Jews". He then shot Ernst vom Rath three times in the stomach.

A spokesman for the Foreign Ministry said that Herr vom Rath's condition was critical, and that the Führer had personally sent both of his doctors to treat his injuries, which were serious.

Grynszpan was apprehended within hours and will face charges of attempted murder. He may face the guillotine.

~~o~~

'This is not good,' the General said, the open paper in front of him as he sipped his coffee. The jam-lathered toast sat on the plate untouched.

'What is it?' Maria asked.

'A young German Jew has walked into our embassy in Paris and shot one of the diplomats.'

'That's terrible. Why would he do that?'

The General glared at her. She flinched.

'I can think of many reasons why he might want to do it,' he said, 'although why Paris?'

'What do you mean? Are you condoning his actions?'

'No. It's the worst thing he could have done. And the poor young man he shot; they say he's critically injured. But it was only a matter of time before some Jewish hothead decided that enough was enough.'

'I'm shocked that you would try and justify someone attempting to murder one of our ambassadors.'

'It wasn't the ambassador,' the General said, 'and I'm not justifying it. I'm just saying that sooner or later, Jews were going react to the way they've all been treated.'

'Just because they've had some restrictions placed on them, it can never excuse attempting to murder someone.'

'A few restrictions? We went beyond that a long time ago. What about the young man killed by the mob while in the custody of the police, here in Kiel?'

'He was in there because he shot a policeman. He was no innocent victim.'

The General could see two red spots, high on her cheekbones. He softened his words.

'I know it was a stupid thing to do, but he thought he was protecting his father.'

'He should have thought twice before shooting a policeman. I'm afraid I have little sympathy for his type.'

The General took a deep breath, and bit back the first reply that came to him.

'All right,' he said, after a few seconds consideration, 'What about Yosef, when he was beaten? They could have killed him. They almost did.'

A shadow crossed her face, and her voice faltered.

'That's different. He shouldn't have been there. He should have known better.'

'Excuse me,' the General said. 'Yosef was there to give his friend some honest support when the National Socialists decided that a boycott of all Jewish-owned shops would be a good idea. Why shouldn't he have been there?'

'You know. He was sticking his nose into things that were none of his business.'

The General sighed.

'I'm sorry you think like that. I'm afraid I can't quite see it that way but we're all different.'

'We are, and I think you sometimes forget that.'

He said nothing, concluding that there was no point in arguing with her. They finished their breakfast in silence and, when Yosef came in with the coal scuttle to fill up the stove, a sullen Maria Kästner glared at her husband and got up from the table.

'I'll be upstairs,' she said.

The General looked at Yosef and shrugged.

'Did you read this?' he said, pointing to the headline.

Yosef glanced at the paper.

'No. Not yet,' he said, 'but I heard about it.'

The General didn't know how Yosef had found out about it but, where Jewish matters were concerned, news seemed to travel around the Jewish community in Kiel with remarkable speed.

'It's not going to help things, is it?' said the General.

Yosef shook his head.

'What are your friends saying?'

'That there will be some sort of clampdown. The authorities will use this as an excuse to round up some of our more vocal young men and increase our taxes.'

'Let's pray he recovers,' the General said. 'If he dies…'

Yosef nodded.

'We are praying.'

~~o~~

KIELER MORGENPOST

Thursday 10th November 1938

GERMAN DIPLOMAT ERNST vom RATH DIES

Ernst vom Rath, the German Diplomat shot in Paris by Polish-German Jew Herschel Grynszpan has died of his wounds. In a personal message to his family, a spokesman for the Führer stated that it was a cowardly act of murder that would not be left unpunished or unavenged.

The Morgenpost incorrectly reported that Ernst vom Rath was a junior officer of the embassy in Paris when in fact he had been recently promoted to Legal Consul, First Class.

DISTURBANCES IN JEWISH NEIGHBOURHOODS

In response to the assassination, there were sporadic outbreaks of spontaneous outrage from the ordinary German people, angry at the Jewish population for their almost universal support for the action of the Polish-German Jew in Paris.

While the Morgenpost cannot condone violence, it can sympathise for actions taken in the name of good German people in the face of this despicable act.

~~o~~

Isaac Stern sat in the kitchen of the Drachensee cottage. Miriam dipped the cloth in the water and dabbed gently at the cuts on his face. He flinched, the antiseptic she'd added to the bowl stinging the raw edges of his wounds.

None of the cuts were too deep, or long, but there were a lot of them.

'You are lucky it isn't a lot worse, my friend,' Yosef said. 'If one of these bricks had hit you, it would have fractured your skull. The glass made a good enough job as it is.'

Isaac, still in his shop a couple of hours after closing, hoping to catch up on his accounts, had heard a noise out the front and, curious and not a little frightened, got up from his seat and hurried through to the counter, where he could see the street.

The sound of chants, singing even, had grown louder by the minute, and he'd lifted the hinged flap and stepped out from behind the counter, craning his neck to look down the road.

To his horror, thirty metres away, he'd spotted a mob of fifty people or more brandishing sticks and carrying heavy sacks. Frozen, in the darkness of his shop, he'd watched as one of the men emptied his sack onto the ground and handed out bricks and pieces of rubble to his companions.

Others in the crowd carrying sacks had done the same.

'Juden Raus! Juden Raus! Juden Raus!'

The chants unnerved him but, looking at their faces, he realised that, in the darkness of the shop, and behind the heaped display, they couldn't see him.

'Jüdische Mörder. Revenge for vom Rath!'

A voice inside had told him to run, but a morbid fascination rooted him to the spot, or perhaps it was the realisation that this was the end of his livelihood, and that he should at least witness it.

The first brick, ironically, had bounced off the glass, but this seemed to incense the rioters further, and a flurry of missiles had hit the window almost simultaneously, smashing it.

A half brick had flown past his head close enough for him to feel the draught of it in his ear, and a blizzard of glass had struck his face and his hands as he tried, too late, to bring them up to protect himself.

Galvanised by pain, he'd turned and stumbled through to the back, grabbing a towel from the small sink in the store on the way to the door at the rear of the building.

Almost blinded by blood, he'd wiped his eyes with the towel and watched with trepidation through the doorway, hoping that the mob would move on.

He'd seen shadowy figures climb through the shattered window, using sticks and crowbars to clear the remaining shards of glass from the frame. The sacks that had held the bricks and rocks were now being used to hold their plunder as the men helped themselves to his stock.

Knowing it would be only a matter of time before they'd follow him through to the back, he'd unlocked the door, opened it a crack, and peered out into the alley.

It was empty.

He'd slipped out, and edged his way up the lane, keeping in the shadows. Just as he reached the end, he'd heard voices not far ahead and he realised, to his horror, that there was another mob milling about on the street the lane opened out on to.

He'd retraced his steps and wondered about trying to hide in one of the small yards at the back of the buildings, but he'd worried that the looters might come looking for him, realising that someone had been in the shop. He'd cursed himself for not locking the back door behind him.

Expecting the mob to spill into the lane in front of him, he'd passed the back of his shop without incident. Inside, he'd heard laughter and shouting, and someone had started up a chorus of one of their filthy fascist songs.

It had pained him to leave the shop to its fate, but he knew that he had to get out, or be killed. He'd remembered only too well the beating they'd given Yosef.

The other end of the lane had been deserted, but he could hear the clamour of rioting to his left and right, and behind him. The only safe route took him the opposite way from home.

Not thinking, he'd headed south, desperate to put some distance between himself and the rioters. Half an hour later, still stumbling blindly, not knowing quite where he was, he'd stopped to take stock. Looking around, he'd realised that he was almost at the edge of town, on the corner of Königsweg and Hummelwiese and that Hamburger Chaussee was just a block away.

With relief, and a little shame, he'd continued along Königsweg until it merged with Hamburger Chaussee and, glancing behind him anxiously, he'd hurried towards Drachensee.

Miriam had answered the door with a gasp but recognising him after a few confused seconds, she'd ushered him inside before sticking her head out the door and looking around.

'Did anyone see you come in?' she asked.

'No, I was careful.'

Yosef had pulled out a chair and had sat Isaac down on it.

'What happened,' he'd asked, pale with shock at his friend's appearance.

'They're rioting,' Isaac gasped. 'The man in Paris died, I heard one of them say. They're taking revenge on us all.'

'Are your family safe? Your house. Did they...?'

'No, no, I was at the shop. They didn't see me. This happened when the window was smashed.'

'So, how did you end up here?'

'I got out the back way and ran. I couldn't get home without them seeing me. By the time I realised where I was, I began to panic about being stopped by the police, or more rioters, and knowing you were close by, I hoped you could help.'

'You did the right thing,' Yosef had said, as Miriam filled a bowl with warm water. 'And you'll stay here tonight.'

As Miriam cleaned his wounds, Isaac had a sudden thought.

'Can you telephone my wife? See that she is all right?'

Yosef checked his watch, then looked at Miriam. It was gone eleven o'clock.

'It's too late to use the phone in the big house,' he said. He threw on his coat and slipped out the door.

When he returned a few minutes later, Miriam had finished patching Isaac up, and was making up a bed for him in the spare room. He sat at the table with some heated-up leftovers and a steaming cup of coffee, his head bowed.

He looked up when Yosef opened the door.

'Are they all right?' he asked.

'Yes, they're fine. They heard nothing but were beginning to worry about you. They were relieved to hear that you were safe.'

'You should get some rest now,' Miriam said from the hall doorway. 'The bed's made, when you're ready.'

'Thank you,' Isaac said, slowly rising from the chair. 'For everything. You have been so kind.'

'Not at all,' Yosef said. 'You did it for me.'

~~o~~

When the knock came, Miriam had already left to prepare breakfast at the big house. Yosef and Isaac looked at each other and froze, then a head peered in the window.

Both men sighed with relief.

'General,' Yosef said, answering the door, 'come in.'

'I don't have to ask what happened to your friend here,' the General said, a little surprised to see a badly disfigured man sitting at the Nussbaum kitchen table. 'I was coming to tell you to stay at home, that there has been rioting all over Germany, targeting Jews. I got a telephone call from Admiral Canaris's office.'

'This is Isaac. From the shop.'

'Oh Lord, Isaac. I'm sorry, I didn't recognise you.'

'Don't worry, sir. I'm sure my own children wouldn't recognise me.'

'The shop? You tried to stop them?'

Isaac laughed.

'It looks like it, doesn't it, but no, this was just being in the wrong place at the wrong time. I just happened to be behind my shop window when the rocks came through it.'

'Do you want me to fetch Doc Speer? You should, you know.'

'No. Please don't. It looks worse than it is. It was mostly flying glass. There's nothing broken, or even bruised, apart from my pride.'

He gave an apologetic smile.

'I ran,' he said.

'You did the right thing, Isaac. At least you're alive.'

The General turned to Yosef.

'Keep the children at home today and, as I said to you, don't go anywhere until we find out what is happening. I'm going to see the mayor and the chief of police to find out what they're doing about it.'

Yosef nodded. 'Thank you, sir.' He glanced at Isaac.

'I'll take Isaac home,' the General said, turning to the injured man.

'Be ready in thirty minutes; I'll get my driver to drop you off on our way.'

'Thank you, sir, my family will be worried.'

'They don't know you're here?' the General asked, shocked.

'I telephoned them last night, sir,' Yosef said.

'Oh,' the General said. 'I didn't hear you.'

'I didn't want to wake you up, sir. I used the public telephone.'

'You shouldn't have,' the General said, a trace of annoyance in his voice.

'And risked Miriam's ire by using your telephone, sir? I'd rather have walked to Isaac's house.'

The General laughed, and Isaac and Yosef joined in, glad of something to smile about. Isaac gave a grimace.

'It's sore to laugh,' he explained.

'Thirty minutes,' the General repeated.

~~o~~

'What did they say?' Dieter asked, the telephone line crackling.

The General waited until the noise subsided.

'Uwe Müller told me that he'd had officers out all over the city, trying to curb any

539

violence. He said that they all reported that it was mainly peaceful protests by a handful of troublemakers.'

At the other end of the line, Dieter snorted.

'Peaceful protest, my *Arsch*,' he said. 'And the only reason the police were on hand was to limit the damage to non-Jewish property. It was the same with the fire brigade. They hosed adjoining buildings to stop the fire spreading and left the Jewish buildings burning.'

'I gathered that, reading between the lines. Jürgen Hoffmann said the same. He told me that they didn't have the manpower to protect every Jew in Kiel. When I asked why he didn't call on the army, he laughed and said that it would make the city look bad if the police couldn't handle a few miscreants who took the law into their own hands.'

'That sounds like Jürgen. As far as I can see, the party, and the authorities, have distanced themselves from this. They're saying that it's an understandable wave of anger and disgust at the death of an innocent German at Jewish hands, that went a little too far.'

'Then why, of all the arrests being made, are most of them young Jewish men?'

'You know this for sure?'

'Yes,' the General said. 'Thousands of them, all over the country. By the Gestapo, assisted by our wonderful police.'

'They'll justify it by saying that there are other Herschel Grynszpans out there, who have spoken out against the government and who must be incarcerated to protect good, ordinary Germans.'

'That was almost their exact words.'

'The bastards. They're using this to their own ends. What can be done?'

'Nothing. Wait and see what happens tonight. Others may see that the rioters and looters are getting away with it and fancy a little bit of that action themselves.'

'I never thought of that. We must warn the Jews.'

'By all means, warn your friends. I've already passed on the message.'

'Right. Of course. Yosef and Miriam.'

'I'll speak to you tomorrow.'

~~o~~

KIELER MORGENPOST

Friday 11th November 1938

KIEL SYNAGOGUE BURNS

In a second night of violence, the synagogue in Goethestraße was set on fire, despite the efforts of police to protect it from an angry crowd, and the fire brigade's presence to extinguish the blaze.

A spokesman for the Rathaus condemned the violence but said that some sort of backlash against Jewish hate had been almost inevitable.

There had been minor skirmishes the previous night in Kiel but crowds, incensed by the lack of condemnation of the murder of Ernst vom Rath by the Jewish community, took matters into their own hands. There were further isolated incidents in the city, but the police said that, in the main, the demonstrations had been peaceful.

Two arrests were made.

~~o~~

[11/11/1938 Friday]

KIELER JÜDISCHES FREIHEITSNACHRICHTENBLATT

Volume 64

17th of Cheshvan, 5699

KRISTALLNACHT - NATIONWIDE ANTI-JEWISH POGROM

On the nights of 9th and 10th November, the country-wide pogrom that has now been coined "Kristallnacht", shocked the Jewish population of Germany and the outside world. Contrary to the limited reporting in national and regional newspapers of "some sporadic and spontaneous outbursts of rioting" by German people outraged by the assassination in Paris of Ernst vom Rath, the German Diplomat, the KJF can report that there was an organised, widespread, and officially condoned series of targeted attacks against German Jews initiated at the highest level.

It is true that the majority of assaults against Jewish homes, shops and synagogues, and against Jews themselves, were committed by ordinary Germans, and that very few uniforms were in evidence, but the violence was so universal and orchestrated that the KJF does not believe the NSDAP's repeated insistence that it was not involved.

In Kiel, as in many towns and cities throughout Germany, the police did not intervene when the synagogue was first smashed and looted, and then set on fire.

Despite reports in local newspapers, the fire brigade did not intervene to prevent damage to Jewish property; they acted only when it was necessary to protect neighbouring buildings. The KJF has also catalogued multiple acts of violence against other Jewish properties and Jewish people.

Fifty-four Jewish shop windows were smashed, and the majority of these shops were looted. Three shopkeepers, in an attempt to protect their premises, were injured, one seriously.

At least 100 Jewish homes were attacked, mostly resulting in broken windows, while many were defaced with anti-Jewish slogans. Around 240 Jews were injured over the two nights, although most did not prove to be serious. Two Jewish men received treatment for extensive burns after they attempted to extinguish the blazing synagogue before the arrival of the fire service.

Two non-Jewish Germans were also injured when they tried to protect a Jewish neighbour's home from being vandalised. They are unwilling to be named.

541

The shooting of Ernst vom Rath, which sparked off the pogrom, took place in Paris, two days before the violence started. The first actions of "Kristallnacht" began within hours of his death.

The KJF has learned that Herschel Grynszpan, the diplomat's murderer, was originally from Hanover, and was a Jew of Polish origin. Friends of his say that he was incensed by the deportation of his parents from Germany to Poland as part of a group of 12,000 "Ostjuden" sent back under the naturalisation laws.

He had lived in Paris illegally for some time, and was threatened with being returned to Germany, and probable incarceration in a concentration camp.

Various Jewish groups came out and deplored his actions and sympathised with Ernst vom Rath's family despite the widespread reports in the national and local press saying otherwise.

In an all too prophetic statement, the Jewish Business Association said that "...this senseless murder will have serious repercussions on Jews throughout Germany".

This has been a black day for Germany's Jews.

~~o~~

'God will smite them one day for this,' Jakob Teubner said in a quiet voice that dripped with anger.

'I'm not so sure,' Yosef said. 'God's face seems to be turning from us.'

'Remember Job,' said Siegmund Eliasowitz, the most pious of the group. 'He did not turn his back on God in his suffering.'

Yosef sighed. 'That was one man. This is a nation of Jews. You think God is doing this to us to make a point to the Devil?'

The man grumbled but didn't argue.

'How bad is the damage?'

'It's not good. It would take a miracle to restore it, especially in these times. And anyway, they'd just burn it again.'

'But what will we do without a synagogue?' the young pious man cried, tears running down his face.

Jakob put his hand on his shoulder.

'We have suffered for countless centuries. We'll suffer for countless more. We will find somewhere to worship.'

'How are Sigo and Louis?' Yosef asked.

'Bad,' Jakob said, shaking his head sadly. 'They are both being treated for serious injuries. Sigo has thirty per cent burns, most of them full depth, the doctors say. Louis isn't quite so bad, but he was hit by a falling beam, and dislocated a shoulder. He also has a few cracked ribs.'

'Where are they now?' Yosef asked.

'Doctor Zember's house. No hospital would take them. A few of the women are helping to nurse them.'

'God help them.'

'They suspect that Sigo was somehow doused in the fuel oil the bastards used to start it. I can't make up my mind if it was brave or foolish of them to try and contain the fire.'

'Probably both,' Yosef said. 'I hope to God they pull through. Then we can tell them they're heroic fools. They saved the scrolls, but little else. The fire damage is extensive, and the building is unsafe. There's nothing left to salvage; anything that had survived the fire had already been smashed. The only thing we managed to retrieve intact was one of the doors of the Ark.'

The Ark contained the revered Torah scrolls. It was a central part of Jewish worship.

'We have craftsmen in the congregation who can make a new Ark,' Jakob said. 'Something smaller and more portable. We can move it around for safety. Perhaps he can make use of the salvaged door.'

'Was anyone else hurt?' Isaac asked.

'Apart from you, Sigo and Louis, there were only minor injuries, as far as we know,' Jakob said, 'but many Jewish shops are ruined.' He looked at Isaac, shaking his head in sadness.

'I went back this morning,' Isaac said. 'The shop has been trashed. All the shelving has been pulled down and their filthy swastikas and slogans are daubed all over the walls. For some reason, they didn't empty the shop – I'd say over eighty per cent of the stock was there, but most of it was spoiled. The Goyim must have pissed on it; the smell of their stinking urine was overpowering. It would take a lot of time and money to get the place all fixed up and repainted, and I'm not sure I have the customers these days to make it worthwhile.'

'What will you do?'

'I'll sell it for a pittance to the first Gentile who makes me an offer,' he said, bitterness and disappointment etched on his face. 'Then leave.'

'Good luck with that one,' Jakob said, 'unless you go to Palestine.'

'We might just do that. Itsik's doing well out there, I hear. He's building a new house.'

'It's not all milk and honey,' Jakob said. 'The Arabs killed nineteen Jewish settlers near the Sea of Galilee, according to Emil Rosenbaum. It's no safer than here.'

Isaac shrugged.

'They say in Hamburg, they arrested thousands of Jews, and marched them down the streets before carting them off to Sachsenhausen.'

'Who's all missing?' Yosef asked. 'They made a lot of arrests here too.'

'Max Weidmann,' Jakob said, 'but that was last week, before this.'

'Nathan Dreilich and Nossen Deller,' Isaac said, between swollen lips. 'They were both picked up last night. Thirteen were detained in Kiel altogether.'

'Are we helping their families?' Yosef asked.

'Yes. We have a lawyer who will still handle Jewish affairs. We've been in contact.'

'It's strange though. They didn't arrest any of our ardent young Zionists that I'd have expected to be picked up. Young Gerstle and Faktorschik, for instance.'

'Ha. The pair of them are as poor as Jewish bookmakers. They wouldn't have had much success trying to shake them down for money if they arrested them.'

They all laughed. Few in the Jewish community gambled, but it was common knowledge that most Jews would offer bribes when arrested. Very rarely did it make a difference to the outcome.

Yosef spoke. 'We must contact everyone in the congregation and let them know where we're going to meet on the Sabbat.'

'We can't. The register is gone,' Jakob said. 'It will be difficult to get in touch with them all.'

'Between us, we will remember most of them,' Isaac said. He hesitated. 'It's strange that the records are all missing, is it not? I mean, who would want them?'

Among the embers, no trace of the congregational register, the list of officers of the synagogue, details of sermons and committee meetings, or the ledger detailing the synagogue's finances had been found.

'We think the SD were here,' Jakob said, 'while the mob were ripping the place apart. We're sure they took them. And my cousin in Hamburg telephoned. They did the same there. They know everything about us now. Who attends the synagogue, who is on the committee, which of us say Derasha, and who speaks out against them.'

They all stood silently. Those who had spoken at the Bimah during services tried to remember what they'd said, and if it would be deemed subversive in the eyes of the Gestapo.

'We may all be arrested by next week,' Jakob said.

'We'll see,' said Yosef. 'Maybe the rabbi was right. We should have left in '33'

'Kristallnacht,' the General said with a sigh. 'That's what they're calling it now. All over the world. In England, *the night of broken glass*; in France, *la nuit de Cristal*. This has tarnished Germany forever.'

'A night of rioting?' Canaris said, shaking his head. 'Hardly. It was bad, but what country hasn't had their troubles. The National Socialists will bend over backwards to distance themselves from it. And there's an element of truth in some of their denials.'

'This was different. Surely there can be no doubt that the party, if not the Führer, was behind it, and that it was targeted only at Jews. And it was nationwide. How can they deny that it was government led?'

'I'll tell you why. The word is that the Führer didn't know about it; it was all down to Goebbels.'

The General gave his friend a look of disbelief. Canaris was in Kiel on his bi-monthly visit to the city and its Naval Headquarters, and he never missed the chance to meet up with Erich Kästner.

'Go on,' the General said.

'Goebbels has been getting frustrated,' Canaris continued. 'A few of his 'great' propaganda coups haven't quite come off; his Sudetenland campaign was moderately successful, but it had no impact abroad. He decided, in the wake of Ernst vom Rath's murder, to spark a backlash against the Jews.'

'And how the hell did he do that without Hitler knowing, or Himmler?'

'Word of Rath's death reached Hitler on the evening of the ninth, during a dinner marking the anniversary of the Beer Hall Putsch. There was a lot of discussion, then Hitler left, visibly upset. Joseph Goebbels delivered a speech, in his place, and told them that, while the Führer indicated that demonstrations should *not* be organised by the party, if they did happen to erupt, they were not to be hampered.'

'So, the party bosses took that as an implicit order to start a pogrom. Clever.'

'Yes. But Himmler was there. He directed Heydrich to send this to all the police chiefs in Germany.'

The admiral handed him a telegram.

DEUTSCHE REICHSPOST

TELEGRAMM

MOST URGENT

From: Police Headquarters, Munich

November 10, 1938, 1:20 a.m.

To all: Headquarters and Stations of the Geheime Staatspolizei (GeStaPo)

To all: Local and Regional Offices of the Sicherheitsdienst (SD)

Urgent! For immediate attention of Chief and his deputy!

Re: Immediate interim measures against Jews

As a result of the assassination of Legation Secretary Ernst vom Rath in Paris, demonstrations throughout the Reich are expected tonight, November 9 to 10, 1938. The following orders should be followed in dealing with these occurrences.

1) Upon receipt of this telegram, the chiefs of the political police stations or their deputies must immediately contact the appropriate NSDAP authorities for their district by telephone to arrange a discussion about the conduct of the demonstrations. This discussion should include the competent Inspector or Commander of the OrPo.

The local NSDAP officials are to be informed that the German police have received from the Reichsführer-SS and the Chief of the German police the following orders:

a) Only such actions may be carried out which do not threaten German lives or property (e.g., burning of synagogues only when there is no threat of fire to the surroundings).

b) Stores and residences of Jews may only be destroyed but not looted. The police are instructed to supervise compliance with this order and to arrest looters.

c) Special care is to be taken on commercial streets that non-Jewish businesses are completely secured against damage.

d) Foreign citizens, even if they are Jewish, may not be molested.

2) Demonstrations in progress should not be prevented by the police but only supervised for compliance with the guidelines.

3) Existing archival material is to be impounded by the police in all synagogues and offices of the Jewish community centres to prevent its destruction in the course of the demonstrations. This material is to be turned over to the offices of the SD.

4) The direction of Security Police operations, both political and criminal divisions, relating to the anti-Jewish demonstrations, resides with Political Police authorities except when orders are issued by Security Police inspectors. Officials from the Criminal Police as well as members of the Security Service (SD), of the SS paramilitary units, and of the General SS may be called upon to carry out Security Police operations.

5) As soon as the course of events during this night allows the assigned police officers to be used for this purpose, as many Jews, particularly affluent Jews, are to be arrested in all districts as can be accommodated in existing detention facilities. For the time being, only healthy male Jews, whose age is not too advanced, are to be arrested. Immediately after the arrests have been carried out, the appropriate concentration camps should be contacted to place the Jews into camps as quickly as possible. Special care should be taken that Jews arrested on the basis of this instruction are not mistreated.

6) The contents of this order are to be passed on to the

competent Inspectors and Commanders of the Order Police and to regional and local sectors of the SD.

The chief of the Order Police has issued the corresponding instructions to the OrPo and to the fire brigades. Close coordination is to be maintained between the Security Police and the OrPo during the implementation of the ordered actions.

Signed: Reinhard Heydrich

SS-Gruppenführer

Chef des Sicherheitsdienst & Sicherheitspolizei

The General bowed his head and shook it slowly from side to side.

'On one hand,' he said, 'Himmler and Heydrich are distancing themselves from the action. On the other, they are using it to further their own agendas. And the Führer can say, in righteous indignation, that he wasn't responsible. It makes me sick. And you still support them?'

Admiral Canaris frowned.

'While they have the levels of support they enjoy throughout the country, there is nothing anyone can do. It's all very well saying the police were told to stand aside but, even if you think the actions were organised by the usual NSDAP thugs, there were significant numbers of ordinary people out there joining in, fuelled by what they call righteous anger, and few, if any, citizens lifted a finger to prevent it happening.'

'A big part of that is fear. I hope there are good German people out there abhorring what is going on, but are just too afraid to act, or even protest. The pessimist in me wonders if that is true, but what can we do?'

'What we are already doing. Making sure we have support in the army and the navy, should Hitler make a mistake. We also need to cultivate influential people away from the Wehrmacht, but that needs more care.'

'Who?' the General asked.

'Some amongst the old aristocracy. A few industrialists who see past the quick profits and massive expansion that the National Socialists are delivering. We have made tentative contact with some of them.'

'Is there not a danger that the Abwehr will be exposed as an anti-NSDAP organisation, and be disbanded?'

'We can always deflect any criticism by saying that we are keeping tabs on dissidents.'

'Is there anything I can do? I was approached a while ago but I did nothing about it. I didn't know how serious they were.'

He told Canaris about his conversation with Maria's countess, about her husband, the count, and about their views on Adolf Hitler.

'You can't be involved,' Canaris said. 'I'll find a way to get in contact with them.'

'But…'

Canaris held his hand up.

'Leave it to me. I need you to concentrate on the Kriegsmarine,' he continued. 'Your only job is to keep close to their top commanders. As it stands, they quite happy to let the National Socialists do what they like while the navy is expanding, and it is being well supported. Do you know that Hitler has made the Kriegsmarine his number one priority?'

'I heard, but I'm sceptical. However, the number of naval vessels they're building is to increase enormously, especially submarines, so there might be some truth in it.'

'Even more than you think, if war comes, I'm told.'

'I can see it. Because Captain Bauer is so heavily involved with the city authorities, we hear about the expansion of the yards at the planning stage. From what I can make out, they'll be able to more than double their output of U-boats next year, and maybe even quadruple it again the year after.'

Canaris smiled.

'Dönitz is very persuasive. He would have us make nothing but *Unterseeboot*; he insists that they're the only things afloat that would help us win a war with Britain.'

'They'll still keep building battleships though. They impress the public more, and that's what Hitler needs.'

'You are becoming too cynical, Kästner. But you're right. And there will be occasions when our surface ships are of vital importance.'

'You still think war is inevitable, don't you?'

'I'll do everything I can to convince them not to go to war, but I think the government, and Hitler himself, are determined to fight.'

'And if we do?'

'Then they're fools, and we'll lose.'

CHAPTER 165

KIELER MORGENPOST

Saturday 12th November 1938

VERORDNUNG ZUR AUSSCHALTUNG DER JUDEN AUS DEM DEUTSCHEN WIRTSCHAFTSLEBEN

The German government has issued the Decree on the Elimination of the Jews from German Economic Life.

This bars any Jewish person from operating a retail store, a sales agency, or from carrying on a trade. The law also forbids Jews from selling goods or services at an establishment of any kind.

In legislation passed in the Reichstag today, German Jews have been pronounced liable to pay reparations of one billion Reichsmarks as a result of the damage to property during Kristallnacht.

This will be collected by a combination of community fines, the confiscation of insurance payments made to Jewish property owners for damages incurred during the riots, and by "atonement" payments from Jewish business owners.

~~o~~

'We'll help you clear the shop,' Jakob said. A chorus of assents came from the other men in the group.

'There's no point. They've banned us from owning or running a business, not that I had many customers left, anyway. They were all too frightened to be seen buying from a Jew.'

Yosef wasn't surprised at the bitterness in his friend's voice. The shop, like Itsik's, had been his father's before him and it had served the family well.

To see it wrecked, in a night of hateful violence...

Yosef couldn't imagine what Isaac was going through.

'Anyway,' Isaac continued, 'what's to say they wouldn't have just trashed it again. At least if I can get an Aryan to take it, it might survive.'

'What will you do?'

'I have a cousin. He has a small factory supplying springs to machinery manufacturers. They're extremely specialised, so he had some protection from the government through the companies he sells to. It fits in with Göring's 'four-year plan'. He'll give me a job for a month or so. His bookkeeper finally got his visa for America, so I can fill in while he finds another.'

'You're lucky the Aryans need your cousin's springs,' Emil Liewermann said. 'I'm only in work because there's no one at the factory who can do my job.'

Rosa's husband was the production manager at a furniture factory.

'At least for now,' he added. 'The owner is one of the good Goyim, but he admits that as soon as he has an Aryan trained up to do my job, he'll be forced to let me go.'

He turned to Isaac.

'What will you do after your month is up?'

'I've applied to go to Palestine,' Isaac replied. 'Itsik is going to find me a small shop to rent in Haifa, close to Abel's place.'

They all started speaking at once, some congratulating him, others commiserating each other that he would be sorely missed.

Jakob summed it up.

'It will be a wrench losing you, Isaac, but it is one family less for the Goyim to harass. God be with you, my friend.'

When the others had left, Isaac spoke to Yosef and Jakob.

'Before we go, we're going to have a small gathering for some food, and to take a little wine with friends. I'll let you know when. We're also going to give away everything we can't take with us so, if there's anything you want, please help yourself. I'd rather it went to someone I know than to these bastards.'

'Sell it then, you'll need every penny the government doesn't take.'

The shopkeeper grinned and tapped his nose.

'We'll be all right. I've taken care of that.'

'Be careful,' Jakob said. 'If you try and smuggle something out and get caught...'

'Don't worry, I have a way. It's as safe as any.'

'Nothing is safe,' Yosef said.

'This is. I've tried it out.'

He reached into his pocket and pulled out a folded handkerchief. He opened it up, and, glancing over his shoulder, showed them its contents.

'A diamond,' Yosef gasped, perhaps a little too loud.

'Ssshhh. Keep your voice down. I have others.'

'So where do you hide them? They'll do a thorough search, you know.'

'I know that, but I have a way.'

Before they could grasp what he'd done, Isaac had placed the diamond on his tongue, and swallowed it.

'In the name of Jehovah. What are you doing?'

'They come through in two to four days, depending on their size. I've tried it.'

'Don't they damage you; make you ill?'

'No. You feel nothing at all. I can't say it's pleasant to retrieve them once they're passed, and I might lose the odd one, but every stone I get to Palestine will make our life there more tolerable.'

Jakob laughed, and Yosef couldn't help but grin.

'What if you have the runs, or you are held for a few days?'

Isaac grimaced.

'I just have to collect them, give them a wash, and repeat the process.'

'Yecchhh,' Yosef said, almost retching. 'That's disgusting.'

'Could you do that, really?' Jakob added.

'Yes. I can, and I will, if that's what it takes.'

'Is anyone else in the family going to do the same?'

'They don't know I'm doing it. I thought it better that way.'

He paused.

'The only people who know are you two,' he added.

'It's safe with us, but don't tell anyone else.'

'I won't. I had to tell someone. In case any of you need to do the same.'

'How did you get hold of the diamonds?'

'My brother-in-law. He's been buying them for me over the last six months, a few at a time. About three quarters of my savings. I'd have bought more, but the government needs to believe it's getting a share of our cash or they might not let us out.'

'So, your brother-in-law knows too?'

'Yes, about the diamonds. But not about the way I'm taking them out.'

'Nisht gefloygen!' Jakob said. *Unbelievable.* 'You're a Meshugener, that's a fact.'

'You may be right about him being crazy man,' Yosef said, after Isaac had gone, 'but it might just work. God help him if it doesn't.'

CHAPTER 166

'It's such a fuss about nothing,' the countess said.

'I know,' Maria said, unnerved by the stab of guilt she felt. 'They shouldn't have killed that poor man Rath. Did they expect people to take it lying down?'

'The people's reaction was understandable, although I find it hard to understand why they needed to do quite as much destruction. The duke's tailor has disappeared, his shop has closed, and the windows are boarded up. It's a real inconvenience.'

'All the Jewish shops in Kiel are shut. It's a shame; they were some of the best shops in the city. That little dressmaker in Holstenbrücke was divine if you needed a frock altered. And she could make one for you, perfectly, if you showed her a photograph. Exquisite stitching.'

'I know the one you mean, although I have an excellent seamstress in Eckernförde and, fortunately, she's not Jewish. I can give you her details.'

'That would be lovely,' Maria said. 'Do you know, I even went to the woman's house, but she wasn't there either. It's so inconsiderate of her to disappear like that. I would have been quite happy to continue using her, even if she were only able to work from home.'

'Maria, darling, you must remember that it is not the done thing these days to be seen to patronise Jewish enterprises.' The countess chuckled. 'But if one's tailor or seamstress is Jewish, what can one do.'

Maria smiled, but on the journey back to Kiel, she couldn't bring herself to engage in conversation with Yosef and, feeling bad, she hoped that Miriam wasn't still around when they got back to Drachensee.

Then she scolded herself.

Why should I feel uncomfortable when I've never asked to be put in this position in the first place?

~~o~~

As soon as Yosef had dropped Maria at the front door on their return, and parked the car, Miriam had called him to come to the big house, telling him that the General wanted to see them both.

'You don't think they're going to dismiss us, do you?' Miriam asked.

'How can you even say that?' Yosef said. 'The General would never do that to us.'

'But she would,' Miriam countered.

'Miriam! That's terrible.' His voice, tense with indignation, faded to doubt. 'Has Frau Kästner said something?'

'No, not to me, but I've heard her on the telephone to her fancy friends, complaining about the General's attitude and how difficult things were becoming *domestically*.'

'It's maybe nothing to do with us. Perhaps the General and Frau Kästner are going through a patch…'

His voice fizzled out.

'They may have their differences but it's not that. I heard her refer to things as *Jüdisches* on several occasions. She's never done that before.'

She watched him. He had a pensive look now and she knew she'd worried him.

'Let's go and see what he has to say,' he told her.

~~o~~

Yosef glanced at his wife, then at his employer.

'Yosef, Miriam,' the General said. 'Now you must act.'

They sat around the kitchen table in the Drachensee house, the General at one end, Yosef at the other. Franz, home on leave, sat on the General's left with Miriam opposite him. Maria had retired upstairs with one of her headaches.

Ruth and Antje were looking after Manny.

'I agree,' Franz said. 'It's imperative that you get out.'

'We know,' Yosef said. The General and Franz glanced at each other.

'I suppose we've been a little insulated living here, under your protection, but last week has brought it home to us how tenuous our position really is, like that of every other Jew in Germany.'

He looked at the Kästner men. He saw the tension in their faces ease a little.

'You're probably wondering why it has taken so long to come to this decision,' he continued, reaching over and taking hold of his wife's hand. 'When Adolf Hitler was convicted for high treason in '24, not one of us thought anything of it; a crazed attempt by a bunch of anarchists to overthrow the government. Little did we know that, nearly fifteen years later, he would one day control Germany with a grip so tight that he could make the German people do whatever he wanted, including victimising their fellow Germans, just because they were Jewish.'

He looked up, his eyes brimming with sadness.

'We should have listened more closely to his speech at the trial, and after,' he continued. 'Since then, his actions have eroded any semblance of democracy, and we've all sleepwalked into it. We accepted the laws he brought in; first, Jews could not be civil servants or part of the army, although many of us had fought for Germany in the last war. Next, we couldn't be doctors or lawyers or teachers, then our citizenship was taken away and he made us change our names. He forced us to declare how much we were worth, to plunder our wealth when it suited him, and taxed us heavily if we wanted to leave.'

He paused. No one interrupted, so he carried on.

'Despite it all, we thought that at some point, the German people would say 'enough is enough' and stop him, that there were enough decent folk in the country who would see through the evil that he represents and call a halt to the nightmare.'

He shook his head.

'They didn't,' he said. 'Last week, a misguided Jewish boy took the deep anger he felt at his parents being deported and turned it into murder; the shooting of one German diplomat shook everyone, Jews included. When the backlash came, as we all knew it would, it wasn't the National Socialists or the government who threw the bricks and lit the fires of Kristallnacht, although they stood back and let it happen. It was the German people who smashed and burned our homes, shops and synagogues.'

Miriam put her hand over his. She nodded for him to continue.

'We've always considered ourselves to be German first, sir, and Jews second but I'll admit there are others who think of themselves as Jews, then Germans. Even so, we all considered ourselves patriots. Now we know that, not only are we not welcome, but we're somehow distasteful to ordinary Germans or good Aryans, as Herr Hitler would have them.'

He paused. They all looked at him. Neither Kästner man had uttered a word.

'So, we must leave Germany. We must abandon our homes, our jobs, our families, and most of our assets. To go God knows where,' he finished, the bitterness in his voice making both Erich and Franz flinch.

He bowed his head and Miriam gripped his hand. Tears ran down her face.

Franz sat, white-faced, staring. It was his father who broke the silence.

'My friends,' he said, his voice breaking, 'I'm ashamed to say it, but you're right. We stumbled like blind men into the mess we're in now and, to my eternal shame, I don't see it getting any better unless we, God forbid, lose another war.'

'If that's what it takes, so be it,' Miriam snapped, unable to look the General, or his soldier son, in the eye.

'Miriam doesn't mean that,' Yosef said, touching Franz's hand.

'Yes, she does, and she's right,' the General said, looking apologetically at his son. 'I just pray that we don't lose too many of our young men if it happens.'

'Where should we go, sir?'

'America would be the best, but I hear that you might wait more than a year to get a visa, if it's granted at all. England would be next on the list; the wait is less than six months, from what I'm told, although there's a risk that Britain may be defeated, and you would end up back under German rule. However, if you get yourselves to Britain, at least you could try and travel to one of its dominions from there. Canada, for instance, or Australia.'

'What about Palestine?' Franz said. 'I hear there's a flood of Jewish people emigrating there.'

'It's easier to get into Palestine,' Yosef said, 'and, at the moment, we could take some of our money. As I'm sure you know, Franz, we have friends there...' He tailed off.

'There's a but?' Franz said.

'I don't want to go,' Miriam stated. 'The Arabs hate us as much as the German people. I want to go somewhere where I don't have to look over my shoulder all the time or worry that my children are safe.'

'I understand,' said the General. 'I hear stories. There was a massacre not long ago, I believe.'

'Yes, there was,' Miriam said, her head bowed. 'It wasn't far from where our friends live. Nineteen innocent people slaughtered, stabbed to death.'

'Miriam gets all the news from Palestine from Esther Weichmann,' Yosef interrupted. 'You'll maybe remember her, sir.'

'I do,' the General confirmed. 'She's been here a few times over the years, at birthday parties and the like. And, of course, I knew Itsik.'

'They're doing well,' Yosef said, looking at Miriam. 'They're building a house for themselves. And they have two shops.'

'That's great to hear,' the General said, 'I'm told that if you're willing to work hard, there are great opportunities.'

This time it was Miriam who interjected.

'That's all right if you have a trade, or a business you can get up and running as soon as you arrive. What are we qualified to do?'

'There must be housekeeping jobs out there, and handyman or gardening jobs,' the General said.

'I don't think so, sir. Everyone out there is starting from scratch; it all seems very... self-sufficient.'

'What about work in England, or America?'

'They're different. Domestic service jobs seem to be much more plentiful,' Miriam said, 'and Yosef could also get a driving job. Even a delivery man's work would be fine until he found something else. We'd have to learn the language first. Ruth's already going to lessons and she's old enough to teach us.'

'Well, whatever you decide is up to you,' the General said. 'I wouldn't completely discount Palestine. It would be your quickest way out and would leave you with the biggest share of your savings.'

'About that, sir,' Yosef said. 'How long would it take you to get our money if we left in a hurry?'

They all caught Franz's puzzled look, and Yosef realised he'd made a mistake.

The General quickly reassured him.

'Don't worry. Franz won't say a word.'

He turned to his son.

'Sorry, I should have said. I'm keeping Yosef's money safe for him, so that the government can't take it from him. Please keep that to yourself.'

'I'll not say a word.'

The General turned to Yosef and Miriam.

'Your secret's safe with us,' he said. 'And I can get your money within a day or two.'

He frowned, then his face cleared, and he smiled.

'I can maybe even help you get your savings out,' he said. 'it would be safer that way. It's perhaps not a bad thing that Franz knows, if something happens to me. Maria needn't know.'

Yosef's body relaxed, and a look of relief came over his face.

'We'll go to Hamburg tomorrow,' the General said, 'To the British consulate.'

Yosef and Miriam looked at each other.

'You don't have to come with us, sir,' Yosef blurted. 'If I can just have a day off, I'll take the train.'

'No, you won't. I'm not sure the train will be safe for you and, anyway, I have some business in Hamburg. You and I can go. Miriam would be better staying here.'

'But, sir…'

'I'll not take any arguments, Yosef. You wouldn't want to lose your job for insubordination on top of everything else, would you?'

Yosef laughed, breaking the tension.

'You're right, sir. Whatever you say, sir.'

'That's settled then. We'll leave at six-thirty.'

He turned to Miriam.

'Don't worry,' he told her. 'We'll sort something out and, after this is all over, you'll always have a place here, if you want it.'

'Thank you, sir,' Miriam said.

~~o~~

[14/11/1938 Monday]

Yosef stood in the long, patient line of Jews that snaked along Harvestehuder Weg from the British consulate. His heart sank as he realised that, at the speed the line was moving, he might not reach the consulate doors by the time they closed for the night.

Two policemen paced up and down the pavement, ensuring that the line of people stretching a couple of hundred metres northwards remained orderly and, in fairness, they were firm but courteous with the diverse mix of Jewish society, from a cobbler and his wife to a Jewish banker, accompanied by two of his sons.

The consulate was one of the many grand houses overlooking the narrow strip of parkland that fronted the tranquil waters of the Außenalster, Hamburg's land-locked lake. In the biting November wind, the people stamped their feet and rubbed their hands to try and stave off the numbing cold, and few took the time to appreciate the refined elegance of their surroundings.

Yosef sighed and resigned himself to the long, cold wait.

~~o~~

The General hadn't lied. He did have business to attend to in Hamburg and he was, at that moment, sitting in his broker's office, receiving Herr Söllner's annual report and discussing the investments he would retain and discard over the following year, and which new stocks might give him the best return.

Arriving in Hamburg just after eight, they'd parked the car in Alsterufer on the lake shore, next to the Bootshaus, and he and Yosef had walked in opposite directions, Yosef taking the path along the lake towards the consulate, the General skirting the smaller Binnenalster to Jungfernstieg, then on to Bergstraße.

As he'd climbed the stairs in his broker's plush building, he'd smiled at Yosef's angst that he had arranged the visit especially for his employee's benefit.

Even if it was true.

'It wouldn't be safe on your own,' he'd told Yosef. 'If the police stop you, there's no knowing what would happen.'

He'd cleared the top steps to find his broker standing waiting for him.

'Still not taking the lift, Erich?' he said, laughing.

'I find that taking the stairs keeps me in shape. At my age...'

The broker laughed again. He'd looked after the General's investments for three decades.

'Come in. Have a seat.'

It took the broker an hour but, eventually, the General gave in to his insistence that a shift to munitions and armament company stock was the best way forward and thanked him for his stewardship of his portfolio.

Leaving the building and, knowing that Yosef would not be finished much before eleven, he strolled towards the Lombardsbrücke, the bridge separating the Außenalster from the Binnenalster. He entered the Kunsthalle, more to get out of the cold than from a great desire to view the painting and sculptures in the gallery but, to his surprise, he found himself drawn to one or two of the more modern works of the type that were getting up the noses of the National Socialists. He was surprised they were still on view.

By the time he'd left the gallery and reached the car, it was almost eleven-fifteen. There was no sign of Yosef, and he frowned, but carried on walking along the lakeside, knowing that it wasn't likely that he'd miss him if his ex-driver was on his way back to the car.

He started to walk more briskly, the cold beginning to seep through his thick coat. The road ran alongside the lake until the pier jutted out into the Außenalster, then it swung left, along the shore. As he reached the corner, he heard the crowd before he saw them. He could only describe it as a loud murmur, even if the long line of people, never more than two abreast, talked in hushed tones, respectful of the quiet neighbourhood the consulate stood in.

Approaching the front of the queue, which tailed away from him, the General scanned the crowd for Yosef's face, but there was no sign of him and, as he walked on, further and further back from the head of the line, he realised that they had arrived in Hamburg far too late; that there had been people queueing since first light, perhaps even overnight, and he wondered how desperate they must be to wait in line through the darkness and the cold, just to put their name down for a piece of paper that would allow them to escape from the country of their birth.

He found Yosef halfway along and, although he hadn't counted, he estimated that there were two or three hundred people in front of his employee and the consulate.

He greeted Yosef, who gave him a shrug and a downcast look.

'I'll be here all day,' Yosef said. 'Maybe longer. Just you go, and I'll make my own way back to Kiel.'

For a second, the General was tempted.

'No,' he said, shaking his head. 'I'll stay and keep you company. We've not had a chance for a good old *Gespräch* in a while. There's a café back at the pier. I'll go and see if they'll let me bring some coffee along.'

'The coffee would be nice, sir, but after that, please don't wait with me. I wouldn't want to waste your day. There's a travelling rug in the boot of the car. If you drop that off before you go, I'll be fine, even if I have to wait here until tomorrow.'

'I'll not hear of it. What do you think Miriam would say if I return without you?' He laughed.

'Sir, she'll be more annoyed if you stay here. If you could please tell her that I'm safe, and that I might be a couple of days, that would be more than enough.'

'I'll get the coffee, then we'll talk about it.'

The General walked off. Even in his civilian clothes, he looked like a military man. He was no martinet, but something in the way he walked gave him a gravitas, and the people in the queue paused their conversation and glanced at him as he passed.

At the coffee shop, the waitress wasn't keen to give him two cups of coffee to take until he left a ten Reichsmark note as deposit and showed her his military identity card.

She gave him a full pot, and two cups, telling him to return for a refill when he wished; she would only charge him for two cups each time, although the pot held more.

He pocketed the cups and walked back, feeling a little ridiculous carrying the coffee pot, but he smiled as he saw people lifting their noses in the air when they smelled the waft of fresh coffee in the cold winter air as he passed.

'Here you go,' he said to Yosef, handing him a cup and filling it from the pot.

'The police are keeping their distance,' he added.

'The only reason they're not hauling us away, sir, or trying to intimidate us to leave is that it's a foreign embassy, and they don't want to be seen to be heavy-handed.'

The General looked around. There were only a couple of policemen in attendance. One stood near the front of the queue where it turned in to the consulate entrance, controlling the number of people waiting in line inside the grounds. The other stood near the back. Every half hour, they would walk towards each other, meeting in the middle. After a brief chat, they would swap over, taking turns to stand near the consulate.

'You're probably right,' he said. 'When did you become so cynical, my friend?'

'When the National Socialists came to power, sir.'

CHAPTER 167

The headmaster looked up from the sheet of paper he'd been instructed to read out and saw the lines of Jewish faces staring back at him in misery, the cold slash of rain and sleet whipping at their legs as they stood, shivering.

He was flanked by four other teachers.

Ruth, Rebeka, and forty other Jewish children stood in the playground. From classroom windows, their fellow pupils craned their necks, trying to see what was happening outside. Some teachers called them back to their desks, others encouraged them to observe the proceedings.

'As from today,' the headmaster said, 'it is not permissible for any Jewish child to attend a German school. You will make your way home. Arrangements must be made by your parents for you to go to a Jewish school, which will be organised and paid for by the Jewish community.'

Part of him was relieved. It had been difficult to turn his face away from what some of the teachers, and pupils, had been doing to these children, but he'd been powerless to act. Now, at least, the burden would not be his and, perhaps, he thought, the Jewish children would be happier in a school of their own.

'Make sure you have everything with you, and...'

He swallowed, his face pale and drawn, and looked at them for a final time.

'...I'd like to wish you best of luck in your future.'

He saw one or two of the older children give small, sad smiles.

Before he could dismiss them, the maths teacher stepped forward, almost shoving him aside. It surprised the headmaster, and he was about to ask him what the devil he was doing but thought better of it. The man was a fanatical National Socialist and would think nothing of making trouble for anyone who got in the way of his own, or the NSDAP's, ambitions.

'Heil Hitler,' he barked, giving a fascist salute, not waiting for it to be returned. He gave the headmaster a dismissive stare before speaking to the group of shivering Jewish children.

'Jewish filth like you should have been expelled from this school long ago, wasting good German taxpayers' money and causing nothing but trouble and disruption, holding back honest and hard-working Aryan pupils from attaining their true potential. But the time has come, thanks to our beloved Führer and the party, that we can finally stop pandering to liberal do-gooders and hound you all back down the ratholes you call homes.'

He clicked the heels of his black boots together and saluted again.

'Heil Hitler.'

The headmaster watched as he stepped back, hating the small man with his self-satisfied smile, turning up every day in his Hitlerjugend uniform, and spitting bile to staff and pupils alike.

The headmaster was, as most teachers were, a party member.

Who would dare not to be these days?

He didn't like the way that education was being subverted by the government but there was nothing he could do about it.

'You can go now,' he said to the children, who stood rooted in disbelief at their sudden expulsion.

~~o~~

Ruth's first care was for Manny. If this were happening to Jewish children all over the city, he would be standing in a playground, just like her, being excluded from school forever. Then she thought of her parents, and how angry it would make them feel.

As the Jewish pupils trudged through the school gates for the last time, Ruth looked back. Despite the taunts, the bullying, and the multitude of ways in which they were unfairly treated, there had been a few decent teachers during her time there, enough to make her school life tolerable. And she'd always loved learning. She wondered if she would enjoy Jewish school as much.

She and Rebeka hurried homeward, not looking left or right in their shame.

~~o~~

It had been pleasant, despite the cold, for Yosef and the General spent the afternoon reminiscing about happier times. Like the rest of the queue, the two fell into conversation with those around them, hearing stories that were becoming all too familiar, but each in their own way unique.

The couple in front were from Hamburg; the man had told Yosef earlier in the day that his wife's brother had settled in England a year ago and was acting as a sponsor for them. He repeated the story for the General.

'It means that our application should go through within a few months. The only problem is our son. We're applying for a visa for him, but he was arrested last week, and we won't leave without him.'

The General suspected that they might have a long wait, but he said nothing.

It's not my place to shatter their lives.

'If you have a relative there,' the man said to Yosef, 'even a distant one, you should contact them. It makes a difference,' the man added.

'We have no one in Britain we can ask,' Yosef replied. 'Nor in America. I wish we had.'

The two men behind them in the queue were brothers from Altona. The General struggled to tell them apart. They were applying to emigrate to Britain with both their families, their children aged from ten to fifteen.

Like Yosef, both had served in the Great War and, when he introduced them to the General, they showed him their veteran's cards and their medals, which they'd brought to the consulate, hoping it would make a difference.

'It will depend on who's interviewing you,' the General said. 'If it is someone who harbours a grudge from the war, it may hinder rather than help. I would wait to be asked before showing them if I were you.'

'I never thought of that,' said one of the brothers.

'If it is an ex-soldier, someone who served at the front, I'd imagine it would be of benefit. There's a general respect between the rank and file who fought in the trenches on opposite sides, having gone through the same horrors. It's just the generals they hate.'

The General joined in the men's laughter. For the next hour they swapped tales of military disasters that had been visited on them by the General Staff. The General had started the war as a major, advancing to colonel by the armistice four long years later, and had seen the worst of the blunders made by those in command who should have known better.

Towards the end of the afternoon, as the queue crept forward one or two people at a time, one of the brothers recounted the story of a two-week period where their company had advanced over the same patch of shell hole and barbed-wire-ridden patch of mud three times, only to retreat a day or two later each time, on *strategic grounds*. As he finished his story, the crowd around them fell silent, and his brother nudged his arm.

Yosef and the General turned round in the direction the two brothers were staring.

An army truck had pulled up on the other side of the road, towards the rear of the queue.

'Perhaps they've brought us soup and bread, and a fine plate of stew,' a man in the queue said, under his breath. In the silence, his voice carried, causing a subdued burst of laughter in a small section of the line.

'They're expecting trouble,' another said, cutting off the laughter. 'Either that or they're going to arrest us all.'

A ripple of unease crept along the line, those at the front fearful that the doors were about to shut within touching distance of their goal, the ones at the back hoping that they would be permitted to stay overnight.

A dozen soldiers jumped out of the back. An officer stepped from the cab and approached one of the policemen and spoke briefly with him. The matter-of-fact way they spoke made the General think that the arrival of the soldiers was part of a routine that had been agreed beforehand. The General noticed that the officer in charge was a lieutenant, but far older than Franz or Johann.

The man barked a command and his men marched behind him in single file. Every ten metres or so, the soldier at the back of the small column would peel off and stop, standing guard. When they reached the gates of the consulate, the officer led the last two men, a sergeant, and a corporal, and stationed them both at the consulate door.

The officer walked back along the line, stopping every so often to say a few words to the people in the queue. When he reached a point twenty metres in front of Yosef and the General, the four men strained to hear what he was saying but could only catch the odd word.

A few minutes later, they saw the officer nod as he finished his explanation and made his way back towards them.

'Now listen up,' the General heard him say, 'The consulate is going to stay open for an extra two hours, to try and get as many of you through as possible, but not all of you will be taken by then. We are here to see that there is no trouble but, if there is, we will not hesitate to take firm action to control it.'

As he spoke, his hand lightly brushed his pistol holster. No one in the crowd mistook his message.

'The consulate will open again at 0700 hours tomorrow morning,' he continued. 'For those of you who decide to queue overnight, you must do so in an orderly and respectful manner. Remember that people live in this street, and do not want to be disturbed.'

The General was impressed by the way the soldiers, and the policemen before them, were conducting themselves, even if it were from political expediency, but he had no illusions that, if the crowd became agitated or unruly, the soldiers wouldn't hesitate to use force to subdue or disperse them.

While they remain quiet and respectful, the soldiers will not intervene.

~~o~~

Yosef turned to the General.

'Sir, I'll not make the entrance by the time it closes, far less the consulate itself. I'd rather you went home.'

'Yosef, I'll think about that when the doors close. In the meantime, I'm going to get another pot of coffee before that café closes.'

He picked up the pot, which they'd sat on the wall, and turned to step out of the line, welcoming the chance for a brisk stroll to warm him up.

He stopped abruptly, coming face to face with the lieutenant. With a start, the General realised that, as part of the crowd, the officer wouldn't take kindly to someone stepping out in front of him, and the officer's grim frown confirmed this.

But as the lieutenant opened his mouth, presumably to reprimand him, he frowned, squinting at the General for a second, then an uncertain smile appeared on the man's face.

'Sir?' he said, hesitating. 'General Kästner?'

'Yes, lieutenant?' the General said, racking his brain for any memory of the man.

'General Kästner, sir,' the man said. 'I'm sorry, sir, I didn't…'

'Don't worry, lieutenant, and please don't salute,' the General said, tilting his head at the people in the queue.

'Yes, sir,' he said, but the General could see curiosity fighting the deference in his eyes.

'You're not…' the man continued, and the General felt sorry for him.

'No, no,' he said, taking the man's arm and leading him gently out of earshot.

'I'm here with a friend,' he continued.

'I see, sir. You're retired now, I believe?'

'Sort of. I still do a little work, but for the Abwehr.'

'Ah, that must be interesting, sir. All that cloak-and-dagger stuff.' He chuckled.

'Quite,' said the General, smiling. A spark of recognition saved him the embarrassment of having to ask the man his name.

'Corporal Vössler, isn't it? You served under me, ten, fifteen years ago. You've done well to make lieutenant.'

'Yes, sir,' the man said, delighted to be remembered. 'I got my promotion a couple of months ago. Now that the army is expanding so fast, there are great opportunities for non-commissioned men to advance.'

'Well, good for you, lieutenant. It's good to meet you again. It's always nice to bump into men who have served under me.'

'Yes, sir. Thank you. You were always good to us.'

'You'll embarrass me now, soldier,' the General said, laughing.

'Those chaps that are with you, sir...'

'Ah. My driver. He's been with me, and my father before me, since I can remember. He was in the same regiment as me in the war. I'm just trying to help him out. The other two are just people we know.'

'Fetch them here, sir.'

'Pardon, lieutenant?'

He called to one of his men.

'These three men, there,' he said, pointing. 'Tell them to come over.'

The soldier walked over to Yosef and the two brothers and motioned for them to leave the line. The lieutenant waited until Yosef and the two brothers stood next to them, shuffling uncomfortably.

'Right, sir. Follow me.'

He marched towards the consulate, the General behind him. He turned to Yosef and shrugged. The three Jews followed the lieutenant and the General, not daring to make eye contact with those they passed, a hundred faces watching them in resentful silence.

When they reached the entrance, the lieutenant led them up the driveway to the door of the consulate and spoke to the sergeant.

The brawny soldier immediately opened the door and waved them through.

'Wait here,' the General's former corporal said, stopping in the hallway. 'You'll be called next.'

'Thank you, lieutenant, I'll not forget this.'

'You're welcome, General,' he said, clicking his heels and giving an old army salute. 'I was only glad to help. For old times, sir.'

The General returned his salute and shook his hand.

When he'd gone, the General turned to Yosef, embarrassed.

'Sorry. I didn't ask, believe me.'

'No, sir. But I thought I was going to die out there, being taken to the head of the queue in front of all these people.'

'They wouldn't be quite sure if we were being allowed to skip the queue, or if we were being taken away to be shot,' the General said.

He turned to the two men.

'Sorry to have involved you in that.'

The two brothers grinned.

'We can put up with a little embarrassment if it means we get out of here today,' one of them said, shaking his head in disbelief.

A door opened, and a harassed embassy official poked his head out into the corridor.

'Next,' he shouted.

'You go first,' one of the brothers said, grabbing the General's hand and shaking it vigorously. His brother insisted on doing the same, and they both clapped Yosef on the shoulder.

'You keep excellent friends,' one of them said.

~~o~~

'Thank God they let us out the back way,' Yosef said, as they left the outskirts of Hamburg. 'I don't think I could have faced these people.'

'No, they'll have a long wait, I fear. It was lucky we bumped into Lieutenant Vössler.'

Yosef shook his head. *It wasn't just luck.*

He knew, from experience, that the General had always been an officer who'd stayed close to his men, where he could see, feel, and smell what they were going through. And he knew that the men loved him for it and would follow him anywhere. And do anything for him.

Yosef had filled out the forms as instructed, but when he'd seen the visa application number, the optimism he'd felt on being called in so quickly had evaporated.

'53,056,' he'd mumbled to himself, appalled.

He'd asked the clerk what it meant.

'We're being swamped at present, but that's the application number for all the consulates in Germany and the embassy in Berlin, not just for here. We're processing applications around the 26,000 mark currently but, even with the extra staff we've taken on, we're only able to process a couple of thousand a month.'

Yosef had done a quick calculation. *Over a year.*

'Even then, there's no guarantee you'll get your visas,' the man had said.

Yosef stared at the road ahead, the white strips of the centre line flicking towards him in the headlights.

'They might speed things up; take on even more staff,' the General said.

It didn't lift his spirits, but Yosef forced a smile.

He must know. He'll have done the arithmetic too.

'We would be as well to have gone to the American Embassy,' Yosef said.

'It will be inundated too. Instead of a year, it could be two.'

'You could be right, sir, which brings us back to Palestine.'

'You'd go?'

'Perhaps, sir, but with reluctance. I'm not sure we could settle there. I know it sounds ridiculous, but some of those fervent Zionists, who extol the virtues of Palestine and our duty to go there; they're as narrow-minded as the NSDAP.'

'Surely not? They only want a place to call home.'

'Don't get me wrong, sir, there are a lot of ordinary Jews emigrating there who're not as political or fanatical but, even if I wanted to go, Miriam is dead set against it.'

'You need to change her mind. Or find somewhere else. I'm not so sure we can avoid war for that long. Herr Hitler seems to be determined to take us into another conflict.'

'I'll keep trying, sir. In the meantime, as you say, perhaps the British will speed up the process, and we'll be in England for spring.'

CHAPTER 168

KIELER MORGENPOST

Monday 14th November 1938

NEW CURBS ON JEWS – EDUCATION. ENTERTAINMENT. SPORTS.

Legislation has been passed barring Jews from all public schools and universities, cinemas, theatres, and sports facilities.

Jewish children must only attend segregated Jewish schools that are financed and managed by the Jewish community.

The changes are effective immediately.

City councils across Germany have been given the go-ahead to introduce designated Aryan zones which Jews are forbidden to enter. We asked Mayor Hoffmann when such areas were going to be set up in Kiel. He told the Morgenpost that the viability of such a scheme was being assessed, and that he hoped that most parks and open spaces within the city, except for the Jewish cemetery, would be set aside for true Germans. He also stated that this would include the promenade on the western shore of Kieler Hafen as far as Wik.

He promised that stiff penalties would be imposed on any Jew flouting the ban and reminded Jews that they must carry their Kennkarte at all times.

Jewish identity cards are marked with the letter 'J' to distinguish them from those carried by German citizens.

~~o~~

Tired from the long day, the General retrieved the plate of food that Miriam had left in the warming oven of the range. They'd telephoned before they left Hamburg, and Miriam had told him that Maria had already left to go to a charity evening with her lady friends.

Now, in between mouthfuls, he sat at the kitchen table reading the *Morgenpost* with horror, wondering if he should go across to the cottage and find out how Miriam and the children had dealt with the events of the day, while Yosef and he were away in Hamburg.

He hesitated, figuring that he'd be imposing on them if he did.

They'll need time to come to terms with the news about their visas, and about the schools.

He read on; the rest of the paper was filled with the usual mixture of dull news and timid speculation. He thought about phoning Canaris, but he knew the admiral was still away; an invitation to Hitler's mountain retreat was not one even his friend could turn down.

~~o~~

Ruth began to cry again. Yosef could hardly bear to look at her; Miriam herself was close to tears. He looked at Manny, but he could only see sullen anger on the boy's face. Almost as soon as he'd got in from Hamburg, Miriam had shown Yosef the paper, and told him about Ruth coming home early from school in tears, with Manny, cold and soaked to the skin, with her.

'So, they marched you out in the cold and wet, and made you stand there while they told you that you were no longer welcome?'

'Yes, Papa,' Ruth said, sobbing. 'We went to the Grundschule, as soon as we could,' Ruth said, 'to get Manny and Fischel.'

'The filthy, rotten…' He bit back a curse.

'Jakob came round,' Miriam interrupted. 'They start Jewish school tomorrow.'

'That was quick,' he replied, a look of surprise on his face.

'He came over to see if you could give them a hand, but I told him you were in Hamburg. They've been given a house, with a workshop beside it, on Kleiner Kuhberg, two doors down from the house we've acquired to use as a synagogue. The man has been put out of business, and he wants us to have it. He's happy for it to be converted into a school.'

'But, how…'

'They're going to start teaching in the house and convert the workshop into classrooms as soon as they can. Jakob says that two or three teachers have already offered their services. You'll remember Frau Epstein; she taught Ruth in Grundschule but was dismissed during the first purge of Jewish teachers. Jakob named the others, but I couldn't place them.'

'I'll get up early and do all my jobs, then take the children myself. I should have time to have a quick word with Jakob then, and still be back for nine.'

Miriam glanced at the clock and told Manny to get ready for bed.

'It's late,' she told him, 'and you'll be up earlier than your usual time. It's a longer walk to school, and you'll want to be on time for your first day, won't you?'

'Yes, Mama,' Manny said. 'Will we be still able to play football?'

'I'm not sure, honey. We'll have to wait and see. You can play when you come home if there's nowhere at school. Have Fischel over, and perhaps a few of your other friends.'

'Yes, Mama,' he said, brightening up at the unexpected treat, hugging both his parents before disappearing to his room.

Miriam turned to Ruth.

'Go and make sure he gets ready for bed. I wouldn't put it past him to go up there and play with his toys.'

'Yes, Mama.' Ruth followed Manny up.

'She's a good girl,' Yosef said, when she'd left. 'She's taken it hard.'

'She said she didn't cry the whole way home, but as soon as I opened the door…'

'She loved that school, despite everything. It'll be a wrench to leave her friends.'

'There are a few Jewish girls in her class. She'll still have them.'

'Rebeka is still here, but Hanne Weidmann was deported with her family, remember. There's a couple of boys, I think, but the rest of the pupils in her class weren't Jewish.'

'She'll settle in. They both will. Manny almost seems to be looking forward to it.'

'He's not taking it as hard as Ruth, but we'll have to watch him. Underneath it all, he's angry, more than anything. I don't want him getting into trouble. You know what boys are like.'

He grinned, despite himself.

'I remember what the General and I used to get up to…'

'I don't want to know,' she said.

'Anyway, you didn't have anything like this to deal with,' she added. 'When young boys are bitter, they can get themselves into trouble. Look at that young man who shot that Rath person in Paris.'

'Manny's hardly going to shoot someone, is he? You're overreacting.'

'Am I? I've seen a couple of posters defaced, and it's only a matter of time before he and his friends will think they can fight back, even in small ways like that. You'll need to have a word with him.'

'I will, if it makes you feel better. He'll soon realise that school is better when he isn't being picked on or called names. And he wants to learn. They both do. This might be a fresh start for them.'

Miriam bit her lip.

'I hope there's no trouble.'

'What do you mean,' he said.

'Well, I wouldn't put it past the government to…'

'No. They'll be safe,' he said, stopping her. 'The government have made a big thing that this is all about segregation, so they'll have to show that it's working, for a while, at least.'

'I only hope so. The children need things to settle down; to put all this behind them.'

'I'm sure it will. Just wait and see, love.'

He reached out and held her hand in his. She gave a tired smile.

'Let's turn in,' he said. 'It has been a long day, and we'll be up before the chickens tomorrow.'

~~o~~

Miriam laughed. It had been a while since they'd kept a henhouse behind the cottage, providing eggs for the Kästners and themselves. In the end, the early morning ritual of the cockerel crowing had worn Maria Kästner down and he'd been dispatched, making one last appearance on the dinner table. The hens had died off naturally over the space of a year, and now the family's eggs were delivered twice a week with the milk.

'You forgot to tell me how you got on,' she said.

'I didn't want to say in front of them,' he said, nodding in the direction of the stairs. 'It's better that we don't tell them too much for now.'

'It might be better to say to Ruth,' Miriam said. 'It will give her something to focus on and let her see there's a way out for us.'

'If you think that's best, I'll have word with her on the way to school. Manny always runs ahead.'

'So,' she said, after a pause. 'What happened?'

'Well, I put our applications in.'

He fished in his pocket and pulled out the receipt from the consulate and handed it to her. She looked at it, then at him, her brow furrowed.

'Look at our allocation number,' he told her, pointing at it.

She paled.

'How can there be that many?'

'The queue stretched for a quarter of a mile,' he said. 'If it hadn't been for the General, I would have been still there, at least until tomorrow, maybe even longer.'

He told her about the soldier who'd served with the General and how they'd been taken to the head of the queue.

'I felt ashamed, passing all these poor people,' he said.

She took hold of his hand and gave him a sympathetic smile.

'So, what does it mean?' she asked. 'How long do we have to wait?'

'They say a year, if not more.'

He could hardly look at her.

'It's not your fault. Maybe we should have tried for America.'

'I don't think it would be any better. The Americans are dragging their heels, for all the size of the place.'

She waited, knowing what was coming.

'There's always Palestine,' he said. 'The General seems to think it's a good idea.'

'I knew you'd bring Palestine into it. And it's easy for the General to say. He and Maria wouldn't be living in a hot, arid, backward country with no water, hardly any trees and Arabs who are hostile to any incomers.'

'All right, but we may have to keep it as an option, if things get worse, or if the British decide to call a halt to immigration.'

'You think they'd do that?'

'No, no. But you can never be sure.'

She looked at him. He didn't seem beaten, but she could see the weight of worry on his shoulders and presumed that she looked the same.

'Come to bed, love,' she said, softly.

I'll give him some comfort tonight, she said to herself, the thought of moulding her soft flesh to his harder body consoling her, too, forgetting everything else save the feel of him within her, two frightened people clinging to each other to shut out the world, and all its pain.

~~o~~

Around ten, the General heard the crunch of gravel, and the soft thump of a car door closing. He got up and made his way into the hall. Maria stood on the front step, her back to him, waving at the departing car. He smiled; as always, the sight of her took his breath away, the marginally fuller figure of her forties suiting her, and pleasing him.

She gave him a terse smile as she opened the door.

'A good evening, dear?' he asked.

'Yes, it was. Grete was kind enough to get her driver to pick me up and drop me off, luckily.'

'I'm sorry about that. The whole thing took an age, and it could have been longer, had it not been for a lieutenant who once served under me.'

'So, they got their visas?'

'No, but their applications are in. They're on the waiting list now.'

She frowned.

'I thought you were going to Hamburg to get visas for them all, so that they could leave. That was the plan, wasn't it? Could they not have applied by post?'

'It's not quite that easy. They're insisting Jews apply in person. There was a short interview just to get on the waiting list.'

'So, when will they get their visas?'

He wondered if he should sugar-coat the truth about the time the process was going to take but, irritated at her lack of empathy, he decided against it.

'It could take up to a year, I'm afraid,' he said. 'They've had a flood of applicants since Kristallnacht.'

'That's impossible,' Maria said.

'I'm afraid not,' he said, with a half-smile that, instead of disarming his wife, infuriated her.

'It's getting to the stage where the Nussbaums could cause a lot of trouble for us, Erich. I don't think you quite understand the seriousness of the situation.'

'Oh, I do understand. Yosef and Miriam, along with every other Jew in Germany, are at their wits' end, not quite knowing what will hit them the next day.'

'That's not what I meant. It might sound selfish, but for our own sakes, we need to be careful.'

'It's not us who're in trouble. It's Yosef and Miriam, and their children.'

'You're making me sound heartless. It's not that I don't care, but my family comes first.'

'Our family's interests are best served by showing some loyalty to our employees who are, incidentally, also our friends.'

'And there's the problem. The countess says that you're too soft on the Nussbaums, and I agree.'

The General bit back a sharp retort and shook his head sadly.

'Maria, we can't just throw them out, after all these years. We owe them our protection.'

'No, we don't, Erich. We owe it to ourselves to look after our children. The Böhms are calling us Jew-lovers behind our backs, and the countess says that it's becoming detrimental to have Jewish staff these days. Grete was just saying that she had to let her maid go last week, and she's been with her since before the children were born.'

'Well, you can tell Antje that you want to turn Ruth out onto the streets,' he snapped, instantly regretting his outburst.

Her face paled, and a cold anger replaced the annoyed frown.

'That's uncalled for,' she said. 'Antje has friends at school now. She doesn't need Ruth. And anyway, the Nussbaums can go and stay with Yosef's parents. In the house that we bought.'

He noticed her emphasis on the collective *we*.

'People don't have friends because they need them for something. You can't just discard them when they're of no further use to you. And Yosef's parents earned that house, and their pension too.'

'Oh, damn you, Erich,' Maria said in exasperation, 'there's no arguing with you. You're always right.'

'Maria,' he said softly, 'I can only follow my conscience. I can't abandon them. We owe them.'

'You do what you have to. I'm going to bed.'

She stormed up the stairs.

'Maria,' he shouted after her, but she didn't reply.

He stood for a few minutes after the bedroom door slammed, then walked through to his study.

He poured himself a whisky and sat at his desk, staring into space.

CHAPTER 169

'We shouldn't be doing this on the Shabbat.'

Siegmund Eliasowitz, the young man who had taken it upon himself to be the guardian of their faith, had spoken out, not for the first time that day.

'Shut up and put your back into it. This is God's work, and I'm sure he'd want us to do it on *his* day,' Jakob said, grimacing.

He was covered from head to toe in dust, turning his beard prematurely grey, giving them a glimpse of how he might look in fifteen or twenty years.

'You're right, grandfather,' Yosef quipped, causing them all to pause and look at Jakob.

While the laughter died, Jakob dusted himself down.

'Right,' he said. 'Coffee break. God also wants us to stay refreshed so that we can do his work efficiently, and without slacking.'

He looked pointedly at the young man who had complained.

They sat down, and a woman, who was working next door in the former residential part of the building, brought a large pot of coffee and a selection of cups and beakers. She poured their coffees, and they helped themselves from the plate of Rugelach she'd laid on a chair. There was silence while they ate, the small, filled bites of rolled pastry, delicious as ever.

'How are you getting on in there?' Jakob asked her when he'd finished.

'Ach, fine. It's coming along. It wasn't the cleanest.'

'Next door housed the owner's workers. They were mostly young men. You know, no mothers to keep an eye on them…'

She laughed.

'Well, it's cleaner now, but the rooms are on the small side for the children. It will be cramped until you've got this place ready.'

'We'll have it done in a couple of weeks, with enough help. We're splitting it into two classrooms. One for Grundschule children, one for Realschule pupils. The rooms in the house will be used for the upper class students and those who have been excluded from university. There's a small yard behind, big enough for a play area.'

She nodded her head and left. Jakob took a seat beside Yosef.

'How are the children settling into their new school,' he asked.

'Oh, Ruth is coping. She misses her Aryan friends though.' He smiled, aware of the irony.

'She'll adjust. She's turning into a fine young woman.'

Yosef smiled.

'Manny has taken to it like a duck to water,' he said. 'He loves it all, wearing the kippah, the Hebrew lessons, and Jewish history. We get a lecture every night over dinner about some battle the Israelites lost, or some miraculous escape of hundreds of Jews from a pogrom during Genghis Khan's reign of terror.'

'We could do with a miraculous escape now. You've applied for a visa to Britain?'

'Yes. If it were just Miriam and I, we'd stay…'

'I know, my friend.'

Jakob hesitated.

'I've made enquiries about Palestine, but we're not going until we have no other choice.'

Yosef nodded. 'We'll be at least a year waiting for our visas. Miriam won't even consider Palestine.'

'Well, I don't know what's the best thing to do, but there's plenty to do here. I do know that.'

He looked around the bare, rubble-strewn building.

'We'd best get on with it then,' Yosef said, standing up.

Jakob put his hand on Yosef's arm.

'I don't know if you heard. Sigo Dember died today. His burns were too severe; he would have had no sort of life had he survived, the doctor said.'

Yosef bowed his head.

'What about Louis Eckart?' he asked.

'He's making progress. They say he'll survive, but he'll be scarred for life.'

Yosef exhaled slowly.

'One day, I hope to see these bastards pay for this.'

~~o~~

[25/11/1938 Friday]

'The Kästner house. Who's calling?'

The General heard his wife's familiar telephone greeting, then, a few seconds later, his name being called.

He made his way from the study and, as he entered the hallway, he saw her gesturing, her face animated, while listening to whoever was on the other end of the line.

'It's Franz,' she whispered, holding her hand over the mouthpiece. 'He's been promoted to major.'

The General feigned surprise. Colonel Schneider had told him a few weeks ago that they were waiting for the posting to come through, but neither Franz nor Maria were aware that he knew.

'That's wonderful. He deserves it.'

'Here, he wants to speak to you.'

He took the telephone from her, watching the spring in her step. The timing was great, he knew. She was attending a gala lunch for one of her charities later that day, and her son's rapid rise through the ranks would be a wonderful topic of conversation.

'Franz,' he said, turning his attention to his son, on the end of the line. 'Congratulations. You've earned it.'

'Thanks. I've known for a couple of months that it was on the cards; it took an age to come through.'

The General gave a short laugh. 'That's the army for you. How did the men take it?'

'Very well. Worried about who'll be next in charge, but they'll be fine. Their new captain is Artur Schweitzer. He's in our company and they know him; he's a good friend of mine.'

'I've met him. Listen, you'll have to come home and let Mama see you with your new epaulettes.'

'I'll be home in a couple of weeks.'

'She'll be pleased.'

'How are things there?' Franz said. 'Are the Nussbaums all right? I heard about Jewish children being excluded from school.'

'They're okay. Just a bit shaken. They've applied to emigrate to England.'

'That's a relief, though you and Mother will miss them. You'll find them impossible to replace.'

'I know. All the good men are being snapped up by the Wehrmacht. Anyway, they'll have to wait at least a year.'

'Oh, I thought it would have been sooner. Well, at least they're going.'

'Yes. I suggested that they should consider Palestine, but Miriam wouldn't hear of it.'

'I can understand that. Those British officers that we met at Kieler Woche a couple of years ago; do you remember them?'

'Yes. What about them?'

'Two of them had served in Palestine. They said it was a hellish place. All dust, sand, and hostile Arabs. They may have exaggerated, but I think the British are sorry they ever took the mandate on.'

'Ha. They're used to it. They control half the world, and most of their colonials can't stand them.'

'Anyway, I don't think it's as safe a place as all that, and if there's a war in Europe…'

'I hadn't thought of that. It might become sucked into the conflict. Perhaps they'd be better waiting. Britain will be safer, providing Herr Hitler doesn't invade.'

'There's talk among the men that we might go to war with Britain and France again. Most of them are for it.'

'I'm surprised their officers aren't urging caution. At least, the ones who fought in the last war.'

'They are, but most of them are senior officers, and the men…'

He hesitated.

'I know,' the General interrupted. 'You can say it. The men think their senior officers are nothing but alte Fürze.'

Old Farts.

Franz laughed.

'I suppose so. But at the end of the day, most of them are itching for a fight too. Unfinished business, I suppose.'

'You could be right,' the General said. 'There's still a lot of bitterness about the way we lost the war, and how we were punished.'

Franz stayed silent for a few seconds.

'We are going to war, you know,' he said.

'Yes, and God help us all.'

CHAPTER 170

'The Ostjuden. They're back,' Erwin Baruch, one of the younger men on the committee said, rushing in to the almost completed school building in Kleiner Kuhberg. They'd finished it in a week, barring a final coat of paint. By working over the Shabbat again, they would have it ready for lessons on Monday morning.

'What? Don't talk nonsense, boy,' Jakob said sharply, regretting his outburst almost as soon as it had left his lips.

'It's true. They all arrived back this morning. They were taken to the border and then nothing happened, so they came back. Max Weidmann is on his way over. They're looking for somewhere to stay.'

Ten minutes later, Jakob saw with his own eyes that Max Weidmann had indeed returned. As soon as he entered the room, Jakob walked over to the big man, who took him in his arms and squeezed.

'You're going to crush me, Max,' Jakob wheezed, laughing.

All the men downed their paint brushes and surrounded Max. A barrage of questions left Max with no time to answer until Jakob raised his arm.

'Let Max speak. He'll tell us everything.'

They brought a seat over and sat Max down. He took a breath and started to speak.

'They came into our houses and dragged us out, putting us into lorries. I told Hanne to hide in a cupboard, but they found her; they must have had a list.'

'I saw them taking you,' Yosef said, his eyes lowered. 'There was nothing I could do.'

'I know, Yosef. I thought I caught a glimpse of you, standing in the doorway. I was glad someone knew what had happened to us.'

He shifted himself in the chair.

'They took us to Hamburg,' he continued, 'to an old warehouse. We stayed there two nights, with just thick blankets to lie on, on a concrete floor. New people were arriving all the time, until the place was almost full.'

In his heavily accented German, he took his time, occasionally searching for a word or phrase that eluded him.

'The next day, they marched us to the station and put us on a train. They crushed us in; everyone who found a seat had someone sitting on their laps; a child, a wife, a brother or sister, or a parent. The rest were standing; we were like salted herrings in a barrel.

'When the train stopped, they told us we were in Frankfurt an der Oder, just across the border from Poland. They put us in two large barns, on a farm. Every day, they'd shout a hundred or so names. It went by what town or village people were being sent back to.

'After a week, there were thirty of us left. It wasn't so bad. The soldiers gave us food – soup, bread, sometimes a stew, and plenty vegetables. We were able to buy milk, eggs and cheese from the farmer's wife.

'Then, the soldiers left. We asked them what we should do. *Go home, Jew*, they said. You're not on the list.'

There was a collective sigh from the men listening. Max smiled.

'So, we came home,' he said. 'It took us three weeks. We got lifts in farm carts, we caught buses and took trains, those of us that they let us on, but mostly we walked. We found places to sleep; we still had some money, so a room in a cheap guest house would suffice for us all. And here we are. Looking for somewhere to stay.'

Jakob was the first to speak.

'You can stay in the attic here for now, until we find you somewhere. There are two rooms; we were going to use them for storage but that can wait.'

He slapped Max on his broad shoulders.

'It's good to have you back; I have only one complaint.'

'What's that?'

'You've come back when the work is almost finished. We could have done with you last week.'

He laughed, handing Max a paintbrush.

~~o~~

[29/11/1938 Tuesday]

KIELER JÜDISCHES FREIHEITSNACHRICHTENBLATT

Volume 68

6th of Kislev, 5699

ALL JEWISH-OWNED RETAIL ESTABLISHMENTS SEIZED!

All Jewish-owned shops have been Aryanised. In a leaked report from the Reich Office of the Four-Year Plan, details emerged that the state had removed all Jewish shops and most other businesses from Jews, but that compensation has been paid. The KJF has learned that this payment has not been forthcoming in many instances and, when it has, it has been a derisory amount, often wiped out by the business owners having to pay the remainder of the fines imposed on them after Kristallnacht.

RESTRICTION ON THE FREEDOM OF MOVEMENT OF JEWS.

The Reich Ministry of the Interior is to implement new rules restricting the movement of Jews. A spokesman for the Reichsminister was quoted as saying that no longer could Jews expect to be able to move round with impunity, endangering the German people with their subversive habits and their thievery. There is much confusion about the new rules; it is expected that they will be enforced ad hoc, and that they will result in an escalation of the arrest and imprisonment of Jews that has been characteristic whenever new laws have been brought in.

JEWS FORBIDDEN TO KEEP CARRIER PIGEONS

A law enacted yesterday by the Reich Interior Ministry forbids Jews from keeping carrier pigeons. The KJF presumes that this ludicrous move is an attempt to stop Jews spreading news abroad about the inhumane persecution of the Jewish population. While the KJF cannot be certain, we cannot find any recorded incidence of this method of communication being used to disseminate such information within Germany, far less across her borders.

~~o~~

'The sky will be full of pigeons leaving Jewish dovecotes, looking for work,' Jakob said, a bitter laugh in his throat.

Yosef smiled. It was one of the reasons he loved being Jewish. Seeing the humour in a dark situation was sometimes the only way to fend off the blackness that had loomed over Jewish communities since Moses led them out from Egypt.

'How do they get these out so fast,' Yosef said, holding the single sheet of the most recent KJF. 'They do a wonderful job.'

'And at great risk,' Isaac said. 'If they get caught…'

His voice tailed off. They all knew the consequences.

'At least we get the truth, however unpalatable,' Yosef said, the other two nodding in agreement.

They sat in one of the small meeting rooms in the Kleiner Kuhberg house that doubled as the synagogue and the administration centre. The three buildings now housed the unofficial organisation that acted as spokesmen for the Jewish population, something that the local authorities and the security services seemed to tolerate.

'Did you get anything for the shop?' Jakob asked.

'I was lucky. I sold it a week before the new law came in. The man paid cash, and for once, he wasn't the greatest admirer of the government, so he was willing to declare a smaller figure than the one he paid. It wasn't much, but it all helps.'

'So, you leave soon?'

'In two weeks. It can't come soon enough, except…'

'You're worried about your diet,' Jakob joked.

'No, I'm putting that in God's hands. It's more that I'll miss you two, and the others. You should speed up your arrangements to get yourselves out. I'll write from Palestine, and I can promise you that if you come out there, I'll help get you settled.'

Jakob held his hand out and gripped Isaac's.

'I might just take you up on that, some day. For now, I need to stay here, and help these people.'

'And I'll be here for a while,' Yosef said, 'at least until our visas come through, although Miriam might change her mind about Palestine now, with these new restrictions coming in. She's seething. That's why I'm here; to keep out of her way.'

Isaac and Jakob laughed. They'd all caught the brunt of their wives' wrath, even when it wasn't of their own making.

'She set off the other day to visit her parents. They stay in Altona, you know. She went to get onto the Hamburg train, but she was stopped. You need a permit, they told her. When she enquired where she would get one, they just shrugged. She asked at the ticket office and they didn't know, or care. She came back home spitting, I can tell you.'

'You have to apply at police headquarters,' Jakob said. 'I was given this yesterday.'

He handed Yosef a sheet of paper. It listed the new travel restrictions for registered Jewish people, including Mischlinge.

'So, you can still travel?' Yosef said when he'd finished reading.

'It would seem so, but I wouldn't count on it. Getting a permit might not be as easy as it sounds.'

He checked his watch and looked apologetically at Jakob.

'Go,' Jakob said, putting his hand on Yosef's shoulder.

Yosef gave him a smile of thanks.

'I'd rather go to the police station myself. Miriam might be a little nervous about going.'

CHAPTER 171

Yosef waited patiently, having been told to take a seat. When he was finally called, he walked up to the sergeant on the duty desk.

'Yes, sir. Sorry about the wait,' the man said.

He didn't look in the slightest apologetic.

'Oh, that's all right. I'm here to ask for a permit for my wife to travel to Altona, to see her parents.'

'When does she wish to travel?'

'I don't know. As soon as possible. She tried to go earlier today, but she wasn't allowed on the train without a permit.'

'Is she a Jew, sir?'

'Yes, she is.'

'Then that's correct. Are you a Jew, too, sir?'

'Yes, we both are.'

'May I see your Kennkarte?'

Yosef showed him his identity card, the large yellow 'J' prominent on the front.

'Well, she would have to apply in person. We can only issue permits to the individual who is intending to travel.'

'Oh. Are you sure?'

'I'm 100 per cent sure. Tell your wife she'll have to come herself. Is that all?'

Yosef mumbled a reluctant thanks and hurried out.

~~o~~

Yosef kept his head down. It was better to make eye contact with no one. He turned the corner onto Sophienblatt and almost collided with a young man. He looked up.

Hitlerjugend.

'Watch where you go, old man.'

There were three of them.

No older than sixteen, Yosef thought.

'I'm so sorry. I wasn't looking…'

It was a mistake. The abject apology.

'I think we have a Jew here,' the taller of the three youths said, grinning at his friends.

'Ask him,' one of his friends said.

'Are you a Jew, old man?'

'Yes, I'm a Jew, but I fought in the war.'

Yosef opened his coat, exposing the three medals that he always wore now.

The three youths peered at them.

'Where did you steal them?' the tall youth said.

'I d-did-didn't. I fought at Passchendaele.'

'Like hell you did, Jew,' the youth said, leaning forward and ripping the medals from Yosef's chest.'

'Hey…'

'What did you say, Jew?'

'Nothing. I…'

'That's better, old Jew. Now run along before I decide that you need taught a lesson.'

Yosef glanced at the medals in the youth's hand, then stumbled on, not looking back.

I can't tell Miriam I've lost my medals.

The three Hitler Youth watched him, laughing.

Yosef looked back as he reached the next corner.

The taller one tossed the medals in the air then caught them, and slipped them into his pocket, basking in the admiring looks of his two friends.

'These Jews shouldn't be allowed on the streets,' he heard the youth say.

~~o~~

Miriam's mood hadn't improved when Yosef told her she'd have to go to the police station herself and by the time they'd walked there together, he had to stop and tell her to calm down before she said something that would get her in trouble.

It was the same sergeant at the desk, and they waited even longer before he motioned for them to come over.

'Can I help you?' he asked.

'I spoke to you a short while ago. My wife wishes to travel to Altona.'

'And when does she wish to travel?'

'As soon as she can if that's possible.'

'We need to know exactly. To put on the permit.'

Miriam opened her mouth to speak but, Yosef, sensing the pent-up frustration in her, gripped her hand, warning her to stay quiet. He replied before she could say anything.

'She wishes to travel tomorrow.'

'I see. I'm afraid that will not be possible.'

'Might I be allowed to ask why?' Miriam said, the cold anger in her voice too obvious to Yosef. He hoped the policeman would take it for politeness.

'Well, you see, it takes forty-eight hours to process the permit.'

'Well, I'll travel the day after,' Miriam said.

The policeman looked at her, unperturbed by her sharp tone.

Without saying anything, he disappeared through the door behind the desk, closing it behind him. Yosef began to sweat. Thoughts of the sergeant returning with a few colleagues to arrest them or, worse still, Gestapo men appearing, began to eat at him.

When the door opened again, the sergeant came through it, alone. He placed a form on the desk.

'Fill this in,' he said.

It was two pages long, and Yosef wondered why the authorities needed so much information for a simple trip to Altona and back.

It took a full ten minutes to complete, but they finally handed it back to the man, and he checked it.

'Come back in two days. It should be here by then.'

They could do nothing but thank him. As they trudged home, Yosef tried talking to Miriam but, when she hardly uttered a word, he gave up his attempts.

I hope it's ready when we return.

~~o~~

[01/12/1938 Thursday]

Esther looked at her calendar. *The beginning of December. It will be getting cold in Kiel.*

She looked at the postmark on the letter. It was dated the fourteenth of November and she hesitated before opening it, worried about what it might contain. She'd read news reports about Kristallnacht but had heard nothing on how it had affected her family and friends in Kiel.

She took a deep breath and read.

13th November 1938

Dearest Esther,

I'm writing now to let you know that you've not to worry; Itsik's parents are fine, and we are too. You've probably heard that the synagogue was ransacked and burned, and that Jewish shops and homes were attacked in two nights of violence they are now calling Kristallnacht. Some of our men, especially the younger ones, have been arrested; most of them seem to have been taken to concentration camps. The NSDAP say they had nothing to do with it; that it was ordinary Germans who were justified in being outraged at the shooting of a German diplomat by a young Jew. Believe that if you will!

I must admit that gave me a fright. Two men were terribly burned trying to put out the fire. They saved the Scrolls but they're both in a bad way. They managed to salvage some other bits and pieces. We are going to hold services in a house in Kleiner Kuhberg in the meantime.

There's talk of a massive fine for the Jewish population, for the damage that's been done to property because of the riots! It couldn't be more unfair. The government are just trying to get our money whatever way they can. You must be relieved that you got your savings out when you did.

Yosef told the General about the problems that Itsik's parents have been having; he said he'd ask some of the Rathaus civil servants with whom he has good relations but, when he did, they all told him that it was outside their jurisdiction; SiPo, the security police, have their grubby hands all over emigration now. He was most apologetic.

However, the General knew that Oskar von Friedeburg had helped Itsik out with the shop, so he mentioned it to him. Honestly, I didn't ask, neither did Yosef, but Oskar has connections within the party so it might be worth a try. Whatever you do, please don't get your hopes up; the security police are a law unto themselves, so it's still an outside chance at best.

By the way, I'm happy to do what little I can for Itsik's parents; it's the least I can do. You would do the same, I'm sure, if the positions were reversed. They're bearing up well but obviously missing you all.

The massacre sounds horrific; I do worry for you and the children. And forty kilometres away from you is nothing. Please take care. Having said all that, you might still be safer in Palestine than we are here.

I don't know if you remember the Weidmanns? Hanne was in Ruth and Rebeka's class at school. They got deported back to Poland. Ruth and Rebeka are devastated, even though they weren't as close to Hanne as they are to each other. I think she was just coming out of her shell. Now she's gone. Yosef saw them being taken by the police and the SA. They're maybe better off in Poland, the way it's going here.

Despite everything, Ruth and Manny still like school. I don't know why. Some of the teachers are horrible to them and, as for the pupils…

Tel Aviv sounds wonderful. It almost made me consider Palestine as somewhere to live, but I can't leave my parents, or Yosef's. I've seen how it has affected you and Itsik.

Manny has sent a letter for Moshe. I had to force him to write it. They don't seem to understand how important it is to keep in touch.

I hope this letter finds you all well.

You're always in our minds.

Miriam.

Moshe,

My mother is standing over me, nagging me to write, so I can't say too much about girls, just in case, but obviously I've kissed one. More than one, in fact.

The next time we meet, we'll have a race. I may not have taken as big a spurt as you, but I'm faster than I ever was. The teacher says I'm the quickest he's ever seen, and it's a pity that I'm a Jew and that I can't join the Hitlerjugend, not that I'd be seen dead in one of their stinking uniforms.

I went with Mama when she visited your grandparents. I said you'd asked me to say hello and your Bubbe cried. Your Sabba must have had a cold because he kept blowing his nose with his handkerchief.

There were riots here. The synagogue was destroyed but they managed to save a few things. I heard some of the younger men say that it was time to fight back but, when they saw me, they said if I told my papa they'd know I was a grass. So, I didn't.

Nothing much happened so they must have changed their minds.

I overheard Mama and Papa speaking about leaving, but they only talk about England and America. England sounds dull, but it is an island, so it might be all right. America sounds great, full of cowboys and Indians, just like in the films, but I'd rather go to Palestine, and we would see who's the fastest. Ha ha!

Got to go now. Mama says no more time, that she's going to Rosa's to give her the letters to send.

Remember the blood of the thumbs.

Manny

CHAPTER 172

'I'll just go straight from the police station to the train,' Miriam shouted. Yosef was fiddling with the car; checking tyre pressures, oil and water levels, and other jobs that he always seemed to be doing.

It was two days since she'd filled in the application for a travel permit. Yosef lifted his head out from under the bonnet of the car.

'I'll be back tomorrow evening,' she told him. 'I'll telephone the big house when I get there, and they can pass the message on to you. Don't forget to make the children do their homework, and the dinner is ready in the larder to heat up on the stove.'

'Yes, dear,' he said, trying to give her a peck on the cheek. 'I am capable of looking after them on my own.'

She dodged away from him, laughing.

'Get away from me, man. You're covered in oil. You'll get it all over my coat.'

She gently leaned over, avoiding contact with his clothes, and kissed him.

'I'll see you tomorrow,' she said, and walked briskly towards the driveway. A few seconds later, he watched her walking along Hamburger Chausee, and marvelled as always at what a wonderful woman she was. He turned back to his work on the car.

An hour later, he'd finished. He had just removed his overalls and was washing his hands at the sink when the door burst open.

'Miriam!' he cried out. 'What are you doing back?'

Her eyes were wide, and there were two glowing spots on her cheeks. She slammed the door behind her.

'These Goy are all Mamzers,' she shouted as she stormed through the kitchen to the sitting room. Yosef rushed to finish cleaning his hands before grabbing a towel and following her through, flinching at her unaccustomed curses.

'They said that it wasn't ready,' she fumed. '"There was nothing they could do", they said. I swear they were laughing at me.'

Her eyes began to well up, but they were tears of anger and frustration and, when he tried to console her, she pushed him away.

'How long are they going to torture us for?' she screamed at him.

Yosef looked out of the window, anxious that someone from the big house would overhear.

She saw his glance.

'I don't care if anyone hears me. I don't think I've ever been so angry.'

'We'll think of something,' Yosef said. 'Perhaps the General...'

He didn't finish his sentence.

'The General,' she shouted, 'what good can he do?'

'Well,' Yosef said, holding his hands up and shrugging, 'he might be able to have a word with Uwe Müller, the police chief.'

'Pah!' she hissed. 'We shouldn't have to rely on other people like this. We have as much right as anyone to go and see our parents.'

He knew she was wrong. They had few rights left, but he thought better of saying it.

'Sit down, and I'll get you a cup of coffee,' he said.

'You think that's the answer for everything. Calm down, have a cup of coffee, talk about it. It does no good. One day, I swear I'll do something and swing for it.'

The same thought had crossed his mind; he wouldn't put it past her if she did react and, in his mind, it would be justified, but it could only result in terrible trouble for her and their family.

'You know we're not in a position to kick up a fuss. None of us are. You've seen what has happened to others.'

Her shoulders slumped, and she started to sob. He saw the fight ebb out of her. She put a hand on the back of a chair to steady herself. He took her arm and guided her to the settee and sat her down. He sat beside her and took her in his arms.

For an hour, he stayed there, holding her, until the sobs died away, and she sat, hardly moving, staring into space. He wondered how long she would remain immobile, but she stirred and rose from the couch and crossed to the sink. He heard the tap running as she washed her face, and when she came out, she put on her apron.

Like an automaton, she moved around the kitchen, pulling out a mixing bowl and measuring the ingredients for a loaf, or a cake.

Leaving her to it, he slipped out of the back door, looking at his watch. He'd make sure he waylaid the children before they bounded into the house after school, to warn them that Miriam might be a little withdrawn or upset, and not to worry.

And he'd have a word with the General, despite Miriam's scepticism.

He almost collided with Frau Kästner, coming round the corner.

'Ah, Yosef,' she said. 'I was just coming to see you. I wonder if you could drop me at the church tonight, about six-thirty?'

'Of course,' he replied, a little flustered at her sudden appearance, 'that will be fine.'

'Thank you,' she said, 'and you'll pick me up at nine?'

'Yes, ma'am,' he said, hesitating, his mind still on Miriam, 'that won't be a problem.'

She moved to go back to the big house, then turned.

'Is everything all right, Yosef. You seem somewhat distracted, and I heard Miriam coming back a little while ago; she seemed upset, and I'd understood that she would be away until tomorrow.'

'Everything's fine, ma'am. Something came up and she couldn't go. I suspect she will serve breakfast tomorrow morning.'

'Oh, good. I'll be able to lie a little longer in bed. I hope it wasn't too much of an inconvenience that she couldn't make her trip.'

She turned and walked off. Although he liked Maria Kästner, Yosef shook his head.

She only sees other people's problems if they impinge on her own life.

~~o~~

By the time he'd talked to the children, warning them that their mama might be upset, and they'd all gone into the cottage, Miriam had almost completely recovered, and he marvelled at her resilience. After they'd eaten, he left to drop Frau Kästner at her meeting at the church, and he was pleased to hear Miriam and the children laughing as he closed the door.

It never bothered him that he often had to be out of an evening; these small inconveniencies came with the positions that he and Miriam held in the Kästner household; he'd been brought up with them. On his return, he saw the General sitting in the kitchen of the big house, so he rapped lightly on the door, and let himself in.

'Yosef, how are you?'

'Fine, sir. I just wondered if I might have a quick word.'

'Of course. Sit down.'

The General looked at Yosef.

'You don't seem fine. You look as if you have the weight of the world on your shoulders.'

Yosef gave a brief laugh.

'Nothing gets by you, sir,' he said with a sigh. He sat down.

'It's Miriam, sir. She tried to go and see her parents the other day, but they wouldn't let her on the train without a travel permit.'

'We need a permit now, to travel on a train?' Erich Kästner's look was one of incredulity.

'No, sir. Only Jews. The new rule came in this week, it seems.'

'I'm sorry. I should have realised. That's terrible. Can she not get a permit?'

'We went to the police station two days ago, and we applied for a permit for her to travel today. When she went to pick it up, it wasn't ready, so she couldn't go. Needless to say, she was distraught.'

'I'd imagine she was. I can't believe they'd do that.'

'I wondered, sir, if you could possibly have a word with Commander Müller. Perhaps it would make getting a permit more likely.'

The General considered the suggestion.

'I could do, Yosef, but it might just be easier if you took the car and drove Miriam to her parents' home. You could be back the same day, or even stay over.'

'Oh, sir. I don't know if I could do that. I mean, Frau Kästner or yourself might need the car.'

'Nonsense. If you can leave it until Monday, I'll make sure my staff car and my driver are available for Maria. Think nothing of it.'

'Thank you, sir. If you're sure.'

'I'll make sure to have a word with Uwe when I bump into him about it, for the next time, but he's a busy man so, on this occasion, this will work better.'

~~o~~

Miriam wasn't as delighted with the news as he'd thought she'd be.

'It's too much to ask, to borrow the car.'

'The General insisted. It's just for now. He's sure he can organise permits, but it might take a while.'

'I worry what Maria will say. She'll not be as disposed to help us as the General is.'

Yosef was inclined to agree with her, but he kept the thought to himself.

'Well, it's agreed, anyway. We can leave on Monday, after breakfast, but make sure we have the evening meal ready.'

CHAPTER 173

KIELER MORGENPOST

Saturday 3rd December 1938

VERORDNUNG ÜBER DEN EINSATZ DES JÜDISCHEN VERMÖGENS

The German government has issued the Decree on the Utilisation of Jewish Property. This builds on the Ordinance to Eliminate Jews from German Economic Life of 12th November 1938.

No Jew can own a business, immovable property, or stocks from 1st January 1939. The profits and securities from the sale of such assets must be deposited in a foreign exchange bank, and the authorities must be notified.

In addition, Jews are no longer free to sell jewels, precious metals and works of art. Under penalty of punishment, Jews must hand them over to state purchasing offices by March 31, 1939.

~~o~~

'How will this affect the school?'

'And the house we use to worship?'

Jakob was touched that his friends' first thoughts were for the children's education and the well-being of their place of worship, even before their own homes.

The role of de facto leader of the committee looking after the schooling of Jewish children in Kiel, and of the religious well-being of his people had, little by little, settled on Jakob Teubner, and he was working ever longer hours trying to juggle all these things, especially as he still worked part time in an Aryan tailor's, a job he'd held since he'd given up his own small establishment a few months previously.

'The authorities have been in touch. The house we are using as the school and one house next door have been acquired by the state. It's the house Father Phillip's soup kitchen was in. They will be used for Jews who have been made homeless. So far, they haven't mentioned number fifteen.'

There was a palpable relief that the makeshift synagogue was unaffected.

'So, we're not being evicted?' Isaac said.

'Surprisingly not. It seems to suit the government to have all things Jewish in the one place. However, we do have to pay rent for the buildings.'

'How kind of them.'

'They did make it sound as if they were doing us a great favour. The Goy I dealt with had the cheek to look magnanimous.'

They all laughed.

'Just out of interest, how much did the current owners receive for the properties?' Isaac asked.

'Let's just say it was well below the market value,' Jakob replied. 'And the rent is well above what an Aryan would pay.'

'At least Nathan Dreilich and Nossen Deller have been released,' one of the other younger Jews said. 'That's a blessing.'

'Yes,' Jakob said, 'but it cost the community a pretty penny, and they spent a couple of months in the camp.'

'Nathan was a bit on the heavy side when he went in,' one of the men joked. 'He came out like a beanpole. It's one way of losing weight, I suppose.'

It provoked a laugh or two, but it quickly withered.

'They said it was tough,' Jakob said. 'Not much food, the work was back-breaking, and the bunks, if you could call them that, were terrible. Sanitation was an open ditch with a seat over it.'

He paused, but the listening men were silent. A few had bowed their heads. Others closed their eyes as Jakob continued.

'There were a lot of deaths too, they said. Every day, at least one poor soul gave up, Nossen told me. They just dragged them out and threw them on a truck. He said it was the most heartless thing he's ever seen. And beatings. The guards hit them with sticks for even the most minor of infringements.'

'Oy vey, what is coming next?' one of the younger men asked.

KIELER MORGENPOST

Monday 5th December 1938

JEWS BANNED FROM DRIVING

Jews are no longer permitted to have their own car or hold a driver's licence. Any Jew found contravening these new rules will be punished severely.

"Anyone buying a car from a Jew is advised to have it serviced by a trained mechanic", a Government spokesman said. "We cannot rule out the possibility of mechanical sabotage of the vehicles that are expected to flood the market from their former owners".

For those who foresee the chance to purchase a car at a knock-down price, it is expected that the government will heavily tax any car that is sold well below its market value.

'Yosef, I'm sorry. I didn't think for one moment that they would ever take your licence away.'

Yosef glanced at the newspaper headline. He'd never seen the General so livid.

'Sir, I would quite understand if my services were no longer required.'

'And what makes you think you would no longer be of use to me?' the General asked.

'Well, sir. I am employed as your driver.'

'I know it will be an inconvenience, but you have other jobs. You maintain the house and the car, and you do most of the gardening, except for the occasional foray by Frau Kästner into growing vegetables to feed the nation, for which she sacrifices one afternoon a fortnight, as far as I can tell.'

'But, sir, how will Frau Kästner get about?'

582

'Well, until we get hold of another driver, or I can get an exemption for you, I will take her wherever she wants to go, or my army driver can do the odd trip where I can't get away. And there are taxis, if all else fails.'

Yosef blanched.

It pained him to think how Frau Kästner would react if she were made to take a taxi.

'Thank you, sir. But at least cut my salary to pay for a new driver. It would make me feel better.'

'Yosef, I'll not hear any more of this.'

Yosef could see that the General was becoming exasperated.

'Sorry, sir, I didn't mean to cause trouble. I just feel bad that I'm not able to do my normal duties, and that I'll still be getting paid for them.'

The General sighed.

'It's through no fault of your own and, if I were to dismiss you, or cut your wages, imagine how hypocritical I would feel after railing against this government's policies.'

'Yes, sir. I see.'

'Well, that's the end of it. Don't worry, I'll find some extra work for you to do.'

Yosef shifted uncomfortably.

'I know,' the General said, beaming. 'I'll get you to build a summer house. Maria has always said it would be nice. Down by the lake.'

'Yes, sir, but it's winter.'

'I know, Yosef, I know. But it will be ready in time for spring.'

'Thank you, sir. Will that be all?'

'No. We have another problem. Until I can have a word with the authorities and make sure you can drive, you won't be able to take Miriam to see her parents.'

'Don't think about that, sir. That's the least of the worries.'

'It's not, Yosef. I'm sure Miriam is desperate to see her parents. Leave it with me, and I'll see what I can do.'

~~o~~

'I tried. I really did.'

Yosef could see that Miriam wasn't impressed.

'I won't accept charity,' she said, her eyes cold and angry. 'We've always stood on our own feet. Anything we've had from the Kästners has been earned by hard work.'

'Listen, woman, for once. He has some projects that he and Frau Kästner have been thinking about for a while, and now I'll have time to do them.'

She gave him a scathing look.

'Like what?'

'A summer house, down by the lake, to start with.'

'I've heard the mistress mention it a few times,' she conceded. 'She did say that it would be nice.'

'Well, there you go. I'll get started on it immediately.'

'It's winter, you idiot. Not even Christmas yet.'

'He wants it ready by spring. It won't go up in a week or two, if it's going to be done right, but it might be better to start laying a foundation base after the festive season is over.'

Miriam shook her head, but the anger he'd seen in her face had subsided and Yosef hoped that she would see the benefits of the General's clever solution. He just wasn't convinced Maria Kästner would see it that way.

'It does mean we can't go to Altona though,' Yosef said, putting the mistress to the back of his mind.

'I realise that,' she said, giving him another scathing look. 'I'll just have to keep applying for a permit. Or perhaps we should try and persuade them to come and live here. We have room.'

Yosef hadn't considered that option. He liked Miriam's family, but he wasn't sure he was ready to have them move in.

CHAPTER 174

Memo: Geh.KdoS. ABW 06/12/38 CAC0695.1

For Attention Only: All senior executive officers, Abwehr.

From: Vice Admiral Wilhelm Canaris, Chef der Abwehr.

The German Reich has agreed to a non-aggression pact with the
Republic of France. It was signed in Paris by the French
Foreign Minister Georges Bonnet and the German Foreign Minister
Joachim von Ribbentrop [END]

~~o~~

'Canaris.'

'Kästner.'

'Can I offer you a drink?'

'A small one, my friend. How are you?'

'Worried. I have two sons who are soldiers, with war approaching fast, and my Jewish staff can't leave the country for another ten months.'

'Tell them to go to Palestine. It's their best option, I'd say.'

'They won't hear of it. At least, Miriam won't. Yosef might be coming round to the idea.'

'So, you don't hold much hope for this pact with France?'

'Not really. Do you?'

'No. It's all about strategy and convenience. A sop to foreign powers, Britain included. It makes no difference in the long term.'

'And how are you, Canaris?'

'I'm doing well, but I'm run off my feet. With so much going on, it's difficult to keep track of everything. Fortunately, they all like to talk to each other, and about each other. Incessantly. And we have ears in strategic places. You'd be surprised at all the subterfuge and back-stabbing that goes on amongst the elite.'

The General laughed.

'It's not funny,' the admiral said. 'They seem to be trying to outdo each other with plans designed only to impress the Führer. There are very few rational thinkers left with any influence.'

'We're in the hands of the rabid fanatics then.'

'I'm afraid so. And it makes war almost inevitable.'

~~o~~

The General knocked on the door of the cottage. When Ruth opened it, he smiled and asked to speak to her father.

'I'm going to a meeting on the other side of Hamburg on Wednesday,' he said, when Yosef appeared. 'I'll be staying overnight. I can drop yourself and Miriam off on the way and pick you up the next day.'

'I'm sure that would be suitable, sir. The children can stay with my parents overnight.'

'That's settled then. We'll leave by nine, sharp. My meeting starts at 1230 hours.'

'Are we travelling in your staff car, sir?'

'No, they're not keen on us using it for civilians. Small journeys, yes, but not for the likes of that. No, we'll take our car.'

'But, sir. I can't drive.'

'No, but you'll find that I can,' the General said, laughing.

~~o~~

[08/12/1938 Thursday]

'Were you not taking a risk letting Yosef drive the car?'

'Yosef didn't drive,' the General said, his mind only half on his wife's question. 'I did.'

'So, now you're driving someone about who is, in point of fact, employed to drive you?'

'Well, I suppose it sounds silly when you say it like that, but the circumstances were exceptional. I'm hoping to get Yosef's licence reinstated shortly.'

'Why didn't your Wehrmacht driver take you? I would have thought if it had been army business, that would have been the logical choice.'

The General missed the tone of disapproval in her voice.

'It might have been, but I wanted to drop the Nussbaums off at Miriam's parents, and the army can be a little funny about things like that.'

'Because they're Jews?'

'No,' the General said, startled at the thought. He wondered if that had perhaps been at the back of his mind. Then he discounted it.

'No,' he repeated, 'just civilians.'

'You seem quite happy to have me ferried about in it, while we don't have a driver.'

'That's different. The odd local run isn't an issue. This was to Hamburg.'

'And if I want to visit the countess, or my mother?'

'Well, there are taxis, and you could travel by train to your mother's.'

'Well, really. You'll take the Nussbaums to Hamburg, but you won't take me to my mother's. And you want me to travel by taxi?'

The General sighed. He realised that he'd made an error, not giving the conversation his full attention.

'Darling Maria. A taxi is a perfectly acceptable way of getting around. If you want to go to your mother's, I'll gladly drive you there. Just tell me when.'

'This weekend, then. I've not seen her for weeks.'

He cursed. A weekend with the old trout wasn't his idea of fun, and he usually managed to get out of it, more often than not.

'And what will the countess think if I turn up in a taxi? I'll just have to wait until we get a new driver.'

He promised he'd start the search for someone to drive her around and allowed himself another sigh.

I should have foreseen this, he thought.

He didn't mind. It had been worth it, just to see the joy on Miriam's face when he dropped them off at her parents' home in Altona.

~~o~~

On the drive back, Yosef had told the General that he'd visited the consulate again, while he was in Hamburg.

'They told me the embassy in Berlin were processing applications a few hundred below the 29,000 mark, sir.'

By the General's reckoning, they were handling an additional thousand a month.
'That's nine months instead of a year,' he said.
'That's how I saw it too, sir.'
He'd felt the weight of worry lift a little.

CHAPTER 175

[12/12/1938 Monday]

KIELER JÜDISCHES FREIHEITSNACHRICHTENBLATT

Volume 72

19th of Kislev, 5699

THE JEWS: ONLY THE STATE SHOULD BENEFIT

Hermann Göring, in a speech made on the 10th of December, declared that the financial benefits arising from the exclusion of the Jews from German Society belongs exclusively to the state. The clarification of the legal basis for the laws passed in November and December was issued to prevent individuals or party organisations from profiting from these Government policies.

NOT ONLY JEWS: GYPSIES TARGETTED TOO

Two days earlier, Heinrich Himmler issued a decree to combat what he called the Gypsy Plague.

The decree centralises the Government's official response to the "Gypsy Question" and defines Gypsies as an inferior race. The Kriminalpolizei have been tasked with establishing a nationwide database, identifying all Gypsies residing in the Greater German Reich. It cites Dr. Robert Ritter's Research Institute for Racial Hygiene and Population Biology as the definitive authority in determining membership of the Gypsy race.

FATE OF KIEL SYNAGOGUE

The KJF has learned that the shell of the Synagogue has been the subject of a compulsory purchased order by the Kiel City Council for 20,000 RM. Despite the destruction of the interior, there was no substantial damage to the building, which was valued at 190,800 RM for insurance purposes.

KINDERTRANSPORT - A CHILD DIASPORA

Great Britain has begun admitting child refugees, primarily Jewish, from the Greater German Reich. It is expected that between 9,000 and 10,000 will be admitted over the next six months.

~~o~~

'Have a look at this.'

Yosef handed Miriam the Jewish newspaper.

'Pah,' she said, 'that's no surprise; we've known for ages that the state wants to rob us of everything we own. They're just saying it openly now, and the gypsies have always had a hard time too. As for the synagogue…'

'No, I didn't mean that. Look at this Kindertransport thing. We could get the children to England now, and we could join them later.'

'Yosef!' she said, frowning. 'How can you even think that?'

He began to doubt the wisdom of mentioning it.

'We should talk it through first before you completely rule it out.'

'There's nothing to talk about. I will not be separated from my children. What if we don't get out? We wouldn't see them for years.'

'At least they'd be safe. What if I'm taken, or both of us?'

'You'd consider sending them to complete strangers, in a foreign country, where they can't speak the language?'

He knew he was in dangerous territory, but something made him push her.

'It would only be for nine months. Then we could join them. By that time, they would both have learned English. And we could write to them, regularly.'

Miriam's shoulders slumped. A tear ran down her cheek. He took her in his arms, feeling awful.

'I just can't,' she said.

'I know,' he said, 'We'll say no more about it. I had to ask.'

~~o~~

Memo: Geh.KdoS. ABW 13/12/38 CAC0703.1

For Attention Only: All senior executive officers, Abwehr.

From: Vice Admiral Wilhelm Canaris, Chef der Abwehr.

SS authorities have opened the Neuengamme concentration camp near Hamburg.

For your information only. No action required. [END]

~~o~~

[23/12/1938 Friday]

The first day Manny left some of his dinner at the side of his plate, Miriam thought nothing of it; perhaps he was a little under the weather. When it happened the next day, too, she began to worry.

Thoughts of him being bullied on his way to school or worse still, being in trouble with the authorities, ran through her mind.

The strange thing was, he was eating food that she knew he didn't like but leaving some of his favourites.

'Are you feeling all right?' she asked him, lifting the third uncleared plate in a row.

They were on their own. Ruth was eating at the big house with Antje, as she did from time to time; they'd remained the closest of friends despite being separated for most of the week, and both were looking forward to the Christmas holidays. Yosef was also over at the big house, attempting to fix a leak in one of the water pipes. He was a good handyman, and the Kästners rarely needed to employ a tradesman, and then only for major repairs or building works.

'I can't eat that,' he said. 'It's not kosher.'

She stopped and put the plate down on the table.

His words hurt, but they also left her with a sense of relief.

589

He isn't in trouble.

'You've always eaten this,' she said. 'I know we're not as strict as we should be, but we've tried to adapt to our life here with the Kästners. We eat nothing that isn't kosher at Passover, and Rosh Hashanah, and we always fast on Yom Kippur.

'My teacher says it's not good enough to be kosher just on holy days.'

She put her hand on his shoulder.

'Your teacher is right. We should be more observant. Perhaps we haven't tried hard enough, but few Jews in Germany stick rigidly to kosher rules.'

'I'm going to. Even if it means giving up things I like.'

'That's good, Manny,' she said, smiling at his stubborn resolve. 'I'll speak to your father. Perhaps we could try a little harder.'

~~o~~

'Well, well,' Yosef said, when Miriam told him, sitting in front of the fire, after Manny had gone to bed. 'In a way it's quite admirable.'

'I know. I can't be cross with him, although I don't know why he suddenly wants to do this. He never came home from lessons at the synagogue saying things like this.

'Herr Joselewicz has taken over the religious studies in both the upper and lower schools,' Yosef said. 'He's originally from Poland; he's deeply passionate about Judaism, and his knowledge is as good as any, even Jakob, and the rabbi, when he was here. The boys seem to like him.'

Miriam let out a hollow laugh.

'The Ostjuden, teaching our children. It's ironic; maybe they were right all along to not become too cosy with the Germans. I mean, what has it done for us?'

Yosef winced but it was hard to argue against. Apart from the General, and a few of his friends, he couldn't think of a single Gentile who would be prepared to lift a finger to help him or his family. And perhaps she was right that the acceptance of Jewish people as ordinary Germans seemed to have been largely superficial.

'Did Manny say anything else?'

'Yes. If they're going to treat him like a Jew, he was sure as hell going to act like one.'

Yosef bowed his head.

Pride and shame battled inside his chest; pride for his son's stance and his words, even if they may have been somebody else's, and shame at his own capitulation to a way of life that would be alien to most Ostjuden.

'We must do it with him,' he said.

'I know.'

~~o~~

When Ruth ran across from the big house, her parents were still up; often, these days, they were in bed before her.

'Ruth, we're going to be much stricter about what we eat from now on,' her mother said, after she'd sat down.

Her father told her of Manny's new-found adherence to stricter kosher rules.

'We've decided to support him,' he said, 'and the easiest way is for us all to do the same. It will mean sacrificing some of the things we all like, but in these times, we feel that Manny is right. It's something we can do to show they're not intimidating us.'

'I'm all right with that,' Ruth said, 'but if I eat at the Kästners' house, or in a café with friends...'

'Yes, we don't have a problem with that,' Yosef said. 'It just makes it easier for your mama to cook if we all eat the same.'

'Thank you, lovely,' Miriam said, smiling at her daughter. 'It will mean a lot to Manny.'

Ruth kissed both her parents on the cheek and climbed the stairs to her bedroom.

There were no kosher cafés in Kiel now, or in Germany. Occasionally, Rebeka, Antje and Ruth would go out on a Saturday to do a little shopping and have lunch. The first time they'd gone, Miriam had shed a few tears.

'They're so grown-up now, just look at them,' she'd said to Yosef, arms folded across her chest, as the three young ladies walked down Hamburger Chaussee.

'I worry about them,' Yosef had replied, frowning. 'You never know these days. I'm glad Antje is with them.'

Unlike Jewish girls over fifteen, young Aryan women weren't required to carry Kennkarte yet but while it was possible that the three girls would be stopped, it was unlikely; Kiel was a relatively small city, and the General and his family were well known. While they were with Antje, it was unlikely that Ruth and Rebeka would be challenged to show their identification, but on their own it was a different story, and they could easily be the target of abuse, violence, or arrest.

1939

'We shall only talk of peace when we have won the war. The Jewish capitalist world will not survive the twentieth century.'

Adolf Hitler.

CHAPTER 176

Afula, 30th December 1938

Dear Miriam,

I'm sorry it's taken me so long to write. I have some news and I wanted to make sure everything was all right before I told you. You and Rosa mustn't laugh. Promise!

All right, here's the thing. I'm pregnant. It was in Tel Aviv. I'm due on the 21st of July. I had a tiny little bleed at the start of December but it's fine now; that's why I held off until now to tell you both.

I'm heartbroken about the synagogue. I loved that old place. I can't believe they could just destroy it like that and then make the Jewish community pay. Our hearts go out to those who were injured, and to those who have been imprisoned.

It is time for you to get out, anywhere, both you and Rosa, before it gets worse. Itsik and I will help you both if you come here, although I don't know what Itsik's parents will do without you.

No matter what you say, you'll be rewarded in heaven, if not on earth, for what you do for them. I dread hearing that something has happened to them, and knowing you are there makes such a difference.

It feels safer here, but the Arab revolt seems to have escalated a little. The British seem to be more or less in control, though, and there are now more Jewish militia who protect the settlements, so that is a comfort.

Our shops are doing exceptionally well. Itsik and Abel say that they could easily open one in Tel Aviv if they had the right person, so tell Yosef that there's a position here for him if he came out, probably with some help from the man who works with Abel until he finds his feet. I've said the same to Rosa about Emil. Maybe they could open two more shops if you both decide to come.

Tell Yosef to thank the General for trying to help Itsik's parents. He was annoyed that the General had asked Oskar von Friedeburg to help, but I'm not. I'm desperate to do anything. Itsik is just feeling bad because he made a promise not to be in touch with Oskar again, but that's just silly pride; it wasn't as if it was Itsik himself who asked. Men, feh.

It's so sad about Hanne Weidmann and her family. I do remember her. She was a rather quiet, serious girl, wasn't she?

Moshe got his letter from Manny. I heard him laughing. He wouldn't let me see it or watch him writing his. I think they are talking about girls. That's the next worry! You can't help but smile at them though.

Please keep writing. It's a lifeline for me.

All my love, your friend,

Esther.

~~o~~

Watching Miriam's face, Rosa couldn't help grinning while her friend read Esther's letter.

She'd been itching to tell her about Esther's pregnancy from the moment Miriam had arrived but had to fight to keep any signs of excitement from her face when she handed her the letter, feeling that the news should come from Esther herself.

'Well,' she said, as Miriam finished reading. 'It's wonderful, isn't it?'

Miriam looked up. There were tears in her eyes.

'It's the best news I've had in ages,' she said, smiling.

'She seems a bit embarrassed. Imagine telling us it happened in Tel Aviv. What a scandal!' Rosa rolled her eyes, the lines at the corners crinkling in amusement.

'It's like a honeymoon baby. She would know we could work it out. She just wanted to get it in first.'

They were both laughing and, before they knew it, they were in each other's arms, hugging tightly, tears of joy streaming down their faces.

'It's good to have something to smile about,' Rosa said, almost forgetting the underlying despair.

For a while, neither woman said anything, allowing the thought of a new brother or sister for Moshe and Shoshana to warm their souls.

It was Miriam who broke the spell.

'I see that we've been banned from being nurses, or dentists.'

Rosa gave a hollow laugh.

'Yes, or vets. I don't think I know of any Jewish vets.'

'There soon won't be any jobs our children can do when they leave school,' Miriam said.

'I know. We had such plans for them too. Lawyers, doctors, accountants, teachers. Now there's nothing for them.'

'Yosef suggested sending the children to England, on this Kindertransport scheme that he'd learned of.'

'I heard about it,' Rosa said. 'We talked it over too.'

'I just couldn't send them away, even if it's only for a few months.'

'We felt the same. Anyhow, it seems to be mostly for children who have no parents, or whose parents are incarcerated, or are somehow unable to cope because of their circumstances.'

Miriam glanced at her friend.

'Don't look at me like that,' Rosa said. 'Emil looked into it, just in case. We didn't seriously consider it.'

'Sorry, I was just surprised, that's all. Still, that makes me feel better. I was fearful that I'd made the wrong decision.'

'I don't think you have, honey. At the end of the day, Ruth and Manny are better off with you, no matter what. And it's only until October, then you can all go.'

'What about you?'

'Emil applied for us to go. He insisted on America. He said...' Rosa stopped.

'What?'

'I'm sorry, I shouldn't have said. He was worried that England might be invaded if war starts; said we would be no better off there.'

'Oh, God, I didn't even think of that. We would be able to get to Canada, or somewhere else, if that happened.'

'Exactly. That's what I told Emil.' The relief in Rosa's voice was palpable. She chided herself for being so tactless.

'How long do you have to wait?'

'Three or four months after you and Yosef leave, at least.'

'There will be no one left at this rate. Isaac Stern and his family left a month ago.'

'I know. What did you think of Itsik's offer?'

'It was more than kind of him, but I can't see Yosef as a shopkeeper and anyway, I don't want him to change his mind, so I'm not going to tell him. Please don't say anything, Rosa.'

595

'I won't. I'm not going to tell Emil either. He wouldn't go anyway; he hates the idea of Palestine even more than me, but it's one less thing for him to worry about.'

'That's settled then.' Miriam got up from the chair.

'It's that time again,' she said.

Rosa looked at the clock.

'I gave Fischel a key. If I'm out, he can let himself in. He's old enough.'

'I should give Manny one. I'd be quite happy leaving him for a while. He's quite sensible, really. But for now, I'll need to go. If I'm not there, he'll go to the Kästner house, and I don't like him to be a nuisance.'

'See you soon, honey,' Rosa said, giving Miriam another hug.

'Yes, on Shabbat, God willing.' She waved as she walked down the path, heading for home.

CHAPTER 177

Memo: Geh.KdoS. ABW 24/01/39 CAC0710.1

For Attention Only: All senior executive officers, Abwehr.

From: Vice Admiral Wilhelm Canaris, Chef der Abwehr.

Hermann Göring has authorised Reinhard Heydrich, Security Police and SD Chief, to coordinate solutions for the forced emigration of Jews from the Greater German Reich. The Central Office for Jewish Emigration has been established in Berlin. [END]

~~o~~

[24/01/1939 Tuesday]

'Right, gentlemen, let's get started.'

Captain Bauer and Chief Petty Officer Neuer had moved the General's desk into the centre of the office and arranged six chairs around it.

Admiral Canaris, who'd asked for the meeting and was now calling it to order, sat at the head of the makeshift table. Around it, in a clockwise direction, he was joined by General Kästner, Vizeadmiral Conrad Albrecht, Commander of the Baltic Sea fleet stationed in Kiel, and Admirals von Exner and Göpfert of the Naval Command.

'Von Exner oversees the commissioning of new naval vessels in Kiel, and Göpfert manages the repairs and refits of naval ships in the Kiel yards,' the General had told Admiral Canaris, just before everyone arrived.

The General indicated that Captain Bauer should take up the remaining seat and asked him to keep minutes.

'General Kästner and I have gathered you here today to pass on some critical information,' Admiral Canaris said, opening the meeting. 'Advance warning, shall we say, of developments that will completely alter the Baltic Naval Command for the foreseeable future.'

A few of the men around the table leaned forward, their interest pricked.

'According to our sources,' Canaris continued, 'the Führer has ordered a massive five-year naval expansion programme of the German fleet capable of defeating the Royal Navy by 1944. The Kriegsmarine, for the first time, is to be given top priority on the allocation of economic resources.'

He paused for a second, then, in an almost conspiratorial tone, he carried on speaking.

'At the present time,' he said, 'it is being referred to as Plan Z, but this could change. It is expected to be announced in the next three to four days.'

He looked over at the General, who got up and walked to the window and nodded at the cranes on the opposite shore.

'Once it is announced,' he said, 'we think there will be a scramble by the yards to expand, in order to fulfil the large numbers of lucrative orders that are to be awarded during the next few years.'

The Kriegsmarine men all nodded, glancing at each other.

'We think that the sudden demand for ships will tempt these companies to maximise their profits,' the General continued, 'at the expense of the exchequer, and we'd like to propose plans to counteract any avarice on the part of our fine industrialists.'

The men round the table smiled. They understood that the navy was completely reliant on the wealthy companies who built the ships, tanks, and planes for the German military, but they'd all seen first-hand the evidence of the financial rewards that could be made from government contracts.

'Before the plan becomes common knowledge,' Canaris said, taking up the thread of the discourse again, 'we feel that the navy, by acquiring nominal leases for vital areas of land on the shorefront and where access to the transport network is critical, can exert some pressure on these companies to work with more efficiency and economy than they might otherwise have done.'

Admiral Canaris turned to the General.

'General Kästner will fill you in on how we can accomplish this.'

'We have close relations with the city authorities,' the General said, 'thanks largely to Captain Bauer's efforts, so we can meet with their key officials immediately.'

Vizeadmiral Conrad Albrecht frowned.

'I can see why you'd want us to do this, but can it be done in time?'

'We have already arranged for us to visit the Rathaus this morning,' the General said. 'That's why I asked you to keep your diary free, sir.'

'What do you require from us?' Admiral Göpfert asked.

'You're here to support Vizeadmiral Albrecht. These meetings, if successful, will generate a mass of administrative tasks. Because we need to keep the number of people involved to a minimum, we need you to personally supervise a few key personnel who you trust to be completely discreet, until the new plan is announced, at least.'

Both the younger admirals nodded.

'Now,' said the General, rolling out a plan of the existing boatyards and the surrounding areas, 'these are the zones we have marked out as being critical.'

He pointed to sections of foreshore adjacent to the already sizeable fabrication yards, towards the mouth of Kieler Hafen.

'These are the most critical areas. If we manage to get these, we can rent them back to the shipyards to force them to keep their profits at a reasonable level. We also need to control the supply of support services, so here, here, and here,' the General said, pointing to areas inland of the proposed new developments, 'we need to get hold of enough land to build oil storage tanks and warehouses. The beauty of this scheme is that, because the Kriegsmarine's victualling facilities at Wik are already under pressure, we can present these acquisitions as an expansion of our current supply facilities, and if it just so happens that we have overestimated our requirements and have tied up the land that the shipyards need, so be it.'

Conrad Albrecht smiled.

'The navy has always had to deal with these people; we do need them to build our ships, but I've always found myself checking my pockets after meeting with them, to make sure that I still have any loose change left. If this goes a little way to redressing that, I'm all for it.'

Admiral Canaris stood, and the others followed suit, shaking hands as they stepped away from the table. Captain Bauer organised transport for the General, the Vizeadmiral and himself, and the two junior admirals left to set up a new office to deal with the administration of the scheme.

'And yourself, Admiral?' Conrad Albrecht asked.

'I'm off to Wilhelmshaven,' Canaris told him. 'We have similar plans there, although our relationship with the local authorities isn't quite as close as they are here. I'm going there for some preliminary talks, to see if we can do something similar there.'

He patted the General on the arm as he left.

'I'll be in touch,' he said.

'Now gentlemen, let's head for the Rathaus,' the General said, turning to Admiral Albrecht and Captain Heinz. 'Our first meeting is with Jürgen Hoffmann, the mayor.'

~~o~~

[27/01/1939 Friday]

By the time the five-year plan was announced in Berlin by Hermann Göring, the Kriegsmarine had tied up all the leases they'd targeted and, with the city council's help, had gained additional land adjacent to those areas from private landowners with the help of a couple of compulsory purchase orders issued by Kiel's city council.

Captain Bauer had rushed round, cajoling officials to expedite his demands, scurrying back and forth to Naval Headquarters with paperwork for von Exner's and Göpfert's teams to work on. It helped immeasurably that he was a popular and well-respected figure in the corridors of the Rathaus, and more than once, his personal intervention prevented the negotiations from stalling.

The General's long relationship with the mayor helped, as did Jürgen Hoffmann's desire to be courted by the naval authorities, pandering to his ego, leaving him open to most of their requests.

The day after the plan had been announced, a meeting was scheduled between the three main Kiel shipyards and the Kriegsmarine. General Kästner was sure that the three rich industrialists would huff and puff before conceding to the navy's demands.

In his office, he offered his captain a whisky.

'Heinz,' he said, 'I know you've sometimes wondered why you were asked to spend so much of your time at the Rathaus. Well, today, I hope you understand how important your part in this process was.'

'Yes, sir. I do. And thank you.'

'Not at all. You deserve it. I would recommend you for a medal, but the Abwehr disapproves of such ostentation.'

The captain laughed.

'If I may ask one question, sir?'

'By all means, Captain. Fire away.'

'Well, sir, how did you know something like this would happen, when you sent me to work with these people at the Rathaus?'

'Ha,' the General said. 'I didn't know that this would come up, but I suspected that, at some point, it would be useful to be on intimate terms with the city fathers. We're like bookmakers, spreading our bets.'

Frau Müller frowned. She left.

Hearing her muttering on the way out, Erich Kästner smiled.

She's right, he thought. *That sort of thing would never have happened in Admiral von Heutschler's day.*

CHAPTER 178

[30/01/1939 Monday]

Adolf Hitler's speech was over two hours long, but in a small room high up in the Kleiner Kuhberg building that housed the school, Yosef Nussbaum and Jakob Teubner stood with the other members of the unofficial Jewish self-help group and listened to the crackle of the radio as it spewed out Adolf Hitler's words.

They looked at each other as the German leader, speaking from the balcony of the Reichstag building, finished eulogising the party, and its extraordinary achievements.

~~o~~

In his office, the General also listened, trying not to show his distaste as the rising, grating howl of the German leader's voice marked a shift in the tone of the speech. He and Captain Bauer sat in horrified fascination as the chancellor blamed the Jews for every ill that had been heaped on the German people; losing the Great War, the hyperinflation of the early thirties and the mass unemployment and economic stagnation that followed.

Frau Müller, ostensibly delivering a document she'd been typing for the General, lingered to listen, frozen by the Führer's hypnotic words. The General looked at her face; her expression reminded him of the classical paintings of Christ's women gazing up at him on the cross, and he swallowed the bile that rose in the back of his throat.

~~o~~

Since 1933, and the devastating fire that destroyed the Reichstag, the German parliament had moved across the square to the Kroll Opera House.

At the corner of the square, in front of the 'new' Reichstag building, Admiral Canaris listened to the Führer's words being relayed by loudspeaker to the massed crowd, and watched them being whipped to a frenzy by the man's sheer force of will, each of their right arms outstretched, as if trying to reach out and touch the Führer inside, to receive a little of the power that emanated from the building or, perhaps, give a little of their strength to their leader.

'...The Jewish people were only intended by God to live as parasites on the body and productive work of other races,' the Führer intoned, softly now, as if he wanted the crowd to lean forward towards him, to catch his words.

Then his voice rose again.

'Judaism will have to adapt itself to steadfast productive activities, as do the people of other nations or, sooner or later, it will succumb to a crisis of unimaginable proportions.'

It's almost sexual in its power, Canaris thought. *All that is left is the climax.*

'Today, I must be a prophet again. If international financial Jewry, both inside and outside Europe, should succeed in plunging the people of the world into war again, then the result will not be the Bolshevization of the earth and thus the victory of Judaism, but the annihilation of the Jewish race in Europe!'

Silence fell for a brief second of time, then the crowd's roar burst around him.

Canaris watched for a second then turned away from the rapturous throng, pushing past the stragglers at the edge to return to his office.

~~o~~

Three hundred kilometres away, Frau Müller sighed, her face still effused with the religious fervour of the NSDAP faithful. She stood transfixed until the General coughed, breaking the spell.

'Thank you, Frau Müller. You enjoyed the Führer's speech?'

'Yes, sir. Don't you just think he's marvellous, sir. So inspiring. I don't know where we'd be without him.'

'I often wonder that myself, Frau Müller,' the General said.

Captain Bauer smiled but the secretary, still in a trance, didn't notice.

'That, my young friend, is the German people,' the General said, nodding in the direction of the outer office, and Frau Müller.

The captain looked embarrassed.

'I was taken in by him, too, sir; you can't blame her.'

'No. This is new. Did you read *Mein Kampf*?'

The captain blushed.

'I started it, sir, but I didn't get far. To be honest, I found it dull to read.'

'Read it, and you'll know why I wasn't surprised by what we've just heard. As for Frau Müller, if she and sixty-five million other Germans can't see the evil in that speech, we're condemned as a people.'

The young captain paled.

'How, sir?'

'By history, Heinz. We'll be condemned by history.'

'But why, sir. Is it not all rhetoric? He can't annihilate all these people.'

The General leaned over, opened a drawer, and pulled out a sheet of paper. It was a memo; the one informing the General of Heydrich's new role in coordinating the forced emigration of Jews.

'Have you seen this,' he asked.

The remaining colour in the captain's face drained as he read the memo.

'No. This means...'

'He might not destroy them, but he's going to make sure there are no Jews left in Germany. Let's only hope they'll all end up somewhere they're welcome.'

~~o~~

Across the city, Jakob Teubner turned to Yosef.

'Isaac did the right thing,' he said.

They both smiled, remembering the bittersweet farewells as Isaac and his family headed for the train, on the first leg of their journey to Palestine. On the cold, mid-December morning, Isaac had looked sick, and Yosef and Jakob had joked that it could have been fear, or perhaps just the weight of the fortune in his gut.

'It's time to leave,' Jakob said, grim-faced.

Yosef nodded.

'Yes. All of us.'

~~o~~

[09/02/1939 Thursday]

KIELER JÜDISCHES FREIHEITSNACHRICHTENBLATT

Volume 73

20th of Sh'vat, 5699

CHILD REFUGEE BILL DEFEATED IN US SENATE

A bill to admit Jewish child refugees to the United States was defeated by a committee in the summer of 1939. The KJF has only recently learned of the attempt by Senator Robert Wagner of New York and Representative Edith Rogers of Massachusetts to introduce the bill to permit the entry of 20,000 refugee children, ages 14 and under, from the Greater German Reich into the United States over the course of two years (1939 and 1940). The children would have been granted entry without reference to the quota system.

CHAPTER 179

[13/02/1939 Sunday]

25th January

Dearest Esther,

What amazing news! B'sha'ah Tovah. It's wonderful that you are pregnant. Rosa and I had a laugh about Tel Aviv.

When I told Yosef that you were expecting, he was pleased for you all, but not as delighted as I am. So, he's a man; how could he understand? When he mentioned it to some of the other men, one of them said it was an auspicious omen; a Kiel Jew being born in Palestine! We are both hoping and praying that everything will go well. What are the medical facilities like out there? Will the women you are friendly with help you?

I only hope that the efforts to get Itsik's parents out to Palestine bear fruit. I spoke to them yesterday, and they are delighted about your news, but sad that they aren't there to help. Oskar von Friedeburg has been trying his best, I hear, but with no success so far, I'm afraid.

The situation is getting worse – Jews are now prohibited from working as nurses, vets, or dentists.

And Jews cannot drive now. Yosef's licence has been revoked, but the General is keeping him on to do some extra work around the house and garden.

An office for Jewish emigration has been established in Berlin but Yosef says that it isn't necessarily a good thing. I hoped (in a small way) that it might speed up our application, but he says it's all about sending immigrant Jews back to where they came from, and it may not be first generation immigrants either, so perhaps more of us are at risk than we think. God forbid we end up in Poland or Russia! Our families have been German for untold generations.

We're not going to panic yet because October isn't too far away. Tell Itsik and Abel to look out for Isaac Stern; he had a grocer's shop in Kiel. You'll remember his wife, Liba. They left to go to Palestine, and I'm sure that they are intending to settle in Haifa.

The children are fine. Ruth is so grown up now, you would hardly recognise her or Rebeka. They are young women now. And Manny has taken a spurt of growth. It makes me feel old.

It's freezing here now. There is sea ice, and deep snow in places. It all looks beautifully crisp but if I'm honest, I would die for a bit of the warmth that you have.

I almost forgot; Hanne Weidmann's family returned to Kiel! It seems that they were taken to the Polish border, then forgotten about, so they just came back, along with a few other families. Maybe the Gestapo aren't quite as efficient as they're made out to be. It lifted everyone's spirits.

I must go now. Rosa and I had a good cry when we read your news, but it was the best day we've had in years. You really have cheered us up.

Look out for yourself, and your little bump.

All my love

Miriam.

Esther smiled and laid the letter on the table. As always, when she heard from Miriam or

Rosa, her eyes were wet with tears. She dried them with the back of her hand and went back to cutting the vegetables.

If anyone sees me, I'll tell them it was the onions.

~~o~~

[20/02/1939 Monday]

'I don't think it's right, Erich, expecting me to do this. You should have asked first. What if we get found out?'

'How are they going to find out?' the General argued, forcing himself to keep any hint of irritation from his voice. 'It will only be a few pieces, of sentimental value.'

The General had assumed that his wife would have no objections to storing a few pieces of Miriam's jewellery and a ring, bracelet and necklace belonging to Ruth, in the wake of the latest decree forcing Jews to hand all valuable objects over to the authorities.

'They'll never be noticed among the amount of jewellery that you have,' he added.

Maria Kästner arched an eyebrow.

'They'll stick out like sore thumbs. Without being unkind, they are of a rather differing quality to mine. Any valuer worth his salt would spot the difference immediately.'

'Put them in Antje's jewellery box then,' the General said. 'I'm sure she has nothing quite as irreplaceable as you have.'

He hadn't meant to sound caustic, but he was annoyed. Fortunately for him, she'd missed the implied rebuke.

'Perhaps that would be more sensible. Antje has one or two nice pieces, but I keep those with mine in the safe. The things she keeps herself are not much better than costume jewellery.'

'Well, there we go. That's sorted.' The General rubbed his hands, pleased with himself.

'Hold on a second,' Maria said. 'Are any of these pieces identifiable?'

'What do you mean,' he asked.

'Well,' she said, looking at him as if he was a small, stupid boy, 'Are their names, or initials, inscribed on them?'

'How would I know?'

'Well, seeing as it's you who has organised this scheme, you should really find out. If they ever checked, and Miriam or Ruth's names or initials are on bracelets or rings, or even an anniversary date, it would look suspicious for Antje to have them.'

'I didn't think of that. They'll never check. They wouldn't dare.'

'Erich Kästner. I can't believe you'd take a risk with your own daughter. Shame on you.'

He couldn't quite work out how he'd become the villain of the piece, but he put that to one side, only caring that the problem was solved.

'We can have any inscriptions erased. They can always put them back, later.'

'And where will you get that done? You are not using my jeweller, before you ask.'

The General smiled.

'I wouldn't worry. There are one or two unemployed Jewish jewellers about. I'm sure Yosef and Miriam will know someone who can help.'

'Well, I don't want to know anything about it.'

Glad that it was settled, he picked up the newspaper.

'Before you get too engrossed,' Maria said. 'There's something else we need to speak about.'

'By all means,' he said, conscious that he'd won a significant concession from her.

'While we're discussing the Nussbaums,' she said, 'Have you found a driver to replace Yosef yet?'

'I have, my dear,' he said, with no small degree of relief. 'It has been almost impossible, with so many men signing up for the army, and factories and stores mopping up the ones that are left.'

'But you have a driver? Definitely?'

'Yes, Maria. He starts a week today.'

~~o~~

DEUTSCHE REICHSPOST

TELEGRAMM

2 MARCH 1939

MADE CAPTAIN. CATCHING FRANZ. MAJOR NEXT. JOHANN. END.

~~o~~

The General smiled when he read the telegram. He put it in the drawer with the last one Johann had sent, three years before.

CHAPTER 180

[06/03/1939 Monday]

16th February

Afula.

Dear Miriam,

You will know already, but I have awful news. Oskar von Friedeburg tried his best but couldn't persuade them to let Itsik's parents come to Palestine. That is the end of it, I think. It has been difficult to accept, even though you told me not to get my hopes up.

As Mama Weichmann has probably told you, the government have taken most of their money, but we have found a way to send them enough each month to get by. Don't ask how but let me know if you think they need more.

So, my baby won't have grandparents here. There's nothing to be done. Itsik and Abel were discussing whether one of them should go back but, in the telegram that he sent, Herr von Friedeburg told us not to come back; that Itsik's parents would be distraught if we did.

I suppose there's always the hope that they can come out when this all blows over, and the NSDAP have gone. They surely can't be in power forever.

I'm sorry about Yosef – he loved his driving. I'm glad the Kästners have been so understanding.

When you mentioned snow, and ice, my heart nearly broke. I loved it at home when the snow fell, and the children miss it too. It is still warm here during the day, but bearable. The biggest relief is that it gets cool at nights, as low as five or six degrees, and we have had five days of rain this month, which we needed to last us through the summer. They are building hundreds of small dams here to irrigate the crops when it's dry. The land was useless and barren before, and it gets greener every year.

Itsik has met Isaac. Abel helped him find a suitable shop and he has opened already. It is not far from our store in Haifa. Isaac said to tell Yosef and Jakob that he had sore guts for weeks after the journey, but he's all right now; apparently, it's a joke between them all, although I couldn't understand what was funny about it.

There are Jews flooding into Palestine from Germany, and all over Europe. You should think of coming.

The baby is growing. I'm showing more every day. By the time it comes, I will look like a hippopotamus!

Moshe just shouted to tell Manny that he sometimes wishes he had snow and ice to have fun on, but he gets to play football every day. I think these boys have forgotten how to write.

I'm missing you both terribly. I don't know if it's the baby, or the weather, or Itsik's parents, but this is the worst I've felt. I shouldn't complain, hearing what's happening at home, but it is so difficult being so far away from you all.

Give my love to everyone.

Your dearest friend,

Esther

~~o~~

'My dear, this is Albert Weisbach, our new driver.'

Maria Kästner shook his hand politely and engaged in enough small talk just long enough to make him feel welcome. The General showed Albert where the garage was.

'Familiarise yourself with the car, Albert,' he said. 'Yosef does most of the maintenance so it might be a good idea to have a talk with him as soon as you can.'

'Of course, sir, and thank you for this. I found retirement dragged in a little.'

The General smiled and returned to the house.

'Where did you find him, Erich,' his wife asked, as he passed through the kitchen.

'Oh, he retired a few years ago but finds he has too much time on his hands, so he wanted to find a driving job that wasn't too onerous.'

~~o~~

[14/03/1939 Tuesday]

Memo: Geh.KdoS. ABW 14/03/39 CAC0725.1

For Attention Only: All senior executive officers, Abwehr.

From: Vice Admiral Wilhelm Canaris, Chef der Abwehr.

The Republic of Slovakia has declared its independence from the Czecho-Slovak state. Jozef Tiso has been appointed as its first prime minister. [END]

~~o~~

KIELER MORGENPOST

Thursday 16th March 1939

BOHEMIA AND MORAVIA OCCUPIED

Following the declaration of independence by Slovakia and the formation of the Slovak Republic, German troops have occupied the Czech part of the Czechoslovak Republic, with only sporadic and limited resistance, establishing the Protectorate of Bohemia and Moravia. It is expected that the Führer will visit Prague within the next few weeks. The close alliance between Germany and the Slovak Republic means that the whole of the former Czechoslovakia is now under the protection of the Third Reich, apart from the small border regions previously seized by Poland and Hungary.

~~o~~

General Kästner finished reading the paper. He'd read a memo about the Slovak Republic, but there had been nothing about the subsequent occupation of Bohemia and Moravia.

He was surprised, but Canaris was due to arrive any minute, and the General knew that

607

the Abwehr chief would fill him in on the situation in Czechoslovakia.

He picked up his telephone and spoke with Frau Müller.

'When Admiral Canaris arrives, send him straight in, please.'

'He's here already, sir,' she said. 'He's making coffee. I told him not to, that I'd do it, but he insisted.'

The General laughed at her indignant tone and walked to the door. Sure enough, Canaris was adding sugar to the three cups of steaming coffee. He saw the General and smiled.

'Here you are, Frau Müller,' he said, handing the embarrassed secretary one of the cups.

'Come on in,' the General said, smiling.

'I made you a cup,' the admiral said. 'Thought you might be ready for it.'

The General pulled a bottle of whisky from his drawer and added a tot to each of the cups.

'It will taste better with this in it,' he said.

'How are you, Kästner?' the admiral asked.

'Fine, Canaris. Yourself?'

'Never been better.'

They each took a long sip of coffee.

'You didn't say much about the purpose of your visit,' the General said.

'Did you not get my memo?' the admiral said, surprised.

'No, I've had nothing since the one about the Slovak Republic.'

'That's strange. You should have had two about the occupation of the Czech lands, and a personal one for you about our meeting today, with the Krupp and Germania management.'

'I've had nothing. I presume this is to thrash out agreements for the yard expansion?'

'Yes. I wanted to congratulate you in person on your efforts here. We weren't quite so successful at Wilhelmshaven; by the time we'd convinced the city council, the news was out, and the councillors saw fit to deal with the shipyards direct.'

'We were lucky. We knew exactly who the best people were to work with, and they knew us.'

'Were our industrial friends annoyed about our little manoeuvre to control the shipyard's excesses?'

'I suspect Krupp wasn't impressed but no doubt we'll find out shortly. It would be imprudent of them to raise a stink about it. After all, what we've done is for the good of the country, and as long as it doesn't jeopardise the contracts going to the yards, they'll still make money.'

'Well, the Kriegsmarine think you are wonderful, Kästner. I've had all its senior commanders singing your praises, and it has reflected well on the Abwehr too.'

'It was nothing.' He picked up the telephone.

'Frau Müller,' he said, 'get me Captain Bauer, will you.'

He put the telephone down.

'We prepared something in readiness for this, fortunately. I'll get Heinz to bring it in.'

The admiral laughed.

'It doesn't surprise me. Your staff are very efficient, but my people have also put something together, just in case. The meeting is in two hours. We'll have a look at both. Conrad will be here shortly.'

When the captain appeared, the General instructed him to fetch the proposals they'd worked on over the previous few days.

'Also, ask Günter to find out why the memos from Abwehr command haven't been getting through,' he added as the young captain left.

He turned to Admiral Canaris.

'While we're waiting, why don't you fill me in on our latest land acquisition?'

'There's not much to tell. Adolf has done it again. Bohemia and Moravia. Another bloodless coup.'

'He's either a military genius, or just lucky.'

'I don't think he's either. He's an extremely shrewd politician and a clever statesman, but he hasn't proved himself militarily yet, because he's never had to win a battle.'

'But a good military leader only fights when he needs to,' the General said with a sigh. 'Perhaps he is a genius, after all, and not as mad as we think.'

'Possibly, but he met with Tiso, the head of the Slovakian Republic and convinced him that he would take care of the Czechs if the Slovaks declared independence and, while the Slovak Republic complied with Germany's interests, his country would remain self-governing.'

'So that took care of the Slovaks. I suspect their independence won't last.'

'Probably not. The next morning, the Führer summoned the Czechoslovakian President, Emil Hácha, to Berlin and informed him of the impending German invasion. He threatened him with a Luftwaffe attack that would destroy Prague, and Hácha had no option but to accept the surrender of the Czechoslovak army. I'm told that the man suffered a heart attack during the meeting, and had to be revived by medical staff. Within an hour, our troops had entered the few remaining parts of Czechoslovakia that were still under Hácha's control.'

'And when is Adolf going to appear in Prague?'

'Later today, I believe. I was invited but managed to use today's meeting as an excuse. Sacrifices for the Third Reich and all that.'

They both laughed.

'We shouldn't laugh. I don't suppose the Jews of Czechoslovakia think it's amusing this morning,' the General said.

'Oh, don't start on that, again. Let's just be thankful there have been no casualties.'

Before Erich Kästner could argue the point, Captain Bauer knocked and entered, followed by Admiral Albrecht.

Admiral Canaris and the General greeted the head of the Baltic fleet as he took his seat.

'Right, gentlemen, let's get down to work,' Canaris said, opening the leather briefcase he'd placed on the desk.

~~o~~

Long after their meeting with the shipyard owners had ended, the two old friends sat, sipping one of the General's malts.

Admiral Canaris had opted to stay over at the Drachensee house and, after a pleasant meal with the General and an especially charming Maria, the two men had retired to the General's study when she protested her tiredness and disappeared upstairs.

'You have a wonderful woman there,' Canaris said, glancing up the stairs.

'You're right, although things are a little strained at present.'

'Really?' Wilhelm Canaris's face showed surprise. 'I always thought you two were the epitome of married bliss.'

'Oh, we'll be fine. Just a few political differences.'

'I try and leave politics at the front door. Anyway, Erika has no strong views, and usually takes my lead. I try and be uncontroversial, so it's easy for her. You, on the other hand…'

The General laughed.

'I suppose I'm a little outspoken, and I don't share the views of most of my fellow countrymen. Maria just wants an easy life, even if that involves turning her back on those who have shown such loyalty to us.'

'Ah. The Nussbaums. They're causing a rift between you?'

'If you think what they're going through is their fault, then yes. I'm just trying to do my best for them, even if it causes us a little inconvenience.'

'I can imagine that your support for them, and others of their type, could cause her some social embarrassment, and that's a part of her life she holds dear. I mean, she is one of the best at it. No one throws better dinner parties or organises charity events so well.'

'See, you're doing it as well. "Their type". They are Germans, just like us.'

609

'Whatever they were, they aren't now. I'm not saying it's right, but that's the reality of it.'

'Well, I'll not accept it, even if I fail. It's not as if I'm trying to keep them here. I've done my best to help them get out.'

'And others, I hear.'

'What do you mean, Canaris?'

'Don't forget, I have ears in many places.'

The General frowned.

'Don't worry,' Canaris said. 'I bumped into your friend, Oskar, the last time I was here. A charming fellow. He chinned me about an old Jewish couple that you'd asked him to help. They wanted to go to Palestine.'

'Ah. The Weichmanns. They're friends of Yosef and Miriam. I did try and help. So did Oskar, but to no avail.'

'He asked me if I could do anything, but I have no influence with regional security services.'

'It's sad. The whole family are out there, making a new life, and the grandparents can't be with them. For what? Spite?'

'I've heard they do that. Keep a few of them back. I believe it's a money-making enterprise.'

The General looked puzzled.

'The ones abroad send money back to those who are stuck here,' the admiral said, seeing the puzzled look on his friend's face, 'and naturally, the government takes as much of that as it can get hold of. Then, there's always the final offer of permission to leave Germany, which comes at a high cost. If they can pay it, it's easy foreign currency for the Third Reich, which we're desperate for.'

'How do they pay it? How is it arranged? I must tell Yosef to get a message to Itsik. They would manage to get the money together.'

'Don't tell them. It'll do no good. You can't approach these people. It must come from them. They might make an offer, they might not. They'll just have to wait. And hope.'

The General's fist thumped down on the desk.

'How can they get away with this?'

'Careful, Erich, you'll wake Maria.'

'She won't be sleeping. She'll be reading. One of her society magazines.'

The General opened the study door and listened.

'She couldn't have heard,' he said, as he returned to his seat.

'To answer your question,' the admiral said, 'who is there to stop them, while he's winning?'

The General's shoulders slumped, knowing Canaris was right.

For a minute, neither man uttered a word.

'Maria has a point,' the admiral said, breaking the silence.

'She has?'

'Yes, you're getting a reputation for, let's say, being a Jewish sympathiser.'

'Well, I'll not deny that. I've never hidden it.'

'It's becoming dangerous these days. If it weren't for your friends in high places, you might have been under a great deal more scrutiny.'

The General arched an eyebrow.

'You? A friend in high places?' he said.

'Oh, I'll always have your back but, no, not me. You are in the unique position of being equally admired by the Kriegsmarine and by the Heer. They see you as almost indispensable. Even Himmler and Heydrich know of your work, perhaps the Führer himself.'

The General laughed.

'Nonsense. I just do what's needed. Maybe I make things run a little smoother, but that's it.'

'Not according to those who know. That's why you're so valuable to me. You keep the lines of communication open.'

'And I thought it was our long-standing friendship,' the General said, breaking into a smile.

'That counts for nothing, these days,' the admiral said, laughing.

'In all seriousness,' he continued, his face grave again, 'this business with your Jews is tolerated as an eccentricity, excusable because they believe you are just trying to hang on to staff you consider irreplaceable. Being honest, they probably don't know about you diverting charitable donations to Jewish soup kitchens or helping with the release of a Jew's body to allow a father to bury him.'

The General's face paled.

'How the…'

'I told you,' the admiral said. 'I have eyes and ears everywhere.'

'Oskar!' the General said.

'He was concerned. He asked me to have a word. The police chief had spoken to him.'

'The bastards,' the General said, his voice taut with anger. 'I thought Oskar and Uwe Müller were friends.'

'Before you go off on one, think about it. They were worried about you. The police chief spoke to Oskar to ask him to have a word with you. Oskar mentioned it to me because he knew that I was your oldest friend, and that you trusted me. They were just looking out for you.'

'I suppose you're right,' the General said, the anger draining from his face, 'but I can't just abandon the Nussbaums, or their friends,' he added.

'Just be careful. Be more discreet and never leave a trail. Be prepared to walk away and deny everything.'

'That will be hard to do.'

'Think of Maria, and the children. Your parents too.'

'Once the Nussbaums get out, it will be easier. Until then, I'll try and be more prudent.'

'That would be wise, Kästner. I don't want to have to bail you out of prison. On the upside, the navy would quite happily put up the money after today. Krupp's face was a picture when he signed the agreement allowing them to expand the shipyard.'

'Ach, he's a businessman,' the General said. 'He'll treat it like any other negotiation. He may even respect us for it.'

'I'm not sure,' the admiral said. 'I don't think you'll be invited to dinner any time soon by the Krupps or the Germania owners.'

'You may be right. Not that I was looking for an invitation anyway. The main thing is that the Kriegsmarine will get ships and submarines built at a reasonable price, Krupp and his friends will still make money, and Kiel's economy won't do badly from it either.'

Canaris lifted the bottle and filled both their glasses. He lifted his and clicked the base against the General's.

'To the new Kriegsmarine ships,' he said.

CHAPTER 181

'Well, I think they're quite right. I mean, it can't be conceivable; a German city separated from the rest of the country just because the Poles demanded a piece of land after the war.'

Maria Kästner looked around at the rest of the ladies at the table. She'd felt vulnerable when someone broached the subject of Hitler's ultimatum to the Polish government, imagining whispers questioning the commitment of the Kästner family to the German cause, and had decided to get her three Reichsmarks' worth in first.

'I quite agree, Frau Kästner,' the mayor's wife said. 'My husband was at a party meeting last night and it was discussed in depth. These Poles need to understand who they're dealing with.'

'They'll just have to learn to be reasonable,' Maria Kästner said. 'The poor people of Danzig have had to live under Polish rule for twenty years, and the German population of East Prussia have been cut off from their homeland, having to travel through Poland to visit their friends or relatives, or even go to work. The Führer has liberated Austria, the Rheinland and Sudetenland. He'll do the same for Danzig.'

'I don't think your husband, *the General*, or your son, are quite as enthusiastic about the Führer's achievements as you, are they?'

Maria didn't have to turn to see who'd spoken. Since Franz and Lise had broken off their engagement, Beate Böhm had rarely spoken to her, and she took every opportunity to smear the Kästner family as anti-NSDAP shirkers.

Maria said nothing. It was Frau Hoffmann who spoke up.

'We all know the General can be a little outspoken, but we have no reason to doubt his patriotism. My husband, the mayor, was telling me the General was instrumental in saving the Kriegsmarine countless millions, which would have ended up in the coffers of the Krupps and their like. He says it will allow the navy to be more ambitious in their expansion. I do believe that the Führer himself commented on what an excellent job he'd done, and Admiral Albrecht was effusive in his praise of the General and my husband, who was influential in the negotiations.'

Maria gave Irmgard Hoffmann a grateful look, although she knew that some quid pro quo would be expected.

~~o~~

Beate Böhm saw Maria Kästner's smile, and her hands clenched in anger. She considered a caustic retort, then thought better of it.

The countess, sitting to the left of Maria Kästner, patted Maria's hand gently, giving her a smile. Catching it out of the corner of her eye, Beate Böhm's stomach twisted.

One day, that smug look will be wiped from your oh-so-perfect face, Maria Kästner.

The countess turned to Beate Böhm.

'I believe that Herr Hitler has demanded that a plebiscite should be held,' she said, 'so that the people of the Polish Corridor can decide for themselves if they want to rejoin Germany. I'm not sure the Poles will ever agree to it though.'

'If they know what's good for them, they will,' Frau Hoffmann said. 'They took advantage of us after the war. It's about time they realised we're a major power again.'

'The Führer has shown time and time again that countries will back down to him,' Beate Böhm said, trying to win back some of the ground she'd lost. 'Poland will be no different.'

Murmurs of agreement came from all around the table.

When the sound had quietened, Maria Kästner spoke.

'Now ladies,' she said, 'we have this year's spring fayre to organise, and we want to better last year's wonderful effort, so let's get down to it.'

She's desperate to steer the conversation away from politics, Beate thought.

She opened her mouth to speak, but all the ladies were watching Maria, and a buzz of animated chatter filled the room.

Maria Kästner looked across at Beate Böhm and smiled.

~~o~~

'Albert, who did you work for before you retired? Was it another family from Kiel?'

The car motored gently along Knooper Weg on the way home.

'No, ma'am. Did the General not tell you? I drove for the KVAG.'

Maria Kästner frowned.

'You drove a limousine for the transport company?'

'No, ma'am. I was a city tram driver.'

~~o~~

'They'll give us what we demand,' Johann bragged, 'but if they don't, I'm ready to fight.'

'I'm not so sure the Poles will roll over like the Czechs or the Austrians,' Franz cautioned, 'and they have a sizeable army, so it won't be a walkover.'

'Pah. We're as ready as we'll ever be. They'll be no match for us.'

'There's a long history of armies winning battles against superior forces because they're fighting for their lives and for their homeland. Don't you remember your military history lessons?'

Johann had hated the academic side of military college and had barely made the grades to pass out. On the practical elements of the course, he'd been a straight-A cadet.

He groaned.

'It's all Scheiße. At the end of the day, it comes down to men; how they're trained, how they're equipped and if they're motivated. And we're the best; you've said so yourself.'

'I know,' he conceded, 'but at the end of the day, fighting is fighting. Talk to father. He'll put you straight.'

'He went to war in 1914. This is 1939, and combat has changed beyond all recognition. You know what we're being trained to do, and it isn't trench warfare.'

'They didn't plan for long entrenched battles in the last war. It happened because there were two perfectly matched opposing armies. The same could happen again.'

'Britain and France won't help the Poles. They hissed and blustered, but they didn't lift a finger to help Austria or Czechoslovakia; it won't be any different with Poland.'

'You might be right, but if they do support Poland, I don't think Adolf will dare attack. We're not ready.'

'Scheiße,' Johann said, 'we're as ready as we'll ever be.'

'No. According to Father, it will be two to three years before the Kriegsmarine is capable of mounting a defensive campaign against the English, far less an offensive one, and a significant proportion of our ground forces aren't fully motorised yet; they're still using horses, even in this day and age.'

'We have enough modern battalions to take Poland. Once we do, we will have all the raw materials we need, and our factories will work from dawn to dusk to supply us with vehicles and equipment. German technology and the German working man are the best in the world.'

'They might be,' Franz retorted, 'or it might be that you believe everything Doctor Goebbels tells you.'

Johann grinned.

~~o~~

Franz looked at his brother and cursed. Johann loved to provoke him and, even when he was right, as he often was, losing his temper gave Johann a minor victory. It was exasperating, but he couldn't help laughing.

'You don't take anything seriously,' he said, 'do you?'

'No. If you do that, you'll worry yourself to an early grave. Talking of which, we're all going out tonight, just in case we're mobilised tomorrow. Are you coming?'

'I might come for a few. Where are you going?'

'The Spiegel Ballhaus.'

'Hamburg.' Franz groaned. The *Mirror Ballroom*.

'Come on. It's time you had yourself some female company. You'll enjoy it. The Hamburg ladies are exceptionally accommodating, you know.'

For Franz, the thought of watching his and Johann's friends attempt to find a girl in the cattle market of Hamburg's premier dance hall didn't appeal to him, but he knew he would go. He would offer to drive if they couldn't wangle an army truck and driver but that was unlikely; Johann had a way of making people go out of their way to help him, even if there was a risk of being disciplined.

'I'll go, but I'm coming back tonight, even if you lot aren't.'

'We'll see,' Johann said, grinning.

~~o~~

'Did you think it funny to humiliate me?'

The General had known he was in trouble before Maria uttered a word by the way she'd walked into the study, and by the pink spots on the cheekbones of her otherwise pale, tight, face.

'Sorry, dear, what are you talking about?'

'Albert. The driver.'

'Ah. He told you?'

'Yes. I'm only glad I asked him when I was in the car on my own. Imagine if I'd had company.'

'You wanted a driver. He's polite, proficient, and safe. For goodness' sake, if he could drive fifty people around on a tram, he can surely drive one or two in a car.'

'A-tram-has-rails, Erich,' she said, her words spitting out like machine-gun bullets. Erich Kästner forced himself not to smile.

'I'm sorry, dear. He has his own little car and has driven for years. I did check up on the man, and made him take me for a drive first, to make sure he was suitable.'

'All the same,' she said, a little mollified, 'you should have told me. It would have saved me the embarrassment of asking him.'

'I'm sorry. I just thought you'd be pleased to have a driver again. He hasn't done anything wrong, has he?'

'No,' she said, flushing. 'No. He's perfectly adequate, if a little slow.'

'There you go. Providing Albert does a good job, does it matter what he did before?'

'That's not the point, and you know it,' she said, turning and walking out.

He smiled to himself, then stopped. It had been cruel of him to keep it from her, but her attitude to the Nussbaums had annoyed him. He shook his head at his own childish conduct.

I'll make it up to her, somehow.

CHAPTER 182

Maria Kästner frowned.

Every Friday, as soon as Antje came home from school, she'd throw her schoolbag in the corner of her bedroom, change out of her school clothes, and tear across the yard to knock on the door of the Nussbaums' cottage. For her, every moment of the weekend, apart from her Saturday morning riding lesson, was time that she and Ruth would spend together.

Other things often got in the way; most of Friday evening was Shabbat, when Ruth ate with her family and attended the evening service, but the Nussbaums weren't strict enough to stop the girls being together outside of these family times.

'Don't run,' Maria would shout, as Antje hurried down the stairs. 'You're sixteen now. You should act like a young lady.'

'Yes, Mama,' Antje always replied, not slowing in the least.

The Friday that school broke up for the Easter holidays, towards the end of March, Maria heard the front door open, and waited for the sounds of the headlong rush up the stairs. She glanced at Miriam, who was putting on her coat, ready to leave to prepare for Shabbat.

'That's strange,' she said. 'Perhaps she's finally decided to grow up.'

Miriam laughed, and opened the back door to leave.

'Everything is ready to serve, ma'am. The soup might need a stir now and again.'

Maria nodded, and self-consciously lifted the pot lid and gave it a stir.

Still puzzled, she waited until Miriam had shut the door behind her, then made her way through to the hall. There was no sign of Antje, but her bag was lying at the foot of the stairs.

She heard voices in the General's study. He'd arrived home early but, as far as she knew, he didn't have anyone with him. The door was slightly ajar and, when she listened, she could hear her daughter's voice, so she knocked politely and walked in.

The General looked up, surprised, and Antje turned. Maria could see the look of anger on her daughter's face, and she drew back, shocked, afraid that it was directed at her, but Antje's face softened.

'What's the matter, darling,' Maria asked.

'It's the BDM,' the General answered for her.

Bund Deutscher Mädel. The League of German Girls, the female branch of the Hitler Youth.

'What about them?' Maria said. 'I thought you enjoyed all the outings and the sport they're so keen on? You're in the BDM horse-riding team at school.'

'I like the horse-riding but despise the rest.'

'Well, sometimes you have to do things you're not that keen on so that you can take part in other ways.'

'They took us to see this,' Antje said, handing her mother a flyer. On a yellow background, there was a caricature of a Jewish moneylender, a whip in one hand, the other open, holding a pile of gold. Maria read it.

Der ewige Jude.

The Eternal Jew.

She'd heard of it. The mayor's wife had mentioned being there when the exhibition opened in Munich. Now it was touring the country.

'Did you see it when you were in Berlin with the BDM?'

'No. It's in Hamburg at the moment. It was terrible. I couldn't help but think of Ruth.'

Maria bit back her anger. There was always some fuss with the Nussbaums, but she dared not comment. Antje had surprised her over the years by remaining completely loyal to Ruth and hadn't made any close friends at school that Maria knew of. She certainly hadn't ever asked to bring any girls from school home, and she'd never stayed over at any of their houses.

'It's best just to ignore it. It's only an exhibition.'

'But people believe it. I could tell. No one said it was wrong.'

'You didn't say anything, did you,' Maria asked, her face blanching.

'I told the other girls that it wasn't true. One of them told our leader. Fräulein Horst. She wasn't pleased.'

'I'm sure she wasn't, Antje. What did she do?'

'I told her that my parents had always taught me to respect people. She became furious and informed me that I was an independent human being and that I should act according to what she taught me and to not let my parents lead me astray.'

'She took Antje to the headmistress,' the General said, his mouth a thin line.

'Antje! You really should learn when you should keep your thoughts to yourself! I hope you said sorry.'

Antje looked at her father.

'Why should she say sorry,' he said. 'She hadn't done anything wrong.'

His voice had softened, but Maria couldn't mistake the cold edge to it.

'She's as pig-headed as you,' she said, angry now. 'I don't think you both realise how serious these people are. What did you say?'

'I told her I wanted to quit the BDM. She said I couldn't.'

'According to Antje, it's now the law for all girls under nineteen to be a member,' the General said. 'It's the same with boys and the Hitlerjugend.'

'So, what did the headmistress say?' Maria asked.

The General grunted.

'The only reason Antje's still at the school is thanks to the fees we pay and because some of Antje's fellow pupils have fathers who are on first-name terms with the Kriegsmarine command, and know my work. But the headmistress and the HJ leadership know that we can only protect her up to a point.'

'I'm to get one last chance, Mama,' she said, but she didn't sound repentant.

'I telephoned the school and asked the headmistress if we'd sent our children to her to be brainwashed. She said she was powerless and that I should impress on Antje that there should be no recurrence of the incident. I had to concede that the woman was in a difficult position but, by God, I wish a few people in this country would grow a pair of...'

'Erich!' Maria said, before he could complete his sentence.

Antje smiled.

'I could leave,' she said, 'and go to school here in Kiel.'

'You will do nothing of the kind,' Maria said, her eyes flashing. 'You will finish your education at the school we sent you to. You're as bright as Eva, if not brighter. You'll go to university as well. You're almost as good at languages as she is.'

'I want to go to art school, Mama.'

To Maria, art school meant bohemian students and even more unconventional teachers.

'No. I'm quite happy for you to fritter away your free time painting but it is not a subject that is suitable for a young lady to study.'

'Perhaps we should discuss that another time,' the General said.

'There will be no discussion. I'll not have any daughter of mine at one of those dens of iniquity. All they do all day is drink, smoke and talk about revolution. It's a wonder they haven't all been arrested.'

Culture had flourished in the more avant-garde spirit of the Weimar Republic, and the world of art, music, and literature, especially in Berlin, had attracted free-thinkers and radicals from all over Europe, but the NSDAP had slowly but surely strangled their freedom, and art schools were being forced to revert to their former remit of teaching only the technical side of painting and sculpture.

'I think that is only in Berlin, my dear,' the General said. 'The Kunstgewerbliche Fachschule in Kiel is much less cosmopolitan. Admiral Göpfert's daughter went there. She now works in an art gallery in Hamburg.'

'So, you've looked into it,' Maria said. Her face had paled and there was a cold set to her jaw.

'Not at all. But Göpfert likes to talk about his children. His son is an Oberfähnrich zur See on a destroyer. Anyway, at least Antje would be at home.'

'Oh, I suppose that's true.'

Although Maria was happy for the children to go away to school, university was a different matter. At boarding school, they were under constant supervision. At military academy, the boys lived in barracks under army discipline. Eva had decided to study modern languages and Maria had dreaded her oldest daughter going to Hamburg, Frankfurt or worse still, Berlin, living in a flat with other students and open to their influence. When she'd chosen Kiel to study at, Maria Kästner had felt nothing but relief.

Now, having Antje at home under her watchful eye seemed suddenly attractive. There were female artists who were respectable, and there were plenty jobs in museums and art galleries for the ones who weren't good enough to make a living selling paintings.

But she wasn't about to give in easily.

'We'll see,' she said, before leaving her husband and daughter to it.

~~o~~

Antje gave her father a grateful smile and made to speak, but the General put his finger to his lips, and she stopped.

He walked to the door and looked out. Maria had gone back to the kitchen. He nodded and smiled at Antje as he returned.

His daughter threw her arms around him.

'Thank you, Papa,' she said, her eyes smiling.

'She hasn't given in just yet,' he warned her.

'But she will,' Antje said. 'I can't wait to tell Ruth.'

'I would keep it to yourself until you know for definite. You might not get in.' He laughed.

'Of course I will. My art teacher has already spoken to a few art schools. It's a year away, but they all say they'd take me.'

The General raised an eyebrow. She was already one step ahead of him. He'd known her work was good and had meant to work on convincing Maria that being an artist was what Antje wanted and that it was an appropriate choice of career for her, but he hadn't had the chance.

'That's wonderful,' he said, 'and I don't want to spoil your excitement, but I must warn you – Herr Hitler would like nothing better than to close down every university.'

The smile left Antje's face.

'He can't,' she said. 'He just can't.'

~~o~~

[01/04/1939 Saturday]

Ruth thought that Manny's reaction to his new Kennkarte was strange, but the more she thought about it, the more she realised it shouldn't have been a surprise.

'You must carry this with you at all times,' Yosef had told him, handing Manny the identity card that the police constable had dropped off at the cottage while Manny was at

617

school.

Far from the resentment and anger Ruth would have expected, Manny seemed pleased when he took it from his father, turning it over in his hands, fascinated.

Later, when Yosef and Miriam had gone over to finish their chores in the big house, Manny showed it to her. Instead of being ashamed of the large yellow 'J' on the card, there was pride in his voice.

'Look, I'm Manny Israel Yosef Nussbaum now,' he said, pointing at his name.

'I know,' Ruth said crossly. 'My card says Ruth Sarah Leonie Nussbaum.'

'I like mine. It means I'm a son of Israel.'

Ruth smiled. Her brother was fast becoming a miniature zealot. Nearly all Jews had Kennkarte by now; Manny was the last in the family, and on his birthday too. The way he was acting, it was the best present he could have been given.

'Just be careful,' Ruth said. 'It's good to be proud of being Jewish, but don't let it get you into trouble. The police will take any opportunity to pick you up.'

'You sound like Mama. I'm not frightened by them.'

'Well, you should be. It would kill Mama and Papa if something happened to you.'

'Don't you get angry about the way they treat us?'

She sighed.

'Of course I do. But there's nothing we can do.'

'We could go to Palestine. I would go in an instant.'

'And leave Mama and Papa? You know Mama would never go to Palestine.'

She watched Manny's face turn sullen.

'I don't know why. It would be better than here. And we belong there.'

'When you're old enough to go on your own, you can make that choice. For now, don't make it hard for them. It will be tough enough for Mama and Papa to leave your grandparents behind when we go to England. If you make a fuss, Mama will feel all the worse.'

'I suppose,' Manny said, still sulking, 'but one day, we will rise up and show them we're better than them.'

She smiled and tousled his hair.

'That's the spirit, Manny Israel Yosef Nussbaum. But keep it inside. For now.'

She gave him a cuddle. She felt the tension in his twelve-year-old body ease, but she knew that in the next few years, the angry young man inside him would gradually snuff out what was left of his childhood, and might yet destroy him.

CHAPTER 183

KIELER MORGENPOST

Sunday 2nd April 1939

SPANISH WAR ENDS. FRANCO VICTORIOUS

The Führer was one of the first world statesmen to offer congratulations to General Francisco Franco on the Nationalist victory in Spain's Civil War. The remnants of the Republican army surrendered to General Franco's forces yesterday, ending the three-year war between the left-wing government of 1936 and Franco's Nationalists.

In a speech in Madrid, attended by Benito Mussolini, General Franco thanked both the Italian and German governments for their help, in terms of manpower and the supply of weapons.

He said that Spain, Italy, and Germany would continue to have close economic and military ties, and that halting the spread of communism required the free nations of Western Europe to have a united front.

General Franco has been declared President of the Spanish State.

Soldiers, airmen and seamen of the Condor Legion, the Reich's contribution to General Franco's forces, will be returning home to heroes' welcomes. It is expected that the Führer will address the massed ranks of the Legion in Berlin, to personally thank them for their service.

Over 300 German servicemen lost their lives in Spain's fight against the Bolsheviks.

~~o~~

'You must be pleased.'

The General cradled the telephone between his shoulder and his ear. It allowed him to continue flicking over documents on his desk, signing them where appropriate before depositing them in the basket labelled *Pending*.

At the other end of the line, Canaris grunted.

'I suppose I am. Our troops will be coming home, and I welcome the end of the bloodshed in Spain. I may even get an invitation to the celebrations. A few days in Madrid would suit me nicely.'

'I'm glad. There were rumours that Colonel Schneider had volunteered his unit to go out to Spain. To harden them up, he said.'

'It would have done them good. There's nothing like a bit of combat to sharpen up men. You should know that.'

'You're right, as usual, Canaris. But I've seen too much belligerence and bloodshed in my time. And for what?'

619

'Better to have their first taste of action in a war like that. The losses were low. A war with France or Britain might not be so kind to us.'

'Canaris, you have a special way of cheering me up. I know what you are saying is true, but I hope that we can avoid war for a few years yet.'

'I wouldn't count on it.' Canaris lowered his voice. The General imagined him looking around, to check he was alone.

'This is strictly for your ears only,' he continued. 'Don't even think about saying anything to Franz or Johann.'

Canaris paused.

'Well, what is it?' the General said irritably.

'*Fall Weiss* is the code name for an attack on Poland they're planning for the end of August.'

The blood in the General's veins seemed to run cold. He caught the telephone handpiece as it dropped from his shoulder.

'You're sure?' he gasped.

'Yes. I've been asked to provide detailed intelligence on the deployment of troops on the Polish border, and their readiness.'

'They let you in on their plans?'

The General was surprised. He knew that the trust between the chief of the Abwehr and Göring, Himmler and the Führer himself was tenuous at best.

'No. They didn't see fit to include me in their plans, but they must have known I'd guess. The details came from my little mole in their camp. Have you heard nothing from your Reichstag source?'

'No, he hasn't been in touch. I'll contact him today.'

'They must be keeping it tight to themselves, the inner circle, and just giving out limited information on a need-to-know basis, to allow the preparations to be made.'

'Will the British and French stand by again and watch another European country fall under our control?'

'I don't know,' Canaris said. 'We have robust intelligence that the British and the French have made a pact with Poland in the event of any action which threatens Polish independence. The British have given the Polish government an assurance that it will lend them all the support in their power, to be announced this week when the Polish foreign minister visits London.'

'So, it will be war.'

'Yes. I can't see any way out of it. Adolf is adamant, from what I hear, but we're two years at least from being ready.'

'That's my take on it too. I don't know about the Luftwaffe, but the talk within the Heer is that there aren't enough fully motorised regiments, and I know the Kriegsmarine are between two and four years away from having a navy that can rival the British.'

'I may have overplayed the readiness and capacity of the Poles in our reports. You know, to make them think twice.'

The General laughed. 'It might work. What happens if they do invade, and find out you've exaggerated?'

'I'll tell them the first rule of field intelligence; assume that it's wrong, double-check it, then still don't trust it. It's not an exact science, and the Luftwaffe haven't been doing aerial reconnaissance for fear of alerting the Poles.'

'Still, it's a dangerous game. I hope you know what you're doing.'

Canaris laughed.

'I was involved in intelligence work when they were still fighting in beer halls. I can look after myself.'

'Just don't underestimate them,' the General said, before hanging up.

~~o~~

620

KIELER MORGENPOST

Wednesday 5th April 1939

LANDESBISCHOF PAULSEN JOINS NEW CHURCH INSTITUTE

Landesbischof Paulsen, regional bishop of the Evangelical Lutheran Church of Schleswig-Holstein, has joined the newly formed Institute for Research and Elimination of the Jewish Influence on German Church Life. During his visits to the Institute's Eisenach base, he will be part of a committee that has been set up to remove any Jewish influence from the church.

It is expected that the committee will review church hymn books and publish a non-judaised translation of the bible to reflect current Aryan religious teaching, and will eventually house a training school for pastors, teachers, and church leaders to implement the latest changes recommended by the Institute.

A spokesman for the Institute stated that it would work in constant close cooperation with the Reich Propaganda Ministry, the Reich Church Ministry, and the Reich Ministry of Education.

~~o~~

Erich Kästner read the *Morgenpost* with disbelief. The last time he looked, Christ had preached tolerance and love of one's neighbour. He supposed he shouldn't be surprised. There had been a long history of men terrorising and subjugating whole nations in the name of Christianity; whole continents even, so why should this be any different?

'I'll not be back at church,' he said.

Maria paled.

'Erich, we've discussed this. Where else would we go?'

'If I were going anywhere, I'd go to the Confessing Church. At least they have the balls to stand up to this government.'

'Erich! Mind your language. And I don't think there is one of those in Kiel and I can assure you that I wouldn't attend a church that defies the authorities at every turn.'

'There's not one in Kiel. I don't even know if there's one in Schleswig-Holstein, but that's not the point.'

'What is the point then, and why this sudden need to change churches? I thought we'd agreed that Father Wengler was a decent man and that we could forget about what the bishop said?'

He showed her the *Morgenpost*. Her brow furrowed as she read it.

'I can see why you're upset but it doesn't change anything here in Kiel.'

'It does for me,' he said. 'I'll not be back. You can go if you wish and take Eva and Antje.'

'What will I tell Father Wengler?'

'You can tell him the truth; that I'm sorry, I can't support a church whose leaders have those views.'

'I will do no such thing. It will be bad enough that you're not there, without making a big issue of it.'

'Well, tell him that I'm being called away for military reasons. Heightened tensions and

621

all that. It's not far from the truth.'

'What do you mean?'

He cursed himself for his slip.

'Nothing, my dear. It's just that with all this expansion of the army and the navy, I'm at the office more and more. You must have noticed.'

He had been getting home later in the evening recently; once or twice he'd missed dinner and he'd been called in on the last three Saturdays to sort out snags with the new yard expansions.

She nodded.

He hoped it was a compromise that she could live with.

He knew that the regular attendance of the family at church was as much part of her social veneer as it was for religious conviction, but he couldn't ask her to cut herself off from something that she deemed so important. Her face reflected a mixture of disappointment and annoyance, and he felt a twinge of guilt that he was the cause of it.

His voice softened.

'That's probably the best way to deal with it. After all, I used to be away for months at a time when I was regular army. Father Wengler will think nothing of it.'

She barely acknowledged his attempt to smooth things over, and he watched as she got up and walked out of the kitchen, her stiffened back and her unwillingness to look at him causing him to flinch and bow his head.

They'd always been able to exist independently of each other; his military career had taken him away so often that they needed to be, but, when they were together, they were a couple who enjoyed each other's company immensely, both in public and in private.

And the General found it hard to believe that, despite being permanently at home, he couldn't remember the last time they'd made love, or the last time they'd kissed, other than a perfunctory peck on the cheek that was demanded by social protocol.

The differences in their attitudes to the National Socialists, and the disparity of their concern for the Nussbaums was driving a wedge between them and he cursed under his breath, vowing to make more of an effort to be kind to her and try to understand her point of view.

But he wasn't going to back down on his decision about the church.

CHAPTER 184

KIELER MORGENPOST

Friday 7th April 1939

ITALY INVADES ALBANIA

The Italian Army has invaded Albania. Early reports suggest that the Albanian Army has offered little resistance and that the country is now almost completely under Italian control.

~~o~~

'It's not just us then,' the General said. 'Our Italian friends have decided to have a tilt at dominating the world as well.'

He and Admiral Canaris sat in the café nearest to the Kriegsmarine Headquarters, looking out over Kieler Hafen to the cranes and sheds of the expanding naval dockyards opposite. In the dry docks, the skeletons of warships rose from their newly laid keels and, covered with scaffolding, the tubular bodies of the latest three submarines being built in the Germania yard sat, squat and menacing, on the quays.

'Yes,' the admiral said with mock gravitas. 'The fall of Albania. I think Mussolini needed something to prove that he was a match for our beloved Führer.'

'It was about as much of a battle as our occupation of Czechoslovakia was, I hear. Sporadic fighting at most.'

'It does seem to have been accomplished with relative ease, but I was talking to an Italian general who is based at the embassy in Berlin. He admitted that the invasion was chaotic and undisciplined, and that it succeeded only because the Albanians were so badly equipped and poorly trained. He was quite scathing. He said that if the Albanians had possessed a well-armed fire brigade, they could have driven the Italians back across the Adriatic.'

Both men let out a laugh, but it sounded hollow to Erich Kästner.

'We shouldn't belittle the result,' the General said, a frown creasing his brow, 'however it was achieved. It gives them almost complete control of the Adriatic and access to the Balkans, should they be stupid enough to try and expand their empire.'

'I'm not sure the Italian Army is up to that,' the admiral replied. 'Besides, the Führer is livid. Mussolini didn't think to tell him about the impending invasion.'

'I'm sure that was reciprocated when we invaded Czechoslovakia. Perhaps Benito thinks that allies aren't required to warn each other about their intentions.'

'Not that it mattered. We knew anyway. The Italians had issued an ultimatum to the king of Albania and had dropped leaflets on the main towns telling people not to resist.'

'I don't think we could count on them if there's a war,' the General said.

'No. I think we need to rely on our own resources, if we have time to put them in place.'

Both men looked across the water. A thousand men scuttled like ants on the ribs of the giant battleship that was growing day by day, but it would be years before their industry could fill the fleet with world-beating fighting ships.

~~o~~

[11/04/1939 Tuesday]

29th March '39

Esther,

I'm so devastated for you. Itsik's mum told me that their last chance had gone, and the General said that Oskar had tried his hardest to reverse the decision, but to no avail. I'm happy to keep an eye on them but our own departure for Britain is only six months away. I'll try to find someone else to look after them once we've gone. I'm so sorry.

We've had a few warm spring days and to be honest, I know you miss the snow and ice, but we'll be glad to see the back of them!

I told Manny that Moshe misses the frost, but he just grunted. I worry about him because he's becoming fiercely religious (I know, it sounds silly to be concerned) and the only things he talks about are Jewish history and the Fifth Aliyah, and about how we should all be going to Palestine, and that it is the only way for Jews to be free of persecution. He even asked in all seriousness if he could go and stay with Moshe, without us! As if I would do that to you.

We are lucky to still have jobs but I'm not sure we would if it were up to Frau Kästner. She acts as if we are a burden, and I've overheard a few remarks which make me think that she is increasingly concerned about what people think of her still retaining Jewish staff. If it weren't for the General, I think we would be 'reluctantly let go', a phrase that we're hearing more and more these days.

People are doing the most menial of jobs just to earn money for food and rent. If they can't afford to pay, they are being put out in the street. The houses in Kleiner Kuhberg are becoming terribly overcrowded, and there is talk of renting another one.

I'm glad Itsik is helping Isaac out. He is a lovely man. He saved Yosef's life once, him and the General. Tell Isaac that Yosef was asking after his health, and that he is a diamond of a friend. (He was laughing when he told me; it must be another private joke between them.) Men. Pah!

I hope you and your little bump are doing well. It's a struggle not being able to see you every day and help, especially when it comes to the birth. It's not long now – over halfway.

That's all for now. Always thinking of you,

Miriam.

~~o~~

[28/04/1939 Friday]

'Did you hear Adolf's latest words of wisdom?'

Yosef looked around nervously. They were standing in Kleiner Kuhberg, on the steps of the makeshift synagogue.

'Sheesht, Jakob. You can be jailed for less,' Yosef said.

'There's no one about. Anyway, did you hear?'

'No, what did he say?'

'He spoke in the Reichstag. It was in the papers this morning. He renounced the Anglo-German Naval Agreement and the German-Polish Non-Aggression Pact.'

'So, war is imminent. Is that good or bad for us?'

'It might take their minds off their *Jewish problem*. Who knows, they may even decide that they need Jewish soldiers after all. On the other hand, there could be shortages, and who do you think will be the first to bear the brunt of them?'

'Us. But what can we do?'

'We must try and buy as much food as we can and hide it under the floorboards. We may as well spend our money now before the government takes the rest of it from us. Medicines too, if we can get hold of them.'

'Medical supplies might prove impossible, but food will be easier. It will have to be canned goods though.'

'Not impossible, my friend. There's a black market developing. You know the Bernheim brothers?'

The Bernheim brothers were a pair of Jewish petty crooks who associated with Kiel's criminal underclass, and were mostly handling stolen goods, and contraband.

'I've seen them. They only show up at the synagogue on Rosh Hashanah, splash a little cash and make themselves out to be as Jewish as the rest of us, then disappear for another year.'

Jakob laughed.

'That's them. And I think we'll see less of them now. They'll not want to be known as Jews these days, I'd imagine. Still, they could be useful. They have contacts.'

Yosef gave Jakob a wary look.

'You've had dealings with them?' he asked.

Jakob sighed.

'Yes. Remember the Frentzen girl, with the blood poisoning?'

'Yes. She survived but lost a foot. It was terrible.'

'She wouldn't be alive if we hadn't got hold of some sulphonamide. They saved her life. It was the Bernheim brothers who procured it for us, at a cost, when we couldn't get it by legal means. Few Aryan doctors or pharmacists are willing to risk involvement with a Jewish patient.'

Yosef knew, with bitterness, that to be Jewish and become ill was a dangerous combination. He regularly prayed that his family stayed healthy.

'And can they get us supplies of medicines on a larger scale?'

'I don't know, yet. We're meeting them today. You and I.'

'Oh,' Yosef said, realisation dawning. 'That's why you wanted me here.'

'Yes. These two are as slimy as a pair of eels. I figured on having some backup. Come on.'

Yosef smiled as he followed Jakob up the steps, and into Kleiner Kuhberg fifteen.

~~o~~

[12/05/1939 Friday]

'Rosa, good luck,' Miriam said, through the tears that threatened to leave her with red-rimmed eyes.

Her friend hugged her tightly as the guard walked past, advising everyone who was travelling to get on the train.

'When do you embark?' Miriam asked.

'We get to Hamburg about four-thirty, and by the time all the formalities are done, we should be on board the ship by seven or eight.'

'And what time do you sail tomorrow?'

'Around lunchtime. Something to do with tide, they said. The children are so excited to be crossing an ocean.'

'I know. They can hardly contain themselves.'

Miriam looked at Rebeka and Fischel's faces, pushed up against the window. From the door of the carriage, Emil, Rosa's husband, called for her to hurry up, that the train was about to leave. In his hand, he gripped the wallet with the tickets and the travel permits for the train journey, and the tickets for the steamship that was going to take them to Cuba.

'What's the name of the ship again?' Miriam asked.

'The *St. Louis*. There's supposed to be 900 passengers on board, and they've told us we'll be travelling in luxury. I'll believe it when it happens. I expect that the Jews on board will be confined to the hold or something but, once we're in Cuba, we've been told that we'll get visas for the United states.'

Rosa and Emil Liewermann had been given only a few days to pack up and say their goodbyes, but they'd had to grasp the chance to get out when it had presented itself.

Miriam felt a stab of jealousy. It was the middle of May, and it would be another five months at least before she, Yosef, and the children could leave, but at least they had a while to get used to the idea, and spend a little time with her parents, and Yosef's, not knowing when they might see them again.

'You'd better go,' Miriam told Rosa, 'before Emil has a heart attack. Write to me from America.'

'I will.' Rosa kissed Miriam and turned away. Emil helped her onto the train and nodded to Miriam, a sad smile on his face.

No sooner had he jumped in and closed the door, then the guard blew the whistle and stepped onto the train. Standing on the platform, waving to Rosa until the last carriage rounded the corner, Miriam had never felt lonelier. Trudging down the platform, she saw through her tears that the police had set up a checkpoint and were scrutinising the identity cards of the people leaving the platform.

Bastards. They would know that, more than usual, the train to Hamburg would have a significant number of Jews on board and that most of the people on the platform were families and friends of these Jews, seeing them off on their journey of hope.

With trembling hands, she fumbled in her coat pocket for her Kennkarte, and found it, breathing a sigh of relief. She joined the end of the queue and watched as people's papers were inspected. People showing Aryan Kennkarte were waved through unchecked, but she was perturbed to see that most carrying the 'J' marked cards were being escorted to an office on one side of the station.

She was glad she hadn't kept Ruth and Manny out of school to see the Liewermanns off. She said a prayer to herself as the line crept forward and she approached the barrier. There were three policemen and two men in dark suits with leather coats.

Gestapo.

Her stomach turned, and she felt an icy barb of fear in her chest. Beads of cold sweat gathered between her shoulder blades and trickled down her spine.

One of the dark-coated men glanced at the identity cards of the older couple in front of her and gestured to the policemen to escort them to the office they'd commandeered in the station buildings. She could hear the husband murmuring to his wife as he took hold of her arm gently, reassuring her that it was just a formality, but it wasn't enough to erase the concern and fear from her face.

Miriam stepped forward, handing the second Gestapo man her card. He studied it for what seemed like an eternity, then looked at her. His gaze seemed to penetrate her skull; she briefly considered the possibility that he could read her mind.

'Your family?' he asked, throwing her completely.

'No, n-no,' she stammered, tasting the bile in her throat as fear threatened to take over. She swallowed and willed herself to speak.

'My friends. They're going to America.'

'More filthy Jews leaving,' the man said, his tone bored and flat, as if he'd said it a hundred times that day.

She said nothing.

'The sooner you all leave, the better. One way or the other.'

He smirked at her.

She felt his gaze drop from her face, and she wished she'd fastened her coat.

'You can go, Jewess. This time. Your papers are in order. If your husband is out of a job, you should consider working on your back. A woman like you could keep a family of Jews in food with no trouble.'

He laughed.

She nodded, mumbled thanks, and walked towards the exit, careful not to break into a run. Turning left at the main entrance, she saw two large black vans parked along the side of the station buildings, next to a door marked 'Railway personnel only'.

She shivered, and walked homewards along Sophienblatt, her head down.

CHAPTER 185

Memo: Geh.KdoS. ABW 15/05/39 CAC0794.1

For Attention Only: All senior executive officers, Abwehr.

From: Vice Admiral Wilhelm Canaris, Chef der Abwehr.

SS authorities have opened a female-only concentration camp at Ravensbrück, north of Berlin.

For your information only. No action required. [END]

~~o~~

KIELER MORGENPOST

Monday 22nd May 1939

GERMANY AND ITALY: PACT OF FRIENDSHIP

Foreign minister Joachim von Ribbentrop has signed the Pact of Friendship and Alliance between Germany and Italy. It was co-signed by his Italian counterpart, Galeazzo Ciano. A spokesman for the government said that this would ensure that the trust and cooperation that existed between Germany and Italy would be continued on a more formal basis.

~~o~~

Memo: Geh.KdoS. ABW 22/05/39 CAC0801.1

For Attention Only: All senior executive officers, Abwehr.

From: Vice Admiral Wilhelm Canaris, Chef der Abwehr.

** HÖCHSTE GEHEIMHALTUNG **

RE: The Pact of Friendship and Alliance between Germany and Italy.

A Supplementary Protocol covering a union of policies concerning the military and economies of both countries was signed by Foreign ministers Galeazzo Ciano and Joachim von Ribbentrop at the same time as the above pact. Knowledge of this agreement is intended to be restricted to ministers of both Governments. The Abwehr has been made aware of this information.

For your information only. No action required. [END]

General Kästner put the memo in his safe and smiled. *Most Secret! How long would it stay that way with the Italians involved?*

~~o~~

[29/05/1939 Monday]

Out of the Kästners' kitchen window, Miriam's heart missed a beat as she caught a glimpse of a figure walking down the driveway towards their cottage. She gave the bread dough a last knead and placed it in the bottom of the range to prove, then rinsed her hands in the sink.

She looked around at the kitchen doorway but there was no sign of Maria in the hall. She dusted the flour from her apron and looked out of the window again.

She vaguely recognised the woman, but she couldn't place her. She hadn't realised she'd been holding her breath until she let out a long sigh. Whoever she was, she didn't look as if she was on official business; her clothes were those of an ordinary housewife, and she didn't have the arrogant bearing of someone in authority.

She opened the back door, looking again to see if Maria Kästner was around. A year ago, she wouldn't have thought twice about it, but she knew that, these days, her employer's wife would frown and ask if anything were amiss, concerned that any unsavoury goings-on would reflect badly on the Kästners.

The woman turned when she called, and Miriam recognised her as Rosa's next-door neighbour.

'Can I help you?' she asked the woman, scrabbling about in her mind, trying to recall her name.

'Hello, you likely won't remember me,' she started.

'I remember you. You're Rosa's neighbour,' Miriam said, relieved.

The woman smiled.

'That's right. Frau Hartmann. Marlene Hartmann.'

She held out her hand, and Miriam took it.

'Come in,' she said. 'We live in the cottage. Can I offer you a cup of coffee?'

'No, no,' Frau Hartmann said, following Miriam. 'I just called to give you these.'

She pulled out a pile of letters.

'Rosa asked me pick up her mail and give it to you.'

'Oh, thank you.' She could understand why the woman did not want to hang around. There was every possibility that what she was doing was in some way illegal.

'It's really kind of you, and I understand the risk you're taking,' she said.

The woman blushed.

'Rosa was a wonderful neighbour. I owe it to her. I'll bring the mail to you as long as the postman keeps delivering it. I have a key, you see.'

'I don't want to appear ungrateful, but perhaps it would be easier for you if I sent my daughter to collect them. It's on her way home from school. It will save you coming here.'

It's a bit of a detour, but Ruth won't mind.

The woman looked relieved and blushed again.

'I'm sorry. It shouldn't be like this, but…'

'I know. I understand.'

The woman smiled, then looked around.

'How do you…' she said, looking around the kitchen of the cottage, then stopped, embarrassed again.

'Our home? Our jobs? We have a determined employer. He refuses to dismiss us.'

'Ah. That's comforting to hear. There are few in this city like him.'

'It's good of you to bring Rosa's mail,' Miriam said, meaning it.

'Do you know, I feel better for having come. One feels so powerless to help.'

Miriam kissed her on both cheeks and showed her to the door. She picked out the letter

629

with the Haifa postmark and slipped it into her apron pocket. As she walked back towards the big house, she looked up and caught sight of Maria Kästner looking out of the kitchen window.

~~o~~

The letter burned a hole in Miriam's apron all day. She'd hoped to get a chance to read it in between her chores but Maria always seemed to be hovering. Then, just before four, she asked Miriam to call Yosef; a floorboard in her bedroom was squeaking horribly every time she stood on it. When the mistress led Yosef upstairs to show him the offending piece of flooring, Miriam sat at the kitchen table and took the letter out of her pocket.

Using a breadknife, she slit the envelope, and poured the contents onto the table. There was a letter for Rosa, which she put aside, and a smaller envelope with her own name on it.

She opened it and started reading.

~~o~~

Haifa,

16th April '39

Dearest Miriam,

Your letters are a lifesaver for me, as are Rosa's. I'm in Haifa for a couple of nights at Abel and Leah's, so that I can go for a check-up, to make sure everything is right with the baby. I am keeping well, so you needn't worry, and my bump is most definitely showing. I had to tell the children, which prompted lots of questions that were uncomfortable to answer. Moshe gave me a funny look which was somewhere between shock and disgust. I guess he knows how babies are made!

It is becoming harder for Itsik to get stock from Germany. He thinks it may be due to a large part of the country's industrial resources being appropriated for the expansion of the military. On the bright side, he has located three small factories here in Palestine that can supply him with some of what he needs; two are in Haifa, run by German immigrants, and one is in Tel Aviv. It is owned by two Jews from England, and Itsik says it is an eye-opener to hear what the British think of the Third Reich. They call them 'Nazis', short for Nationalsozialistische Deutsche Arbeiterpartei.

Miriam smiled at Esther's underlining. Nazi. She'd read it somewhere before. She said it a few times and thought that she might start using it. In private. It would be her own small way of belittling the NSDAP, the cause of their troubles.

She read on.

The British are convinced that Hitler is gunning for a war and they are worried that they will be dragged into it. There has been a sudden scramble towards rearmament, but most feel that they might have left it too late.

There is outrage in the British press about Adolf Hitler and his policies, especially towards Jews, which is good, but there is still a reluctance to let refugees in, despite pressure from British Jews in the government. The man said that it was the same in the USA.

Jews are pouring into Palestine, despite the British trying to limit it. They come from all over Europe, but mostly from territory the 'Nazis' have taken over, and we are starting to see a few from Poland now; they fear that they will be next.

630

Manny would be welcome, but I know it would be impossible for you to be separated from your children, so I've told Moshe not to say anything more about it, not that they write much anyway.

I'm sorry to hear that Frau Kästner is being less than kind to you. The General is a wonderful man, and we do appreciate the efforts he and Herr von Friedeburg made to get Itsik's parents permission to travel. I also can't tell you how much it means that you are still able to look after them. It will be hard for them both when you leave but for your sake, I dearly hope it comes sooner rather than later. If you could find someone to keep an eye on them, that would be wonderful. We could send money if it would help to get someone reliable.

There is still some violence here, but you get kind of used to it, and the British mostly keep on top of the trouble and, more and more, there are Jewish defence forces in every settlement who give us a feeling of relative security. Itsik takes his turn at guard duty and they taught him how to shoot a gun. Moshe, not surprisingly, is desperate to do the same, but they won't let him until he is sixteen. I'm dreading it! At least it is a few years away.

I must go now. We are going out for something to eat with Abel and Leah and the children. That's what is wonderful about here. You can do normal things without a second thought. Always remember that there is a place for you here with us if you change your mind.

All my love,

Esther.

CHAPTER 186

There was a strange atmosphere at the 1939 Kieler Woche. No one in Kiel could ignore the massive naval backdrop to the races. Destroyers and frigates berthed two and three abreast on the moles of Wik and at Tirpitzhafen, and newly launched ships lay on the shipyard jetties being fitted out, the skeletons of others rising behind them in the dry docks. Three submarines lay alongside one of the smaller wharves, their decks awash with Kriegsmarine uniforms and dockyard workers' overalls in preparation for the vessels' handovers.

And the noise never ceased. The clamour of riveting guns and the whine of drills merged with the thudding of enormous engines being put through their paces and the rumble of coal being dropped into ships' fuel bunkers by giant cranes, lifting it in five-tonne-bucketfuls from heaps on the quayside.

One of the new frigates lay patiently at the oil berth, the umbilical tubes filling her tanks with fuel oil, readying her for sea.

In the stands, a buzz of excitement that had little to do with the racing was tempered with an unsettling air of trepidation; the crowds weren't talking only of war, but it was at the front of most of their minds.

Franz sat with his father in the bright morning sun, watching the Star class yachts race in the inner part of Kieler Hafen; he'd won the event a few years before but, now that he'd graduated to the eight-metre boats, they raced in the outer fjord beyond Friedrichsort, and his next race wasn't until the afternoon.

'You're in a good position,' the General said, sipping his coffee. 'One point behind with two races to go.'

'Yes. Schulze hasn't made any mistakes this year, and his boat is just a tad faster.'

'You've done nothing wrong either. I get the impression that whoever blinks first will lose.'

'I hope so. It will all come down to the last race. And we'll win. Especially if the wind blows hard. My crew are the best they've ever been, and we have more experience in heavy conditions.'

The General smiled.

'You smell it?' he asked.

'What, the storm?' Franz replied, glancing at his father. 'I think we'll get it tonight or in the morning.'

'As long as they don't cancel the race.'

'It shouldn't get too fierce, this time of year. Just a stiff blow, hopefully, with a good hard chop to make it interesting. Oh, here we go.'

They watched the start of the race in silence. When it settled down, the General turned to his son.

'How are things in the regiment?'

'Good. My new rank certainly comes with its own set of problems. I'm beginning to understand why the higher you rise in the army, the higher the pay!'

The General laughed.

'It doesn't always work that way. By the time some of them get above Oberst, they've perfected the art of delegation. I knew a general whose adjutant ran the show for him, while he did nothing but drink gin, like the British, and play patience.'

'There are still some like him,' Franz said. 'Colonel Schneider has no time for those types.'

'How is the colonel?'

'Pushing us hard. Without meaning to brag, our battalion is one of the best in the army.

He told us that war is coming, and he says that our only chance of surviving it is to be the best soldiers we can be.'

'That's a good philosophy.'

The General smiled. He remembered telling a young Lieutenant Schneider the same thing two decades earlier, during the last years of the Great War.

'It's getting close, isn't it?'

'Yes,' the General said, his voice heavy. 'Are you worried?'

'I'd be lying if I said I wasn't, but I'm ready to fight if I need to. I did sign up for it.'

'You signed up to serve your country. You weren't to know what Germany would turn into.'

'No. But I'm in it now and I'll do what I have to.'

'I know it's a big ask but try and keep an eye out for Johann.'

Franz raised an eyebrow.

'Why?' he said.

'I just worry he might get carried away, trying to be a hero. It's in his nature to act first and worry about the consequences later.'

'I suppose so. He's a good soldier though, and he leads his men well. But I'll watch out for him. During training, the colonel usually keeps our units close to each other. He seems to think we work well together.'

The General smiled.

'It doesn't surprise me. You sail well as a team. There's no reason that wouldn't spill over into your army service.'

Franz looked at his watch and stood up.

'Here comes Johann. It's time to teach Kapitänleutnant Rainer Schulze a lesson.'

CHAPTER 187

[03/07/1939 Monday]

2nd June '39

Kiel.

My dearest friend,

I feel so alone now. Rosa and Emil had the chance to go early to America, so they took it. They left with the children on the 13th of May, on the St. Louis, bound for Cuba. From there they'll travel to Florida. It all sounds wonderful, but I miss her so much already.

Her neighbour brought me your letter. She was so nice about it, and she says she would keep bringing them but perhaps, for her sake, it would be better if you send your letters to me via Itsik's parents. I'm there twice a week anyway, so it seems sensible.

It's alarming that Itsik needs to carry a gun and even more scary that Moshe will need to do the same in a few years, but I suppose it's the same here when young men leave school and join the army.

Say hello to Abel and Leah. Is there no sign of them starting a family, especially with you being pregnant?

We get harassed at every turn now. It's quite a thought to go anywhere at present. You are likely to be stopped and asked to show your Kennkarte, and they make any inspection as unpleasant as possible, but you just have to stand there and accept it. The only saving grace is that the children have been left alone so far on their way to and from school.

Part of me would love to come and stay with you, more so now that Rosa is gone but I know I wouldn't feel comfortable there. One day, we will be able to visit.

All my love,

Miriam.

~~o~~

[04/07/1939 Tuesday]

KIELER JÜDISCHES FREIHEITSNACHRICHTENBLATT

Volume 74

17th of Tamuz, 5699

REICHSVEREINIGUNG DER JUDEN IN DEUTSCHLAND

A new body has been set up by the National Socialist Government. The Reich Association of Jews in Germany is now the sole legal Jewish organisation in the country. Its members have been hand-picked by the German Security Police for their "suitability" and will act as liaison between the authorities and the Jewish population.

The local representative for the Kiel area is Hans Leo Dampf.

~~o~~

'He's a patsy,' Jakob Teubner grumbled. 'They all are. The Germans have filled the organisation with Jews who will do their bidding without a word of argument.'

'We'll have to deal with him though. The Germans will not speak directly to us now.'

'He might as well be in bed with them. Did you hear him?' Jakob said, grimacing. '"I'm here to help",' he said, mimicking the Jewish council official, '"the authorities are only doing their best in a bad situation".'

Yosef laughed. Jakob had aped the man's condescending whine almost perfectly.

'It will be no different from working with the Goyim.'

'But he's a Jew. How can he live with himself?'

'Don't worry. He'll be able to justify it to himself. These people always do.'

~~o~~

[10/07/1939 Monday]

The General switched off the radio and turned to Admiral Canaris. The news bulletin had just reported the British prime minister's latest speech.

'So, has Chamberlain finally found himself a pair of balls?'

'I doubt he'll be any more willing to go to war for the Poles than he was for the Czechs,' the General replied.

Neville Chamberlain had reaffirmed his support for Poland and had made it clear that Britain did not view the Free City of Danzig as being solely of German and Polish concern. He'd promised that Britain would intervene on behalf of Poland if hostilities broke out between the two countries.

'This is different,' the admiral said. 'Even the British will know that any occupancy of Poland by our forces would give us the raw materials we need to grow our industrial and military strength, and the food we require to avoid our people starving if there is a war, with a blockade by the British Navy.'

'And he can't afford to let that happen, or we will be the strongest power in Europe, besides Russia.'

'No word from our Soviet friends?'

'Nothing at all. Comrade Stalin is playing his cards close to his chest.'

'No help for Britain there, then. What do you think they'll do?'

'I'm not sure. I've told Adolf and Hermann that the British will declare war if we were to occupy Poland, to see if it would shock him into reconsidering his plans.'

'And...?'

'They laughed. Then Adolf cursed the British as cowards and weaklings.'

'What did you say?'

'I told him not to underestimate them. They've been fighting since the end of the war, in one way or the other, to keep their empire intact. We might have a well-trained and better equipped army, but they have something you can't write off. Soldiers who know what it is to fight.'

'Was he not annoyed that you brought up the subject of an invasion of Poland?'

'No, he'd asked me my opinion on the Polish Army, and what Britain would do. He must have known I would guess his plans from his line of questioning.'

'And have you heard anything more from your informant?'

'Only that the plans are being refined and finalised. They're still talking about the 25th of August.'

'It's getting closer,' the General said. He shivered.

'Oh, by the way, we have a new section in the Abwehr, one that I'm not fully in control of.'

'Oh. When did that happen?'

'As of today, we now have an executive branch. The Geheime Feldpolizei. They have a remit to carry out security work in the field. I'm trying to populate it with our people where I can, but there will be a significant number of outsiders, and in positions of significance.'

'I'm guessing they'll be called the GFP,' the General said, laughing. 'They do like their acronyms. What will their role be?'

'Counter-espionage during military actions, mopping up resistance, etcetera, etcetera. They could be a bit of a thorn in the flesh.'

'These outsiders. They're party men?'

'Yes. We'll have to be a little careful.'

CHAPTER 188

[13/07/1939 Thursday]

The postman handed Miriam the letter, watching her suspiciously for any reaction. She smiled, politely thanked him, and closed the door as if letters postmarked Antwerp arrived on a regular basis. She tore it open, and recognised Rosa's handwriting.

Her first thought was that her friend had posted a letter when the ship had stopped in Belgium to pick up passengers. Then she saw the date.

She began to read.

19th June.

Dear Miriam,

We didn't make it to America. We are back in Europe. We got within touching distance, but we were turned back. We are all shattered by the experience.

The journey out was lovely, and exciting. The captain was a wonderful man and despite all the rules and laws forbidding it, he treated us Jews like ordinary passengers. We could swim in the pool and eat in the restaurant with the few non-Jewish passengers who were on board; the crew treated us like real people for a change. I nearly cried, it was so different from what we'd been used to, and I thought that, once we got to America, it would always be like this.

But it didn't last. When we got to Havana, the Cubans wouldn't let us off. They'd changed their laws a month or so before to keep out the flood of refugees from Europe. The captain pleaded with the authorities but to no avail, so we left, and the ship headed for America. Emil and a few others became friendly with one of the ship's officers and he told him that the captain was constantly on the radio, trying to negotiate with them to let us off the ship, but they refused. The man said the captain had even considered running the ship aground, then they'd have had to let us off but there were small naval vessels watching our every move and staying inshore of us so, in the end, the ship was forced to return to Europe. We arrived in Antwerp two days ago.

We were terrified the ship would return to Hamburg; we were sure they would put us all into concentration camps if we did, but the captain got permission to dock in Antwerp. By that time, a few countries had agreed to take us in. About a third of the passengers were sent on to Britain; I tried to get us on the list as I thought you would be going there soon, but we weren't chosen. We've been allocated to stay in Belgium, and we've found a room in a flat to rent in Antwerp for the moment, but Emil has already been to the American embassy to see if our original application, at the consulate in Hamburg, will still be valid so that we can try again later.

We may have to return to Kiel and try and resurrect our visa application there; part of me thinks we should return anyway as we are using up our savings renting this room, but Emil is adamant that we should stay here; that we'll be safe until we can sort out our papers for the United States.

Rebeka and Fischel are devastated; we'd promised them so much once we got to America, but they are good children, and will cope, I'm sure. Emil has some short-term work gluing packing boxes in a small factory round the corner, so at least we have a little money coming in. I'm looking for work as a waitress (don't laugh) or a cook in one of the cafés when he is home, as the voyage used up quite a bit of our money.

If you can write, our address is C\O Hemmerechts, Haarstraat 21, Antwerp. I'll try and keep

637

you up to date with what is happening. Keep me posted on how Esther is doing. I've written to her, but God knows if she'll get it.

Sending all my love.

Rosa.

Tears of disappointment for her friend blinded her as she finished reading. The one thing she'd hoped for through the pain of losing Rosa was that she and her family were safe and sound in America, away from all the horrors of 'Nazi' Germany.

She sat down to write a reply. She knew, at all costs, that she had to persuade Rosa not to return to Kiel.

~~o~~

Memo: Geh.KdoS. ABW 24/07/39 CAC0837.1

For Attention Only: General Erich Kästner, Abwehr, Kiel office, Abwehr.

From: Vice Admiral Wilhelm Canaris, Chef der Abwehr.

This, and all subsequent command Memorandum will be directly addressed to you. It is your duty to destroy these communications once you have read them. Routine communications should be dealt with as normal. [END]

~~o~~

[17/08/1939 Thursday]

Miriam climbed the stairs to Itsik's parents' flat as fast as she could, wondering what the matter was. Itsik's mother had shouted something from the window when she'd rang the bell, but the noise of traffic had drowned out the older woman's voice.

By the time she'd reached the penultimate landing, she found herself short of breath. Itsik's mother stood at the bannister, looking down at her climbing the last flight. She was crying.

'What's up,' she gasped, catching hold of the old lady's arm, concerned.

'Here,' she said, handing her a letter, tears running down her face. 'Esther's had her baby.'

Miriam, a sense of relief flooding through her, ripped open the envelope.

~~o~~

23rd July

Haifa Jewish Hospital.

My dearest Miriam,

Itsik and I have another daughter. Miriam Rosa Weichmann. 3.2kg. She was born two days ago.

Miriam's eyes filled with tears. They overflowed onto her cheeks and dripped onto the letter. Itsik's mother placed her hand on Miriam's wrist and squeezed.

'She called her after me and Rosa,' Miriam said, her voice choking.

'I know. I only found out today,' the older woman said, still crying. The two women hugged for a minute without speaking.

'Are they both well?' Miriam asked, breaking the silence.

'Yes. Come in and read your letter. I'll make you a cup of coffee.'

Miriam followed the older woman through. She hugged Itsik's father and congratulated him, but she worried at the man's lukewarm response. She'd noticed him becoming more and more withdrawn over the last few months and she thought that, if a new grandchild couldn't bring him out of his misery, nothing else would.

She sat down and finished reading Esther's letter.

We are both well now although the labour was harder than with the other two, which is why I've taken two days to write. I've been sleeping most of the time since, and the nurses have been feeding the baby for me. I hope it wasn't too much of a shock about the name. I was going to ask you first but thought it might be bad luck, so I decided to wait and see if it was a boy or a girl. And before you tut-tut and say the baby shouldn't be called Miriam, after you, remember that you are my oldest friend and have supported me above and beyond what I should expect, especially in giving me peace of mind about how Itsik's parents are being cared for. And I couldn't call her after you without giving her Rosa's name too.

Anyway, I'll always think of you two when I shout her name.

I should get out tomorrow. Abel and Leah are in Afula looking after the children, so we'd better get back before they get too spoiled. And anyway, the longer they have our children, the more likely it is that they will never have children of their own. I think they are trying, but nothing has happened yet. I hope it does soon. It would be nice for Miriam Rosa to have a little cousin to play with now and again.

I'm sorry that you're all on your own now. I know what you mean. Family are everything to me but sometimes you just need a true friend. Still, you'll get out soon and perhaps even join Rosa, eventually.

I feel sad that you, Rosa, and Itsik's parents can't come and see little Miriam. I only hope the National Socialists are ousted soon, and Germany gets back to what it was.

Even if it did, I don't think I could ever go back. Not after the way people treated us. I would never feel safe or welcome again, and I wouldn't want this little one to feel different from everyone else.

Anyway, the British have debated a new deal for Palestine in parliament and they intend for it to become an independent country. They really want out, truth be told, but if it happens, it will be a place where Jews all over the world can come to, and that would wonderful, even though the British want to have a curb put on open immigration. I hope the Arabs, like some of ours, can be part of it, too.

I must go. I need to feed the little one again, and Itsik is coming to visit soon, so I can give him your letters to post. I've sent one for Rosa. Mama Weichmann will give it to you. Can you forward it to her if you have an address for her? It was a good idea to send your letters to the flat. You always were sharp at coming up with answers to our problems.

All my love,

Esther.

CHAPTER 189

Miriam signed the letter she'd just finished writing and reread it. It was the first moment she'd had a chance to reply since hearing about the new baby.

20th August

Kiel

Dear Esther,

It was heart-warming to hear your wonderful news – Itsik's mother was over the moon although we were both saddened that we couldn't just nip over and see you and the baby. Is there any chance you could send her a photograph of her? I'm sure that would help.

I'm so touched that you have called her after me. I never expected that! I'm sure Rosa will be thrilled too.

Talking of Rosa, the news is not so great. She is back. Not in Germany, but in Europe at least. They wouldn't let them in to Cuba or America, so the ship returned across the Atlantic, landing in Belgium. She is still hoping to get a visa and try again. She did talk about coming back home but I wrote to her telling her not to return to Kiel, despite being so close to her parents and Emil's parents, and to me.

It is heartbreaking, and they are all bitterly disappointed but, hopefully, they'll still get to America and, even if they don't, they'll be safe enough in Belgium.

Everyone here is talking of war; of Germany attacking Poland. If the British join in, it will be impossible for us to get to England. Fingers crossed, nothing happens until October, when we should have our visas.

I've found a couple who are happy to look after Itsik's parents once we leave. I told them you would be happy to pay a little and they seemed pleased. I'll take them up to the flat next month to introduce them.

Your letter took almost a month to get here! Yosef says that if war comes, the post might not get through.

Anyway, I can hardly write I'm still so excited. You must be delighted that it's all over and the baby is well. Moshe and Shoshana will be over the moon to have a new little sister and I'm sure Itsik is overjoyed and relieved.

All my love, especially to the little one,

Miriam.

She sealed the letter and put it in her bag. She would post it along with the one that Itsik's mother would give her when she visited the next afternoon.

~~o~~

Memo: Geh.KdoS. ABW 23/08/39 CAC0842.1

For Attention Only: General Erich Kästner, Abwehr, Kiel office, Abwehr.

From: Vice Admiral Wilhelm Canaris, Chef der Abwehr.

In addition to the parts of the non-aggression agreement signed yesterday by foreign ministers Joachim von Ribbentrop and Vyacheslav Molotov announced today, we have learned that a hidden protocol, as happened with Italy, has been agreed, allowing for the joint occupation of Poland by Germany and the Soviet Union, and the Soviet occupation of the Baltic States, Finland, and Bessarabia. In the light of the breakdown of the tripartite talks between Britain, France, and the Soviet Union two days ago, this protocol removes the threat of Soviet intervention during the proposed German invasion of Poland. [END]

~~o~~

KIELER MORGENPOST

Thursday 24th August 1939

HISTORIC PEACE AGREEMENT SIGNED WITH RUSSIA!

A non-aggression agreement between the Third Reich and the Soviet Union, the Molotov-Ribbentrop Pact, was signed yesterday. In light of the recent belligerence of the Polish Government and its armed forces, this is a welcome affirmation of the friendship between Germany and the Soviet Union. The Morgenpost believes that this agreement will increase pressure on the Polish Government to resolve its current dispute with Germany and remove the threat of war between our nations.

It affirms our opinion that the Führer, Adolf Hitler, is one of the greatest statesmen Germany, and the world, has ever known.

~~o~~

In a way, it pleased the General that the Soviets were out of the picture. The knowledge that his sons would likely be involved in an invasion of Poland, with the threat of a Soviet intervention hanging over them, had worried him more than he'd admitted, although he didn't by any means take the threat of Polish resistance lightly.

But any hopes that a conflict might be averted had been dashed, and he was almost certain that, in three days' time, the country, and Europe, would be at war for the second time in his life.

~~o~~

[25/08/1939 Friday]

'Father, we've been mobilised. We've been moved to Stettin, but we leave for the border tomorrow.'

The telephone line crackled, but the General could hear a nervous excitement in

641

Johann's voice.

'I know,' the General said. 'We had notification of all the troop movements yesterday. I saw that your regiment were involved. Have you spoken to Franz?'

'Yes. He couldn't get away. He asked me to telephone you if I got the chance. I can't speak for long.'

'That's fine. It was good that you called. The best of luck to you both. Remember to keep a level head. It's easy to get caught up in all the turmoil but the best leaders keep their emotions under check. That's how I survived the last war.'

'I know. I hear people talk. I should have taken the chance to ask you more, but it's too late now.'

'Don't worry. The colonel said you were both top soldiers, and he's not the type to flatter people. You'll be fine. I'll tell Mama you called.'

'Yes. I'll telephone her from Warsaw.'

The General heard his son's laughter at the end of the line, and it didn't sound forced. He hoped it wouldn't be the last time he heard it.

'Goodbye,' he heard himself say, 'And God bless.'

'See you soon. Goodbye.'

The line went dead, and the General replaced the receiver on its cradle.

CHAPTER 190

'Erich, there has been a delay. I just thought I'd let you know.'

'Thanks for telephoning, Canaris. The boys' regiment is involved. In a way, it would have been better if it had gone ahead. The wait will be frustrating for them, and me. What reason did they give for it?'

'Ha. Our friend, Il Duce, is dragging his heels. I'm told he telephoned the Führer and said that he would not honour the Pact of Steel if Germany attacked Poland. They've postponed the invasion for five days. Sources say the Italians will come round; old Mussolini needs us too much if he wants to further his ambitions for the region.'

'I heard the British have beefed up their support for Poland.'

'Yes. The two countries signed a mutual assistance treaty yesterday, but they'll not have time to send any troops, and I guarantee that they'll not send their navy into the Baltic, which would be suicide for them if hostilities break out.'

'They will declare war though?'

Canaris sighed.

'They will. They've backed themselves into a corner. France will follow suit.'

'Herr Hitler takes a risk. France could attack us to support Poland.'

'We have substantial military strength in the Rheinland. I doubt the French will risk attacking without significant help from the British.'

'So, we take Poland or, at least, half of it. What then?'

'That depends on what Britain and France do. But I suspect that we'll just wait, growing stronger by the day, economically and militarily.'

'And after that?'

'He means to conquer Europe. He might just do it.'

~~o~~

Memo: Geh.KdoS. ABW 31/08/39 CAC0842.1

For Attention Only: General Erich Kästner, Abwehr, Kiel office, Abwehr.

From: Vice Admiral Wilhelm Canaris, Chef der Abwehr.

The British fleet has mobilised; all leave has been cancelled and all naval ships have been made ready to go to sea. [END]

~~o~~

Memo: Geh.KdoS. ABW 31/08/39 CAC0842.1

For Attention Only: General Erich Kästner, Abwehr, Kiel office, Abwehr.

From: Vice Admiral Wilhelm Canaris, Chef der Abwehr.

An ultimatum to Poland concerning the Polish Corridor and the Free City of Danzig has been issued from the office of the Foreign Minister. It states that if Poland does not concede to the demands of the German Government, Germany will have no option but to take the appropriate action to protect all its citizens living in the disputed zone. [END]

~~o~~

[01/09/1939 Friday]

Colonel Schneider looked around. All his platoon leaders were there, and two of his four majors.

They'd set up field tents the day before and he could hear the subdued murmur of chatter from his enlisted men in the rows of canvas tents surrounding his command quarters.

'Right, men. Let's begin.'

Their eager faces looked towards him, a mixture of uneasiness and anticipation etched on their features in the faded light of the hissing paraffin lamps.

'We finally have our orders. Some of you were involved in our small campaign in Sudetenland. Forget about that. It wasn't a war, or anything like it. At 0450 hours we will cross the border, and we will be at war with Poland. Others may choose to fight on the side of the Poles, but we are ready for any of them.'

A buzz of excitement spread around the tent, and he waited until it had subsided. He flipped over the sheet of paper that covered the military map clipped to a board, set up like an artist's easel. He used his swagger stick to point to it.

'The 4th Army have been given orders to cross into Poland here,' he said, tapping the map, 'and fight towards the Vistula River which we will cross at Chełmno, then move southeastwards towards Warsaw. Our battalion's immediate orders are to take Chojnice, a small town a few kilometres inside the border, within the first twenty-four hours. Any questions?'

He looked around and saw that one of his lieutenants wanted to ask something. He nodded at him to speak.

'Herr Oberst, why is it called Konitz on the map?'

'Good question. These maps were prepared from our existing ones and have been updated where necessary. Before the last war, this town belonged to us, and its German name was Konitz. It will be again.'

He waited until the buzz of approval died down.

'Before we attack, the Luftwaffe are going to bomb and strafe the defending positions. This will start at 0430 hours, during which time we will move close to the Polish border.'

He knew that none of them would sleep; not on the first night at least, but he wanted to get them into a routine.

'In preparation for this,' he told them, 'we will strike camp at 0200 hours, so I suggest you arrange for your men to get a few hours' sleep and for the cooks to have something warm prepared for them at 0100 hours. Does everybody understand?'

'Yes, sir,' a chorus of voices yelled back at him, and the sounds in the tents around the field fell silent.

'Go and brief your men. Major Kästner and Major Breit will remain here. Dismissed.'

The officers, mostly in their twenties, trooped out, eager to tell their men that they were about to go into battle.

'Here we go, brother,' Johann said, grinning, as he passed Franz, punching him on the arm.

When the tent had emptied, the colonel motioned for his two senior officers to join him at the folding table that was set up in the corner. He unfolded and laid out a low-scale map of the town of Chojnice.

'Major Mandel and Major Dressel have taken a squad each and are scouting the border area. I never completely trust intelligence that I've not confirmed myself, where possible. You two will command the first units into Chojnice. Get your men to wrap something over their heads until the bombing stops; they'll think clearer and hear better. The Polish troops will be

644

in shock so the quicker we hit them, the better. They'll never have been in a bombardment before, so we will have a few minutes' advantage before they realise what's happening.'

The Colonel pointed to the map.

'Franz, you take four platoons and hit the Polish troops that are guarding the main road into town. Magnus, you do the same with your men but circle round and take the western approach road. Major Mandel will loop to the north and cut off any retreat to the east. Major Dressel and I will bring the trucks and half-tracks in once you have secured the roads, and we'll mop up the stragglers in the centre. When we've done that, follow us in. You know how to secure any prisoners. Leave as few men guarding them as you can. Medical support will come in behind us. Any questions?'

'Sir, just a suggestion but if you could keep two empty trucks with the medical team, we can bring in any casualties and prisoners with us when we bring up your rear.'

'Good call, major. I'll do that. Now, go and update your platoon leaders with your orders, and make your final checks. Be brave tomorrow, but don't be stupid.'

'Yes, sir.' Both men saluted and left. The colonel opened the chest that sat in the corner and took out a bottle of brandy. Pouring himself a glass, he looked around, and smiled. The last time he'd seen real action was in 1918. He'd been a junior officer, serving under one Colonel Erich Kästner. He thought about the General, himself, and the old man's two sons.

It's a funny world.

~~o~~

At the end of the day, they loaded the last of the prisoners onto the waiting trucks on the first stage of their journey to the hastily erected prisoner-of-war camps being set up in eastern Germany.

The bulk of the battalion were camped in a field outside Chojnice but Colonel Schneider and two of his senior officers were billeted in the headquarters they'd set up in the town's police station, to be at the centre of things. Franz and Magnus Breit were at the camp, sorting out the men for the next day.

The colonel had taken Franz aside before he left.

'Franz, I have to stay here and meet the town officials and wait for the staff officers and men to arrive and take over from us when we move on. I want you to keep the men busy and have us ready to leave at 0600 hours tomorrow. Take Major Breit with you. Break out a tot of Schnapps for each of the men; they deserve it after their first day in action but keep them in camp and get them settled early. This war is all about moving fast, keeping the enemy stumbling in front of us, just like in training.'

'Yes, sir. What will I tell them?'

'We're making for Chełmno, the other side of the Vistula. I aim to be there in two days, but the Poles may pull back behind the river and if there is no resistance tomorrow, we could easily be there by mid-afternoon.'

'So, we'll set up camp when we arrive?'

'Perhaps. I'll send a scouting party ahead. Depending on the situation, we may attack as soon as we get there. Don't tell the men where we're going but prepare them to fight tomorrow.'

'Oh, and on your way,' the colonel added, 'send one of your squads to go and paint over the town signs before we leave. Change them back to Konitz.'

Franz pulled all the officers together as soon as he had reached the camp. They'd almost finished building it, and the cooks were already preparing the men's evening meal. Franz told them of the colonel's plans for the next morning and left them to brief their platoons in their own time. He grabbed a plate of food from the mess as soon as it was ready, and headed back to his own tent, sending Private Knef, his own personal aide, to fetch his brother.

'What did you think?' he asked Johann, when he'd finished the stew, cabbage, and potatoes that he suspected would be his diet for the foreseeable future.

'Good,' Johann replied, munching on a piece of bread and jam he'd purloined. 'Our casualties were low; the men did exactly what they've been trained to do, and the air strikes; have you ever experienced anything like that? It's no wonder the poor bastards didn't know what was happening.'

The Polish Army had fought hard, but without a cohesive strategy, and it had been almost clinical, the way the colonel's plan had worked. Three men had been killed on the German side, with a smattering of injuries from the minor, and sometimes absurd, to the life-threatening and life-changing ones that ended a soldier's war, one way or the other.

The Poles had suffered far heavier casualties, and they'd been so outnumbered and outmanoeuvred that they'd surrendered before the sun had risen for more than an hour.

When the Stukas had screamed in above Franz and Johann's heads, diving low to drop bombs on the enemy's machine-gun emplacements, the men had scrambled to cover their ears and watch the ground in front of them in horror as it seemed to bulge and heave into the air, the shock wave rolling across the fields separating them from the Polish positions like a swell on a grassy sea.

The planes followed their bombing strikes by flying along the enemy lines, strafing their positions with large-calibre machine-gun fire, so low that the noise was almost painful to listen to. Franz had looked up and had seen the pilot of one plane give him a thumbs up, which he returned.

He hadn't waited for the smoke to clear. Shouting an order to the men, he broke cover at a low run and made for the heaped earth of the bomb craters, hearing Johann and the other platoon leaders echo his command.

It had taken just ten minutes of intense fighting to extinguish the pocket of resistance that remained guarding the road, and none of his men had been killed. He'd called for a medic for two injured soldiers and told his radio operator to inform the colonel that the road was open.

'Tell him that there is some bomb damage to the road, but that it is passable with care.'

The town had been taken an hour later, and it only remained to round up the fragments of the defending Polish units and the local policemen, before setting up a perimeter, installing a makeshift civilian administration and putting a curfew in place.

'The colonel knows his stuff,' Johann said, swallowing the last of his crust. 'It went just like he said it would, and afterwards, he just seemed to know exactly what to do to make the town safe, and under control.'

'He told me that he learned most of it from Father, but I'm sure that's a bit of an exaggeration. He's his own man. I like him, and he knows the men.'

'I used to resent him, you know, for always pulling me up for mucking around but, today, when we were in the thick of it, I was glad he'd rode down hard on us, because everything we did out there seemed like second nature.'

A brief smile flitted across Franz's face, then disappeared as fast as it had materialised.

'Were you frightened?' he asked.

Johann looked up, relieved that Franz had brought it up.

'Yes. When the planes arrived, I suddenly realised that people were dying too easily and that I had to be party to it or be killed myself. It hit me hard for a minute or two, but as soon as we started moving, I felt as if I were outside my body. Everything became automatic. And then, after it was all over, when I saw the dead and wounded and thought that it could have been me, or you, or one of our friends, I started to shake.'

Franz smiled again.

'I was the same. I don't think fear left me all day, but I managed to keep it under control. It was as if I could put it in a box, but know it was still there.'

'You didn't look frightened. You were the first man to charge the Polish positions.'

'I couldn't ask the men to do something I wasn't prepared to do myself, and I knew that you were all covering me. And the Poles were stunned, the ones who were still alive.'

'It won't always be as easy as that. We'll not always have the element of shock on our side, but we are better trained, and equipped. Did you see their machine gun? It was probably used in the last war.'

Franz laughed.

'We still have some old gear too, but most of it is up to date.'

They didn't speak for a minute, then Johann broke the silence.

'How do you think father survived four years of this?' he asked. 'It is unimaginable.'

'What he went through was much worse, from the little he's said about it. The trenches, the artillery, the gas, the mud. And so much death. This war will be fought differently, wait and see.'

'I hope so,' Johann said. He looked at his watch. 'I should go. I need to debrief the men and prepare them for tomorrow.'

Franz nodded.

'I have to report to the colonel, and then try and get some rest. We have an early start. We'll have to break camp around five, to be ready to move at six. Get some sleep.'

They hugged.

'Tomorrow,' Johann said, as he left.

~~o~~

[02/09/1939 Saturday]

Memo: Geh.KdoS. ABW 02/09/39 CAC0852.1

For Attention Only: General Erich Kästner, Abwehr, Kiel office, Abwehr.

From: Vice Admiral Wilhelm Canaris, Chef der Abwehr.

In a meeting attended by Heinrich Himmler, his deputy Reinhard Heydrich, Adolf Eichmann, and the head of the Reichsbahn, Julius Dorpmüller, it has been confirmed that one of the main functions of the rail network is the deportation of Jews from Germany to Poland. [END]

~~o~~

Memo: Geh.KdoS. ABW 02/09/39 CAC0853.1

For Attention Only: General Erich Kästner, Abwehr, Kiel office, Abwehr.

From: Vice Admiral Wilhelm Canaris, Chef der Abwehr.

The sustained and substantial bombing of Warsaw has begun. We expect reports of heavy civilian casualties. [END]

CHAPTER 191

THE LONDON EVENING TELEGRAPH

LATE EDITION

Sunday, September 3rd, 1939

BRITAIN AT WAR WITH GERMANY

"I am speaking to you from the Cabinet Room at 10, Downing Street.

This morning the British Ambassador in Berlin handed the German Government a final note stating that unless we heard from them by 11 o'clock, that they were prepared at once to withdraw their troops from Poland, then a state of war would exist between us.

I have to tell you now that no such undertaking has been received, and that consequently this country is at war with Germany".

These were the words of Prime Minister, Neville Chamberlain, yesterday.

Since the German invasion of Poland two days ago, the British Government has called for a withdrawal of German troops from Polish territory and it issued the ultimatum earlier today.

The Government has started civilian evacuations from London and the naval fleet has been mobilised. The Prime Minister has appointed Winston Churchill as the First Lord of the Admiralty. The former Home Secretary and Chancellor of the Exchequer, who held the post in the last war, has long been an advocate of rearmament and has opposed appeasement in parliament on numerous occasions.

In preparation for war, the army, navy and air force had already been mobilised. All leave has been cancelled and the civilian reserves have been ordered to report for duty.

In addition, 600 high-risk male Germans resident in Britain have been interned. It is expected that the German authorities will reciprocate by arresting those Britons who did not manage to leave Germany before the declaration of war.

~~o~~

'Finally, Marjorie, we are standing up to this martinet.'

'Herr Hitler, you mean?'

'Of course,' Major Anthony Plenderleith said, scowling under his bushy eyebrows. 'Who else did you think I was talking about.'

'I was reading the *Woman's Weekly*,' his wife said, tutting. 'I wasn't paying attention.'

'Well, you should. We're now at war.'

'Oh dear.'

~~o~~

[04/09/1939 Monday]

'Where's Yosef?' Maria said.

The General looked up from the paper, its pages full of the progress being made by the German forces in Poland.

'I gave him the day off today. He took the last train to Hamburg last night. We managed to get a travel permit. He'll be back later this evening.'

'For goodness' sake, I wish you'd told me. I was going to dig up the carrots today. There's a collection for home-grown vegetables tomorrow at the church. We're distributing them to poorer families.'

'You'll have to do it yourself. It was essential that he visited the British consulate to see if there's any chance that they'll still get their visas for Britain, and to find out if they can get there via one of the low countries, or Denmark. I would give you a hand, but I've got a meeting I can't get out of. I felt bad that I couldn't drive Yosef down there myself, but I had to be in Kiel.'

He didn't say it, but he had briefly considered offering Albert to drive down with Yosef, but for Maria it would have been one step too far, having taken so long to find a replacement driver.

'Oh. I see. I suppose he had to go. It's just not great timing. Do you think they will still get to Britain?'

'I doubt it, but he's going to try the American consulate if the British can't help.'

'Won't that take much longer? Can't they go somewhere else?'

'They could, but Yosef had such a job persuading Miriam to consider going in the first place, and he didn't want to jeopardise her decision by pushing other options too much.'

'It would be better for them, and us, if they got away sooner rather than later.'

'I'm sure they're trying their best, dear,' he answered, keeping his voice level, if a little dry.

~~o~~

It had been a terrible trip; one of the worst forty-eight hours he'd had since being beaten by the SA thugs at Isaac's shop.

His travel pass, which the General had procured for him, had been checked three times on the journey. At the station barrier, the guard had scrutinised it for what seemed like a lifetime before showing it to his superior. In the end, they'd let him through, but it had been checked on two further occasions on the train, with similar thoroughness. Each time, Yosef had shown his identification and had made sure his veteran's card was prominently displayed, as the General had advised.

On reaching Hamburg, he'd made his way to Altona, where he'd been warmly welcomed by Miriam's parents and given a bed for the night.

In the morning, he'd risen at four, and walked to the British consulate, remembering the queues of previous visits.

The road along of the shore of Außenalster was closed off by barriers tended by policemen, so he had to divert a couple of streets away before being able to cut down to the front again.

The British consulate building was closed and empty. His heart sinking, he read the hastily printed sign on the gate.

> Due to the state of war existing between Germany and Great
> Britain, this consulate will be closed until such hostilities
> end. British citizens seeking consular support should visit the
> consulate of the United States of America.

Yosef had almost cried, despite having known in his heart that the British would be gone, but he'd hurried along Harvestehuder Weg, hardly seeing the grand houses on his right and the lakeside on his left. When he turned the corner into Alsterufer he realised why the shore road had been closed. The US consulate, halfway along, was engulfed by a crowd numbering in the high hundreds, maybe more.

They were being barely corralled by a score of baton-wielding policemen, one of whom Yosef assumed was in charge, as he was using a loudhailer to harangue the crowd with warnings of the consequences if order was not swiftly restored.

From behind Yosef, an army truck suddenly appeared out from the morning gloom and, as he stood aside, behind a tree, he watched as a squad of reinforcements jumped out from the back as soon as the truck screeched to a halt.

The milling crowd seemed to freeze for a second as the soldiers' boots hit the ground, then panic set in as the new arrivals charged at them, batons raised.

In the melee, Yosef saw men and women trampled and others clubbed, blood running down their faces.

Knowing he could do little to help, he ducked out of sight and retraced his steps back towards the British consulate, and skirted the closed streets, making his way back to the centre of town. He found a telephone box and called the Drachensee house.

~~o~~

Miriam was the only one in the house. When the telephone rang, she answered it, as she'd been instructed to do when the mistress and General Kästner were out.

It was a shock when she heard Yosef's voice.

'The consulate is closed,' he said, the words rushing from him, not giving her a chance to ask questions. 'There's a riot at the American one. I'm going to stay here tonight, at your parents, if I can, then try again in the morning when the authorities should have restored order.'

'But…'

He interrupted her.

'I've got to go. Just tell the General when he comes home. Don't say anything to Frau Kästner. She wouldn't approve.'

'Yosef…' she said, but he'd gone.

Worried, she wondered if she should try and contact her parents, but she would have to slip out later and use the telephone booth in Hamburger Chaussee; she would never consider using the Kästners' telephone for personal calls.

Her parents didn't have a telephone so she would have to call her brother, who'd had one installed by his employers, and she doubted it would still be connected, now that he'd lost his job.

She returned to her chores, Yosef never far from her thoughts.

~~o~~

The General opened the cupboard door and stood back to let Admiral Canaris see.

'Ah. So that's why you wanted the detailed reports from the field. I wasn't surprised that

650

you wanted the information on the 4th Army, but on the entire campaign? I began to wonder if you were thinking of passing it on to the British.'

The General laughed. A map of Poland covered the inside of the cupboard door, and a series of card shapes were pinned to it, indicating the positions of the various regiments that made up *Fall Weiss*, the code name for the operation to occupy Western Poland.

'It's partly out of a fascination for this new way we're waging war, but it's mostly out of a need to know where my sons are, and what sort of action they're involved in.'

Canaris put his hand on the General's shoulder.

'I understand, old friend. And what is eating you up is that you can't be out there looking after them, instead of being stuck here in an office.'

'The memos gave such a sparse overview of the situations. It was driving me insane, not knowing the detail. Thanks for arranging for the reports to be sent. I hope it didn't cause any trouble.'

'Not at all. I told Heydrich that you were one of my most useful analysts; that you were regarded as one of our more astute generals and that it would be a shame to waste your knowledge and experience.'

Canaris picked up his own memo from the pile on the table and read it.

Memo: Geh.KdoS. ABW 04/09/39 CAC0861.1

For Attention Only: All senior executive officers, Abwehr.

From: Vice Admiral Wilhelm Canaris, Chef der Abwehr.

The Wehrmacht is making excellent progress on all fronts, although the Polish Army is showing sporadic resistance. Advances are rapid in most areas and although some Polish units have managed to pull back, the speed of our advance has cut off large numbers of their troops. By yesterday, all main Polish air bases had been destroyed. This gives the Luftwaffe complete control of the air.

Although a few minor skirmishes occurred at the border of the Saarland with France, the French Army did not intervene in any substantial or meaningful way. The British have sent repeated demands for our withdrawal but have taken no action to support the Polish armed forces directly.

RAF Bomber Command carried out a raid on the battleship, Admiral Scheer and the cruiser, Emden, in the Helgoland Bight, with 29 Bristol Blenheims and Vickers Wellingtons during the hours of daylight. The Admiral Scheer was hit by three bombs but was undamaged when they did not explode. The bow of the cruiser Emden was damaged by the wreckage of a crashed Blenheim. Five of the attacking aircraft were shot down by our fighters. [END]

~~o~~

'I see what you mean about sparse,' he said. 'There's not much detail there but, in my defence, most of my heads of station don't need any more than that.'

The General picked up the pile of detailed battle reports.

'I shall provide you with incisive analysis then. I wouldn't want Heydrich to think you weren't getting your money's worth.'

Canaris laughed.

'You probably should. It would make it easier if questions were ever asked. How are the boys doing?'

'I've heard nothing specific, but casualties in their regiment have been light, so no news is good news, as far as I'm concerned.'

'How much progress have they made?'

'They took the small town of Chojnice the first day, without too much resistance, and reached the Vistula two days later. That's 100 kilometres.'

'It's a different war, Erich, and we don't even have the best motorised military equipment in the world. We haven't even used our panzer regiments to their full potential yet.'

'What do you mean?'

'They're still fighting an infantry war. Granted, they can move units, and even regiments, quickly and efficiently, and with the half-tracks, they can move across country if needed, but the fighting is still man against man, and gun against gun.'

'But we have complete control of the air, and our bombers are supporting the troops where needed.'

'Yes, yes, and that is making a big difference, but most of the bombers are targeting Warsaw, and a few of the other larger cities. Our tanks should be punching holes in defensive lines and the infantry should follow them through. At this point in time, it's the other way around. Have a look at the reports yourself.'

'I will,' the General said, a thoughtful look on his face. 'Did you come up with this?'

'No, I have to admit that I didn't, but I could clearly see it once it was pointed out. I have a couple of extremely smart young men on my staff who seem to have a good grip of what modern warfare should look like.'

'It seems that we have a lot still to learn. Is there any way we can get this information to the men on the battlefield?'

'We've informed the staff command. It's they who make all the decisions. We can only advise.'

'But that's ludicrous. If this sort of information would make a difference, it should be acted on.'

'In an ideal world, it would. As it turns out, we are comfortably winning without risking our tanks, so it might not be a popular suggestion. Providing they understand our concerns, and use the lessons learned when we have to fight against a better-equipped and better-trained opponent, it will be worth it.'

'I hope so.'

The General turned back to the map.

'The boys have crossed the Vistula,' he said, pointing, 'and their battalion is currently trying to take Chełmno. It would be nice if some of these panzers would lend a hand.'

'I could get you posted out there, if you like,' Canaris said, laughing again.

'I'm too old and set in my ways. You and I both know that war is a young man's game.'

'I just hope that our young men come out of it better than our generation did.'

'Amen,' the General said, closing the cupboard.

'I'm going to Poland, next week,' the admiral said.

'You are? Where?' the General asked, surprise in his voice.

'To Warsaw, if we have it by then, or as close to it as I can get.'

'Why you?'

'We've had reports, and I need to go and see for myself.'

'Reports? What reports?'

'I'll speak to you when I get back. A couple of our agents have asked to see me in person, and they're posted in Poland. Heydrich says I'm a fool to be going into a war zone, but I think he's secretly impressed that I should be willing to risk it. He doesn't know about our contacts, obviously.'

The General hesitated.

'At the expense of sounding like an old woman, if you happen to chance on Franz and Johann…'

'I will look out for them, but it will be difficult.'

A knock on the door interrupted them, and Günter Neuer entered.

'Your car is here, Admiral,' the chief petty officer said.

The General shook his friend's hand.

'Good luck,' he said.

CHAPTER 192

The morning after the disturbance at the American consulate, and long before daybreak, Yosef made the journey back to shore of the Außenalster, walking much of the way after a Gestapo officer had boarded the tram he was travelling on.

The crowd had been dispersed overnight, with many arrests, and hadn't gathered to quite the same degree as it had the day before. A policeman checked his papers; the letter from the General and his British visa application seemed to convince the man that he had a bona fide reason for visiting the embassy and, surprised, Yosef thanked him for letting him through, and made his way to the end of the queue. By mid-morning, the snaking column of people had grown behind him, but the police had it under control, and there was no repeat of the previous day's violence.

Just before lunchtime he was seen by a harassed junior embassy officer, who told him that, much to his sorrow, they could do nothing for holders of British visa applications, but he handed him a printed letter that the British consulate had prepared. He waited patiently while Yosef filled in an application for United States visas and told him that they were trying their best to expedite processing, but that it would be at least nine months before Yosef would receive an answer.

'Even then,' the young American man had said, in passable German, 'only one application in five is successful.'

Seeing the shock on Yosef's face, he frowned.

'Congress has blocked a bill to let more refugees in. We all think it's terrible; they just can't see what it's like here on the ground. If it's any consolation, we're trying our best for you all, and I know the ambassador is applying as much pressure as he can.'

Yosef thanked the man and left. The queue had now snaked its way back and forward twice along the road and he kept his head down as he hurried along, not wanting to catch the eye of any of the poor souls at the back of the line.

At the station, he approached the barrier with trepidation, hoping his travel pass was still valid. The policeman barely glanced at it, and there was only one cursory check on the return journey to Kiel.

He read the hastily printed sheet he'd been given at the embassy on the way back.

He arrived home just after lunchtime, but Miriam was busy, helping Frau Kästner to pack away the summer clothes and bring the warm winter ones down from the attic, so he didn't get the chance to speak to her until they'd finished their chores after dinner.

'Well,' she said, when they were finally alone, 'Any news.'

'The British have gone,' he told her, his eyes barely able to meet hers. 'I visited the American consulate and talked to a nice young man there. He helped me fill in an application, but we're back to square one. Nine months to a year, he said.'

'And there's nothing we can do about our British visa? What if we travelled somewhere else first?'

He handed her the letter.

'I was given this. It's from the British, saying that it is unlikely that other countries will let us in and, even if they do, there's no guarantee that our visa application will be transferrable.'

'They don't want flocks of German Jews turning up at their embassies and consulates all over Europe in desperation, trying to get their visas,' Miriam said, her shoulders slumping.

'It might be worthwhile trying Holland or Belgium. They're not at war.'

'We'd have to get visas for either of those countries.'

'Or slip over the border to Denmark,' Yosef said, glancing at her to see her reaction.

'No. If we failed, or if we were sent back, we'd risk being sent to one of the camps.'

'I'll have a word with the General. He might be able to help.'

'He was all for driving to Hamburg last night when I told him you were staying overnight, but I managed to convince him that you were safe enough.'

'Did he tell Frau Kästner where I was?'

'Yes, although I think he said that your train was cancelled. She didn't speak much yesterday and looked a bit cross today. She wants you to help her in the garden.'

'After that journey, and the two days in Hamburg, I'll be happy to have a day in the garden.'

She squeezed his hand.

'Tell me all about it,' she said...

~~o~~

Esther almost grabbed the letters from the postman. She glanced at the handwriting and lay the one from Itsik's mother to the side. She tore open Miriam's letter and read it.

There was nothing about the war; they'd only heard news of it on the radio a few days before but, although the Palestine Broadcasting Service was heavily slanted towards the British perspective, they could gather much of what was happening back home.

She gasped when she read that Rosa and her family hadn't made it to the United States, and because of the war, she knew Miriam and Yosef's hopes of getting to Britain were now dashed.

After she'd finished Miriam's letter, she read the one from her mother-in-law. She frowned at the older woman's despair about never seeing her latest grandchild and at her dismay that Miriam would be leaving them shortly; that the new people wouldn't be as nice, or as trustworthy.

That won't be a problem now.

She sat at the table and, although she knew that she, her husband, and their young family were safe, she felt the weight of the world heavy on her shoulders.

She sat down to reply to their letters.

She'd written a page of Miriam's letter when she sat bolt upright.

The letters. The British are at war with us. How will they get to Germany?

~~o~~

[07/09/1939 Thursday]

The General sipped his coffee in the kitchen of the Nussbaums' house. Miriam busied herself laying out a spread of home-made biscuits and cakes on the table, before sitting down to join Yosef and the General.

'You shouldn't have gone to this effort,' the General said, smiling at the polite normality of it, despite the extraordinary times they were living in.

'It's no bother, sir. It's kind of you to give up your time to talk to us.'

'Not at all, and please, at least here, call me Erich.'

The Nussbaums both blushed.

'I don't know, sir...' Miriam said, and they all laughed, breaking the tension.

'Yosef told me about Hamburg,' the General said, broaching the subject that none of them wanted to talk about. 'It was inevitable, I'm afraid. It's what you do now that's the important thing.'

'What can we do, sir, other than wait.'

'There are other options, and you'll have to consider the possibility that the United States will be drawn into the war, sooner or later, although for now, it seems unlikely. The political will on the opposite side of the Atlantic to intervene in another European conflict seems almost non-existent.'

'I think you're right, sir,' Yosef said. 'In spite of calls from Jewish groups over there, they don't seem to want to know about our problems, or even increase Jewish immigration to help, far less come to our aid. Even so, we still feel that a US visa is our best chance.'

'There must be some way of getting you out of Germany to somewhere neutral, then continuing your application for a British visa. Your names will surely be on record.'

'I don't think we are much of a priority for the British either. They aren't lifting a finger to help the Poles, despite their declaration that they would support them if the Wehrmacht invaded, so why would they bother with us?'

Yosef handed the General the printed sheet he'd been given by the American consulate on behalf of the British. He read it and frowned.

'They certainly don't want you to appear at any of their embassies outside Germany,' he said. 'That doesn't mean they wouldn't deal with you if you turned up.'

'We thought of that. It might just be possible to get permission to travel to the low countries, but there's no guarantees we would get our visas there, for Britain or America.'

'If you got as far as Belgium, it wouldn't be hard to travel on to France. You'd be safe enough there. The French haven't rushed to the defence of Poland, but Herr Hitler would think twice about taking on their military forces. France is a different kettle of fish from Poland, in that respect.'

'We thought about France, sir. We can all speak a little of the language, but I hear their economy is in crisis, and refugees have virtually no chance of a job. We know no one in France who would take us in, so we'd be dependent on our savings, sir, if we could access them.'

'What about Denmark? There will be an embassy in Copenhagen.'

'It's nearly impossible to get permission to travel to Denmark unless you have a relative there. Even then, they're only letting a few through. We've made enquiries.'

'Maria has relatives there. I'll see if there's anything I can do.' The General hesitated for a second.

'You could just slip over the border,' he said.

He noticed the Nussbaums glance at each other.

They've thought about it.

'Sir, we know no one there, so it would be difficult to find somewhere to hide and, anyway, would the British issue a visa to people who are in the country illegally?'

'Perhaps not, but you could stay in Denmark. We might be able to find you somewhere to go into hiding.'

The General could understand their reluctance. The Danes wouldn't want to upset the German authorities and would possibly feel under pressure to hand back any German Jews who tried to cross the border. He'd made enquiries himself, and he knew there were documented cases of that happening.

And the consequences of failure would be dire.

'If you wait for the Americans, there's no guarantee you'll get visas,' he said, seeing their uncertainty.

'I know, sir. We can't allow ourselves to think like that. The man in the embassy said they would pull out all the stops to help.'

The General sighed to himself at their naivety. Despite the official's best intentions, the machinery of international bureaucracy left no room for sentiment.

Yosef's voice interrupted his thoughts.

'What about Switzerland, sir? We'd need your help.'

'The Swiss have closed the border, unless you have tens of millions of Reichsmarks in your Deutsch Bank account.'

Yosef gave a bitter laugh.

'Show me a Jew with any money in the bank…'

It was the General's turn to blush.

'Sorry…' he said.

'It's all right, sir. There probably are some wealthy Jews with accounts in Zurich, but I suspect they have all left already.'

'I'll make enquiries,' he told them. He hesitated.

'If we could get the children out…' His voice tailed away. Yosef looked at Miriam before answering.

'We've already decided that we couldn't separate the children from us, sir. There was some talk of that with the Kindertransport.'

'Ah, yes. I heard about that. No, I was thinking about people I know abroad, who would be willing to look after them.'

Yosef glanced briefly at Miriam again and the General saw her give an imperceptible shake of the head.

'It's not that we don't trust your judgement, sir,' Yosef said, a little hesitancy in his voice, 'but we feel that the children's place is with us,' he finished, the resolve in his voice returning.

'I had to ask. What about Palestine? Are you still ruling it out?'

'Yes, sir, we are.' Again, the General spotted his glance at Miriam before he replied.

'It's not an option now, anyway, sir,' Miriam said. 'All emigration to Palestine has been stopped.'

'I know the Haavara Agreement was suspended at the outbreak of war,' the General said, a little truculence creeping into his voice, 'but I hear there are other ways.'

'What do you mean, sir?'

'Well, we could get you a visa for a third country, like Turkey or Greece, then you could enter Palestine from there, legitimately or otherwise.'

The Haavara Agreement was the reason 60,000 Jews had reached Palestine from Germany by 1939, with only modest emigration taxes. Designed by the National Socialists to help rid Germany of its Jews, it had been axed when the invasion of Poland had begun.

'Is there any guarantee that we would be permitted to enter Palestine, sir?'

'Well, no, but there are ways to get there.'

'What are they, sir?' Miriam asked, curious despite her misgivings about life in Palestine.

'Well, you know that I hear things in my position,' the General said. 'I've seen reports that an organisation calling themselves the Haganah have started smuggling Jews into Palestine. Have you heard of them?'

Yosef's eyes briefly shifted to the floor, then back again.

'I have, sir,' he said. 'They're Zionists, sir.'

'I know that. Does it matter? The thing is, do you know how to contact them?'

'I could find out,' Yosef said, looking down.

The General frowned.

Yosef shook his head, barely, and looked up again.

'I'm sorry, sir, it would be possible for me to get in touch with them,' he admitted, appalled at the lack of trust he was showing. 'It would be risky though. If it was just Miriam and I… but the children…'

'Keep it in mind,' the General said, rising to leave. 'It might be your only option if all else fails. In the meantime, I will make inquiries about your chances of getting to Switzerland or Denmark, and maybe even to France or the low countries.

Canaris will know. He has contacts everywhere.

~~o~~

Miriam saw the General out. She stood at the door until he reached the big house.

'I'll not forget this,' she said quietly to herself.

657

CHAPTER 193

Memo: Geh.KdoS. ABW 08/09/39 CAC0869.1

For Attention Only: All senior executive officers, Abwehr.

From: Vice Admiral Wilhelm Canaris, Chef der Abwehr.

Troops of the 3rd Army from East Prussia have reached the
approaches to Warsaw. It is expected that units of the 4th
Army, moving eastwards from Chełmno, taken two days ago, and
the 10th Army, currently fighting for Wyszków, will reach
Warsaw within three days to link up with the 3rd Army.

In preparation for the assault on Warsaw, air attacks have been
increased. Today's bombing of the parts of the city on the east
bank of the Vistula River, the heaviest to date, involved 140
Junkers Ju 87s of the Luftwaffe. A second wave of aircraft
bombed the Polish Army positions in the western suburbs. Large
parts of the city are in flames. [END]

~~o~~

[09/09/1939 Saturday]

'I'm sorry my friend,' Yosef said, his hand on Jakob's shoulder.

'Ach. It's maybe for the best. There's plenty for me to do here. Anyway, I'm not sure I would have liked the heat and the dust.'

Yosef smiled. He knew Jakob would not let his disappointment at failing to reach Palestine show, or get in the way of what needed to be done, but to be so close to getting him and his wife to safety…

'There are other ways of getting in, you know,' Yosef said, remembering the General's words.

'The Haganah,' Jakob spat. 'They're nothing but Zionist troublemakers. They stir up our young men and women with talk of a new Israel, and how they should kick back against the authorities. It's why so many of them are getting arrested. All it takes is a silly remark to one of these bastards in uniform, or a zealous Goy overhearing careless talk about Jewish resistance.'

'Still, if you really wanted to go, I hear they can get you and your family through. I'm told that thousands are getting in that way.'

'To be stateless, an illegal immigrant, even if it is away from this verdammt place. Is it worth it?'

'No. Not for me, or for Miriam. We briefly discussed it, and to my surprise, she did give the idea some consideration before discounting it.'

'Enough talk about Palestine. Our chance is gone. It's forgotten about. We have work to do.'

'You wanted to speak to me about something?'

'Yes. Before the meeting of the whole committee. The city has purchased the last two houses in Kleiner Kuhberg that are Jewish owned. The first is number fifteen, but we knew that was coming. They didn't mention anything about us using it as our synagogue, but they suggested that it would facilitate the housing of more Jews who might become homeless because of the new home ownership laws.'

Yosef grunted. 'They did, did they? And I suppose we'll have to rent that, too, and make any necessary changes out of our own pockets?'

'As always. We will have to make it one family per room,' Jakob said, 'and perhaps utilise the Cheder as accommodation and find somewhere else for Bronisław Joselewicz to teach his Torah. I'll need your support on that when I bring it up.'

Yosef cringed. It bordered on slum housing, and the children's religious teacher wouldn't be happy losing his classroom, but he nodded.

'Of course. You didn't have to ask. What about the other house?'

'The Weber's house? It's further down the street. They didn't go into details, but I'm sure they have plans for it. A holding pen for people earmarked for the camps, I'd imagine.'

Yosef closed his eyes and shook his head.

'Where will it all end?' he asked.

~~o~~

[10/09/1939 Sunday]

'What's the name of this place?'

Wilhelm Canaris stared, his face impassive, as the heavy wooden doors of the synagogue were slammed shut. The SS-Sturmbannführer turned the large key, removed it from the lock and, with a grin, handed it to the white-faced rabbi. A crowd of around three or four hundred stood watching, guarded by half a dozen SS storm troopers, their machine pistols held ready despite the subdued nature of the captive audience.

'It's called Będzin, sir. The men inside are all Jews suspected of taking part in resistance against the occupation,' Captain Schwarzhul said, his voice low enough not to carry. 'I've seen this dozens of times during this campaign. I thought you should observe it yourself.'

Hauptmann Janik Schwarzhul had been assigned to be Admiral Canaris's driver and guide on the Abwehr chief's visit to the front line, supposedly to show him the Wehrmacht in action first-hand. It was a cover. Captain Schwarzhul was one of Canaris's best agents; working in the communications and administration section of the 14th Army, his duties took him almost everywhere the regiment operated, giving him the chance to see and report on much of what transpired in their sector of the Polish campaign.

'Schnell! Schnell!' Three of the SS men began to pour petrol onto the doors and through the open windows, hurrying so as not to displease the Sturmbannführer. In the watching crowd, the sounds of a woman wailing split the stillness of the courtyard.

'Jews,' the Sturmbannführer barked at the crowd. 'This is what happens to Judenscheiße who think they can oppose the might of the Third Reich, and our beloved Führer.'

He turned to his men.

'Light it,' he commanded. A spate of cries rang out from wives in the crowd, and a child screamed. From inside the synagogue, Wilhelm Canaris could hear the drone of men praying, their gentle chanting a stark contrast to the agitation of the crowd outside.

The first match broke, and the young storm trooper cursed. He drew another one from the pack and this time it flared. He tossed it through the window. He repeated his actions at the door, and the other window.

Admiral Canaris made to move forward, and open his mouth to call out, but the captain held his arm with a vice-like grip.

'You can't stop this,' he hissed. 'It is more important that you do not give your feelings away, sir, until you can talk to someone who can do something about it.'

Canaris glared at him, and the captain let go. He bowed his head.

'My abject apologies, sir, but...'

'No, you're right,' the admiral said, his mouth set in a rigid line. 'I'm not sure I quite believed your report. I do now. I'm going to take this right to the top.'

More screams came from the crowd as the flames licked up around the door and smoke began to billow out from each of the windows. Through the soft crackling of the flames, the sound of praying grew louder.

'Esâ' `êynay 'el-hehâriym mê'ayinyâbho' `ezriy.'

The admiral knew a little Yiddish, but not Hebrew.

'Ezriy mê`im Adonay `osêh shâmayim vâ'ârets.'

'Why are they chanting?'

'It's the 121st Psalm, sir.'

Canaris glanced at him. He remembered the verse.

I lift my eyes to the mountains ¬– from where will my help come?

My help will come from the Lord, maker of heaven and earth.

'Are you Jewish, Captain?' the admiral asked under his breath.

'No, sir, but my brother married a Jewish girl. I pick up languages easily,' he said, shrugging. 'I recognised it from her father's funeral service.'

'Your brother's wife. Is she safe?'

'Yes, sir. She left Germany with her mother. They went to America.'

'And your brother?'

'He will join them when all of this is over.'

The admiral turned back to the synagogue. Flames were creeping from the eaves and he could see the roof timbers smoking. A window high up in the building exploded outwards, and the crowd let out an agonised gasp.

'Mimma`amaqqiym qerâ'thiykha Adonay,'

The chant continued but the voices were ragged, and racking coughs and the roar of the flames would have almost drowned it out, but he realised, over the weeping and the wailing, that the crowd outside had taken up the chant, and he felt the hairs on the back of his neck rise.

'That's the 130th Psalm now, sir.'

Canaris whispered it, and he heard the captain join him, almost inaudible.

'Out of the depths have I called Thee, O the Lord.'

The two men stood with their heads bowed, unnoticed by the SS men, and softly intoned the words of the psalmist in their mother tongue.

'O Israel, hope in the Lord; for with the Lord there is mercy, and with him is plenteous redemption.'

The roof had caught light now, and groans and cracks came from the burning timbers.

'And he will redeem Israel from all his iniquities.'

Admiral Canaris couldn't be sure if the words of the prayer still came from the burning building, or if it were only the crowd they could hear.

The Sturmbannführer barked an order and two of the storm troopers fired their weapons into the air above the crowd.

For a few long seconds, the chanting stopped, then, from somewhere in the middle, a lone voice took up the chant again. Then another joined in, and another.

The admiral held his breath as the SS men lowered their guns to aim at the chanting Jews.

They looked around at the Sturmbannführer for the order to fire. Admiral Canaris stepped forward, but before he could speak, the roof of the synagogue, with a rending crack, crumpled in on itself, and the front wall collapsed outwards.

The crowd screamed as they scrambled backwards towards the river, away from the falling masonry. For the storm troopers, closer to the blaze, self-preservation overtook their anger, and they stumbled to follow the fleeing Jews.

Admiral Wilhelm Canaris bowed his head in sorrow and shame. He watched until the flames turned to smoke, and all that was left of the synagogue were embers, and a half-standing corner, pointing to the sky like an accusing finger.

'How many?' he asked the captain.

'I counted 200 this time, sir. Often it's more.'

'Come. I have a train to catch.'

CHAPTER 194

[11/09/1939 Monday]

They hugged and cheered each other like old friends, though they'd never met.

On the eleventh of September, ten days after the invasion had begun, Colonel Schneider's battalion, crossing Poland from the west, met up with the men from the 3rd Army who'd entered the country from East Prussia on its northern border. They'd already had contact with messengers from the 10th Army, sent across the Vistula River in the south, to coordinate the encircling of Warsaw.

The vice-like grip that the city was now held in should have left no room for hope in the minds of the last vestiges of the Polish Army, but it continued to resist both in Warsaw itself and in a few isolated pockets dotted around the country.

The Kästner brothers' units, on the east flank of the positions the 4th Army had taken within sight of the western suburbs, were billeted within hailing distance of their counterparts from the 3rd Army and, after the men of the Wehrmacht set up offensive positions to place Warsaw completely under siege, they had, for the first time in almost two weeks, been allowed a few hours' leave.

As soldiers do, they chose to find the nearest village with a bar in it and persuade the Polish landlord that, now that he was in occupied territory, he might as well continue his trade and make the most of a bad situation.

Franz, Johann, and the close group of friends they'd been with since they'd joined the regiment, sat in the crowded inn, drinking the local Żywiec beer, the soldiers of each regiment taking turns to regale the other with stories of their advance to Warsaw.

The capture of Chojnice and Chełmno were recounted by the six friends, and the officers of the 3rd Army countered with tales of their own actions at Pułtusk and Wysków.

Of Franz and Johann's Kompanie, only Fritz Aumeier was missing, injured in action.

'He fell over a wall, and broke his foot.' Johann laughed, explaining to their opposite numbers that they'd suffered low casualties, despite a couple of days of fierce fighting, the worst of which was at the crossing of the Vistula at Chełmno.

'He'll be back in a month, once it's healed,' Maxi Grabner said. 'He just wanted a holiday, in hospital with all those lovely nurses running after him.'

'From what I hear,' Artur said, 'some of these army nurses are fierce. Bed baths with scouring pads, they say, to discourage any ideas of a sexual nature.'

The men laughed.

'How about you?' Franz asked. 'Many casualties?'

'No, fairly light, so far,' a first lieutenant with a thick mop of red hair said. 'The Poles pulled back quickly after they realised that they were outnumbered, and that their weapons and equipment were inadequate.'

'They seem to be putting up a sterner resistance now,' Heinrich Öhlman said. 'I heard that after the fourth panzer division had taken the suburbs of Grójec and Radziejowice, they tried to take Ochota, the next suburb on. They were pushed back by the Poles and, despite air support, they failed the next day too.'

Franz was about to add that he'd heard that one of the barricades, erected at the crossing of the Opaczewska and Grójecka streets, had been defended by a regiment of Polish fighters made up almost entirely of children, and that they'd fought off the panzer troops with the help of two cleverly placed anti-tank guns.

But something held him back. The Army Command didn't look favourably on talk of defeats and difficulties and, although they could never stop soldiers engaging in idle gossip, the legacy of the Hitlerjugend had meant that there were enough NSDAP whistle-blowers in the ranks to make sure that any derogatory comments about the performance of German troops could land the miscreant in trouble.

And while talk of a setback against stiff Polish resistance was just about acceptable, defeat by a unit made up of children would be deemed humiliating.

'Did you hear what happened in Kaliska Street?' Johann said.

Franz tried to catch his eye, but his brother didn't look his way.

'These panzer boys,' he continued, 'they think they're invincible, surrounded by armoured steel; they treat us like dross, as if they can win the war on their own. It's we infantrymen that win battles, street by street.'

The other officers nodded, grunting their approval at Johann's assessment of the tank crews.

'So, what happened?' one of the 3rd Army's officers said, leaning towards Johann.

'Well, four or five of them drove down the street towards the barricade; there were no anti-tank guns in sight. The unit commander ordered those on the barricade to surrender.'

'There was a seventy-five-millimetre gun hidden in the barricade, or in one of the buildings, right?'

Johann looked at the young lieutenant who'd spoken.

'No,' he said, shaking his head and closing his eyes for a second, imagining the scene. 'There was a turpentine factory in the street, and the Poles had flooded the street with the stuff, just before the tanks entered it. They set it on fire. One of our boys managed to reverse out of it, but his crew had terrible burns. None of the others made it.'

'The dirty Polish bastards,' Heinrich Öhlman spat. 'What a way to die, cooped up in a metal box, engulfed in flames. It would be like being in an oven.'

'The ammo went off in two of the tanks,' Johann continued. 'They said the turrets blew off and landed in the next street.'

'Are you sure about all this?' Franz said, wishing Johann would take his hint, although all the soldiers from the 3rd Army seemed just like them. Heer, through and through.

'Yes,' Johann said. 'A couple of my men heard it from two of the medics who treated the boys from the tank that made it out, and I spoke to a runner from the panzer regiment HQ, who told me the same story.'

Franz, as usual, wondered why complete strangers always took to Johann, chatting to him as if they'd known him for years. It had been like that since they'd been children.

'We'll make the bastards suffer, don't worry,' the young lieutenant said, 'even if we have to flatten Warsaw.'

Franz wanted to tell them.

They're only doing what we would do if someone invaded Germany.

But he didn't, because they would be shocked, and wonder about him.

They would argue that Germany was only occupying Poland because the Poles would not be reasonable about the East Prussia situation, and to save the ethnic Germans in the Polish Corridor, but he knew that it wasn't true. He sometimes felt that he was the only person who thought like that, and he longed to speak with his father.

He shook his head and, instead, warned them that the Poles might not be as easy to crush as they thought.

'Scheiße,' said Artur. 'They'll not last three days. Our bombers will have them hiding in their cellars and when we move in with our men and our tanks, they'll be glad to come out of their holes and give themselves up.'

'You want to wager, Franz?' Artur asked, grinning.

'I don't bet on stuff like that,' Franz replied, uncomfortable with the line the conversation had taken.

'Oh, go on, Franz. You've made a prediction; all we want to see is if you have the balls to put twenty marks on it.'

'I'll take your money,' Johann said. 'He's got a horrible habit of being right.'

'All right. Since your yellow-bellied brother won't take my bet, you're on.'

Johann grinned and shook Artur's hand. Franz laughed, not taking offence.

He was still smiling when the door of the inn opened, and Private Stein, Franz's orderly, caught his eye. Franz hurried over to him.

'What's the matter, private?' Franz asked, now alert, despite the few beers he'd consumed.

'Nothing, sir. You have a visitor. I said I'd come and tell you.'

'My father...' Franz said, regretting the slip.

'No, sir,' the private said. 'It's Admiral Canaris, sir. He said he'd also be delighted to see your brother as well.'

'Where is he? Back at camp?'

'No, sir. He's outside. In a jeep. With his driver. He said that he isn't here for long.'

'Thank you, private. You can go back to camp.'

Franz called to his brother and gestured for him to come outside. Johann followed Franz out of the inn, grumbling at losing precious drinking time.

'What is it?' he asked.

'Wait and see,' Franz told him, walking towards the Kübelwagen parked a few metres along the road. As they approached, the door opened, and Admiral Canaris stepped out.

'Uncle Wilhelm,' Johann shouted, his eyes lighting up. 'What the hell are you doing here?'

'I think you'll find that the current protocol is Admiral Canaris, and a salute,' the older man said, giving Johann a hug first, then Franz.

'But what are you doing here, sir?' the older Kästner brother asked, rendering an over-the-top parade-ground salute.

The admiral returned his salute without the flamboyance and laughed.

'I recognise sarcasm when I see it. And after me coming all the way to see you!'

'Like hell you did, sir,' Johann said.

The admiral laughed again, and thumped Johann on the shoulder.

'I'm here on official business. Your father knew I was going to be in your vicinity, so he asked me to check on you. He's turned out to be quite a mother hen when it comes to your military careers.'

'What do you mean, sir?' Franz asked.

'Let's just say he worries about you both more than he ever worried about himself.'

'So, he sent you to check up on us, eh?' Johann laughed.

'That's about the nub of it. He just thought it might be nice for me to look you up, seeing as I was a few miles away. How is your war going?'

'Very well, so far,' Franz said, 'We've had few casualties, despite a couple of heavy engagements.'

'Ah. Chełmno. I saw the reports. You acquitted yourselves well. And Chojnice. You took that without much fuss.'

'Do you see reports from all the regiments, Admiral,' Johann asked.

'Most of them. Why?'

'How are we doing?' Johann said, the thirst for information etched on his face.

'It's going much as expected,' the admiral said. 'Warsaw will be a harder nut to crack, and there might not be much left of it by the time we take it, but other than that, all of Poland west of the Vistula is in our hands.'

'That's what Franz thinks,' Johann said, 'don't you, brother?'

He turned to Admiral Canaris. 'I have some money riding on his being correct,' he said, 'so it's good to hear you agree with him.'

'You bet on the outcome of the battle?' the admiral asked, shaking his head.

'Ach, it was one of the boys who thought we'd take Warsaw within a few days. I disagreed and before I knew it, Johann had twenty Reichsmarks riding on it.'

'Soldiers will be soldiers; sailors will be sailors. If it keeps you sane...'

Franz laughed.

'I don't think you could ever consider Johann or our friends sane, but the army is where they best fit in.'

The three men laughed together easily, almost forgetting where they were.

'Have you seen anything you weren't happy with?' the admiral asked. It was said in a casual manner, but Franz got the impression that his father's friend had intended to ask the question from the beginning.

'Nothing,' said Johann. 'The command has been excellent; the men have lived up to expectations; all that training has paid off. Some of our equipment is a little past its best but compared with the Poles', it's state of the art.'

'That's good. Your father says that Colonel Schneider is an exceptionally capable soldier.'

'He is, sir, but why do you ask?' Johann said.

'No reason. Just checking you are happy with your lot. Your father will be looking for a full report, you know.'

Johann laughed again.

'Get back to your friends, boys. I hear this is the first time off you've had since it all kicked off. Make the most of tonight. I need to get going.'

Johann shook his hand and hurried back into the bar.

Franz turned to Admiral Canaris.

'You'd be welcome to come in for a drink, sir. It would give the boys quite a start to see someone like you turning up to have a beer with us.'

'Franz, I could see why that would be fun to spring on your friends, and I would like nothing better than to sit and have a drink with you, but I really do have to go. I have a train to catch.'

He took Franz's hand.

'There was one thing, sir. You asked…'

Franz looked towards the admiral's driver.

'You're safe enough with Captain Schwarzhul, Franz. Go on.'

'Well, sir, at Chełmno, on the day we moved out, I saw an SS unit, which had moved to the town the night before, rounding up civilians and putting them in trucks. When I asked one of their officers what they were doing he just laughed and told me to fight the battles, and they would deal with the Jews.'

'Did you see where they took them?'

'No, sir. We were moving out. I only spoke to him briefly.'

'And did you see that happening anywhere else?'

'No. But I'd seen the same SS unit before. They arrived in Chojnice the day we left. And a unit of army reservists; older men, they were, had also moved in to take over the control and administration of the town, so I thought nothing of it, although it did strike me as unfair that the SS weren't doing their share of the fighting.'

'Ha. You're right about the SS. So far, they've not seen much action but they're poorly trained compared to the regular army, so maybe it's a good thing.'

Franz stared at the admiral.

'I thought they were supposed to be the elite,' he said.

'Well, yes, they are, but not in the way you or I would judge. Politically, they're all fanatical supporters of the Führer and the party. They're all certified 100 per cent Aryan and few of them are married.'

'They sound like priests. Married to Adolf Hitler, their own Jesus Christ.'

The admiral laughed.

'They aren't necessarily celibate. They're encouraged to impregnate young Aryan women from good German stock, for the Third Reich's citizens of the future.'

Franz's jaw dropped open.

'A breeding program?'

'Sort of. Some of them marry, as long as it's to a good Bund Deutscher Mädchen.'

Franz thought of Lise, marrying her SS officer.

'So, what do they do if they're not fighting, or when they're not making little Hitler youths?' he asked.

'The SS are being used in a number of roles. All the concentration camps are run by the

SS. They call themselves the SS-Totenkopfverbände.'

Death's head units. Typical NSDAP.

Franz's attention snapped back to the admiral, as the older man continued.

'The SS are also being used in actions against civilian agitators, and in repatriating immigrant Jews.'

'I thought that was the Gestapo's job?'

'It is. They're part of the SS too, but they all work closely together, especially during larger operations.'

'So, none of the SS units are going to fight like us?'

Admiral Canaris shook his head.

'No, they will. Eventually,' he said. 'The Waffen-SS will be fighting soldiers, like you, but they aren't yet quite up to speed in combat. They should be bloodied over the next few months. If a full-on war comes, they will eventually be expected to live up to the myth that has been created for them, that the SS will throw themselves at the most dangerous objectives and die for the privilege of serving their Führer.'

Franz shook his head.

'You couldn't make this up,' he said. 'Why not just use some of our more experienced units for that sort of thing?'

'The regular army doesn't have the level of fanaticism that the SS units have. In addition, having these SS units integrated with the regular army is one of the ways the National Socialists will try to control the Wehrmacht, your father thinks.'

'Through fear,' Franz said, as slow realisation dawned.

The admiral nodded.

'Your father. You're like him,' he said. 'A lot.'

'My father? What do you mean?'

'You think about things; you don't simply accept them, and you evaluate everything you see and hear. You have a sound military mind. Your father was the same at your age.'

Franz blushed.

'I've known him for most of my adult life,' Canaris continued. 'We have our different views, but we understand each other, and I'm beginning to think that he's right about some of the things we disagreed about.'

Franz was taken aback. He'd always got on well with *Uncle Wilhelm*, but he'd never talked with him, like this, so candidly.

'Listen, Franz,' the admiral continued, 'there will be things that take place in this skirmish, and in the bigger war that is coming, that won't sit well with you. Don't try and stop them all; they will squash you like a bug. Make a note of them, and tell only me, or your father.'

Franz's stomach tightened, and he tasted bile at the back of his throat.

'The Jews,' he said.

'Yes,' the admiral said. 'And others. But mainly the Jews.'

~~o~~

After he'd left, Franz returned to the bar.

'What kept you?' Johann asked. 'Did you bump into a little Polish Fräulein out there?'

He laughed, and Franz joined in, but part of his mind remained hung on the admiral's words.

'Don't look so serious, Franz. We might only have one night to enjoy ourselves. Let's make the most of it.'

Franz looked around. *What the hell.*

He picked up his beer glass and drank deeply, letting the sounds of men blowing off steam engulf him and help him forget, at least for a time.

CHAPTER 195

[12/09/1939 Tuesday]

On the evening of twelfth September, Admiral Canaris stepped onto Adolf Hitler's headquarters train. It sat on a siding outside a small town he couldn't remember the name of, in the province of Silesia. He was met by the chief of the Oberkommando der Wehrmacht, General Wilhelm Keitel.

As supreme commander of the armed forces, Keitel had the ear of the Führer, and was responsible for the Wehrmacht's progress during the invasion of Poland.

'I have a dossier here,' Canaris told Keitel, 'and I have seen with my own eyes that mass executions are taking place in Poland under the nose of the armed forces, perhaps even with their complicity. Amongst others, they're killing members of the Polish aristocracy and church clergy, and Jews.

'One day,' Canaris continued, before Keitel could interrupt, 'the world will hold the Wehrmacht responsible for these atrocities, since these things are taking place under its jurisdiction.'

Keitel paled for a second, but his face hardened, and he warned Canaris not to take the matter further.

'This is war, you fool. For us to succeed, we must not only beat the enemy, but crush him, so that the next army that dares to face us will do so with fear in their hearts. Everything you have spoken about here, including those actions not directly associated with the Wehrmacht, have been sanctioned by the office of the Führer. You would be unwise to persist.'

'I'd still like my objections to be noted,' the admiral said.

~~o~~

After the head of the Abwehr had left, Wilhelm Keitel placed the piece of paper in a buff folder and, instead of putting it in the tray to be typed up, he tucked it underneath the pile of files to be archived.

No need to drop Canaris in it. He could still be useful.

CHAPTER 196

[13/09/1939 Wednesday]

Less than a mile away from where Franz and Johann were billeted, units of the SS-Verfügungstruppe Germania regiment, contrary to the admiral's assertions, had taken part in some of the initial probes against the Warsaw defenders, but they were both reckless and ineffective, in keeping with the information the admiral had received, and had been beaten back by ferocious fire from the Polish defenders.

SS-Untersturmführer Rudolf Mey, Lise Böhm's new husband, stood and watched with a smile on his face and his hands shaking with excitement as a new wave of bombers flew over their positions and, almost at once, opened their bomb doors. They flew high enough to make it difficult for the guns of the Polish air defence corps to hit them, but low enough for Rudolf to make out the markings on the aircraft and identify them as Heinkels, Dorniers or Junkers Ju 88s.

Stukas.

They were Rudolf's favourites.

As the black projectiles tumbled earthwards, Rudolf's eyes followed them with eager anticipation and, when they landed and exploded less than a quarter of a mile from where he stood, his fists balled, and he had to suppress a shout of pure joy.

The evening sky lit up with flames as the shattered buildings of the suburb burned.

'Those Polish defence units won't be so cocky now, Untersturmführer,' he heard a voice say.

He jumped and turned in fright.

Hauptsturmführer Eicke laughed.

'You're nervous, Kamerad. Perhaps it was our action earlier. We're all a little jumpy.'

'I enjoyed it, sir,' Rudolf said.

'Yes, you did. I was impressed, truth be told. Some of the others weren't quite so, shall we say, steady.'

'I wouldn't like to comment, sir,' Rudolf said.

'But I will. We were ill-prepared and ragged. Too much gung-ho individualism and not enough teamwork. We were lucky we didn't lose many men.'

'You were wise to pull back, sir. We'd stretched our lines too much.'

The Hauptsturmführer looked sharply at the young officer, then smiled.

'As a rule, I don't appreciate advice or praise from my junior officers but, seeing how well you acquitted yourself today, I'll make an exception.' His voice hardened. 'Just don't think you can do it in front of the men.'

'No, sir. I wouldn't.'

'We'll be better next time,' the Hauptsturmführer said. He turned his eyes in the direction of the burning city.

'It's a rare sight, Untersturmführer, is it not?' he said.

Rudolf's eyes shone as he followed the Hauptsturmführer's stare.

'Yes, sir. It's wonderful,' Rudolf said, his voice almost breaking. 'They can do so much damage in so little time. Those Polish scum will be buried or burned to ashes. We'll mop up the rest tomorrow, if we get the chance.'

The Hauptsturmführer stared at him.

'We're the same, you and I. We're made for this.'

'Thank you, sir.'

'How did you find our little job the other day?' he asked, and Rudolf noticed a change in his voice; less sure, perhaps.

'I must admit, at first it was a little disconcerting, but I steeled myself and, in the end, I found it easier, and more enjoyable than I'd expected.'

They'd rounded up 100 male Jews from a town the Wehrmacht troops had taken. Putting them in lorries, they'd taken them out to the edge of a forest and lined them up in tens. The Hauptsturmführer had made them all take turns at shooting the captives, before throwing their bodies deep into the wood.

'Some of the men were sick, and I'm sure there were a few that aimed low or high on purpose.'

'I suppose so, sir. Some of our troops are young, and they lack experience.'

'That's no excuse, Untersturmführer. They have all been personally chosen for this regiment. Remember our oath.'

'Meine Ehre heißt Treue,' Rudolf intoned, his eyes shining with pride. *My honour is loyalty.*

'They will follow orders without exception, or I'll have them shipped out, to shovel horseshit in one of the cavalry regiments.'

'Yes, sir. That would be fair. We are the Schutzstaffel, sir.'

The Hauptsturmführer clapped him on the back, laughing.

'We are indeed. Perhaps I should recommend you for a promotion. Your beautiful young wife thought it would be a good idea.'

Rudolf's chest constricted, and his breath came in short gasps.

'She said something to you, sir?' he said, hardly believing it.

The Hauptsturmführer laughed.

'Yes. At your wedding. She's a remarkable woman. You must miss her.'

'I do, sir,' Rudolf said, unsure of himself now.

'You're a lucky man, I'd say. I hear the men talking. They envy you.'

'I'm sure they don't, sir,' he said, trying to sound modest but knowing it was true.

'It either gives you an edge, or blunts it, that envy. It all depends what you let it do.'

'What do you mean, sir?'

'Don't let thoughts of her get in the way of your mission, soldier, but remember, if you get a promotion, having a woman they covet gives you one more thing that your men will look up to you for. I should know. You think my wife is hot, Untersturmführer?'

Rudolf knew he was in the verbal equivalent of no-man's land.

'I've heard the men say she's beautiful. I'd have to agree.'

'Clever answer, Untersturmführer. She is indeed, but sometimes it's not enough. A man has needs that one woman can't always satisfy. Don't ever give up a chance for some fresh meat. It keeps you sharp.'

'Yes, sir,' Rudolf mumbled, not knowing how to respond.

His commanding officer thumped him on the back again, laughing at his discomfort.

'Don't worry, Untersturmführer Mey. I'm winding you up. You're newly married, to one of the most desirable women in the Third Reich. It's only natural you should feel that you want to stay true to her. I admire that, but we'll see how long it will last.'

The Hauptsturmführer paused, and looked at him, as if gauging his reaction.

'Do you trust your wife, while you're away?'

Rudolf flushed deeply.

'Of course, sir,' he replied, unable to keep the anger out of his voice.

'That's good, soldier. I just hope, for your sake, you aren't disappointed.'

The Hauptsturmführer turned to leave, then hesitated.

'You know, this,' he said, pointing to the burning city, 'is like sex.'

'How is that, sir?' Rudolf asked, frowning.

'The first time is always the best.'

The Hauptsturmführer turned away again, laughing, and this time, he continued to walk down between the piles of rubble, turning the corner, out of sight.

Rudolf Mey let a long, low breath out.

He pulled his wallet from his inside pocket and opened it. He looked at the photograph of Lise, and shivered.

'Yosef, how are you, my friend?'

'Ach, you know. The usual. What's with the long faces?'

Yosef nodded to each of the men sitting on the back step of Kleiner Kuhberg fifteen. In addition to Jakob, he recognised Erwin Baruch, Nossen Deller and Siegmund Eliasowitz, three of the younger men on the unofficial committee that managed the various Kleiner Kuhberg houses.

'We were just talking about these new ration cards,' Erwin said.

'Oh, we haven't got ours yet,' Yosef replied.

The young man reached into his jacket and pulled out a small cardboard folder. He handed it to Yosef.

'There are cards for sugar, butter, milk and meat,' he said, as Yosef opened it and pulled out the cards. Each was of a different colour, and they all had a large red letter 'J' stamped on them.

'I'm guessing the allocation of each product is less for a card stamped like this than on an Aryan's card,' Yosef said, a bitter edge to his voice.

'We don't know,' Jakob replied. 'We haven't seen one, but we suspect that will be the case. We thought Miriam might know, in her dealings with the supplies for the General's house.'

'She didn't say anything, but I'll ask her.'

'This will just be the start of it if the war escalates. The more materials and goods that are required for the armed forces, the more they'll take from us.'

'There's already a black market for medical supplies. There will soon be one for everything else, and no doubt the Bernheim brothers are involved.'

They all laughed.

'The Goyim in the government have already taken our money. How do we pay black market prices?'

Jakob raised an eyebrow.

'We're Jewish. There's no one better than us at hiding money. We've needed to do it for hundreds of years but, yes, it will run out if this goes on too long.'

'We have our reserves,' Yosef said, thinking of the crates of canned goods they'd purchased. 'Did that last shipment arrive?'

'Yes,' Jakob said. 'Two days ago. We have it stored away safely, but it's for emergencies and for those who have nothing.'

'And the medical supplies?' Nossen Deller asked.

'Yes. They weren't cheap, but we have them well hidden, in two or three different locations, just in case.'

Yosef looked at his friend. Jakob was showing the strain of holding the Jewish community together. It seemed to him that the older man's face was more lined, and he had developed a slight stoop, as if the weight of the world were crushing him, millimetre by millimetre.

They all looked up as the door opened, and a breathless Nathan Dreilich appeared.

'Bronisław Joselewicz has been deported back to Poland. So have Max Weidmann and his family.'

Bronisław Joselewicz was one of the Orthodox Ostjuden, who had taken charge of the religious teaching of the community's youth.

'When did this happen?'

'Last night, late.'

The Weidmanns had been living in the attic above the makeshift synagogue but had moved to Kleiner Kuhberg twenty-one when a larger room had become available.

'Where did they take them?' Jakob asked, scrambling to his feet.

'Nobody knows, but I don't think they're in Kiel. We've tried all the usual places.'

'They're gone then. We can't help them. There's little chance they'll be sent back a second time.'

'They're not even escaping the National Socialists' clutches. The whole of Poland will be occupied by the time they arrive.'

'We need somebody for Cheder,' Jakob said. 'The children need to be taught the Torah, and about our history, especially in times like these.'

Cheder, the room in the synagogue where religious education was given to Jewish children, was on the floor above the one used for worship. The children were usually, but not exclusively, taught by a rabbi or by a cantor. At the current time, it was occupied by two families, but the teaching took place in the corridor outside.

'I'll do it.'

Yosef groaned to himself. Although Siegmund Eliasowitz was young, he was in some ways the oldest amongst them, the one who always pointed out if religious observances were not being strictly adhered to.

The men called him a Nudnik, and it was apt; he could be a bore, and a nag.

And Yosef knew he would be just as narrow-minded and fervent as Bronisław Joselewicz had been, indoctrinating Manny with his conservative views without the other man's humanity.

'That's a fine offer, Siegmund,' Jakob said, 'and I will consider it. You are a little inexperienced, though, I have to warn you.'

The young man bridled. 'I'm as prepared as anyone for it, and you know it. Who else will do it?'

Jakob did not show any sign of irritation, and Yosef smiled at his self-control.

'That may well be, but I will still have to consider it, young man. I had thought of someone older, like Yosef, or myself. But I will think about it.'

It was Rosh Hashanah, and Yosef knew that Jakob would not have to make the decision until the two-day Jewish new year celebrations were over.

'What do we have to look forward to for the next year?' Yosef said, trying to steer the conversation away from the topic of the children's religious well-being.

'More of the same, unfortunately,' Jakob said. 'If Britain and France enter the war, or Russia, or all three, it could be over within months, and Hitler and his lackeys will be ousted. That's our best hope.'

'But the Third Reich, as Herr Hitler is calling it, will become more powerful by the day,' Erwin Baruch argued. 'With the addition of Poland's agricultural and mineral resources, a defeat in a European war might not be a foregone conclusion. And the British and French haven't shown any enthusiasm for getting involved yet, despite their promises.'

Jakob shrugged.

'Ach, people like us will never know what is really going on,' he said. 'The propaganda ministry tells us that German U-boats and our magnificent Sturzkampfflieger are breaking the British blockade in the North Sea, and that our ships are getting through, but then we find we have rationing. Who do you believe?'

'You're right. I hear it being called the Ministry of Lies,' Yosef said. 'But I know that the dive bombers have been a big success in Poland, so perhaps the rest of it is true.'

Jakob raised an eyebrow, and Yosef flinched. The General had mentioned the Luftwaffe's success when he'd spoken about the boys. Yosef knew that he shouldn't have repeated it but if Jakob had any suspicions that he was betraying a confidence, he kept them to himself.

'The authorities say that there have been minimal casualties,' he said, 'but a cousin of mine lives close to Fliegerhorst Stargard-Klützow. He helped build the airfield in '34 and he lives close by, in the small village of Warnice, which is not far from the end of the runway. It served as an assembly and refuelling airfield for the bombing campaign during the invasion. The first week, he counted the bombers out, then back in again. He says at least fifteen aircraft didn't come back over the first two days.'

'They could lose, then?'

Jakob Teubner sighed.

'Some days, I wake up and I think that this regime will implode, and we'll be rid of them by Passover. Other times, I worry they'll get their thousand years.'

CHAPTER 197

KIELER MORGENPOST

Monday 18th September 1939

SOVIET UNION INVADES POLAND FROM THE EAST

Yesterday, armies of the Soviet Union crossed the border into Poland, creating a state of war between the two countries. Conservative estimates of the Soviet forces range from 500,000 to 1,000,000 men.

Only light skirmishes have been reported and it has been assumed that Polish forces have been ordered to retreat towards Warsaw.

The German Government has cautiously welcomed the Soviet action. A spokesman said that Polish intransigence and agitation of the Baltic states were sufficient reasons to justify the invasion and expected that there would be significant cooperation between the military forces of the two allies.

The recent peace agreement between the Soviet Union and Japan has removed the threat of Japanese invasion in the east of Russia and has freed the Soviet Army to concentrate on their campaign in Poland.

Around Warsaw, the forces of the Third Reich have won control of two further suburbs on the south and west of the city, where fierce fighting has been reported.

~~o~~

[19/09/1939 Tuesday]

General Kästner told Frau Müller, his secretary, to finish early.

'You deserve it, for all the hard work you do.'

He knew she'd seen through him immediately, having watched an ashen-faced Admiral Canaris being ushered in by Captain Bauer, and she itched to listen in to their conversation.

He saw her as a bit of a busybody and, so far, he'd made sure to be a great disappointment to her, taking care not to discuss anything of significance in her hearing, unlike the old admiral, who'd treated her like a trusted confidante.

He ushered her out and she left, huffing. At the General's command, Heinz Bauer stood guard in the anteroom to prevent the General and Admiral Canaris being disturbed.

In his office, the General reached for two glasses and poured a generous measure into each, and laid a hand gently on the admiral's shoulder, before sitting down opposite him. His stomach had lurched when he'd seen his friend's colour.

Please God, don't let it be one of the boys, he prayed.

He couldn't bring himself to say the words, to ask the question.

Canaris finished his drink in three deep gulps. The General reached over and refilled his glass.

He lifted his eyes to the General.

'Erich, my friend, you were right.'

The General couldn't remember ever hearing anyone speak with such a depth of sadness. He let out a long, slow breath of relief.

It's not about my sons.

'About what in particular?' he asked, his voice steadier than he expected.

'Everything, my friend. The National Socialists. Adolf Hitler. The Jews, the Gypsies, and the communists. The only thing you got wrong is the scale of their plans.'

The General said nothing. It wasn't the time for smug satisfaction. The admiral continued, his head bowed, unable to look him in the eye.

'Germany will never be forgiven for this, for a thousand years. We're finished, unless he's stopped.'

'What did you find?'

'That the reports I was getting were true. Massacres are going on all over Poland, in our name.'

'My boys,' the General said, his voice cracking. 'Are they involved?'

'No. No. Definitely not.' The admiral looked up. 'I'm sorry, Erich. My heart is so heavy I didn't even think. Your boys are fine. I met them, briefly and no, they're not a part of this; at least, not directly, but the Wehrmacht will be held responsible, if we let it go on.'

'Tell me all of it,' the General said, replenishing his own glass, and the admiral's.

For the next fifteen minutes, Canaris told him everything he knew, from the initial reports of the atrocities received from his field agents to his first-hand experience of the burning of Będzin's Jews, and even Franz's account of what he'd seen going on behind the advancing army.

The General listened, occasionally interrupting with a question to clarify a detail or two.

Canaris managed a grim smile describing his visit to Franz and Johann.

'They're real fighting soldiers now,' he said, 'and Colonel Schneider has done a great job with them all.'

The General let a little of the pride he felt show on his face. Canaris nodded.

'They're a credit to you.'

He smiled again, and took another gulp from the whisky glass.

'I went to Hitler's field headquarters,' he said, the smile wiped away, 'on his special train, in a station in some God-forsaken backwater in Silesia. It took a bit of finding. He wasn't there, but I spoke to Wilhelm Keitel. I told him what I'd seen and heard. Do you know what he said?'

'I don't know, but don't you think it was a little foolhardy to blaze in there and let him know how you felt?'

'Perhaps I was naive to believe that they'd take any notice, but I doubt Keitel will try and ruin me, just as I'm sure he'll not take my concerns any further. He told me that I shouldn't persist. It wasn't advice; it was an order.'

'I would do as he says, for now, at least.'

The admiral didn't reply. The silence lengthened, and the General watched with concern as the admiral sat opposite, head in his hands.

Then he lifted his eyes to the General.

'Do you know what I did on the journey back from Silesia?'

'No. But I can't imagine you slept.'

'No. You're right. I read *Mein Kampf*. The copy you gave me.'

'Ah. I see.'

'You do, don't you. You have all along.'

'Well, I always thought that at some point, enough of the German people would wake up and put a curb on his madness, but I'm still waiting.'

'I should have listened to you. You could always see the big picture.'

'So can you, Canaris. But none of us get it right every time. You've done more than your fair share to prevent this war.'

'Yes, but the war is only part of it. It's what went on in peacetime that I chose to ignore. And I'll admit, I've never been the biggest fan of Jews in general. Perhaps most Germans are like me, and that's why no one has spoken out.'

Erich Kästner didn't argue with him. He'd come to the same conclusion long before.

'So, what can we do about it?' the admiral said.

'I don't know. I've spent the last few years trying to figure that out.'

'I don't see that there's much we can do, while everything *Der Führer* does is successful.'

'It is uncanny,' the General said. 'First, the Saarland, then Austria, the Sudetenland and Czechoslovakia; now Poland. He's either had the most incredible luck, or he has an extraordinary ability to read his enemies' minds. On each occasion, the British and the French, so full of indignation, have stood back and watched while we've stomped all over Europe, claiming it for our own. And that from a position of terrible weakness just five years ago.'

'That's part of his appeal,' the admiral said. 'Versailles was so deeply unpopular here, and in a few short years he reversed all of its unfairness and its restrictions, and made Germany a nation to be feared again, if not respected.'

'What do you think will happen?'

'We would have defeated Poland anyway, but now that the Soviets are involved, she will be crushed within weeks. You had my memo about the Molotov-Ribbentrop agreement and the secret adjunct to it; the Soviets get a chunk of Eastern Poland and the freedom to do what they like with the Baltic States, and we get what we wanted without having to fight all the way to the Russian border or worry about the Soviets jumping into the fray.'

'What next? Will Adolf be happy with that?'

'No, but he'll do nothing for a while. He'll continue to consolidate, continuing to build our army, navy and air force for the real war, the one against Britain and France. I've seen the plans.'

'We won't march into France as easily as they did in Poland. The French Army is larger, better prepared, and their defensive line is much more heavily fortified.'

'I'm not so sure. The French and the British may still believe they can win this war like the last one, by attrition and blockade, but war is now different; we've seen that in Poland.'

'I hear this Blitzkrieg mentioned. Is that what you're talking about?'

'It's partly that. The combination of aerial power, mechanised battalions and infantrymen trained to cross terrain rapidly on foot, or using modern transport, is going to be a potent mix; I believe the Wehrmacht Command are calling it total war.'

The General nodded. It was an extension of the training that he'd delivered during the last years of his army career.

'So, we wait?' he said, shaking his head, 'and do nothing?'

'That's all we can do, until he slips up, but we can work behind the scenes, to be ready if he does.'

'What do you want me to do?' the General asked.

'Nothing. Just keep doing what you do best. Keep the navy out of their hands, as much as possible, and with us. One day, we may need them.'

'And the army?'

'Do what you can but leave the army to me. I have a few key officers I can count on.'

'It's ironic; an admiral keeping the army on side, and a general maintaining the support of the navy. The world has gone mad.'

For the first time, the admiral laughed.

'We live in bizarre times. Who knows where it will end?'

The General poured another measure into each glass.

'I have a small favour to ask,' he said.

'Fire away,' the admiral replied, dully.

'I need to get the Nussbaums out. What are their chances of getting into Switzerland or Denmark or, if that's not possible, France or the low countries?'

'It's going to be almost impossible. Have they applied for an American visa? The United States won't be sucked into a European war again. There is no appetite for it; quite the opposite, in fact.'

'They have applied, but it may take a year.'

'The Americans aren't letting more than a trickle of Jews in. Only one in four applications are successful, I hear, but it's still worth trying. I'll ask around about Denmark, Belgium, and the Netherlands. Switzerland is out. The border is virtually closed, other than to people who make large deposits of cash in their banks.'

'Let me know. I need to know they are safe, because their position with us, and their place in German society, is becoming increasingly tenuous.'

'I'll see what I can do, but you might not like the answers, Erich. The border with France is closed and all the other countries are nervous about taking refugees or antagonising the German government. They might want to think about China. I hear Shanghai are still letting Jews in, and Bolivia, of all places.'

'I'll tell them. Miriam will be the tough one we have to sell it to. She was reluctant to leave and, when she finally relented, she would only consider Britain or America.'

'She may have to get over her obstinacy or remain in Germany.'

'I know.'

CHAPTER 198

'Papa, have you heard how Franz and Johann are getting on?'

The General smiled at his daughter. Antje was growing up fast, and was turning into a beautiful young lady, despite her attempts to sometimes act like a boy.

'They're stationed just outside Warsaw. They're doing fine. Uncle Wilhelm saw them last week.'

'Will the war be over soon? Everyone is saying we will win, and Poland will be under our control.'

'The operation to occupy Poland will end soon, but we are now at war with France and Britain over it. It all depends what they do now.'

'When will Franz and Johann be back home? Mama was crying the other day. She worries about them.'

'She didn't say anything to me. I'll speak to her. The boys should get some leave once the Polish business has settled down. Thanks for telling me about Mama.'

~~o~~

'Maria, come with me.'

She looked startled.

'Why? Where are we going?'

'Just follow me.'

He took hold of her hand and led her into his study.

'I want to show you something.'

'What is it,' she said, 'I've got things to do, Erich.'

'I know. This will only take a minute.'

From his briefcase, he pulled out a cardboard folder.

'I probably shouldn't have taken these home, so if they court-martial me…'

'Really, Erich! What are you going on about? I don't have time for this.'

From the folder, the General extracted two large maps, and unfolded them on top of his desk, one on top of the other.

'This is a map of Poland,' he said. 'I want to show you what has been happening with Franz and Johann.'

He saw her eyes widen, and her features soften a little. She almost stumbled, and he caught her arm.

'The Second Division, including Colonel Schneider's battalion, entered Poland here, eleven days ago.'

He pointed to the red line that denoted the border and showed her their short advance to Chojnice.

'After capturing the town, they moved on the next day, towards the Vistula.'

He showed her on the map how the river acted as a natural barrier, which the Polish troops retreated behind.

'It took them almost a week to fight their way over the river and take Chełmno.'

'Was the fighting fierce?' she asked, a tremor in her voice.

'Chojnice was more of a skirmish, but there was heavy fighting before Chełmno was captured.'

'But Franz and Johann are safe?'

'Yes. Canaris met up with them, briefly, near Warsaw. Casualties on our side were light.

677

We were better equipped and better trained; we have Colonel Schneider to thank for that.'

'He served under you in the war, didn't he?'

'Yes. I'm surprised you remembered.'

'You said he was the most promising of your junior officers, back then.'

'He was,' he said, even more astonished.

'So, where are they now?'

'Ah. They're here,' he said, pointing again to the map. 'On the outskirts of Warsaw. They had to cross the Vistula again, where it curves round to the north of the city. They arrived there about a week ago.'

'And they're still there?'

He lifted the top map away, revealing a larger scale map of Warsaw and the surrounding countryside.

'The Poles have barricaded the city and are defending it with large numbers of troops,' he told her. 'Franz and Johann's units, along with the rest of the 4th Army, the 3rd Army and the 10th Army, are taking it suburb by suburb and street by street. They're being supported by the Luftwaffe and by the panzer regiments. I've been told the Poles are fighting valiantly, but that it's only a matter of time.'

'Are they in a lot of danger?'

'War is always dangerous, but Colonel Schneider doesn't risk his men unnecessarily, and they are trained to fight in a way that minimises casualties. With the Soviets attacking Poland from the East, it should shorten the conflict considerably. And Franz will look after Johann, I promise.'

She smiled, but he could see a tear running down her cheek, and his heart went out to her. He reached for her and drew her to him. She buried her head in his shoulder and clung to him.

'I should be used to this, but it's different now,' she sobbed.

'I know,' he said, 'I feel the same. I was never nervous for myself but with the boys...'

She pulled her head back and gaped at him.

'I didn't know...' she said, her voice trailing off.

'As you say, it's different. We were young, and we knew no better. You had the children to worry about.'

'I used to worry about you too. It's not that. I always felt you would come home to me, deep in my heart. With the boys, I keep getting a ghastly feeling that something is going to happen to them.'

'Nothing will happen to them,' the General said, praying that he was right. If war broke out all over Europe, there was no saying how safe they would be; even in the Polish campaign, although the odds were heavily stacked in favour of the Wehrmacht, it would only take one stray bullet. Or two.

'It's the not knowing that's the worst bit, even if the news from the war is favourable.'

'I'm sorry, darling. I should have kept you up to date with their progress. I thought you didn't want to know the details.'

'I thought that myself. But I find that I need to know. Did you say Canaris was in Poland?'

'Yes. He was invited to see the Wehrmacht in action. While he was there, he made a point of looking in on Franz and Johann.'

'That was good of him. The boys would be pleased to see a familiar face.'

'Yes, I'm sure they were. Canaris said they were both in excellent spirits but looking forward to getting home after the hostilities are over.'

Maria smiled.

That night, in bed, for the first time in months, she turned towards him.

~~o~~

She gave him a smile at breakfast.

He judged that he would never have a better time to ask.

'Maria,' he said. 'You have relatives in Denmark, don't you?'

'Yes. Two second cousins. I haven't seen them in years. I'm not even sure if they're still alive. Why do you ask?'

'I need a favour.'

He paused and took a breath.

'There's just a chance the Nussbaums might need to go to Denmark, to get out, and they'd need someone to act as a guarantor to be allowed in. They may have to stay with them for a few days. Do you think your cousins would be willing to help?'

She laughed. 'I doubt it. If they're still alive, they'll be in their late eighties or early nineties and I don't think they'd take kindly to lodgers.'

The General forced himself to breathe normally and keep his voice calm.

'It would only be on paper. We could find somewhere for them to stay; a hotel or guest house.'

'I haven't spoken to them for years. It would look bad if I just wrote to them out of the blue, asking them to vouch for complete strangers.'

'But the Nussbaums aren't strangers to us. I'm sure they'd take your word as to their character.'

He could see irritation in her face.

'It's a little unfair to ask, Erich, really.'

'I'm only doing it out of desperation. I would never have mentioned it otherwise.'

Her eyes softened.

'Oh, all right,' she said, letting out a long sigh. 'I'll ask. But don't expect miracles.'

'Danke,' he said, letting out a long breath.

~~o~~

[22/09/1939 Friday]

'Mama, why must we have fish all the time?'

It wasn't like Ruth to complain, but Miriam knew how she felt. If anything, the rich smells and look of the food she prepared for the Kästners made it even harder to take.

'You know why,' Miriam said. 'We agreed to be stricter with kosher food for Manny's sake.'

Ruth groaned.

'Could Manny not just eat kosher on his own? We used to eat such nice food. And anyway, why can't we eat meat?'

'You do understand, young lady, that our meat ration is pitiful and it's nearly impossible to buy kosher meat anyway.'

'Could you not just buy ordinary meat, and tell Manny it's kosher?'

'Of course not. That would be lying.' Her indignation covered a sense of guilt. It had crossed her mind to do exactly that, and pass some of the leftover meat from the Kästners as kosher.

She was still able to use cheese, bread, eggs, and vegetables from the Kästner kitchen, so the rationing that had blighted the dinner tables of most of her Jewish friends had not hit them so hard, and she pointed this out to Ruth.

'I know, Mama. It's just…'

Since she'd got married, and had come to work for the Kästner family, it had always been agreed that all the food they needed was provided as part of their stipend. Often, she just made enough of whatever the Kästners were eating to feed her own family too, but she could also order additional items for the cottage, and they would arrive with the deliveries to the

679

Drachensee house.

Now, she had to visit the shops every couple of days to buy extra food, as the Kästners' household purchases were controlled by ration cards too, even if the allowances were far more generous.

Fish was still plentiful, and not rationed. It was cheap too; Two smoked herrings were only twenty pfennigs and they were kosher, so she felt that she had to make the most of it, even if it did get monotonous at times.

Whether by accident or design, the Kästner rations still included coupons for Franz and Johann, who were rarely home, and she was sure that the General received supplies of luxuries such as coffee and wine as a privilege of rank, or through the black market. She'd seen a new bottle of one of the General's favourite malts when she'd been cleaning his study, and she knew that could only have been purchased illegally.

'You're a lot better off than most of your friends. You'll just have to put up with it, I'm afraid.'

She looked around, expecting an answer but Ruth had disappeared, probably upstairs, more than likely reading a book, or studying. She smiled.

She was the best daughter a mother could have, and Miriam could put up with the odd complaint.

~~o~~

Memo: Geh.KdoS. ABW 22/09/39 CAC0895.1

For Attention Only: General Erich Kästner, Abwehr, Kiel office, Abwehr.

From: Vice Admiral Wilhelm Canaris, Chef der Abwehr.

** HÖCHSTE GEHEIMHALTUNG **

In a meeting held yesterday at SD Headquarters in Prinz-Albrecht-Straße, Berlin, Reinhard Heydrich issued the following directives to the heads of all SiPo and SD divisions, re: Jewish and Gypsy deportments.

[1] Poland's Jews will be concentrated in the larger cities, close to major rail termini.

[2] All of Germany's Jews will be resettled in Poland.

[3] All of Germany's Roma (Gypsies) will be resettled in Poland.

[4] Reichsbahn freight cars have been deemed appropriate for the transport of Jews and Roma.

No Action Required. For information only. [END]

~~o~~

KIELER MORGENPOST

Monday, 25th September 1939

HEAVIEST BOMBING OF WAR BRINGS WARSAW TO ITS KNEES

Over one thousand aircraft took part in the latest heavy bombing of Warsaw by the Luftwaffe that started yesterday and continues today. Our war correspondent reported that large parts of the city were burning, the flames reaching hundreds of feet into the sky.

An intense bombardment of central Warsaw by Wehrmacht artillery units compounded the terror for the city's defenders and inhabitants.

An army spokesman stated that while the destruction was unfortunate, the Polish Army's refusal to surrender had left the commander of the German armed forces, General Wilhelm Keitel, with no option.

He added that further territorial gains had been made but that the implicit difficulties of fighting in the close confines of city streets meant that our soldiers had to advance cautiously to avoid unnecessary casualties.

CHAPTER 199

SS-Obersturmführer Mey sat outside his billet, watching the city's destruction. He touched the insignia on his shoulder, the newness of his promotion reflected in the unblemished stitching on the shoulder tag, with its single gold star, denoting the step up in rank equivalent to a first lieutenant in the Heer.

He was desperate to get on with the fighting, to pound the lousy Polacks into the ground, get out of this dump and back to Kiel to see Lise and tell her about his promotion. He hoped that she might have some news for him; they'd used no protection in their lovemaking during his last short home leave before he returned to his battalion. Since then, there had been no chance of getting furlough in the run up to the invasion and during the offensive itself.

She'd said nothing in her letters.

'Hey, Obersturmführer, you want another drink?'

He nodded and the Untersturmführer who had been promoted to Rudolf's former rank, recorked the bottle and threw it to him. He caught it expertly and pulled the cork out before taking a sizeable swallow of the rather good red wine they'd plundered from a well-to-do house in one of the outer suburbs, the owners having fled. The locks had been no match for the butt of a submachine gun. He'd watched as his men had raped the three Jewish servants they'd found cowering in the cellar, emboldened by the vocal encouragements of the squad members and the wine they'd consumed, so conveniently stored within touching distance of their wretched victims.

Rudolf Mey hadn't taken his squad's offer of first go with one of the women, but even a bottle of Chablis hadn't dulled the uncomfortable erection he'd had while his men took it in turns to mount the three women, their initial screams dying to plaintive sobbing as their ordeal drew to a close. Each had been dispatched with a bullet through the head once the squad had finished with them.

His men had plundered the cellar and, while they held position outside Warsaw, waiting for the call to clear an area of Jews and other undesirables, or take part in one of the assaults, they hadn't been sober.

At first, Obersturmführer Mey had resisted their constant offers to top up with one of the vintage wines they'd stolen, but when Hauptsturmführer Eicke dropped by to tell him that his men could stand down for another twenty-four hours, he had accepted the nervously proffered bottle of superior port from one of his men and handed it to his commanding officer. The Hauptsturmführer had proceeded to pull the cork, take a large swig, and hand it back to Rudolf. They'd finished the bottle together.

That was two days ago, and apart from a solitary mission to pick up and dispose of a captured squad of Polish soldiers, all of whom were Jewish, they'd received no orders to move, and had remained in an almost constant state of inebriation.

Rudolf sat and watched the flames of Warsaw's destruction roar into the early evening sky. The Hauptsturmführer was right about something; watching a city burn was like sex, but he was wrong about the lust dulling. The second time, and the third time were as good as the first. Just like with Lise. And he wouldn't let her down, no matter how satisfying it would feel to stand over one of these Jewish sluts and undo his belt buckle…

~~o~~

'Have you read the papers? The people will think there's nothing but success,' the admiral said.

At the other end of the telephone, the General tensed.

'Why, what has happened?'

'They're calling yesterday's air raids decisive, but there are no signs of Polish capitulation. And we may have killed more of our own troops than the Polish have. Fools.'

'What do you mean?' the General asked, desperately hoping his sons weren't among the dead.

'The smoke and dust from the first wave of bombing obscured most of the city and, instead of aborting the subsequent missions, the stupid bastards dropped them on the suburbs our boys had taken yesterday.'

The General's knuckles whitened. He forced himself to relax his grip on the receiver.

'What suburbs?' he gasped.

'In the north-west.'

'That's where Franz and Johann are.'

'No, they're not, they're on the other flank, which has moved round to assist the 3rd Army, who have come under heavy fire. You had the reports, did you not.'

The General felt relief flood through him.

'They haven't arrived yet,' he told Canaris, his mind still numb.

'Erich. I do apologise, but if anything had happened to Franz or Johann, I would have told you.'

'I should have known that, but you gave me a fright, my friend, and at my age, that's not necessarily a good thing.'

'I'm surprised, to be honest. The Luftwaffe had enough training in Spain, supporting Franco's civil war. I would have thought they would have got their strategy right by now.'

'I don't suppose they carried out bombing on this scale. Nobody has.'

There was silence at the end of the line for a moment.

'I almost cried when I saw Warsaw in flames,' the admiral said. 'I visited it, you know, a few years ago. It was a beautiful city. I dread to think of the damage we've done to it, not to mention the civilian casualties.'

'Are we allowed to do that?'

'It seems so, because the Polish defensive positions are in the parts of the city we're bombing. It's a sad way to fight a war though.'

'There's no good way to fight a war, Canaris.'

~~o~~

Memo: Geh.KdoS. ABW 26/09/39 CAC0908.1

For Attention Only: All senior executive officers, Abwehr.

From: Vice Admiral Wilhelm Canaris, Chef der Abwehr.

In what is hoped will be the final push, the 18th, 19th, 31st and 46th divisions have joined the 2nd and 3rd divisions of the 4th Army to attack the western parts of Warsaw earlier this morning. At the same time, the 32nd, 61st and 217th divisions are supporting the 10th Army on its advance into the eastern suburbs.

In the east of Poland, the Soviet Armies are making significant gains. There are still pockets of resistance; around Modlin, to the west of Warsaw and, in Kock, in the south of the country, where fighting is still fierce. [END]

~~o~~

Obersturmführer Mey finally got his wish. On the last day, Hauptsturmführer Eicke volunteered his squad to storm a machine-gun enclave that refused to surrender, despite being surrounded on three sides. It guarded an important junction on the road into central Warsaw, and its young commander had cleverly positioned it where it was almost impossible for a German tank to get a clear shot at it, and the German infantry did not have sufficient faith in the Luftwaffe's accuracy to call a bombing strike in on it without risking collateral damage to its own troops.

The Hauptsturmführer, on a reconnoitre trip with Rudolf, offered the use of his squad to clear it, to Rudolf's horror.

'They're still drunk, sir,' he said, on the way back to their billet, knowing that he and the Hauptsturmführer weren't much more sober.

'Ach, don't worry, Rudolf. They will fight without fear with a little wine in their blood,' he'd replied, laughing, and they had.

The watching men of the 3rd Infantry Division said afterwards that it was the bravest piece of soldiering they had ever seen. It was also the most foolish and ill-conceived military manoeuvre they had witnessed. Disdaining the use of covering fire, or the utilisation of the buildings lining the street for protection, the SS men charged the Polish position without thought for their own lives, or for the lives of their colleagues.

~~o~~

By the time they stood in front of the smoking and silent emplacement, screaming the glory of the SS, the Führer, and the Fatherland, their numbers had been diminished by over fifty per cent.

The Hauptsturmführer looked around for his Obersturmführer but could not see him. He frowned and imagined visiting the grieving widow to tell her of her husband's brave sacrifice and saw the advantages in having to console her through the difficult months that would follow.

He heard two shots from deep within the building that the machine gun had been sited in and made a quick motion for two of his surviving storm troopers to follow him, running ahead of them into the darkness.

He rattled down a flight of iron steps and, not waiting for cover, ran along a dark corridor, seeing a light ahead in a doorway at the end of the passage.

His two companions struggled to keep up, so it was the Hauptsturmführer who burst into the room first.

From a hole in the ceiling of the cellar, light from the street dimly lit the room, and the SS man barely managed to stop himself shooting at the armed figure in the middle.

Three of the enemy soldiers sat propped up against the wall, blood welling from each of their chests and from their mouths. Their lifeless hands still held their weapons across their laps. The figure in the middle of the room watched the three Polish soldiers as the last crimson bubbles of breath left them.

'Obersturmführer!'

The barked words from his commander broke Rudolf's trance. He turned to face the Hauptsturmführer.

'Yes, sir,' he shouted. 'I heard the sound of running footsteps on the stairway, sir. I followed them down.'

The Hauptsturmführer laughed, and clapped Rudolf on the back.

He nodded to the two storm troopers who had followed him down.

'Search the other rooms. Kill anyone you find.'

The two men left, kicking open doors as they went, the beams from their torches lighting up the corridor.

'Write in your report that these men tried to resist.'

'As you wish, sir.'

'That was very clever, Obersturmführer.'

'Sorry, sir. What was clever, sir?'

'When they surrendered, you shot them in the chest, not the head. It looks like they died in combat. Most of my men would have put a shot in each of their foreheads.'

'That wasn't why I shot them in the chest, sir.'

The Hauptsturmführer frowned.

'Then why, Kamerad Obersturmführer?'

'If I'd shot them in the head, they would have died instantly, sir. I wanted them to know that I'd killed them.'

Hauptsturmführer Eicke tilted his head back and let out a roar of laughter and shook his head.

'Do you know, Obersturmführer Mey,' he said, his hand on Rudolf's shoulder, 'You and I will go far in this war. The Führer needs men like us.'

He put a fatherly arm around Rudolf.

'Come. We will help those two Dummköpfe before they kill themselves.'

~~o~~

Memo: Geh.KdoS. ABW 27/09/39 CAC0913.1

For Attention Only: General Erich Kästner, Abwehr, Kiel office, Abwehr.

From: Vice Admiral Wilhelm Canaris, Chef der Abwehr.

** HÖCHSTE GEHEIMHALTUNG **

Heinrich Himmler has ordered that the offices of the Security Police (Gestapo and KriPo) and the SD, are to be formally brought under the control of one organisation, the Reich Security Main Office (RSHA). This formalises the arrangement that is currently in place, and it will be headed by Reinhard Heydrich, the current head of both organisations.

Reinhard Heydrich is succeeded as Director of the Gestapo by Heinrich Müller.

Adolf Hitler has entrusted the RSHA with coordinating the resettlement of German Jews, and those in the occupied territories of Austria, Czechoslovakia, and Poland. [END]

~~o~~

Memo: Geh.KdoS. ABW 28/09/39 CAC0915.1

For Attention Only: General Erich Kästner, Abwehr, Kiel office, Abwehr.

From: Vice Admiral Wilhelm Canaris, Chef der Abwehr.

** HÖCHSTE GEHEIMHALTUNG **

The Führer has signed an authorisation, backdated to September 1, 1939, that exonerates the Reich's physicians from future prosecution in relation to euthanasia of German citizens living in institutions with mental and physical disabilities, whom the participating physicians deem incurable and thus unworthy of life. [END]

CHAPTER 200

KIELER MORGENPOST

Friday 29th September 1939

WARSAW SURRENDERS

Late yesterday, the commander of Polish forces in Warsaw, General Walerian Czuma, surrendered the city to the German Command. Troops of the Wehrmacht will enter central Warsaw today. It is expected that the Führer will visit the city next week.

A spokesman for the Reich Ministry of War said that the campaign had been a tremendous success for the German Armed Forces and the German people, with extremely low casualties among its soldiers and airmen.

He stated that Germany had strived to solve its international difficulties with Polish aggression through diplomacy, and that the Wehrmacht had attempted to minimise civilian casualties where it could.

The spokesman added that the few remaining pockets of Polish resistance were expected to surrender over the next forty-eight hours.

~~o~~

[07/10/1939 Saturday]

'Sir, does that mean we have complete control of Poland now?'

'Yes, it does, Heinz. At least, the part of Poland agreed with the Soviets.'

The last pocket of Polish resistance, at Kock, near Lublin, had finally surrendered on the sixth of October, the day before.

'It seems only yesterday that the National Socialists won the election on a ticket of anti-bolshevism, and now they are our allies.'

The General laughed, but it had a hollow ring to it.

'Captain, you are right. And despite thousands of his communist comrades being imprisoned in our camps, it suits Stalin to accept a peace with Adolf Hitler, to further his own plans to expand Soviet borders.'

'At least our casualties were low, sir. You must be relieved that your sons are safe.'

'More than I should admit. But the government have been a little disingenuous about our losses.'

The General lifted a sheet of paper from his desk and handed it to Heinz Bauer.

'These figures are for Luftwaffe alone.'

~~o~~

Memo: Geh.KdoS. ABW 06/10/39 CAC0930.1

For Attention Only: General Erich Kästner, Abwehr, Kiel office, Abwehr.

From: Vice Admiral Wilhelm Canaris, Chef der Abwehr.

** HÖCHSTE GEHEIMHALTUNG **

Fall Weiss casualties – Luftwaffe.

Killled:189

Wounded: 126

Missing in action: 224

Aircraft lost: 285

[END]

~~o~~

'Around the same number of aircraft sustained sufficient damage to be written off or required major repairs,' the General said, as Heinz Bauer finished reading.

The young captain flinched.

'I didn't realise, sir. The newspapers and the wireless didn't give any indication.'

'I told you to read the newspapers, but they're only a small part of the truth.'

'What about the army, sir? How did it fare?'

'Considering the scope of our successes, there were surprisingly few casualties, although I hear the SS suffered far more losses than the regular army, despite seeing less action.'

'They're being spoken of as heroes, sir. Even the Führer made a point of mentioning their bravery.'

'I believe they did make some critical assaults, but there are also reports that they carried out some terrible acts of brutality.'

'Surely not, sir. They swear an oath to the Führer. *Obedience until death.*'

'It all depends on what they're ordered to do.'

The captain lowered his eyes. For a few moments he said nothing.

The General put his hand on the young man's shoulder.

'Talk to Franz when you get the chance,' he said.

'When do they come home, sir?' Heinz Bauer asked.

'We'll need to keep a sizeable detachment of troops in Poland,' the General said, 'so it may be a while, although I hear that General Keitel is hoping to use reserve troops to relieve those who took part in the invasion, to let them home to see their loved ones.'

'I'm sure you must be proud of them, sir.'

The General sighed.

'We now have an army that is second to none in Europe, an air force that is to be reckoned with, and the Kriegsmarine is fast catching up with the Royal Navy. Our soldiers performed magnificently, from what I hear, and the Polish Army were no match for them but, abroad, I fear that Germany is fast becoming an international pariah. I am proud of my sons, Captain Bauer, but I'm not sure I'm happy with what they're fighting for.'

'Yes, sir. It must be difficult.'

He paused. The chimes of church bells echoed through the open window.

'The celebrations on the streets of Kiel are just starting, sir.'

'I know. The general population doesn't care if a few liberties are taken. All it wants is for Germany to be great again; to have pride in themselves. The question is, Captain Bauer – what price will they pay for it?'

Memo: Geh.KdoS. ABW 08/10/39 CAC0938.1

For Attention Only: General Erich Kästner, Abwehr, Kiel office, Abwehr.

From: Vice Admiral Wilhelm Canaris, Chef der Abwehr.

** HÖCHSTE GEHEIMHALTUNG **

The announcement of a ghetto in Piotrków Trybunalski, Poland, was made today by Reinhard Heydrich, in a joint statement made with Hans Drexler, who has been appointed Oberbürgermeister of the town.

The appointment of the Judenrat, a Jewish-German collaborative administration agency, will assist in the relocation of Jewish residents of the city into the designated ghetto area. [END]

CHAPTER 201

[11/10/1939 Wednesday]

Miriam waited until she got home before opening the letter. She felt bad, but she hadn't wanted Itsik's mother to know what Esther had written, when so much of Miriam's correspondence discussed the older Weichmanns.

She smiled at the postmark franked on the envelope.

```
Shanghai
```

She began to read.

7th September.

Afula

Dearest Miriam,

Thank you for your letter and your kind wishes about little Miriam Rosa. She is beautiful, and we are both doing well. And whatever you say, you deserve to have her named after you. You are a wonderful friend to me.

I have enclosed two photographs; one of the baby, and one of all of us in front of our new house, which is almost finished; Itsik had it ready for us to move into when we brought little Miriam back from Haifa, although there are a lot of little jobs to do, and Moshe and Shoshana are having to share a room for a few weeks until his own room is ready.

I've started working on our garden, although I have a young Arab man to help, who does all the heavy work. Most of the work in the house was done by Arabs and I must say, they did a great job, and you couldn't meet nicer people, but Itsik says that not all the Arabs are as friendly, and that I should never completely trust them.

I was terrified when the war started that the fighting might affect you and Itsik's parents but, from the little I've heard, the German Army seems to be advancing quickly into Poland and Itsik says it seems unlikely that the Poles can mount any sort of effective resistance. I hope it takes the government's mind off harassing you.

I'm devastated for Rosa, but at least she can try again, and she's not back in Germany. Please keep me in touch about her progress. I haven't heard from her.

Moshe is giving us a little trouble. We can't stop him mixing with some of the older boys; one of his friends has an elder brother who is eighteen and Moshe and this friend of his are forever hanging around them, running errands for them and learning all the stuff I didn't want him to know.

He constantly comes home and talks about what is happening in Germany (I think he knows more about it than us, sometimes) and I have to impress upon him to be quiet about the camps, Jewish resettlement in Poland, and the security services, in front of Shoshana.

One good thing might come out of it. These older boys seem to have connections with an organisation called the Haganah, which organises Jewish fighters to protect the settlements, and it also smuggles Jews into Palestine now that the British have reduced the amount of legal immigration, so Itsik had a word with them and he's been put in touch with a man in Haifa with a view to getting Itsik's parents here.

I feel bad asking, as you have done so much for us already, but can you do a big favour for me?

Can you help persuade Itsik's parents to accept the help of the Haganah, if we can arrange it? And if it does go ahead, can you give them a hand to prepare for the journey; it won't be easy and they'll be able to bring almost nothing with them, and you know what Mama Weichmann is like about her things'.

You should also consider it yourself. The Haganah don't charge for bringing people in and are eager to have families like yours settling in Palestine, although most people donate what they can afford.

Our offer of a job for Yosef is always open, and you could have our old house until you get on your feet, or you could get somewhere in Haifa.

Itsik is worried that his last remaining German suppliers will dry up completely, although it's amazing how quickly factories and other businesses are springing up here, and he can still purchase goods from other countries.

I hope you get this letter. The post office say they can't deliver it because Germany and Britain are now at war. Itsik is going to give it to old Herr Bacher, next door, who travels to China on business; he will post it for me.

I must go now. Little Miriam Rosa is crying to be fed.

All our love

Esther.

~~o~~

[20/10/1939 Friday]

They lay, spent, in the bed of the small flat that had been Lise's home since their honeymoon. Their lovemaking had been heavy with the pent-up release of two people whose craving for each other's flesh had burned fiercer every day they were apart.

They had been denied all but the most fleeting days to lose themselves in each other; Rudolf had been home only twice in their first year of marriage; once for five frantic days in December and then for an inconsolably wonderful weekend, just as spring was melting the ice of Kieler Hafen.

Lise was relieved at her willingness to wait for Rudolf on each occasion, and not to give in to her needs. She attracted unremitting interest from other men, despite the gold band on her finger, but she found the strength to resist their advances. She spent much of her time at her parents' home, knowing she was safe from temptation there.

And it wasn't just the protection and comfort of home; her mother understood her and was the only person who didn't ask her the irritating questions that well-meaning friends and other family members did.

Was the pitter-patter of tiny feet in the offing? Was good news on the way?

Even Rudolf had hinted at it in every letter he'd sent. She'd hoped he would realise that the passionate and sensual nature of their union would disappear if they had a child and, anyway, the thought of despoiling her almost perfect body with a child repulsed her; the stretched belly, the engorged and vein-filled breasts, and the untold damage to the place between her thighs that she knew drove men wild with desire.

Rudolf reached out and took a long sip from his glass of wine. Lise frowned.

'You drink a lot more than you used to,' she said.

She felt him stiffen.

'I'm on leave,' he said. 'I'm just enjoying it to the full.'

She detected more than a hint of irritation in his voice.

'I just wondered why you need alcohol, when you have this,' she said, leaning back on the pillow and showing herself to him.

He looked, and his eyes gorged on the rich curves of her body, and the bush of hair between her legs, still damp from their last furious devouring of each other.

He closed his eyes, but her comment had annoyed him, and he couldn't let it go. She'd done the same yesterday, stopping him from opening a third bottle of wine after dinner.

'I want both,' he said, draining his glass and dribbling a little wine from his mouth into the valley between her breasts. The little rivulet ran down her belly and, pausing to puddle for a second in her navel, rolled onwards. He followed it with his tongue, meeting the soft springy hair of her pubis.

Lise wanted him to keep going, to feel him tasting her; losing himself within her, but she frowned, wanting the wondering, passionate and subservient Rudolf back; not this arrogant version of her husband, who wanted his cake, and to eat it, too.

'Am I not enough for you?' she asked, 'that you need to be drunk to be with me?'

He lifted his head and stared at her. It was a look she'd never seen before and it frightened her a little, but the fear suddenly sparked a warmth in her loins again and she clutched his hair and forced his head down, pressing his lips against her.

He responded, and she felt his tongue on the place that she'd taught him to find. And her body arched once more.

~~o~~

Later, as she walked along Hamburger Chaussee, her arm through his and proud of the fresh epaulettes on his shoulders, she smiled as she thought of the pleasure it would give her parents when they told them of Rudolf's new rank.

'Lise,' he said, breaking her reverie, 'I've been wanting to speak to you about something.'

Hoping it was a suggestion that a larger and slightly more luxurious flat could be rented on his Obersturmführer's more generous pay, she smiled at him.

'I thought you might be, you know…'

'What?' she said, taken aback for a second. Then it hit her. He was asking her why she wasn't pregnant.

She'd been ready for the question earlier but now it caught her by surprise, and she fought to keep her anger and fear under control.

'I was hoping we might have a child by now,' he said, spitting it out as if it had been stuck in his throat.

'I know, darling,' she said, her voice easy now as she quelled the nausea in her belly. 'It will come in time, don't worry.'

'It's not as if we don't…'

Again, the sudden shyness. If she hadn't been so angry, she might have found it endearing.

They'd used protection on their honeymoon; she'd told him that she was too frightened of getting pregnant so young, but he'd insisted before he left that they should try for a baby on his next visit home.

She'd purchased a 'Dutch Cap' and had prayed ever since then that it wouldn't come out at some point during their lovemaking, or that he'd burst in on her putting the thing in place before they made love.

It hadn't been easy to procure; the National Socialists had all but outlawed contraception, wanting to encourage the birth rate to rise, and populate the expanding Third Reich. They had even introduced an award for prolificacy in German women; those who bore multiple children would be awarded the *Ehrenzeichen der Deutschen Mutter*, in bronze for a fourth or fifth child, silver for a sixth or seventh and gold for an eighth.

The Cross of Honour of the German Mother, Lise thought, frowning. *Not for me.*

But she was running out of excuses to disappear for a few minutes just as their passion ignited, so she'd resorted to keeping her cap in for hours beforehand, just to avoid discovery. She didn't know how he'd react if he found out.

'It will happen when God decides it will,' she said, marvelling at her own ingenuity.

'I suppose it will,' he said.

It was with relief that she realised they'd reached Drachensee, and that they were almost at her parents' home. She glanced at the Kästner house and chided herself, wondering when she would stop thinking of Franz every time she visited her parents.

~~o~~

Beate Böhm's eyes widened for a second when she opened the door and saw Rudolf's uniform, but it didn't register with the young Obersturmführer. Beate glanced at her daughter and saw a fleeting look of curiosity cross her face.

'Come on in,' she said, giving Rudolf a hug, then Lise.

'Eberhard, Rudolf and Lise are here,' she shouted.

'Look Mama, Rudolf is an Obersturmführer now,' Lise said, pointing proudly to Rudolf's collar patches.

'Oh,' Beate Böhm said. 'That's lovely.' She turned as her husband came into the hallway.

'Eberhard,' she said. 'Rudolf has been promoted. Isn't that marvellous?'

'When did this happen?' Lise's father said, slapping Rudolf on the back.

'Three or four weeks ago.' Rudolf beamed. 'In Warsaw. I didn't write, so that I could surprise Lise when I came home.'

'Wonderful,' Eberhard Böhm said. 'This calls for a drink.' He took Rudolf's arm.

'The only other task you need to take care of is giving Lise's mother and I a grandchild,' he said, as he led Rudolf down the hallway.

Beate saw Lise's eyes narrow.

'Ignore him,' Beate said to Lise. 'Take as much time as you want.'

Lise gave her mother a quick smile of gratitude.

'You didn't seem surprised by Rudolf's news,' Lise said.

'It wasn't much of a shock,' Beate said, colouring a little. 'Rudolf is an excellent young officer and good soldiers are being rewarded with promotions while this war is going on.'

She hoped Lise hadn't noticed.

'Oh. I suppose that's true,' Lise said with a shrug.

'Your father will be pouring drinks. Let's go through.'

Beate Böhm followed her daughter into the lounge. A delicious ripple of guilt and pleasure ran through her and she allowed herself a smile.

It had all started a couple of months ago.

She'd been in the house, alone, when the telephone rang. The maid answered it and told her that there was a gentleman who wished to speak with her and, no, he hadn't left his name.

Intending to rebuff the expected insurance salesman or some other cold caller, she'd picked up the handset.

'Who is this?'

'Frau Böhm, you might remember me,' the man had said, his voice one that she recognised but couldn't put a name to.

'Sorry. I think you must be mistaken. What did you say your name was?'

'I'm teasing, Frau Böhm. It's Hauptsturmführer Eicke. I was passing through Kiel and thought I might say hello.'

Beate Böhm had felt her stomach twist, and she'd taken a sharp breath. For a second there had been silence on the line.

'Frau Böhm?' It had seemed to her there was a hint of laughter in his voice.

'Sorry. I was just a little surprised,' she'd said, her voice a shade breathless.

'If it's not convenient...'

'No, it's not that. It's just a little...'

She'd paused.

'... irregular,' she said.

'So, you'll meet me?' he'd said, and she'd been sure that there was amusement in his tone.

'Not here. Not in Kiel.'

'Where? Do you have transport?'

'You can pick me up.'

She'd told him to meet her in Elmschenhagen. She had a friend there.

She'd put the telephone down and stood for a minute, waiting for her breathing to return to normal.

Climbing the stairs to her room, she'd found what she wanted to wear, then, in her bathroom, she'd ran a sink of water. She couldn't risk a bath, with the maid in the house, so she'd washed herself and sprayed a little perfume. In her bedroom she'd looked at herself in the mirror, standing in her brassiere and panties. She'd dressed, and told the maid she was visiting her friend, Frau Baumann. She'd be back by six.

A twenty minute taxi ride later, she'd stood outside a small café in Elmschenhagen's main street, pretending to wait for her friend.

A terrible dread that Frau Baumann would suddenly appear had been dispelled when the Hauptsturmführer's car had drawn up. She'd glanced around, just in case but, when he'd leaned over and opened the door, she'd jumped in.

'You look wonderful,' he'd said.

She'd blushed and smoothed her dress across her knees. He'd looked down at her hands, held clasped on her lap.

It was a knowing look, she thought.

'Where are we going?' she'd asked.

'Preetz,' he'd said.

She'd racked her brains, trying desperately to recall if she knew anyone there.

~~o~~

Beate sat half-listening to her son-in-law tell of his unit's attack on the machine-gun emplacement in Warsaw, but her mind drifted back to that first afternoon with his commanding officer.

They'd talked in generalities on the way to Preetz, and in the restaurant of a small hotel in the main square where they ate a buffet lunch. She'd glanced around anxiously, expecting to be tapped on the shoulder by someone she knew, or by one of Eberhard's friends or acquaintances.

'The Hotelbesitzer is very discreet,' the Hauptsturmführer had said, smiling at her, nodding at the waiter as he passed.

'You're terribly presumptuous,' she'd replied, but there had been a smile at the corner of her mouth.

'I knew at Lise's wedding that if I called on you, you'd come. Your husband is a fine man, but has not excited you for years, if ever. You are a woman who deserves to be aroused, to be awakened, to be lusted after.'

And she had been aroused; she'd wished she'd slipped fresh panties into her handbag; her journey home would be uncomfortably damp.

Afterwards, on the way back to Kiel, they hadn't talked much. He'd spoken briefly of Rudolf's promotion, and it had been a slip not to appear more surprised when Lise had told her about it later.

694

He'd dropped her off at the same place, and she found that she couldn't return home immediately. She'd sat drinking coffee, sure that everyone in the café knew what she'd been doing all afternoon.

But she didn't care. She hadn't been made to feel like that for... she thought back, trying to remember the first days of her marriage.

... forever. She realised she'd never experienced anything like that with Eberhard. The Hauptsturmführer had been masterful, and she'd forgiven him for his cruelty and arrogance for the pleasure he'd given her, and for the pleasure he'd taken from her. And even if he'd made no pretence to hold her afterwards, or whisper endearments in her ear, she hadn't cared.

It suited her; she was fond of her husband and even more in love with her position in society, and she didn't want any complications.

'I'll be back in Kiel every few months,' he'd said. It would be enough, she'd thought, but she found herself counting the days until they next met.

And each time he'd been on leave, the Hauptsturmführer had paid Beate Böhm a visit. And he'd made her feel Lise's age again.

CHAPTER 202

[27/10/1939 Friday]

'Canaris.'

'Kästner.'

The General looked at his friend. He was more like the Canaris of old. He'd aged, it appeared, but he'd recovered some of the sureness that he'd always had.

'How are you, Canaris?' the General said, pouring the obligatory glass of malt.

'More worried than ever, but this is the only place I can afford to let it show. The last time I was here, I made a terrible error.'

'You did? I hope you're not having second thoughts on what you witnessed in Poland.'

'No, no. Definitely not. That is seared on my mind forever. What I mean is, how trustworthy are your staff?'

'Mixed, I'd say. The captain, I'd almost certainly trust with my life, and the chief petty officer too. My other military staff will do as they are told. Frau Müller, on the other hand, I'm not sure of.'

'That's the problem. The last time I was here, I was in a state.'

'You did cause a stir when you arrived. You looked as if you'd seen a ghost.'

'Did I blurt it all out in front of her?'

'You said nothing until we were on our own. I sent Frau Müller home, and Captain Bauer held station in the outer office while we talked. I'm sure he wouldn't have tried to listen in, but Frau Müller would have. I don't know if she's just a gossip, or if she has been tasked with keeping an eye on me. It's hard to tell, but I'm always careful around her.'

'I should have composed myself before coming to see you. She must have known something was wrong.'

'I wouldn't worry. I told her the next day that you had lost a close friend in the fighting. She seemed convinced and asked me to pass on her condolences. I wouldn't worry about the captain. He sees things our way.'

'That's clever, Kästner. You seem to have taken to this intelligence business like a duck to water. We'll make a spy out of you yet.'

'So, that's out the way. Have you any more news?'

'You have been destroying the memos; the most secret ones?'

'Yes. As you asked.' The General pointed to the ashtray. 'It's the only time I use it. I think Frau Müller thinks I'm a heavy smoker.'

'Good. I have a fancy shredding machine. It rips it into strips. The children love to turn the handle on it and feed paper into it.'

'Why do you ask?'

'Well, I'm not even sure it's safe to put any of that sort of information on paper. From now on, we'll only discuss it face to face, or by telephone. Even then, I'll use a public telephone to contact you, if I need to talk. I'll telephone here, or your home, and give you the number I'm calling from, but I'll swap the last two digits. Find a public telephone, then telephone me on that number.'

'Are you not being a little overdramatic, Canaris?'

'Perhaps, but there's a fine line between paranoia and good field technique. They often overlap. It may be overkill, but it's a wise habit to get into.'

'All right. I'll humour you. Now you're here. What is bothering you?'

'Three things. You got my memo about the RSHA?'

'Yes. Himmler and Heydrich control the entire security service now but, if I'm honest, it's nothing new.'

'That's true, but they've now been given complete charge of coordinating the resettlement of Jews from Germany and the occupied countries.'

'They've been repatriating Jews for a while now. That's no surprise either.'

'This is all Jews we're talking about here, not just immigrants. And that will include the Nussbaums.'

The General stared at the admiral for a second.

'That can't be right. Surely they wouldn't…'

He stopped.

'I must have misread it,' he said, realising that Canaris was right.

'Next,' Canaris continued. 'On the twelfth of October, the Führer issued a decree establishing the Generalgouvernement für die besetzten polnischen Gebiete. It came into force yesterday.'

The General Government for the Occupied Polish Territories.

'I believe, for brevity, they're just calling it the Generalgouvernement,' he added.

'Is that not just the National Socialists' usual love of titles?'

'No. Poland has been split up into three zones. The Russian one, which we already know about, and two separate defined areas under our control.'

'Why split it up?'

'I don't know for sure but I suspect that it's down to the ethnic German population. The western parts of Poland, the area surrounding East Prussia and the Polish Corridor, have been annexed to Germany, like Austria, the Saarland, and the Sudetenland. A significant percentage of the people in these areas are of German origin.'

The General nodded, but didn't speak.

'Central Poland,' Canaris continued, 'has been set up as a semi-autonomous territorial unit with its own administration, and Hans Frank has been appointed as the governor of the Generalgouvernement.'

'He was Hitler's personal lawyer, wasn't he?'

'Yes, and the party's legal adviser. He was Minister of Justice for Bavaria before he took this post. The Generalgouvernement region includes the cities of Cracow, Warsaw, Radom, and Lublin with a total population of twelve million, of which one and a half million are Jews.'

'And hardly an ethnic German, I would imagine,' the General said. 'Why keep it separate though?'

'That brings us to the final piece of the puzzle. On the twentieth of October, the security services deported just under 4,000 people from Austria, Czechoslovakia, and the annexed part of Poland to a makeshift camp near Lublin, in the Generalgouvernement.'

He looked at the General.

'Don't you see what they plan to do?' he said.

The General's eyes closed as everything clicked into place.

'They're going to use the Generalgouvernement as a dumping ground for all the Jews in Germany and the occupied countries,' he said. 'It will be one big ghetto.'

'That's the conclusion I came to. It will make the concentration camps look like small potatoes. Do you know they have a name for it?'

'No. But the National Socialists do like to label everything.'

'Judenrein.'

The General's head slumped.

Cleansed of its Jewish presence.

'There won't be a single Jew left in Germany, Austria, or Czechoslovakia,' the General said, looking up at Canaris and shaking his head.

'No,' the admiral said, his face gaunt and pale. 'And what will conditions be like for the Jews, and even the Poles, in the Generalgouvernement zone? The overcrowding will be unbearable.'

'The Nussbaums,' the General said, his hand on his forehead. 'I must get them out.'

'I asked around for you. Switzerland is out. Denmark is a possibility if they know someone they can stay with.'

'I'm working on that. Where else?'

'Belgium, the Netherlands, but there are rumours that they might not be safe for long. They're in his war plans, I'm told.'

The General raised an eyebrow.

'How likely is it to happen, and how soon?'

'There's no telling what Hitler's ambitions are, or the timescale he has in mind. If I were the Nussbaums, I would get as far away as possible, whether that be Palestine, China, South America or the United States, it doesn't matter.'

'And what about you? What are your plans, Canaris?'

'There's nothing for it but to carry on. Work away, keeping an eye on what's going on, trying to limit the damage.'

'And I've just to continue as I am doing?'

'Yes.' He held out his hand to the General. 'Until the next time.'

~~o~~

Miriam stood in the queue. She was fourth in line and watched as each person ahead of her purchased rationed items like cheese, bread, sugar, and milk. It was a slow process and, although the grocer worked steadily, by the time she reached the front of the queue, ten minutes had passed, and this had been the third shop she'd had to wait in that morning.

She moved towards the counter, nodding politely to the woman leaving the shop, and placed her ration cards on the counter.

The man looked up.

'Please wait over there,' the man said, pointing towards the other end of the counter.

'I'm sorry?' she said.

'Wait there,' he repeated, pointing again.

'Why do I have to wait,' she asked.

'Du bist Jüdin,' he said. *You are a Jew.*

She was about to argue, but his glare, and the irritated cough of the person in the queue behind her, undermined her resolve. She stepped to the side, and waited, staring at the bottles, cans and dry goods lining the shelves on the back wall, tears of shame stinging her eyes.

Glancing, she watched the grocer serve two customers, tearing off the coupons from their ration books, the absence of the large red 'J' stamp guaranteeing prompt and polite service.

Once the counter was clear, she stepped back in front of the grocer and placed her ration book on the counter for the second time. The man failed to look up, tallying a row of figures in a small notebook on the counter, so she gave a polite cough.

He looked up at her.

'Wait a minute. I'm busy.'

She drew in a sharp breath but said nothing. She looked around anxiously, knowing that, if another customer appeared, the vicious little man would serve them first. If she said something to him, she suspected he would just make her wait longer.

The minutes ticked by, and she could feel the blood pumping behind her temples, and she would have liked to do nothing better than to walk out of the shop, but it would take her ten minutes to walk from Sophienblatt to Danische Straße, and it was a much longer trudge home from the old quarter.

The man looked up again. She was just about to speak when she heard the door open behind her, and her head slumped as a woman entered the shop.

She looked back at the grocer, just in time to see a hint of a smile on his face. He lifted his hand, and moved it sideways, indicating that she should return to her spot to wait.

Miriam did as she was told, filled with disgust for the spiteful bigot.

'Can I help you, madam,' he said to the woman. She pulled her ration book from her shopping bag and undid her headscarf as she handed the sheaf of tokens to him.

The woman pulled back the hair from her face and Miriam wasn't sure what she noticed first; the disgusted snort of the grocer or the spark of recognition she suddenly had for her fellow shopper.

She turned towards the counter and saw the red 'J' on the ration book and the anger on the man's face.

The grocer glanced towards the door, but it stayed firmly closed.

Miriam proffered her ration book to the man and the other woman stepped back and apologised, giving Miriam a look of recognition.

Miriam asked the owner for her allowance of cheese, milk, butter, and sugar, and waited patiently while he wordlessly weighed out the allotted amounts of each.

While she waited, she turned to the woman.

'You're Jakob Teubner's sister, aren't you, from Schleswig?' she said.

'Yes, we've met before, haven't we?'

'Yes, at the synagogue. I'm Miriam, Yosef Nussbaum's wife. My husband and Jakob are good friends. Are you visiting?'

'No, we've come to stay with Jakob,' she said, lowering her eyes to the floor.

Miriam cursed herself.

'I'll wait for you,' she said, pulling out her purse to pay the grocer, who had placed Miriam's purchases on the counter.

She paid the man, and thanked him, gratified to see his face tighten. She left, nodding to Jakob's sister. As she opened the door, she stood back and let another woman in. Closing the door behind her, she looked through the glass and was dismayed to see the new customer being served before her fellow Jew, who was now standing in the same spot where Miriam had been a few minutes earlier.

Jakob's sister looked up and shook her head, signalling with her hand that Miriam should go. As she walked away, she kept looking back and, a few minutes later, saw the other customer leave the shop. She turned round once more at the end of Sophienblatt, but as far as she could tell, no one else had gone in or out. She smiled, relieved.

As she trudged home in the bitter cold, she vowed that she would never be back in the man's shop; even it meant an extra ten minutes each way, she would gladly make the journey to Danische Straße.

CHAPTER 203

Maldon, England.

'*Working for the Kästners, my parents had been, to some degree, shielded from the worst of the humiliation that their fellow Jews had to face every day of their lives. It wasn't until Mama had to shop for us, independent of the General's family, that she realised just how bad it had been for Rosa and her family, and Jakob, and every other Jew who'd stayed in Kiel.*'

Ruth shook her head, the anger at her mother's shame etched on her face, even after fifty years.

'*You'll wonder how I knew about all this,*' she said.

I must have looked surprised, so she explained.

'*Mama would tell me about her troubles; I was seventeen by then, and my parents had started to treat me more like an adult, and I heard things at school, from the other children. We talked about it a lot.*'

'*It must have been tough being a teenager during those times,*' I said.

'*It was tough for everyone but, yes, I suppose I lost my teenage years. The dark shadow of the National Socialists shaded every part of our lives. Even Manny and his friends, who could disappear into their own imaginations, and forget about the world around them, were often subdued, infected by the tsuris of my parents and I.*'

Tsuris. I smiled. It was a word that summed up the worries and woes that Jews had suffered throughout their history.

'*Yes,*' Ruth said. '*It helped Mama accept that we should leave Germany, even if it meant leaving my grandparents behind.*'

700

CHAPTER 204

Oskar was the last man to join the group. He shook the hands of the other three and sat down at the table.

'We're just about to order,' the Doc said, handing Oskar a menu.

'I apologise for the Doc,' the General said, 'he has no patience.'

The four men who made up the crew of the *Snowgoose* met up every three or four weeks, just to keep in touch, and because they each enjoyed the others' company.

'The summer seems so far away now, and we're not even at Christmas yet.'

'Don't worry. After the turn of the year, I'll expect you all to appear, sleeves rolled up, to start preparing the boat for spring, if the ice ever thaws.'

Oskar held up his hands.

'Erich, I think you have the wrong idea about me. I don't get my hands dirty.'

They looked at his nails. They were spotless, and manicured.

'I'll give you gloves,' the General growled, and they all laughed, even Oskar.

'It's part of the fun,' Erich Kästner added.

'He used to be able to press-gang his sons into slave labour,' the Doc said. 'Now they're gone, he's looking for new victims. It's the only reason he took us sailing this year.'

The General enjoyed their good-natured ribbing, and he knew all three of his friends would turn out to help sand, paint, varnish and sew to have the boat ready for the start of the season.

'Antje will help. We'll leave the fiddly bits of painting to her, I think. She's a dab hand with the brush.'

The waiter arrived and took their order, replenishing their drinks.

'Did you hear about the Führer? He's lucky to be alive,' the General said.

'No. What happened?' The Doc stared at him.

'A bomb. In the Bürgerbräukeller in Munich. He was delivering his usual speech on the anniversary of the Putsch. He'd left a few minutes before it went off.'

'Who did it?'

'They don't know. The bomber had left the building, but eight were killed and there were hundreds injured.'

'It's a pity they didn't succeed, whoever they were,' the Doc muttered.

'Verdammt, Doc, keep quiet, man.' Oskar looked around anxiously.

'It's true,' the Doc said, barely lowering his voice.

'You don't say it though,' Oskar hissed. 'They have ears everywhere.'

The others laughed nervously, but the General could see on their faces that they knew Oskar was right.

'They'll hang if they're lucky, those who were involved,' Dieter said.

'And their families, no doubt,' the General added.

Oskar turned each way in his chair, looking around.

'Dining out with you three isn't good for my nerves. Can we please change the subject?'

'Certainly, Oskar. What would you like to talk about?'

'Anything. Just not politics or war. I want to get through this evening without having a heart attack.'

They all laughed again.

'Well, what about women…'

As Oskar groaned, the General smiled. The conversation would start in general terms but would eventually come around to when Oskar was going to settle down.

'I'm going to stop coming to these informal evenings of yours, Herr General,' Oskar said.

~~o~~

'What have you heard about the attack, Dieter?' the General said, when the two men were alone.

'I asked around; I knew you would be interested but I didn't want to say when the others were there. An unemployed munitions worker, Johann Georg Elser, has been arrested. As far as anyone can tell, he seemed to have been working on his own.'

'I wondered if it was the communist underground.'

'He was a member of the left-leaning Federation of Woodworkers Union but, although he joined the Red Front Fighters Association, he wasn't an active member, and they had no knowledge of his plans. These organisations are not very discreet. That's why so many of their members end up being arrested, but, whatever the reasons behind it, the Doc was right. It's a great pity he failed. They were all there. Hitler, Goebbels, Heydrich, Hess, and Himmler. It would have destroyed the National Socialists.'

'Perhaps,' the General said.

'He was thirteen minutes away from ridding Germany of them for good. The only reason they left early was because of the fog. Hitler wanted to stay until the end and fly back to Berlin, but because of the fog, they had to go by train, so they left sooner than they'd intended.'

'How did he get in?'

'Meticulous planning. For months before, he'd slip in to Bürgerbräukeller towards closing time, every night, then hide. He worked away, packing the pillar nearest the stage with explosives he'd filched from the factory he worked in before he was made unemployed.'

Dieter shook his head and lifted his glass.

'To a brave bastard. God rest his soul.'

The General lowered his voice.

'There will be a purge. Watch yourself.'

'I'm safe enough. I have no official connection with any of these organisations, although they all know that I'm sympathetic to them, and that I can get information into the right hands.'

'Look after yourself, Dieter,' the General said, draining the last of his drink.

'You too, my friend.'

~~o~~

[10/11/1939 Friday]

Erich Kästner turned to Corporal Lubinus.

'You can leave us now, Corporal.'

'Yes, sir. If either you or the admiral needs anything, just give me a call. I'll be in the corridor.'

'You're dismissed, Corporal,' the General said, not unkindly. 'There's no point in you standing around. Go and have a cup of coffee in the mess.'

'Yes, sir.'

He saluted and left.

'A corporal, eh?' Wilhelm Canaris said. 'I had him down as a private all his days.'

The General laughed.

702

'It's true, he has no ambitions, other than to serve, but he's immensely useful to me and I thought giving him the stripe would give him a little more clout, when he's doing things for me down here in Plön.'

'How long has he been with you?'

'Oh, twenty years, or thereabouts.'

The admiral got up and opened the door. He stuck his head out and looked right and left, but the corporal hadn't hung around, and there was no one else in sight.

He sat back down.

'You're making me nervous,' the General said.

'These are strange days. It pays to be cautious.'

'I suppose you are right. What was so urgent, and so secretive, that you wanted to meet me here?'

'I knew it would be secure, and I wanted to ask you something, which you must answer with complete honesty.'

Erich Kästner hardly flinched, but inside, his friend's distrust hurt.

He didn't need to say that.

'Of course. I'd give you nothing else.'

'Unless you thought it was for my own good.'

The General grimaced.

He's right.

'Go on,' he said.

'Did you have any part in the attempt on the Führer's life.'

The General almost laughed, but he stopped himself when he saw the deadly serious look on Canaris's face.

'No,' he said firmly, 'that's a ludicrous thought. What made you think…?'

'You have contacts with the communists.'

'Hardly. And anyway, so do you.'

'But I knew I had no part in it,' Canaris said, the dryness in his voice almost causing a smile to appear on the General's face.

'My connections with the communists are tenuous at best,' he said. 'And besides, I heard that the culprit worked on his own.'

'Where did you hear that?'

'My contacts,' the General said, matching Canaris's earlier sharpness.

Wilhelm Canaris laughed, breaking the tension in the room. There was a knock on the door.

The General opened it and let Corporal Lubinus in.

'I thought you might need some lubrication,' the seasoned soldier said, putting a tray down on the desk. He poured two coffees and handed them to the two older men.

'Thank you, Corporal.'

Once he'd gone, Canaris leaned forward again.

'I had to know,' he said, his tone apologetic now. 'I was worried that you'd let your heart rule your head, and I didn't want you at risk.'

'Or to put the Abwehr at risk,' the General said.

Canaris gave his friend an embarrassed smile.

'There is that too,' he said. For a moment, neither man said anything.

'I worked out why they set up the Generalgouvernement,' Canaris said, breaking the silence.

'Why?'

'Once they've dumped all the people they don't want in the Reich, it will leave the rest of Poland as Lebensraum for German *Volks*. You know, Jews and Gypsies, communists, dissenters, homosexuals, initially, but perhaps, in time, the Poles themselves.'

The General closed his eyes.

Lebensraum. Living space. The extra land that Germany has always believed it needed to survive.

'Their minds,' he said. 'I just can't fathom how they work.'

~~o~~

'Go on, Obersturmführer. She's a virgin.'

The Hauptsturmführer laughed, pulling up his trousers. 'So was this one,' he said.

Rudolf could see his men, strung out along the side of the clearing, watching him. He could swear they were laughing at him.

If she wasn't a Jew...

He knew it mattered. There were laws against it, but he could hear the Hauptsturmführer's words in his head, when he'd plucked up the courage to ask.

Taking one of these Jew bitches isn't verboten. They don't count. The law exists to stop Jewish sluts from seducing good young German men.

He understood, but then there was Lise.

'Don't be a pussy, Obersturmführer. It means nothing.' The Hauptsturmführer laughed again.

'Fresh meat,' he added.

The girl was no more than fifteen and she lay, whimpering, on the floor in front of him.

'We left her for you, sir,' his Untersturmführer said, grinning. 'Some of the others weren't as ripe as her.'

It was true. Of the fifteen women in the group, only the two girls the squad had reserved for him and the Hauptsturmführer were under forty, and in any way attractive. It hadn't prevented the others from sharing the fate of these two, but at least they would have the privilege of being defiled by officers, Rudolf thought.

'Your wife will never know,' the Hauptsturmführer said, his tone mocking.

Angrily, Rudolf tore off his belt and knelt in front of the girl. She squirmed away from him, so he pulled out his pistol and held it to her head.

'Let me,' the Hauptsturmführer said, taking the pistol from him and pushing it into the girl's mouth, forcing her teeth apart. She stopped struggling.

Rudolf reached out and gripped the top of the girl's dress and pulled hard, ripping it in two. He looked at the pubescent breasts and her threadbare cotton panties. He took his bayonet from its sheath and, as the girl's eyes widened, and a whimper came from her mouth, he placed the tip of the knife against her leg and under the thin cloth and sliced upwards. She gasped, but the knife had cut only cotton.

He reached down and undid his buttons. He looked at the largeness of him and the size of her and smiled. The cheers of his men rang in his ears as he entered her, drowning out her screams.

After he'd finished, and wiped the blood from himself with her dress, he shot her, like the others.

'How many dead Jews is that today?' the Hauptsturmführer asked.

'Three hundred and twelve, sir,' the Untersturmführer said. 'Fourteen if you count the two pregnant whores.'

When they'd returned to Poland, their depleted squad was absorbed into one of the new elite Einsatzgruppen units formed by Reinhard Heydrich at the start of the invasion to travel in the wake of the German Armies, mopping up the partisans and Jews who'd escaped the advance of the regular troops.

These were the SS units Franz had seen entering Chełmno as they were leaving.

Since Rudolf and his squad had joined them, they'd travelled slowly through the western regions of Poland, eliminating those who were declared a risk to the fragile security of the latest lands annexed by the Third Reich.

The day had been a particularly bloody one. They'd only just heard of the attempt on the Führer's life that morning and the search for Jews had been more brutal and thorough than usual.

They hadn't found any partisans, but that wasn't unusual. That required a degree of expertise and a level of sobriety that the Einsatzgruppen unit lacked.

'I don't think you can count the unborn,' Rudolf said, laughing, opening a bottle of almost undrinkable Polish brandy and taking a long swallow, before passing it to his commanding officer.

'I don't see why not,' the Hauptsturmführer said. 'We've stopped two more Jews from polluting this earth. Why the hell shouldn't we count them?'

CHAPTER 205

'Sir, Admiral Göpfert is here.'

'Show him in, Captain. Please remain and take notes.'

'Yes, sir.'

When the admiral, in charge of repairs and refits on the Kriegsmarine command staff, was seated, Captain Bauer took his place and lay his pad in front of him.

'General Kästner, we are being stymied at every turn, and it's all the fault of these blasted railways.'

The General wasn't surprised that Admiral Göpfert had come to him, but he was astounded that Kriegsmarine were having issues with the railways. The Reichsbahn had a reputation for being extremely efficient and, even when they were called upon to play an important logistic role in supporting the rapid movement of the troops of the Wehrmacht, in Austria, Sudetenland, Czechoslovakia and Poland, the trains in Germany still ran with clockwork precision.

'Is the problem moving naval personnel around?'

'There may well be, but that's not my remit, General. It's spares, materials, and fuel that are the problem. I currently have three ships lying far too long in dock. One is waiting for a new turbine, which was promised a week ago, and we urgently need 20,000 tonnes of plate steel before we can start on the bow modifications for the two class 1938 destroyers. The vessels ship too much water. The designer should be taken out and shot.'

He'd heard rumours that the Kriegsmarine's new destroyer fleet was proving problematical. Radical new engines which were too complicated to maintain, and a flawed bow design, led to severe restrictions being placed on their use.

The admiral continued.

'Von Exner says that the yards are having the same problem with new ships, although Krupp and his fellow shipbuilders seem to have a bit more influence when it comes to bullying the Reichsbahn into upping their game.'

The General nodded sympathetically.

He's just glad to vent his frustrations to someone who'll listen to him, he thought.

'How can I help?' he asked.

'I've come to you,' Admiral Göpfert replied, 'because I've tried everything; even the threat of hanging the Reichsbahn directors from the yardarm didn't work, and I know you are a man who can work miracles with verdammte bureaucracy.'

The General smiled.

'Miracles I can't do. I leave that to the powers above, but I'll try my best to find out what the problem is. Have one of your staff send me over the details, and leave it with me, Admiral.'

Once the Admiral left, the General instructed Heinz Bauer to dig into the specifics once the papers had been sent over.

'And get my driver. I'm going to see a man about a train.'

~~o~~

Matthäus Brück showed the General into his front room. Looking around, he could see that the man was proud of his lifetime as a railwayman; the room was full of pictures and Reichsbahn memorabilia.

The General peered closely at the photographs while his host went through to his small kitchen to put the kettle on. Matthäus Brück was in most of them, either as part of a group of workmates or standing alone in front of a locomotive. In two of the pictures, he was being presented with an award. The remaining photographs were of stations and goods yards where he'd worked at some point in his life.

'That's quite a collection you have, Matthäus,' the General said.

'Ach, it was Frau Brück who insisted on putting them all up, while she was still with us. But I do miss it since I retired.'

'You were with the Reichsbahn a long while, weren't you?'

'All my working life, man and boy. I started as an apprentice on the shunters and worked my way up. I was a driver on most of these.'

He pointed to the different locomotives.

'I didn't realise that you were a train driver. I assumed you'd always been in management.'

'I have, for nearly twenty years, but I started as a driver. I had a bad injury, and when I returned to work, I found that I struggled with driving; my back, you see. They gave me a desk job, and to my surprise, I found that I had a knack for organising and filling in forms. Before I knew it, I was a manager of a small goods yard, in Neumünster. Three years later, they offered me the main Kiel marshalling yard and I ran that until I retired.'

'And you joined the Rotary when you came to Kiel? That's why I always knew you as a yard manager.'

'No, that was later, in the early thirties. You were all so welcoming, I must say. I did enjoy my time in the Rotary. It's a scandal that it had to stop.'

'I know. But we had no choice. I hear a few of the members still go for lunch once a month.'

'I went once, but it's not the same. They don't seem to have a sense of purpose.'

The General smiled.

'I should have made the effort, but I've been so busy. Still, it's nice to see you, Matthäus.'

'You too, Erich. You sounded very mysterious on the telephone. You wanted to ask me some questions about the Reichsbahn, is that correct?'

'Yes. As you know, I retired as a front-line general a few years ago, but the army found me a job doing liaison work with the Kriegsmarine, of all things.'

'I see. But what does that have to do with the railways?'

The General told him about the navy's transport difficulties, and about the major delays it was causing.

'I could have a word, Erich, with some former colleagues. Unofficially, you understand.'

'That would be great, Matthäus, but perhaps you could explain to me first how the system works, if that's not too much to ask. Even just an outline.'

'No problem, Erich. It would be easier if I gave you a little bit of background first. In 1924 the Deutsche Reichsbahn-Gesellschaft took over most of the divisions of the German Länderbahnen, that's the individual railway companies, which then acted as intermediate authorities within the Reichsbahn structure...'

Half an hour later, the General's head was spinning, but he had grasped the central tenets of how the Reichsbahn was coordinated and organised.

'I might be able to help,' the retired railwayman said. 'I'll introduce you to the new marshalling yard manager in Kiel. He's a real supporter of the Kriegsmarine, so he should be keen to help. The thing is, trains can be prioritised within the rail network by the yard managers. They can't abuse the system, but because it's at their discretion, there's a good chance he could improve your delivery times.'

'I'd appreciate that,' the General said. 'Just let me know when you can set up a meeting.'

'I'll be in touch.'

Matthäus Brück was a man of his word. Within a week, he accompanied the General to the larger of Kiel's two marshalling yards, out at Eichof, to meet Christian Junge, a surprisingly young-looking man of forty who managed the goods facility.

They discussed the General's problems and, as the retired manager had said, the current incumbent of his old job was happy to help.

'Do your trains go straight to the naval yards and the shipbuilders?' Herr Junge asked.

'Some of them,' the General replied. 'Others are part of larger shipments and go to one of the goods yards first, and then they are split up, and taken to where they're needed.'

'Part trains can be slow. They might sit in a yard in Hamburg for a few days waiting for another few waggons coming to Kiel. And your direct trains are routed by central handling; local yard managers have no control over these trains so we couldn't prioritise them.'

'Is there anything you can do?'

'Yes. Come to me with all your delivery schedules and requests. Part trains I can prioritise with no problems. It will put them at the front of the queue in every yard they pass through.'

'What about the direct trains. Our fuel, steel plate and sections?'

Christian Junge rubbed his chin.

'It might not work, but it's worth a try. Instead of having these trains go direct to the naval yards, we'll make sure they come to the yard here or, even better, to our smaller yard down by the Bahnhof; it's closer to where they're needed.'

'How does that help?'

'They're under my control, so I can prioritise them, and I can assure you that they'll not sit in my yard. You'll get them right away.'

'If you can do that, the Kriegsmarine will be eternally grateful.'

The three men stood up, and the General shook the hands of the two railwaymen warmly.

'Danke.'

He turned to go.

'Oh, by the way, you'll be dealing with me personally, or my adjutant, Captain Bauer, or my chief petty officer, Günter Neuer. They're both good men.'

The yard manager nodded and opened the door for the General and his predecessor.

'Oh, General. There's just one thing,' he said, almost embarrassed.

'Yes, of course. What is it?'

'I'm a big admirer of the Kriegsmarine. Would it be possible to get a look around one of the warships?'

The General laughed.

'I can do better than that. The Prinz Eugen starts her sea trials next week. She'll be in and out for a month. If you can speed up these trains of ours, I'll see if I can get you on one of her test runs.'

1940

'I would say to the House, as I said to those who have joined this government: I have nothing to offer but blood, toil, tears and sweat.'

Winston Churchill.

'The battle beginning today will decide the fate of the German nation for the next thousand years.'

Adolf Hitler.

CHAPTER 206

'Happy new year, Canaris, and congratulations. I feel as if you've made it at last.'

'Very good, Erich. At least my star is in the ascendant. I count at least three promotions since your career has stagnated.'

They both laughed, and the handshake was held for longer than usual.

'You must be doing something right, in their eyes, for them to finally make you a full admiral.'

'I supply them with quality intelligence. Admittedly, it does tend to be on the cautious side, but they may just put that down to my careful nature and, if there is the odd inaccuracy, that is understandable given the difficult nature of intelligence gathering.'

The General smiled, shaking his head.

'One day, this will all catch up with you.'

'Quite possibly. We'll cross that bridge when we come to it.'

'So, what do you have to tell me, that necessitates you delivering it in person and, incidentally, reducing my stocks of malt at the same time. Do you know how hard it is becoming to replenish my supplies?'

The admiral grinned and took a sip from his glass. Then his face clouded.

'The failed assassination plot – the bomber is still alive, in Dachau, I hear. He quite willingly told them everything, and it does seem that he worked alone. Incredible.'

'If only he'd succeeded.'

'Others would have stepped in, but with the big four out of it, I think you're right. It would have imploded. There will be others,' the admiral said.

The General cocked his head.

'I hear things,' the admiral said, shrugging.

For a minute, both men sat deep in their thoughts.

'What else?' the General asked, breaking the silence.

'Well, you heard the Soviets invaded Finland. That was the last part of the agreement they reached over the partition of Poland. They won't touch Sweden. We need it to supply us with all the iron we require.'

'Between his escape at Munich, and everything else falling into place, Herr Hitler must think that God is looking down kindly on him.'

'And everyone stepping aside to let him do as he likes. Does he have divine premonition, or is he just lucky?'

'I don't know. And when will Britain or France act? And if they do, will it be too late?'

Canaris said nothing and sat, deep in thought.

'What?' the General said.

'Not quite. They have already taken some action, and in my defence, I had a part in it.'

The General frowned and couldn't keep a doubtful look from his face.

'It was a month ago,' the admiral said, seeing the General's sceptical look. 'I'd seen Hitler's plans and the British were stricken with indecision. I had an agent leak plans for the 'Dutch War' that Hitler was planning; an invasion of the Netherlands in February with the aim of using their airfields to launch a strategic bombing offensive against Britain, bringing the country to its knees.'

'Hitler had planned to do that, as early as February?'

'No, but I made it look convincing. The British sent ground troops to help defend France and the low countries later that month.'

'So,' the General said, thumping the table, 'an invasion of France will be more daunting, and any move on the low countries will have the British directly involved.'

Then he frowned again.

'What's wrong?' the admiral said.

'If they ever find that out, they'll kill you. Either side.'

'They won't. Until I told you, only two other people know about it. One is in England, for the duration. The other is me.'

~~o~~

The General stood back, keeping out of the way. He'd been on a few test runs before, but it was always a thrill to be on the bridge of a warship travelling at top speed. Wrapped up against the bitter chill of the exceptionally cold winter, he glanced at the railwayman standing next to him and was rewarded with a grin.

'Well, what do you think?' the General said to the wide-eyed railwayman standing next to him.

'This is wonderful. I can't thank you enough.'

'Don't thank me. This one's down to Captain Herzog and the crew of the *Gneisenau*. And anyway, it's us that should be thanking you. The admirals are astounded at the improvement in the speed with which we're getting our supplies delivered.'

Christian Junge smiled and shrugged.

'It was a simple task and, if it helped the Kriegsmarine, it has been my privilege.'

He paused and looked around.

'It's an experience I'll never forget.'

The General smiled to himself. It had taken all his powers of persuasion to stop Admiral Raeder recommending that the General should receive a medal for his services to the Kriegsmarine. To his relief, the admiral had reluctantly conceded that he was right.

CHAPTER 207

Miriam opened the door and gasped in shock.

'Rosa!' she said, frozen still for a second.

'Are you not going to give me a hug? Come here, you.'

Rosa threw her arms around Miriam, the two women standing in the biting cold, the tears frosting on their cheeks.

'Come in, come in,' Miriam said, breaking away for a second. They stepped inside and hugged again.

'What are you doing here?' Miriam asked, her face pale.

'It's my mama. She's ill. Really ill.'

'Oh, Rosa, I'm sorry. I didn't hear.'

'She kept it hidden. Papa knew there was something wrong, but he couldn't get help for her. Then, last week, he mentioned it in a letter. I had to come, to find her a doctor.'

Miriam sighed. 'I understand,' she said, 'but you're taking a risk, are you not?'

'Pah. They're not going to bother with one stroppy Jewish *Froy*. They have too much on their plates.'

'Don't be so sure, Rosa. People are being deported every day.'

Rosa shrugged. 'I arrived late last night. I had to see Mama. And I couldn't come without seeing you.'

'Are you going back?'

'Yes, but I'll stay until we find out about Mama. We're trying to find a doctor today.'

'I'll get Yosef to ask Jakob Teubner. He'll know.'

'I have another favour to ask.'

'Anything, Rosa. You know that.'

'I know you look after Itsik's parents and I feel bad, but once I've gone, could you look in on Mama occasionally?'

'Of course I will, Rosa. You didn't have to ask. I'd have gone earlier if I'd known. Your parents always seemed so... capable. I didn't see any need.'

Rosa let out a deep breath and hugged Miriam again.

'Thank you,' she said.

'You must come and eat with us, while you're here. Share a glass of wine,' Miriam said, laughing.

'Don't worry, I will.'

~~o~~

She never did. On the third day, the Gestapo picked her up.

The first Miriam knew of it was when she called round to ask after Rosa's mother, on the way to Shabbat service on the Friday, with Yosef and the children.

When she knocked on the door, a fearful voice asked who was calling.

When Rosa's father opened the door, he told them it wasn't safe for them to be there.

'Rosa's been taken,' he said, before closing the door.

At Kleiner Kuhberg, after the service, Yosef asked Jakob if he'd heard anything.

'No,' he said, 'but I'll try and find out.'

'Do you know of a doctor, for Rosa's mother?'

'Leave it with me. What's their address?'

Yosef gave him a slip of paper.

'She shouldn't have come back, you know. As soon as she crossed the border, her name would be on a list. It was only a matter of time before she was taken.'

'I know. She just turned up. If they'd been further away, she wouldn't have.'

~~o~~

[31/01/1940 Wednesday]

'Rosa Liewermann is in Neuengamme.'

Miriam's face drained and she let out a gasping sob.

'Can we do anything?' Yosef asked.

Jakob Teubner faced the Nussbaums across the kitchen table at the Drachensee cottage. He'd called in with them as soon as he'd heard.

'I don't think so. Sometimes, with money, and a lawyer who's willing to take the case on...'

'I'll write to Emil,' Yosef said, 'or send a telegram. That would be better.'

'If he and the children come, they will arrest him too. Maybe even the children.'

'Perhaps he can pay for a lawyer,' Miriam said, drying her tears.

'It's not just the lawyer, Miriam. You must pay a bribe, too, and there's no guarantee that it will be successful. Even if it is, she may not be able to leave the country. But my advice is for Emil to stay put and send some money, and I will try and find them a lawyer.'

Miriam looked at Yosef and nodded.

'Thanks, Jakob. You're a good friend.'

'I do this every day for someone's wife, brother or son. You might have to do it for me, some day.'

'Don't say that, Jakob. It's you who holds this community together.'

'With help,' he said, touching Yosef on the shoulder.

When he'd gone, Miriam looked at Yosef.

'Can we help?' she asked.

'A little. We can give a little.'

~~o~~

Miriam signed her name at the bottom of the letter, and began to read it back to herself, not wanting to have left anything out.

3rd February '40

Dear Esther,

I'm heartbroken. I'm sorry to have to tell you, but Rosa has been arrested, and is in a camp, at Neuengamme, near Hamburg. Her mother was ill, so she travelled from Belgium to see her and was arrested by the Gestapo within a few days.

We have organised a lawyer to see if we can get her released and send her back to Emil and the children in Antwerp, but Jakob is not optimistic. He, along with Yosef, to a lesser extent, have been involved in trying to get others released. The lawyer has been allowed to speak with Rosa briefly, and she told him to say to Emil not to return, but to get out if he can and she will join them later.

You will have noticed that this letter has come from Denmark. I apologise for not writing sooner but there is no mail now from Germany to Palestine because of the British, and the war, and it wasn't until Yosef asked the General if he could help, that I was able to write.

I doubt that I'll be able to send any more, though, so if this is my last letter to you for a while, I want you to know that I love you, and you have been the best friend I could have wished for, especially after moving to Kiel all these years ago and not knowing a soul, other than you.

So much has happened since we last spoke. Poland has fallen, without drastic losses, and there are some worrying rumours that Jews are being deported there in larger numbers than before, and not just those that came from Poland in the first place.

Yosef and the General, bless him, are trying to find ways to get us back on track with our British visas, maybe through Denmark or Belgium or France. We don't even know if our applications were even processed but we'd have to get out of Germany to find out.

The photographs are wonderful. You all look so happy and healthy. And that house! It's wonderful. You deserve all the happiness you get.

Little Miriam Rosa (I get a warm feeling every time I say that) looks beautiful, and she's big! Moshe looks like a young man now, and Shoshana has changed so much. I suppose I can say the same for our two; you can make up your own mind as I have enclosed a photo of us all that Antje took with her new camera. (How the General got it with all the shortages, I don't know.)

Itsik's parents are fine. Mama Weichmann asked me to enclose a letter for you, which I've done. The baby seems to have given them a lift and, when I mentioned your suggestion about getting them out there using the Haganah, they didn't immediately discount the idea.

I've previously said I wouldn't come to Palestine. Now, a small part of me wishes I'd taken your offer more seriously. If I hadn't liked it, we could always have moved on. And we could have sent Manny out to you, but it would have broken our hearts, and destroyed your peace. Anyway, what's done is done, and I don't think we could risk exposing the children to the dangers that would be involved in a journey organised by the Haganah.

I'll try and write again sometime, and hope that this gets to you, and that you can still write.

If not, we will catch up when this horror is all over,

Be'ezrát Hashém.

With all my love.

Miriam.

She added a line at the bottom of the letter.

PS Itsik's Mama says the postman gave her a strange look when he handed her your letter. Shanghai indeed!

She folded it, then shook her head and flattened it out on the desk again. She scribbled another line.

PPS. Someone will call at your shop in Haifa each week and ask if there is any mail. Get Abel to give him your reply. The General says that it will get to me, but he says that it will be for one time only.

Satisfied, she placed it in the envelope along with the letter Itsik's mother had given her, then sealed it.

She walked over to the big house and, putting on her apron, she placed the letter in the pocket. When the General retired to his study after dinner, she took him through a cup of coffee, handing him the letter at the same time.

He took it from her, nodded without saying anything, and put it in his briefcase.

CHAPTER 208

KIELER MORGENPOST

Friday 9th February 1940

GNEISENAU FINALLY MOVES

Repairs to be completed at Wilhelmshaven

The battleship Gneisenau, the sister ship of Scharnhorst, the most modern battleships of the Kriegsmarine fleet, has finally been freed from the thick ice which caused damage to her plating and her screws. Yesterday, two ice-breakers cleared a route to the sea locks at Holtenau, and she entered the Kaiser-Wilhelm-Kanal. She is expected to arrive in Wilhelmshaven, which is not ice-bound, tomorrow, where she will enter dry dock for repairs.

The extreme cold, which has gripped most of northern Europe since the turn of the year, shows little sign of easing. It is expected that the Baltic ice field will persist for up to two months longer than normal.

An increase in the death rate among the elderly has been attributed to the bitterly cold spell.

~~o~~

[12/02/1940 Monday]

'It was so kind of you to organise this, Erich, especially with everything else the Kriegsmarine is having to deal with.'

As usual, Jürgen Hoffmann simpered when he was surrounded by generals, admirals, and air marshals, who sat around the large table in the conference room at Naval HQ, along with a group of city officials.

It had a splendid view over Kieler Hafen but, apart from the mayor, none of the others present took any notice of the scenery. Erich Kästner looked across the thick ice that had gripped the whole Baltic coast.

'It's not a bother,' he said, the two men standing a little apart from the others. 'The Kriegsmarine has a vested interest in protecting Kiel from any aerial attack, and both the Luftwaffe and the Heer will be heavily involved in putting together the air defence network for the city, the harbour, and the shipyards. You, the police and fire chiefs, and your civil servants in charge of transport, housing, and civil engineering, are here to help us coordinate shelters, warning systems, and the emergency services response strategies.'

'All our people are here. I made sure they were all up to speed on matters concerning their roles and responsibilities.'

'Good. Over the next six months, we'll see the fruit of what's decided here today. Concrete bunkers will spring up all over the city, with anti-aircraft emplacements around the periphery. The aerodrome out at Holtenau is to be beefed up to provide fighter cover, and a screen of barrage balloons will need to be deployed overhead.'

'Do you really think there will be an aerial war? Will they bomb Kiel?'

'In case it has slipped your mind, we are already at war with the British and the French. If they do decide to move against Germany, you can be sure Kiel, as our largest naval base, will be first on their list of targets. We must prepare now, just in case.'

'I know we are at war, but nothing is happening,' the mayor blustered. 'I was just wondering if you had some inside knowledge of when it might all start.'

'I have no miraculous insight, I'm afraid. If I were a betting man, I'd say sooner rather than later, if we continue to be the aggressor. I'm sure that they'll be forced to act before long.'

'Where else are we likely to invade? I was told our military actions have been to protect the German people, home and abroad.'

'I don't know, Jürgen, but it would surprise me if we didn't pursue this expansionism further. Now, if you'll take your seat, we should call this meeting to order.'

~~o~~

[19/03/1940 Tuesday]

Up until the point he hit her, it was the best sex Lise had ever had. A little rough in places, but she could handle it for the sheer exhilaration of taming Rudolf, of making him cry at the end of it.

Each time, she'd cradle his head as their rasping, jerking breaths returned to normal.

He'd been home for two days and, apart from a visit to her parents, they'd hardly left the apartment, or even their bed.

He'd even drank less, until that afternoon, when he'd suddenly become morose, dreading leaving her again, and had finished a bottle of Schnapps he'd brought back with him in the space of two hours. He'd fallen asleep, but when he woke up, he saw her lying next to him, watching him, and he'd become instantly aroused and she'd responded.

But the alcohol was still coursing through his bloodstream and his passion turned to force.

'Rudolf!' she shouted, 'Stop!'

But he'd kept going and had placed his hand over her mouth as he thrust himself harder and harder into her, muffling her steadily more frantic protests. She was hurting now, and not in the way she liked, those little slaps and the odd pinch that she encouraged.

She tried to hit him, but he grabbed her wrist and twisted, hurting her more. She was too angry to cry. She made herself go limp and, although he continued for a while, without her struggling, he seemed to lose interest and fell off her, grabbing for the bottle.

'It's empty,' he said, hurling it across the room. It smashed against the wall.

She looked down at her thighs. They were blood-smeared and she could feel the sharp sting of the cuts inside her.

'Don't you ever do anything like that again,' she hissed at him, her face white.

He hit her across her face with the back of his hand, and her head snapped back, unprepared for the blow. For the first time, she started to whimper. It seemed to sober him up.

'Lise, Lise. What have I done?' he said, reaching out for her.

She cowered away then she saw the strained anguish in his face and knew that whatever had possessed him had gone, and she allowed him to embrace her.

'I'm sorry, I'm sorry, I'm sorry,' he repeated, mumbling her name.

She started to cry.

For the rest of his leave, he didn't drink. And he was, once again, the gentle but passionate Rudolf that she'd married. But during the night, she'd awoken to hear him crying out in his sleep. She touched him to comfort him, but his body was rigid and dripping with sweat. In the pale moonlight, his face was a mask of terror, or maybe anger; his lips were drawn back over his teeth and his eyes stared madly at nothing, even while he was sleeping. She stroked his chest until he began to relax and breathe easily again.

It happened two or three times again that night, and the next. On the last night, he drank a bottle of wine in the evening, and slept like a baby.

~~o~~

[20/03/1940 Wednesday]

'Scheiße.'

Johann stood with his mouth hanging open, looking out of the French windows, down to the still frozen lake.

'Johann!' Franz hissed. 'Miriam or Yosef might hear you.'

'But when did she get to look like that?'

Franz walked quickly over to the door of the drawing room and closed it.

'She's always looked like that. It's Ruth.'

'No, you fool. She has curves now. And look at the way she moves.'

'For God's sake, Johann, she's a young woman now. What do you expect? I mean, look at Antje. She's as striking as Eva.'

Both the girls had gone from being awkward teenagers to startling young women in the space of a year, but the boys hadn't been home on leave for a while, and it was the first time Johann had taken notice.

'I suppose, but they're my sisters. How old is Ruth?'

'Johann,' Franz said, a warning tone in his voice.

'What? I was merely asking.'

'Too young for you, so don't get any ideas.'

Johann held up his hands. 'All right, Papa,' he said, grinning at Franz's frown.

'What did you think of Eva's beau?' he said, eager to change the subject.

'He seems personable enough, and not too high-minded for an aristocrat.'

'Yes. He has a sense of humour which is quite down to earth.'

Maria had warned Johann to be on his best behaviour when Frederick, Eva's young man, had been invited over to meet the family. Eva had been nervous but, when the time came, Frederick had made a good impression on them, and had fitted in well.

'He's very devoted to her,' Franz said.

'Yes, a bit like a puppy-dog sometimes though,' Johann said, screwing up his face.

'Johann, you're terrible,' Franz said, shaking his head.

Johann laughed, and gazed down towards the lake again.

~~o~~

[24/03/1940 Sunday]

The General waited until Maria left for church. He slipped out the kitchen door and crossed to the Nussbaums' cottage. Yosef let him in. He told them both to sit down, that he had something to say.

With puzzled frowns, they did as they were asked.

'Yosef, Miriam, listen to me. Don't ask me how I know, but I have found out things that mean you have to get out of Germany as soon as possible. Not next year or the year after that. Now.'

'Sir, you're putting the fear of God into us. Is it that bad?'

'Yes. If you don't wish to end up living in a ghetto in Poland, you'll have to get you and your children out. Only last month, a thousand German Jews from Stettin were sent to Lublin in the Generalgouvernement.'

They both gasped.

'What about our parents?'

'Ask them what you should do,' the General said, with no attempt to disguise the harshness in his voice. 'I know what they'll tell you.'

'They already have, sir,' Yosef said, bowing his head.

'Sir, we've tried everything,' Miriam said. 'We even considered Palestine again, through these Haganah people, but we heard about three families who had been shot trying to get in, and countless more who were caught and sent back, ending up in concentration camps.'

'I can understand that, but staying could be just as dangerous, believe me. Do either of you know anyone in Denmark?'

'No, sir.'

'Maria has a cousin in Copenhagen. I'll put her address down on the travel permit. When you get there, make for the synagogue and find one of your own people to hide you, but watch out for the Gestapo. They may be keeping an eye on it and remember, neither Maria nor her cousins know anything about this, so say nothing.'

The General didn't like deceiving Maria but, after all, he wasn't involving her surviving cousin in anything of note, and the Nussbaums weren't going to turn up, looking for shelter.

He thought back to the conversation he'd had with his wife, the day before. She'd been almost relieved when she told him that she'd had a letter back from her cousins' housekeeper; one of the old ladies had died, and the other was in a home. He'd nodded and told her he was disappointed.

It hadn't made much difference to his plan.

'Once you're there, Yosef should go to the British embassy, and find out about your visas. Make sure you take all your papers with you. If you can get the visas, get on the first available ship to England. They sail daily from Esbjerg to Harwich. You'll have to catch a ferry train from Copenhagen to Esbjerg.'

'How do we get our money out, sir.'

'I'll take it to Denmark for you.'

'Is that not risky for you?'

'Don't worry about me. I still have friends and anyway, travel is still allowed for the likes of me. Why shouldn't I visit my wife's relations?'

'If you say so, sir. What if we don't get out of Denmark?'

'Find someone who will rent you a room or two while you learn Danish, then get your own place to hide, and wait until all of this is ended.'

'You think it will end, sir?' Miriam asked. 'Everyone is talking about a thousand-year Reich.'

'There won't be. The world will not stand for it, even if Germany will.'

The Nussbaums looked at each other.

'You really think it is necessary to leave now, and not wait for our American visas?' Yosef asked.

'Yes, I do. If you stay, you will end up on a train to Poland.'

A signal seemed to pass between Miriam and Yosef.

'When would we have to go?'

'It will take me a little while to arrange the travel permits. Let's say a fortnight.'

The General reached into his pocket and pulled out his diary.

'Let's make it the sixth of April. That will give us sufficient time.'

He saw the look on the Nussbaums' faces.

'What's up?'

'Manny's Bar Mitzvah is that day. He's been preparing for it for months, and our whole family will be there; Miriam's parents and Manny's uncle and aunt are travelling from Altona, if they can. It will be their last chance…'

'We can make it the next day then,' the General said, shrugging.

719

He looked at the calendar and shook his head.

'That's a Sunday,' he said. 'There won't be many people travelling that day. Better make it the Monday.'

He pulled out a map.

'From Kiel, you get the Reichsbahn to the border at Padborg, where you will transfer to a Danish train. You'll change at Fredericia for Copenhagen.'

'How will you find us there?' Miriam asked.

'Every day, one of you should go to the synagogue at six in the evening. I'll send someone or meet you there myself. Have you got all that?'

'Yes, sir. Thank you. We're sorry to be leaving you.'

'I know, Yosef. But it's the only way.'

~~o~~

[26/03/1940 Tuesday]

'Mama, it has been wonderful,' Johann said.

He and Franz were back in uniform, kitbags by their feet. Albert, the Kästners' driver, waited patiently to take the boys to the station. The train to Stettin, to their barracks, was leaving in thirty minutes.

'I've hardly seen you, Johann, but it has been lovely having you and Franz home, all the same.'

She gave him a hug.

As was usual with Johann, most of his time on leave was spent in the company of friends, or with his latest flame. He rarely brought any of his girls to the Drachensee house, and the current one had been no exception.

The General shook Johann's hand, then Franz's.

'Are you going back to Poland?'

'We haven't been told,' Franz said. 'We'll be briefed when we get back. The colonel is careful to keep us informed, unlike some of the commanding officers.'

'We'd better go if we're to catch this train,' Johann said.

Maria and the General stood at the top of the steps, waving. As the boys got into the car, Maria shouted, 'Take care, the pair of you.'

'We will,' they chorused, before slamming the doors.

Their parents watched until the car was out of sight.

'At least it's all quiet for now,' Maria said.

'And long may it remain that way,' the General replied.

~~o~~

[04/04/1940 Thursday]

'Hello, operator. May I have Kiel 3457, please.'

Franz heard various clicks on the line as he waited patiently for the connection.

'Please hold, sir, we're trying to connect you,' the woman's voice informed him.

He idly wondered what she looked like. She sounded pretty, and he knew that, if it had been Johann on the line, he would be flirting with her.

'I'm sorry, sir, we seem to be having some difficulty connecting you to that number. Could you please check that it's correct?'

'Yes, it's correct,' Franz said, trying to keep the irritation from his voice.

Again, the line clicked and popped, and he thought he could hear a distant ring.

'I'm sorry, sir. I can't seem to connect you at this time. Would you like to try again later, or try another number?'

Franz looked at his watch. There was still a chance his father would be at his office.

'Get me the Naval Headquarters in Kiel, please.'

'Certainly, sir, please hold,' the woman said.

He heard the line click once and then again, a few minutes later.

'I'm sorry, sir. It isn't connecting. It's rather strange. I've spoken to my colleague and there seems to be some problem in the Kiel area. I would advise you to try again tomorrow.'

'Thank you,' he said, 'but I won't be able to do that. It doesn't matter.'

He stepped out of the telephone booth and made for the bar Johann and his friends were in. It wouldn't be a late night as they all had to be back in barracks by ten.

'Did you get him?' Johann asked when Franz joined them.

'No, there's a problem with the telephone lines to Kiel. It doesn't matter anyway. I'm sure he knows what's happening before we do.'

Johann laughed.

'My father the spymaster,' he said, grinning.

'Shussh,' Franz said, frowning. 'We're not supposed to talk about it. I would have liked to speak to him, though, and tell him where we're going.'

'Probably going, Franz.'

'Why else would they ask for those of us who could ski well, eh?'

'I take your point, but that doesn't necessarily mean Norway. It could be Switzerland. Or France. And anyway, they have mountain divisions; why do they want more soldiers who can ski?'

'That's the only place it makes sense. Most of the Norwegian soldiers are in mountain battalions, and there's still a lot of snow there, especially in the north, so every German soldier who can ski will be a bonus.'

'I suppose so. And we are shipping out by boat. There's a rumour that we're using proper warships, rather than troop transports.'

'Where did you hear that?'

'Oh, just some of the men. It would make sense, though, if it were Norway, getting us up the west coast, fast.'

'It has to be Norway if that's true. The only other place would be Finland, but the Soviets have taken that, and we'd be fools to attack them.'

'We'll find out soon. What was the little snippet of gossip you were going to tell me before you went out to telephone the old man?'

'I don't deal in gossip, like you. I know for a fact that the 15th and the 12th have been deployed near Flensburg, and the 8th and 9th are moving further west.'

'We're going into Denmark as well?' Johann gasped.

'Yes. That's what I wanted to tell Father. Not that it matters; he'll know soon enough anyway.'

CHAPTER 209

[06/04/1940 Saturday]

Manny missed Bronisław Joselewicz. It made him sad, not knowing where he was, or what had happened to him.

He remembered the first time the strange Polish Jew had taken the three boys the same age aside and sat them down together in the synagogue in Kleiner Kuhberg.

'Boys,' the religious teacher had said, his voice dry but insistent, 'you are coming to the age of Bar Mitzvah next year, which signifies that you have become men, and fully-fledged members of the Jewish community, with all the privileges and responsibilities that come with it.'

The three young Jews had sat, not moving, their whole concentration on the tall, bearded man in front of them.

'You'll be expected to have a moral responsibility for your own actions, to be worthy to be called to read from the Torah and to lead or participate in a minyan; you'll have the right to be legally married according to Jewish law and to possess personal property. You'll have a duty to follow the 613 laws of the Torah and keep the halakha and you'll have the ability to testify as a witness in a Beth Din case in a Jewish court. These are all important, but the most fundamental of them all is that you become a fully-fledged son of Jacob and, no matter where you are in the world, you must remember Israel.'

They'd studied for more than six months; twice a week they would stay on after school to learn Hebrew, Torah cantillation, Jewish history, and to pray. They would also, on occasion, help in the soup kitchen, and at other charitable functions, as part of their religious development.

And now the day had come. And Bronisław Joselewicz wasn't here with them.

Siegmund Eliasowitz had, against the elders' wills, he thought, been given the job of finishing their preparation, and of teaching religious studies in the school.

For Manny, and the other two boys, he didn't bring things to life the way Bronisław Joselewicz had. His teaching of the Torah was dry and academic, with no reference to the daily struggle of Jews in Germany or an aspiration to a Jewish homeland in Palestine, and his voice lulled rather than inspired, leading more than once to a sharp crack with a ruler when they inevitably nodded off in his lessons.

'Now, my young men,' he'd said to them, on the day before the Bar Mitzvah was to take place, 'remember this reflects on my teaching, on God, your family and on yourselves. Don't let me, or them, down.'

When Manny had stood on the Bimah, reading the Torah, he'd seen the pride shining on the faces of his parents, his grandparents, and his sister; even on old Jakob Teubner, standing with Yosef and the other men.

He saw Siegmund Eliasowitz standing next to them, smugly nodding at Manny's faultless reading, but he imagined the tall figure of Bronisław Joselewicz standing behind him, closing his eyes and listening to the chant of the Torah, and thinking of Jerusalem.

~~o~~

Maria Kästner had been visiting her mother with the two girls the weekend of the Bar Mitzvah, but the General had attended both the ceremony, sitting at the back, and the Seudat Mitzvah, the celebratory meal after the ceremony with family, friends, and a few members of the Jewish community in the Drachensee cottage.

'You read very well, Manny,' the General said, shaking his hand.

'Thank you, sir. I had a good teacher.'

Jakob smiled, knowing the tribute was for a man now somewhere in Poland.

Yosef and Manny continued to move around the cottage, accepting congratulations and small gifts from the guests. Jakob and the General watched, smiling.

'It's a happy day, but tinged with sadness,' Jakob said.

The General turned towards him, frowning.

'Yosef spoke to you?'

'Yes. But don't worry. It's safe with me.'

'It's for the best. You should get out too.'

'I hear that. I just wonder what information you have that makes you so certain.'

'You know I can't say much but, for what it's worth, warn as many of your people as you can to get out while there's still a chance, by whatever route. If they don't, they are going end up in Poland, in some form of ghetto.'

'You've seen concrete plans for this?'

'I've seen enough to be worried. Some of it has been guesswork, but it's all beginning to look ominous.'

Jakob sighed.

'I'll trust your judgement, Herr General. I know you have done more than most to help us in the past.'

'I help when I can, but this…' He struggled to find the words. 'But this is beyond help,' he finally said.

Jakob shrugged.

'We are Jews. We know about pogroms and ghettos. We have survived them before. But it will be hard.'

The General felt a chill in his stomach.

'Jakob, you cannot repeat what I'm about to say to anyone. I'm only telling you because you are in the best position of any to persuade your people to leave. There have been massacres in Poland. Of Jews.'

Jakob bowed his head.

'I've heard rumours. You have proof?'

'Yes. I know for sure of one such horror, but I believe the reports of others.'

Jakob reached out and put his hand on the General's shoulder.

'Thank you for the information. I won't mention your name, but I will pass on your warning, and add my own.'

'And Jakob. Get yourself and your family out. If you can.'

Jakob looked at the General, sadness etched on his face.

'I was going to leave. I'm not sure I can now.'

'Then send your family.'

~~o~~

[08/04/1940 Monday]

'Auf wiedersehen, my friend, and good luck. We may meet in Copenhagen.'

The General took Yosef's hand, and shook it, then hugged him, kissing him on both cheeks. The two men held each other for a few seconds.

Both turned away, not wanting the other to see how close they were to tears.

The General kissed Miriam.

'I'm sorry Maria isn't here,' he said, 'but perhaps it is better this way.'

'Thank you, sir. For everything.'

He turned to Ruth.

'Antje is going to be devastated that she wasn't here to say goodbye, so I'll say it for her. She'll miss you terribly.'

Ruth pulled a small envelope from her pocket and gave it to the General. It was addressed to Antje.

'Would you give her this,' she sobbed, making no effort to hide her tears.

Miriam put her arm round her and gave her a handkerchief. Manny stood on the other side of his mother, saying nothing. The General tousled his hair.

'I've ordered you a taxi to drive you to the station,' he said. 'It will be here any moment. Albert is away with Maria and the girls, or he would have driven you. Will your mother and father be there to see you off, Yosef?'

'No, sir. We thought it better to say our goodbyes yesterday.'

'Ah. I can see the sense in that. Now, do you have everything? Tickets, travel permits, passports?'

'Yes, sir,' Yosef said. 'And thank you, sir.'

They all heard the crunch of gravel as the taxi arrived.

Yosef shepherded his family out, and down the steps.

The General watched as the taxi turned onto Hamburger Chaussee and he waved for a last time.

He returned to the house to pick up his jacket and briefcase and, closing the door behind him, made his way to his staff car that was parked to the side.

'The office, Private Zimmer, please.'

EPILOGUE

Memo: Geh.KdoS. ABW 08/04/40 CAC1021.1

For Attention Only: All senior executive officers, Abwehr.

From: Admiral Wilhelm Canaris, Chef der Abwehr.

Final preparations for Operation Weserübung, the invasion of Norway and Denmark, are in place. A combined naval and army operation will land Wehrmacht forces in Narvik, Trondheim, Bergen, Oslo, Egersund, Kristiansand and Arendal on the morning of the 9th of April.

Seven divisions of the 11th Army Corps, under General Nikolaus von Falkenhorst, including one mountain division and additional units from the 2nd Army, will be transported to Norway by two battleships, one heavy cruiser, two light cruisers, fourteen destroyers, and a variety of support vessels.

Two further battalions will cross the Danish border from Schleswig-Holstein at the same time, supported by simultaneous landings by the Kriegsmarine of troops at strategic positions in the Little Belt, the Great Belt, and in Copenhagen.

Air support for the naval forces and ground troops of both campaigns is to be provided by the Luftwaffe.

This action has been sanctioned as a preventive manoeuvre against the proposed Franco-British occupation of Norway. The invasion of Denmark has been deemed necessary to provide bases for air support for the occupation of Norway and to secure the approaches to the Baltic through the Skagerrak and Kattegat. [END]

The end.

Flight of the Shearwater, the second book in the *Sturmtaucher Trilogy*, picks up the story of the Nussbaums and the Kästners as the new decade, still in its infancy, unfolds, and the crisis for Europe's Jews deepens.

For further information, visit www.alanjonesbooks.co.uk/sturmtaucher_trilogy.html

ACKNOWLEDGEMENTS

Although writing a novel, more so a trilogy, is a lonely, solitary task, there are times when a writer needs to reach out for support, for help with research, and for feedback. Here is the list of people who all had a hand in the making of the Sturmtaucher Trilogy. Please forgive me if I've left anyone out. Let me know and I can add you to the list.

John Gale, for the wonderful Shearwater illustration. www.galleryofbirds.co.uk

Catrin Jeans and Fraser McDonald, for their advice and input regarding the covers

The National Library of Scotland and The British Library, for their wonderful collection of maps and sea charts, and the British Newspaper Archive for such a vast collection of newspaper from every corner of Britain.

Gav Don, for recommending that I read Victor Klemperer's Diaries

Kirsty McKerrow and Iain Russell, from the Edinburgh Whisky Academy. www.edinburghwhiskyacademy.com/

Graeme Crawford for advice on German motor vehicles.

Tom Cunliffe, for being easily approachable for advice, and for his book *Hand, Reef and Steer*, my bible for gaff-rigged sailing.

Ute Kühl, Schwentinetalfahrt, Kiel for local knowledge

Steffi Blix and Anja Manleitner, from the wonderfully curated *Mahnmal Kilian bunker*, Kiel. www.mahnmalkilian.de/

Dr. Julian Freche, *Kieler Stadt- und Schifffahrtsmuseum*, Kiel, for taking the time to speak with me during my visit to Germany.

The Railways of Germany Forum for pointing me in the right direction for Reichsbahn information.

Harvey L Kaplan MA, Director, the Scottish Jewish Archives Centre for information on Jewish religious practices

Anne Cater, Random Things Tours for the blog tour. www.randomthingsthroughmyletterbox.blogspot.com/

The blog tour participants. All the blog tour participants: Bookchatter @cookiebiscuit, Reflections Of A Reader @LeahJMoyse, The Magic of Wor(l)ds @MagicOfWorldsBE, Steph's Book Blog @sjroth21, By The Letter Book Reviews @sarahhardy681, The Book Magnet @thebookmagnet, Beyond The Books @ShazzieRimmel, Wild Writing Life @wildwritinglife, Cal Turner Reviews @calturner, Hair Past A Freckle @karlou, Cheryl M-M's Book Blog @mm_cheryl, Berty Boy 123 @arabat

The dedicated book bloggers who have supported me and my books over the years, doing an amazing amount of hard work and asking nothing in return but a story.

All my remarkably loyal readers, especially Val Spencer and Susan Hunter, who have been unremitting in their enthusiasm for my writing.

Sharon Bairden and Noelle Holten, 'The Twinnies', for having my back, and for advice and support ad nauseum.

Sarah Hardy, for much advice and support, for being the first blogger to read 'The Gathering Storm', and for being so enthusiastic about it. https://bytheletterbookreviews.com

Michael J Malone and Douglas Skelton. Ross Greenwood. Authors helping authors.

Ask an Editor Facebook group, especially Bernadette Kearns, for advice on the difficult permissions issues.

The Book Club on Facebook, and its Reviewers Group, for once again finding me so many beta readers.

The Historical Fiction Novel Society, who's members enthusiastically responded to my request for beta readers.

My wonderful beta readers for their time, patience, encouragement and critical feedback. As a self-published author, I couldn't do it without them. They are, in no particular order:

Gill Lynch, Stuart Clachan, Teresa Murphy, Susan McDonald, Ian Mclymont, Rob Lee, Gordon Smith, Gabi Gerganova, Marc Kelly, Mary Jeans, Simon Caldecut, Marion Simmons, Kenny Stirling, Katrina Taylor, David Petherick, Fraser McDonald, Sapna Chamaria, Lauren Cohen, Fiona McCormick, Sally Stackhouse, Theresa Webber, Amanda Williams, Susan Hunter, Sydney Clark, Amanda Nellist, and Breffni Martin.

In addition, there were a handful of beta readers who also turned out to be my *technical support* section:

Mark Jardine, for gaff-rigged sailing expertise. www.boattripsiona.com/

Pauline Mullender, for German proofreading, a former resident of Kiel.

Olaf Meys, for advice on the Wehrmacht, and National Socialist document translation.

Charlotte Bidstrup, for Danish proofreading.

Nigel and Lia Court, for their input on Jewish religion, language and culture, and for proofreading the Yiddish content, and for their humbling enthusiasm for the books.

Madeleine Black, whose father was a Holocaust survivor. madeleineblack.co.uk/

Ian Skewis, for proof-reading with great patience. www.ianskewis.com/

My wife Mary, for support and forbearance, and watching me disappear for five years into my 'writing hole'.

My children, and my grandchildren, and to all my extended family and friends. In the words of Erich Kästner, if it weren't for them, none of it would matter.

REFERENCES & ATTRIBUTIONS

ICRC (International Committee of the Red Cross) The third Geneva Convention, the Convention Relating to the Treatment of Prisoners of War (1929)

03/03/1933 Hannukah Menorah Photograph inscription and story. Rachel Posner. https://www.yadvashem.org/artifacts/museum/hanukkah-1932.html

13/03/1933 Die Fahne hoch, 'Horst Wessel song'
Translated by author and Olaf Meyes from original German version: public domain, Wiki Commons. commons.wikimedia.org/wiki/File:Die_Fahne_Hoch.gif

13/07/1934 Adolf Hitler speech, Röhm Affair, Reichstag.
Public domain, Library of Congress.
www.loc.gov/rr/frd/Military_Law/pdf/NT_Nazi_Vol-II.pdf

15/09/1935 Adolf Hitler Speech, Reichs Citizenship law.
Public domain, The Speeches of Adolf Hitler, I, London, 1942, N.H. Baynes, ed., National Library of Scotland B000252727

11/02/1936 Document: Neither the instructions nor the affairs of the Gestapo will be open to review by the administrative courts. Public domain, Library of Congress: Amendments To The Federal Tort Claims Act : S. 2117 Thursday , January 26 , 1978 U.S. Senate , Subcommittee On Citizens And Shareholders Rights And Remedies , And Subcommittee On Administrative Practice And Procedure Of The Committee On The Judiciary , Washington , D.C.

01/04/1938 Adolf Hitler Speech - Anschluss
Public domain, The Speeches of Adolf Hitler, I, London, 1942, N.H. Baynes, ed., National Library of Scotland B000252727

22/04/1938 Der Giftpilz extracts, Ernst Hiemer, Nuremberg Stürmerverlag, 1938.
Public domain, Nazi Conspiracy And Aggression, Volume IV, Office of United States. Chief of Counsel For Prosecution of Axis Criminality
www.loc.gov/rr/frd/Military_Law/pdf/NT_Nazi_Vol-IV.pdf

20/08/1938 Oaths to Adolf Hitler
Public domain, Nazi Conspiracy And Aggression, Volume IV, Office of United States. Chief of Counsel For Prosecution of Axis Criminality
www.loc.gov/rr/frd/Military_Law/pdf/NT_Nazi_Vol-IV.pdf

10/11/1938 Deutsche Reichspost Telegramm Krystallnacht Gestapo\SD Orders: USHMM, Public domain https://www.ushmm.org/information/exhibitions/online-exhibitions/special-focus/kristallnacht/historical-overview/role-of-the-police/document-page-2

30/01/1939 Adolf Hitler Speech, The Jewish question. Translated by author and Olaf Meyes from original German version: ghdi.ghi-dc.org/pdf/deu/German35.pdf

BIBLIOGRAPHY

LITERATURE

Although this is not an exhaustive list, they are the books I referred to most often during the writing of the Sturmtaucher Trilogy.IBM and the Holocaust *Black, Edwin*

I Shall Bear Witness: The Diaries Of Victor Klemperer 1933-41 *Klemperer, Victor*

To The Bitter End: The Diaries of Victor Klemperer 1942-45 *Klemperer, Victor*

Language of the Third Reich *Klemperer, Victor*

Ordinary Men: Reserve Police Battalion 101 and the Final Solution in Poland *Browning, Christopher R.*

The Holocaust: The Jewish Tragedy *Martin, Gilbert*

Reeds Nautical Almanac 1944 *Watts, Oswald M., Ed., Adlard Coles*

Hand, Reef and Steer *Cunliffe, Tom*

Heavy Weather Sailing *Bruce, Peter*

The Windfall Yachts - a legacy of goodwill' by *Cudmore, Michael*

Documents on the Holocaust *Arak, Yitshak; Gutman, Israel; Margaliot, Abraham*

Sexual Violence Against Jewish Women During The Holocaust *Hedgepeth, Sonia M. and Saidel, Rochelle G.*

Battleships of the Scharnhorst Class: Warships of the Kriegsmarine *Koop, Gerard, and Schmolke, Klaus-Peter*

Jane's fighting ships of World War II *Preston, Antony*

Minenschiffe 1939-1945 *Kutzbelen, Karl. V. ; Schroeder, William; Brennecke, Jochen*

German Battleships 1939–45 *Williamson, Gordon*

Camp 21 Cultybraggan History *Cultybraggan Local History Group for Comrie Development Trust*

Camp 21 Comrie *Campbell, Valerie*

German Railroads and the Holocaust: Uncovering the Tracks *Ben-Horin, Lisa*

Jewish women's sexual behaviour and sexualized abuse during the Nazi era *Beverley*

Chalmers www.utpjournals.press/doi/pdf/10.3138/cjhs.242-A10

Conti Atlas für Kraftfahrer. Deutschland 1 : 500 000 mit den Reichskraftfahrbahnen. *Conti. - Ed.*

Baltic Pilot *Stan Townsend \ Adlard Coles*

Heil Hitler, Das Schwien ist Tot *Herzog, Rudolf*

Admiralty Tidal Stream Atlas North Sea Eastern Part Admiralty *UK Hydrographic Dept.*

Yiddish-English English -Yiddish *Michael James*

Road Atlas of Great Britain *John Bartholemew*

WEBSITES

As well as the books I used in my research, I trawled through thousands of websites over a five-year period, too numerous to mention individually, but I found myself going back to a few sites again and again. Here is a short list.

HebCal - Hebrew date convertor www.hebcal.com/converter

Historical US Dollars to German Marks currency conversion
marcuse.faculty.history.ucsb.edu/projects/currency.htm

Measuring Worth - Purchasing Power of the Pound.
www.measuringworth.com/calculators/ukcompare/

Wikipedia en.wikipedia.org/wiki/

Jewish Virtual Library www.jewishvirtuallibrary.org/

Railways of Germany Forum (English) www.tapatalk.com/groups/germanrailfr/index.php

United States Holocaust Memorial Museum Holocaust Encyclopedia
encyclopedia.ushmm.org/

US library of Congress www.loc.gov/collections/

Yad Vashem www.yadvashem.org/

Kiel municipal website www.kiel.de/

Kiel WW2 Bunker list www.bunker-kiel.com/

Air strikes Kiel kiel-wiki.de/Luftangriffe_auf_Kiel

Konzentrationslager-Gedenkstaette-Neuengamme www.kz-gedenkstaette-neuengamme.de/en

British Library - Maps and Charts explore.bl.uk/primo_library/libweb/action/search.do

Danish overlaid historical Maps - The Danish Agency for Data Supply and Efficiency sdfekort.dk/spatialmap

Mapster (Poland) German Historical Maps 1:25 000 igrek.amzp.pl/mapindex.php?cat=M841W

National Libarary of Scotland map collection maps.nls.uk/

The University of Texas Libraries - Maps legacy.lib.utexas.edu/maps/

Kiel Municipal photograph Archive fotoarchiv-stadtarchiv.kiel.de/

Traces of War (Information World War Two Foundation) www.tracesofwar.com/default.asp

World Time Date - Sun and moon calculators www.world-timedate.com/astronomy/index.php

Heinrich Böll Foundation -Sexual Violence in the Holocaust: Perspectives from Ghettos and Camps in Ukraine www.boell.de/en/2020/05/18/sexual-violence-holocaust-perspectives-ghettos-and-camps-ukraine

Comrie Development Trust - Cultybraggan POW camp comriedevelopmenttrust.org.uk/

RAILSCOT | Crieff Junction Railway www.railscot.co.uk/Crieff_Junction_Railway/index.php

AKENS (Arbeitskreis zur Erforschung des Nationalsozialismus in Schleswig-Holstein) www.akens.org/

ABOUT

Alan Jones is a Scottish author with three gritty crime stories to his name, the first two set in Glasgow, the third one based in London. He has now switched genres, and his WW2 trilogy will be published from August to December 2021. It is a Holocaust story set in Northern Germany.

He is married with four grown up children and four wonderful grandchildren.

He has recently retired as a mixed-practice vet in a small Scottish coastal town in Ayrshire and is one of the coxswains on the local RNLI lifeboat. He makes furniture in his spare time, and maintains and sails a 45-year-old yacht, cruising in the Irish Sea and on the beautiful west coast of Scotland. He loves reading, watching films and cooking. He still plays football despite being just the wrong side of sixty.

His crime novels are not for the faint-hearted, with some strong language, violence, and various degrees of sexual content. The first two books also contain a fair smattering of Glasgow slang.

He is one of the few self-published authors to be given a panel at the Bloody Scotland crime fiction festival in Stirling and has done two pop-up book launches at previous festivals.

He has spent the last five years researching and writing the Sturmtaucher Trilogy.

To find out more, please visit www.alanjonesbooks.co.uk/

GLOSSARY

A freylekhn geburtstag....Yiddish, Happy birthday. Literally 'a good birthday'
Abaft....Behind. 'Abaft the beam'
Abeam....To the side. 'A boat-length abeam'
Absender....Sender
Abwehr....German Army intelligence
Admiral....Kriegsmarine, Admiral
Aft....In front. 'Aft of the mast'
Ahnenpaß \ ahnenpass....Certification of being Aryan
Akvavit....Scandinavian spiced alcoholic drink. 'Water of life'
Aleichem Shalom....Reply to Shalom, 'Peace'
Alter furz....Old fart
Alter\alte....Old
amidships....Towards the centre of a ship or boat
Anschluss....Political union of Austria with Germany
Appell....Roll-call in POW or Concentration camp
Appellplatz....Roll-call Square
Aquarelle....Watercolors
Arbeiter....Worker(s)
Arbeitskommando....Work detail
Arbeitsscheue....Work shy, targetting the unemployed
Arsch....Arse, profanity
Arschleckern....Arse-licker
Arschloch....Asshole
Aryan....Germans of Nordic type, untainted
Aryanised....Process where non-Germans deemed suitable to be classified as Aryans
Auf....On
Auf wiedersehen....Goodbye
Auffangslager....Reception camp, transit camp
Aufstehen....Get to your feet, stand up
Aus....Out
Auschwitz....A Nazi concentration camp near Oświęcim in southern Poland
Ausland-SD....The Reich Foreign Security Service. In 1944, it took over the functions of the Abwehr
Ausschaltung....Elimination, often a euphemism for murder by the state
Auswanderung....Emigration, often a euphemism for deportation to Ghettos and camps
Autobahn....Motorway
AWOL....Absent without leave
Babka....sweet braided bread or cake which originated in the Jewish communities of Poland and Ukraine
Backstay....Part of the rigging, from the top of the mast to the stern of the boat.
Bahnhof....Railway station
Bar-mitzvah....The initiation ceremony of a boy into adulthood at the age of 13
Bataillonen....Battalion, typically commanded by a lieutenant colonel, divided into companies
Bat-mitzvah....The initiation ceremony of a girl into adulthood at the age of 13
Bauernhof....Farm
Baumhangen....Punishment: to be hung from a pole by hands tied behind back
BDM....Bund Deutscher Mädel, girls' wing of the Nazi Party youth movement, the Hitler Youth
Be'ezrát hashém....God willing, with the help of God

Beam....To the side. 'on the beam'

Beauftragter....Representative

Beer hall putsch....Attempted coup by Adolf Hitler and his party in 1923

BEF....British Expeditionary Force

Belzec....a Nazi German extermination camp southeast of Lublin

Bergen-Belsen....Nazi concentration camp in the northern Germany

BerlinerTageblatt....German liberal newspaper, shut down by the National Socialists in 1939

Besetzten....Occupied

Beyz....Evil

Bier....Beer

Bight....A bay or recess in a coastline, also a loop of rope

Bimah....A raised platform in a synagogue where the Torah is read from

Binnacle....A vertical wooden stand that holds the boat's wheel

Birkenau, Auschwitz-II-Birkenau....Expansion camp, adjacent to Auschwitz in southern Poland

Bitte....Please\You're welcome

Blitzkrieg....A military tactic utilising speed, surprise, excellent communications and air support.

Blockführer....SS concentration camp guard in charge of a prisoner barrack

Blut....Blood

Blut und boden....Blood and Soil. Used as slogan for NSDAP campaign for German citizens to grow food for the nation

Blutschande....Blood shame', the adulteration of German racial purity by intermarriage with other non-Germanic races

Boche....British derogatory name for the German Army or German soldiers.

Bohemia....Western region of Czechoslovakia, part of Austrian empire before WW1

Bolshevik....Radical left wing party associated with the Soviet Union

Boom....The spar that supports the bottom of the mainsail

Bootshafen....Boat Harbour

Bootshaus....Boathouse

Bow....Front end of a boat

Bratkartoffeln....Fried potato dish

Bratwurst....German sausage

Brigadeführer-SS....SS-Brigade Leader, Brigadier General

Broaching....A sudden change of a yacht's direction due to loss of control in strong winds or following waves

Brownshirts....Sturmabteilung, SA, so called because of their brown uniform

Brücke....Bridge, gangway, pier

Bubbe....Yiddish, grandmother

Bubbeleh....Yiddish term of endearment for a child

Buchenwald....A Nazi concentration camp near Weimar in central Germany

BUF,British Union....British Union of Fascists. Formed in 1932 by Oswald Mosley. British Union from 1937.

Bund Deutscher Mädel....BDM, Girls' wing of the Nazi Party youth movement, the Hitler Youth

Buoy....A floating marker for navigational or racing purposes

C\O....Commanding officer

Caserne....Barracks

CB....Confined to barracks

Challah bread....Braided loaf, with part of the dough, or Challah, set aside as an offering

Chametz....Leavening foods, forbidden on the Jewish holiday of Passover

Chamudah....Yiddish term of endearment, 'cutie-pie'

Chanukkah....Jewish festival commemorating Jerusalem's recapture and the rededication of the Second Temple

Cheder....A traditional school teaching children the basics of Judaism and the Hebrew language

Chef der....Chief of (Police, Abwehr, etc.)

cleat....A necked deck or spar fitting for attaching lines or warps to

Clubkapitän....Club captain

Coamings....The raised protective barrier around a yacht's cockpit

Cockpit....The recessed area for the crew in a yacht, and the steering position.

Comintern....The international wing of the Soviet Communist Party

Cresting....Waves that are breaking. They are very dangerous to vessels

Crosstrees....The spar crossing the mast which holds the shrouds away from the mast

Cutter....Sailing vessel with two foresails

Dachau....A Nazi concentration camp near Munich in southern Germany

Dankgottesdienste....Thanksgiving service

Davits....Arms used to hold and lower a lifeboat or launch on a ship

Deck-stepped....A mast whose base sits on the keel deck, supported by bulkheads below deck

Depowering....Letting a sail flap loose to lose its drive. Also luffing or stalling

Der Stürmer....Nazi newspaper famous for its rabid antisemitism

Derasha\derashah....Sermon

Deutsche\en\er\es....German

Deutschland....Germany

Deutschnationale Volkspartei....DNVP, a German Nationalist political party in coalition with the National Socialist Party in 1933

Deutsch-ostafrika....German East Africa

Deutsch-westafrika....German West Africa

Diaspora....A scattered population whose origin lies in a separate geographic locale. Historically, it has often referred to the dispersion of Jews

Dinghy....A small sailing vessel or rowing boat

DNVP....Deutschnationale Volkspartei, a German Nationalist political party in coalition with the National Socialist Party in 1933

Dornier....German aeroplane manufacturer

Downwind....Sailing with the wind directly behind the boat, or close to it

Drogue....A small canvas open ended cone used to slow a boat, to prevent broaching by following waves

DSO....Distinguished Service Order (DSO) is a British military decoration

Dummkopf\dummköpfe....Idiot

Dumplingwurst....German term of endearment. Literally 'Dumpling sausage'

Ebb, ebbing....The outgoing tide

Ehre....Honour

Ehrenzeichen....Badge of honour

Ein....a

Eins. Zwei. Drei. Vier....A count to four in German

Einsatz....Mission

Einsatzgruppen....SS death squads in Nazi Germany responsible for mass killings during WW2

Entschuldigung....Excuse me \ sorry

EP....Estimated position, using course, speed, time and tide

Erbhöfe....Hereditary farm

Ersatzkaffe ....Substitute coffee, used when real coffee became unavailable

erschossen....Shot

Esterwegen....Nazi concentration camp in the northwest of Germany

F1-12....Beaufort scale, Force 0 (windless) to Force 12 (hurricane)

Fachschule....Technical school

Fähnrich....Sub-company Sergeant Major

Feh....A Yiddish expression of disgust or disappointment

Feldpolizei....The secret military police of the German Wehrmacht
Feldwebel....Wehrmacht, Company Sergeant Major; Kriegsmarine, Petty Officer
Fischhafen....Fishing Harbour
Flossenbürg....Nazi concentration camp near the Czech border in Germany
Förde....Fjord, narrow inlet of water
Fore....Towards the front of the boat
Fore-and-aft....Front and back of the boat. 'Fore-and-aft rigged'
Forecabin....The accomodation at the bow of the boat
Foredeck....The part of the deck in front of the main mast
Foremast....Furthest forward mast in multiple-masted boat
Forepeak....A small locker at the bow of a boat
Fore-reaching....Setting sails amidships and lashing the rudder over for unhanded sailing
Foresail....The sail, or sails, set in front of the mast, usually on the forestay
Forestay....Rigging wire or rope that holds the mast vertically from the bow
Forward....Towards the front of the boat. 'forward of the mast'
Four-tonner....British Army lorry
Frau....Mrs,salutation
Fräulein....Miss, salutation, or a young woman
Fregattenkapitän....Kriegsmarine, Frigate captain, Commander
Frei....Free
Freiheit....Freedom
Freiheitsnachrichtenblatt....Freedom news sheet. 'Kieler Jüdisches Freiheitsnachrichtenblatt'
Friedhof....Cemetery
Fritzies....British derogatory name for the Germans
Froy....Yiddish, woman
Führer....Leader
Führerhauptquartiere....Command post of Adolf Hitler as Commander in Chief of the Wehrmacht
Funkmessgerät....Radar
Für....For
Furz\fürze....Farts
Furzmaschinen....Fart machines
Gaff....Spar supporting the top of a sail, usually at around 30° from mast
Gaff-rigged....Sailing set up incorporating at least one gaff sail
Gärtnerei....Nursery
Gauleiter....Regional governor under Nazi rule
Gebiete....Areas
Gebietsführer....Area leader
Geburtstag....Birthday
Gefangenschaft....Captured
Gefilte....Jewish poached fish patties
Gefreiter....Lance Corporal
Gegen....Against
Geh.kdos....Abbreviation for Secret Command, For senior officers only
Geheime staatspolizei ....Gestapo, German secret police
Gehinnom....A place to go after death to atone for one's sins. A jewish version of purgatory
General der Infanterie, Artillerie etc....Lieutenant General, commands Corps
Generaladmiral....Kriegsmarine, Admiral
General-Feldmarschall....Field Marshall, commands Armies
Generalgouvernement....Part of Poland not incorporated into the Third Reich. Governed by Hans Frank, destination for the bulk of Europe's Jews during WW2
Generalissimo....Leader of the armed forces, specifically General Franco, Fascist leader of Spain
Generalleutnant....Major General, commands Division

Generalmajor....Brigadier, commands Brigade

Generaloberst....General, commands Army, Armies

Gentile....Hebrew term for a non-Jew

Germanisation....Resettling of Germans to occupied countries; indoctrination of acceptable foreign children

Gesellschaft....Company, industrial

Gesetze....Laws

Gespräch....Conversation, chat

Gestapo....Geheime staatspolizei, German secret police

Gestorben....Died

Giftpilz....Toadstool, 'The poisonous mushroom'

Gimballed....Instrument or appliance suspended on arms allowing it to stay level despite the heel, or tilt, of a yacht

Glockengeläut....Church bell ringing

Gooseneck....The connecting joint between the mast and the boom

Goose-winging....Sailing directly downwind with mainsail and foresail set out on opposite sides of the yacht

Goyim....Yiddish, non-Jews, not complimentary

Großadmiral....Kriegsmarine, Admiral of the Fleet

Großer....Greater

Ground....To Ground a boat is to touch the bottom, to run aground

Grundschule....Infant School

Gruppenführer-SS....SS-Group Leader, Major General

Guardrail....Usually wire, they stop crew falling overboard

Gunwale....the upper edge or planking of the side of a boat or ship

Guten Abend....Good evening

Guten morgen....Good morning

Gybe....Turning a yacht with the wind crossing behind the stern. Can be a dangerous manoeuvre if uncontrolled

Haavara agreement....A German scheme to encourage Jewish emigration to Palestine from 1933 -1933

Hafen....Harbour

Haganah....Jewish paramilitary organization in the Palestine Mandate 1920 - 1948

Haggadah ....The Jewish text that sets forth the order of the Passover Seder

Halakha....The collective body of Jewish religious laws derived from the written and Oral Torah

Half-tracks....Military vehicle with front wheels and tracks behind

Halyards....Lines on a yacht that are used to hoist sails and spars

Hank....to attach the jib to the forestay by it's hanks, allowing it to be hoisted by the jib halyard

Hannukah....See Chanukkah

Hashém\hashem....Jewish name for God

Hauptamt....Main office

Hauptbahnhof....Main railway station

Hauptmann....Captain, 2nd-I-C to Major (Company)

Hauptscharführer....SS-Head Company Leader

Hauptscharführer-SS....SS-Head Company Leader, Master Sergeant

Hauptsturmführer....SS-Head Storm Leader

Hauptsturmführer....Head storm leader

Hauptsturmführer-SS....SS-Head Storm Leader, Captain

Havn....Harbour in Danish

hawsepipe....A right angled pipe set through the deck to take the anchor chain to its locker

Heer....German Army after 1935

Heeresleitung....Army command

Heil....Hail
Heinkel....German aeroplane manufacturer
Herr....Mr, Salutation
Himbeerschnitt....Raspberry shortbread
Hitlerjugend, HJ....Hitler Youth, National Socialist organisation for boys
Hoch....High
Höchste geheimhaltung....Maximum confidentiality (Top Secret)
Hof....Court, often used in hotel names
Höhere....Higher
Hora....Hebrew group dance, usually done by men
HQ....Headquarters
HSSPF....Regional Security Representative directly accountable to Heinrich Himmler
hydrophones....Listening device on a submarine for ships engines
ICRC....The International Committee of the Red Cross
Im yirtzeh hashem....God willing
Innenhafen....Inner Harbour
Jachtclub....Yacht Club
Jawohl....Yes sir
Juda....Jewish peoples
Jude, Juden....Jew, Jews
Judenfrage....Jewish question
Judenfrei....Free of Jews
Judenhaus\ Judenhäuser....House(s) set aside to accommodate Jews made homeless by Nazi
laws
Judenhund, Judenhunde....Jew dog
Judenjagden....Jew hunts, carried out by Einzatzgruppen
Judenjäger....Jew hunters
Judenknecht....servant of the Jews
Judenlaus\ Judenläuse....Jew-louse\Lice
Judenliebhaber....Jew lover
Judenmörder....Jew Killer
Judenrat....Jewish council, appointed by Nazi authorities to control Jewish populations
Judenrein....Cleansed of its Jewish presence
Judensau....Jew-sow
Judenscheiße....Jew-shit
Judenschwein\Judenschweine....Jew-pig(s)
Jüdische \ Jüdisches....Jewish
Jungvolk....Young people
Kaddish....Jewish spoken hymn, often refers to mourner's Kaddish, a prayer for the dead
Kaffee....Coffee
Kaffeeklatsch....Coffee gossip
Kaiser....German emperor
Kamerad\Kameraden....Friend(s), comrade(s)
Kampf....Struggle, Fight, battle
Kapitän zur see, captain....Captain
Kapitän zur See, Captain....Kriegsmarine, Captain
Kapitänleutnant....Lieutenant
Kapitänleutnant....Kriegsmarine, Lieutenant
Karte....Card
Kartoffelkopf....Potato-head
Kartoffelpuffer....Small potato pancakes served with an apple sauce
Kauf....Purchase
Kedge anchor....A second anchor, usually at the stern, to hold a vessel aligned to the sea or the
wind

Keel....Lowest part of a boat
Keelboats....Yacht with an inbuilt Keel
Keel-stepped....A mast whose base sits on the keel and penetrates the deck
Kennkarte....German Identification card
Keriah....A strip of cloth ripped during a funeral, symbolic of rending of clothing
Ketch....Two masted sailing vessel with the mizzen mast in front of the rudder
Kibbutz....A collective community in Israel traditionally based on agriculture.
Kinderlandverschickung (KLV)....The evacuation of children in Germany during the World War II
Kindertransport....Trains used to transport thousands of Jewish children from Germany to Britain just prior to WW2
Kippah....Brimless hat worn by Jewish men as a head covering
Kirche....Church
Kirchenfest....Church festival
Knödel....Savoury dumplings
Kommodore....Kriegsmarine, Commodore
Kompanie....Company, a unit of soldiers, around 100 - 150 men, usually commanded by a Major
Konteradmiral....Kriegsmarine, Rear-Admiral, Counter Admiral
Korvette....Corvette, a small naval fighting vessel
Korvettenkapitän....Kriegsmarine, Lieutenant-Commander
Kosher....Food that complies with the strict dietary standards of traditional Jewish law
KPD....Communist party of Germany during the Weimar Republic
Kriegsakademie....Naval academy
Kriegsmarine....German Navy after 1935
Kriegsschule....Navy college
Kriminalassistent....Criminal Assistant, Gestapo, rank 2
Kriminalassistentanwärter....Criminal Assistant Guard, Gestapo rank 1
Kriminaldirektor....Criminal Director, Gestapo rank 6
Kriminalinspektor....Criminal Inspector, Gestapo rank 4
Kriminalkommissar....Criminal Commissioner, Gestapo rank 5
Kriminalpolizei, KriPo....Criminal Investigation Department CPD
Kriminalsekretär....Criminal Secretary, Gestapo rank 3
Kristallnacht....The night of broken glass', a pogrom against Jews in response to the assasination of a German diplomat in Paris
Kübelwagen....German equivalent of a jeep or landrover
Kuchen....Cake
kugel....A potato dish
Kunsthalle....Art Gallery
Künstlerspaint....Artist's paints
Kvell....Yiddish, Proud
Lagerführer....Camp leader
Länderbahnen....Regional railways
Landesbischof....Archbishop
Landespolizei....National Police
Lashed....Tied down
L'Chaim....To life, Hebrew toast
Lebensborn....Nazi breeding program for unmarried mothers. The resulting babies were to be raised by the Reich
Lebensraum....Living space', the concept of German territorial expansion to provide homes and resources for German citizens
Lebensunwertes Leben ....Unfit for life', disabled, the old and the mentally ill, euthanased by the Nazi authorities
Leberknödel....Small liver dumplings

Lederhosen....Traditional leather breeches

Leech....The front edge of a sail, attached vertically to the mast or to a stay

Leeway....The amount of sideways drift of a vessel due to wind

Leutnant....2nd Lieutenant

Lieblingsmädchen....Term of endearment, 'favourite girl'

Lines....Ropes

Lt....Shortened form of light, or lighthouse, used in navigation

luff....The rear edge of a sail

luffed....An unfilled, or stalled sail

Luftwaffe....German air force

Mädchen, Mädel....Girl

Maginot line....A series of defensive fortresses that guarded the French border with Germany

Mainsail....The primary sail flying from the main mast, with a swinging boom at its foot

Mainsheet....The rope that controls the boom, and hence the mainsail

Majdanek....Nazi concentration camp near Lublin in Poland

Major....Major, commands Company: 100-150 men

Mamzer....A person who is born as the result of certain forbidden relationships or incest

Marineunteroffizierschule....Naval NCO school

Mark....Short for Reichsmark, currency from 1924 to 1948

Markt....Market

Marktplatz....Market place, market square

Marzahn....A Nazi concentration camp in Berlin that housed mainly Gypsies

Matjes....Pickled herrings

Matratzen....Mattresses

Matrose....Kriegsmarine, Ordinary rating/seaman

Matrosengefreiter....Kriegsmarine, Able rating/seaman

Matrosenhaupgefreiter....Kriegsmarine, Leading Hand

Matrosenstabsgefreiter....Kriegsmarine, Petty Officer

Matzah....Unleavened bread, eaten during Passover

Matzah ball....Jewish soup dumplings

Maultaschen....Pasta dish

Mauthausen....A Nazi concentration camp near Munich in upper Austria

Menorah....A nine-lamp candelabrum used on the Jewish holiday of Hanukka

Mentsh....Yiddish, a good person

Meshugener....Yiddish, a crazy person

Mettwurst....A strongly flavored German sausage made from raw minced pork preserved by curing and smoking, often with garlic

Meydaleh....Little girl

Mischling, Mischlinge(pl)....A person of mixed Jewish blood

Mizzen....Primary sail on the mizzenmast

Mizzenmast....Second, smaller mast aft of the main mast on ketch or a yawl

Morgen....Morning

Nase....Nose

National socialist party, NSDAP....Fascist party of Adolf Hitler, shortened to Nazi by Western Allies

Nationalsozialistische....Nationalsozialistische Deutsche Arbeiterpartei, National Socialist Party

Near-gale....Force 7 on Beaufort scale, wind 28-33 knots

Neuengamme....Concentration camp close to Hamburg

Nisht gefloygn....Yiddish, unbelievable

NM....Nautical mile, equal to 1.15 statute miles, 1 minute of latitude

Non-aryan....Not conforming to racial stereotype required in Nazi Germany

Nordmark....Work camp at Hassee, near Kiel, northern Germany

Nord-Ostsee-Kanal....The canal that runs from the Elbe estuary in the north sea to Kiel on the

Baltic

Nordsee....North Sea

NSDAP....Nationalsozialistische Deutsche Arbeiterpartei, National Socialist Party

Nuremberg....City in Bavaria, in south of Germany, home of some of the largest Nazi rallies and birthplace of the Nuremberg race laws

Oberbannführer....Hitler Youth, Senior Banner Leader

Oberbürgermeister....Lord Mayor

Oberfähnrich....Division Sergeant Major

Oberfähnrich zur See....Kriegsmarine, Midshipman

Oberfeldwebel....Kriegsmarine, Chief Petty Officer

Oberfeldwebel....Battalion Sergeant Major

Oberführer-SS....SS-Senior Leader, Colonel

Obergefreiter....Corporal

Obergruppenführer-SS....SS-Senior Group Leader, Lieutenant General

Oberkommando der Wehrmacht....OKW, High Command of the Wehrmach

Oberleutnant....Lieutenant, commands Platoon \ Trup\ Unit :30 men

Oberleutnant zur See....Kriegsmarine, Sub-Lieutenant

Oberpräsident....High President, usually of one or more of the Reichs's regions

Oberscharführer-SS....SS-Senior Company Leader, Sergeant 1st Class

Oberschütze....Private 1st Class

Oberschütze-SS....SS-Head Private

Oberst....Colonel,Brigade\ division, command or 2nd-I-C

Oberstgruppenführer-SS....SS-Supreme Group Leader, General

Oberstleutnant....Lieutenant Colonel, commands Sub units of up to 650 men

Obersturmbannführer-SS....SS-Senior Storm Command Leader, Lieutenant Colonel

Obersturmführer-SS....SS-Senior Storm Leader, 1st Lieutenant

OKW....Oberkommando der Wehrmacht, High Command of the Wehrmach

Oog....Island

Orcas....Killer whales

OrPo....Ordnungspolizei, 'Order Police'. Uniformed police force

Österrreich....Austria

Ostjuden....Eastern Jews, usually emigrated to Germany from Russia due to pogroms in late 1800s, early 1900s

Ostsee....Baltic Sea

Oświęcim....Village in Southern Poland, close to Auschwitz-Birkinau death camp

Outhaul....A line that tensions the mainsail out along the boom

Pah....German expression of disbelief or frustration

Palmach....Elite fighting force of the Haganah, the Jewish underground army in Palestine.

Paradeplatz....Parade square

passage-making....Sailing a yacht from one destination to another

Pentateuch....The first five books of the Torah, and the Christian bible

Pfennig....Penny, German currency

PHM....Port hand mark, a buoy marking the left side of the channel

Platz....Place, Square

Poch....A German card game

Pogrom....Organised violence aimed at the massacre or expulsion of an ethnic or religious group

Polacks....Derogatory term for Polish people

Polnischen....Polish

Pooped....Yacht's cockpit filled with water, usually from a wave crashing over the stern

Port....The left side of a vessel, looking forward

Purchase....Two wooden blocks, or pulleys, with a reduction gear of 3 or 4 to one, to exert greater pull on a rope.

Purim....Jewish holy day, 'The deliverence of the Jews'

Putsch....Coup

R\T....Radiotelephonic communications

Rassenschande....Racial disgrace

Rathaus....Town hall

Raus....Out

Ravensbrück....Concentration camp 90 km north of Berlin

Reaching....Sailing with the wind across the deck, often the fastest point of sail

Realschule....Secondary school, equivalent to comprehensive school

Regatta....Sailing race festival

Reich....Realm, empire. Used by National Socialists for Germany and all territories occupied during WW2

Reichsadler....The eagle insignia of the Third Reich

Reichsbahn....German railways

Reichsbank....National bank of Germany

Reichschancellery, Reich Chancellery....The office of the Chancellor of Germany

Reichsführer-SS....SS-Command. Heinrich Himmler

Reichsheer....German Army prior to 1935

Reichskanzler....Chancellor

Reichsmarine....German Navy prior to 1935

Reichsmarks, RM....German currency from 1924 to 1948

Reichsminister....Minister of the German government

Reichspost....German national post office

Reichstag....German parliament

Reichsvereinigung....Reich Association

Reichswehr....German Armed forces prior to 1935

Rheinland....Rhineland, a region of Germany ceded to France after WW1 in the Versailles Treaty

Rigging....The wires or ropes that hold up the mast or masts on a yacht

Rinderrouladen....Rolls of stuffed beef

RNVR....Royal Naval Volunteer Reserve (RNVR), to utilise amateur sailors during wartime

Rosh Hashanah....Jewish new year

Rottenführer-SS....SS-Band Leader, Corporal

RSHA....Reichssicherheitshauptamt, Reich Security Main Office

Rugelach....A filled pastry product originating in the Jewish communities of Poland

Rührer....Stirrer

Running Backstay....Paired backstays on both sides of mainsail, used alternately. Changed over when gybing

Running fix ....A way of fixing a boat's position on the chart with only one point of reference

SA....Sturmabteilung

Saar, Saarland....A region of Germany administered by France after WW1 in the Versailles Treaty

Sachsenhausen....Concentration camp 35 km north of Berlin

Samson post....A strong metal bollard at the bow or stern of a vessel to tie lines to

Sandtorte....German cake, very popular in Schleswig Holstein

Sardinenpackung....Sardine packing', the method of shooting Jews to stack more into a mass grave

Sauerbraten....A beef dish marinated for days, then slow-cooked for twelve hours

Sauerkraut....Pickled Cabbage

scandalising....Lifting the boom of a sail to depower it quickly

Schadenfreude....The deriving of pleasure, or relief, from someone else's misfortune

Scharführer-SS....SS-Company Leader, Staff Sergeant

Schatzi....Sweetheart

Scheiße....Shit, shite, faeces

Scheißkerl....Shit guy, literal - general insult

Scheißköpfe....Shitheads
Schlagball....Similar to the British game of rounders
Schleswig-holstein....Most northern of the German states, borders with Denmark, with whom the territory was historically disputed
Schloss....Castle or palace
Schmeckel....Yiddish insult. Penis
Schmendrick....Yiddish, Ineffectual, foolish, or contemptible person
Schmutziger....Dirty
Schnapps....An alcoholic beverage that may take several forms, including distilled fruit brandies and flavored liqueurs
Schneebälle....Snowball', a shortcrust pastry treat
Schneegans....Snowgoose
Schnell....Fast, quick
Schnitzel....Thin slice of meat, usually breaded before frying
Schule....School
Schütze....Private
Schütze-SS....SS-Private
Schutzstaffel ....SS, National Socialist political armed wing
Schwachkopf....Bonehead, imbecile, halfwit
Schwarze....Black
Schwein\Schweine....Pig(s)
Schweinhund....Pig-dog
SD....Sicherheitsdienst des reichsführers-ss, German Security Service, part of SS
Seacock....A through-hull valve for the expulsion or intake of water
See....German for a body of water, lake or sea
Shabbat....Jewish Sabbath, from just before sunset on Friday to nightfall on Saturday
Shalom....Jewish greeting, 'peace'
Shalom aleichem ....Peace be upon you
Shanah Tovah....Greeting on Rosh Hashanah, 'have a good year'
Shanah Tovah Umetukah....Happy Jewish New Year
Sheets....Lines that control sails on a yacht
Shema....A prayer that serves as a centerpiece of the morning and evening Jewish prayer services
Shiksa....Yiddish, Gentile woman
Shkoyekh....Yiddish, thankyou
Shlaym....Yiddish, scum
Shleger ....Yiddish, Bully
SHM....Starboard hand mark, a buoy marking the right side of the channel
Shoal....An area of shallow seabed
Shrouds....Rigging wires or ropes that hold the mast vertically at each side. Often in pairs
Sicherheitsdienst des reichsführers-ss....SD, German Security Service, part of SS
Sicherheitspolizei(SiPo)....Nazi state political and criminal investigation security agencies
Sieg....Victory
Sippenhaft....Law making family share the responsibility for a crime committed by one of its members
Sonderkeller....Special cellar', Nazi euphamism for gas chamber
Sonderkommando....Work units made up prisoners, usually Jews, to aid the loading of of gas chamber victims
Sounding....Taking a depth reading, usually with a lead line in the 1930s and 40s
Sparkasse....Savings bank
Spars....A wooden pole used in the rigging of a yacht to support its sail. Includes yards, booms, and masts
Spindrift....Spray blown from cresting waves during a gale
Spinnaker....A large sail for downwind sailing that flies from the front of the yacht

SS....Schutzstaffel, National Socialist political armed wing
Staatsgeheimnisse declaration ....Similar to signing the Official Secrets Act
Staatspolizei....State Police
Stabsfeldwebel....Regimental Sergeant Major, Heer; Chief Petty Officer, Kriegsmarine
Stabskapitänleutnant....Kriegsmarine, Lieutenant
Stabsoberfeldwebel....Kriegsmarine, Warrant Officer
Städtische....City, urban
Standartenführer-SS....SS-Standard Leader, Colonel
Starboard....The right side of a vessel, looking forward
staysail....A second foresail set aft of the Genoa or Jib, in parallel or alone in high winds
Stillgestanden....Stand still. Stand to attention
Stormtrooper....SS soldier
Strafing....Aerial attack of ground targets using mounted automatic weapons
Strandkörbe....Beach chairs
Straße....Street
Streuselkuchen....Crumb cake
Stücke....Literally 'pieces', The number of Jews killed on an Einsatzgruppen aktion
Stuka....Junkers Ju 88s. German dive bomber
Stukas....Junkers Ju 87, a Luftwaffe dive-bomber
Sturmabteilung....SA, Paramilitary wing of National Socialists. Eventually superceded by SS
Sturmbannführer-SS....SS-Storm Command Leader, Major
Stürmerkasten....Street-corner billboards for the public to read Der Stürmer
Sturmmann-SS....SS-Storm Man, Lance Corporal
Sturmscharführer-SS....SS-Storm Company Leader, Sergeant Major
Sturmtaucher....Shearwater
Sudetendeutsche....Ethnic Germans from the Sudeten area of Czechoslovakia
Sudetenland....The Sudeten area of Czechoslovakia, ceded to the Czechs after WW1
Tacking....The process of sailing upwind by making a series of legs at 45° angle to the wind
Talmud....The central book of Rabbinic Judaism, the source of much Jewish religious law
Tell-tails....A piece of yarn or fabric attached to a sail, a stay, or any rigging to indicate wind flow
The hard....Concrete or stone slip for launching small boats, usually at a yacht club
Topmast....A small spar at the top of the main mast to carry the topsail
Topping lift....A halyard that holds the boom up when not supported by the mainsail
Topsail....A small sail that fits between the mainsail's gaff and the topmast
Topsides....Part of the hull between the waterline and the deck
Torah....The Hebrew Bible, often refers to the five books of Moses, but can include up to 24
Totenkopfverbände....SS Death's head units
Tsuris....Yiddish, worries
Tyrol....Historical region in the alps, split between Austria and Italy
Über....Over
U-boat....Submarine
Ul.....Abbreviation for Ulica, street in Polish
Ungarnaktion....The deportation and killing of Hungary's Jews
Unnütze....Useless
Unterfeldwebel....Platoon Sergeant Major
Untermensch\Untermenschen....Sub-human(s) Term used for Jews in Nazi Germany
Unteroffizier....Sergeant
Unterscharführer-SS....SS-Under Company Leader, Sergeant
Unterseeboot....U-boat, submarine
Untersturmführer-SS....SS-Under Storm Leader, 2nd Lieutenant
Veer....Usally refers to the wind, swinging round to clockwise on the compass
Verboten....Forbidden
Verdammt....Curse. Damned

Vermögens....Riches, property, fortune

Verordnung....Decree, regulation

Versailles....Town in France where the Treaty of Versailles at the end of WW1

Vierjahresplan....The Four Year Plan was a series of economic measures overseen by Hermann Göring

Vizeadmiral....Kriegsmarine, Vice-Admiral

Völkischer beobachter....The newspaper of the Nazi Party (NSDAP) from 25 December 1920

Volksempfänger....The 'People's Receiver', a subsidised German state radio set

WAAF....Women's Auxiliary Air Force

Waffen-SS....Military branch of the SS

Warps....Ropes used to secure a vessel to the shore

Warps....Ropes securing a vessel to a harbour wall or jetty

Washboards....The removable boards closing off the companionway on a Yacht

Watches....The splitting up of the day into 4-6 hour periods to rotate crew on deck

Watchkeeping....To be on watch, to navigate the yacht and keep a lookout

Way....When a vessel is moving under control it has way on

Wehrmacht....German armed services after 1935

Wiener schnitzel....Thin, breaded, fried veal cutlet

Winch....A drum shaped mechanical device used to control halyards and sheets

Windlass....A winch on a ship, often for hauling an Anchor on a yacht

Withy sticks....Tall willow sticks used to mark the sides of small little-used channels

Wolfsschanze....The Wolf's Lair , Adolf Hitler's first Eastern Front military headquarters

Wunderbar....Wonderful

Yirtzeh Hashem.....God willing

Yom Kippers....Affectionate name given to interned Jews by Isle of Man residents for their love of smoked fish

Yom Kippur....Day of Atonement, the holiest day of the year in Judaism

Zoologischer....Zoological

Zurückgehen....Move back

Zyklon-B....Gas used in gas chambers to kill Holocaust victims